A new twist to an old legend
The She

"[Kluger's] carefully rendered   nd his portrayal of the degradation and   edieval women...is sensitive and affecting....Mr. Kluger has creaᴛᴇᴅ   pansive, realistic picture of an age in which brutality and corruption were the norm."   —*The New York Times Book Review*

"An earthy, richly textured revisionist tale....Kluger weaves a magnificent medieval tapestry of near-Chaucerian zest and complexity."
          —*Publishers Weekly*

"It may be difficult for some to accept that one of history's truly hated characters has been transformed into this very likable and just figure, but in his telling of the tale, Richard Kluger completely held my attention in a most enjoyable way."   —Brian Jacomb, *The Washington Post*

"Highly recommended."   —*Library Journal*

"A lively, vivid and informative book that nourishes like history but moves like a novel."   —*New York Newsday*

"*The Sheriff of Nottingham* is a work of genuine excellence that explains the things that really matter—then and now."
          —*Philadelphia Inquirer*

"A compelling view of what life must have been like in the thirteenth century."   —*Dallas Morning News*

"Kevin Costner wouldn't recognize the Robin Hood that Richard Kluger presents in...his elegant and entertaining retelling of the tale. [The sheriff] is a sympathetic, flawed, complex man whose story is told against the fascinating, tumultuous age in which he flourished."
          —*San Francisco Chronicle*

"Mr. Kluger is quite adept at the blending of fact and fiction, and there is an aura of authenticity in his narrative....The past comes alive in these pages."   —*King Features Syndicate*

PENGUIN BOOKS

THE SHERIFF OF NOTTINGHAM

Richard Kluger, a former journalist and book publisher, is best known for his works of social history, *Simple Justice* and *The Paper*, winner of the Polk Award, and the novel *Members of the Tribe*. He lives on the rural western edge of New Jersey, where the deer, he reports, are more numerous (if less picturesque) than in Sherwood Forest in its primeval glory.

Richard Kluger

The Sheriff of Nottingham

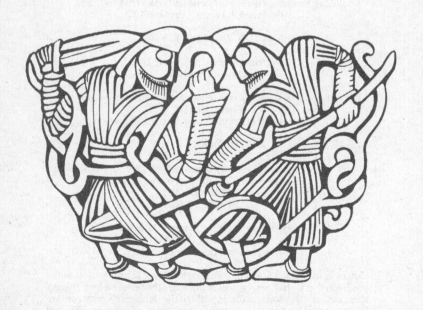

PENGUIN BOOKS

PENGUIN BOOKS
Published by the Penguin Group
Viking Penguin, a division of Penguin Books USA Inc.,
375 Hudson Street, New York, New York 10014, U.S.A.
Penguin Books Ltd, 27 Wrights Lane, London W8 5TZ, England
Penguin Books Australia Ltd, Ringwood, Victoria, Australia
Penguin Books Canada Ltd, 10 Alcorn Avenue, Suite 300,
Toronto, Ontario, Canada M4V 3B2
Penguin Books (N.Z.) Ltd, 182–190 Wairau Road,
Auckland 10, New Zealand

Penguin Books Ltd, Registered Offices:
Harmondsworth, Middlesex, England

First published in the United States of America by
Viking Penguin, a division of Penguin Books USA Inc., 1992
Published in Penguin Books 1993

1 3 5 7 9 10 8 6 4 2

THE LIBRARY OF CONGRESS HAS CATALOGUED THE HARDCOVER AS FOLLOWS:
Kluger, Richard.
The Sheriff of Nottingham / Richard Kluger.
p. cm.
ISBN 0-670-84022-X (hc.)
ISBN 0 14 01.7703 5 (pbk.)
1. Sheriff of Nottingham (Legendary character)—Fiction. 2. Great Britain—
History—John, 1199–1216—Fiction. I. Title.
PS3561.L78S54 1991
813´.54–dc20 91–50240

Printed in the United States of America
Set in Century Old Style
Designed by Francesca Belanger

For Jacqueline and John Bogart

But wherefore do you droop? Why look you sad?
Be great in act, as you have been in thought.
Let not the world see fear and sad distrust
Govern the motion of a kingly eye.
Be stirring as the time; be fire with fire;
Threaten the threat'ner and outface the brow
Of bragging horror. So shall inferior eyes,
That borrow their behaviours from the great,
Grow great by your example and put on
The dauntless spirit of resolution. . . .

—*King John*, Act V, scene i
WILLIAM SHAKESPEARE

Foreword

CAN IT BE HISTORY'S SENSELESS HAPPENSTANCE that but a single king of England has borne the name of John? That one, who came to the throne nearly eight hundred years ago, wished mightily to be a great king like his father, Henry II, and a heroic warrior like his brother, Richard I. Instead, he earned a high place only in the annals of infamy.

King John is remembered best for agreeing, toward the end of his reign, to halt certain of his practices found tyrannical by the ranking lords of the realm and granting them a great charter of liberties. His name is popularly linked as well with the golden-hearted outlaw Robin Hood, whose existence is altogether lacking in credible documentation but whose antic adventures, particularly in their modern retelling, are often set in King John's day.

Darkest of the figures in this luminous legend is The Sheriff, chief royal officer at Nottingham, a few miles south of Sherwood Forest, where Robin and his raffish band of brigands were said to operate in rollicking disregard of the king's peace. The Sheriff is never given a name, and so posterity has taken him for the faceless embodiment of generic villainy, one of folklore's enduring stock characters.

In truth, the crown began to keep careful records at about this period, and thus we know more than their names about the men who presided over the king's castle at Nottingham. Of these officers, by far the most competent—and the one who served throughout the years when the legend may well have taken root—was a soldier of fortune who began his service at Nottingham in the ninth year of John's reign. He came there at an unusually troubling time. For three years the king and the pope had been

quarreling over who should succeed Hubert Walter, that master of pomp
and governance, as archbishop of Canterbury and prime spiritual authority
of the kingdom. The king's choice was a former crown secretary, John de
Gray, then bishop of Norwich. Pope Innocent III's preference was Cardinal
Stephen Langton, among the leading theologians of the age and by any
standard save one—namely, unswerving personal loyalty to the monarch—
the infinitely better-qualified candidate.

Efforts to negotiate the deepening dispute came to naught. And so
in June of 1207 the pope summoned Langton to Rome and invested him.
King John, sorely aggrieved at this papal affront to his royal prerogative,
threatened to hang the newly consecrated archbishop the moment he set
foot in England. The pope, no less aggrieved at this lay intrusion upon his
hallowed terrain, responded in March of the following year by imposing
an interdict, ordering the English clergy into idleness. Such failure to
perform their spiritual services, the king ruled in turn, nullified every crown
grant and charter to the church; all holy houses and estates, comprising
a full quarter of the land mass of England, were thereupon declared to be
royal property. To make them so in fact as well as name was a thornier
thicket.

Thus matters stood in August of 1208 when King John ordered a
number of new sheriffs into his shires in the hope of tethering them more
tightly to the royal will and mastering the seditious clergy. For five months,
no bells had sounded, no doors had opened in any parish church or cathedral, no worshiper was shriven or marital vows spoken or earthly
remains laid to rest in consecrated ground. The dead were placed in
roadside ditches or still less fitting repositories. At Nottingham, they were
being stored in the cool darkness of the hillside caves that encircled the
town. . . .

A.D.
1208

· I ·

"Ho, hawk!"

The bellow raced up the hillside to where the reeve, astride his motionless dappled gray, had been addressing the condition of the manor fields. Their grain was nearly ripe now under the unstinting August sun, and Blake, the reeve, had just placed their likely yield at a satisfactory nine bushels to the acre. The mews-master's sharp cry from the hollow below caused the reeve's horse to shift uneasily beneath him and the rider's glance to turn heavenward.

Styx, at the apex of her ascent, appeared no larger than a swallow from the ground. Well established in her fourth season as the keenest peregrine ever raised at Swanhill, she hung transfixed for an instant at the signal from her trainer. Moments earlier, her prey had been roused from the pond, its huge concave wings and light body in motion at the first sound of the dogs. The heron rose rapidly in small, jittery circles, as if fully aware of its sacrificial role. Only when the larger bird was well under way had Thomas de Lambert, lord of Swanhill, given the falcon, tautly balanced on his fist, a final stroke of mingled affection and arousal before deftly unhooding her. The light briefly stunned her fierce, dark eyes, and then, with a narrow scan, they were absorbing in minutest detail the full play of earth and firmament. The next instant she was off in blood pursuit.

At first it looked an uneven contest. The heron, with its headstart, was spiraling swiftly away as Styx, with her denser body and shorter wings, launched slowly, as if on an unrelated errand, tracing a wider circle and gliding into the wind. From the ground she seemed thoroughly indifferent to her mission until the great chest muscles began to work the powerful wings at full beat. In another moment she was racing down the wind and climbing up into it at heightening velocity. Soon her gyre had compassed the heron's waning route of escape and left it enmeshed in the vortex below as the falcon arrived pridefully at her point of maximum ascent, waiting on in suspended expectation for her master's cry. "Ho, hawk!" it came a second time.

Squinting against the sun, the reeve focused on the dark dot as the peregrine tucked her wings beneath her and became a sleek-feathered wedge dropping at a speed that left her slowed prey without hope of evasion. All at once the unearthly shriek of air forcing through the slitted bells tied to the predator's legs assaulted Blake's ears. It was surely what Hell must sound like, the reeve thought—the perfect accompaniment to the horrific vision he used to confront at Mass each Sunday hanging on the cracked wall of the Rainworth parish church: leaping flames and capering demons who wielded savage hooks to strip the putrid flesh from the melting bones of the damned. Always his eyes shrank from that insistent threat of pitiless torture and wandered to the wall opposite where the dove of the Holy Spirit was pictured, plunging earthward much like Lord Lambert's peregrine at that very instant, but with altogether different intent. The doves he knew, though—the ones that came each spring at planting time from Sir Thomas's dovecote to shadow the sowers and then swoop down to feast on their broadcast seed—seemed anything but angelic, let alone emanations of the Heavenly Father. Did a bird's color or habits, or both, or neither, determine if it partook of the divine or the infernal, he wondered, until the piercing ring from above grew so unbearable to his ears that his mind shredded.

Styx struck with explosive force, her talons like tridents sinking into the vitals of her quarry. The heron fell stone-dead from the sky, a flurry of feathers in the wake of its sheer descent. The falcon followed in a leisurely slope, alighting on her victim as gently as a butterfly. She was licking demurely around the heron's gaping wounds when the hunting party drew up in admiration.

"Splendid creature, our Styx is," said the steward, Stryker, who had ridden up silently through the daisied meadow behind the reeve on his way to join the hunt. The steward's goshawk, a bird as notoriously cross as its owner, perched on Stryker's gauntlet, ready to bloody hares all afternoon.

The reeve, caught unawares, turned with a startled bob of his head and groped to remove his cap in deference to his agate-eyed superior.

"She's never missed yet."

"Never while I've watched, sire."

"Let that be a lesson to you, sweet Diana," the steward said, cosseting his bird with several airborne kisses before readdressing the reeve. "Anyway, I'm glad to catch you here idling, Master Blake. There are several things I need to mention."

"Sire?"

"I've discussed it with Sir Thomas, and the lord agrees entirely that the manor will no longer recognize the Feast of St. Lawrence as a holy day. It's a minor festival, the priest assures me—of no special devoutness. It's an excuse, really, for a day of idleness, if you'll be honest with me, Sir Reeve. And we cannot afford another day of idleness in the midst of the harvest season. I expect to see your people in the manor fields that morning."

Since the steward declined, as usual, to look directly at Blake while delivering a spiteful edict, he failed to observe the reeve's poorly concealed frown. "I fear they'll prove a surly lot that day, Master Stryker. The feast has become customary."

"Yes—and so they customarily avoid the church and crowd the alehouse, grousing, dicing, wrestling, drinking themselves into a fine stupor— don't deny what I've seen with my own eyes—which leaves them good for nothing the next three days but rutting like swine." He had recently toted up the holy days on which the villeins were excused from serving the manor, the steward went on, and the figure was eighteen, not counting the long interlude at Christmas. "It's time that we unaccustomed them to St. Lawrence. Tell the pious to light a candle for him at eventide instead."

Was there a steward in all the world who was not overmighty, Blake wondered, with eyes averted lest Stryker now detect his bitter disapproval. "May I say, sire, that I think it an unfortunate step—and unnecessary. The work gets done regardless—it is my charge, and there's no evidence of our ever having fallen short."

"The lord is expecting a larger harvest, in view of the newly assarted fields—not to mention the expanded common you whined about for years. For your own people's sake as well as Swanhill's, the added work day is needed. Nor is it a matter for debate." His goshawk emitted a screech in corroboration.

"Sire."

The steward made placating sounds at the bird through sly, wet lips. "Then there is the further matter of the dung, Master Reeve."

"Which dung would that be, sire?"

"The dung that is the lord's by right but that he's not been getting." For weeks now Stryker had observed two flocks on the common for several hours after sun-up whereas the manor's fallow fields, as the reeve hardly needed to be instructed, were in urgent need of manuring.

"The sheep you speak of surely belong to Morris and Peters—and they have paid the lord to graze their holdings till noon three days of the week." And paid dearly at that, Blake wished to add but did not.

"I recall no such arrangement."

"Nevertheless, it was thoroughly bargained and is duly recorded on the manor roll. I watch to see that the terms are not exceeded."

The steward's head gave a small, feigned recoil. "I stand corrected—since I know you to have all these items engraved upon your scrotum. Still, it sets a bad example; it should not be renewed."

"Sire." But he will forget, the reeve thought; the man lies awake at night inventing peeves, to be superseded in a week by a new set.

"And tell the shepherds to make it up by gathering whatever manure resides on the village road and carting it straightway to the fallow fields. Sir Thomas is entitled to every dropping."

Stryker the dungmaster; indeed, the greater part of him had turned to excrement—and the balance, to bile. "Sire."

The steward's steed, dark as onyx, began to move off. "And don't forget about your beloved Griggs. The whole of his arrears plus what is ordinarily due by Michaelmas, or out they go. We have extended him quite long enough—Swanhill is not in the credit business. Let the churl go to the Jew." He gave a derisive snort.

"Griggs is ever on my mind, sire," Blake said to the retreating steward. "He is no malingerer, but I doubt he'll have the rent. He's a broken man—though one of our best."

Stryker had no hope to offer, only dispossession. "Very grievous," he called over his shoulder. "I'll have the groom drop you off a hare or two from our takings—if that would suit you, Sir Reeve."

"You are generous, sire," Blake called back to him, and replaced his cap as the steward's black stallion stepped diagonally down the embankment toward the hollow.

A sad case, Griggs, thought the reeve. You could count every rib on the scrawny ploughman's sweat-soaked chest the few days a month he was well enough to work. His humpback son tried to fill the void but made a pitiable spectacle, while his wife, Susan, and their two daughters could produce no income. Blake himself, out of pity, had directed that one of his teams tend to a third part of Griggs's acreage in the common, but he could do no more; the village would cry rank favoritism if the reeve's oxen were long put to such use. There would be no end to unfulfillable calls upon him, and what dubious sway he held over them would be lost. He was, after all, but one of them, risen higher through their sufferance no less than their lord's, so it behooved him to have a care whom he smiled upon, and how often he smiled at all.

Blake wheeled his small gray mare away from the blood sport and its haughty players and traveled along the hedgerow heavy with hawthorn and lilting with birdsong until he reached the stream that bisected the manor. While his gray paused to lap the rushing waters, the reeve gloried in the gentle fragrance of the wild thyme that clustered in the moist verges. Why did men take pleasure teaching birds to kill other birds for the sheer spectacle of it, he asked himself, when there were so many other harmless sources of delight at the ready? He put it to himself thus each time he went to watch the majestic Styx soar and stoop and strike. But why, he asked as well on this limpid afternoon, did he himself join the watchers, even at a furtive distance? He had not just happened by that vantage point.

At the third pang of hunger he reached into his saddlebag for a crust of brown bread and, while chewing it gingerly to avoid the persistent ache in his next-to-last lower molar, headed up the path over the heather-sweet knoll. At its summit he cast a look southward across the green and golden patchwork of shallow valleys and hilly glens, bringing his keen eyes to rest on the dark stub he knew to be the great tower of Nottingham Castle, a league distant. He had seen it up close countless times but never been within the hulking royal citadel. Only yesterday at the alehouse, all the talk was of the reported successor to the disgraced and dismissed Vieux-pont as the king's master of the shire. The new sheriff was already on his way north, it was said, and word had it that he was a commoner—a soldier of modest renown but long service to the crown in the French fighting. A peculiar choice if true, thought the reeve. But titled or not, how could he prove worse than the rest who had occupied that commanding crag? Sheriffs were sheriffs; it was their nature to inspire dread as it was their function to oppress. Indeed, in that regard, they were remarkably similar to stewards: the less seen and heard of them, the better.

As he proceeded down the easy slope toward the village, the reeve's attention was arrested by a sudden tumult a furlong or so to the west, where a hunting party crashed thunderously through the leafy wall of chestnut and sycamore that marked the end of the Swanhill warren. The party of young knights, dames, squires, pages, and grooms, led by Sir Thomas's spirited son Guthrie, broke into the clearing and, in response to a volley of blasts from the huntmaster's horn, veered leftward in a loose arc that would lead the riders back to their sanctioned hunting ground. In their path lay the newly expanded fields of the common; in their wake a moment after, the reeve saw as the dust settled and the din receded, perhaps two acres of oats and peas had been trampled by the madly churning hooves.

A similar incident had occurred in the spring, just after planting time, a few furlongs north along the warren's edge. In that case there had been an excuse: the hunt had collectively forgotten the newly reduced perimeter of the warren and was unable to rein in before they were upon the fresh-sown fields. But there had been time enough then to replough and replant; now the destruction was beyond remedy. Was the act deliberate or merely wanton, the reeve wondered, futile fury rising within him. Either way, it came to the same thing: it was merely serf land, and there would be neither regret nor recompense forthcoming from the manor house. For three years Blake had beseeched Sir Thomas to increase the common, and the lord had at last succumbed to his petition the past winter. The reeve had then to persuade his own chronically disgruntled people that a dozen new acres to cultivate as they wished were far better than none. And now, in a mindless moment of youthful exuberance, a portion of the precious increment had been wasted. The act seemed mute testimony to the grudging nature of the concession.

Four furlongs to the north, mounted on his magnificent Gascoyne roan, Thomas de Lambert, master of Swanhill barony, looked downward from the edge of his manor house lawn, across a vast, cupped incline of bursting cropland to his bondsmen's common fields and witnessed the same act of destruction. It did not please him. Nor did it move him to remorse, for the occurrence had been entirely foreseeable.

From the outset of their pleading he had told the reeve and the hayward that a more ample border of waste was needed between the warren's end and the beginning of the common, but they had persisted with tales of too little tillable acreage and too many mouths to feed. He was not the one who had created those mouths, and he was thus not obliged to feed them, he replied. In the end, though, against his steward's counsel, he had relented because he wished the tenants and bondsmen of Swanhill to be contented. In foul humor they would labor but fitfully for him, and the manor would flourish the less.

Such calculated benevolence had served his purpose; if there was a more bountiful estate per acre in Nottinghamshire than his own—in all of England, for that matter—he did not know of it. His people were adequately clothed, sheltered, and nourished and were asked in return only to work with reasonable diligence under God's eye, and his own, with every chance thereby for gaining their eternal salvation. It was a fair bargain, made more equitable still by his occasional indulgence of the reeve's incessant pleadings in their behalf. Such yielding was rare indeed, though, for if Sir Thomas knew one thing in life, it was that the lord overly solicitous of those who served him would be repaid only with their contempt.

"Our Guthrie is both headstrong and carefree," Sir Thomas remarked to his stablemaster, who sat mounted beside him. "It's a dangerous combination. Do me the favor of speaking with him sometime—he should be cautious where he tramples."

"Yes, my lord," said the stablemaster. It was not the first time he had been so charged—more nearly the hundredth. "I suspect, though, sire, the point would be better brought home coming from his father."

From any other retainer, even the steward, such forthrightness would have skirted too near to impertinence. The stablemaster, though, had been at Swanhill longer than Guthrie's whole life span and knew the yoked joy and curse of the lord's possessing a son who was the apple—nay, the whole orchard—of his father's eye.

"No doubt you're right," Sir Thomas countered.

But in the great hall at Swanhill that night, where the hunt party was feasting on fresh venison and pheasant and the free flow of godale and rich wine turned young spirits raucous, the lord of the manor gave scant thought to cautionary words. Guthrie was about the manor all too rarely as it was, now that he had attained an age and bearing that warranted his overseeing the lesser Lambert holdings in shires north and east. A wasted acre or two of serf corn was hardly cause to provoke a quarrel with his playful heir.

· II ·

"WE SHALL HAVE TO POSTPONE the rose window for a year or possibly two," said Prior Clement, gazing up at the wondrous device lately installed on the balcony overlooking the cloister court. "But the clock is well worth it. The convenience of it in guiding the use of one's time is priceless. And the accuracy—it is infinitely superior to the sundial, of course, functioning as it does without reference to the sky, and after dark as well, you see. It is all accomplished with weights and pulleys and chains—they have shown me the innards and explained it all a dozen times, but I'm a perfect dunce when it comes to mechanisms. They assure me that the one they have at Canterbury has worked splendidly for half a dozen years, so ours should do no worse, provided it is properly attended each day." The prior's bony shoulders sagged a bit over the nuisance of it, but then he brightened. "Nevertheless, it is a vast improvement on the hourglass, which must be reversed at the very instant it expires or it—"

"Yes, Father—I'm familiar with its limitations," said Sir Mitchell of Rainworth, hoping not to disclose impatience with the prior. His enthusiasm for every acquisition, whether vessels and vestments to celebrate the Mass more grandly or volumes for the already bulging cupboards lining the cloister alcoves or added pastures for his fecund flocks, seemed to dim not in the least with age. Each new object, he never tired of stressing, somehow or other served the greater glory of God—and of Lenton Priory but incidentally. In what manner his new clock might please the Lord, Father Clement declined to speculate, suspicious as he was that punctuality might well be redundant to the author of creation.

"I must confess," the prior continued, as the clock hand crawled ever closer to the numeral III on its shiny tin face, "I'm sorely tempted to invite the most reverend chancellor here to see our new installation. He'd likely denounce it as the devil's work—and then begin scheming for one of his own the instant he's back at Southwell. They say the merest hint of our transcendence induces a week of flagellation in the man."

A classic case of the pot calling the kettle black, thought Sir Mitchell, coroner of Nottinghamshire, liegeman of the earl of Derby and, as such, permanently designated knight-protector of Lenton Priory. For of the dozen other religious establishments that had risen in the county during the century past (bespeaking a confluence of unconscionably rich men fearful of their heavenly prospects), none provoked greater dismay in Prior Clement than the splendid bulwark of Southwell Minster.

To invite comparison with the minster was, on the face of it, absurd of the prior; Southwell was not a monastic house at all but a subcathedral of the archbishop of York, with dominion over the southern sector of that prelate's vast see. Anchored in massive solidity at the heart of the shire some fifteen miles to the north of Lenton Priory, Southwell was a hub of learning and clerical training (some said dissipation as well), a busy clear-inghouse of administrative tasks, and a magnet for Whitsun pilgrims by the thousands. Their offerings went toward completion of the minster's great nave, with its massive columns and profusion of arches that achieved a monumental dignity unmatched by any church in the north of England. How the master of Lenton Priory envied those Whitsun offerings!

Yet in terms of accumulated wealth, no religious house in Nottinghamshire could match the graceful Cluniac monastery over which Clement of Beaupré presided. Lenton Priory stood a mile west of the king's castle at Nottingham, within a sharp bend of the Leen, where that burbling stream entered the Trent. It had been built in the opening years of the twelfth century by the magnate William Peverel, a ranking countryman of the Conqueror himself, and was munificently endowed from the first—no doubt in expiation of Peverel's having advanced the Norman cause throughout the English north country by entirely leveling it. The priory's riches bought Clement influence, and influence might purchase a bishopric—possibly at Lincoln, although the great see at York was not beyond his contemplation. At least remotely aware that he was neither the most pious nor the most politic of priors, Clement had labored to make of his abbey a masterwork of holiness, thereby hoping to advance his ecclesiastic ambitions. Thus, Lenton now numbered among its possessions thousands of acres of rich fields, upland pastures, and stout woods spread over six shires; enough sheep to clothe half the kingdom; a small mountain of jewelry and plate in its subterranean vaults; a promising collection of relics (though nothing yet to rival Reading Abbey's piece of the True Cross and hand of St. James the Apostle); and now, a clock . . . which just then clanged three times and caused Sir Mitchell to jump.

"Extraordinary!" said the coroner. "Alas, you'd better muffle that bell by the archdeacon's next visit or he'll have the papal legate on your neck. Is there another functioning church bell in all England?"

"But it summons no worshipers," the prior answered hurriedly, having well considered the point before approving of the clock's installation. "It is more a bell that happens to be in a church than a church bell—if you grasp the distinction. And, of course, the priory is not precisely a church within the truer sense of the Interdict. The pope has not ordered his vicars into paralysis—merely to cease ministering to the laity. What has a clock at a priory to do with that? It is simply a convenience to—"

"With all due respect, Father, it is an arguable question."

"Perhaps. And perhaps the king will come to his senses before it must be confronted."

"Would that I could agree that he has deserted them," the coroner replied. "Rather, the quarrel appears much in the king's interest. It rallies the commoners to him as nothing else has—they may venerate the Holy Father in their various ways, but he is not their king. Even the baronage slackens in its animosity to John. He at least is approachable when they wish to buy a canonry or a vacant abbotship for a son or a friend. The pope is remote—though, I grant you, he is said to ask more reasonable prices."

The prior's waxen flesh grew taut over his high cheekbones. "The king is misguided. Any temporary advantage to him will give way to disaster. The issue is irrevocably drawn—it is the pope's lot to determine the church's officers. If Rome defers to the crown in an egregious case such as this, we will be saddled forever with shadows and sycophants like this John de Gray—without a liturgical bone in his body, a mere secretary, a cleric in name only, the king's errand boy—installed at Canterbury. Holy Church quite simply cannot permit it."

"I grant you the principle. Reality is another matter."

"The reality is that Langton is perhaps the most thoughtful Englishman in cassock. Who better for Canterbury?"

"An Englishman in name only."

"What? Born not forty miles from here—"

"But a resident of France for decades—in the bosom of John's archfoe—and, arguably, he has absorbed French thinking and French ways."

"Nonsense. He has eternal questions on his mind, not the petty quarrels of vain rulers." The prior reached for the flask of malmsey on the table between them and poured them each a half-cup. "Why, just two nights ago I found renewed pleasure from reading one of Cardinal Langton's discourses. He has such a supple mind. He was examining the question of whether transubstantiation takes place if the wine is not mixed with water. Truly a fascinating topic for the orthodox celebrant." The prior gave his cup a little shake lest the ruby liquid turn viscous. "A lesser mind would leap to judgment, but Langton declines to commit himself. On the one hand, he notes authority for concluding that it does occur, provided the priest intends no heresy—yet he must be punished. On the other hand, he notes that Cyprian the martyr speculated that perhaps the wine of Palestine was so heavy that it could not be drunk unless mixed, which is why the Lord gave such to His disciples at the final supper." Clement lifted his dram and savored a swallow. "Thus, the suitability of sacramental wine might be said to depend less on its degree of dilution than the volume of sediment produced by the local—"

"An astonishing symposium, I agree." Sir Mitchell drank the prior's health and emptied his cup before setting it down. "Meanwhile, your marvelous clock is by law the property of the king—and from what I gathered at the castle yesterday, he'll soon have your revenues, too."

Father Clement grunted. "That remains to be seen."

"You think that bunch at the castle is pliable?"

"Well, not that officious little pagan Sparks whom your friends at the castle sent over to visit with us the other forenoon."

"I have no friends at the castle, only acquaintances, and they all suspect me of having a hand in Vieuxpont's departure—as well they might. Believe me, Father, I intend to shield you from the new sheriff as best I can, especially at this trying time. Brother Jocelin put his underling on you only because Westminster sent word to get on with it, and he is too frail a reed to temporize longer."

The prior nodded. "Well, there's nothing frail about Master Sparks. Beneath that meek exterior I sense the latent arrogance of the unbeliever. His animus to Holy Church is patent. But what else would one expect of an unordained clerk? I can't think why Jocelin ever engaged him in the first place."

"A treasury clerk longs for efficiency in his apprentice, not religiosity—which is to say someone trustworthy enough to relieve him of his burdens. So now Jocelin sleeps half the day, when he's not counting the king's pennies and helping himself to an occasional shortweight. Practically speaking, Sparks has succeeded his superior."

"There is danger in that for us. He marched in here with nary a thought of genuflection, as if this were some sort of abattoir, poked his letters patent under my nose, and said the crown required payment in full from us by Michaelmas. Then he asked if he might tour our planted fields and view our flocks—something about a preliminary appraisal—as if there were a suspicion we should be less than entirely forthcoming."

"It borders on sacrilege."

"Under the circumstances, I thought it prudent not to press him on what the crown means by 'payment in full.' Surely it cannot include bequests to our endowment or the revenues that accrue to us from them. And what sort of allowance will be left for the priory to maintain itself? Shall our brothers be required of a sudden to abandon contemplation and prayer for the drudgery of the hoe and the trivia of domesticity?"

"Did you put that to Sparks?"

"He said it is all to be negotiated by the new sheriff."

Sir Mitchell fingered his cup, vaguely gauging the sediment in its contents. "That may not bode well, either. At the castle they say he is a fierce warrior—ordered the survivors at Loches to drink the blood of the fallen rather than yield the besieged castle to thirst. No doubt an apocryphal account, but it hints at a certain level of brutishness."

"Brutishness can be cozened, we have found in the past. Honeyed words accompanied by a sacred gift that every sheriff would cherish—a reliquary with gilt chasing, perhaps, or a jewel-handled dagger. The crucifix and cruciform, you see, are interchangeable to the military mind."

"I wonder if Sparks isn't the better bet for—considerations."

"Can one trust an infidel with church matters?"

"I doubt he's that. Our Father Ivo says Sparks is more doubting than faithless."

"Your chaplain is obtuse—per usual. I know Sparks's sort. His manner reeks of ill breeding."

"Indeed—he's a serf's son, albeit a smith. Even after a dozen years of polishing, a certain roughness remains indelible."

"My inclination would be to throttle him rather than offer appeasement. A churl is likely to confuse a small token of gratitude for an outright bribe. Perhaps if you were to hint of his tarnished character to the new sheriff and suggest that a clerk not in holy orders necessarily suffers from dubious virtue . . ."

"Meaning?"

"Say that he steals. He must—they all do, from what you tell me— Brother Jocelin most of all. Some clerk of the royal treasury!"

"Only Chaplain Ivo doesn't dip into the castle collections, so far as I can determine—which makes him our gravest menace." The coroner drank again, wondering as the wine coursed down his throat how its taste compared with that of blood. "Incorruptible men are prone to be thoughtless of others."

· III ·

HIS HAND REACHED OUT reflexively until his fingertips skimmed the surface of the wall as he passed along the corridor paralleling the great hall and emptying into the bailey. The wall glistened with a perpetual sheen that seemed to give it the character of living tissue. The dampness, though, varied with the season. In autumn it was rather like a fine film, the merest patina, as if a decorative glaze, displeasing to neither eye nor touch. In winter it turned gelatinous, like a congealed coating to shield the tissue beneath from the infiltrations of the brittling cold. In spring it ran in rivulets of sap, coursing down every vein and fissure in the thawing rock—a harbinger of fresh life and hope. And now in summer it had turned clammy and clinging, like a sort of vegetative sweat about to metamorphose into moss.

Why were these walls so preternaturally wet? The chaplain liked to suggest, with a nasality to his tone betraying archness, that it was the castle shedding tears for all the evil and sorrow it had witnessed within. The barber, who preferred to call himself surgeon (though but rarely called upon to excise or amputate much more than a tooth), conceived of the moisture as a kind of mineralized perspiration that kept the organism healthy and helped heal its wounds. The steward's explanation was less fanciful. He traced the dankness to seepage from a hundred cracks in the roofing and battlements that there was never money enough to fix, given the priorities of sheriffs and the uncertainties of their tenure.

Of these speculations Jared Sparks was most inclined to credit the chaplain's. Indeed, Father Ivo, for all his shortcomings, was the only occupant of Nottingham Castle—besides himself—whom the little clerk found estimable. No doubt this appraisal had stemmed from the chaplain's willingness to accept Sparks as an outcast from the seminary at Southwell without pressing for reasons or supposing a lapse of faith. It was Ivo who had prevailed on Brother Jocelin, the shire treasurer and receiver of taxes, to accept a clerk no longer in pursuit of final orders, citing as qualifications the chancellor's assurances that the lad wrote an excellent hand, was adept with numbers, and possessed no obnoxious personal habits. There had been, as well, the endorsement of the chaplain's old friend Honorius, the minster chronicler, who vouched that young Brother Sparks, to judge by several exchanges with him over the two years he had been at Southwell, had a lively and perceptive mind, if a bit prone to wander from received wisdom. Now, ten years afterward, Brother Jocelin had still not formally pronounced Master Sparks's probationary period at an end, but he was installed, for all practical purposes, as clerk treasurer for Nottinghamshire and Derbyshire. Throughout, Ivo had been his counselor, less as a priest dispensing dogma than as a kindly uncle willing to trade confidences and convictions without need to mold the nephew in his likeness.

This enduring communion between them, the clerk thought as he hurried to the rendezvous for their nightly stroll along the riverbank, was the more remarkable in light of his own ill-concealed disaffection from Holy Church. The clergy, Sparks long ago had become persuaded, thrived by fervently cultivating the fears and ignorance of the laity, forever threatening with eternal hellfire whoever withheld from it the full measure of devotion—and his tithe. Every service rendered, every sacrament celebrated had its price, he judged, going by his own experience with the coarse parish priest to whom he had been sent by his father, the smith at Swanhill manor, to learn to read and write in exchange for a precious penny a week. The priest, Father Theodorus, would promptly pocket the coin and order the indigent parish deacon to provide the lesson. The cleric was similarly delinquent in all his duties. Mass, when he bothered to say it, was a rush of Latinate mutterings with a discordant hymn or two interspersed; he had not the wit to fashion a sermon. The little church itself was a monument only to neglect, its few benches broken, its candlelight sputtering, its roof a gaping invitation to the elements, its nave littered with droppings by the sparrows that lived in the eaves (and were periodically threatened by the priest with excommunication for their irreverence), its churchyard fencing in such disrepair that swine and geese wandered godlessly among the gravestones.

These abuses notwithstanding, the priest would rhapsodize, as the alms plate passed, upon the efficacy of giving: all donors' crops would flourish, pains ease, and prospects for salvation multiply; those who begrudged God their penny did so at their peril. On their deathbed he pursued his parishioners most tenaciously of all, soliciting bequests as if their conduct of a lifetime had not already sealed Heaven's judgment of them. Only in the company of his two hearthmates, one a devoted crone who fixed his porridge and mended his soiled vestments, the other a plump maid who tended his other fleshly needs, did he evince a humor unclouded by torpor.

Southwell was a different matter, but no less troubling to Sparks. He had been given the privilege, rare among lads of low birth, of attending the grammar school at the minster upon his father's payment of an onerous fine for the manor's loss of the boy's services. It was, at first, a thrilling place for him, full of collegial verve, alive with music and song, alluring with sweetmeats and succulent salmon and other foods he had never known, an endless supply of books and manuscripts, and the spectacle of soaring stonework and statues of saints and martyrs carved with remarkable fidelity to nature. Yet languor and luxury pervaded all, so that even as a novitiate, Sparks had begun to grasp the point of the epigram that mankind, like all Gaul, was divided into three parts: those who fought, those who worked, and those who prayed. At Southwell, there was indeed prayer, but still more of smugness, and it was not long before he came to despise those parasitic inmates who bought their temporal ease and comfort at the laity's expense while making exclusive claim upon the sacred heart.

Over time, Sparks revealed these sources of his estrangement from Holy Church to Father Ivo, who, surprisingly, would not deny an element of insufferability among his fellow clerics. In particular, the chaplain questioned whether fine vestments and immense cathedrals better promoted the adoration of the Almighty or the ennoblement of the priesthood. But Ivo would not overcredit Sparks's doubts about the clergy as a whole. Whatever lamentable lapses or excesses the younger man had witnessed were not conclusive grounds, he argued, for denial of Holy Church's embracing mission. "Our most faithful practitioners," Ivo said, leaving open his membership among them, "bring to mankind the gifts of love, understanding, and consolation for all the woes that flesh is heir to." For the chaplain, this earthly life, whatever station one occupied in its course, was intended as an ordeal for determining one's eternal destiny; ergo, Holy Church at its best was humanity's devoted usher, guiding and comforting it through the travail.

Sparks considered this facile cant, though he refrained from denouncing it as such. "If I must do everything with reference only to whether it will or won't advance my cause in the Lord's eye," Sparks suggested to the chaplain in one of their early exchanges, "then all charity is a sham, all benevolence a travesty—and self-sacrifice the slyest of hypocrisies."

Father Ivo pinched the bridge of his nose at this onslaught and asked in response merely, "What is wrong with forming each act of your life in a manner to please God?"

"But what puny mortal can know for certain the will and pleasure of the Almighty?"

"Precisely why He sent His Son to earth and dispersed the Apostles."

"They were exemplars—they cannot live our lives for us."

"But by their teachings we are to be led—and where they are not altogether clear, I see no harm whatever in our acting in a manner we *suppose* likely to please the Lord."

"But don't the Mohammedans and the Zoroastrians and doubtless the Jews as well suppose *their* actions pleasing to the Lord? Yet we name them infidel and declare Heaven closed to their foul ilk."

"As indeed *our* Heaven is. Perhaps they have some other."

In this concession Sparks detected the soul of enlightenment and withdrew from the attack. But there was no shortage of other subjects on which they chose to disagree. Of these by far the most compelling was that high and sacred enterprise to which all Christendom had rallied not yet twenty years before—and the king, now nine years dead, who had led it. The Lionheart, for Ivo, was the outsized champion of the church militant: his exploits in the Holy Land had thrilled his kingdom and justified all their risks and costs, his own ransom not the least of them. To Sparks, that same Richard was but an overgrown child, a war lover who had visited an indecisive bloodbath upon Palestine and meanwhile sacrificed all to his passion. Every office in England had been put up for sale to finance the crusade—he would have sold London itself, it was said, had he found a buyer—and the kingdom left in the hands of rascals.

"Than whom none was more unworthy than his brother," Ivo sniped, "now our anointed king, Heaven help us."

"If the prince was misguided," Sparks answered, eyes burning, "the Lionheart was more so. You do not triumph over the heathen by slaying him but by precept and compassion—that is what the Gospels teach. To descend to butchery is to defile the temple of God, not to reclaim it."

To Ivo, though, the choice was clear between the brother monarchs.

The present king was and always had been a schemer, and never more so than when his brother slew in the name of Christ, placing the kingdom of God above his own, while John stayed home and plotted with the epicene and guileful king of France to usurp Richard's throne. The prince went so far as to seize the royal castles in the six counties whose revenues Richard had generously assigned him—Nottinghamshire among them—though the castles themselves had been forbidden him. Worst of all, John withheld the ransom money collected in his shires with the forlorn prayer that his brother might rot in German captivity. But the sprung Lion made straightway for Nottingham, where he spared the renegade garrison at the castle only because Ivo fell to his knees before the king. They had been held captive by John's party till it fled at the first word of Richard's return, the chaplain abjectly explained—and then revealed the hiding place of the withheld ransom money. Bankrupt as usual, Richard took the bait and embraced the chaplain in forgiveness. Little wonder Ivo cherished his memory, though the Lionheart was never again seen at Nottingham, and only rarely on English soil.

John's presence, though, was another matter. By the time Richard had died on a fool's errand in the Limousin five years later, Sparks had already come to work at the castle, helping draft writs and summonses and delivering them in the company of the bailiffs. So the little clerk had been on hand when the new king's entourage arrived at Nottingham in the midst of a bitter winter the first full year of his reign at the beginning of the thirteenth century of the Christian era. And the sovereign had come almost annually thereafter, each time leaving Sparks admiring and exultant.

Largely it was the panoply of his arrival. The great baggage train clattered endlessly over the Trent bridge and wound up to the castle precipice, four royal hornblowers in the lead, the king's guard of knights and sergeants just behind, then the marshal and the constable, archers and huntsmen, squires and pages, grooms and footmen, clerks and messengers, carters and carts and half a hundred pack horses, hunting dogs and a prized Norway falcon. In the rear came cooks and personal attendants, including the king's own hearthman, who set the fire each night precisely to the royal liking; Florence, the royal laundress; and William, the royal ewerer, minister of the king's bath. Though each of the six-dozen crown castles and lodges maintained a royal apartment for his exclusive use, John's ever-roving court traveled with all the trappings of domesticity (save the queen, who was spared the rigors of the rutted highway). Wide-eyed, Sparks would watch the spectacular clutter in the bailey as the royal train halted and unpacked, starting with the king's featherbed, linen sheets, and fur coverlets, then on to his bathtub, portable library, personal urinal, wardrobes of the finest woolens and silks and miniver, chests of jewels and barrels of silver pennies (sole coin of the realm), stores of rich foods, canisters of precious sugar and almonds and ginger, and cases of wine from as far as Lesbos and Iberia. And when the tumult subsided, the throng parted and in rode His Majesty, fresh from an overnight stay at Lincoln while his baggage train had been preceding him for three days at a torturous pace. He dismounted without assistance and embraced the waiting sheriff, setting off a roar of welcome from the gathered castle staff—a decided contrast from the sullen greeting tendered him on the streets of the town.

John was a short but powerfully constructed man, a less imposing figure than his larger and ruddier father and brother who had preceded him on the throne. That he was the last of the eight children born alive to Henry Plantagenet of Anjou and Eleanor of Aquitaine, and therefore perceived throughout his youth as exceedingly unlikely ever to reign, seemed to have shaped his determination every waking moment as king not merely to reign but to rule. To judge by his stays at Nottingham, he was an engine of perpetual activity. He received the barons, knights, and prelates of the region, sought their counsel without promise of heeding it, collected their debts and fees, levied fines, listened to complaints and chided malcontents, presided over a judicial eyre, questioned the sheriff at length about problems within his jurisdiction, gathered gossip (the more infamous, the better), hunted on a Friday (for which sin he distributed an extra portion of alms), played chess (winning all his matches, curiously enough), heard and told bawdy stories, hosted a banquet, danced with the prettiest of his vassals' ladies, diced, drank bottomlessly, went to bed with somebody else's wife, and, in the middle of the night, in order to calm a royal bellyful, read a bit of Pliny.

Sparks, bearing the shire rolls, had twice come within a dozen feet of the monarch but no closer. The royal attendants were more accessible, and lavish in their fondness for the king, who was a model employer, to hear them tell it. He knew their names, even their children's in some instances, remembered their birthdays (or had a clerk remind him), saw that they were tended when sick, gave them generous gifts at the Yuletide (even the royal archers' wives were remembered with new dresses), and paid them justly by the standards of the age; for fixing the royal bath, all of Nottingham Castle heard, William the ewerer got sixpence.

Yet to Sparks's puzzlement, the king remained unloved by his subjects. His quick intelligence and dexterous use of the new tools of government the Chancery had perfected counted little with the multitudes when weighed against his bootless military expeditions to France and the draining taxes that fueled the ever busier activities of state. Richard at least had prowess as a warrior—even if he was nothing more than that and had bankrupted the realm. Engaging as John could be during visits to Nottingham and on other forays across the hinterland, he nevertheless was said to suffer generally from a charmless intensity in the conduct of his duties. All craft and no grace, grudging of the benevolent gesture toward his vassals, his every policy move transparent in purpose, he acted as if persuaded that money and loyalty were equally (and even simultaneously) extractable from his subjects. Majesty thus eluded him. To Father Ivo, John the king was still Henry and Eleanor's unredeemed bad seed.

Over the years Sparks and the chaplain had resolved their differences thus: Ivo served not so much Holy Church, with all its conceded imperfections, as the Lord Himself, who by definition had none, and his disparagement of the crown was not treason but merely his aspiration, as it were, for a more exalted temporal ruler. Sparks, for his part, served not so much the king, with all his acknowledged blemishes, as the kingdom, and his sourness toward the church was not heresy but disappointment. Throughout the years it took them to effect this compact, the castle that employed them both was in the charge of mean and greedy men, so the pair of them toiled quietly, finding solace in their bond.

A soft mist, tinted by the vermilion sunset, had stolen across the river and enshrouded Father Ivo by the time Sparks reached him on the path that fringed the meadow. The chaplain's face, when the clerk got close enough to read it, wore a look still more brooding than usual. He had just heard from Chief Bailiff Manning that the new sheriff was indefinitely delayed in the Welsh Marcher counties—the usual restlessness required his presence, especially now that the two most powerful Marcher lords, William de Briouse and William the Marshal, were estranged from the king. In his stead and due at the castle the very next day was the new undersheriff. "And he sounds even worse," Ivo rasped through his evening catarrh.

Gerard d'Athiés, the sheriff-designate of Nottinghamshire and Derbyshire, was one of those mercenary captains in the king's French service
who had fought desperately in the defense of Touraine three summers
earlier but finally surrendered. The grateful king had ransomed the most
valorous of the lot and brought them back to England as a kind of elite
royal officers' corps, assigned to the most vital, and vile, tasks of law
enforcement. When the Welsh situation worsened and John needed a man
of unalloyed allegiance to administer the frontier counties, Gerard was
rewarded with the sheriffships of Gloucestershire and Herefordshire. His
tenure had begun promisingly enough to ask him to take charge as well
at Nottingham Castle when Vieuxpont was deposed for misfeasance, with
the understanding that the deputy of d'Athiés's choice would bear the main
burden in that midlands bailiwick. D'Athiés chose as undersheriff a colleague from Touraine about whom virtually nothing was known, Ivo added,
"except that he is not even a knight."

"Not a knight?" The clerk's words had the lift of incredulity to them.
"To serve as de facto sheriff?" It did not sound promising. A Frenchman,
not even Norman, a common soldier of fortune, with no knowledge of
England, probably a smattering at most of English, the flimsiest familiarity
with the intricacies of taxation, and surely even less with the protocols of
fealty and the interlocking genealogies of the British baronage. Why send
such a man to Nottingham, the clerk asked, "unless Westminster thinks
any rattlebrain can oversee our two shires?"

Likely it was that, they agreed as they paced through the encroaching
twilight. After all, Derbyshire was not a populous place and placidly endured
the firm dominion of William de Ferrers, earl of Derby and unshakable ally
of the king. Nottinghamshire itself, the prime object of the sheriff's attentions, was occupied one-fourth part by church holdings, one-fifth part
by Sherwood Forest, and another goodly portion by royal estates under
direct custodianship for the crown. Thus, the county may have looked
docile to Westminster's eyes. But the churches of the shire were famously
acquisitive and not a little fratricidal. Sherwood, with the fairest game in
England, was notorious for violations of the forest laws committed within
its borders. The royal estates were a thicket of contentious subtenancies
with chronically delinquent rental payments. And the remainder of the
shire was notable for the fierce pride of its landholders and the surliness
of its peasantry. In short, it would have been a sheriff's graveyard, assuming any one of them had ever set out in earnest to keep the king's

peace and exact only his just revenues. Oppression was easier and more lucrative. But a man utterly foreign to the shire, without lineage, property, allies, or even the trappings of chivalry to gild him, was going to meet with resistance if he swung too heavy a truncheon.

"He'll be in sore need of counsel," the chaplain commiserated, his thoughts directed toward the captain due on the morrow. "Who would be best—for all our sakes?" he asked Sparks.

"The earl, without a doubt. But he won't be bothered—and the Frenchman probably lacks connections to him."

"Then I suppose Lord Lambert would be best."

Swanhill was the largest estate in the county not held by the crown or the church, and its holder, accordingly, was the ranking layman. Sparks, who was born in thrall to the manor and had devoted much of his life to avoiding return to it, knew the political currents swirling about the place. "Sir Thomas harbors grievances toward the crown—and his taxes remain in intentional arrears. Intimacy with him would likely hurt our Frenchman if the king caught wind of it."

The chaplain nodded as the last pale remnant of daylight receded from the sky and they began to retrace their steps before darkness overtook them. "The chancellor would have been an inspired choice, but the Interdict has placed Southwell out of bounds. Possibly there is someone at the castle itself. . . ."

"You can't mean the coroner? Sir Mitchell is his own perennial contender for the sheriff's job—too treacherous to be trusted." Sparks shook his head emphatically. "The constable plunders the place and brought the last undersheriff to ruin. He should be dismissed forthwith, not consulted for guidance." The rest were no better. The steward excelled only as resident sybarite, more concerned with which castle maid would share his bedding that night than with the maintenance of the king's citadel. Brother Jocelin, the treasury clerk, was too frail now and remote from the realities of power. The bailiff was able, if stolid, but a dim beacon to follow. "There is only yourself, Father—precisely the right choice. You know the shire—you're skeptical of the king, but within tolerable bounds. You've seen the extorters and malingerers come and go at the castle. . . ."

"You jest."

"Not in the least. Nobody else makes sense."

The priest thought a moment and then shook his head. "Our newcomer is said to be a trained killer—a bloodthirsty soldier of the crown. He's unlikely to heed the dubious wisdom of an aging cleric."

"Our sainted Lionheart was a trained killer as well—yet he let men of the cloth run his kingdom."

"But Richard was unquestionably a man of the Cross, working for God's greater glory. This—this foreigner will no doubt seek only to cover his own hide and offend the crown as little as possible. Which may make him an unholy terror, devoid of all civility, grossly antagonizing the shire—"

"All the more reason for his enlisting your counsel."

The chaplain fell silent again as the castle lights flickered across the meadow, already aglisten with the evening damp. "I doubt we even speak the same language. His Latin is surely execrable—or nonexistent. I'd have to master his native dialect." There was an antic catch in his tone. "But I have no ambition for that, Master Sparks—that or much of anything else."

"Precisely why you must be the one, Father. Now to set our minds on how we can guide this brutish captain to the same conclusion."

· IV ·

ANGELIQUE'S STRAW BONNET, too large for her head but securely strapped to her chin to keep the wind from taking it, bobbed rhythmically beneath him as she braved the last morning of the ordeal without complaint of the heat, dust, hunger, or the demands of her small bladder. Doubtless the child had savored the sensation of sharing her father's saddle with him when they had set out from London a week earlier, but he lacked the patience to keep responding to her chatter and had no aptitude for quieting her by crooning as her mother did. As the novelty of his comforting closeness wore away, she lapsed into long, unwonted silences, to the point where he now feared that she might be falling ill from the rigors of the journey.

Their party of twelve had left Leicester town at daybreak: he and Angelique on his big bay; Anne on her palfrey; their younger daughter,

Julia, and the nursemaid on a straw pallet in one of the carts; a second cart for the balance of their belongings; his older brother, Reginald, and sister-in-law, Helene, sharing an ancient charger; Reginald and Helene's grown son, Geoffrey, leading a pair of packhorses that bore their family's things; and at the rear, his younger brother, Peter, lugging a blunt lance good only for discouraging highwaymen. Ordinarily, he would have had the carts and sumpter horses leave several days in advance so the rest of the party could make better time. But the remainder of Anne's dowry, in jewels and coin, was hidden among their possessions and could not be risked on the road without a proper guard, which they could not afford. So their train had to move at the wearing pace the carts could manage over the rutted route.

The sun was nearing its zenith when he calculated, by the map he had thought to have copied at the Chancery, that they had crossed the county line into Nottinghamshire. He signaled the ragged cavalcade to follow him off the highway into a cool dell, and while they ate bread, goat cheese, and pickled calves' liver and washed it down with fresh perry, he spread the map in front of them and indicated the point they had reached, as if it were the gateway to a promised land. Guiding Angelique's finger, he traced the contours of the shire, some fifty miles from north to south and nearly half as wide, and noted that it lay in the geographic heart of England. Nottingham Town, still four hours' travel to the north, held the strategic key to the great midlands plain, which gave way at that point to rolling uplands that grew into an ever more formidable obstacle to the movement of armies.

They had halved the distance to their destination by the time they drew up a gentle rise and won their first glimpse of the silver Trent, cutting a serpentine diagonal across the southern portion of the shire. "It's the third-longest river in England," he said to Angelique, hoping to arouse the child's interest.

She considered the information for a moment and then, her head pivoting sideways, asked, "How do they know?"

"They measure—somehow."

"But it curves about so."

"They count the curves—somehow."

"A sheriff should know such things."

Philip Mark smiled and touched his child's cheek. "I'm only an under-sheriff, *ma petite*. Undersheriffs aren't required to know everything."

"What if Captain Gerard never comes?"

"Then I'll have to learn how to measure rivers."

That satisfied her but only for a moment. "Is it salt or fresh?"

Philip spurred his flagging mount. "Here it would be fresh."

"Where does it go?"

"To the sea—eighty miles distant." He extended his arm over her shoulder and pointed northeast.

"Away from France."

"Yes."

Her small head nodded. "It's just as well."

He bent and kissed her cheek, then turned to steal a look at Anne, whose oval face and delicate features, normally pale and composed, were flushed from so many long, broiling hours in the saddle. She masked her fatigue with a quick smile and nodded as he gestured toward the river so she would know the end was nearing. How he wished to believe that this supremely lovely countryside, so much more strikingly sculpted than the valleys of the Loire, where he had passed most of his forty years, was beckoning to him, promising refuge, dignity, and the chance of modest reward for service honorably rendered. Yet he was entering it as the agent of an unbeloved sovereign and knew not a soul dwelling there. The faithful discharge of his duties, moreover, was as likely to cost him his neck as advance him in the crown's esteem—a fickle and irritable crown, at that.

Anne's anxiety could have been no less than his own, he knew, watching her eyes swing away from the horizon line and fall pensively on the perspiring neck of her mount. Yet she had come willingly, even cheerfully, vowing never again to be separated from him as she and the infant Angelique had been during the final two years in Touraine. At first he had thought she was feigning delight with his assignment to Nottingham, which he himself suspected of being a demotion. But she speculated that it would soon enough become his very own command—Gerard's hands would be full in the Marcher counties, and he would have to cede Philip practical dominion in the north. Nottingham Castle would be their haven as no other place had been, and he would prosper there when the people came to value his mettle.

But for him a castle, especially a royal one, was hardly congenial to domesticity. Castles were, above all, military bastions, and the one at Nottingham was of particular value because of its site astride one of the two main routes north from London to York. It stood just above where the Trent was forded by a bridge three hundred feet across and a dozen feet wide, resting upon seventeen mighty oaken arches. Such a bulwark could not be readily bypassed in time of war, for it would thus endure as a rallying point with a garrison that could form raiding parties perpetually threatening to fall upon the enemy from the rear. No, a castle like Nottingham had to be stormed, and few fortresses on earth, to judge by the maps and drawings of it they had shown him at Westminster, were better suited to withstand siege.

Philip's service at Nottingham, though, was to be less as the king's captain fending off an implausible foreign host than as his chief civil magistrate, and in that connection the castle held manifold challenges novel to him. It was the king's provincial palace and the royal court whenever he chose to make it so; the administrative seat of government for two shires; the crown treasury for coin and jewels and collection depot for taxes; the repository for shire deeds, charters, grants, and archives of every sort; a court of law; headquarters and supply house for bailiffs, foresters, and other keepers of the king's peace, and a gaol for its violators. Such an array of functions and responsibilities might have daunted any officer lacking the combined skills of Solomon and Caesar, let alone one tilling amid alien corn.

For the purpose of schooling himself in the complex task ahead of him, Philip had haunted the halls of the Chancery and Exchequer at Westminster for a week, absorbing what he could from clerks and deputies. While there, he was granted an interview with one of the king's closest counselors and his acknowledged authority on the sheriff's art—the redoubtable William Brewer. For thirty years he had served Plantagenet rulers, the first of them as sheriff of Devonshire under the second Henry, then additionally as one of four members of the baronial council monitoring the royal government during Richard's absentee reign, and currently under John as the prime baron of the Exchequer. In this last office Brewer sat implacably for a fortnight at Eastertide and Michaelmas while the royal auditors scrutinized the ledgers for every shire; it was he who recommended which sheriffs ought to retain their posts, which to be removed, and which to be fined, gaoled, or possibly maimed. The king, engaged now in quarrels with the pope, barons bristling over royal tax exactions and withheld privileges, and chieftains in the restless outlying regions of the realm, had lately asked Brewer to serve as sheriff of no fewer than five additional counties.

"You've done well to seek me out, Captain Mark," Sir William had said upon their meeting. "But don't think for a moment our auditors will go any easier on you as a result—they're hawk-eyed predators trained to pounce."

"So I am told, my lord," Philip replied. "I seek no favors—only guidance."

Brewer formed a sizable bulk seated behind the long table piled high with documents betokening his rank as royal counselor extraordinaire. Even in that heavily guarded precinct, he kept his sword girded to him and a red-eyed mastiff half the size of a lion stationed at his heel. He had not risen to greet the slender Frenchman, whom he must have thought a dubious candidate to grapple with the thorny labors of a sheriffship in the midlands.

"Then you must understand, *mon capitaine,* that these Plantagenets we serve are harsh and gifted masters," said Brewer. "This one most of all. He is much more like his father than his brother was—though I mean in that no lack of affection or awe for the Lionheart—he was one of God's noblemen. Had no head for figures at all, though, beyond how many men, horse, and engines he needed to flatten a castle. His father, on the other hand—a genius—retained every face and fact he ever encountered—knew every language spoken from the Hebrides to Byzantium—read voraciously—always in motion. John is like that—the brain is ever at work, assessing. But not a man to cross."

"I have heard tell, my lord."

"Your education is well launched, then, Master Mark. What else have you heard, Captain—about me, pray tell? That I am a monster, no doubt— an abuser of men claimed by misfortune. There are advantages, you know—or should know—in being preceded by a hateful reputation. Fulfilling it when required arouses less resentment that way, whereas any display of leniency is met with gratitude."

Philip Mark's discreet inquiries at Westminster had yielded the consensus that Brewer was a decided improvement on those dreaded early Norman sheriffs from whom the office had evolved—the shire reeves. Mounted high on a fine white stallion, the haughty outrider of a terrifying conqueror from across the waves, the shire reeve was the first royal officer truly to wield absolute police and financial power over his county, ranking just below the earl, who held military and judicial supremacy, and the bishop, its spiritual head. He traveled his shire imposing order and governance, despoiling church lands, robbing from the royal demesnes in his control, gathering taxes and exacting fines as caprice dictated, extorting, taking bribes, and generally reaping a fortune that he came to perceive as his mandated right. The second King Henry, reigning a century after the Conquest, sought to curb these plunderers by appointing a new breed of sheriff, professional and often unlanded retainers of the crown who were expected to place the king's needs ahead of their own.

Brewer was of this latter breed. He gathered up the shire tax quota methodically, using force selectively and not by reflex, and faithfully forwarded it to the crown treasury—but not a penny beyond. He was rewarded with a rich harvest of custodianships and escheated estates; and once he took hold of other men's property, he was a wizard at draining every last penny from the entitlement. When finally ordered to surrender it, he did so reluctantly and belatedly even if the rightful owner had paid full penance—and then only when Brewer was paid a bribe, else he would keep finding legal grounds, often of the most dubious merit, to delay the transfer. Officially, he was careful to observe the letter of the law down to its minutest serif. Yet he was said not to cavil at the extralegal when it suited his ends and was safely undetectable—such as the time his son contended with another man for title to an escheated manor within Sheriff Brewer's jurisdiction, and while the legal dispute raged, the contender against his son disappeared without a trace.

"Your range of chores is very broad," he now instructed Philip, "from serving writs' of summons to hanging felons. But above all others, the sheriff's chief duty is to see to it with pea-brained singlemindedness that the crown receives every penny due it from every conceivable source. You have no need to be loved, only feared, for you cannot serve both your sovereign and his subjects in equal measure. You must choose between them—and the choice will be plain to all."

It was this creed that had prompted newly ransomed King Richard to assign Brewer to Nottinghamshire. The sheriffship there, as elsewhere, had been ill used after the Lionheart auctioned off nearly every crown post to raise money for his holy war, so what better model for reforming the office than that supreme crown loyalist, William Brewer? In those closing years of the twelfth century Baron Brewer solidified his reputation as a surpassingly fierce magistrate. He was known to have ordered the fingers chopped off a woodward caught wasting a royal park, had a whole hand removed from a royal moneyer and hammered to the door of his mint for issuing debased coins, and in the next-to-last year of the Lionheart's reign, proposed enactment of harsher forest laws: to wit, for the first taking of the king's deer, blinding; for the second offense, castration; for the third instance, death. His monarch, never squeamish about bloodletting, approved the cruel code.

"Greed is your worst enemy. Bardulf proved to be greedy—and possibly a fool," Brewer went on, referring to his successor at Nottingham at the onset of John's reign. Sir Hugh Bardulf had sat with Brewer on Richard's council of advisors and seemed a reliable choice for sheriff. But upon his death three and a half years later, many men were found to be in his debt, suggesting that he had been either overgenerous with his private funds or had employed his surplus of crown revenues in clandestine usury. The latter was held more likely. "Greed I can understand, if not condone," the baron remarked, a momentarily faraway look in his eye. "It's only a sin and can be forgiven—at a price. But stupidity is inexcusable."

And so Brewer was reassigned to Nottingham to clean up the mess Bardulf had left. By then the full dimension of the financial dilemma besetting the crown had been borne home to its wearer. Richard's crusading, ransom, and subsequent wars in France had bled the treasury dry. That stark financial fact darkened John's joy upon ascending the throne and contributed heavily to his decision to make what some thought a shameful peace with France, accepting Philip Augustus as liege lord for his French territories and a fine of twenty thousand pounds on top of it. "Softsword" they called him after that, but others judged it prudent statecraft.

The resulting peace allowed John greatly to improve the governing of England. The Chancery and Exchequer were established at Westminster as the nexus of an orderly royal administration. Careful records of all crown transactions were made and kept for the first time. Judicial eyres were held more frequently, the king himself presiding on occasion. The currency was reformed as the old mill-edged silver penny, so easily clipped and thereby debased, was replaced by one with a smooth protruding rim. And the king with his court moved incessantly about the realm, the better to grasp its problems, minister to its needs, and solidify his hegemony, if not his place in the hearts of his countrymen.

All these efforts proved costly. Costlier still were John's provocative renewal of hostilities on the continent, the loss of Normandy and his Angevin holdings, and his subsequent delusionary attempts to rewin them.

Defeated abroad, the king now insisted on strengthening his island fortress lest the French invade or stir the Scots, the Welsh, and the Irish to rise against him. A navy was built, a standing militia organized, and castles were constructed or reinforced, especially on the perimeter of the homeland.

Compounding these heavy expenses was an unprecedented inflation, fed in large part by a sharp rise in demand for luxury goods from the Levant—a byproduct of the crusades—and burgeoning mercantile activity throughout Europe. This development heartened the merchants and land-holders of England, in particular the latter, whose crops fetched ever higher prices without a corresponding rise in the cost of their enslaved laborers. The king's growing army of retainers, however, and the supplies they consumed had to be paid for—and since it cost twice as much to keep a knight in the field as in his brother's day, the severity of his dilemma was soon manifest.

There was but one solution; and the king's chamberlains, chancellors, and clerks labored mightily to devise variants on it. Royal fees that had once been optional, like charter renewals upon the succession of a new king, were made mandatory. Inheritances now became dependent upon payment of a duty often set sky-high and varying with the inheritor's distance from the king's favor. Fines and amercements grew likewise arbitrary, sometimes punitively so. The scutage tax, in lieu of military service due the crown, and the tallage of tribute that every landholder owed his lord—both heretofore imposed only now and then—were levied habitually. Taxing of incomes and chattels, once strictly an emergency measure, was deemed a patriotic necessity. And taxes never before applied, like import duties and an impost on wine, were introduced.

To see that this intricate system was properly expedited in the shires, Brewer was recalled from Nottingham and installed at Westminster as royal watchdog. His place in Nottinghamshire was taken by Robert de Vieuxpont, the younger son in a junior branch of a noble Anglo-Norman family who had risen rapidly in the crown's favor from a sergeant in Richard's forces defending Normandy to sheriff with vast holdings in the troublesome shires along the Scottish border. Vieuxpont agreed to provide the crown one hundred pounds beyond the traditional tax "farm" for Nottinghamshire and Derbyshire; but when he fell repeatedly behind, more likely from lax oversight of the castle staff than from cupidity, he was heavily fined as an object lesson and removed from his post.

"And Vieuxpont, bear in mind, is a favorite of the king," Brewer underscored as he drew himself up and regarded his student with deadly intensity. In neighboring Lincolnshire, he added, where Thomas of Moulton, less beloved by the crown than Vieuxpont, had similarly contracted for the sheriffship, failure had recently led not only to a fine and removal from office but imprisonment as well. "As I say, this is not a king to cross lightly."

"I thank you, sire."

"I doubt you'll be thanking me for long—it's not an enviable assignment, Captain, however vital. You've been given it—you and d'Athiés and de Burgh and that little mad dog Fawkes and the rest of our French heroes—because it's become ungodly hard to find capable men of suitable standing to take the job. But I think you'll find it preferable to languishing in a Capetian gaol."

"My gratitude to the crown is boundless, sire, I can assure—"

"Yes, yes, but make no mistake—you were rescued not merely to repay your fortitude at Loches but because the crown has its uses for men of steadfast devotion to it." The baron rose, his physique a reinforcement of his iron voice, and placed his left fist over his heart and his right hand upon the hilt of his broadsword. "May God go with you to Nottingham, Philip Mark." His glower lightened momentarily and his voice softened. "It's not a bad place when you get to know it."

But could he endure it long enough to gain that pleasure? The question was much with him as he caught sight of the castle now for the first time. The dark, hulking mass of it, stout ramparts a ghostly gray, stood anchored to an immense crag of red sandstone, aflame in the late-afternoon sun. Then all their eyes were fixed upon it. His older daughter stirred uncomfortably in the saddle she shared with him, knowing without his telling her that this fearsome fortress was their new home.

"I thought it would be beautiful," the child said.

"And so it is," her father said. "You'll see."

As the highway dipped toward the river, the plainer it became to him why the Conqueror himself had picked this overlook "to bridle the English," as tradition had him saying. The enormous rock table holding the citadel was unapproachable on its southern and western flanks, where it towered above the valley of the Trent and the stout bridge that opened the way north. To shield the castle on the east, where the terrain was undulating but negotiable, and on the north, where it was level, a great moat had been dug and massive earthworks molded and strengthened over the decades. No castle was impregnable if besieged long enough, but this mighty bulwark looked to him a fair bet to weather Armageddon.

The road from Lincoln joined theirs at the south end of the Trent Bridge, still choked with carts bringing grain to town from the alluvial farmlands east of it and bearing away charcoal from Sherwood and dyed wool spun from the finest flocks in two shires. When their party had safely crossed to the Nottingham side, Philip signaled to his bachelor brother, Peter, who, having consigned his lance to one of the carters, drew up alongside and carefully hoisted the tired but unprotesting Angelique from her father's saddle onto his own. Stone castles needed hard men, not adoring fathers, in charge of them.

"Be brave now, pet," he called to her as her uncle's horse fell back.

"You be brave, too, Papa," the little girl piped.

Half a mile farther, the huddled masses and blunt towers of the town rose up to meet them, and to the west they could distinguish the crenellations on the castle breastworks. Philip turned to the groom and instructed him to unfurl the royal pennon—a purple field with three golden lions rampant—that sheriffs and their deputies bore with them in traveling the realm. A moment after the ensign was hoisted, an answering series of shrill, triple-noted blasts sounded from atop the donjon tower and rolled in quavering volleys down upon them across the intervening meadow.

ANNE MARK KNEW WELL the charmlessness of castles, having endured several where her husband was stationed. But this one, on first encounter, was particularly dispiriting, if only because of the apparent solidity of the scum encrusting the moat that lay before its formidable gates. No would-be invader tumbling into it by misfortune, she judged, could long survive the foul effluvia. And what unspeakable water creatures lurked beneath, ready to dismember the intruder? Surely the royal keepers of Nottingham Castle might from time to time skim that thick coverlet of green slime.

Within, conditions did not much improve. The rushes strewn about the floors were gritty with bits of bone, bread, dried meat, and vermin feeding off the foregoing and appeared to have gone unchanged since Pentecost, possibly Easter. Devereaux, the castle steward, was nonplussed by her disapproving surveillance. "A more pleasing cleanliness and fresh greens had been planned," he remarked, "but we were advised the sheriff's arrival had been delayed."

"And does not his deputy as well warrant such preparations, sire?" she asked with pique at the steward's hauteur.

"Our undersheriffs generally have more urgent concerns than tidiness, Madame Mark, and rarely reside at the castle *en famille.*"

The larger debris at least was gathered into the corners of corridors and chambers, awaiting—Devereaux assured her—fortnightly disposal and meanwhile emitting a nice variety of aromas of decay. These were nothing, though, compared to what greeted her as they advanced to the second storey. There the garderobes were clustered about a shaft emptying into a cesspit, which sent up a stench that set her nostrils aquiver; it could not have been mucked out since the king's last visit—or the one before that. "It is the heat, madame," the steward said in dismissal of the rank air as they approached the residential apartments. "A fresh layer of straw will be put down the pit in the morning."

"I fear," she said, "that something more drastic may be required."

The halls and chambers, a good deal darker than in other castles of her acquaintance, hinted of indifference to all amenity. What torches there were produced a markedly resinous and smoky effect in betrayal of the raw quality of wood used. Even the few hearths where fires had been set burned with a low flame, so that the gyrating shadows their small party cast in passing through those gigantic halls were of such sinister size and blackness that her little girls gripped the edges of her bliaut in terror.

The undersheriff's apartment was but half the size of the sheriff's, and while this no doubt accorded with protocol, it made no sense whatever to her. There was no telling when, if ever, Gerard d'Athiés would come, and the likelihood of his bringing his family, in view of the demands on him elsewhere, was remote. Still, she could not protest the cramped, spartan quarters or the droppings of the last occupant's goshawk that formed a petrified mound in one corner. Nor was she at liberty to remark on the state of repair of the great hall when they arrived there to sup. Of imposing dimensions, the vaulted ceiling was badly stained at one end and said by the page who served them to leak visibly in inclement weather for lack of funds to fix it. The condition of the food was not so readily explained. The meat was unchewable and just this side of spoiled; the fowl, pink to raw, with pinfeathers still in place; the wine, thick, sour, moldy, and smacking of pitch from the casks. The ale at least was potable—a product, they were told, supplied by the Inn of the Trip to Jerusalem, an establishment carved out of the base of the southern flank of the castle rock and renowned locally for its fare. "Alas," Anne remarked on learning of it, "that I do not attend alehouses!"

After shepherding her children off to sleep with their nursemaid, she saw to it that the accommodations assigned to her brothers-in-law were tolerable. The steward, not having bargained for an entire colony of Marks, had tucked Peter and Reginald and his family into the paltriest of servants' quarters adjacent to the sheriff's apartments. It would have to do while Philip explored how to put his brothers to use. Their worth to him was marginal at best, but they were not bad sorts, really. Reginald, the older, was taciturn, possibly slow-witted (he did not say enough to tell for certain), but kindly withal and able enough with a mace. Peter, by contrast, was almost too voluble, even brash at times, excelling only in self-indulgence and prone to shirk. Philip's solicitude for them, Anne thought, went beyond fraternal affection at times. What had been the need for bringing them over from France? Their endangerment there had been more in Philip's imagining than in fact. Frankly, they were just so much excess cargo so far as Philip's fortunes were concerned. Hadn't he quite enough burdens as it was, settling in a new country with her and the children? His nature was entirely too noble for his own good—and hers as well, perhaps.

The groom helped her arrange their few furnishings while Philip was off acquainting himself with his new subordinates. The task accomplished, she dismissed the lad and drifted to the far end of the apartment, where she pushed open the oiled-hide window. A light breeze flew in, only faintly redolent of the congealed moat. She looked out but could see little under the new moon. Suddenly out of the enveloping dark the premonition assailed her that this forbidding place would prove a prison for her every bit as horrid as the one Philip had escaped through the merciful offices of his king and the silver of his father-in-law. But she would not yield to the foreboding, for to do so would have been tantamount to confessing she no longer believed that Philip was overseen by a providential star.

It was less the sense of imperishability about him than one of self-command that had drawn her at once to him when he first appeared in her family's parlor in Tours. The newly designated seneschal of the royal castle there, he had come as the guest of her father, the town's leading importer of spices and other exotic comestibles, who was eager to make the acquaintance of so useful a purchasing agent. Philip Mark was slender as a marsh reed, with a veiled muscularity to his lank frame and a fineness to the features of his narrow face. He had a thin mustache and thinning sandy hair above a wide, high brow and kept his beard short, indeed almost too precisely shorn. The smallish dark eyes had a way of gauging carefully without staring and remaining in direct contact not an instant longer than needed to establish the intensity of his purpose. His tenor voice was mellow, with a slight sibilance to his speech and an exactness of diction that revealed a mind honing each phrase and calculating its effect before it was uttered. Everything about him bespoke an introspective man with a tensile, coiled quality to him, as if he feared the free play of word or gesture or emotion would somehow undo him. Even so, there was a decided grace to his movements, although it would have been unkind to call him dashing, for his left leg had been malformed or injured and caused him to walk with a slightly irregular gait. He compensated for this with an admirable uprightness of bearing, narrow shoulders thrust back and a hand playing over his scabbard as if in constant vigil. She sensed a defensive quality in this posture, not the tendencies of a ready killer. This Philip Mark, something told her, was a soldier in name only.

While they dined, he was responsive but reserved in meeting her father's polite inquiries. Of his origins he revealed only that he was native to the region between the Cher and Indre valleys, not a full day's ride below the Loire, and the second son of a lesser liegeman of the viscount of Touraine. Primogeniture made him an unlikely heir to his family's modest manor, but he would have been a still less promising husband for Anne or her older sister had the captain revealed the entire truth of his circumstances.

Strictly speaking, he was indeed the second son of a minor nobleman, but he was born to the seamstress of the manor, not to his father's wife, who had proven barren. The same was true of Philip's brothers. Their father chose to allay his disappointment by siring progeny out of wedlock with the comeliest of the maidens in his service. This compensatory practice did not escape his wife's notice, and, far from countenancing it out of guilt for her failure to fulfill the role nature had intended for her, she took his wandering lust most unkindly. Whatever hopes he had harbored of legitimizing the issue of his and the seamstress's loins were dashed by his wife's replenished rage at each new gurgling arrival. She wished the infants banished from sight and their mother carelessly eviscerated. But Seigneur Marque (as his name was spelled) would neither appease his anguished wife nor dignify his sons by making them his heirs against her fierce objection. He acknowledged their existence only to the extent of providing them and their mother with marginal comfort and presenting her at each birth with a small gold crucifix on a chain, to be affixed to the infant as soon as he was unlikely to swallow it. The lads were not allowed to tarry about the manor house lest they take on airs of gentility; instead, each was set, the moment he was robust enough, to physical labor—Reginald as a swineherd, Philip as a stableboy, and Peter to help the smith. Of them only Philip displayed more than loutishness. On his thirteenth birthday, his father arranged through the village curate, and a sizable bribe, for the boy to be removed from the manor and employed as a groom at Château de St. George, the royal castle Henry of Anjou had built at Chinon, some twenty miles distant.

Doubtless fearful that Anne would reject him as unfit, possibly degenerate, had she the knowledge of his illegitimacy, Philip had never disclosed it to her. She was told of it one night a year or so after their marriage when Philip was off on royal business and his younger brother had come to Tours to visit, overindulged himself, and blurted the truth. Sober by morning, Peter begged her never to disclose his lapse—and she never had. But in exchange she demanded of him a full account of Philip's youth, which he himself had but sparingly shared with her, likely as much from modesty as from shame. In bits and pieces over many a year he had disclosed the details to his brothers, for whom he felt an abiding love surely stemming from the shared pain of their unacknowledged paternity. Anne listened transfixed to the rest of Peter's revelations.

At his new home in the royal castle at Chinon, Philip thrived in the stableyard under the tutelage of the childless marshal, who lavished on the lad the father's dotage he had never known. The boy worked dutifully, rising to set the smith's fire before cock-crow and never slacking the day long. In time he became a precocious judge of horse flesh and horsemanship, a deft handler of tack and armor, and knowledgeable about weapons and fodder. The marshal's clerk taught him to read and write his native tongue, with a touch of Latin for good measure. Soon he was the most accomplished and devoted groom at the castle, having several times been of service to the visiting King Henry, whose broad shoulders and huge round head were no more than five feet from him. For respite the boy would attend the tourneys of the region, dazzled by the snapping pennants, the phalanx of knights chanting as they passed the pavilion on their caparisoned chargers, the dash and surge and brute impact of the dusty combat, the glory of the prancing victors, and the bereavement of the sprawled and dented vanquished.

One day while exercising a charger in the castle's outer ward, Philip was quick to intercept a runaway mount carrying the seneschal's daughter. Her grateful father saw to it that Philip was offered the position—and the certain adventure accompanying it—of groom to the seneschal's nephew, a lackluster knight badly in need of tending. Philip leapt at the chance to serve even so hapless a paladin as Sir Simon des Nuages. The lad's zeal was such that after completing his own tasks, he took on as well the ones neglected by Sir Simon's palpably contemptuous squire and page. Soon the knight's shaggy charger was properly curried, his caparison clean and tack in good repair, his armor polished, weaponry honed, and supplies ample. Philip even saw to it as no one else had that Sir Simon left enough time to journey to the tourneys in which he was entered and never managed to arrive at before the melee. His reward for these exertions was the steady abuse of Sir Simon's squire, who took pleasure in addressing Philip as "Pond Scum" and reminding him at every opportunity that one who was to the cesspit born could never become a knight.

Lacking both prowess and resolve, Sir Simon fared poorly at tourneys and struggled to preserve his knighthood. When his squire, humiliated by association with a knight manqué, abandoned him, the page soon followed. Sir Simon took consolation in Philip's faithfulness and designated him squire, page, and groom rolled into one overworked bundle. And it saved the knight money. Now Philip also shaved and bathed him, fed and sobered him, dressed and armed him, devotedly wrapped a cloth around his head and fitted his helmet gingerly over it before he entered the lists, and tended the wounds and bruises that he inevitably acquired in the fray.

To survive in the field, Sir Simon took to pillage, at which—since he was heavily armed and his victims were not—he excelled. Philip would look on glumly from afar as his master enlisted in raiding parties, ostensibly defending the interests of the king and viscount. They assaulted castles and manors delinquent in taxes or chary of tribute, laid waste the fields of gentry and peasantry with impartiality, stole from abbeys that did not promptly pay them welcome, and torched rebel towns more for the joy of the spectacle than any tactical advantage.

On one foray against an adulterine castle of more wood than stone in nearby Maine, Philip rode in the wake of the raiding party as it readily broke through the gates and systematically slaughtered the defenseless commoners within, lancing some, heaving others off the ramparts, leaving still others drawn and quartered or blinded and emasculated—or all of those—to crawl about in a bloody mass until they expired in a puddle of their own making. The defending knights and resident gentry, by contrast, were spared and taken off for ransom. It was not chivalry's shining hour, Philip thought as he gathered booty among the dead and dying. Recognizing as never before the central fact of life in his world—there were only masters or servants, nobles or commoners, and the latter in each instance counted for little this side of Heaven—he swore to himself then and there somehow to contrive entry into those exalted ranks against whom butchery did not go unanswered.

On one of Sir Simon's bloody outings, his party was surrounded and taken prisoner, but Philip eluded the captors and rode furiously through hostile countryside to King Henry's camp, which he knew to be four leagues distant. A rescue mission was dispatched at once, and the freed Sir Simon shortly concluded that his life could better be spent in the mastery of chess and minstrelsy than at feckless knight errantry. His parting gift to Philip was an appointment as royal messenger for Touraine, circuiting among the castles at Chinon, Tours, and Loches. He proved swift, clever, and observant at this occupation, all the while familiarizing himself with the habits of speech, thought, and civility of the titled and their retainers.

Fortune interceded in Philip's second year at this task when he one day was required to deliver a letter of diseissin to a tenant of the crown who had for too long withheld his tallage. Unhappy at the prospect of dispossession but unable to pay what he owed, the nobleman took out his frustration on Philip by forcing him to eat the punishing message, waxen seal and all. This act of craven defiance, which the decidedly dyspeptic messenger at once reported, was met with a bristling reprisal party of knights and men-at-arms, whom Philip was invited to accompany. But they were waylaid by a still larger party gathered around the unremorseful delinquent, and all at once Philip found himself beside the unhorsed and disarmed leader of the royal band, who was about to be ridden down by a mace-wielding foe. Philip scurried for a loose sword and at the last moment thrust it into the steaming flanks of the onrushing attack horse, sending its rider flying and sparing his intended victim. Alas, another mounted attacker turned his fury on Philip and dealt him a fierce blow of the mace, which caught and shattered his left leg. The royalists managed to rally long enough to gather their wounded and make an orderly retreat.

At the castle Philip was hailed a hero and much fussed over while his leg mended, a bit shorter than the other, reducing his nimbleness and causing him pain while he rode that would not subside for years. Told to name his reward for the courage he had displayed, Philip asked only to be made a squire. But the wish was not granted. At first he was told the rejection traced to his injury, which would prevent the full performance of a squire's duties. When the plucky lad struggled to disprove the charge, it was left to the seneschal at Chinon to concede the truth to him—that his low birth disqualified him from candidacy for the knighthood, as Simon's squire had cruelly forecast.

He wept to himself long into the night. Yet by dawn he had not succumbed to despair simply because the shortest pathway to acquired gentility was denied him. Instead, he vowed to conduct himself from that moment forth as if in fact he were already a knight of the most valorous order; in a wolfish world he would abide by a code of the highest rectitude, finer than any he had ever witnessed in practice. If his virtue were rewarded, he would know serenity. If reward were delayed, he would persevere. If his destiny were to be naught but anguish and degradation, perhaps there would be recompense, as they said, in Heaven. But the prospect of Heaven seemed to him chancy at best—Paradise was likely to prove as devoid of bliss as of pain.

They made him head groom and then deputy to his beloved marshal at Chinon. By way of advanced military training, Philip worked long and hard to perfect his skills as an archer; the bow was no weapon for a knight, perhaps, but none was more essential for a defender of castles. The chaplain taught him serviceable Latin, and he grew at ease in his intercourse with gentry. The once unprepossessing stableboy knew his worth now and saw to it by grace of word and virtuosity of performance that no one would ever scorn him again.

As it happened, half the knights of Touraine were off on the great crusade when the marshal succumbed to apoplexy, and with such a dearth of candidates to succeed him, scant objection greeted the viscount's appointment of Philip Mark, an esteemed commoner (and illegitimate at that), as the marshal of Chinon. At twenty-four, he was an officer of rank in the royal service of Richard Coeur de Lion.

Unexceptionable devotion to his post for the ensuing seven years had won him the added title of captain by the day the king fell in the Limousin and Prince John arrived breathless at Chinon, having fled the clutches of those surrounding his nephew Arthur, his sole rival for the throne. John had turned instinctively to Chinon to help himself to the royal treasury at the castle; money would arm him against whatever contingencies lay ahead on the road through Maine and Normandy to Westminster. Emboldened by the drama of history on his doorstep, Philip proposed to the prince's marshal that the royal party take the entire garrison of the castle with them as far as Rheims to protect the head that would wear the crown. He added that as a safeguard in the event of mishap, the five thousand pounds of bagged silver pennies they were to bear away ought to be hidden in a compartment that could be attached to the underside of their wagons. Anxious to be off but persuaded of the good sense of the proposal, John's marshal asked how long such a safeguard would take to install. Philip promised that it would not exceed an afternoon—and by application of every hand and tool in the stableyard, including his own ten fingers, the task was accomplished.

The prince had then thundered off to his destiny without so much as a nod his way, so Philip grew reconciled that he could expect no reward for merely performing his duty to the royal Plantagenets. But four months later to the day, he was in receipt of letters patent from London designating him seneschal of the castle at Tours, a day's ride northeast of Chinon and a far more metropolitan setting than any he had known. Within three weeks, he found himself a guest in the imposing stone house of the town spice merchant and at table with his two daughters. It was the younger one, with her fair face, pleasingly low voice, and darting smile, who beguiled him.

Growing up in Tours, long a center of trade, amid the bustle in one of the town's more prosperous mercantile houses, Anne caught all the currents of the age: news of fratricidal battles for succession in this county, the appalling crop conditions in that duchy, the latest alignment of the Rhenish principalities, rumors of perversion on the Ile de France, at the papal court, in Saladin's realm, even in Araby, where men were said to take many wives and fondle them seriatim. She was tutored in faith and literature by monks from the nearby collegiate church school, taught to mend, tidy, sing, lay a table, speak demurely, chew with refinement, and otherwise bear herself like a titled lady, for the family nourished hope she might become one. By thirteen she could recite whole cantos of the *Chanson de Roland* from memory for the amusement of her parents' guests. Against her mother's wishes she even became a fair match for her father at chess and backgammon, and twice she accompanied him on the five-day ride to Paris to see the great city and the sublime cathedral rising in its midst. All in all, Captain Mark had never encountered a more knowing and spirited young woman of quality. Her occasional sauciness infiltrated his carefully staid demeanor and brought laughter to his taut lips.

Philip's visits grew more frequent, along with purchase orders from the castle for her father's goods. All suggestions, though, that the captain accept a small percentage of the purchase price for his considerateness were politely declined. He had but one gift in mind for the family to bestow.

Whether Anne would have wedded Philip with full knowledge of his parentage was as uncertain as whether he would have had her if he had been informed in advance of her own dark secret. The particulars as she reviewed them in her mind grew less heinous with the passage of time; they were no more, really, than the mindless exuberance of youth.

As she was growing to womanhood, she would take occasional pleasure in self-arousal, which in the first instance was dutifully confessed to the priest. He seemed little distressed by her disclosure, perfunctorily granting absolution upon her pledge to abstain forthwith and pray for God's forgiveness. On reflection, Anne wondered how this small private act could have been of the slightest interest to the Almighty and why, furthermore, He might have provided her with such an anatomical arrangement if it had not been intended for use. Concluding that she had debased herself only in the priest's eye and not the Lord's—and least of all her own—she renewed the practice and omitted its mention in the confessional.

It was not a long leap from regularly gratifying this impulse to the one of being pleasured by another, at first with a young housemaid and then—more perilously, as she well understood—by a bulky youth who toiled at a nearby atelier devoted to the fashioning of stained glass. He had the face and physique of an Olympian god, she told herself (although in truth she had but the shallowest basis for conjuring the image of any Greek, divine or mortal). She took to slipping out of her house and into his workshop, even when he was there late and alone, and in admiring his craftsmanship she did not shrink from coquetry, then more overt intimacies, culminating one sultry summer twilight in the ultimate act.

Aware that its nature was more repugnant to the Lord than any offense she had yet committed, she begged Him for mercy and then, still more abjectly, that He might spare her the full penalty of a seeded womb. When her fervent prayers were answered, she rejoiced in this sign of renewed grace yet felt her expiation could not be complete until knowledge of the liaison had been shared. She chose as confidante her older sister, Adrienne. This proved unwise. On the premise that Anne needed to be insulated from her own sordid impulses before her ruin was final—but more probably from envy of her sister's fairer face and form—Adrienne told her mother, who, in the full flush of hysteria, prescribed the convent as her younger daughter's only route to purgation. When Anne resisted, saying she saw no reason why her lapse need be advertised to the world, her mother embroidered lavishly on the primal value of the maidenhead: no man of position was likely to accept a damaged woman in wedlock. Unable to reveal that that critical membrane had been worn away by her earlier engagement with self-pleasuring, Anne said only that she would confront the problem herself when and if need arose.

In the event, Philip proved gallant enough not to mention her small lacuna—unless he was merely obtuse, which she doubted, or embittered by this violation of her assumed warranty but powerless to undo their plighted troth. Lacking pedigree himself, though, was he in any position to demand such purity? At any rate, he adored her; and besides, she came with a not inconsiderable dowry of two hundred pounds. She found him more than tolerable in every way and hoped, in time, to turn her fondness into passion. Her family, sure their soiled daughter could make no better match than a civilized if landless crown officer, blessed the union.

Their rhapsodic wedding night gave way to the harsher reality that she had married a military officer and that barracks life, even at a castle, was far more austere than the vibrant existence Anne had known. Privacy was awkwardly managed, and Philip's duties required him to be less attentive to her than she had hoped. At his suggestion she began to divide her time between the castle and her family's home, so that their hours together, while reduced, gained in congeniality.

In their second year of marriage, Philip was appointed seneschal and deputy castellan of the royal castle at Loches, a long day's ride southeast of Tours. Dutifully she followed him to the bleaker outpost, where the

sole point of cultural interest was the pair of huge stone pyramids sur-
mounting the nave at the church of Saint Ours in the monastery complex
around which the little town had grown. Cold and obdurate as she imagined
them to the touch, the pyramids nonetheless struck her as a far more
suitable emblem of man's aspiration to perfect piety than the crucifix, which
was more truly a memento of human folly and barbarism. She dared to
pass on this conceit to the curate, who stared at her in bewilderment over
so blatant a heresy. Thereafter she avoided speculations on iconography
and all other spiritual matters until, finding herself gravid and dreading
God's delayed wrath for the sins of her youth, she took to attending both
morning and evening prayer. In between she amused herself by watching
Philip drill the castle garrison in the deadly art of the crossbow, at which
he demanded accuracy from three hundred meters.

It was a wearying existence for her and surely no place to bring a
child into the world. Conditions grew still less hospitable when the fragile
peace between John and Philip Augustus was broken and the Bretons in
the west, the fickle Poitevins and the irascible Lusignans to the south,
and the probing outriders of the Capetian crown from the northeast turned
the territory between the Loire and Aquitaine into a vast no-man's-land
of rapidly shifting loyalties. Anne went home to bear Angelique, and Philip
rode to Tours two days afterward, joyfully embraced mother and babe,
ordered them to remain among the comforts of home, and within the third
hour of his arrival, rode off again to tend to the fortifications at Loches.
She saw him but once monthly after that as the fighting in Normandy
reached new levels of intensity, atrocities both military and civilian became
commonplace, and John of England's Angevin hegemony waned by the
week. Touraine, though, remained a zone of relative safety due largely to
the efforts of Captain Gerard d'Athiés, whose battalion of mercenaries
patrolled the county and, by bloodying the waverers, kept it from defecting
massively to France.

After two draining years, Normandy was lost, John's English barons
and knights had abandoned the Continent, and the forces of the French
king turned south, linking with the Bretons and the Poitevins, who now
pledged unmitigated fealty to Philip Augustus. Touraine was marooned
and in imminent peril so long as it resisted. And resist it did. For months
the French forces harassed John's castles at Chinon, under the resolute
command of Hubert de Burgh, and at Loches, where Gerard d'Athiés's
troops were now garrisoned and Captain Philip Mark supervised the de-

fense. Harassment turned into full-scale siege as the summer of 1205 lengthened, and no more messages reached Anne in bypassed Tours. She braced for the worst.

Chinon fell first after Hubert's garrison, supplies and resolve depleted, abandoned the fortress and tried in vain to fight its way to safety. Loches, more amply supplied, thanks to Philip's indefatigable preparations, struggled on, a tiny island surrounded by a pounding sea. The long hours of drill he had imposed were vindicated by the punishing toll his crossbowmen exacted. But the enemy redoubled its efforts, showering the fortress with flaming missiles for weeks without letup. Sleepless vigilance, unremitting resistance to the siege engines, and gravely cut food stores wore the garrison down to its last ounce of strength—and then there were no arrows left to loose.

When the battered gates at Loches at last gave way, the foot soldiers and villagers who had taken refuge within were hacked to pieces by the French king's vengeful legions. Only Captains d'Athiés and Mark and a handful of other castle officers were spared—Philip, in defeat, had achieved at least the victory of survival accorded the master class—and carted off to imprisonment in Angiers. It took Philip's last coin to send word to Anne that, amidst the debacle and butchery, he still lived.

But that life was tenuous indeed, confined to a filthy dungeon, where even royal captains were denied all dignity, and made endurable only by the companionship of Gerard and Hubert and his lingering hopes for reunion with Anne and the infant daughter he scarcely knew.

The captives were duly offered for ransom, but for two months no reply came from Westminster. Ordered to write letters to London pleading for their rescue, they refused their gaolers and suffered near-starvation rations in reprisal. Philip's courage dwindled and self-sorrow bloomed. He had labored long and assiduously at every station he had drawn in life, obeyed his superiors to the hilt, dealt justly with his subordinates as he acquired them, painstakingly mastered the science of defensive warfare, and, when called upon at Loches, fought without stinting in a forlorn cause. And for his travail, he found himself in his thirty-eighth year in a godforsaken pit, likely abandoned by his king, and nearly conceding that his embrace of unrequited virtue had been the rankest of follies.

It was then that the king of England offered to buy the freedom of his heroic captains. But the price did not suit the French, so Anne Mark prevailed upon her father to supplement the crown's tender. Philip at first balked at Anne's intervention; it was King John's place to redeem him, he wrote her, not the obligation of a merchant of Tours. Immediately upon receipt of his letter, Anne hurried aboard the first boat down the Loire to Angiers, demanded and won a brief audience with her husband, swallowed her horror at his wasted appearance, and, summoning iron to her voice, said, "Your pride or your life—which is it to be?"

"I'm a soldier—and have my honor," Philip whispered, tears in his eyes at the sight of his beloved.

"You're a man as well—and a husband and a father. And there is no dishonor in purchasing your life from thieves. Don't play the fool a moment longer."

He yielded to her, insisting only that the terms of his liberation provide as well for passage to England of his brothers, detained at Tours, where they had served at the castle through Philip's influence. He feared, he said, for their persecution because of his feats. The ransom price rose accordingly, but Anne's father met it, and a month later the Marks were in England, Anne's dowry intact, courtesy of precisely the same deception in packing their carts as Philip had prescribed for Prince John en route to his throne six years earlier.

For three years Philip and his rescued confreres moved about England, captains without fixed duties, of use whenever a show of military force was tactically desirable, while Anne had her second child near Windsor at the apartments set aside for the French refugees. She had grown disheartened by this makeshift life when the crown's growing need for utterly dependable—and dependent—sheriffs brought relief. Gerard was assigned to the Marcher counties, Hubert de Burgh to Lincolnshire, and Philip to Nottingham as Gerard's deputy.

She sensed him behind her now as she drew a final breath of night air and reached back to give his cheek and beard a slow caress. "How is it with them?"

"They're all very guarded—it's to be expected. The bailiff especially so. He's used to instructing the undersheriff, I suspect—not receiving orders."

"He'll change."

"Not too soon, I hope. I'm in need of instruction just now." He encircled her waist from the rear, drew her tight against him, and stared out into the blackness. "They say the dead are being left in the caves above the town, because of the Interdict. They say it's a bad time."

"They probably always tell that to newcomers. And at least these dead weren't slain." She swiveled toward him without breaking his grip. "Oh, Philip, I'm so weary of wars and warring!"

"It's what soldiers do."

She nodded, then fell pensive for a time. "I think this sheriffing will be better. It suits you." She brightened then. "But you must see to their crossbows."

·VI·

BEING THE JUNIORMOST of the castle clerks and perhaps the last member of the entire staff to be summoned to the sheriff's closet off the lesser hall, Sparks approached the doorway with brimming anxiety. His palms were moist, his heart hurrying, and he had devoted the previous quarter of an hour to subduing a persistent case of the hiccoughs.

The sight of the French captain bent over the shire rolls, apparently in deep study, did nothing to lessen the clerk's concern for his fate at the hands of this outlander, slim and neat as a dagger—and perhaps just as deadly. Philip Mark could read, which ipso facto made him more intellectually accomplished than any previous undersheriff Sparks had dealt with, and thus likely less pliable. There would be too many questions if he remained vigilant longer than a month, which was the usual span of attention for occupants of the office; thereafter, their own share of the castle receipts invariably became the concern overriding all else. What turmoil this Captain Mark could wreak if he—

"Ah, Master Sparks," he said, glancing up as the clerk soundlessly materialized on his threshold.

"You sent for me, sire?"

The undersheriff rose and directed Sparks to the bench opposite him. "I thought it might prove useful for me to become a bit acquainted with you, as the others. Please seat yourself."

"Thank you, sire, but I prefer standing before my superiors."

"As you wish." The undersheriff, though, also remained standing, then moved off to the window and appeared to glance out of it at the activity in the inner ward. "They tell me at Westminster that you are of high competence but perhaps questionable piety."

The remark threw the little clerk off his precarious balance. He had least anticipated that a foreigner might have familiarized himself in advance with the minutiae of the castle regimen and personnel. "I—don't—know what . . ." Words left him.

"Do you deny the appraisal?"

"I—would not have thought . . . Westminster has so much else—to bear in mind that . . ."

"Come, come, Sparks. Surely you take no offense at the Exchequer's regard for your workmanship."

"It—merely—surprises me, sire, that I am recognized."

"Your modesty is becoming, to be certain. But what of your allegedly impious nature—a slander, no doubt, because you are not in orders?"

The clerk's mind spun. Why these quick, deep probes into his very core? "I—it is quite an old story, sire, going back to my youth."

"Tell it to me."

"I would not impose it on your time or good humor, sire."

"They wish to be imposed on."

Cautiously, yet pleased by the attention, Sparks recited the main points: his escape from serfdom at Swanhill by entering holy orders; his enrollment at Southwell Minster school; how he flew through the trivium, mastered Donatus's grammar, read hungrily from Aristotle to Augustine, perfected his writing hand by apprenticing with the second copyist, advanced fearlessly to the quadrivium—arithmetic, geometry, astronomy, and music—and even timidly made the acquaintance of Honorius, the minster's celebrated chronicler, who deigned to speak with him on more than one occasion of the crusades and other great events of the age.

"You are well schooled, then, Master Sparks."

"My academics were not at issue, sire."

"Only your faith?"

"Or so it was said."

"And how was this supposed faithlessness manifested?"

"I—it was long ago, sire—the details elude my memory."

"Recapture them." The undersheriff swung about toward him, making it plain he would brook no evasion.

This probing perplexed the clerk, but he sensed in it some purpose not inimical to him. "I asked too many questions—wondering aloud . . ."

"By way of example?"

"Oh, smallish things—of merely ecclesiastical concern. Such as the rule that monks should not eat rich, delicious fish like pike or salmon, since they are to follow the example of John the Baptist, partaking only of austere foods. I asked why, then, are rich fish of this kind, so much more succulent than, say, mutton, not explicitly prohibited on fast days. I was instructed that when Adam sinned, the earth but not the water was put under a curse, and fish of course are born of water, which is a purifier, and so are not proscribed. I found the explanation unpersuasive—and erred by saying so."

"That's all?"

"There were other such instances."

"Namely?"

"I recall the parable of the monk well supplied with victuals who meets a starving man on the high road. I was instructed that the cleric was not obliged to share his blessings because, though it is true the goods of Holy Church belong to the poor, they cannot be demanded at will by just any wayfarer. I thought that unworthy of our Saviour."

"And said as much?"

"Alas."

The corners of the undersheriff's mouth edged into a smile. "Your deficiency seems to have been in the area of tact rather than faith."

"In truth, sire—there was some of each. I delved into sacred dogma—of peculiar meaning to me. You would find it too tiresome . . ."

"Tell me."

The interrogation began to drain his strength. "It is written in the Thirty-Seventh Psalm that the meek shall inherit the earth, and I inquired if this did not in fact allude to the poor and forecast that they would inherit Heaven rather than the earth—that is to say, even the serfs have immortal souls worth saving. And since we impoverished comprise substantially the larger part of humanity, I thought it a question of some moment. It was greeted with consternation. In the end I was told that of course it was so, the psalm had reference to life everlasting and not any change in the laws of inheritance. And so then I asked whether, if Heaven is thus truly retributive, the rich and the poor are not mingled there—indeed, should the rich not serve the poor, reversing the order of things on earth? Still greater consternation followed. I was finally told that the accommodations of eternity are not for mortal knowledge in advance of salvation—that the rich, moreover, who are admitted beyond the heavenly portals must have comported themselves admirably in life, coping with the blessings of providence—and so it was spiteful to expect that the social distinctions on earth should be reversed upon arrival in Heaven. When I ventured that it was not spite at all but habitual humiliation that prompted my inquiry, the discussion was summarily closed."

"So," said the Frenchman, not displeased with this narrative, "you thought too deeply and spoke too much?"

"There are other things as well—from my end. The objections were not one-sided. Advances of an intimate nature from some older brethren that I repulsed. Couplings in the wood on the Sabbath of men in orders and women of feral appetites. The impassioned embrace of statues not as icons but as the living embodiment of the only Son of the Heavenly Father— in a word, idolatry. My disillusionment knew no bounds." Sparks's head slumped from the effort of recounting. "It was no surprise—a relief, frankly—when the chancellor of the minster himself drew me aside and said it was plain I was not suited to holy orders, that the chronicler had spoken of me to the chaplain at the castle, an erstwhile colleague during the latter's stay at the minster, and it was arranged that I should apprentice with Brother Jocelin—thank the Lord."

"And plainly, after this passage of time, Jocelin is pleased with you?"

"Tolerates me, I should say. I'm useful to him, but he remains incorrigibly suspicious of clerks who have abandoned holy orders."

The undersheriff reflected for a time and then moved back toward him. "Tell me, if you will, Master Sparks—who here is honest?"

"Sire?"

"Is the question murky?"

"I—why . . . I should say everyone here is honest, sire."

"Should you? Then why is it that Sheriff Vieuxpont was dismissed?"

"I cannot say, sire—possibly for reasons of state or politics."

"At Westminster they gravely suspect that much money is subtracted here before the receipts ever reach the royal treasury."

"I—only enter and keep the records of what funds are brought in to the castle by the bailiffs. Beyond that I know of no . . ."

The undersheriff took two steps closer to the little clerk so that no more than six feet separated them. "To be specific, Sparks, I have been told that you yourself are something of a petty thief."

His head swam and heart pounded from sudden dread. "I—I—I— should like to be seated now, sire, if it is still permitted."

"As you wish."

For years he had known the other clerks were clipping edges off the silver pennies that flowed through their hands by the thousands and having the shavings melted down to pay for the small comforts of life that their meager wages did not permit. Only when Jocelin finally entrusted him with a key to the treasury, a catacomb off the oblique tunnel they called the Hole to Hell in the deepest bowel of the castle, did he begin to dip into those neatly arrayed hundred-pound bags and barrels of pennies and do likewise. But then the assize of money had been promulgated by the Chancery, declaring any coin shaved by one-eighth below the standard weight to be outlawed. Much furtive weighing ensued lest the shire be found guilty of shortchanging the crown upon presentation of its tax collections. Since the year before, though, when Nottingham was made a full-scale royal repository, the situation had improved. With so many more coins at their disposal, his fellow clerks, Brothers Timothy and Gabriel, would disappear for long hours in the afternoon, methodically clipping the old pennies within the prescribed weight and sharing the fruits of their industry with Brother Jocelin. Sparks the infidel, Sparks the outsider, was excluded. A more wily subterfuge was called for on his part. He began inserting an occasional numeral I before a V or X in summing columns for the shire ledgers and thus could now and then filch a whole shilling without high risk of detection at the audit. He thought himself clever until he discovered that Jocelin, with too heavy a stroke of the quill to escape his assistant's eye, had been doing the same, probably for years.

He fought for breath and waited for his head to clear. "I deny the slander," Sparks said slowly and in obvious discomfort, "beyond a bit of penny-shaving—and that well within the standard of the law. It was a universal practice with the old coins, sire—there would be hardly a clerk left in England if all the coin shavers were gaoled. Our pay is so slender there is no alternative if one wishes even the most modest of life's pleasures—a visit to the alehouse, a new garment at Easter. . . ." The words tumbled from him lamely; he feared the crown's imminent wrath.

All the undersheriff said, though, was "Good day, Master Sparks. I feel we are well enough acquainted for the moment."

That same evening, unable to sleep from growing apprehension over his fate at the hands of this tormentor of an undersheriff—why had he revealed so much to him?—Sparks arose in his dormitory compartment and made his way to the top of the donjon tower, there to commune with the stars in Heaven and soothe his soul in the summer night. He rapped three times on the underside of the trapdoor to the roof, the signal to Ryder, the night watch, that a friend sought access. He heard in reply a slightly nasal demand for his identity. "The king's clerk Jared Sparks," he said almost jauntily, not recalling the last time a castle lookout had been so vigilant. Then the door creaked upward, and Sparks found himself face to face once more with Philip Mark.

"Sire—I—had no . . . Sergeant Ryder—is he not . . . ?"

"He's in the gaol." The undersheriff stepped aside and let Sparks clamber up the ladder; retreat was impossible now.

"What was his offense, sire?"

"I came here as you did—no doubt to breathe the air and drink in the night sky—and was not challenged. I found him fast asleep."

In the pale light that played over them from the crescent moon, he thought he could detect more sorrow than anger in Mark's expression. "Surely he has committed a grievous offense, sire. But need you stand his watch yourself?"

"For a time at least—it clears the brain." The Frenchman moved toward the parapet, and Sparks found himself drawn along. "Shall I dismiss him?" the undersheriff asked.

The clerk was startled by the question; Sheriff Brewer would by now have had the offender pitched directly off the tower. "You would not be faulted for it, sire."

"You beg the question, Sparks."

The tormentor was at him again. "In mitigation, sire, he has been a devoted servant of the crown. . . ."

"If inept."

"He's growing old. Perhaps another task might be found for him."

"A lesson must be made of his slackness."

"No doubt. But might not he be spared the ultimate indignity of—"

Mark's head turned dismissively away and toward the pinpoints of firelight broadcast over the vast blue-black blanket of countryside far below. After a moment he spoke anew with studied candor. "I was not entirely satisfied with our exchange this afternoon. I sought your appraisal of the honesty of the castle's people, and it was not forthcoming. Your answer was too quick and unpersuasive—no doubt protective of your colleagues."

His choice now was denial or concession. Perhaps he could slither in between. "With all due respect, sire, is that not understandable?"

"Yes—but no help to me whatever. I need counsel, Sparks—people whose judgment I can rely on. I thought that perhaps, given your learning and aptitudes, you might . . ." His voice trailed off, then regathered force. "I'll repeat it now, under the privacy of darkness. Who here is honest?"

Something about this man, so peculiar a meld of sternness and civility, reached out to Sparks—the vulnerability of his position as a foreigner, perhaps, and the directness of his attack—and penetrated his own protective armor. He had become so inured to trafficking in deceit in the interest of survival that he had failed at first to assess the potential gain in purveying its opposite to a needy customer. "If, sire, you mean scrupulously honest," he said, parceling each word with care, "then I should revise my earlier reply. We are all culpable—though some more grievously so."

"Need I press you for which ones?"

"I will not volunteer them, sire."

"Then speak of the bailiff first."

"There are many bailiffs—the castle houses a dozen with the chief, and each of the districts has its own."

"I had Master Manning in mind."

"The chief is—stolid—relatively efficient, I should guess—though the niceties of justice are said to elude him at times."

"He is an oppressor, then?"

"As oppressive as needs be, I should suppose."

"What need—whose need?"

"The demands on him by the castle."

"Demands? Whose demands?"

"The crown's, directly or not—the quantity of greed manifested."

"The bailiffs are extortionate, then, at the behest of the sheriff?"

"I should not put it quite thus, sire. It's more a relative thing—bailiffs need to live, too, and the crown provides but poorly for them. If they did not extract their pelf on their own, the crown should have to levy still higher taxes to pay them, so it would in any event come to the same thing. I shouldn't be overly harsh in my prejudgments, sire, if I were you."

Mark rubbed the knuckles of his left hand. "What of Master Aubrey?"

"The constable is lethargic—but few demands for improvement have been made upon him. We have had no sheriff in permanent residence within my ten years at the castle—and to the undersheriffs, all else is generally a matter of indifference so long as adequate revenues are gathered."

"Does he at least keep the castle militia in good order and on alert?"

"The nonperformance you witnessed by the watchman, I should think, bespeaks the mock state of military readiness here, sire. The funds allotted for it, I fear, find other, more private uses. But in mitigation, there is little perceived need for armed might beyond assisting the bailiffs now and then with a nasty case of diseissin. It would surprise me if the men-at-arms have their weapons sharpened from one year to the next."

The undersheriff reflected afresh on the delinquent watchman. "I think we'll leave Sergeant Ryder to languish in gaol for a week and then give him one chance to redeem himself."

"Probably more charity than he deserves—but I doubt he'll survive a week down there."

"Are the conditions of confinement so appalling?"

"They are as Master Plunk chooses to make them. He is a professional turnkey—cruelty is his nature."

"Can he be bribed?"

"I believe, sire, that everyone can be bribed—beginning, if you will forgive the blasphemy, with the king himself."

Mark smiled. "Now you are too candid by half, Master Sparks. Tell me of the steward."

"You ask me in entire confidence? I must live with these men—who would as soon have me boiled in lead as—"

"You have my word—the Lord is my witness."

Sparks breathed deeply and then proceeded, less slowly now, as if eager to make a clean breast of it all. "Master Devereaux is said to be yet more felonious than most of his calling. The prices he pays the castle vendors are for goods of the premium grade, but what we receive is often detectably inferior—mutton gone rank, half-wild chickens too tough to eat, fish with more bone than flesh. He likely pockets the difference. On top of that, he is a voluptuary. The maids of the castle vie for which of them will be pleasured in the steward's private apartment—which, I'm told, abounds with the trappings of luxury."

"The marshal?"

"A good hunter, I hear—but as to the castle stable, it is indifferently tended. The animals often turn up lame for want of shoeing."

"The barber?"

"Surgeon, he prefers—he cuts too close and with too dull a blade. He blames the smith for incompetence at the bellows."

"Your fellow clerks?"

Sparks hesitated. "Betrayal is not my vocation."

"If there's something in need of betrayal, I'll uncover it shortly."

"Perhaps that would be best."

"Don't toy with me, Sparks, or you'll join the watchman in irons."

Lip service to honor paid, Sparks expanded his indictment with relish. "Brother Jocelin is—well, clerkly."

"Meaning?"

"Dull—mechanical—at best marginally fit for the task of *receptor*—and his flatulence increases with age. But he is otherwise not notorious in any regard. As to Brothers Timothy and Gabriel, it is hard to distinguish them. The *receptores brevium* heed the rest of the world scarcely at all—and each other intently."

"They're efficient, though?"

"They have not been tested in that regard. The work here gets done all in good time—or not, as the case may be. There is little urgency about the castle's business."

"I'm told the coroner is different."

"To a fault. He covets the sheriffship and so makes it a point to alert Westminster of the worst irregularities—all under the delusion he will be rewarded with the office himself. Sir Mitchell has a venomous tongue."

"Why would he have used it against you in my interview with him?"

"Because I am a product, however flawed, of Southwell, and he is leagued with Lenton Priory through his knight's fee—an intimate of the prior, they tell me, and there is no love lost between the priory and the minster. Sir Mitchell might be said to perform his duties for the castle both adequately and mischievously. He avoids assassination by those he betrays only because his victims have already been removed from office by the time the coroner's role in their undoing is suspected. It was thus with Vieuxpont."

The undersheriff gave a series of short nods, peered out over the battlement, and idly ran a hand over the top of a merlon worn smooth by the elements. "And what, finally, of the chaplain?"

"I cannot speak of him with dispassion. I owe my presence here to Father Ivo's intercession. He is an altogether different sort of being from the rest—more mindful of enduring things—more troubled by the nature of life. I should value his counsel above all others, sire—if you can extract it. He tends to view sheriffs and their deputies as the king's licensed looters. And I have been unable to disabuse him of the thought."

In the morning, Brother Timothy, his glee barely contained, was the first to advise Sparks that his replacement was already being sought. The undersheriff had asked the coroner—who was ebullient in his disclosure of the inquiry to the clerk, Timothy slyly inserted—to consult with Prior Clement about a suitable candidate to assist the *receptor* in Sparks's stead. Brother Jocelin himself was said to be but minimally aggrieved by the impending loss.

Soon called to the sheriff's closet to receive the coup de grâce, Sparks could not mask his rage at this French viper's exploitive treachery and his own gullibility. "You look the victim of a sleepless night," Mark said to him with the faintest edge of irony and no hint of remorse.

"It was not the night that has undone me but the news that greets me at the dawn," the clerk blurted, omitting the honorific "sire."

"Ah, yes—I've quite forgotten the virulent contagion of castle gossip. No doubt you've already heard there is to be a new *receptor secondus?*"

Sparks nodded, eyes glazed.

"I thought it best to move swiftly, with the approach to Michaelmas. You will of course assume supervisory powers over your replacement as well as over Brother Jocelin and the amorous *receptores brevium.*"

"Sire?"

"You see, Sir Mitchell was so taken with my request that he seek the prior's counsel as to your successor—I thought it useful to enlist his confidence in this delicate matter—that he spun on his heels and set to it before I could tell him the rest. Namely, you have been advanced to the newly devised post of first clerk to the sheriff and undersheriff." His right arm reached down and grasped Sparks's left shoulder. "You will attend me closely, I trust."

·VII·

ON THE MORNING OF THE TENTH DAY of Philip Mark's service at Nottingham, a castle bailiff came to his closet to say there was a woman from Linby who had been begging to see him for some time. "She would not state her business, sire, so the gatekeeper would not admit her to the bailey."

"What is it she wants?" asked the undersheriff, who had a dozen matters awaiting his attention.

"She still will not say, sire. But the keeper thought it best to admit her—lest you think him unduly harsh."

Philip nodded his consent, and the bonneted woman, her skirt badly frayed at the hem, was brought before him, gave her best approximation of a curtsy, and the moment the bailiff left the chamber, related her tale of woe. For nearly two months her husband, Harold, the wheelwright of Linby, had been languishing in the castle gaol to await a hearing before the presentment court in their district. The foresters had found him hiding in Sherwood not far from a hart with a slit throat, and they charged him with the crime. In fact, said his wife, Harold had gone to the wood in search of his runaway horse and, upon hearing the royal foresters approach, tried to hide because his cottage lay about a mile outside the boundary of the forest, and so by strict reading of the law he was a trespasser. The imprisoned wheelwright, his wife went on, struggling for composure in the company of the mighty, was being starved and tortured at the castle— "They're melting him down, sire!" she cried, voice husky with grief—in hope of extracting a confession from him. When the presentment court last convened, as it did in Linby every sixth Monday, Harold was not brought before it to state his defense. And when his wife came to the castle to learn the reason, she was told to go away. Only when she offered the gatekeeper two silver pennies was she admitted to the bailey, where she was told that Harold's case was delayed because all matters of justice in the shire were awaiting the arrival of the new sheriff. It cost her sixpence more to be taken to see her husband, whose suffering he tried manfully to withhold from her, but there was no mistaking his shriveled form or missing toes where boiling water had been poured repeatedly onto his boots. "And my Harry's as innocent o' mischief as a newborn lamb, sire," she concluded, tears copious. His only offense had been to refuse the arresting foresters' demand for a bribe to let him out of their clutches.

"And did you have to pay the gatekeeper to admit you to the castle this morning as well?" Philip inquired gently after she had fallen still.

"Aye, sire—and the bailiff as well to tell you of my presence."

Since the wheelwright's wife was the first commoner he had encountered from beyond the castle since coming to Nottinghamshire, the undersheriff thought it might prove useful to inquire of her on diverse matters relating to the maintenance of the king's peace. What, after all, could the woman gain by fabricating? Indeed, truth was the only lever she could work if she hoped to obtain justice for her beleaguered spouse. He asked Sparks to have wine and cheese brought for the woman's refreshment and then to attend their exchange, which was to last the better part of an hour. At its end, he had her escorted to the gate with the firm instruction to the keeper that she was henceforth to be admitted to the bailey without need of gratuity.

"Her words are unsettling—if they are to be credited," the undersheriff said to his clerk. "Are you in any doubt of them?"

"None, sire."

"Then why have you not fully apprised me?"

Sparks searched the floor. "It seemed unduly forward—to volunteer—when I had no firsthand knowledge—only reports of—"

"Call Master Manning—and stay to bear witness."

The bailiff-in-chief, a mountainous man with a temper to match, was fiercely proud of his charge. He declared his deputies to be the rock upon which all law and order in the shire were founded. The oft-uttered claim that the bailiffs, both those from the castle and the ones posted in the districts, abused the populace was flint to his ire. If anyone could justly be accused of plundering, he would say to those few in whom he chose to confide, it was the sheriffs and their underlings; they came to mine what they could and left, in no way having improved the shire, whereas the bailiffs abided.

"I must familiarize myself with the methods of your officers—and the extent to which you countenance them," Philip said. "I ask only for your complete honesty and assure you in return that no harm will befall you or any of your men for whatever actions have been taken before my arrival."

"I know no language but complete honesty, sire."

"Nor do I suggest the contrary, Master Manning." The undersheriff then related the particulars of the case of the unfortunate Harold as the wheelwright's wife had given them and inquired into their accuracy.

The bailiff crossed a pair of powerful arms in front of his mailed chest. "They all claim their innocence, even the ones caught with their faces in the animal's still-steamy blood. And they all say the foresters ask them for money not to prosecute their crimes. This Harold of Linby might have been released on bail, but the only chattel he owned of sufficient value was the missing horse he said he had been looking for in the wood. The bailiff at Linby found the animal tethered to the wheelwright's shed, but his wife, doubtless thinking its discovery would destroy his alibi, claimed this was a second horse and it couldn't be sold or the family would have to travel on foot. As to the ordeal of pain he has suffered in our gaol, it must be expected. At the very least, the churl was trespassing in the forest—and at the worst, committed a crime gravely offensive to the crown. I instructed the turnkey and the hangman to try loosening his tongue a bit and generally making him weary of life. Often it succeeds. In this case the man has resisted."

"Perhaps with good reason."

Manning looked doubtful. "It was at my command, at any rate, that this Harold was not brought to the Linby presentment court at the first opportunity—there is no requirement that the matter proceed in haste, and I believed that the additional weeks in captivity would speed a confession."

Philip glanced past the burly bailiff into the yard. "A trial by ordeal, one might say."

"Quite so. If he is innocent, God will give him strength."

"And if he is guilty, why should the Lord need bailiffs to mete the villain his punishment? I myself am loath to suppose there is divine intervention in matters of temporal justice." He gestured to Sparks to fetch them some ale, signaling that the interrogation was not likely to be brief. "Let me press you, Master Manning, on some other matters that concern me as well."

"As you wish, sire," the bailiff said, but his pouchy face disclosed that he did not welcome the procedure.

"I am told that the bailiff in each district collects an aid of sixpence a head per year—rather like the sheriff's aid in the same amount."

"And for the selfsame purpose, sire—to defray the costs—"

"Westminster is fully familiar with the sheriff's aid, but no mention was made to me of any bailiff's aid. Who authorized it?"

"Who? I—it's—the custom, sire. There's no secret about it."

"Except, possibly, to Westminster. My understanding is that the sheriff's aid is divided fourpence to the sheriff for defraying the castle's expenses of operation and tuppence to be pooled among the bailiffs for their living. You concede now an additional sixpence a goes to the bailiffs—under what division, may I ask?"

"Four to the district bailiff, two to the castle contingent. It's entirely necessary, sire, to maintain our—"

"It is also entirely unauthorized by the king, Master Manning."

"I know nothing of that, sire. It has always been done, and I'm—"

"I'm also told the district bailiffs hold an annual scotale at their nearest inn, with attendance mandatory or a fine is levied. I thought the scotale was reserved for the foresters as a money-raising scheme?"

The chief bailiff's arms knotted tighter in front of him. "It's an informal business, sire—not the universal practice among our officers. I'm not aware, though, that the device has been forbidden to us."

"I see. And what do you say of the reported commandeering of commoners' horses and carts whenever the bailiffs choose—and fodder for their animals and food and drink for themselves—and clothing and lodging—all without recompense?"

"When it is necessary, yes—of course."

"And when it is not? When they take away a villager's cart because they are too lazy to bring their own—and sleep where and when they choose without regard to the convenience of—"

"They are permitted only what is necessary, sire, and are entitled to it. Beyond that, it's in violation of the rule."

"And what is the rule with regard to accepting gifts in order not to collect a tax or a fine—or deliver a writ of summons? What rule pertains to soliciting a gift in exchange for protecting a person from harm—or in return for not levying a false charge or not making an unwarranted arrest?"

Fire flashed in Manning's eyes, and his low, bulging brow grew furrowed. "All that ilk are irregular and beyond my knowledge."

"The bailiffs do not extort?"

"The bailiffs in the districts are paid but one shilling a year by the crown, sire. How else are they to subsist except by certain exactions and gifts? It's true as well with the castle bailiffs, but they at least get victuals, clothing, a dormitory bed, and their weapons. But how else are they to sustain a wife and brood except by—by—"

"Living off the people?"

"Sire, the king himself may be said to live off the people."

"But his takings are made known and applied universally. Here we seem to have each bailiff as his own king. It troubles me."

Later that day the undersheriff appeared unannounced in the donjon and made straightway for the turnkey's apartment. Its squat occupant was sitting astride a bench and gnawing on half a haunch of mutton. His bulbous, hairless head had no neck beneath but an angrily enlarged goiter that left him resembling nothing so much as a malevolent toad. His repast fairly flew out of his greasy hands at the sight of the visitor. "Rest easy, Master Plunk," said the undersheriff, retrieving the fallen joint of meat and handing it with a smile to the bowing and circling gaolkeeper. The fellow was plainly unused to receiving guests. "When your meal is done, I'd like to see your arrangements here."

"Arrangements, sire?" Plunk asked, tossing the mutton leg onto the straw-covered pallet in the corner that served as his bed.

"The gaol and the prisoners."

"You want to go down there—is that it?" He wiped his mouth against his sleeve and anxiously tried to fathom the undersheriff's motive.

"I do, Master Plunk—unless there is some reason for me not to."

"No, sire—only it's . . . not very . . . cozy . . . down there."

"Then I'll not be disappointed. They tell me your gaol is a model of uncoziness, Master Plunk."

"I'll vouch for it, sire," said the turnkey, brightening.

Two torches, one each on opposite sides of the great vaulted chamber, cast a somber light on the three dozen half-naked wretches strewn about the cold stone floor, alive with rivers of excrement. Coughs, moans, and mutters echoed continuously in the rank air. The sole amenity beyond a few precious bunches of befouled straw was a large jar of water with a tin dipper that sat in the center of the octagonal room. After a gagging moment or two, Philip nodded, and Plunk led him back upstairs and into the chamber adjoining his apartment where the instruments of persuasion were applied.

"This is the one I'm most partial to—there's less screams," Plunk said, indicating a chair made entirely of iron except for wooden strips at the top and bottom of the back panel. "Master Sunbeam grips it at these places," the turnkey explained, referring to the shire's hereditary hangman and ex officio torturer, "and shoves it a foot closer to the hearth every so often. With a good blaze going, it sets their blood aboil in about two hours. If we strap 'em in too tight, though, they faint dead away, so it's nice and easy on the lacing, but not too loose. . . ."

A less subtle technique, Plunk explained with an upward gesture, were the rings suspended from the ceiling through which the hoisted prisoner's arms, raised behind his back, were firmly secured while lead weights of up to twenty stone were tied to his feet. Excruciating dislocation of the limbs followed within an hour, accompanied by endless screams and voiding of the bowels. "The screams unsettle me," said the gaoler, who preferred to administer the rack, located in the far corner. It achieved the same effect more swiftly, but it brought the inflicters unpleasantly close to the afflicted. Most insidious of all the items in his satisfying inventory, Plunk pridefully concluded, was the water device, a large, downturned jug hung just below the ceiling, the contents of which escaped a drop every ten seconds through a puncture in the cork stopper and landed with explosive force on the bared abdomen of the carefully positioned prisoner. In time, his musculature gave way to the softer tissue beneath it, hemorrhaging ensued, and the vital organs were destroyed one by one. "If they vomit too much blood, they choke to death, but that's no doing o' mine." He rubbed his hands together exculpatorily. "It works wondrously well on the testicles also."

"I should imagine," said the undersheriff. And had Master Sunbeam in fact poured boiling water onto the toes of the prisoner Harold of Linby? The question was put with no more than clinical interest.

"Onto the fronts of his boots, sire—directly onto the flesh would be inhuman."

"Isn't the leather eaten through soon enough?"

"Oh, you get down to bone by the fourth dose or so—but all feeling has been killed by then. The whole business works worse the longer it lasts. Still, it weakens the resolve of the prisoner—except for this Harold. He suffered in silence. I think he must not be guilty."

That same evening, Philip walked the parapet in the company of Father Ivo, whose alliance he had not hitherto solicited. The question of his usefulness was linked in the undersheriff's mind not merely to whether Sparks's judgment of the priest was reliable but to how any man could equally well serve both the king and the pope when the two were locked, as now, in monumental combat over who should be archbishop at Canterbury. The chaplain's allegiance, in the last analysis, could not be in doubt. The more severe test was for Philip to determine whether the chaplain was truly a man of God or merely a creature of Rome.

"There is a task I would ask you to undertake," Philip said after they had stood silently awhile contemplating the crescent of moonlit hills and cliffs that surmounted the town like a crown glowing pearly against the northern sky, "provided, of course, it does not violate the Holy Father's Interdict."

"I fear it's impossible—by definition," the chaplain said softly. "You serve the king—you are his direct surrogate. How can I perform any useful task at your behest in these circumstances?"

"You continue to recite morning and evening prayers in chapel."

"Only because no one attends them. For all intents, they are a private meditation. I have no parishoners for the nonce."

"You have them, Father, but they are sufficiently saddened by your enforced idleness that they elect not to remind you of your plight by attending. In the meantime, they commune with the Lord in their own awkward fashion—doubtless availing them little."

"I would not demean the efficacy of private prayer, Master Mark. Indeed, I commend it to you—though I can do but little more. If holy service is what you seek, I must beg forgiveness. . . ."

"I wouldn't call it that."

"Call it what you will, but it cannot amount to ministering to the souls of mankind."

"Not their souls, Father, but their tortured bodies," Philip said and proceeded to elaborate the task he had in mind for the chaplain.

Ivo pondered it for several moments, trying to gauge both the manner of man this French newcomer was and the thornier aspects of his proposition. "They might well set upon me in their desperation," the priest mused aloud, "and hold me hostage down there."

"They might."

The chaplain reflected further, then asked, "And if I decline your request?"

"Then I should be hard put to justify your continuing residence at the castle. The rest of us are here to perform duties."

Ivo sighed, and his chest rattled at the swift passage of air. "You cannot coerce service from a holy man, Master Mark. It must be rendered from faith and charity."

"It's not the holy aspects of your calling that I appeal to, Father. You are a man as well as a priest, and it is a manly task I ask of you—without imperiling your profound commitment to Rome."

The chaplain's habitually dour countenance lightened. "In truth, I should like to be of service—idleness ill suits me. And your purpose is admirable enough."

"Weigh it overnight. I won't presume to urge your enlistment of divine guidance."

Ivo smiled for the first time. "Now the laity ministers to the clergy. The Lord's ways are ever instructive."

At noon on the morrow the bailiff-in-chief was resummoned to the sheriff's closet.

"The question, Master Manning," the undersheriff began in the presence of his clerk, "is whether your officers are defending the king's peace or exploiting it for their own betterment. I fear it's more the latter." Undeterred by Manning's grimace, Philip spelled out the changes he was ordering forthwith. "The so-called bailiffs' aid, this help-yourselves exaction, is to be no more." The bailiffs' and sheriff's aids, which together had come to a shilling, were to be converted into a single sheriff's aid of nine pence, five going to the sheriff, two to the castle bailiffs, and two to the bailiffs in the districts.

"It will not do, sire!" Manning blurted. "The money is required—my officers cannot subsist on such a pittance. It is unjust and—"

"If the castle succeeds in operating economically, then your men will receive a share of the sheriff's aid."

"That's very uncertain. It amounts to a sharp reduction in the bailiffs' assured pay."

"Your officers have been invoking the king's name to line their own pockets. If they can't survive under this arrangement, we'll find new bailiffs in their stead."

"Good bailiffs don't grow on trees, sire."

"Then we'll have to beat the bushes for them. At any rate, I already have a worthy new recruit for you. Unless there is objection, I ask that my older brother, Reginald, be added to the roster of castle bailiffs. He has served the king well and faithfully for many years as a sergeant-at-arms in France as well as here. I should like him to tour the districts to counsel the bailiffs and, not incidentally, to make sure their exactions are as I've prescribed."

"In short, he is to be your spy among us."

"I would not put it thus, Master Manning. He will first serve the king and then the shire—and his brother last of all."

"Still and all, he's likely to be viewed as—"

"Reginald is a large, powerful man and can hold his own in any company. Should he come to woe, though, the bailiff-in-chief will answer for it." Nor was that all. Any further extortionate or oppressive behavior by the bailiffs was prohibited. Gifts of food, drink, clothing, or coin were equally forbidden; a bribe by any other name was not thereby gilded. "And with regard to fees and taxes due the crown, the bailiffs are to take no more than is owed—but no less, either. All debts to the king are to be paid in full."

"In full?" Manning simmered. "It's quite impossible."

"And why is that?" Philip asked, voice arching.

"Ask that pismire of yours," the bailiff shot back with an ugly glance toward Sparks, whom he suddenly conceived as the mastermind behind these hateful directives.

"I urge you to keep a civil tongue, Master Manning. My clerk has done you no harm."

"Someone has been whispering rotten words into your ear."

"Not he—and the source, at any rate, doesn't alter their truthfulness." Philip turned to Sparks. "Now what does the bailiff mean that it's impossible to collect all crown debts in full? Isn't that our primary function?".

The little clerk took a few steps closer to the undersheriff. "Not so much impossible, sire, as ill-advised—perhaps even a disservice to the king." Some of the debts, Sparks confided, were intentionally onerous, like the inheritance duties imposed on those of dubious loyalty to the crown. Even certain fees willingly contracted for, like those for a plump custodianship, were no longer set at the traditional price but at the limits of the purchaser's greed or foolhardiness. "Westminster may not have conceded the point to you, sire, but it is tacitly understood to be crown policy—the greater a lord's debt to the king, the more abject his submission to the royal will, and hence the stronger his supposed fealty. Once the debt is entirely discharged, the crown loses its hold on the debtor and invites his disloyalty. This way—with the bailiff collecting no more than a respectable portion of the debt each year—the debtor remains at liberty only through the king's sufferance." If, on the other hand, payment in full were demanded of a debtor unable to meet it, his land and his chattels would escheat to the king, "but then, sire, the crown would have forfeited both the debt and the loyalty it purchased. And if you imprison the debtor, you'll have the man but lose both his payments and his services. So what is wanted is just enough payment to quiet the Exchequer yet keep the currents of government churning."

Manning nodded, his anger beginning to abate. "The ant speaks wisely. I apologize, Master Sparks, but all this is deeply—"

"Moreover, what harm is there, sire," the clerk hurried on, addressing the undersheriff, "if the bailiffs accept a small gift from these heavy debtors for not pressing them to the hilt?"

"The harm," said Philip, "is that it is outside the law, and I do not know about it."

"Hence, you cannot be held accountable for it by Westminster. And the crown, the debtor, *and* the bailiff are all equally served."

"But that way I am in collusion with the bailiffs and gain nothing for it."

"Save their devoted service," Sparks countered.

The undersheriff withdrew into his thoughts. "There is a large element of perversity in all of this," he said finally. "I'll take the last point under advisement." He turned back to the bailiff. "As to the matter of Master Harold of Linby, I want the wheelwright released at once and dealt with in the normal fashion at the next presentment court."

"He still must pay the bail."

"I'll bail him myself," said Philip.

"On what ground?" Manning demanded.

"That he is falsely charged, in all likelihood."

"You cannot know that, sire!"

"But I can suspect it—and will pay for the privilege."

"It's most irregular, and not in keeping with—"

"It cannot be done under the law, sire," Sparks cut in. "In the case of one not resident of the forest, only the king himself or the presentment court may permit the trespasser to be bailed."

Chagrin quieted the undersheriff. "You are well schooled in these legal matters, Master Sparks. Would they were honored as much in the practice as in the breach." Philip rose and met the bailiff's momentarily triumphant mien. "Be that as it may, Master Manning, I demand that all bodily punishment of this prisoner cease at once. Moreover, the gaol is a sty of unspeakable filth—there is no need for the inmates to wallow in their shit and vomit. Let them gather it up and have the turnkey dispose of it. Let them have clothing against the damp and cold. Let them be fed so they do not teeter on the very brink of starvation. Let there be straw enough for a semblance of bedding." Philip raised his hand as the bailiff's renewed fury threatened to unleash a mammoth blow to the under-sheriff's mouth. "Finally, the chaplain has consented to visit the gaol each forenoon to lend what succor he can and, not incidentally, to learn which of the inmates may be abused for no purpose beyond the amusement of their keepers."

"I fear Father Ivo's too frail for the task," said Sparks, surprised that he had not been asked to serve as intermediary to the chaplain in the matter.

"He has not said that to me."

"Then he has not dwelled on the reality, sire. It is quite a—"

"I cannot vouch for his safety," Manning inserted.

"He knows it—and is nevertheless willing."

"It's . . . unseemly," said the bailiff.

"Don't speak to me of what's unseemly! The gaol is barbaric. We are supposedly Christians."

"Criminals are to be punished, sire—not pampered."

The undersheriff placed a solitary finger against the bailiff's hauberk and pressed it home. "I daresay, Master Manning, that I have passed more time in gaol than you and know the cruelty of it better. It is doubled when the imprisonment is unjust. You will see it is done as I order, or we shall have a new bailiff-in-chief."

Not long after this encounter, a certain reaper in the village of Linby ran away when the bailiff in that district happened by his croft and dis-covered a trail of blood leading to it. His search yielded a dismembered hind, its head intact and its throat slit in the same manner as the hart found in the forest near the unfortunate Harold. The reaper's hut, more-over, was still closer to the forest than the wheelwright's. The investigating bailiff theorized that the reaper may have been interrupted in the earlier felony by the foresters before he could remove the slain deer for which Harold was then taken into custody. Upon hearing of this turn of events, Master Manning ordered the wheelwright to be set free, and at the next shire court the fled reaper was declared an outlaw.

· VIII ·

AUBREY, THE CONSTABLE, was dumbstruck by the question. "How *many* weapons, sire? Within the castle stores, or at the ready, or in actual use—which do you mean?"

"All in all."

"All in all? I . . . cannot say . . . with precision. Perhaps an approximation, sire, if that would serve to—"

"I wish to know the exact numbers by nightfall as well as the state of repair for each category—swords, spears, daggers, axes, maces, bows and arrows—to the last arrow—crossbows—"

"We have no crossbows, sire."

"Why is that?" the undersheriff asked.

"There are but few of them in England. I'm told they are commoner in France, but very cumbersome and slow—not well suited to our needs."

Philip eyed the constable coldly, swallowing his contempt for the fireside warrior. "In truth, it is a heavy weapon, Master Aubrey, and takes some manipulation, but its penetrating power is fearsome. I have seen it pin a man to a wall like a skewered bug from a thousand feet away. There is nothing like it to slow an onrushing knight and his charger. And given the protection a castle lends for the reloading, the crossbow is the ideal weapon for defending against siege."

"My experience is narrow, sire. Forgive me—I meant no—"

"I should like to know as well what supplies we have of boulders, lead, and pitch—they're also cumbersome and slow but highly useful, the latter two in particular when brought to a boil and poured onto those who would scale our walls."

"I'm familiar with their—"

"Do we have such materials, then, and cauldrons to contain them?"

"I—cannot say—for certain."

"By nightfall, Master Constable."

The totals, for a castle aspiring to even a semblance of military readiness, were pitiable. Anticipating as much before he had departed London, the undersheriff had argued at the Chancery that it made little sense to have designated Nottingham Castle a repository of crown funds the previous year—one of only six in all England—without a simultaneous strengthening of the structure and its garrison. Accordingly, Philip was granted authority for his first year at Nottingham to divert whatever portion of the revenues was needed, once the crown's established quota from his two shires was reached, to improve the castle fortifications. Every outlay, of course, had to be justified and accounted for to the penny.

"To begin with, every blade within the castle walls or carried by the men on their person is to be honed at once," he ordered the constable, "and is to be re-examined every second month and resharpened as need be."

"Aye, sire." Aubrey was attentive if weary from the prospect of such unaccustomed labors. "Does that include the kitchen cutlery as well?"

"A splendid thought—and one with a point to it."

The jest eluded the constable. "The smith cannot accomplish this work and his other duties as well."

"He must have another helper, then—two if required. And you will see promptly to the manufacture of four dozen crossbows from oak and iron of the first quality—I'm told of an admirable ferrier at Lincoln—and five thousand arrows of the appropriate sort, as well as three thousand additional arrows for the longbow—our supply is hopelessly inadequate."

"Forgive me, sire, but what need have we for four dozen crossbows when there are but ten archers in the castle complement?"

"A further splendid observation, Master Aubrey. The answer is that every able-bodied castle occupant, starting with you, is to be trained with the crossbow the moment they are obtained. In case of siege, every man available will use one. There will be twice-weekly drills—I'll preside over the instruction at first, and then you—using the butts at ground level and later firing down through the loops." The roof of the castle, Philip went on, consulting the list he had made on a parchment scrap, required repair in dozens of places where the iron sheeting had separated or worn away, exposing the timbers below to seepage, rot, and fire from pitch catapulted onto it by attackers. "You will need laborers from the town—enlist enough so that the work is accomplished by Lent."

"Aye, sire." The constable's eyes were beginning to spin. "Would that be the beginning of Lent or the end of it, sire?"

"If we say the beginning, we may make it by the end." Further, the pointed finials atop the merlons on the castle battlements were broken or missing at fifty-seven locations. "You'll need masons and stonecutters. Seek the counsel of the chancellor at Southwell Minster—they've em-

ployed such artisans in quantity for twenty years now." The iron capping
on the portcullis was gone in places and also required immediate repair.
"I judge half the horses in the stable too old for heavy riding, and the rest
show signs of improper grooming. The marshal must see the condition
corrected before the month is out—or leave us." Finally, the intricate
webbing of tunnels throughout the great sandstone crag on which the
castle sat needed careful examination; as it had grown, the labyrinth invited
infiltration from below—in the very fashion that the king had lost his jewel,
Château Gaillard, and with it, the last hope of retaining Normandy. "It will
need blocking off at certain junctures," the undersheriff ordered, "and I
fear we must seal the Hole to Hell forever." That precipitous corridor
through which casks of wine and barrels of ale to slake the castle's thirst
were regularly trundled from the Trip to Jerusalem Inn at the base of the
castle rock made an ideal thoroughfare for furtive invaders.

"Then how will the spirits be transported up from the Trip?" asked
the constable, benumbed by now under this torrent of directions.

"By cart the roundabout way—as with all our other provisions."

"It will prove more costly, sire."

"Tell the innkeeper to reduce his profits—or we'll fetch our ale from
elsewhere."

That daunting assignment left the constable still further dispirited.
"And as to the cost of all these other matters, sire?"

"It will please you to know that in undertaking these labors, you will
have the assistance of my younger brother, Peter, who will serve as the
deputy constable. He will keep careful track of the money, so I may be
assured it falls within the totals I've arranged for with Westminster—
assuming, of course, Peter meets with your approval. He's a man of great
good will."

"I have no doubt of it, sire." Aubrey's downcast eyes belied his words.
"If I may be so bold," the constable ventured when it was clear the
undersheriff had no further directives to bedevil him with, "against whom
are all these precautionary measures directed? Nottingham is far from the
coasts and frontiers of England."

"You are most perceptive, Master Aubrey. But the king, I regret to
point out, has his enemies. Is he not locked in a mighty war even now
with Pope Innocent?"

"A war of words, perhaps. The pope has no legions."

"But the French king has, and he curries favor with Rome. Should the pope declare John excommunicate, who is to say he will not commission Philip Augustus to reclaim England for the Cross?"

Aubrey was doubtful. "But Nottingham is far from Paris."

"And the Indus was much farther still from Macedon, but that didn't deter Alexander from fording it and gaining unthinkable victories."

The undersheriff's interview the next morning with Devereaux, the steward, was no less pressing in nature. The quality of the castle food and its manner of preparation were so far from satisfactory, the steward was advised, that the cook's neck was flirting with the hangman's noose. The whole castle, moreover, was dark as a catacomb and in dire need of added torchlight. Fresh rushes or straw was to be put down on the floors no less than monthly. The hearths were to be more amply fueled and better attended. And the steward was to see to it that the castle food stores were massively augmented with enough sacks of corn, sides of dried mutton, giant cheeses, casks of wine, and cords of wood to endure a six-month siege.

Devereaux's usual grand manner fled him at the enormity of the tasks prescribed. "How can the cellars contain so large a . . . ? The moisture . . ."

"Use pallets and coverings against exposure."

"The rats . . ."

"Get cats—they're needed throughout the castle. My younger daughter was nearly bitten by a rat two nights ago. I believe Mistress Mark spoke with you on the subject."

"Yes, sire—and I intend without fail—"

"By nightfall, Master Devereaux—let the castle sing with meows."

The corpulent steward bowed to the extent his girth permitted. "And as to the cost of these added stores, sire?"

"You will begin by applying the surplus regularly returned to you by the castle provisioners—and thereafter consult with the new deputy constable, who will be monitoring your every expenditure from this time forth." The undersheriff rose and handed the large roll bearing the steward's accounts back to him across the tabletop. Devereaux took it glumly with no word of protest and began to retreat. "And may I add," said Philip, "that it behooves you to devote rather less of your while charming the castle cleaning maidens and more of it attending business."

"Yes, sire." Devereaux pursed his glistening lips wistfully. "The maidens, sire," he said after a moment's reflection, "they're wholesome wenches—quite clean—not the whoring sort."

"I'm pleased to hear of it."

"It occurs to me, sire—if perchance . . . you would not take it unkindly . . . or misconstrue my purpose . . . it would be my pleasure . . . I could recommend which of them . . . you would find . . ."

Philip restrained a smile; he could not recall a less guileful, and more misguided, attempt to ingratiate. "You are kind, Master Devereaux, but I suggest that you limit your procuring to the castle staples."

Not all of these sundry commands and innovations were gladly taken up by the castle's officers. Since they entailed greater labors and a curbing of ill-got gains, resentment had been all but guaranteed. A small portion of this displeasure was registered at the Trip to Jerusalem, a second home for denizens of the castle who could afford the fare. Stirred by its superior libations, the talk in that shadowy, timbered cave was generally unrestrained and even boisterous, but it had turned dark and more guarded since the arrival of Philip Mark. An attentive listener could detect an undertow of insurrection.

"The crossbow is a coward's weapon," hissed Sir Mitchell of Rainworth upon hearing of the undersheriff's instructions to the constable. "It kills from afar and more by chance than adroitness—whereas the soul of chivalry is hand-to-hand combat, so you may look your foe in the eye before bloodying him." The coroner shook his head. "This all stems from our Master Mark's being no knight. He naturally prefers the bow, a churl's choice of arms."

Bailiff Manning directed his barely muted fury at what he took for the undersheriff's intent to impoverish him and his officers. "He's a babe in the woods if he thinks he can browbeat us into submission," he muttered. "And his brother Reginald—now there's a lummox for you. It wouldn't surprise me if this pack of Marks were gone by the new year or dismissed by our phantom sheriff soon upon his arrival—whichever comes first."

The constable was less certain but more acid, styling the undersheriff "a monstrous taskmaster" whose sole distinction as a military commander was the protracted nature of his defeat at Loches. The steward called him "a decadent Frenchman" for asking the castle kitchen to provide him and his brood with delicacies on a nightly basis. And the marshal wondered if this foreign interloper knew one end of a horse from the other.

These calumnies were regularly overheard by Bartholomew le Gyw, proprietor of the Trip, who, unknown to the gallants uttering them, appeared one evening in the undersheriff's apartment, through the intervention of Master Sparks, and reported their substance. "My allegiance is to the crown, sire," said Master le Gyw after disgorging his unsavory intelligence, "and whom it sends to command the castle. My livelihood—the inn's charter—depends on the good opinion of me held by the sheriff of the moment." He was thus prepared to inform on whoever revealed aloud, within the confines of the Trip, alien sentiment toward the undersheriff.

Philip thanked the innkeeper but added at once, "I cannot be a party to eavesdropping. It goes against my nature."

"I do not stoop to that, sire. I mean to report only words plainly spoken."

"Still, I cannot sanction it—and surely will not pay for it, if that's what you may be—"

"Not one penny, sire. It's my patriotic duty."

"Then I commend you. Yet there is something distasteful—"

"It is in your own interest, sire—and at no exposure."

Except, Philip calculated, to leave himself beholden to a rascal (for no man of probity would make such an offer). What, though, was so objectionable about the innkeeper's proposal? Merely that it was underhanded. *Merely?* The essence of treachery was its covertness; to triumph by stealth was as great a villainy as victory in behalf of the wicked. And what profit was there in his knowing who his detractors were or how savagely they disparaged him? He had acted not to gain their favor but to advance the crown's standing; Brewer had memorably counseled him that the two ends were incompatible. What mattered was that they obey him, like it or not. Insubordination was the cardinal sin; disgruntlement, merely the state of nature for subordinates. But mutiny sprang from compacted grievances—and innkeeper le Gyw might stand guard at the threshold between the two, or at least supply an early inkling of the tendency. Was he trustworthy enough, or more likely to use his listening post to advantage himself? Sparks had told him that while the innkeeper was a pleasing character, le Gyw was half a Welshman, and that the Welsh were a people often said to wander from the English standard for truthfulness. Doubtless, the English said the same of the French, the Venetians, and the Bulgars. . . .

All these musings contorted the undersheriff's brain and defied easy resolution. To dispel them he embraced the rationale that it was no sin to consort with purveyors of soiled goods so long as it was done at one remove. "I cannot prevent you from hearing what you will, Master le Gyw," he said at last, "or sharing what part of it you choose to with my clerk. Your disinterested patriotism will be duly noted."

"He's a prig and a half, isn't he?" the innkeeper commented to Sparks after they had departed the undersheriff's quarters. "An overflow of righteousness may be worse than none at all."

"It's not a choice we've been offered by others of his rank," said the clerk.

"I salute your loyalty—but fear his artifice. I can't tell if he's a wolf in sheep's clothing or the other way around."

"And I worry because he feigns nothing—and thereby risks everything."

· IX ·

THE SHERIFF'S PURPLE PENNON, tied on just below the point of a lance sunk into the ground business end up, caught the autumnal wind that raked lightly through the stand of sycamore beside the churchyard at Rainworth. The castle party, consisting of the undersheriff, his clerk, his chief bailiff, ten men-at-arms, the receiver of taxes, a clerk of writs, and Sir Mitchell, the shire coroner (Rainworth being his home district), had assembled there at noonday and would not disperse until nightfall, or later still if their purpose was not yet accomplished.

By custom, the sheriff made his tourn of the shire twice yearly, visiting each district to adjudicate disputes, hear pleas to the crown, collect the sheriff's aid, and make the view of frankpledge, whereby every villager swore to uphold the king's peace and raise the hue and cry against its violators. Attendance was obligatory at some point on the day the sheriff's itinerant court appeared; truant villagers were fined. This royally sanctioned penalty had proven irresistible in the past to corrupt sheriffs and their bailiffs. Tourns would be scheduled more often than needed, perhaps three or even four times in the year, frequently on short notice, with the prime purpose of harvesting fines from those who failed to appear.

On this occasion, though, word had preceded the arrival of the castle party that the new undersheriff had decreed not only that tourns would be strictly limited to two per annum but also that the sheriff's and bailiffs' aids were henceforth to be combined, reducing the total bite by 25 percent. Accordingly, a certain festive air animated the assemblage at Rainworth Parish. Choice pigs were roasting, ale tumbled freely into tankards hoisted to the king's health, maidens jumped rope, lads wrestled in the mire at the roadside, and traveling merchants who shadowed the sheriff's company on its fortnight-long circuit of the shire hawked their bright and pungent wares on the fringe of the gathering.

Keenest interest naturally centered upon disputes between commoners and their rich neighbors; the vaster the holdings of the latter, the less likely, it was supposed, for the sheriff to find against them. But since the castle, for the moment at least, was in the control of a slender Frenchman apparently unfamiliar with the normal order of things, excitement stirred with the wind as the pleas began.

Among the early complainants was the widow of a vassal holding fifty acres of a certain pugnacious lord who had claimed custody of the property until the deceased's son and heir came of age. The widow, charging that she had thus been denied the income from the land and her dower, had won an order six months earlier from the king's judicial eyre requiring the lord's surrender of the custodianship. Control, though, had not yet been returned to her, and the widow now asked the undersheriff to enforce the crown judgment in her favor.

It seemed to Philip a simple enough matter of bullying and, despite a reprimand, continued defiance of the king. But the lord in question was Ralph de Greasley, a potent warrior who had taken the Cross and gone with Richard to the Holy Land; such piety militated in his favor. Sir Ralph's steward appeared before the tourn, moreover, and stated that custody of the property had been withheld from the widow until the harvest could be taken off it lest she prove incapable of managing the fields and thus paying her tallage.

"But in the meantime, the woman and child cannot subsist," said the undersheriff. "Your lord holds against them without royal sanction."

"Temporarily, sire. The harvest will be gathered anon."

"The timing is of your devise, not the crown's."

"Sir Ralph has his rights."

"The widow is not in default—your lord merely anticipates it and so acts the oppressor." Philip turned to Bailiff Manning. "Instruct your officer in the district to see to it that custody and an amercement of five shillings, to compensate the widow for lost income, pass to her by sundown on the morrow—and if this not be done, he is to seize and hold a dozen of the lord's best sheep. And if a week passes and it is not yet done, the sheep shall be forfeit to the widow—and worse shall be in store."

A murmur arose and enveloped the audience. "It is excessive," Sir Mitchell whispered anxiously into the undersheriff's ear. "You impugn Sir Ralph's virtue—it is enough to order the eyre's ruling enforced without resort to the fine and threat of seizures."

"Your counsel is welcome," Philip said drily to the coroner, "but the king's bench may not be defied with impunity."

"The steward noted the mitigating reason."

"Sheer filigree." He signaled the clerk to enter the order. "Let us proceed."

A yet mightier lord, Baron Thomas de Lambert, holder of Swanhill Manor, was shortly the object of complaint. A certain villein of the manor had been dispossessed of his team of oxen on the ground of default of service and charged that the taking was unjust. The ague had laid him low, the serf contended, and each time he had tried to work too soon, a relapse left him still weaker. Without his oxen he could not attend his own fields or feed his family properly or fulfill his work days for Lord Lambert, whom he loved dearly. His words, barely audible above the persistent hum of the throng, carried with them the conviction of the sorely put-upon.

In place of the steward, who would normally have justified the taking from the villein, the reeve of the manor, a fellow serf named Blake, appeared and gave the lie to the complaint. "For years he's been a slacker, sire, and though repeatedly warned of his deficiency in work due the manor, has nonetheless gone his way," the reeve recited, his cap doffed in tribute to the undersheriff. "On six occasions he was found ploughing his own fields when obliged to work the lord's. As to his sickness, he repairs regularly to the alehouse to take the cure."

"The reeve lies!" the suddenly invigorated villein declared. "He despises me because I've spoken against him for years as the steward's pawn. He's no champion of ours but seeks only to butter his own bread."

The reeve disclosed no emotion at the outburst. "It must also be said," he continued, "that this person has repeatedly despoiled the common spring in the village, has been chastised by the manor court for it and fined, and yet persists in the unspeakable habit. His fellow peasants thus have a still stronger grievance against him than Lord Lambert does. This is a knave, sire, in need of chastening."

Asked by the undersheriff to explain his locus of excretion, the churl dejectedly replied that he had befouled his own small parcel to the point of saturation, that the forest was forbidden to him, likewise the lord's stream because of the fish weir, that his neighbors naturally resented his encroachment, and that he had supposed the common spring would rapidly bear away his wastes.

"Don't be rash," Sir Mitchell said behind a cupped hand as the undersheriff sat back a moment to ponder the case. "Swanhill ranks behind only Peverel and Tickhill among the shire estates, and Lord Lambert is our foremost magnate. Do not offend him on so puny a matter."

Philip turned from the coroner without acknowledgment and leaned toward his clerk. "Was Swanhill not your birthplace?"

"Aye, sire—my mother dwells there still, though she's ailing."

"How fierce a master is Lord Lambert?"

"His steward is your standard oppressor," said Sparks.

"Grievously so?"

"Grievous enough to earn his keep—a gyrfalcon of a fellow."

"And this Blake?"

"Nobody loves a reeve—but this one, they say, is able. He bends before his lord's retainers only as required—and sometimes less."

The undersheriff slapped the table edge in front of him. "The lord's taking is upheld, and the case is quit," he said, indifferent to the coroner's nod or the fresh wave of murmurs, astir with disapproval, that now rippled through the onlookers.

Easily the most important matter to come before the tourn that day was the charge of malfeasance against the tollkeeper of the little bridge at Rainworth. England's roads were adequate in number and condition but notoriously ill-provided with bridges. The crossing of a tributary of the Trent at Rainworth, which saved nearly a full day's journey by allowing travelers to bypass Nottingham town, was thus a well-used facility and much prized by the residents of the vicinity. It brought news from the world to their remote region and yielded welcome revenue to the innkeeper, the smith, and the stableman among other proprietors. The bridge was held by Utley of Throways, who paid the king a fee of not less than two pounds yearly and agreed to maintain the crossing at all times. Notwithstanding that Utley's charter provided the tolls not exceed a penny per rider and tuppence per loaded cart, his tollkeeper, one Alan Little, a bruiser of mean disposition but enviable attentiveness, now stood accused of exacting a good deal more from defenseless wayfarers. Out-of-county riders were regularly asked tuppence and carts were taxed as the tollkeeper's caprice dictated, often including a small portion of the cargo— an armload of firewood, say, or a barrowful of quarried stone. A canon of Worcester with a load of books was reputedly detained three days for failure to surrender one of the volumes, and a pilgrim en route to Southwell from Derbyshire was said to have been relieved of a shilling before gaining passage.

"And why has such conduct gone unchecked before now?" the undersheriff asked a carter from Worksop who headed a group of complainants against Alan Little's alleged deprecations.

"Many reasons, sire. The people of Rainworth fear this Alan Little, and fear even more the loss of the bridge if he is not there to maintain it—and still more, the loss of commerce if the crossing is closed."

"Has complaint not been made to the bailiff of Rainworth?" Philip asked, indicating the officer not ten paces to his left.

"Often, sire—but it's availed us naught. Suspicion is rife that the bailiff partakes of the keeper's tolls and so is a party to the abuses. This likelihood was spoken of at tourns past, but no sheriff or undersheriff has been moved by our pleas."

Philip looked to Sparks for confirmation. "It is an old sore, sire," the clerk said.

The accused himself was far from contrite. Upkeep of the bridge the year 'round was costly, he said—there were food and lodgings for him, a helper, and a man-at-arms and the cost of labor and materials to maintain the hard-used timbers of the crossing bed. And since half of all the tolls was payable to the lord of Throways, the heavy financial burden sometimes required the keeper to charge whatever the traffic might bear. "But the poor are never penalized as a result," Master Little asserted truculently to a chorus of hisses from the crowd.

"And do you withhold from Sir Utley any portion of the tolls due him?"

"Never, sire. One half of them all is his."

"What is the total of your takings, Master Little?"

"I could not say for certain, sire. I remit his half to Sir Utley by the week, and from the balance maintain the bridge and take what sustenance I can."

Sparks slid the castle copy of Utley's charter under Philip's eyes and noted that it specified the crown was due half the profits once the holder's fees had been recouped and the upkeep deducted. The point was not lost on the undersheriff. "Tell us, then, Master Tollkeeper, what your collections amount to per week?"

"That would be difficult, sire—it varies so with the season."

"Even so, I ask you to gauge it for us."

"It's very difficult, sire."

"Surely the tollkeeper can count. Is it a shilling? Is it five shillings? Ten shillings? Or ten pence?"

"I cannot say with accuracy, sire."

"Cannot, or will not?"

The question hung in the air as the tollkeeper's silence provided eloquent testimony for the gravamen of the charges. "Moderation now, sire," was all the coroner spoke into Philip's ear. Whereupon the undersheriff ordered the tollkeeper to cease and desist forthwith from abusing his commission and to maintain from that day on a record of his collections, to be rendered to Sir Utley, who in turn was to show them on demand to the sheriff or his deputies and remit to the crown all profits as required by his charter. Master Manning, moreover, was told to see to it that any collusion between the bailiff at Rainworth and the tollkeeper be put to a stop.

This ruling was received with groans and hoots of derision. Why was there no amercement for past offenses? And once the castle officers departed the scene, the complainants told one another, the abuses would go on unabated. The Frenchman's bite had no teeth—and if there was anything worse than a corrupt sheriff, it was a weak undersheriff afraid to offend the mighty. As the tourn crowd disbanded under torchlight, the fragile seed of reform that Philip Mark's earlier actions were thought to have planted lay crushed and strewn about the Rainworth churchyard.

Upon the undersheriff's return to the castle three days hence, he found awaiting him letters patent from Westminster, advising that Gerard d'Athiés was consumed by the demands of overseeing the other two shires of which he was sheriff—and thus Philip Mark was duly elevated to the

sheriffship of Nottinghamshire and Derbyshire, with civil authority pleni-
potentiary in all matters affecting the crown. The document bore the king's
seal and the signature "Iohannes rex." Philip wrote at once to thank his
gracious sovereign and sent his nephew, Geoffrey, employed as the castle
messenger, flying south to deliver the note.

His wife, Anne, naturally elated at Philip's advancement, saw promptly
to the family's transfer to the sheriff's larger apartment. "For the first
time," she told her husband beneath their coverlet that night, "I feel we
are Englishmen. The castle is truly ours now, Philip."

"The castle," he said, drawing her to him, "is the king's, and the
moment I forget it is the day we are stripped of it." He kissed her mouth
and nose and eyelids. "In the meantime, let us make the most of it."

"You'll be, bar none, the most splendid sheriff in all of England."

His splayed fingers firmly enclosed her breasts, the still-supple full-
ness of which much pleased him. "And how will they measure my
splendor—by which among us is the least grasping?"

"Your grasp is not entirely innocent, sire," Anne said with an easy
laugh, and untwined her legs for the new sheriff to delve between in
celebration.

His first act the morning afterward was to dispatch his brother Peter,
wearing carter's motley and driving the most battered cart in the castle's
fleet, to the bridge at Rainworth with instructions to cross it in the guise
of a dry-goods engrosser from Lincolnshire. The cart was temptingly piled
with a miscellany of cargo. The incorrigible tollkeeper took the bait, charging Peter thruppence and helping himself to a bolt of wool lately dyed with
the excellent fastness of Lincoln green. Peter sought out the elusive bailiff
of Rainworth, lodged a complaint with him against the tollkeeper, was told
the charge and the taking were standard for outlanders, and made his way
back to the castle with the incriminating report.

Master Manning, two deputies, and four men-at-arms were shortly
in Rainworth to relieve the bailiff—one of the castle deputies was to
serve until a permanent replacement could be enlisted—and to take Alan
Little into custody. But word of the sheriff's ruse had reached him before
Manning's squadron, and the tollkeeper disappeared into the forest, not
to be seen again. Utley of Throways was served with a writ of summons
to the shire court to answer charges of withholding funds from the bridge
tolls that were rightfully the king's. And Philip wrote to Westminster
recommending the bridge charter be transferred to a suitable holder

and the tolls be scrupulously collected in the meantime by the villagers of Rainworth, at peril of the crossing's destruction if they abused the trust.

Shortly after this episode, the new sheriff found himself under heightened scrutiny for the manner in which he carried out a common duty of his office—seizure of a convicted felon's property in behalf of the crown. The felon in question was the salt merchant of Nottingham and perhaps the richest Christian of ungentle birth in the whole shire. Alas, a portion of his wealth had been ill-got through his covert arrangement with a certain cooper for the manufacture of false-bottomed barrels in which a lead wafer had been inserted, enabling the merchant to short-weight his customers for years. But the day came when the cooper was threatened with disclosure of the subterfuge by one of his laborers unless paid for his continuing silence; soon thereafter, the would-be taleteller was found floating face-down in the Trent midway between Nottingham and Newark. The ever-alert coroner, noting a sizable dent to the rear of the deceased's skull, suspected foul play and empowered the bailiffs to investigate; in no time the whole tawdry skein came unraveled, and the murderous cooper was hanged in the town marketplace. Final sentence for the salt merchant had awaited the new sheriff's arrival, and so, in presiding over the shire court for the first time, Philip meted the prisoner a ten-year stay in the castle gaol—four years longer, it was said, than anyone had yet survived the ministrations of turnkey Plunk and hangman Sunbeam.

Within hours of the salt merchant's tearful farewell to his family, the sheriff, the bailiff-in-chief, and a sizable body of castle retainers arrived at the felon's fine stone-and-timber house, which for months had been under close surveillance lest it be emptied of its contents. Under law, the crown was entitled to all a felon's possessions; by custom, a variable portion was taken as booty by the castle, which accounted for the whole to the Exchequer in any manner the sheriff chose, for who would be the wiser? In this instance, the lure seemed irresistible: finely carved tables, chairs, and bedsteads, brightly painted linen hangings, a wardrobe of furs and silk, and in the cellar a caliph's cache of jewels, plate, spices, and eight barrels each holding one hundred pounds in pennies.

The bailiff's opinion was that since his officers had played an essential role in the investigation of the crimes responsible for the merchant's imprisonment, a portion of the seizure ought rightly to be allocated for their needs. The coroner, too, argued that some part of the taking ought to be deployed for the maintenance of his office. And whatever portion of the balance scruple did not consign to the royal treasury, all agreed, belonged fit and proper to the sheriff himself.

But Philip ruled otherwise. To the crestfallen bailiffs went only some perishable foods, several items of durable clothing, the few armaments in the merchant's house, and a shilling each for meritorious service. Four shillings went to the coroner's office and one splendid mastiff to its holder—for which Sir Mitchell professed gratitude. The merchant's dozen horses were transferred to the marshal, along with four stout carts much in need around the castle. The felon's library of nine books was to be divided equally among Southwell Minster, Lenton Priory, and Newstead Abbey. And the rest, including whatever price the house fetched when offered for sale, would go to Westminster to help meet the quota for Philip's two shires and defray the high cost of his ambitious plans to improve the castle. "Except," said the sheriff, "twenty pounds shall be set aside for the prisoner's wife and children, and the unfortunate woman may choose one fine garment to keep."

"And what of yourself, sire?" asked Manning, torn between admiration and loathing for the sheriff's unalloyed allegiance to the crown.

"The castle will benefit."

"But you must have something for yourself, sire," said Sir Mitchell, finding such a surfeit of altruism unbearable. He fingered over the merchant's books. "At least take some of these—I'm sure the church libraries have copies. I know for a fact that Lenton has this of Horace's. And these poems of Ovid—they are said to be aphrodisiac, to the point the prior has grown sheepish of their retention. And St. Augustine's *City* they all have, of course. . . . Oh, and this I commend to you personally, the parables of Aesop. They would delight your little girls—stories of talking animals—which sounds a nonsensical sort of business, but they're very instructive, you see, and most—"

"You're very kind," the sheriff said to him, "but I don't think it fit to take seized property for my personal enhancement."

"Then set the volumes in a special niche, sire, for the delight and edification of visitors to the castle."

"I'll think upon it," said Philip. "For now there's much to do here." He turned to Sparks. "Every item is to be accounted for, without exception." His flashing eye caught the chief bailiff's somber demeanor. "I'm not unmindful of your officers' needs," he said, taking Manning to one side. "Let us see where the accounts stand at year's end. But it's my place to determine a fair reward—not the bailiffs'."

Word shortly began to spread about the town and sift out through the countryside about the ungreedy nature of the new sheriff. Some said his very newness was the cause and that he would soon become like the rest; others attributed it to his ignorance of English custom; and still others said it was a trick to lull the shire while he hatched dark plans to gull both the crown and its subjects. Aubrey, the constable, was overheard at the Trip to speculate that the sheriff might simply lack the courage to exploit his office and risk the ire of Westminster. "Somehow or other," the coroner remarked, "there is perversion in all this uprightness—I can smell it."

This perceived excess of virtue grew yet more unsettling when a delegation from the Nottingham Town Council of Burgesses appeared in the sheriff's closet and attempted to present him with a gift of one hundred shillings—"for your good will and support in maintaining our liberties," they explained.

"Most kind of you—I'm deeply moved," Philip said at once. "But you have the sheriff's good will to begin with. There's no need to purchase it. As to your liberties, my pledge of office holds that I—"

"But sire, it is the tradition," said Simon Welles, the angular president of the fullers' guild and acting spokesman for the burgesses. "We vote to give it each year, out of respect—and admiration."

"As sheriff, I ask only that the townsmen support me in sustaining the king's peace and meeting the crown's cost of governance. For that you'll have my profound gratitude; beyond that you need not venture."

Dejection writ large upon his face, Master Welles asked that his delegation be excused a moment. Its members filed out in glazed silence. On their prompt reappearance, the fuller cleared his throat and gingerly raised the size of the proffered gift to one hundred fifty shillings. "We cannot go higher, sire." Hope swam in his imploring eyes. "Please do not reject us out of hand."

Philip by now was queasy with acute embarrassment. "Master Welles—good gentlemen of Nottingham—you quite misconstrue my meaning. I cannot take a gift merely for performing my duty. And as I am new in your midst, you know me not—and may yet judge me harshly. And for my part, I cannot be beholden—"

"Sire, your hesitancy only reinforces our eagerness to be of aid," said

Master Welles, groping for a reprieve. "We ask that you reconsider the matter and delay your final answer for a week."

To do less would have been rude. And so Philip reported the exchange to his wife that evening at supper. "Your response was no doubt the right one and entirely commendable," she said. "But if you reject them in the end as well, they may think you haughty—which might be still worse in their eyes than being mercenary."

"Anne, I cannot . . ."

She placed her warm, gracefully long hand upon his wrist. "I know. I'm only saying you may lose more by being—"

"I cannot calculate the matter that fine."

"All right," she said, reflecting a moment. "Then why not—rather than antagonizing the burgesses by seeming to denigrate their gesture— accept it on the condition that it not benefit you personally? Let the money go toward beautifying the castle in some manner or other, even as the salt merchant's volumes now grace our guest quarters?"

He kissed her mouth for forming so sensible a solution. But the burgesses, on their revisit, registered dismay at it. "It was not our intention to decorate the king's castle," said Master Welles, "but to comfort the sheriff's life—a rather different proposition."

"I say not," the sheriff replied. "I say they are one and the same."

Seeing the Frenchman's iron resolve, the fuller turned to his colleagues and, palms upward, relented. "Very well," he said, "we gladly accept your condition of acceptance—but we wish to add one of our own." Would the sheriff consent to attend, as guest of honor, the burgesses' annual banquet on the eve of the Nottingham town fair the next year?

"I can see no hardship in it," said Philip with a smile. "I should welcome the pleasure of your company."

"Alas, your predecessors, men of vast holdings and far-flung responsibilities, have rarely been on hand for the occasion. It is, of course, the civic and commercial highlight of the year for our townspeople."

"Then it shall have my highest priority."

Master Welles looked pleased. "In that case, sire, let me say as well that we are hopeful the castle will see fit to safeguard the populace during the event. In recent years the marketplace has been preyed upon by beggars, thieves, charlatans, prostitutes, and every manner of importuning low-life throughout the course of the fair, greatly detracting from the pleasure of the occasion."

"Haven't the bailiffs maintained order?"

"Master Manning sought a steep price that we elected not to meet. The protection, as a result, has been negligible."

"I'll see to it," Philip said and no more.

Thus, the burgesses soon added their conviction to the growing sentiment that there now sat at Nottingham an honest sheriff. And while many feared he was too good to long endure or suspected he was far more devious than met the eye, the novelty of a paragon in command of the castle was as welcome as it was perplexing.

· X ·

"THOUGH IT BE CALLED SWANHILL—and we have both the mute and the whooper variety in abundance—they make equally fine eating if singed precisely right, as our cook has mastered the skill over the years—what we truly pride ourselves on, Master Mark, is the quality of our sheep. They are remarkably hardy, which is not characteristic of the species, and free of the murrain." Thomas de Lambert cocked his lavish, snow-white head of hair toward the unfurling prospect of hillside pastures and pale gold fields that the great manor house commanded. "You know, I never fail to be amazed at the Lord God Almighty's benevolence in giving man so miraculously useful a creature as the sheep. Think on it—its every particle has a purpose—its flesh and ewe's milk to nourish us, its coat to warm us, its skin to record our thoughts and our business upon—even its droppings to enrich our soil and increase our bounty. And they are docile. Could Adam have asked Heaven for a more suitable beast to assure his own and his progeny's survival?" Lambert's head straightened and his arm shot out in an encompassing sweep. "We have nigh ten thousand of them, and I would wish for ten times that and forget the crops. But then we should become a nation of shepherds and bush warriors like the Welsh." He smiled and dismissed the conceit. "You French have the better of it, though, so far as the tastiness of your sheep goes."

Philip smiled back. "I am French now in name only, sire," he said, taking pain that his words not bear the tone of rebuke. "But if memory serves, the distinction in taste lies all in the preparation. As to the fleece, the French sheep are no match for the English. The difference must lie in the richness of the grasses. The greenness here is so much more vivid."

"Would that our wines as well were a match for yours—for *theirs*, I should say, you being an official Englishman now, and a ranking one at that."

There was an elegance to his patronizing, as with the rest of his speech and, indeed, his entire bearing. Well into his sixth decade, the baron's step was lively, his back straight, his eyes hard and clear, his manner brisk and purposeful as befitted a true bearer of blue Norman blood even at a remove of several generations. Three greyhounds, one white, one tawny, one more silver than grey, looped about him in sinewy arabesques like a pack of lazy attendants. "The rank is new," Philip replied, "and precarious."

"Rank is always thus," said Lord Lambert. "You will grow into it. Now tell me why our busy sheriff comes to Swanhill. I suspect it is for more than to make the acquaintance of its holder—though the pleasure, I assure you, sire, is mine."

The first clerk to the chancellor of England had come from Westminster two days prior, on a circuit of the shires, with the instruction. To advance the king's seizure of all church property, in the wake of the papal Interdict, from merely asserted dominion to accomplished fact, each sheriff was to choose a council of leading landholders from his shire. Under the eye of said council, each church or monastic establishment was to be given into the custody of a neighboring lord; this worthy would see to its tending and that its harvest be taken in good order (and none of it wasted to spite the crown), that it bring a fair price at market, and that after subtracting for custodial services and suitable living allowance for the resident clergy, the balance of the revenues be forwarded to the king. The special shire council, moreover, was to exercise extreme vigilance that the clergy be guarded in life and limb and that whosoever might direct a hand or weapon against a man of God while idled in his calling by papal command be hanged from the nearest stout oak.

Philip understood at once that this complex task presented the opportunity to gain favor with those awarded the plump church custodianships and, at the same time, to rewin for the crown the loyalty of those lords and lesser liegemen hitherto soured by the king's policies. In fact, John's vassals by and large resented the imposition on the realm of foreign authority, however divinely inspired, and saw in the papal Interdict a sundering of the feudal ties that bound in place the entire social order. For if the clergy could retain its holdings of the crown in spite of mass default of service, the very same could happen, in turn, with each vassal and villein among the king's tenants and subtenants—and soon nobody in the kingdom would be working at all, wealth and privilege would atrophy, and only anarchy would reign. No, the system had to be defended. But which of the men of the shire ought the sheriff to enlist to do the king's bidding in his war with Rome?

"I'd start at Swanhill," said Sparks. "Lambert is the bellwether."

Sir Thomas had come honestly by his estrangement from the crown, the sheriff's clerk recounted. The baron had served honorably in combat by the side of the estimable second Henry while he solidified his Angevin empire and repulsed the brash uprisings of royal sons too impatient for their father's death. When Richard succeeded to the throne, Lambert served him dutifully as well until the Lionheart fixed his lance point on the Holy Land; Sir Thomas retired from the wars then and there, rendering scutage as required, and with the crown off crusading and the headless body beneath it wobbling, Swanhill flourished under the baron's exacting hand. He met without complaint all the king's ensuing financial demands; for Richard's ransom, for his futile wars to hold Normandy, even for John's still more forlorn campaigns in France, including the hateful levy of one-seventh the value of all the movables in the realm. His son Guthrie fought valiantly with John's forces throughout the bitter debacle. But when the king had decided three years ago, against the preponderant consensus of his counselors and the baronage, to strike afresh across the channel to regain his lost ancestral empire, Lambert parted company with the crown. It was one thing to fight for Normandy, but that duchy was now an unbreakable bastion of Philip Augustus—and beyond it, what stake did the English nobility have in Anjou and Maine, in Poitou and Touraine, or even in Aquitaine now that the queen mother was gone? It was madness, it was delusion, this great amphibious assault, and while Sir Thomas continued to pay his scutage to avoid open rebellion, he forbade his son to join the fray. When the expedition was canceled on the brink of departure, the lord of Swanhill breathed easier, thinking the king had at last come to his senses. But then John maddeningly set sail for La Rochelle the following spring and demanded yet another scutage. The baron made his revulsion manifest; he sent half the fee required of him. To compound his delinquency, he answered the king's call the next year for one-thirteenth of his movables by paying only a small fraction of what had been taken by the property tax four years before. In short, Thomas de Lambert, lord and master of Swanhill, was a tax evader, arguing along with a growing number of his peers that he owed the king neither feudal service for combat in foreign wars of no vital interest to the realm nor ruinous exactions from his subjects' holdings simply to gratify the royal mania.

In answer, therefore, to the baron's questioning the purpose of his visit, the sheriff said he thought perhaps Sir Thomas would be willing to look beyond his differences with the king; it would serve both his own and the crown's interests for him to accept custody of Newstead Abbey, which directly bordered his manor on the west and to which he had tithed two hundred acres over the years. "As well, I invite you to join three other lords of the shire who will sit in council with the sheriff and assure the orderly maintenance of all church properties as long as the Interdict may require it."

Lambert flicked the underside of his beard in brief contemplation. "Whom else have you asked to be your councillor in this matter?"

"I begin with you, my lord, as the leading holder of the shire—and I do not pretend there may not be as much drudgery as reward in this service. But who better or more suited to bear the responsibility?"

Lambert eyed him laterally for a moment. "And have you consulted Westminster about my suitability for this distinction?"

"I would not presume to, my lord, before consulting with you."

"Then you are naive—and waste both our time, Master Mark. The crown will not accept me as things stand between us."

"Which is precisely why I begin by approaching you on this vital matter."

"Killing two birds with one stone, as it were . . ."

The sheriff's design was quickly apparent, and so intended. "Perhaps."

". . . provided that I acquiesce?"

"I would not put it thus, my lord."

"That seems your drift."

"I would stress, rather, the opportunity for reconciliation, and not dwell on the protocol of it, as to who begins the healing process."

"Perhaps I'm less moved by a need to reconcile than you suppose."

Philip slowed his tongue. "Forgive me, sire, but I cannot conceive how a protracted quarrel with your liege lord is in your—or, for that matter, anyone else's—interest."

Lambert wheeled upon him as his hounds crouched in concerted reaction. "You presume too much, Master Mark, by marching in here and declaring what my interests are!" His weather-lined face darkened. "You're a stranger to the realm—you're new to the shire—you hold no land or rank—and have no standing whatever among us except as the paid retainer of a king who thrives on the degradation of his vassals!"

"I meant no impertinence, my lord, only to—"

"Our king has no understanding whatever of how to gauge loyalty. He supposes all who question his dementia to restore the Angevin dominion in France are ipso facto his enemies. The very opposite is the case. I demonstrate my loyalty to king and crown precisely by urging him off this lunatic squandering of his resources—and these harsh policies in support of a feckless ambition."

"All of that seems past, though, my lord. The king has much else on his mind nowadays."

"For the moment—and only because the pope is not so easily browbeaten as we lesser holders of the crown—though I little love Innocent. In this quarrel, John is right for once. But he fails to inspire confidence. A king who as a prince strove to steal his brother's throne . . ."

The sheriff smoothed his mustache and gathered his thoughts before so withering an onslaught. "Yet John paid dearly for it, as I understand, with years of flawless penance. And dare I add that his brother was ill suited to rule?"

"That could not have excused the conspiracy—and was not knowable until well after the treachery had been hatched. Richard had character, at least—and balls. John has only craft."

"Some would call it statecraft, my lord."

"I prefer balls on my monarch. John had no need to reach a dishonorable peace with France by buying it, if that's what you call statecraft. Nor to abduct the affianced of one of his French vassals and make her his queen. Nor to slay his nephew on the pretext—"

"The marriage was hardly an abduction, my lord—and there were valid reasons of state behind it, alliances to fasten—"

"It was conduct ill suited to a knight's vows—to steal another's dame. I hear the real reason is that this Isabelle is a Jezebel whom the king fondles most ardently when the tide of battle crests. Alas, his prowess is all between his legs—and by no means limited to the queen. They say he chooses whom he wishes among the ladies of the realm—and what female subject has the fortitude to resist a randy king?"

Philip lowered his eyes. "Discretion seals my lips in this connection, my lord—royal philandering is no concern of a sheriff. As to the king's nephew, it was surely more than pretext. Arthur was in open rebellion against him, claiming the throne—"

"He was a child, being used by ambitious elders. John needn't have had him slain." Lambert halted his pacing and came to rest in front of Philip. "All this, though, is secondary. My chief grievance—and it is hardly mine alone—is that the king destroys the feudal compact by these endless and uncustomary demands for money. He thinks silver the touchstone of his dominion—as if he can purchase majesty instead of winning it by character, by wisdom, by high example, by dealing justly with his subjects and separating friend from foe through discernment instead of trial by ordeal."

The sheriff nodded. "But the king faces severe problems, sire, that require sums of money without precedent."

"I think otherwise, my good sheriff. I think he uses the problems, seizes upon them, magnifies them, *invents* them even, as an excuse to add to his hoard—and does so arbitrarily and punitively. I say it is unkingly—and ignoble."

There was an aura about Lambert such as Philip had not before encountered up close in any lord of the realm. It was variously composed of lineage, the rank and wealth it bred, courage, muscle, manly beauty and bearing, and the power they all conspired to gain for their possessor. In the presence of such potency he felt himself yet further reduced to the unstinting application of wit and tact and industry to gain but a modicum of standing.

"I cannot be the winner, sire, in debating with you the king's virtues or lack thereof—we come at the question from different vantage points. I sought only to remedy the situation, and hoped I might serve yourself and the shire as well as the crown by enlisting you to help combat the Interdict, which you concede to be against the—"

"Westminster will not approve your plan for me unless I first clear my debt. I owe yet on the last scutage—and intend, frankly, to parcel it out by the pennies to make my point."

"I'm told there is the matter of the thirteenth of last year as well, my lord, if I may risk being indelicate."

"What of it? I discharged my duty for that."

"In your fashion, sire."

Lambert's sapphire eyes narrowed. "Leash your tongue, Master Mark. I paid what the manor inventory justified, no more, no less."

"The payment, I'm told, was minimal—however it was arranged is not my place to say."

"Then don't say it!"

"I don't mean to harp on it, my lord, just to note that the matter has not been overlooked. I have a larger purpose in mind—which is to say you've registered your point with Westminster. Your protest is known and recognized, if not entirely appreciated. How do you gain by prolonging it?"

"I calculate no gain—only establishment of a principle."

"You've succeeded—and now if you make a gesture of good will to the crown by clearing your debt, my hope is the crown will reciprocate by granting you custody of Newstead, toward which your benevolence cannot be questioned, and in that fashion acknowledge that your views are not taken lightly and that you are indeed a baron to reckon with."

Lambert tossed his snowy mass of hair backward and gave a throaty laugh. "You have a deft tongue, Master Sheriff—but it does not conceal the tenacious tax collector behind it." He encircled Philip's upper arm within his iron grip. "This good will you speak of must run both ways. So let us approach it the other way 'round. If, withal, Westminster sees fit to grant me Newstead in custody—which I hardly covet but would undertake, as you put it, in loyal service—and approves my place on your council, I will end the quarrel by doing what you propose, yet not forfeit my right to protest anew if the crown resumes its captious policies."

"My lord chooses to stand on ceremony. Westminster is not likely to yield first. Why not settle with the crown—and receive your just reward from it?"

"I seek no reward—you've come to me trying to peddle one, and thereby advance your own standing in the crown's eyes. I have no need to number the king among my friends, nor any of his retainers. I wish you Godspeed, Master Mark."

The sheriff proposed the baron's bargain to Westminster and within the fortnight was advised that a king who would not submit to the pope was hardly prepared to yield to the lord of Swanhill—indeed, might strip him of his barony if his debt was not soon cleared. Philip duly sent word of this outcome to Sir Thomas, tactfully omitting the threat of seizure. He received in return a worn but still lethal battle sword and, wrapped about it, a note that read: "I used this when I rode with the king's father. It better belongs now with one who rides for the son. May it long protect you and defend the realm we both serve under God's beneficence.— Lambert."

·XI·

"MY HEART WEEPS FOR ENGLAND—and us all," said Clement de Beaupré, embracing the sheriff while taking care not to bless him. "That we should meet under such circumstances of duress and rancor instead of loving kindness . . ." His voice trailed off in studied lamentation.

"I fully share your regret, Father," Philip replied. "But I trust we may conduct our business with each other honoring every courtesy. I am no foe of Holy Church."

"Alas, our king has so cast himself," said the prior with a cluck of the tongue that edged him toward combativeness. "And the pity is that Langton has the makings of so superb an archbishop for us all."

"The issue cannot be resolved between us, Father, or it would be speedily done, I suspect. My concern just now is the future well-being of Lenton Priory."

Once again Westminster had changed its mind regarding how the crown should administer the seized properties of the church for the duration of the Interdict. The Chancery had finally determined that the best solution was to invite each religious establishment to recover control of itself provided that it agreed, first, to pay a fine for the privilege and, second, to transmit to the crown all revenues in excess of a fairly determined living allowance.

To implement this arrangement, reliable numbers were required by the crown, but church officers had been less than forthcoming with such data. This was especially so at the large monastic houses, with their substantial endowments of both land and money, producing income of unknown magnitude from rents, crops, livestock, and other sources—all of it necessary, they stated, for their devoted service to God and mankind. Because the Exchequer suspected the churches of understating their revenues and inflating their claimed expenses, a careful auditing had now been ordered. Toward that end, the sheriff had led a party from the castle to each of the larger holy houses in his shires, bringing with him his clerk, the *receptor*, the chaplain, two bailiffs, and three men-at-arms. Nowhere were they received with more patently feigned innocence than at Lenton Priory, a short ride from Nottingham Castle.

"I share your concern to the utmost, sire," Prior Clement said, "but let us enjoy a brief respite before addressing these worldly matters." He led them to a refectory table generously laid with platters of sweetmeats, fruit, nuts, five varieties of cheese, French wines of freshly pungent bouquet, and flagons of ale spiced with either ginger or nutmeg. "The pears are a special delight," the prior noted. "Our orchards have been unaccountably bountiful this season—perhaps out of divine compassion for our troublous state." He smiled thinly to indicate the remark was meant as a barbed pleasantry.

More from courtesy than appetite, the sheriff partook of the food, especially commending his pear for its meaty sweetness. "I've never had a finer one," he said between wetly appreciative chews.

The prior beamed. "I hope, then, Master Mark, that the priory may have the pleasure of your company at supper one evening soon. Our cook prepares a superb trout and a surpassingly tasty rabbit stew."

"The pleasure would be mine, Father," Philip encouraged him, and the discussion dwelt for a time on equally airy matters. The prior had heard that Hubert de Burgh, lately installed as sheriff in neighboring Lincolnshire and Philip's erstwhile companion-in-arms in Touraine, was a lineal descendant of Charlemagne, and he wondered whether Sir Hubert had ever broached the subject. "If it had been on his mind at all," said Philip, "the irony must have been borne home to him during our long weeks together as prisoners of the king of France. But he did not broach it— and I saw fit not to, though I had heard the same report as you. To judge by his prowess as a warrior, I should not have been surprised to learn Hubert's ancestry traced back to Vercingetorix."

Clement's eyes widened. "Ah, so you know the *Gallic Commentaries*. I have heard you are a learned man."

"Hardly that, Father. For a soldier I have perhaps read more than some, but beyond that . . ."

"Then you must avail yourself of our library—it's very extensive for a house our size. Any manuscript of interest to you we would allow to be removed to the castle for a time, provided only that you vow to protect it with your life." Another wan smile to convey the prior's measured benevolence.

"You are most kind, Father."

"I must confess to you, however, a certain reluctance to lend the pre-Christian works. Holy Church ought not to encourage dissemination of words and thoughts conceived by pagans and idolaters."

Silence greeted this profound nullity. To break it, Father Ivo ventured, "With all due respect, Prior—they did not know they were pagans."

"In what way does that excuse the impurity of their doctrines?" the prior asked, casting a sidelong look at the castle chaplain as if he had not the wit to warrant being addressed directly.

"Does the prior mean to imply," Ivo countered, his mournful features unaroused, "that no man ever had a thought worth our contemplation until the Heavenly Father sent His Son to earth?"

"I say such thoughts were sullied. Only sacred texts ought to command our study and reverence."

"Would that not preclude the Decalogue?" Ivo wondered.

The prior scented a trap and retreated. "Perhaps I would partially exclude the writings of the Israelites from my proscription."

"But do we not deem them infidels, Father," Sparks inquired, "every bit as objectionable as Saladin?"

The prior's glance fell upon the sheriff's clerk with amazement that a satanic insect should display such boldness. "No, not as much—they are not pagan." The prior turned away from the clerk. "It is their stubbornness that promotes revilement. So long as they will not adore the Son as the Father, they sin greatly."

"What has any of this to do," asked Ivo, exasperation filming the edge of his voice, "with the worthiness, let us say, of Aristotle's thought? His wisdom was no less divinely inspired than Solomon's, can we not agree?"

Before the prior could further entangle himself in spurious dogma, the sacristan intervened and led the castle party on a tour of the great religious house and its grounds. Throughout, Father Clement could not restrain himself from continuous commentary upon the priory's many excellences—its lawns and gardens, its fields and flocks, the marvelous new clock in the cloister courtyard, its golden honey and beeswax candles of superior brilliance, the ecstatic harmonies of its choir, and the effulgent grace emanating from its latest relic. For his rarefied holy house Clement de Beaupré failed to claim only the transcendent power of its prayer.

All of this proved highly instructive to the sheriff, who had come there, in effect, to tax the priory to the utmost—a point apparently lost upon the prior amid his orgy of self-enshrinement. Nor did Philip fail to observe that the physical labor at the priory, from the field work to the lawn tending to the barbering to the laundering, was performed entirely by indentured servants; no one in cassock discomforted himself in such a fashion.

"More than half our brethren spring from gentle birth," the prior noted in a final spasm of immodesty. "That's most uncommon in any monastic house nowadays—though I do not mean to dwell on distinctions between the social classes. Still, we must endure what providence hath wrought in this regard." Six Lenton monks, he added, had once held knighthoods—three Templars, two Hospitalers, and a Sempringham. "Yet they tell me you yourself are not a knight," the prior said to Philip with deft deployment of the non sequitur. "How is it that one of such refined speech and gracious manner failed to undertake chivalric vows?"

The question stung the sheriff, as much for the casual cruelty of its directness as for its implied reprimand. "I am a humble soldier and no more," he answered with muted voice. "The circumstances of my upbringing did not conspire to permit—"

"It's of no consequence whatever," the prior intruded with an abruptness that said he did not wish to protract the insult, merely to lodge it.

Philip, undiminished, turned now to business. If the priory would reclaim itself from the crown's hold, he said, it was necessary for the pair of them to concur with regard to its quantity of revenues, the permissible cost of its operation, and the size of the fine for the king's relinquishment. The prior grew flushed. "A fine—for the privilege of administering ourselves and relieving the king of the task? Preposterous!"

"It is the royal prerogative, Father," said the sheriff. "Westminster, moreover, feels the fines must be applied against any errors, accidental or otherwise, in the revenues and expenses anticipated."

"In short, you do not trust our figures."

"Let us say, Father, that they may be open to varying interpretations by laymen and clerics."

"Which is still to say the crown distrusts the church."

Courtesy had been strained to its limit. "If you say so, Father."

The prior grunted testily at the concession. "And if we do not agree to the fine you set and the figures your auditors propose for our maintenance?"

"Then you'll be subjected to the whims of a custodian."

"So—it is to be coercion, not a negotiation." He shook his head. "Then why should the king ever deal in good faith with the pope if Holy Church is thus at the crown's disposal as a fatted calf? We relieve John of all his financial burdens."

"It is the pope who imposed the Interdict, not the king. Now if you will be kind enough, Father, to permit Master Sparks and Brother Jocelin to examine the priory ledgers—all of them, including those that pertain to your endowments and the uses to which they are put."

Clement's jaw contorted in angry reflex. "I cannot! Such records are for clerics' eyes only. The church must remain sacrosanct in—"

"You must submit, Father, although I know how it pains you."

"You ask to violate a sanctuary. It is sacrilege—"

"It is arithmetic, Father—there is nothing metaphysical in it. To resist is to invite the suspicion you have something to hide, and I cannot believe that to be the case."

The prior was momentarily assaulted by shortness of breath, which drew a look of alarm from the sheriff. Soon the cleric raised a hand to allay his onlookers' concern and gathered himself up. "All right, you will have the ledgers—but they must first be assembled and put in order and— your clerks will not be able to understand them—which could lead to unfortunate—"

"With some guidance from your own clerks, Father, they'll manage."

"Tomorrow—you may have them tomorrow—they must be or- dered—"

Philip eyed the prior coldly. "Now, Father—not tomorrow."

"It's impossible."

The sheriff turned to the bailiffs. "Then we will confiscate them and return them to you when we have done."

"No—they must remain here."

"Very well. Let us proceed, then."

"It will take many hours—no, days—for your people to grasp it all."

"My clerks will remain as long as necessary—along with the bailiffs and men-at-arms."

The prior donned a look of wounded dignity. "No harm will come to your people, Master Sheriff—I can assure you. This is a house of God."

"It's not they I fear for," said Philip.

"You cannot mean . . ."

"The ledgers will remain in our care at all times."

A day and a half of record-combing produced a pair of revelations that Sparks reported in detail to the sheriff. The first was that the priory was actively engaged in the moneylending business, and very profitably so. The church documents did not call it such, referring instead to what was loosely translated from the Latin as "rent charges." By such device the priory purchased for perhaps two-thirds of a property's value whatever annual rent and other revenues it gleaned from crops or livestock or tolls or any licensed income whatever that ran with the deed; this purchase price—in all but name a loan—was repaid over twenty years and yielded the priory some 15 percent annually. Furthermore, the castle clerks' audit disclosed how heavily freighted the priory's expenses were with the upkeep of its servants.

Confronted by these revelations, Father Clement grew hotly defensive. "The rent charges are no different from the direct purchase of property, which is entirely permitted," he said. "Only this way, the money is of greater service to the needy, who may yet retain their holdings—a destitute knight going on crusade but in want of funds, or an estate owner whose crops have failed and yet must meet his debts. . . ."

"It is nonetheless money let out at interest—at rates close to usurious," Philip said calmly. "It is not derived from honest toil or the sale of legitimate wares, and so all such of your proceeds will be diverted to the crown."

"You—you vilify us—you liken us to the Jews—a monstrous slander—"

"The numbers speak for themselves, Father—they do the indicting, not I. As to the provisions for your laborers—"

"What would you have us do with them, Master Mark—cast them out into the cold and damp, where they can remain idle and starve?"

"I would have you perform your own labors in keeping with the vow of poverty by those who take the cloth—and not dwell in exceeding comfort like so many nobles in cassock."

"You—you profane Holy Church, Master Sheriff!"

"I leave it to higher powers, Father, to judge who does the profaning. In the meantime the crown must disallow the costs for so gross a luxury as all these servants. They are but another form of profit the priory realizes."

"We have no profit, only a margin of safety. And what you call luxury is a necessity—how else would the brethren have time and strength for study, prayer, and contemplation? You see, this is why the laity cannot be permitted to intrude upon our way of life!"

"The numbers are incontrovertible, though we may argue over their justification."

In sum, the sheriff had set the priory's fine at three hundred pounds, and its living allowance, servants excluded, at not quite twice that amount, with all revenues exceeding it to redound to the royal treasury.

"Rank piracy!" the prior exclaimed, a rosy glow suffusing his usual pallor. "It cannot be!"

"I take no pleasure in your distress, Father."

There was no soothing him. "When the king is declared excommunicate," he thundered, "as surely he will be, you who torment us, too, must be prepared for a similar fate!" He looked away from the sheriff. "I will speak of this at once to Sir Mitchell."

"The coroner serves the same king as I."

"But not so slavishly—no knight could."

·XII·

ALL IN ALL, Sparks was greatly gladdened by the improvement in his position, though it had not come without a price for him.

Before the new sheriff lifted him from obscurity, he had been but another silent stone among the multitudes composing the enormous edifice of the castle—and more pebble than boulder, at that. As a literate commoner and conscientious workman amid a den of largely unlettered slackers, he was alternately resented and ignored. As a faceless functionary of the law, he had nearly reached the point of relishing his anonymity. There was security in being a pebble—people neither tripped over you nor were inclined to boot you with gusto.

Now it had all changed. His constant access to the sheriff meant that the little clerk could no longer be treated like a wedge of sod. Everyone knew who he was, and their eyes lingered on him in recognition. But with respect also came envy and, as the hound follows the hare, loathing. People minded their words around him, fearful he would betray any slighting remark to the potentate who, for the moment anyway, ruled the castle. For the first time in his life Sparks was tasting the power that inspired dread, and he found the flavor more to his liking than he would have supposed. It left him lonelier than ever, though, and keenly aware of the dangerous game he had entered upon.

Father Ivo remained his sole confidant, yet even he had retreated from their prior intimacy. Rather than exploiting it to enhance his own position with Philip Mark, the chaplain had hung back, uncertain how to gauge the astringent newcomer. Indeed, Sparks himself was unsure. By comparison with his predecessors—the devious terrorist Brewer, the wolfishly prosperous Bardulf, the grossly negligent and largely absent Vieuxpont—the Frenchman had so far been the very model of efficiency, civility, and forthrightness. But would he prove masterly enough to sustain the authority of the office? And what flaws remained hidden behind that tightly fitted mask of rank, Sparks could only guess at. The clerk's prime concern was the sheriff's occasional tendency to impulsiveness—which was to say that he sometimes acted without seeking Sparks's counsel. Yet even those occasions, on investigation, seemed to have been governed more by shrewd design than by spontaneity. Why, for example, had Mark risked antagonizing the chaplain by assigning him the thankless task of regularly visiting the gaol? "To test his nature," the sheriff told him when Sparks grew bold enough to ask, "and to learn if there were kindliness and piety within him, as you gave me to believe—and whether I could depend on him as a man among men, not merely a spectral presence." If Ivo had felt degraded by the grim vigil, he gave no sign of it to the clerk, who guessed the chaplain was secretly pleased to be of service.

But if, by Sparks's reckoning, the chaplain seemed to be ever more favorably disposed toward Philip Mark, however sparing Ivo's praise of him, they undeniably held differing views of the sheriff's wife. Sparks, quite simply, was smitten with her.

There was, at first encounter, Anne Mark's sheer physical radiance.

She was nearly as tall as her husband and more animated, with a voice less flat and nasal but low and musically resonant. Her face was a pallid ovoid with an ethereal evenness to the features and lack of angularity that made its character seem to emanate all from within—or to be artfully applied, as with the blush of color always at her cheek. She moved with an almost stately deliberateness, head high but gaze demurely downcast unless she was directly addressed—and then the large eyes, of a brilliant blue and widely spaced, utterly arrested whomever they fixed upon. Her presence was still more striking for the manner in which she costumed herself. In summer her partiality was to shimmery sendal silks of daffodil and peach-pink and sky-blue or a pelisson of multicolored thread from the fairs of Champagne; now in the cooler season her preference was Flemish and Picard wools of more sedate tints. Over these she wore a close-fitting bliaut that her maid laced in place with a girdle of woven silk cords that served to enhance her long, voluptuous form.

Beneath this compelling surface Sparks had discovered a well of rarer qualities that threatened to afflict him with infatuation. Her formidable intelligence armed her to converse, when invited, on a breadth of subjects from which most women would have shrunk. She could engage the castle surgeon, to cite but a single instance, on everything from the healing power of herbs to the therapeutic value of bloodletting (of which she was dubious, arguing that if it were so, women, whose blood was let by nature each month, would be the detectably healthier sex); furthermore, she could bind a wound nearly as deftly as he. Her piety could not be calculated by the regularity of her attendance at Mass, which had been suspended by the Interdict, but her most prized possession other than her children was a finely illustrated psalter. Many of the hymns in it she had committed to memory, and several she had given soaring voice to during a lay service that she had asked Father Ivo's consent to hold in the chapel at Michaelmas for the people of the castle. She rode with vigor, having learned to hunt since coming to England; played chess with a certain impatient daring that unnerved her more contemplative opponents (save her husband); and loved to dance, albeit the infrequency of occasions to do so reduced her to performing by herself or with her daughters in the privacy of their apartment. By all reports she was attentive to her children, who were rarely seen in the public portions of the castle, and unfailingly courteous to the servants, even the maids, whose exasperating love of gossip she sought to curb—with but middling success.

Upon attaining the station of a true chatelaine, Anne no longer hesitated to press the steward regarding the household amenities. With so much else to attend to now, her husband had gladly deputized her to see to it that the living quarters were passably clean and liberated from guano, that the sheepskin windows were replaced by glass to brighten the interiors, that two dozen more flambeaux were fastened to the walls and lighted each night, and that rushes and straw were spread throughout and flowers and greens displayed to soften the austere aspect of the bastion. At her instruction, herbs and garlic and mustard brought flavor to the barely tolerable cuisine, a garden and orchard were planned for the spring on the castle grounds to ensure a ready supply of vegetables and fruits, and the freshly caught game was now more carefully salted and preserved. The great hall itself took on a cheerfulness and coloration it had not known. The aisle piers supporting the repaired ceiling were artfully painted to resemble marble; the long supper table on the dais was covered with linen dyed Montpelier scarlet (a contribution from Anne's own trousseau), and the wall behind it was graced with a huge *mappa mundi* drawn on canvas under the personal supervision of Honorius, the chronicler of Southwell, whom Father Ivo had been prevailed upon to enlist from the minster. The living quarters as well she had caused to be transformed. Walls were plastered and whitewashed, in some cases painted and marked with red lines to resemble masonry blocks and decorated with floral patterns; and in the king's and sheriff's apartments wainscoting of Norwegian fir had been introduced and painted green, with an overlay of scintillated gold in the royal bedchamber.

All of these charms, aptitudes, and accomplishments notwithstanding (or perhaps because of their very abundance), the chaplain confided to the sheriff's clerk on one of their walks along the banks of the Trent that he found Anne Mark offensive to him. Not a keen admirer of womanhood in general beyond his adoration of the unthreatening Virgin Mother, Ivo had remained a steadfast celibate who found in that blessed state the core of his faith; the lures of libido, the pangs of unrequited yearning, the distractions of family—all, he said, would have drained his strength and left him prey to the manifold corruptions of the laity. Like many a holy man, he saw women as creatures moved largely by lust and vanity, Mistress Mark unexcepted. But his displeasure with her went well beyond that. Whereas a wife should be retiring, this one was too bold in almost every respect—her bearing, her speech, her dress, how she painted her face with rouge and vermilion, the way she was domesticating the castle (as if it were her own château on the Loire!), and how she indulged in certain mannish recreations to burn up her pulsating energies. There was more than a touch of the infernal about the woman. Nor had her few transactions with the chaplain eased his mind toward her. When she requested his permission to celebrate Michaelmas in the chapel, what choice had she really left him under the circumstances? And why had she asked him to enlist his friend Honorius, who was a historian, not a geographer, to authenticate the map of the world being painted in the great hall when he himself had sufficient learning to do so? And still again she had come to the chaplain, doubtless believing he would be appeased, with the notion that apropos her endeavors to embellish the castle, the chapel might be enhanced by the addition of stained-glass windows. Since the burgesses of Nottingham were eager to pay tribute to the sheriff and had agreed to do so by some gratis work of artisanry, what could be more appropriate? She went so far as to suggest that the chapel windows might depict the warrior saints of Britain and France—George and Martin—along with other assorted paladins of the Cross. In every regard this proposal of hers won Ivo's hearty disapproval. He told her politely he was opposed to all gaudy displays of craft that many in the clergy mistook for veneration; purity of design and simplicity in rendering were for him the height of religiosity— thus, clear glass, by his lights, was holier than tinted. With due respect to her husband, moreover, he did not wish to dedicate the chapel windows to the glorification of war and warriors. To which Anne replied, "Philip is no warrior, Father, but a defender of the faithful." The chaplain, though, was not to be mollified. It troubled him, too, that she had been the one to broach the idea instead of the sheriff, whose approval she must have solicited beforehand—and if not, she should not have wasted his time on a whim.

The woman, all this was to say, simply could not please him.

Sparks was mindful of these abrasions when word arrived from West-minster that every sheriff in the realm was to seize forthwith and hold for ransom what the Chancery termed the clergy's "mistresses, hearthmates, and lady-loves." The particulars of the process, including the size of the ransom to be demanded and how to distinguish the implicated categories from the innocent female servants within each rectory, were left to the sheriffs' discretion. All that mattered was to flaunt the hypocrisy of those purportedly above and beyond the seductions of the flesh and to make them pay for it with Mammon's currency.

The sheriff shook his head upon receipt of the order. "It's unmanly—unchivalrous—and unnecessary," he said more to himself than to his clerk, and then, conscious that his words might be taken for open disparagement of crown policy, added, "I fear the king has more to lose than to gain by so heavyhanded a rebuke."

"It originates with Brewer—the Chancery messenger told me as much," Sparks reported. "He specializes in such punishing arrangements. There are three prongs to this fork, the fellow said. It harasses and demoralizes the clergy, holding them up to general ridicule and thereby undermining the Interdict. It extracts money from them for the crown in the bargain. And nobody can complain about the exorcism of such blatant impurity among the chief propagators of the faith—least of all Holy Church herself. They say Brewer is dancing with ecstasy at the perfection of the scheme—and the king is appreciative, as usual, of the baron's cruel ingenuity."

Philip nodded at this prodigy of statecraft but allowed that he had little stomach for it. In that case, asked Sparks, why not place supervision of the delicate task in the joint hands of the chaplain and Mistress Mark, who could be relied upon to deal mercifully with all concerned? Their sharing the responsibility would have the added virtue of binding their alliance, which stood in need of repair.

Philip mused on the suggestion, another of the sort by which the little clerk was proving himself invaluable. "But couldn't it as easily make matters worse between them?"

"Perhaps—but less likely if you consulted Father Ivo first and seemed to make him a party to her enlistment."

Summoned to the sheriff's closet, the chaplain expressed his full accord with the crown order to flay the unchaste. Resplendent in his own exemplary abstinence, he regretted only that the flagellation was being conducted by the laity. As to his active participation in the ingathering of concubines, Ivo was reluctant, feeling it would violate the Interdict by causing him to minister in one fashion or another to the tainted women.

"I suspect the Holy Father in Rome would secretly applaud the measure," said Philip, "even as you do."

"Be that as it may, sire, it would prove awkward. Still, I might offer counsel behind the arras, as it were, if that would be of—"

"Splendid, Father. I'm at a loss, though, to know who else might deal directly with these unfortunate women in a kindly manner." Philip raked the fingers of his right hand through his thinning hair. "I wonder," he went on cautiously, "at the propriety of asking Mistress Mark to help us—under your guidance, of course, Father. Conceivably a female sensibility in attendance might soften the blow—which is directed, after all, less at the consorts than the priests."

"I suspect she would find it beneath her dignity, sire—they are in some cases coarse women habituated to sin."

"Mistress Mark is no frail flower, Father, though I appreciate—"

"Then I suppose it would not be inappropriate, sire," said the chaplain with muted enthusiasm.

"Let us see if she's receptive—and would serve our needs."

Anne's face grew flushed, matching the spot of color on either cheek, at the disclosure of the order from Westminster, and her indignation was immediate. This served, at least, to persuade the chaplain that her involvement had not been prearranged.

"It's an unkind thing," said she, forehead ridging. "Why punish the women for the priests' self-indulgence? Is the immorality theirs?"

"Westminster is likely indifferent to the question," said Philip.

"Then it speaks ill for the compassion of the crown."

Philip cast her a quick, cautionary look; they were not in the privacy of their apartment. "The women are but the visible instrument for the exercise of a transparent policy. We thought, therefore, that in view of your sympathetic nature, you might be—"

"These women are already denied the dignity of betrothal. Why deepen the wound by treating them as inanimate objects?"

"I am not invited to debate the matter with Westminster, madam," Philip said stiffly.

"Nevertheless, it is callous and heartless—and a very bad joke."

"But you would make innocent bystanders of these women, madam," the chaplain remarked, surfeited with Anne's indignation. "Would you deny they are willing accomplices in these more or less permanent trysts?"

"I cannot speak of their willingness, Father—a woman's lot on earth has much of the involuntary about it. But I cannot think they are the prime movers in these sordid relationships."

"But hardly immaculate victims of clerical oppression."

"I cannot say, Father—although as domestic companions, I should suppose the clergy to be less violent than the general run of men."

"I thank thee, my lady, for the boon words," the chaplain said, a rare barb to his tone, and bowed stiffly. Sparks's eyes rolled heavenward at the growing sharpness of the exchange.

"At any rate," Philip interceded, "do you concur, at least, that the women ought to be treated gently—leaving aside the question of their respectability?"

His wife and the chaplain exchanged glances and nodded in unison.

"Then let us proceed together."

The sheriff put down three principles to guide them. He would instruct Bailiff Manning that his officers were to avoid brutality in shepherding the women to the castle, even if some of them had to be forcibly removed from the rectories and parsonages. The ransom charges, furthermore, were to be modest—from sixpence to a few shillings. Finally, the captives were to be given the choice of liberty if they wished to escape from their illicit unions; Anne and the chaplain would counsel them and try to arrange alternative havens for those who wished them.

Great speed and industry were required in the undertaking lest word of it spread ahead of the castle's officers and the hearthmates be hidden from them or temporarily sent off. Anne labored to ready the great hall for the women's arrival, equipping it with extra benches and straw bedding for their repose, food and drink to sustain their strength, chests for their belongings, serviceable garments if theirs were threadbare, rags for their indisposal, and slop jars for their relief.

The collection process began at dawn, with every horse, wagon, law officer, and soldier in the castle garrison pressed into the effort. The comings and goings were endless, producing such a tumult of cries and clatter of carts that the sheriff ordered the portcullis left open. Finally assembled, the women numbered nearly one hundred, many of them tearful upon their arrival, professing ignorance of what transgression they had committed against the king; less uncertainty prevailed as to how they may have offended Heaven. Others objected to the indignity of the occasion, having been plucked up like so many soulless, negotiable chattels and roughly handled in several instances, resulting in sizable bruises and ripped garments—fully warranted, the bailiffs testified after Anne carried these cases to the sheriff. She and Father Ivo interviewed each arriving woman to determine, as her nature permitted, the strength and depth of the bond with her cleric. In view of these findings, along with each priest's likely capacity to pay and the wealth or impoverishment of his religious house, the two of them jointly suggested the ransom prices to Bailiff Manning, whose officers conducted the negotiations when the clergy were admitted to the castle two days later to reclaim their lady-loves.

Because he was forbidden by the Interdict to hear the confessions of even the more contrite among those being held, Father Ivo's role was restricted to general commiseration, yet he heard enough to jar his predispositions. With more latitude, the sheriff's wife seemed to be everywhere at once, in attendance all day and late into the night, sparing herself for only a few catnaps—a marvel of compassion, good sense, and rectitude shorn of sanctimony. She sought to minimize the women's discomfort and feelings of degradation by listening with an open heart to those who chose to ventilate their grief. Commonest among their plaints was that they had entered upon their relationship in order to serve God, supposing it the closest they might approach to His ministry. This initially spiritual bonding grew carnal only with propinquity, and as it became knotted with age, they found themselves less and less able to extricate themselves from it. Their consciences were partially salved, most of them said, by the consoling words of their masters, who reassured them that there was no scriptural bar to cohabitation by clerics and that even Holy Church's strictures against it were mitigated by the history of licentiousness at the papal court.

Perhaps half the women whom Anne counseled spoke of being unjustly used and soiled in both body and soul. Some openly applied for relief from their hateful submission. To others who felt trapped in their parsonage by fear and habit, Anne stressed that they had taken no holy vows and were thus free to pursue a new life, with the castle promising succor in the quest. To those riven by remorse and eager to rededicate their lives in absolution, she spoke of the convent, starting perhaps in the scullery or some other mean station while Father Ivo worked to gain them admission to orders. To those deeply committed to their priests but certain—as were the clerics—that the bond was sinful, she raised the possibility that their men abandon the cassock and that the couples then seek a life together in the lay world. And to those defiantly defensive of their role as consort and scornful of the king's intrusion upon it, she prescribed only that in seeking God's understanding of their lot, they prevail upon their holy lovers likewise to solicit heavenly sanction.

Even at the height of the ordeal, the sheriff's wife stood vigilant against abuse of the captives, whom she viewed for the most part as pitiable creatures. When it came to her attention that several of the castle officers were mocking the women beyond her earshot—speculating as to whether they copulated gymnastically upon the altar and genuflected at the climactic moment—she flew into a fury and apprised Master Manning at once of the misconduct. He ended it with a full-throated upbraiding. Her ceaseless efforts wrung from the chaplain, shortly before midnight on the second evening of the shameful captivity, the quiet concession to her that "our prisoners, it is plain, are no temptresses."

The ruler of Lenton Priory appeared at the castle in high dudgeon the next day, intruding upon the sheriff's dinner in order to register publicly the degree of his wrath over these events. Armed with the certitude of the righteous because none of the women held for ransom was drawn from his establishment, Prior Clement charged that the abduction was yet another outrage by the crown, this one lacking even the pretense of justification that had accompanied the earlier seizure of church property. It was precisely the kind of harassment the king had warned the laity to abjure, threatening death to all who tormented the clergy over the Interdict; and yet here were the sheriff and his henchmen themselves perpetrating the selfsame sort of offense.

"I must disagree with you, Father," said the sheriff, putting his trencher aside and standing to confront his accuser. "The taking of the women was in no sense a punishment but rather a rite of purification, so to speak, against a practice universally acknowledged as sordid."

"It's not the king's place to stand in judgment of churchmen and their practices, however reprehensible." The prior leveled a finger at the sheriff across the void of twenty feet between them. "Holy Church tends to its own business."

"Do you mean to say, Father, that the laity may not judge Holy Church?" Philip asked as the others in the hall sat frozen in astonishment at the encounter, "even when it stands condemned for violating its own precepts, and steadfastly turns its back on the transgressors?"

"I mean, Master Sheriff, that the laity is not anointed by the Lord to police His custodians of faith on earth."

Before Philip could respond, Anne Mark rose and implored in a firm voice free of rancor, "Please do not blame the sheriff, Father, or the others of us here in the king's service for your own flock's immorality, which violates the teachings of the Apostle Paul and St. Augustine—and, so I understand, the earnest preachments of the saintly Bishop Hugh of Lincoln, long your mentor in Christ."

The prior's ire only intensified. "I do not address Mistress Mark," he said to the sheriff, refusing to dignify his wife with a glance, much less a reply.

"Then you would do well to," rasped Father Ivo from his seat, "for it is her sex that Holy Church permits its officers to exploit and degrade."

"You betray the Cross!" the prior shouted, turning his fury from the sheriff to the chaplain. "You and that godless little weasel of a clerk beside you—both of you in league—feeding this—this excrement to this—this—this swaggerer of a sheriff—and his wife!"

"You strike out in anguish, Father," the sheriff said, reclaiming his seat and thereby signaling that his patience was exhausted, "but it cannot alter the moral balance. You are free to stay and see to it that these consorts of your brethren in orders are gently tended under our roof."

But the prior declined the invitation, spun about, and led his entourage from the hall, trailing vapors of enmity.

"The prior's charms elude me—the more so with each encounter," Philip whispered into Anne's ear, "while the chaplain's begin to grow on me."

The sheriff's wife and Father Ivo persisted in their task until but one abducted hearthmate remained unclaimed—a certain Margot, the strapping housekeeper at Blyth Priory and known to be the beloved of its celerer. At first Margot denied the relationship and her own unchastity, insisting she had been taken in error. When Anne urged her to confront the reality of her life, the woman grew fierce and said the abbot would shortly appear in her behalf and vouch for her purity. But neither the abbot nor the celerer came, and Margot's defiance waned. As the other women were reunited with their companions or withdrew from their state of fallen grace, she grew forlorn and then despondent, taking no nourishment and refusing to speak at all. When it was at last clear she had been forsaken, the big, trembling woman broke down in Anne's arms. Not only had she long submitted to loveless coitus with the celerer but she had endured torture as well—she bared her breasts and showed Anne scar tissue about the nipples where they had been singed by votive candles. Asked why she had not fled her abuser's clutches, Margot said she feared yet worse treatment, then added in a voice wretched with self-hatred, "and I deserved to be disfigured for my sins."

In the middle of that night Anne was summoned to Margot's side; she had drawn a table knife across her wrist, inflicting a grievous but not quite fatal wound. Anne and Ivo took turns nursing her back to health, arranging finally for her employment in the castle kitchens.

One morning not long after their patient's recovery, Ivo encountered Anne close by the chapel and said with a crooked little grin, "Though I am forbidden to hear confession, I know of no restraint upon my making one." He asked that she hear him that afternoon on a walk across the meadow below the castle. She consented without a word but with the most radiant of smiles.

The meadow, a gentle incline of dun stubble in that wintering season, became a brilliant carpet of crocuses each spring, the chaplain began—"It will delight you to the quick"—and then abruptly cast aside the pleasantry to say he was doubly troubled.

"It grieves me to think so, Father," Anne replied.

"I have too poorly esteemed my lady," he said, "and misconstrued the quality of your mercy and loving nature. I would ask that you—"

"We are new among you, Father—and, at any rate, I am undeserving of excessive praise. I have the fault of impetuosity at times, I know, and have no doubt seemed to you—"

The chaplain reached out with a bony hand, clutched her closer one, twice gave it a fervent squeeze, and returned it to its owner. The former chasm between them thus bridged, he spoke then of his profound regret that a dozen women from Southwell Minster had been among those implicated in the recent ransoming of clerical lovers. While he had long since left the minster, unable to make a world for himself in its midst but finding one instead within himself, still he harbored friendships there and tender memories.

"But you cannot fault yourself for the minster's sins."

"In truth, my lady, I spoke against these sexual preoccupations while I was yet enrolled there. It won me little favor."

"Then you are to be commended."

"Alas, no. Rather than sustaining the battle, I abandoned it—and now, long afterward, I give the bailiffs the names of the perpetrators." His eyes locked to his footsteps. "They would not otherwise have known who among them had women—and which women."

"You were commanded by your king."

"Not to inform—only to lend comfort. I might have feigned ignorance, yet I avidly provided the incriminating—"

"You would not have been true to yourself."

"The truth is that I spared myself and betrayed others—except my beloved Honorius."

"The chronicler is your great friend. People often favor their friends, Father. It is not the worst human trait."

"But a priest has no more business playing favorites than betraying even blatant sinners."

"They were defilers of your former holy house."

He would accept none of her apologies for him. "I defiled that house as well. Honorius's woman, you see, was—"

She guessed the rest and hastened to ease his distress. "You sought only to spare her as well in not naming . . . well, surely a forgivable—"

"Thus compounding my sin."

"It is long past, Father. No doubt you have done penance—perhaps she has as well."

"I think not—it was not in her nature."

"Was she a wanton woman, then—and you blame yourself for—?"

"No."

"Did she spurn you for another—for Honorius—and so the memory is repellent to you?"

"No, it wasn't that way. And the memory is painful, but not repellent. Indeed, that was the issue. Our brief bond was so ardent that I finally had to flee from it—and her—and the whole place." His rheumy eyes sought hers and the reassurance that she did not revile him. "I fear this informing against the minster was some hateful form of vengeance." When she shook her head dismissively at that, he sighed. "I fear all my motives—and take balm only from knowing that the fires within me have long been banked."

She reached for his hand now and gave it a single strong squeeze. "Would that it were not sacrilege, Father, else I should pronounce '*Ego te absolvo.*' "

Their pace quickened thereafter, spurred by a chill wind gusting up from the river, and they concluded their walk in soothing silence.

·XIII·

THE REEVE'S STOMACH ROILED as he turned up the road past the churchyard and headed toward the better end of the village. Despite every intention of quelling his appetite, Blake nevertheless managed to overeat at Sunday dinner—it was his memory's fault for too vividly retaining the years when the food on his table was far less plentiful and varied. The awareness that he and his family were more abundantly blessed than their neighbors (the miller excepted) left him little conscience-stricken, though, for the reeve's duties were incalculably more taxing than those of any other man at Swanhill. Whatever happened there outside of the manor house he was answerable for—the field work, care of the stock, repair of barns and carts and fences, the health and conduct of those in bondage to Lord Lambert and the upkeep of their dwellings, even the deployment of dung on every arable acre. He earned his full stomach.

Still, he could not blunt a sharp pang of sorrow over the woes of the widow Griggs and had brought along a basket of leftovers from his own table—a wedge of green cheese, four eggs, a third of a loaf of brown bread, and a few oatcakes—that he knew would sustain Susan and the three children for several days. But as he neared her cottage, he saw tied to a tree nearby the shaggy old warhorse that belonged to the beadle. Jadwin's presence could mean only more trouble for her, as if her life had not been brimming with it for the past two years, ever since Griggs's once stout body began to fail before all their eyes.

The ploughman had been among the hardest-working, if least winning, men on the manor. His life was a perpetual struggle to tend his twenty-seven acres, spread over twice that number of selions in the common, while fulfilling his duties to the fief. He got scant help from his humpback twelve-year-old, who could do little more than spell the shepherds for an hour or two each day; nor did Griggs ask or expect any from his women. The older daughter, fifteen now, served as a milkmaid in the manor barn, while the other, two years her junior, put her dexterous hands to weaving for hire. His wife, Susan, busied herself with the cottage and feeding them; but beyond some small effort from her at harvest time, he did not want her soiled and broken by the demands of field work. So he labored feverishly in the common, knowing that if he were not ever-vigilant, the stone markers separating his field strips from his neighbors' had a way of shifting against him. More than half his week was spent at manor work, to which he submitted with no overt sign of truculence. Indeed, he ploughed and sowed and harrowed with uncommon skill and speed, carried dung uncomplainingly from the stables and cowsheds to spread upon the manor fields, scoured ditches and built fences and carted hay till harvest season, and from St. Peter in Chains to Michaelmas was in ceaseless motion, up well before the dawn and dragging himself back to Susan's gladsome greeting hours after the sun was down.

The fruit of Griggs's prodigious labors was a level of well-being decidedly above subsistence. His fields yielded enough oats, rye, barley, beans, peas, and vetches to stave off hunger even in lean years, with the excess allowing the family to maintain a team of oxen, a horse, a milk cow, a few pigs, and some chicks. In the eight years Blake had been reeve, moreover, never had he brought Griggs before the manor court for laziness, lateness, impudence, drunkenness, nightwalking or eavesdropping, theft or adultery, violating his neighbors' person or keeping his cottage in a dilapidated state or taking from the wood more than he was entitled to by hook or crook. No less than once a month did he hie himself to the parish church to confront the painted phantasms of eternal damnation that surely awaited him if he strayed into sin (and possibly, even if he did not). Griggs, in short, was the perfect serf.

As such, it followed that he was wanting in comeliness of manner. Habitually sour and suspicious, forever fearful from a lifetime of incessant servitude, he had nary a glad word nor any tiding beyond his perpetual bemoaning of the weather. On his occasional visits to the alehouse, he was a torrent of vituperation, reviling his God, his church, the lord of his manor, and those of his neighbors who worked less but had more than he. The anger within the ploughman, as Blake gauged it, never slackened except toward his Susan, who soothed him without complaint and never forgot to bless him for what he provided. Toward the reeve himself, Griggs was neither kindly nor hatefully disposed but saw in him a gain over Jadwin, Blake's predecessor as reeve until ordained as beadle of the manor. Jadwin, the bloodthirsty bastard, once drove a dung fork through the chest of a slacker, killing him on the instant, and caused the village drunkard to be hanged for filching sixteen eggs from the manor henhouse. If the reeve was no monster by Griggs's reckoning, Blake supposed the ploughman nonetheless saw him as a parasite who asslicked the lord and his steward to preserve his privileged status; who else but the reeve among the commoners was paid for doing no physical labor, was charged nothing for rent or firewood or having his flour milled, was permitted to pasture his animals on the lord's fields, and was granted a share in the bounty of the manorial harvest? It was that very reeve who assigned him his work and stood in judgment of its performance—a man of no gentler birth or freer soul than his own. How could he harbor other than resentment toward such a taskmaster?

This seething bitterness Blake instinctively sensed and forgave, appreciative that Griggs met his every duty without need for the lash. And so when the consumption began to wrack his sinewy body and caused his smoky cottage to fill with bloody coughs, the reeve took mercy on him. Susan came to Blake as the disease wasted her husband's fiber and, without his knowledge, begged the reeve to ease Griggs's burdens, offering to do anything she could to compensate so they would not lose their dwelling or chattels. The reeve, stating it was only temporary surcease, assigned him the least taxing chores on the manor—hedge-trimming, fence-mending, carting without carrying—and even had his own team brought to the common to plough and plant perhaps a third part of the ailing churl's selions. But Griggs knew he was being pitied and could no more bring himself to thank the reeve for his kindness than to damn God for afflicting him, though his eyes, receding into his gaunt face, said that he wished to do both.

His family got by for the first year of his sickness but not without duress. His fields, improperly watched and weeded, produced less, and it became necessary to sell off their livestock by stages, with their diet suffering as a result. The tallage went unmet, threatening them with dispossession, and the wood-penny as well. The miller, who was entitled to a sixteenth of Griggs's corn for grinding his flour, was cranky over the ploughman's reduced harvest and serviced him badly. The sole relief in the second year of his decline was the Interdict, for which Griggs blessed the pope; worshipers were not obliged to tithe for holy services that went unperformed. During much of the year Griggs could not rise out of bed; yet he would not allow Susan to ask help from their neighbors, nor, in any event, would it likely have been forthcoming. Charity did not overflow from their worn bodies and pinched souls—rather, they had nibbled at Griggs's neglected fields in the common, appropriating perhaps a fourth part for their own.

Thus, when harvest time came, he roused himself, knowing that if his work were not done, debt would overwhelm the family and ruin lay just ahead. He pushed his frail body to its limit, and beyond; a fortnight shy of Michaelmas, sweat beading on his shrunken chest, the heart within it burst just as he brought in the last wheat.

Inconsolable for a week, his widow recovered her wits sufficiently to ask the reeve to attend her when Stryker, the steward of Swanhill, came to her cottage accompanied by the beadle, Jadwin, enforcer of Lord Lambert's will, and the new bailiff of Rainworth district to collect the death tax. The three of them lingered outside her door for a time, like hovering creatures of prey, to examine the condition of the ox and the horse, the only stock remaining to Susan. Upon finally entering, they registered cold condolence as their eyes roved about the interior in swift appraisal. Blake's unwelcome presence was acknowledged with the merest of nods.

The heriot entitled the manor to take a widow's best beast, Master Stryker stated woodenly, "and that would be your ox—though there's little enough service left in those sagging bones." Ordinarily, he went on, the church's mortuary would have claimed the second-best beast, but since the Interdict had meant the cancellation of all church takings, she ought not to mind unduly that the manor must have her horse as well to meet the eight shillings of rent now due the lord. It was necessary, too, to resolve the matters of a substantial default of service to the manor for the two years of Griggs's illness, the unpaid wood-penny, and the short multure to the miller. "Half your household implements must also be forfeit— though the lot of them isn't worth it. The lord, you see, wishes to be kind."

"The manor is harsh," the reeve spoke up. "You leave them bereft of means to survive—of any hope to—"

"The manor follows the law and custom," the steward said, nodding toward the bailiff. "She'll have a year to try to gather the rent and provide the labor owed the lord—but with the boy a cripple, I can see no likelihood the women will make it up."

"I'll work the fields myself," a tearful Susan offered.

"You're not fit for it—and if you try, you'll go the same way Griggs did." The steward turned to the reeve. "The only answer is for her to remarry as soon as a suitable husband is found."

"I'll marry as I choose! . . . He must be kind," Susan declared, suddenly stifling her sobs. "I'll not submit!"

"Then you must pay the lord for the manor work undone—and the rent and every other fine—or yield the cottage to those who fulfill their duties. It's a forlorn hope, Mistress Susan—it would be far better for you to—"

"Nevertheless, I'll try."

Susan soon after asked the reeve to seek permission for Judith, her older daughter, to work outside the manor while the younger, Sarah, roughened her soft hands spelling Judith as a milkmaid. Susan herself would look for weaving work to take in and a ploughman to plant and harvest the family fields in return for half their yield; in-between time she and the boy would tend the crops as best they could. But when Blake put the matter to Stryker, even offering to ease Susan's plight by finding her light field chores, the steward snapped, "Let her be less proud—they should move to a shack and seek alms from the manor until there is a husband." To release Judith for work off the manor, he added, would entail a fine of two shillings. Even without that added burden, Susan's woes intensified when her boy was caught by the woodward taking down a small tree in the waste for firewood. The fine of sixpence was suspended at the lord's sufferance in view of the family's dire condition, but the terrified little humpback was threatened with the stocks if he repeated the offense.

Susan found herself left but one choice if the family was to avoid beggary—and she, a hateful marriage. She began to grind her own corn from the last harvest on a quern, a small hand mill that had lain unused for years in a corner of the cottage, and to do the same for some of her neighbors who wished to avoid going to the miller. This course, though, was laden with peril, for the miller alone was licensed to perform any and all grinding done on or for the manor, with the lord extracting his share of the fee. Thus enfranchised, the miller had long since grown overbearing and abusive, giving currency to the manor's best known riddle: "What is the boldest thing in the world?—A miller's shirt, because it grasps a thief by the throat every day of the year." This popular assessment traced to the way he was known to adulterate the flour with water and wood dust, allow his dogs and chicks to wander about the grinding room (with a resulting admixture of filth), underweigh the grain due him from each villein's harvest, and fail to keep the mill in good repair, often causing those who had laboriously carried in their grain to have to haul it away and return another day.

The miller's meanness was particularly manifest in the zeal with which he saw to it that those who tried to avoid his services paid dearly for the slight. Whoever brought his flour to the manor baker without having first taken the grain to the mill was presumed guilty of hand-milling it at home— and whoever failed to patronize the baker was held doubly suspect, inviting a sudden visit from the beadle. The quern would be confiscated and charges pressed for its surreptitious use; heavy fines at the manor court regularly resulted.

Thus, Susan proceeded with extreme caution, digging a hole to hide the hand mill in, and each time she ceased her exhausting labors, dragging over it the great chest that held what few belongings remained to her.

Her baking she did in the middle of the night, hoping whatever telltale aromas escaped her oven would go undetected. For several weeks she continued in this fashion as her dread of being caught yielded to the prayerful hope that the family's predicament had inspired leniency among the authorities.

This delusion ended one afternoon when Jadwin rapped rudely on her door and, before she could open it, pushed his way inside. Fortunately she had not been milling at the time, but the beadle was not to be gulled. It took him scarcely a minute to deduce the hiding place. He stalked about the cottage in triumph, then paused in front of her and placed a hand familiarly on her shoulder. "This must end at once," he said, softening his voice while heightening his menace, "or the consequences will be terrible for you." His hand brushed across her breasts as he added, "Accept this warning as Christian charity and think well of the beadle."

She related the incident to the reeve and, though wary of enlisting his complicity, asked if he might intervene. Blake judged the beadle as likely to relent as the tides. The reeve would have to appeal directly to the miller in the hope a granule of mercy lurked somewhere within him. So he brought a load of his own barley to the mill for grinding but found on hand only Lot, the miller's son, who explained that his father had gone to Lincoln with the steward to buy a new millstone. When he was done with Blake's load, Lot asked whether his father set down the service in the tally book he kept, even though the reeve was not charged for the labor. That such a ledger even existed—and, as Lot confided when asked, was transferred each week onto a master list held by the steward's clerk— meant that Stryker himself was thus fully aware of likely offenders against the manor rules on milling and baking and advised the beadle accordingly.

Blake cautioned Susan on this systematic surveillance and, by way of discouraging her from the risky practice, had his wife bring her some of their own foodstuffs—"just to help," that good woman said, "until things go better with you." Torn between gratitude and shame over accepting such dependency, Susan resumed the hand-milling.

Within the fortnight, the beadle was back, this time granting her the choice between a fine of sixpence or lying with him on the straw. It was so long since she had been with anyone but Griggs that the latter possibility quite startled her. Had the invitation come from a source less vile, it might even have gratified her, for she had ceased to suppose that, as a ploughman's faithful wife, she could yet be an object of desire to another man.

But how could the act, performed with such a partner, prove other than a bestial coupling? And the offhanded way in which it was put to her—as a quick job of rogering to stave off yet worse consequences—made the prospect doubly offensive. She chose to be fined instead, adding to her ever longer list of arrears.

Whereupon the reeve revisited the miller and, finding him at his task and in spirits less balky than usual, solicited his kindness toward Mistress Susan. "Why would I?" the miller snorted, as if it had been put to him to swallow a salamander whole. "Griggs always tried to cheat me in the multure—but I could count better than him."

"But you claim the same of everyone, allowing you no choice—as you tell yourself—but to adjust your scale against them. The hayward and I are not fools."

The miller managed a lopsided grin. "I must look out for myself," he said. "They all have it in for me."

"If you showed a little kindness sometimes, maybe that would change."

"When kindness is first shown to me. Meanwhile the widow cannot be permitted to endanger my livelihood."

Thus stood Susan's tribulation that Sunday as the reeve rode out to deliver her another basket of victuals from his own larder, only to find the beadle's horse beside the cottage, expiring great plumes of hot breath into the chill air. Had she rashly kept on hand-milling in spite of all? Even in her growing desperation, could the poor woman have been so foolhardy? Or had Jadwin just come to torment her—or worse? Ought he to fly to her rescue at once, or would his intrusion only drive the beadle to extremes and aggravate the never easy dealings between the two men?

Blake chose discretion and rode on a way, biding his time until finally dismounting in a copse just off the road to await the beadle's departure. It took perhaps an hour, to which he added ten minutes out of politeness before returning to the cottage. Within, Susan's soft weeping was unmistakable. Sensing the cause, he grew taut with emotion and knocked insistently. A long minute lapsed before the red-eyed widow wordlessly admitted him but would not meet his glance.

The reeve dropped his gift basket of food onto the table and saw on the corner opposite a half-empty bottle of malmsey and two tin cups. His eyes traveled to the mussed straw bedding by the hearth and then to the quern on the floor beside the chest; in front of it, a powdery mound of flour sat upon a cloth.

"You supposed the beadle would not be stalking about on the Lord's day—is that it?" Blake asked, struggling to sustain a civil tone.

"Yes." She receded into the darkest corner of the cottage.

"Why weren't your children with you?"

"I sent them off," she said, her voice small and quavering.

He could not still his anger. "I see you've been celebrating the Sabbath with fine spirits. I had no idea that your circumstances have so improved that you're able—"

"He offered it to me—as a kindness."

"A kindness!"

"I was so afraid he'd—take the mill—that I—"

"Thought you'd conciliate him by drinking his health?"

"He—was being—less horrid than before, so—"

"So you played his game—and soon found your resolve weakening."

"I . . . yes . . . the wine . . ."

"It's good wine, isn't it?" The reeve's voice was thick with rage.

"Yes."

"And you debased yourself?"

Snapping embers in the hearth made the only sound in the cottage until Susan finally said, "I had no choice. It was that or he'd have—"

"And was it to your liking?"

She lowered her face into her hands and began to weep afresh. "If you're my friend," she said, gasping to regain her voice, "you won't be harsh with me. I have no—"

"Because I am your friend, I will be harsh!" He took two long strides across the cottage, seized the little flour mill off the floor, lifted it as high as he could over his head, and brought it crashing to the compacted ground.

Susan spun around in time to see the millstone in a thousand fragments. "You—terrible—*shit!*"

"Someone had to stop you—since you can't stop yourself!"

She sent up a wail of fury and moved purposefully toward him.

"He'd have kept coming back to you for more, if I didn't . . ." His own spasm of fury was spent now and began to yield before hers.

She reached the table and grabbed up the bottle of malmsey.

"Or do you want him to keep coming to you?"

"Ohhh!" she screamed and pitched the wine bottle at him with all the force in her. He leaned aside and let it sail past, shattering against the door in as many particles as the little millstone near it and leaving a jagged garnet stain at the point of impact.

"I'll attend to the beadle," Blake said, taking his leave before she chose to lunge at him with one of the shards, "and you attend to your virtue. If you must sell it finally, set the price dearer."

When Blake confronted him the day following by the main gate to the manor pasture, Jadwin was riding at a jaunty pace with the white wand of his office tucked beneath his arm. The reeve, not being a man to spend his courage idly, knew full well the beadle's proneness to violent expression of his wrath and that even those far from fainthearted often cowered at his approach. Yet a limit had to be fixed to his brutal ways—he had terrorized the manor for too many years now—and who else was there to stand against him? The prospect had given Blake a sleepless night; either the issue had to be joined or he should quit his office—and the latter step would only feed Jadwin's tyrannical habits.

On foot, the reeve gave away two stone and four inches to him, but mounted as they were at this encounter, the beadle seemed a less formidable Goliath. "I urge you, Master Jadwin," he said without preface or bluster, "not to violate the widow Susan again, or you'll sorely regret it."

The beadle's eyes widened, then turned to slits radiant with contempt. "She submitted of her own accord—and what bloody concern is it of yours, anyway, *Sir* Reeve?" His voice dripped sarcasm.

"Every churl on the manor is the reeve's concern—and you well know it."

"The reeve should worry over their pisspots, not what's between their legs. Besides, she's just another dirty, degenerate slattern—what do you care for her?"

"Her plight moves me."

"You'd like her moving under you, is what I think—and envy me for having got to the widow first. Fart up your nose, Master Blake—and if you threaten me one more time, you'll wake up with a dung fork planted in your bung."

Heart thudding and throat suddenly dry, he pulled immediately alongside the beadle and looked him hard in the eye. "Nobody licensed you, Master Jadwin, to fuck the world to your heart's content," the reeve said evenly. "Touch her again, and I go straight to the steward."

"Ha!" said Jadwin, fixing the beadle's wand firmly in his grip, as if ready to bring it slashing down onto the reeve's brow. "Stryker would as soon see Susan's sweet cunt carved to pieces and fed to the hounds."

"Then it's Lord Lambert himself I go to. He'll not tolerate your savaging a helpless woman."

The beadle hawked up half a mouthful of spittle and sent it flying past the farther ear of the reeve's mare. "Our lusty Susan is anything but helpless—and Sir Thomas wouldn't waste so much as a good belch over the fucking habits of the manor's indigent widows."

"The new bailiff, then."

"Too late—he's already safely in Master Stryker's pay. If anything, he'd arrest you for destroying the widow's hand mill and bottle of malmsey because she wouldn't submit to you. You have a nasty little temper there, Master Blake."

His temples pounded. "How do you . . . ? She couldn't have . . ."

"The whole manor knows what transpired—I made certain. You're less beloved around here than I am just now." The beadle snickered. "You see, I'd forgotten to take my wine with me and, not wanting the widow to sicken herself with it, I turned back—only to find the reeve's horse beside the cottage. So, compassionate fellow that I am, I revisited Susan after you'd left to see what mischief you were up to."

Venom surged through the reeve's veins. "The sheriff, then—I'll go to him. I've seen him—he's a just man. He'll put a stop to your vicious ways—"

The beadle threw back his head with a laugh that turned readily to a snarl. "The day you fly to the castle to tattle, Sir Reeve, is the day you seal your doom." He jabbed a booted heel into his ancient warhorse's underbelly and rode on. "Anyhow," he called over his shoulder, "they say your counterfeit sheriff will be mincemeat by Twelfth Night. So have a care, old cock."

A.D.
1209

·XIV·

"I HAVE NOT SEEN A WOMAN go at a gallop quite so fiercely as you, madam," Lambert declared as he drew up alongside her for the last leg of the ride back to the manor house.

The hunt appeared not to have disheveled a lock of his leonine hair, whereas Anne felt herself damp all over from the exertion. Did Sir Thomas suppose a woman who was assertive in the saddle to be lacking in refinement? Ought she to have hung back in the chase with Guthrie's pretty little magpies, who rode as if pained by the challenge of controlling such a mass of muscled power between their legs? "Is that a fault, then, sire?"

"Not in the least, my dear. I find such spirit enchanting in a woman." He reined his mount down to a walk so his words needed not be shouted.

"Now I fear I've truly made a spectacle of myself."

"Of a not displeasing sort. The hunt is as close as any woman comes to martial combat, and most pale at the prospect—yet you rally to it. I suspect you'd have made a splendid warrior."

She slowed her pace to his. "I have thought so myself at times," she said with a small smile yet without fully meeting his look, "so long as bloodshed were not required." Reaching forward to give her horse an appreciative rub on the side of his damp neck, she searched her mind for a topic to deflect his attentions. "I regret Lady Cicely's absence, my lord. I trust her indisposition is brief."

"It's chronic whenever there's a hunt. She prefers to take life's pleasures indoors."

Indeed, Lady Lambert was known to suffer from a certain delicacy of constitution and engaged in no exercise more strenuous than playing the harp—at which, as it happened, she excelled. For their first social engagement of consequence since arriving at Nottingham, Anne Mark wished to commit no gaucheries and thus had thought it prudent to make discreet inquiries about the master and mistress of Swanhill. Lady Lambert, she readily discovered, was the prime source of the family's lofty standing. Her husband was merely the second son of a third son of a Norman baronet; she was the sister and sole sibling of the earl of Hampshire, a choice prize conferred upon Sir Thomas by the second Henry for his battlefield prowess and grace as a courtier. The Lambert barony had since grown to more than five thousand acres parceled among seven estates, of which Swanhill was the jewel. Besides Sir Guthrie, the oldest of their surviving children, Cicely had borne a second son, now a deacon at York cathedral, shortly to be advanced to canon, and a daughter married into the third-best family in Warwickshire. Having done her conjugal duty, she was said—probably because Lambert, in moments of drunken unrestraint, blurted as much—to have lost all interest in the joys of the bedstead, preferring to pluck at musical strings and dally over needlework.

"A sedentary life is not an unsensible course for a woman," said Anne. "Alas, our own family's existence has been too transient for me to adopt such a course. And travel is so wearing."

"Then may your tenure at the castle prove enduring," said Lambert.

"It has already endured longer than I gather some had anticipated— or even might have preferred. Your hospitality toward us is thus the more pleasing, my lord."

"It is to the shire's interest not to begrudge you welcome, even while it tries to fathom your husband's ways. I have told others as much."

Anne had never attended a grander manor house than Swanhill. No detail among its fineries escaped her notice: the beading on the timbering, the soft hues and careful brushwork on the wainscoting, the carving on the chests, the massiveness of the silver candelabra, the dyed leather coverings on the benches, the lively scenes so exquisitely embroidered onto the wall hangings (several of them said to have been of Lady Cicely's own device). The food at dinner was well prepared and abundant; the minstrel's playing was unintrusive (if a shade too dirgelike for Anne's taste); and the great hall was comfortably draught-free yet not overly smoky. The company, as if selected to put at ease a sheriff without aristocratic linkage or high standing at the royal court, was for the most part a family gathering: the ebullient host and austere hostess; their son Guthrie and two high-humored friends of loosely bridled decorum; Cicely's ancient aunt, who could hardly see what was on her trencher but heard every syllable uttered from one end of the table to the other; Lambert's corpulent cousin and his wife from Lincoln, where he owned a dyeworks and half the freemen of the town; and the ascetic abbot of Newstead, who before the Interdict had sent a monk to say Mass each morning in Swanhill's little chapel in consideration for Sir Thomas's generous patronage of the abbey. The sole outsider of rank on hand was the widower Ralph de Greasley, whose steward the sheriff had found it necessary to rebuke at his first tourn the previous autumn. Yet Sir Ralph, celebrated for having gored at least a dozen Saracens at Acre (and done next to nothing since), proved far from resentful.

"As it was told to me, you were altogether in the right," he conceded almost the moment after their introduction, "if perhaps a touch excessive in your reprimand. The crown had spoken plainly of the widow's rights, and my steward had thought to slip around them, supposing my consent. Stewards are known to do that if not cautioned."

"My duty was clear," said Philip, "and your understanding of it is greatly valued, sire."

"Our sheriff has fast won renown for his dutifulness to the interests of crown and shire alike," Lambert put in good-naturedly. "Let us pray those interests never diverge—with the usual appalling consequences."

"I see no prospect but concord between them," Philip countered, "and I'll not sally out to look for incitements."

"Hear, hear," said Lambert with a light clap to the sheriff's shoulder. "Let us drink the king's peace."

Toasting the king's health was another matter, though. Over dinner Lambert referred only obliquely to the problem by remarking to the abbot, "We sorely miss Brother Aloysius's daily intervention in our behalf with the Heavenly Father. Mornings without Mass leave us feeling pagan. But then the whole kingdom, I suppose, is in the same boat with us."

"Not quite," said Greasley. "Your craft is sturdier."

The table laughed, but the abbot turned up his palms defensively. "They tell me the king, alas, will not bargain in good faith so long as he holds the English church captive and thereby funds his government."

"What I fail to understand, though, Father," said Lambert's cousin, wolfishly disposing of the last of his lark wings, "is why the pope deprives all us bystanders of the clergy's services when his quarrel is with the king alone."

"No doubt Rome hopes his deprived subjects will convince the king of the error of his ways." The abbot shook his head. "It is a painful policy, I grant you—which is why I frankly suspect that unless Westminster sues for peace soon, excommunication is nigh."

"And how will that soften our most sovereign John?" Lambert asked. "Given his nature, it's likely to make him still more obdurate."

"It will also render him officially godless—and cause his subjects to fear they may be similarly damned through continued fealty to an outlaw of the faith." The abbot turned to the sheriff. "And forgive me, Master Mark, but I fear insurrection could follow."

"Possibly," said Philip as all eyes turned upon him. "Or possibly the opposite might occur, Father. If the king is perceived to have been sundered from the faith unjustly, his subjects may side with the outcast, leaving Holy Church to suffer the graver loss."

Such weighty matters were cast aside for the remainder of the evening as countless flagons of wine fed the prevailing mellowness of mood. Following the meal Lady Cicely stroked the harp, further soothing temperaments and transporting several of her guests to the nearer shore of Nod. The men thereafter engaged in chess and the women adjourned to the mistress's parlor to admire her needlework and suffer her withering tongue. The latter surprised the sheriff's wife, who took Lady Cicely's brevity of comment at table for a withdrawn nature that matched the unbroken iciness of her appearance. The pale pillbox crowning her coif was fixed so tightly by the strap beneath her chin that it was a wonder any words at all escaped from the intervening face. Presiding in her own parlor, however, she proved both voluble and caustic. "You are very beautiful, Mistress Mark," she said after disposing of her obtuse Lincoln cousin with a snide epigram, "and your costume equally so."

"My lady is kind," said Anne, knowing full well that her best garment was no match for Lady Lambert's blue cyclas, with its silver embroidery in the shape of little swans about the neckline and her cape of ermine lining. "But I pretend to no fashion and can afford little extravagance."

"You are too modest. The wife of a soldier must be clever indeed to manage such a wardrobe—or is the booty of war as lavish as it's said?"

Anne could not be certain whether the remark was in jest or rife with intolerance for a commoner who would consort with nobility. "As to the wherewithal," she said crisply, "my own family is not entirely destitute— or loath to supplement a soldier's pay for the benefit of a grateful daughter. As to booty, the sheriff assigns it to the category of pillage and rapine— the proper business of barbarians only."

"No doubt," said Cicely, addressing her embroidery. "But the tendency is not unknown among mercenary captains—not to mention our sheriffs past."

"A misfortune, my lady."

She brought the cloth closer to her eyes. "Your accent is charming, madam. Tell me your native county—you are from the Midi?"

"Not so southerly, my lady. Touraine—the town of Tours."

"Ah, a provincial setting! So your speech is unspoiled by—"

"Less remote than Nottingham, my lady," Anne put in, "and astir with yet more commerce." She checked herself lest she appear to be embracing persiflage and demurely asked the way to the garderobe.

On her leisurely return, she passed through the great hall and found it abandoned save for the lord of the manor, who was teetering blearily over a chess table. Her rustling passage awakened him. Guthrie and his cronies had ushered Greasley and the sheriff to the trophy room, he said—"to see the old man's killing tools from his days at the king's side and to take a little target practice with the long knives. Come join me for a chess game—your husband says you're the better player."

"He can be excessively gallant. I'm passable at best."

He took her hand and guided her onto the stool opposite his; there was no escaping. "You're a woman of many rare talents, I see."

"Small talents but wide interests, sire. My fondness for the game, I fear, far outstrips my aptitude."

She was in fact no match for him, even in his somewhat muzzy state, and made no effort to protract the contest. That he was playing with a woman interested him far more than the outcome, and he looked disappointed when she surrendered. "Don't be so hasty to sacrifice your pawns—they have their uses," he said, returning the pieces to their opening positions. "And be more deliberate with your play—you seem more eager to have the game over with than to win it. Enjoy the combat as your husband seems to, though he managed to lose to me—most discreetly and, let me say, unnecessarily—almost as if he feared I'd not forgive his victory. When he can play to win and not merely to avoid offending me, he'll truly be my sheriff."

"I'll impress your sentiment upon him," she said with a smile, "discretion in this case being the poorer choice than boldness."

There arrived at the castle the week following a superb chessboard with inlaid squares of yew and chestnut edged in silver and gilt. The accompanying note to the Marks was a reminder of their visit to Swanhill with an amusing prayer that they attend more raptly to their game. At its close, it begged the pleasure of their company for an afternoon of hawking at the manor ten days hence. The invitation, while still more pleasing than the earlier one since it signaled an acceptable level of compatibility, left Philip cautious. "I fear he may expect something in return that the sheriff cannot—and should not—provide." As the date neared, Anne wrote to say that her husband's duties would prevent his attendance but she herself would welcome being initiated into the mysteries of falconry.

"It's only the female of the species, you see," said Lambert, manifestly delighted at the renewed sight of the sheriff's wife, "that is properly called a falcon, and her character is quite the opposite of the human female's as generally conceived. The falcon is the stronger and more aggressive side of the breed, yet calmer in temperament. It is the tiercel that is the more edgy and emotional—although I confess to knowing some men of that disposition."

In the mews-house she marveled at the compact, athletic form of the baron's favorite, Styx, as the bird perched motionless on his arm except for the nervous bobbing of her head, with its intimation of high intelligence, and the darting play of her large, bright eyes which bespoke such lethal potentiality. Expertly tailored for her purpose by nature, Styx was ornamented with a helmetlike cap of gray, yellow edging about her eyes and bill, and plumage of a bluish, metallic luster much resembling knight's mail. "She is so fiercely beautiful," said Anne as one of the falconers placed a hood with golden embroidery on it over the bird's head for the ride to the hollow.

"You cannot bully them—you can only coax them to obedience," Lambert said as Styx's little silver bells tinkled in time to his horse's gait. "It's as if one must have some of their same feral blood coursing through one's veins to work well with them." The whole skill was in accustoming the bird to man's ways and needs without extinguishing her wild nature— "as with the best soldiers," he added. The process of training took months, even years, of patience. Just to keep her from flying off her perch and not biting at her jesses and bells or scratching at her hood meant endlessly gentling her, unruffling her; then you taught her to sit still on your arm and ride along with you in disregard of the horse's motion and, finally, to master the skills to match her instinct to kill. "It's truly an art form, the falconer's profession."

"Not, I think, unlike a sheriff's," she said, "in terms of truculence encountered."

Styx sat becalmed at the hollow while Anne watched a falconer train another bird to return to him by means of the lure, a pair of crane wings lashed together with a thong. A long leather cord had been tied to the end of her leash as the trainer hung on tight to the gyrfalcon's jesses and cooed to her while feeding the bird a piece of crane's heart; then he fastened the rest of the morsel to the lure, unhooded the bird, and had an assistant move off, keeping the lure always in her sight and finally placing it on the ground with the meat removed. The tethered bird, once released, flew straight for the lure and, finding no reward, waited until the assistant reappeared with the meat. Feeding was to commence at the falconer's pleasure, not the bird's. "Next time, if she has mastered this lesson, the lure will be whirled through the air for her capturing on the wing," Lambert said. "But our progress is often slow."

"And do they misbehave?" she asked.

"Worse than children—and they are prone to bad habits if not quickly arrested. Some lazy ones, though never my sweet Styx, are fond of sitting on the ground or taking a stand in a tree or flying too low or raking out too far instead of well overhead so they can properly spy their prey below." He stroked the peregrine's breast plumage. "And they must be bathed twice weekly, else when they are let go, they may fly off to seek water on their own—and never return."

Moments later Styx performed her deadly aerial feat with customary precision, taking a crane with such furious impact that Anne looked away as the victim dropped to earth. "Didn't the bells warn it?" she asked, a hint of sorrow in the question.

"Too late," said Lambert as they rode to retrieve the predator.

"Then is it ever a fair contest?"

"If the falcon is improperly trained—or less than precise in her movements."

"Barring those, it's simply a blood sacrifice?"

"Not 'simply' at all. The sport is in the difficulty of the achievement—to bring the hawk to such a level of performance at the expenditure of so much time and effort, knowing that at her next release she might ride up into the wind and disappear on you forever. You must savor the grace of the flight and the perfection of the kill rather than speaking of an equal contest."

Anne nodded. "Yet I find it as unsettling as it is enthralling—as if I were attending a ritual execution."

"You're not wrong, but it's a question of how you perceive it. The whole undertaking, you see, is about mastery—the falcon's over her prey, and ours over her. So much of life is taken up with mastery and subservience. This sport is but a variation on it—and more beautiful than the rest."

She still saw more terror than beauty in it but chose not to say as much lest he suppose her unappreciative of the spectacle or the costly diversions of the lordly class.

He walked with her for a time through the manor orchard after they had taken refreshment with Lady Cicely, who was cordial enough without in any way seeking to prolong the occasion or deepen their acquaintance. Lambert evidenced the opposite tendency, though without the slightest betraying impropriety.

"I should like you to know," Anne said as they toured among the pear trees, "how greatly we are taken by your generosity—not only for the splendid chessboard, which has awakened my powers of concentration on the game, but as well for the sword you presented Philip last autumn. While I know he sent you his thanks, you cannot be aware of the special place it occupies in his thoughts. He keeps it beside the sheriff's chair of office, less for his immediate protection, I think, than for its powers as a talisman."

"I didn't know it had any."

"Perhaps not for you—since you hadn't the need. But I suspect that he secretly thinks—and you must not scoff—that its magical potency may someday make him a great lord like the one who gave it to him."

The baron professed no false modesty about the flattering conjecture. "Is that his wish—or yours?"

"I can't speak for Philip with any authority whatever—there's much of the enigma about him, even to me. Surely he would not put the proposition so baldly, being the diplomat he is."

"Then it's your own hope for him?"

She shied from the question. "Do you know what I call your sword," she asked by way of an answer, "the one you gave him? You must not laugh at me, but I refer to it as Durandal."

"Roland's sword?"

"I see a smile lurking in you. You must promise—"

"I'll refrain."

"That's just how I think of Philip—cast in Roland's mold. They are both brave, honorable, and supremely loyal to their king. Philip lacks only for noble lineage."

Lambert paused to examine the buds on the nearest tree. "No doubt the comparison is attractive," he said, "and grounded in your deep affection for Philip. But bear in mind that Roland was something of a simpleton—too trusting, too easily used—"

"I'd not press the parallel beyond a—"

"—and was betrayed in the end, just as our Lord and Saviour."

"You read me too literally. I withdraw the silly—"

"Your Philip, furthermore, is an ambitious man, is he not? I sense that in him as much as the virtues you proclaim—and I in no way question. He wishes for the rewards and insignia of the nobility—you concede as much in confiding your suspicions to me. Roland was practically ethereal by contrast."

"Roland is hereby renounced, sire. Nor do I think Philip aspires to more than a modest estate of his own—nothing grand. It's the idea of it, you see—to be his own master and not forever a dependent retainer."

"But we are all dependent, my dear, to whoever our liege lord is."

"There are degrees of dependency. May not one long for a self-sustaining existence?"

"The king, I'll warrant you, will be in no hurry to grant Philip such a status. Land, as you say, makes a man his own commander to a greater or lesser degree, with delusions, even, that he is gentry. The last thing His Majesty wants in his royal retainers are airs of grandeur—it makes them the less manageable. Your Philip's most plausible and immediate pathway to wealth, short of extortion and other corruptions—which are the usual route of sheriffs—is the award of crown custodianships. I doubt the king will bestow them lightly on his commoner captains, even the most devoted ones. Only the sheriff's satisfying some extraordinary demand on him is likely to speed the process."

Anne's face clouded at this melancholy prospect. "In the meantime, there is something other than an estate that Philip craves. It may be of still more importance to him, though I cannot gauge such matters with precision."

"Namely?"

She hesitated, suddenly fearful now of having miscalculated Lambert's trustworthiness. Yet how to extricate herself? "Forgive me, my lord—I am indiscreet to broach such confidences. We are newly met and, for all your kindness, I cannot mistake the chasm between our two stations."

"As you wish, madam."

They neared the end of the orchard, and impulse overtook her, albeit of the calculated sort. "He wishes a knighthood, sire—though he would likely flay me for revealing it. The circumstances of his birth and upbringing did not permit it, yet he has prevailed over them—and is a most knightly man. Still . . ."

"It haunts him."

"It does, my lord."

"Well, it is readily enough attainable for a man in his position—with a certain outlay of effort."

"He would not risk exposure to ridicule, I suspect, by publicly undergoing the ritual aspects of the procedure—and has little time for them, at any rate."

"Then it troubles him less than you may imagine."

"Perhaps. But I think he would dearly wish to be dubbed for services rendered the crown, here and in France."

"The king would have to be apprised. Or might the earl of Derby do as well for him?"

"I should think. The trouble is that Philip would never solicit it."

"Such modesty speaks well for him, but puts a greater burden on whoever would champion him. How does Philip get on with the earl? Ferrers can be a prickly sort."

"Their relationship is correct but cool, I should say. The earl likely views him as an upstart mercenary. Philip rides to Derby every so often, and they do their business there. The sheriff naturally gives him wide ambit in his own lair—all Derbyshire seems the earl's fief."

"Yet your Philip has the one thing Ferrers covets."

"I—cannot imagine . . ."

"A castle. Without one he is merely another baron—yet the king withholds permission and thus keeps the earl on a short rein."

"It seems preposterous."

"But true. It's why Ferrers rarely comes to Nottingham."

"He could hardly blame Philip."

"The sight of him is reminder enough of his own deprivation."

Anne shook her head. "Suppose Philip tendered him ready access—offered him the run of the castle—honored the earl with a banquet. Would all of that ease or compound the matter?"

"It's impossible to say."

"Perhaps a banquet for him would be the most natural first step in winning him—or would he find the gesture presumptuous of an untitled and unlanded sheriff?"

"My guess is he'd be flattered, but he has been known to take offense unduly. As I say, a prickly man, though not without saving graces."

"You know him?"

"Oh, quite well. He spends Easter with us every second year, and we go to Derby the odd one."

Anne looked at the ground, retreating decorously, and fell still.

"Would you like me to ask him, my dear madam?"

"Only if you don't think me or the notion itself overly forward?"

"Your forwardness is matched by your ingenuousness—and I find them both entrancing. But I think you'd best inquire of the sheriff about your scheme before I undertake the mission for you."

"That may prove a still more delicate task, though of course you're entirely right."

"Just apprise me of the outcome."

She beamed at him and brushed a hand across his upper arm. "I—cannot begin to thank you, Your Lordship, adequately."

"You can begin by calling me Thomas."

"I could not take the liberty, sire."

"Sir Thomas, then—but nothing grander."

"Very well. And I must be Anne, then—between us. Plain Anne."

"There is nothing whatever plain about you, madam," he said, and touched a hand momentarily to her cheek. "Perhaps Anne of Tours?"

She smiled. "I should like that—but only between us."

· XV ·

No more deferential being could be found in all of Nottingham than its royally licensed usurer. The Jew Ephraim lived near the Castle Gate in a two-storey house of stone, as much a fortress for his family's safety as a testament of his assiduously gathered gains. There he was said to guard with his life a chest buried in the basement and holding the bonds and contracts of his ungodly business. Neighbors reported—on what evidence, it was impossible to say—how he unearthed it once a week amid guttural incantations in the darkness of his Sabbath night and counted each instrument in a prayerful chant of woe. By daylight, he scarcely looked to be among the forsaken of Jehovah—just a small, neat, olive-faced figure gliding unhurriedly along the street, gaze downcast, stepping aside whenever there was not ample space to pass a Gentile on his way to the little synagogue west of Lister Gate. And now he had presented himself in the sheriff's closet with an earnest petition for renewal of the king's services in his behalf.

"Thank you for admitting me, sire," said Ephraim, "but I had hoped my audience with you could be a private one." He cast Sparks a look that applied for understanding even as it registered discomfort.

"I have no secrets from my clerk," said the sheriff.

"I understand, sire. Nor do I have anything nefarious in mind, for I believe I seek the selfsame ends as your own—the well-being of the kingdom and obedience to its lawful obligations. It's just that on occasion some matter arises that is more readily spoken of when—"

"Master Sparks's presence is in your interest. Indeed, he has instructed me at some length on the history of your dealings with the crown. I am no abuser of your people, Master Ephraim, but neither am I ignorant of your practices."

"*My* practices?" The Jew looked mournful. "They are only what the crown ordains—and because no one else besides my people will overtly undertake them, since we are left with few other means of survival."

"I meant no accusation," said Philip, "only to say I'm familiar with your lot in life—and don't envy it much."

Ephraim of Nottingham was the nephew of Aaron of Lincoln, who was said to have been the richest man in England when he died twenty-three years earlier. That Aaron had abetted Ephraim's father in establishing his trade was not in doubt. What befell Aaron's fortune, and subsequent events involving English Jewry, had greatly affected Ephraim's livelihood and left him persuaded that if his people had been chosen for anything at all, it was to endure torment.

The second King Henry, in need of funds to keep his half of France from Capetian clutches, had confiscated Aaron's hoard in its entirety at his death and sent it aboard ship bound for the Angevin treasury at Rheims. The craft sank in the Channel off Dieppe—surely a sign to even the most virulent Jew-hater in Christendom that those who abused the dispersed remnant of the ancient Israelites did so under the eye of a seriously retributive God. The lesson lasted only briefly, though. Within three years the crusaders were on the march, little discriminating between the heathens of the Levant and the unbelievers at home. Jews were assaulted in London on the day of the Lionheart's coronation; they were massacred in York shortly afterward; and all debts to them were forgiven by the crown for those who took the Cross and left for Palestine.

At Nottingham, Ephraim and his family lay low, prospering modestly until his father's death in '93, when the crown seized a full third of his holdings as the inheritance duty. Ephraim had largely recovered from this exaction when King John levied his infamous Seventh of '03 against all the movable property in the realm to finance his French operations—and then excused debts to the Jews of all lords and knights who served on the battlefield with his forces. By then, too, Ephraim faced covert competition from monastic houses like Lenton Priory, which let out its endowment funds at interest but in sanctimonious guise, and from the sheriff himself, Hugh Bardulf, who was wondrously lax in pressing his debtors. How could an honest moneylender thrive amid such conditions?

They grew still worse in '05, when the pope decreed that all Jews were doomed to perpetual servitude for their complicity in the Crucifixion. Added to earlier prohibitions against their holding land (and thus farming for a living), joining craft and trade guilds unless they took an oath on the Holy Trinity (and thus denied their faith), and employing Christians in any capacity, this condemnation by Innocent III yet further imperiled the standing of Jews as certifiably human. Finally, the king had begun of late to impose special tallages against them, such as his taking a tenth part of the value of their bonds in '06, and to forgive debts to them of those whom the crown wished to reward.

For all these official acts of church and state against him, Ephraim could not have remained in business without the crown's sanction. It took one essential form: for 10 percent of the yield, the king's men enforced the debt obligations to the Jews of all those except whom it was the monarch's pleasure to excuse. Absent such royal intervention, Ephraim was powerless to collect his due. But therein lay his dilemma. To qualify for the crown's services in his behalf, Ephraim was obliged to register his every transaction with the sheriff's clerks; failure to do so was ground for arrest, with no torture rated too cruel to extract the withheld records. His full compliance, however, meant the crown knew Ephraim's wealth precisely and could expropriate at will whatever portion it fancied with no justification beyond that it was only Jews' money.

"Given your understanding," Ephraim said to the sheriff, "I should greatly welcome resumption of the castle's efforts to require the payments owed me by contract and duly filed with the castle. I have prepared a list of the most delinquent cases, knowing as I do that your men have many other duties. Yet since each collection your officers make goes toward accumulating the shire's quota at the Exchequer, I pray you will view our interests as coinciding."

Philip took the list and glanced over it. "How long have you held these in abeyance?"

"Since several months before your arrival. The bailiff advised me his officers had no time for me—and I thought it inadvisable to trouble you before now, sire, given all the other demands on you."

"I see. And this is an opportune moment?"

"In truth, sire, I can no longer afford the luxury of waiting." His eyes flicked toward Sparks, and his voice dropped. "And it is only fitting, my lord sheriff, that you yourself as the presiding officer of the shire ought to have—beyond the crown's regular commission—a small portion of what is received—by way of showing my gratitude for your supervisory efforts."

"I see."

"Shall we say six percent?"

"Is that customary?" the sheriff asked.

"I have gone as high as seven and one-half, sire—under duress."

"I see. So you are testing my level of greed?"

Ephraim lowered his face. "I would not put it thus, sire. I conceive it as a kind of surtax."

"But isn't it the crown's duty to collect such registered debts?"

"The crown has many duties, sire—and the sheriff's men have other pursuits."

"And do you think a bribe the proper way to advance your needs amid the press of other crown business in the shire?"

"I meant no offense, sire—only to honor the practice of your predecessors. For me not to have done so might well have struck you as subterfuge. Any way I turn there are unlovely choices, you see."

Philip gave a single nod and then folded his hands together on the table in front of him. "Just so you will understand, neither I nor my men are entitled to extra considerations for performing our lawfully appointed tasks."

"I see—now. And do you include the bailiffs, sire?"

"Prominently."

Ephraim looked crestfallen. "Then I fear nothing whatever will be accomplished in my behalf. The work is obnoxious to them, so the bailiffs have come to expect a personal benefit."

Philip turned to his clerk, who assented to the moneylender's claim. "To the bailiffs' way of thinking, sire, it is one thing to enforce debts to the king," said Sparks, "and an altogether different matter for them to demand that Christians repay an infidel. That the crown benefits in both cases is immaterial—or nearly so—without, as Master Ephraim states, some added inducement to them." He reached for the Jew's proffered list of truants. "And many of these are hard cases." There was, for example, a certain knight from Kirkby who had borrowed from Ephraim to ransom his son, a captive of the French during the fighting in Normandy in '04. The knight's fields had not produced enough to meet his payments—and his freed son turned dissolute and became in all ways a heartache to the family. Yet the Jew was entitled to be paid. And then there was the slightly avaricious Lord Everett, who had hoped to profit on the differences between the cost of his loan from Ephraim and the return on a custodianship to a part of the king's estate at Peverel. But the property had been obtained too dearly from the crown, and the lord was well behind on the transaction. There were as well several borrowers who claimed their debts had been voided because they fought in France with the king—even though their loans from Ephraim were taken *after* they returned from the wars. Finally, there were some who borrowed simply to pay their taxes, relying on the demonstrably correct premise that the king's bailiffs would work harder to collect debts to the crown than to a Jew. Whatever the particulars, all these debtors had proven ruggedly resistant to Ephraim's claims against them.

"Our bailiffs," said the sheriff after hearing out his clerk, "are not hired to enjoy themselves but to exercise the crown's rights and perform its duties." He turned to the moneylender. "Your matter will be attended to, Master Ephraim—for the usual royal commission and no more."

Bailiff-in-chief Manning did not rejoice at the news. "You miscalculate the obstinacy of these debtors," he told the sheriff. "They often offer my men a bigger reward *not* to collect from them than the Jew offers them to win compliance. It's the principle of the thing."

"There is only one principle here, Master Manning—no bribes from any source may be accepted," said the sheriff.

"What's the harm in my men having a piece of the Jew's takings?"

"Because once such practices are permitted, there will be no end to them. Moreover, the Jew will no doubt raise his rate of interest to compensate for what he pays the bailiffs, so it is Christian money we are speaking of." He handed Ephraim's list to the bailiff. "I want these cases prosecuted with vigor."

Manning thrust the sheet of parchment aside without a glance. "My men are greatly harried nowadays, sire. All in good time, but I cannot in full faith promise when."

Philip's eyes narrowed. "You will set aside one afternoon each week for this purpose and assign three officers to it."

"You're being precipitous, Master Mark. The Jew will endure."

"It's a command, Master Manning! Pick up the Jew's listings."

The bailiff let it sit for a moment longer on the sheriff's table. "I know it from memory—a loathsome business."

"But you will execute it."

Manning breathed deeply and exhaled slowly. "As you say—sire."

"Your word is your bond, is it not, Master Manning?"

"It is—sire."

"You render me obedience, like it or not?"

"I do—sire." He picked up the Jew's list.

"But you have little or no respect for my tenets. Obedience without respect is an empty vessel—it is grounded more in fear than love."

"I neither fear nor love you, Master Mark. I carry out my duty as you do yours—with professional devotion. As I would not presume to inquire whether you love the king while carrying out his designs, neither ought you to require high regard from me so long as I do what I am instructed. My liking it or nay is tuppence."

"Quite so," said the sheriff, moving toward the window. "But like the king, I seek a loyalty in my ranking officers that runs beyond methodical devotion to duty. Loyalty, not mere obedience, may spell the difference between victory and defeat in any close encounter." He turned to glimpse the activity in the bailey. "Had you tendered me loyalty, Master Manning, I should this moment be elevating you to the position of undersheriff, which I've waited these several months to fill—in the hope you would—"

"The idea never crossed my mind, sire."

"I gather." The sheriff wheeled on him. "And I commend you for not dishonestly altering your nature. But without loyalty to me personally or regard for my values—and in view of your lingering resentment of me, which I sorely regret but am powerless to erase—I must choose another man, one who I can confidently feel will serve me with love as well as wit and devotion. My brother Peter will fill the vacancy in the morning."

"Peter!" The bailiff looked as if an axe had just separated his shoulders. "You cannot!" he cried out.

"And why is that?"

"He—has no . . . Governing the shire is—no mere family business, sire. You will do yourself a disservice by—"

"Peter has served with distinction as the constable's deputy—and kept the steward honest."

"He has a certain native intelligence, I grant you, Master Mark, but his assignments have been more clerical than commanding. He has shown no capacity whatever for undertaking serious—"

"He'll come by the aptitude faster than you have learned loyalty."

Manning blinked back his disbelief. "Have you considered how Westminster will view such an appointment, sire?"

"Westminster says I am the sheriff and may deputize whom I wish."

The bailiff shook his head slowly. "It will not sit well with the shire—mark my words."

"I mark them well—and you mark mine. If you are heard henceforth, as you've been in the past, to speak against me on any ground whatever—starting with the choice of Peter as my deputy—your service to the crown will terminate. So long as you do not flout my instructions, I'll continue to prize your skills. Not a moment longer, though, Master Manning—not a moment longer."

Peter wept with gratitude that evening upon learning of his advancement. "You'll begin," said Philip, escaping from his brother's wet embrace, "by overseeing these listed debts to the Jew. But I implore you, Peter—you must not be tempted, in this matter or any other, to veer from your duty for money."

"God's blood," said Peter, wiping his nose on his sleeve.

"He'll bear watching like the rest," Anne Mark told her husband beneath their coverlet that night, "brother or no brother."

·XVI·

FOR THE ANNUAL GOOSE FAIR, Nottingham's great market square became
a tumultuous bazaar drawing celebrants and curiosity-seekers from as far
away as York. Every inch of the vast plaza, where the old Saxon settlement
to the east converged with the newer Norman community that had grown
out from the castle to the west, seemed to come alive with gaudy colors,
rich aromas, and the brash cacophony of vendors proclaiming the virtues
of their wares. The prime attractions, as always, were the exotic foodstuffs
and rare Levantine articles—silks and spices and implements with intricate
patterns (no doubt pagan iconography) incised—along with row upon row
of carts heaped with dyed woolens from throughout the north of England.
Every guild in Nottingham operated a stall for the display of its skills and
products—the weavers and fullers, the butchers and tanners, the silversmiths and ironmongers, the fletchers and coopers, the joiners and masons—while pipers, jugglers, acrobats, mimes, and an assortment of other
entertainers played to the crowds, beseeching pennies at the close of each
brief performance. More sordid elements worked the throng no less in-
dustriously—herbalists, soothsayers, dicers, prostitutes, shrill mounte-
banks who hawked their nostrums from the steps of idled St. Mary's
Church. And at every turn, cripples, lepers, and less pitiable beggars
offered palms upraised for alms.

As pledged, the sheriff was on hand, the honored guest of the Town
Council of Burgesses, who sponsored the festive event on which so large
a part of Nottingham's economic well-being depended. More to the point,
the sheriff had seen to it that a full complement of bailiffs now patrolled
these goings-on, monitoring rowdiness and thereby encouraging a spirited
pace of exchange. Minor disputes were settled and petty crimes prosecuted on the spot at a makeshift bailiffs' court beneath a tent at the edge
of the square. Master Simon Welles, on behalf of the burgesses, commended the sheriff for the new sense of orderliness that prevailed even
amid the push and clangor of the throbbing marketplace.

The high point of the festivities on the closing Saturday were the
afternoon competitions held on the meadow below the castle. Contestants
flocked from far and wide. The winner of the wrestling matches was to
be awarded a plump steer from the king's flock at Peverel; the victor in

the quarterstaff bouts, a whole oak from the royal stands in Sherwood; and the nonpareil of the archery contest, a silver arrow with a golden tip, to be presented by Sheriff Philip Mark, whose renown had begun to spread beyond the two shires he commanded.

The sheriff's wife had hesitated at first to bring their two small daughters to watch the climactic games, even as she had not exposed them to the bright frenzy of the marketplace for fear some harm might befall them. In the case of the games, Anne was reluctant to let the girls watch the rough-and-tumble of half-naked men grappling and blunting one another to the accompaniment of drunken japery. But the sheriff reassured her that she and the children would be seated in a small pavilion with the castle contingent and the burgesses, at a sufficient remove to insulate them from any unpleasantness among the mob. Anne thus relented, drawing a smart clap from Angelique, who taught her tiny sister to do likewise.

Their mother's apprehension had not been groundless. Bodies flew every which way across the sawdust circle where the wrestling was carried on to uproarious volleys each time a bare-chested competitor chewed, clawed, kneed, and wrenched his rival into agonized submission. When the bloodied, sweating winner, genitals partially exposed, was proclaimed, he drained half a tun of godale and fed the remainder to his new prize steer as the thunderously approving onlookers pelted him with clover. A certain Owen Saffron, reputedly a lapsed mendicant from Mansfield, excelled all others with the quarterstaff, manipulating the stout shaft as if it were no bigger than a twig, cracking pates with a practiced forehand lunge, jabbing groins with an excruciating backhand flick, feinting and dodging so nimbly all the while that his final and most dogged foe tired at length, inviting a wicked whack across the belly, and fell puking in the dust. Mistress Mark and the sheriff lifted their daughters onto their laps for a better view only when the archers swarmed over the greensward to begin their meet.

Philip leaned toward Constable Aubrey, seated behind him in the pavilion, to express the hope that one or more of the castle archers might excel in the contest, given the emphasis that had been placed of late on improved marksmanship among the garrison. "I fear," said the constable, "that our stress on the crossbow, however prudent a defensive tactic, has blunted our shooters' skill with the longbow. They've become better soldiers, no doubt, but poorer sportsmen."

This appraisal was borne out as the field slowly winnowed itself to sixteen, none of them, much to the sheriff's chagrin, from the castle corps. His interest was whetted, though, by the sight of a beardless, broad-shouldered young fellow, already gone a bit to suet though not yet out of his twenties, who was in the second of the four-man groups from each of which the best shot would qualify as a semifinalist. The lad wore a dark patch over his left eye. This apparent impediment to his performance drew a few curious comments at first but then a wider chorus edging toward disbelief when the one-eyed entrant claimed, as he toed the mark for his first shot, that the middle one of the three rings drawn on the clout two hundred yards distant was slightly lopsided.

Laughter and heckles from the crowd encircling the butts greeted this claim, but when the complainant appealed to the master of the games to look for himself, the noise swelled into an anthem of ridicule. The chief judge, in no way mean-spirited, obliged the monocular (and surely mistaken) entrant by trudging to the clout and inspecting it minutely. To the astonishment of the throng, he nodded emphatically and ordered a fresh clout affixed to the butt post.

Nothing riled by the earlier taunts nor gloating now over his proven charge, the cyclops had his turn. His technique, the sheriff noted with care, seemed none at all, so effortlessly did he take his stance and retract the bowstring, sustaining it at the point of utmost extension for such a protracted moment that when the arrow at last took wing, it appeared to travel of its own volition, as if the shooter were inseparable from the shot and the target but incidental to the act. His first shaft landed within a mouse-tail of dead center and gained him inclusion among the final four contenders.

"Who is he?" Anne asked her husband, who shrugged and turned to his clerk, per usual, for enlightenment.

"A lout from upcounty named Stuckey Woodfinch," Sparks replied. The Trip had been abuzz for days over wagers being placed on him by habitués at the Leaping Stag, a notorious alehouse on the Great Road North by Blyth. "He's employed there in a variety of capacities and is said to be something of a favorite with the ladies."

"Odd credentials for a marksman," mused Philip.

"There's a bit more of him than that, I'm told."

This Stuckey was in fact the son of a woodward of legendary skills on a manor adjacent to Blyth Priory. The father, who was reputedly able to spy a fawn in deep brush from two rods off, taught the boy everything there was to know about the flora and wildlife of the wood, the trails that wended through it, the bounds of every estate and warren and chase in that sector of the shire, how to track and shoot game, how to skin and bleed and gut and cure it, all the laws of the forest—and no doubt the art of abridging them without detection. Father and son would wander Sherwood together, master and apprentice, intimates of the royal foresters, passing them word of likely violators of the king's code yet steadfastly declining to pay them tribute money in their own behalf or in the name of the lord for whose manor they labored. In time there was nothing more for his father to teach the young Woodfinch (as the woodward's son came to be called), and so he grew to manhood, yearning to strike out on his own instead of waiting for his father's energies to flag and the hereditary position to pass to him.

When he caught wind of a vacancy in the ranks of the royal foresters, Stuckey applied for the position, which, after payment to the crown of a six-shilling annual fine, was said to throw off a goodly living from fees, reliefs, scotales, bribes accepted, and tributes extorted. The deputy forest warden, who somewhat resented the woodward and his lord for their high propriety, was quick to double the price of the position upon learning of Stuckey Woodfinch's interest in it. Thanks to promised help from his lord, Stuckey was able to meet the charge, but the post was nonetheless awarded to the nephew of one of the forest regarders, a knight from Mattersey of dubious standing.

The unsuccessful candidate, greatly grieved at being passed over despite his merits, began lingering at the Leaping Stag, the inn nearest his home, to drown his sorrow. But this wallowing in self-pity (not to mention the prohibitive cost of same) soon lost its allure for him, so Master Woodfinch applied to the innkeeper for work and found himself engaged as carter, remover of patrons who misbehaved, provider of fresh game from the wood, and resident jester. His recompense for these sundry roles was room and board, all the ale he could down, and gratis servicing by the house wenches (but only after the paying clientele had done with them).

Stuckey's entry into the Goose Fair contest for bowmen grew out of a dare one roistering evening at the Stag: if he lost the competition—and the odds against him were astronomical—he would provide each bettor one haunch of venison; if he won, he could roger each bettor's wife or lady-love to a fare-thee-well, but one time only. "Or so they tell it at the Trip," Sparks concluded.

"Cheeky devil," said the sheriff. "And what ails his eye that he wears a patch—some hunting mishap, I suppose?"

"I've heard nothing of a patch. Perhaps it's some temporary condition."

"What's 'roger'?" asked Angelique, whose attention her father had thought to be clamped to the flight of the arrows across the meadow.

Philip winced and ducked his wife's scalding glance. "A boy's name," he said, and frowned at his clerk, who bit his lip in apology. "Now see how they're moving the clout back twenty yards for the next round?"

"To make it harder?"

"Exactement."

"Don't speak French, Papa," the girl whispered. "People will hear."

Woodfinch was pitted next against a royal forester named Godfrey Gos, who shot first and well; but the lusty fellow from Blyth, without seeming to try hard, came a fraction closer to the center with each of his first two arrows. On the third and final round, in which both made their best effort, Stuckey's shot appeared to land equidistant from the middle with the forester's; from the pavilion, the issue was very much in doubt. The target judge examined the clout closely and then bellowed back that Master Gos had triumphed.

Woodfinch whirled about and shouted toward the notables in the pavilion. "I am wronged, sires! My arrow is closer!"

Given his earlier feat of visual acuity, the crowd grew hushed instead of deriding the declared loser for his ill grace. The burgess who was serving as master of the games shrugged helplessly and pointed back to the target judge, as if to say that his was the last word.

But Woodfinch would not yield. "It's politics—because Master Gos is a forester of the king and I'm a simple commoner, they rule against me!" He took three steps toward the pavilion as the judge approached the clout to clear it of their arrows for the other semifinal match. "Stay his hand, good gentlemen, and send one of your own to measure!"

Master Welles, as the presiding burgess, leaned forward to seek the sheriff's eye. Fearing riot by the murmuring crowd, which was not partial to royal foresters and had taken a fancy to the one-eyed archer, Philip nodded his approval. A shout ran down the butts and froze the judge, who had come within three feet of the clout. "Send one of the bailiffs," the sheriff instructed Master Manning.

"No, none of the bailiffs!" Woodfinch called out. "They are hand in glove with the foresters. I ask a neutral judge—the sheriff himself."

The throng reacted with swelling approval. But Philip sensed he was being mocked by a disrespectful boor and his high office diminished. "I do no man's bidding but the king's," he said only within earshot of those seated in the pavilion. "My clerk will do as well as I," he called out, "but you must abide by his finding without protest."

"Gladly, my lord sheriff," Woodfinch said with a deep bow as his supporters whooped in glee.

Sparks borrowed a spare bowstring from one of the archers and scurried down the shooting course to the clout, where he applied the string with care to measure the distance the last two arrows had landed from the center. Then he hurried back as fast as his short legs could carry him and whispered the results to his master. The sheriff in turn whispered them to the chief burgess, insisting that since the entire proceedings were a municipal function, the townsman announce them. "By a goodly inch," Master Welles cried aloud, "Master Woodfinch of Blyth has prevailed!"

The cheering had not yet died when the clout was set back for a final time, and the two best archers at the fair stood side by side. Stuckey's opponent was the disdainful Walter fitz Adderfang of Skipwith, who had gained the silver arrow of victory the year before and was regarded as one of the keenest shots in England from the midlands north. He would not so much look at his upstart foe.

As the defending champion, Adderfang chose to shoot first. His arrow, loosed at a distance of 240 yards, hit between the middle and inner rings; Woodfinch quickly matched it. But on Adderfang's second shot, the arrow faltered midway down the butts as one of its feathers fluttered free and the clothyard bit the earth. The crowd loosed a collective sigh of disappointment. His plucky rival, though, wished no unfair advantage, so as he took his stance for the second shot, he eyed a crow flying close by and, in a movement so swift that few could follow it, he took the bird with a flawless shot. It landed twenty feet in front of the contestants and drew a great roar of approval from the spectators.

With the outcome now entirely dependent on the final shot, Adderfang slowly edged against the mark and prepared his bow with great deliberation. Even as he was doing so, Woodfinch casually shifted the dark patch he wore from his left eye to his right. The gesture brought the assemblage to stone-still silence, causing Adderfang to glance up. What did the maneuver mean? That the archer's ailment, whatever it was, had suddenly transferred from one eye to the other? Or that he had no ailment whatever and was, so to speak, ambidextrously one-eyed? Or was it, as some in the crowd snickeringly detected, the patch-wearer's tacit declaration that he could shoot better with one eye—and it didn't matter which—than anyone else with both? Dissonant murmurs, broken by occasional guffaws, grew on every side, so distracting Adderfang that his mind flooded with fury over his opponent's perplexing gambit. His final arrow overflew the clout entirely.

Blinking his left eye repeatedly as if to accustom it to the sunlight, Woodfinch offered his shattered foe a nod of condolence, then sailed his last arrow swift and straight down the course; it took the clout a fraction off dead center.

"Stuck-ee! Stuck-ee!" his claque shouted as they scooped up the victor (who had by now discarded his patch altogether), doused him with ale, hauled him on their shoulders to the pavilion, and unceremoniously dumped him, drenched and tattered, and not a little dazed, in front of the tier of dignitaries. Master Welles, with full attention focused on the spot, chose that moment prior to the presentation of the silver arrow to launch a speech on the marvels of Nottingham, its merchants, and craftsmen, but his words were soon drowned in the din. Stuckey, partially recovered from his rough handling and comically poised on all fours, feigned attentiveness to the droning oratory. But nature shortly overtook him, and he crawled around the corner of the pavilion, out of its occupants' sight but not the crowd's, stood to relieve himself, and crawled back to his former place of honor as the laughter at his antics crested. Master Welles surrendered the stage in frustration and gestured toward the sheriff.

Philip rose with the full dignity of his rank and waited patiently for the noise to ebb. It took a minute or more while Stuckey slowly cranked himself upright and presented his damp and dirtied personage to the king's ranking officer in those environs. "I am as overcome with admiration for Master Woodfinch's marksmanship," said the sheriff to the hushed multitude, "as I am with sadness for his ill manners." Whereupon he tossed the silver arrow betokening victory so that it landed at its recipient's feet, then without a further word led the castle party from the little grandstand as the bailiffs cleared a path.

A month later Stuckey Woodfinch once again found himself before the sheriff, but in drastically altered circumstances.

Two foresters had arrested him for allegedly abusing the king's peace by posting a confederate just within Sherwood's border and having him bang loudly on a drum to drive from cover all manner of game: Woodfinch, bow at the ready, was said to have been stationed in the open, waiting to bag them. The royal officers produced Stuckey, his bow, and the purportedly offending drum—but no accomplice, who they said had fled at their approach.

While the accused miscreant was languishing in the castle keep and awaiting bail, Bailiff Reginald, the sheriff's brother, happened by a certain alehouse frequented by the foresters and heard several of them boast of the plot they had fashioned to punish the reprobate archer who had shamed their fellow forester Godfrey Gos at the Goose Fair. In receipt of this intelligence, the sheriff had the prisoner, looking even worse for wear than when last seen, brought to his closet. "What have you to say for yourself, Master Woodfinch?" he asked sternly.

"That I am wronged, sire—and very hungry."

"The hunger can be attended to. The wrong is a harder matter."

"My arrest is plainly an act of vengeance by the foresters. They laughed in my face after taking me and offered to sell me my freedom—it's their custom, in case the practice has somehow escaped your notice."

"The foresters' work is beyond my jurisdiction. In any event, they appear to have succeeded in dampening your usually antic humor."

Woodfinch studied the sheriff somberly. "So you approve of their oppressive tactics?"

"Perhaps they meant no more than a jest—rather like a fully sighted archer wearing an eyepatch to disarm his rivals."

The prisoner shook his tousled head. "I can't believe the sheriff is party to such business. I did you no wrong at the fair, sire—indeed, was grateful for your intervention in my behalf. If I was not quick to humble myself at your feet and those of the other officials, it was due to the merriment of the moment. I deserve no pillorying for behavior that was perhaps a shade too playful."

"Yet the foresters caught you with your bow and the drum."

"The bow I had outside the forest boundary—it was no breach of the law. The drum they had brought with them to entrap me."

"It's their word against yours."

"My word is the truth. They're habitual extorters."

"Then the reports I've received that you're a dissolute brawler who takes the king's deer at your pleasure and supplies their flesh to your employer—surely they must be in error."

"I take deer only when they are at liberty—never in the forest."

"You are keen, then, at determining its precise boundaries at all points—and the exact location of the animals' hooves the very instant you bring them down?"

"By long practice, sire."

"I am relieved to hear it."

"As to my other conduct, I confess only to a bit of merrymaking now and then, like any other wholesome fellow—nothing worse."

"So much the better."

"I swear to it, sire. The rest is calumny."

"In that event," said the sheriff, "I have a proposal for you." He took up the broadsword that stood against the wall just behind his chair and traced a finger down its flat side. "I need a peerless marksman among the castle archers, Master Woodfinch—my men must be better trained. You would serve me additionally as a royal huntsman, providing game for the castle. And I'll match whatever pay they give you at your disreputable inn."

The prisoner's eyes widened. "You jest, sire!"

"Sheriffs do not jest, Master Woodfinch." He turned his sword on edge and examined the blade for keenness. "Of course, the castle's ale ration is not bottomless, as yours is said to be, and we are somewhat short on wenches—whose favors you would have to vie for with the steward, though I should think you'd have no—"

"Then I am truly at liberty, sire?"

"Will you serve at the castle as I ask?"

"At the castle? As a royal retainer? Sire, I'm a free spirit who dearly loves to roam—and to revel when the mood—"

"You'll do little roaming or reveling in gaol—and free spirits generally rot there. What do you say now?"

"You would conscript me by duress, sire?"

"Not in the least," said the sheriff, laying the sword aside with a small clatter. "The choice is entirely yours—freedom under my employ or gaol until you can be bailed, a trial with the testimony all against you, and then probably indefinite confinement—with no wenches and less ale."

"I—it's not something I—have ever—"

"Then think about it overnight, Master Woodfinch—though I may well have changed my mind by morning."

The prisoner's confusion slowly yielded to a wide grin. "Long live our noble king," he said, holding up his manacles to be unbolted, "and his nobler sheriff!"

"Master Sparks! Food and drink for our newest recruit!"

·XVII·

AMONG THE DEBTORS of the Jew Ephraim whom Peter Mark was pressing in the crown's behalf, one case in particular defied his strategems and forced him to consult with his brother. "This woman has the grace and form of an angel and the wiles of a Circe," the undersheriff reported. "She says the king unjustly persecutes her and begs to see the sheriff. I think it worth your while."

By her own account, Olivia Pendrake was at the brink of ruin. Her husband, Stephen, before his untimely death from being pitched headlong off his horse at full gallop, was among the ranking lords of Nottinghamshire; his manor was nearly the size of Thomas de Lambert's, though his holdings elsewhere were more modest. His widow, still spirited and attractive with a young daughter, was entitled by law to a third part of the revenues of her husband's holdings so long as she did not remarry. And worse than anything, Lady Olivia dreaded a hateful remarriage, which the king nevertheless had the right to impose on her. To forestall such a possibility— indeed, it was a likelihood, since the crown had few more valuable rewards to bestow upon a loyal subject than the hand of a rich and comely woman— she had offered to pay the king a fine for the privilege of selecting her own new husband, pending royal approval; meanwhile, her estate would be held under a royal custodianship. The king was receptive to the widow's appeal but, in granting it, set her yearly fine for remaining unwed at the burdensome figure of two hundred pounds. To make it worse, Olivia's fee could be paid only from the widow's third part of the Pendrake revenues, the balance to be held in escrow until the crown got around to naming a custodian to tend the monies.

Hopeful that her quest for an acceptable husband would be short-lived, Lady Pendrake did not protest the onerous fine the crown had set. To do so, she calculated, would be to risk trying the king's patience and speeding the appointment of a custodian who would surely exercise the right of such practiced usurpers to plunder their holdings. Thus, for the first year of her widowhood, she had met the heavy payment to the king with the help of a loan from the moneylender of Nottingham. But now he was harrying her for repayment with interest, which she could not manage, and the king's retainers in the shire had come to reinforce Ephraim's claim against her.

"But why has the king taxed her so heavily to remain unmarried?" the sheriff asked his brother. "It seems unduly mean-spirited."

"You must judge that," said Peter. "Apparently, she was a bystander to events that greatly riled our gracious sovereign."

Stephen Pendrake's sin, the one for which his widow was being forced to pay so dearly, was that he had not sided with the king in a dispute with his foremost counselor, William the Marshal, easily the most admired man in the kingdom. Son of the hereditary member of the king's household in charge of military arrangements (in an age when the ruler had no standing army), William had begun his rise as a landless knight-errant and soon proved himself the most adept wielder of sword and lance of any combatant on the jousting fields of Europe. The strength of his arm was reinforced by a loyalty of heart, quickness of wit, and grace of manner that early earned him the leading place among the second King Henry's personal retinue of knights. In that capacity he helped groom the crown princes in chivalry and, when necessary, obedience. The latter he did most famously the time young Richard rebelled against his father and, in head-to-head combat with the Marshal, found himself unhorsed and within a sword's point of death; William slew the prince's horse instead. On succeeding to the throne, Richard made the Marshal one of the guardians of the realm and added to his holdings, which were already immense through his marriage to the daughter of the earl of Pembroke, then the second-richest heiress in England. His timely intervention later in support of John's claim to the throne still further enhanced William's standing. A titan of the west country, with vast property as well in Normandy and Ireland, the Marshal had become the king's most trusted military, administrative, and diplomatic advisor. And then it all went awry.

The fault resided in how the king and William differently defined loyalty. When Normandy had been all but lost in '04, John sent his most faithful and potent retainer to seek peace terms with King Philip of France; in the process and out of the wreckage, the Marshal hoped to retain his own Norman estates. To do so he would have to pay homage to Philip, but such a step without King John's concurrence would almost surely have cost William his far larger British holdings, so he sought the king's approval and got it in writing. "I know you to be so loyal," John reportedly said to him, "that no consideration would draw your affection from me. I wish you to do the homage to save yourself from loss, for I know the more land you have, the better you will serve me."

William's efforts as peace negotiator, undermined by those in England opposed to settlement with France, came to naught, but the Marshal managed to salvage his Norman property by pledging Philip "liege homage on this side of the sea." The vow was understood to mean a division of allegiance whereby William was John's man in England and all matters British and Philip's man in France and its continental involvements. Left unsettled was whose man he was in the event the two rulers warred anew with each other.

The question was called into play the following year when John prepared to embark on an expedition to France to re-establish his ancestral claims. William argued vigorously that the military effort was doomed— Philip had all the advantages of geography and manpower—and would greatly deplete England at precisely the time the king needed to strengthen his home base. When John persisted, the Marshal declined to set sail with him, citing his homage to Philip. John saw only deceit and disloyalty in the refusal, charging that William was devoted solely to feathering his own nest. The Marshal, insisting he had acted only by the king's leave, claimed full knightly propriety for his stand. Whereupon the king turned to the other barons and lords who were attending him in Portsmouth Harbor as the great war fleet collected in the Salent, and proposed that they resolve the bitter argument. Among them was Lord Stephen Pendrake.

Though more powerful than any of the magnates there assembled, the Marshal bowed to the proposal that they arbitrate but told his fellow noblemen, "Attend closely to the king, for what he plans to do to me, he will do to all of you—and worse yet if he can."

Faced with two mighty and irreconcilable disputants, the attendant lords of the realm did what any wise men would—they shrank from their charge and rendered no judgment. All took this for exoneration of William, thus infuriating the king still further. He stripped the Marshal of his English castles and government offices, demanded two of his sons as hostages against his future loyal (which was to say, compliant) behavior, and effectively sent him into exile in Ireland. That the king had not forgotten and sorely begrudged those who would not stand by him in his clash with William was manifest in his conduct toward Lady Pendrake when she was widowed three years after.

"You are gracious to attend me, Master Mark," she said on greeting the sheriff in her parlor. "I know your duties elsewhere to be arduous."

He could not recall encountering another noblewoman who appeared outside her private quarters without a headdress. Olivia Pendrake's raven hair was drawn back and fixed in a single thick braid that reached just short of her buttocks. A slender woman of moderate size, she met his eye directly and spoke with a throaty edge to her voice that befit a larger frame. "Not so arduous," he said, "that I cannot try to be of service to a troubled lady of the shire."

She ran her eye over him in slow appraisal. "They say you are a man not entirely devoid of compassion for those who have been wronged."

"Be that as it may, my lady, I am the king's man and cannot blithely assent to your opinion of him."

"Surely not. I don't ask for your assent—only your grasp of the problem."

"A grasp can be a slippery thing, madam, but let me try."

Her eyes narrowed shrewdly. "Our king, you see, has but a single grave failing. He assumes it altogether just and proper to pursue his own self-interest to the utmost, yet he takes any such tendency in others for a deformity of nature—and calls it treachery. The Marshal was guilty of no more than that."

"I grant you, my lady, that some find the king immoderate in—"

"And my Stephen did nothing whatever to him, I assure you."

"My understanding is to the contrary—that the king asked his support, but it was not forthcoming. To him, apparently, this was not nothing."

"Therefore, oppress his widow with an unseemly fine for an arguable error of omission?"

"Oppressive or otherwise, it is the prerogative of the crown. I do not defend it—and am not called upon to."

"Only to enforce it, sire—which comes to the very same thing, does it not?" She sighed and turned her face from his. "Ah, but I accost you unduly when you were so kind to come here. Let me extend the hospitality of our house." She drew him toward the porch, remaining close by him so that he could detect her perfumed sweetness. Refreshments awaited, and while they partook of them, she cast aside all reference to her travail and inquired instead regarding Philip's years in France, the nature of his military career, and how he found the life and people in Nottinghamshire. "To me there are charms in our remoteness," she said, "but I should think a man of your travels might find the shire a tedious backwater."

"Not at all," Philip replied, glad for the less combative tone the interview had taken, "though to tell the truth, castle life is insular by its very nature, so tedium is an occupational hazard with me. Touring the shire is welcome refreshment. Even hearing grievances such as yours, while not my favored pastime, has its compensations."

She smiled for the first time and seemed to warm to his laconic manner. They walked and talked for the better part of an hour as the formality between them waned, and at the end she ventured to ask whether he was at all familiar with the fables of Aesop. The castle had only recently come into possession of a copy, he told her, but he had had neither the time nor the inclination to take it up. "My wife, though, reads from the stories to our daughters and assures me of their worth."

"Has she spoken of the tale of the wolf and the heron?"

"If so, I've not retained it."

A wolf, having swallowed a bone, went about looking for someone to dislodge it, Lady Olivia recited. Encountering a heron, he offered it a reward to remove the bone. The intrepid bird put its head down the wolf's throat, pulled out the bone, and then claimed the promised prize. " 'Are you not content, my friend,' " Olivia quoted the wolf in her best imitation of lupine menace, " 'to have got your head safely out of a wolf's mouth without demanding a fee as well?' "

Philip waited for more, but there was none. "I see," he said noncommittally.

"But do you? The point, I think, is well taken—and rather puts me in mind of my sheriff's awkward position."

"The point? Is it other than that wolves are mean creatures not readily trifled with?"

She searched his face to fathom how much she might risk with him. "Aesop puts it thus by way of instruction: " 'When one does a bad man a service, the only recompense one can hope for is that the villain will not add injury to ingratitude.' " She tapped his wrist once as if to punctuate the moral. "Now do you see my point?"

"The king is villainous—and those of us who serve him will be lucky not to be devoured by him in the end?"

"Just so."

His wariness returned; he feared entrapment in her charming snare. "I cannot concur."

"That he is an oppressor?"

"Or that his loyal retainers' only reward will be their destruction."

She sighed anew, and her breasts heaved in concert. "Riding an ill wind can prove a risky game. I fear for your safety, Master Mark. You seem to me a man of kindliness—a quality our sovereign little prizes."

"Danger runs with the sheriff's trade—and the soldier's—no matter who is king. The nature of my office breeds resentments. As to kindliness, it's a cheap enough commodity—and easily enough feigned. In your delicate position, gentle lady, I should be most wary of honeyed tongues."

She sensed his withdrawal and struggled to hold his ear and pry open his heart. "It's not tongues I fear, sire, but lashes. Your fluid words do both of us a disservice. You fail to heed my message: we are likewise victimized, yourself unwittingly."

"I promise to deliberate on it, madam. The only remaining question between us now is what service I can perform for you without disavowing my oath to the crown."

She fell back defeated onto a cushioned bench and curled her legs beneath her. "You could forestall the Jew—I should welcome it." She swallowed from a wine goblet on the small table beside her, little hiding her agitation at his growing coldness. "You could also intercede with the king, asking that my fine be reduced to a humane level so that I can sustain myself." She folded her hands, trying to regain composure, and managed a wan smile. "And you could especially comfort me if you would ask that a kindly custodian be named to manage Pendrake manor—one who would not sell off my stock and equipage and despoil the place, making me the less attractive to a suitor." She sat up and fixed him with her quick, clever eyes. "A custodian like you, sire, would be ideal."

Philip considered the list item by item, fully understanding now the course Lady Olivia had been pursuing. "I may be able to prevail upon Master Ephraim to accept partial payment," he said after a moment, "but you would only be buying time. The amount must be made up."

"Time may ease my dilemma—especially if the king can be prevailed upon to reduce my fine. It is unconscionable."

"And on what ground other than alleged injustice might I intercede in your behalf?"

"Is injustice not a suitable ground for appealing my case? Or do you doubt I'm punished without due cause?"

"The fine is plainly punitive—and so intended. For me to argue it is without sufficient cause would be received at Westminster as high impertinence. You vastly mistake my leverage with the crown."

"Mmmm—and you'll not risk your neck on so trivial a matter."

"If you ask me to play the heron in the wolf's throat, then I'll abide by Master Aesop's counsel and your own. Furthermore, it would get neither of us anywhere—indeed, could worsen your plight."

She crossed her arms over her bodice and worriedly rubbed the upper part of each with the hand opposite. "Might you not argue to Westminster that the Pendrakes are prominent in this shire—and it is not to the crown's interest to be perceived as oppressing the innocent widow of such a clan?"

"My lady, it's precisely because the Pendrake name is well known and honored that you have been selected for punishment—even as the Marshal was. But you gave less provocation, without a doubt. Far less."

Her eyes suddenly filled with tears she fought to control. "Honeyed or not," she said, "your words bespeak comprehension of my case. Yet it does not move you. Can you not see tortured flesh and blood before you?"

"To understand your grievance, my lady, is not to judge it. There is little I can do, in truth, except to stymie the Jew for a time—and not long at that."

She rose and moved close to him. "Would I greatly offend you, Master Mark, if I offered to pay for your help? I badly need it—yet I sense behind your eloquence a decided callousness to the troubles of the propertied. Perhaps if I, too, had risen from modest origins to your present august station, I should feel the same."

"You don't offend me, madam, so much as you disappoint me. You fail to credit my words and then suppose me purchasable."

"I suppose nothing, sire. I'm only asking because you leave me with no recourse."

"Your condition is not of my making."

"But you will do very little to alleviate it. Is it that you distrust me, Master Mark, and therefore will not entertain my proposal? Do you think I would disclose the transaction if silver passed between us?"

"The question demeans us both, my lady. I must beg your leave."

· XVIII ·

EXCEPT FOR THE ROYAL VISITS, Nottingham Castle had not in years witnessed preparations so extensive as those for the banquet being tendered by the sheriff a fortnight past Michaelmas to honor the earl of Derby and Lady Ferrers. The planning was left largely in Anne Mark's hands, for the idea had been hers, whereas Philip, while conceding the possible value of the event, had feared that if it were to prove less than congenial to the guest of honor, their fragile relationship might be ruptured irreparably. Anne was determined, therefore, that all must go right.

The most sensitive matter was of course the guest list and, equally important, the seating arrangement thereof. Other than the earl and the sheriff, who were naturally to sit side by side at the center of the dais, the custom of the shire left the precise deployment of guests to the design of the hostess. Tactful inquiry, though, soon impressed upon Anne that arbitrary placement would likely prove disastrous, for the garden of civility through which the gentry's lives played themselves out hid within it a tanglewood of thorns and sticker bushes. Social slights and deeper grievances abounded, and the sheriff's wife struggled to familiarize herself with them.

Ralph de Greasley, by way of example, could not be seated close by—or perhaps ought not even to lay eyes on—Evan of Yardley, since the two of them were feuding fiercely over ownership of fifty acres of scraggly pastureland. The deed supporting Sir Ralph's long claim to them had been lost, and when it was reissued by the Chancery soon after King John's coronation, title had been miraculously transferred to Sir Evan as part of his charter—the result, Greasley charged, of a bribe to a well-placed clerk. Each, in the ensuing years, had attempted to plant the contested acreage, only to have the other trample it from spite. Nor would either of them leave it fallow, for fear the disuse would be taken as surrender. So the land was leeched and denuded as their stock jointly grazed it in uneasy tenancy while their owners regularly threatened each other's skewering.

How to juggle such antagonists within the same room without inviting mayhem had at first reduced Anne to despair. But Steward Devereaux, puffed with pride over the coming event, rallied her courage, and Sparks, that walking compendium of lords and estates in size order, helped her chart the hall in a manner well suited to maintain decorum. To gratify the palates of the nobly overfed, the castle kitchen was ordered to spare no cost. The banquet menu thus included trout soup, juicy gray goose and whooper crane, peacock and partridge fresh from Sherwood, carp and eel plucked from the Trent, candied suckling pig, stag roasted to a crisp and topped with steaming pepper sauce, five kinds of bread and crackers, three kinds of pasties, and for dessert a compote of baked pears and apples, mounds of dates, figs, and peeled walnuts. This substantial fare was to be washed down with tuns and tuns of the best available French wine, most of it from Bordeaux and Auvergne, aquilian from Spain, several varieties of Rhenish, and a river of Master le Gyw's home-brewed spiced ale trundled up from the Trip to Jerusalem Inn. For entertainment Anne enlisted an earthy minstrel named John-a-Dale and a brightly clad troupe of Breton jongleurs who came with lutes, flutes, viols, and castanets to cheer the banqueters as late into the evening as any of them remained conscious. To commemorate the occasion, the sheriff commissioned the silversmiths of Nottingham to fashion a dozen drinking cups in the shape of a griffin, that mythic embodiment of fused strength and grace, for presentation to the earl at the height of the festivities. Anne, at her most adroit, had prevailed upon the burgesses to bear the cost of the cups in lieu of their annual gift to the castle, suggesting to Master Welles, "They will surely help broadcast word of the town's exquisite artisanry." He yielded to her at the price of banquet invitations for three of the burgesses and their wives (who were assigned a narrow table close by the pantry door).

As her final act of preparation, Anne forcefully instructed Philip to say nothing whatever that would remind the earl he had no castle of his own, only a shire. Herself she told repeatedly to be in no way forward with Lady Ferrers; Philip's dream of one day gaining a knighthood—the rationale, after all, for the whole undertaking—might depend on her earning the woman's esteem.

William de Ferrers, earl of Derby, was a bantam rooster of a man who arrived for the banquet wrapped in loose folds of deep red velvet, like an undersized emperor of Rome, and wearing a heavy gold pendant with a ruby amulet nearly the size of his fist. If he had nursed any hesitance over being received as the guest of one so greatly his social inferior, the earl artfully cloaked it beneath the surety of his own grandeur. Indeed, he adopted a tone so cordial in conversing with the sheriff that Philip wondered why he himself had so inclined toward the reverential in his prior dealings with the earl. "You know, my good lad, I held your job once—for seven weeks," Ferrers remarked at the outset of the evening. "Were you aware?"

"Only that the shire rolls testify to it, my lord, but I know none of the circumstances."

"In '94 it was—the Lionheart was just freed and en route home, and John and his party had run off from Nottingham with their behinds bare— it was the prince's darkest hour, beyond a doubt—and the castle and the shire were in chaos, so the king's council asked me to step in for the time being. Richard wisely assigned Brewer up here at the first opportunity— he was the man for the job, not the likes of me. I've no head for all the pettiness—and the dirt. Not an easy job, yours, or very likable, either." Having made the office sound more janitorial than magisterial, the earl recouped somewhat by adding, "I'm glad it's being handled more professionally now by your likes—more neutral, less passionate men—true servants of the crown. They tell me you passed the Michaelmas audit at the Exchequer with flying colors—even bringing in a surplus. Brewer and the chamberlain are said to be delighted."

"Thank you, my lord. It was my good fortune to be able—"

"And Longsword says he's inspected for the king and you've worked miracles with the castle—that it's now more legitimately a fortress than ever."

"The crown was persuaded of the necessity."

"But you raised the money."

"Our bailiffs have been heroic."

"I've heard they shit purple if you so much as look at them."

"It's news to me, my lord."

"Why so? Dread is the fodder of good governance."

"I should rather have enthusiasm than cringing compliance in my men—though I concede they seem to respond more to snarls than to smiles."

The earl grunted and drank deeply from his goblet. The wine continued to flow into him so ceaselessly thereafter that Philip began to suppose as the meal lengthened that not only were both His Lordship's legs hollow but his entire internal cavity as well, the brain pan not excepted.

As his blood vessels dilated and spirits warmed, he grew more hortatory. "You must not be reluctant to make your impress, Philip," Ferrers asserted. "Where and how you have derived your power matters far less than how you exercise it. You may not be of the gentry, but at least you're a Frenchman—nearly a Norman—and it is our heritage of mastery that has built this kingdom and brought it order and prosperity. Without force it would fly apart. The Saxons could never have sustained it—they have a thinner blood and natural bend of the back, and yet a decided surliness that infects the commonality and needs constant draining. Strength is wanted in those of us with sway if a greater Britain is to be achieved, as His Majesty is admirably attempting." He spoke then of the bloodless triumph the king had gained only two months before, ending with William the Lion, king of the Scots, in abject submission. "The nerve of that old fart, having advanced outrageous claims all these years to the northern counties and withheld tribute—and lately granting haven to a bunch of addled bastards with insurrectionist leanings against the crown! There was only one way to deal with him: take an army to his border, threaten to chop him to pieces—and mean it. The king did it beautifully. Let it be a lesson to you, my good sheriff."

Philip listened dutifully to all this and at the end asked quietly, "Is there evidence, my lord, I'm wanting in the proper use of force?"

"It's *how* you're using it that I fret over—indeed, overusing it against those who should be your natural allies while cosseting the rest. You've needlessly made a foe, as an instance, of our Prior Clement."

"Forgive me, my lord, but the prior would have looked unkindly on any officer of the king who fulfilled his commands during the Interdict."

"He complains that you have been excessively methodical in your harassments."

"I take that for a compliment."

"Perhaps a bit more politesse than rigor is wanted where Holy Church is concerned—the fight with Rome will not last forever. I have in mind as well your ruling in shire court not long ago wherein you voided a deathbed bequest to Clement's priory by a wealthy Templar still perfectly in his senses."

"Deathbeds rarely promote clearheadedness, my lord, nor were there any witnesses from the family present—only clerics."

"Their word generally goes unquestioned."

"The practice is unseemly, and the crown is discouraging it in the course of the Interdict."

"Still, he senses animus in you."

"I cannot shrink from my duty, whatever the prior's feelings. In candor, I think him an intemperate man of God."

The earl helped himself to half a platter of eels even while noting the gastric commotion they induced in him. Then he returned to a cautionary vein. "You have another enemy in Greasley, I'm sorry to learn. Some petty squabble, I believe, where you ruled against him on the tourn?"

"He was plainly in the wrong, having disregarded a judgment by the king's eyre. He's acknowledged his steward's error to me."

"Has he? Then he's two-faced, for he tells me otherwise. Thinks you a misguided weakling for trying to curry favor with the rabble. And the coroner has little good to say of you, either, slurring you equally for low birth and high airs—which I take to mean you haven't gone out of your way to flatter the silly bunghole. On the other hand, Lord Lambert speaks well of you—and you could want no sounder ally in the county, though I differ with him some on the king and his ways."

As if the mention of his name were a stage cue, the lord of Swanhill himself loomed over them the next moment and, having overheard the earl's last few words, asked, "Am I being invoked in vain?"

"Ah, Thomas—I've just been reviewing the world with our young colleague here—in particular how the king pulled our Scottish Lion's dewlaps. I hope you're thinking better of him nowadays."

Lambert spoke with approval of the king's humbling of the Scots but doubted the wisdom of the peace terms. "He knows no magnanimity in victory. Wasn't it enough for John to take the Lion's castles and levy the fine of ten thousand? Lord knows where he'll get it—he's already in debt to the Jews up to his kidneys. But why did he demand his two daughters as well? He does it all the time, egregiously so with the Marshal's sons—and sought the same from your uncle Briouse, igniting this lethal feud between them. To take children as collateral against their parents' good behavior is a ruler's confession that he is insecure in his strength. As a means of extracting obedience, let alone loyalty, I find the practice reprehensible."

"Balls!" said the earl. "It's just plain hard politics and good sense. Besides, the king doesn't abuse the hostages—I see no harm in it. As to my uncle, the matter was far more complex than my aunt's refusal to turn the boys over to the crown."

In the years before the king had detected defiance and ingratitude in William de Briouse, he had built up that vassal into a force every bit as powerful as the Marshal and a counterweight to his dominion on the Welsh frontier. To tame the native tribes, Briouse had been awarded as many as sixteen castles in the south of Wales and well over three hundred knights' fees—"a force unto himself," Ferrers had once observed somewhat acidly.

"But it was the king who made him overmighty," said Lambert, "and then picks a quarrel to reduce him. Is it seemly?"

"It was a necessary retrenchment and served the king's purposes. Besides, Uncle William needed reducing." The earl faded off momentarily into squinting reverie. "It's—quite remarkable, you know—the man had all those castles but no earldom. I have the earldom yet not a castle to my name." He sighed mightily and drew his small frame upright. "No doubt that's the king's genius—keeping us all on the threshold of discontent and thus habitual suitors for his favor."

"Yet his folly," said Lambert, "is that he is forever testing us all for loyalty and inevitably finds us all wanting. Will anything satisfy him short of groveling subservience?"

Ferrers gave his glowing head a fierce shake. "You touch on but the outward signs. The origin, I tell you, is that he wishes mightily to be loved, as he conceives his father and brother before him were, yet he knows not how to play the suitor. Kings are not used to soliciting."

"Perhaps someone should tell him," replied Lambert, "that to earn love, one must evidence some. He husbands his all for himself."

"I'll pass your sentiment on to him," the earl said waspishly, "along with full payment of your next scutage."

The dancing began with an intricate galliard and proceeded to the faster *tourdion,* which called for more stamina than nimbleness. The youthful heroics that had shattered the sheriff's leg and left him with a slight stiffness of gait made him a reluctant dancer except in the most private of surroundings. His wife, however, relished the chance to disport with Gallic flourish amid the fusty Anglo-Norman gentry gathered in her castle— it seemed far more hers, on this festive night at least, than the king's— and thus much welcomed Thomas de Lambert's request to be her partner. The baron moved, she thought, with surprising ease and in close tempo to the music, and she commended him accordingly. "My lady of Tours is too generous," he said. "The social skills of my youth have rusted, I regret to say. Happily, they dance more suavely in Normandy, where I was taught, than in Nottinghamshire."

His social skills were plainly still abundant, she told him with a smile—

"and without them, this evening would not have materialized." His diplomatic approach to the earl and subsequent counsel to her on the treacheries of local protocol were of inestimable value, she added.

"My part was a speck in your grand design. You've carried it all off splendidly, Anne. Lady Ferrers, you should know, is entirely charmed by you—and she is not alone."

Her smile broadened. "I did no more than nod at the right points in her lectures to me—and wiped my mouth only on the napkin."

"Nevertheless, you're on your way to a triumph."

Anne's flush deepened as the jongleurs paused between dances. "Forgive my impertinence, Sir Thomas, but I cannot help noticing you choose not to dance with Lady Cicely. I trust there is no rift . . ."

"The choice is hers. She cares not for dancing."

"Does she care that you attend me?"

"I didn't inquire. Should she?"

"I sense that she views Philip and me as belonging to the lower orders of humanity—and thus it's perhaps beneath your dignity to—"

"You mistake a certain remoteness in Lady Cicely's manner for disdain. You must not be too quick to take offense—it's the sign of one new to social rank. If you did not please us, we wouldn't be here."

"Is it both of you we please—or only you, Thomas?"

He appraised her closely, though her eyes fled from his. "I've not considered the distinction," he said.

"Then I ask you to."

"Well, I'm more aware than she of the value of befriending the sheriff. And I find Philip engaging."

"And the sheriff's wife—of what use is she to you?"

He glanced about him to see if they could be overheard, but the music began anew just then, reducing the likelihood. "If you are in doubt," he said, taking her hand to begin the dance, "I'm not indifferent to the loveliness of Anne of Tours. More need not be said. Now leave me to hear the players, or I'll go trippingly to pieces."

Within the hour, the mood of merrymaking fled. Geoffrey, the sheriff's nephew, had arrived disheveled from London with stunning news that he whispered to Philip. Uncertain for the moment whether to report it to his guests and thereby shatter the evening's festive air, he saw on swift reflection where his duty lay.

"Honored guests and fellow subjects of our liege lord, the king," the sheriff called out after gesturing the musicians into silence, "I have sober tidings from Westminster." The pope had excommunicated John of England and called upon all his bishops there to abandon the realm. The king was said to be regretful and had taken at once to consulting holy texts for spiritual guidance; beyond that, he was unmoved.

Even as this somber advisory spread gloom through the gathering, the guest of honor climbed onto his bench and commanded every eye. "Lords and ladies, gentles and dames," rasped the diminutive earl of Derby, "I ask you to join me in toasting the king's health—and urge us all to pray for his soul in this, his hour of travail. We must share the crown's ordeal."

The room rose in obedience, drinking vessels in hand, save for the clerics in attendance—the chancellor of Southwell, the priors of Lenton and Blyth, the abbot of Newstead, and the castle chaplain. The five of them remained seated with eyes closed in prayer, as if acting in premeditated concert. So startling was this spectacle of passive defiance that the rest of the hall hesitated to follow the earl's directive, fearful as they were that the papal wrath would descend on them as well the next instant.

Rather than witness the earl suffer the indignity of drinking alone after so solemn a tender, thus turning the whole occasion to ruin, the sheriff broke the embarrassed silence of the hall by declaring, "I intrude only to ask the understanding of the holy fathers among us—no disrespect is intended by this gesture of solidarity with our monarch. We are laymen and not—"

"This is the king's sanctuary, Master Sheriff, not the pope's!" the earl shouted at him. "You have no need to apologize for me—or the crown. Show your grit, man!" He turned back to the hall and raised his goblet still higher. "To the king, I say—to the king!" he roared, and swallowed hungrily. Then, with lips still wine-stained, he stepped down from his bench and marched from the hall, Lady Ferrers and two footmen scurrying in pursuit.

·XIX·

BLAKE THREADED HIS WAY between the strips of the common, high now with barley, and whistled the most tuneful passage from his favorite hymn. Its precise subject he had never been certain of but knew to be at least partially concerned with the blessedness of salvation. That promise, its pearly luster having grown fainter in his memory, interested him far less than the sound passing through his own lips that caused his little mare's ears to prick. He wondered, in the full warmth of the day, whether the anthem he trilled was more pleasing to his horse than the low drone of the insects that rose up from the fields. Or did it seem just a louder and more discordant form of birdsong and thus more abrasive to her? Whatever his mount's judgment of the sound, the reeve decided, he whistled better than he sang, and for sparing her his unfortunate croak the animal ought to be grateful.

As he whistled, he admired how much more variable his song was than the insects' sustained note, which, at best, seemed to alter only every now and then and never turned to melody. This led him to ponder how many insects were contributing to the soft, ceaseless hum that filled the moist air. Hundreds? No, thousands it had to be. How many thousands? How many on the whole manor? In the whole shire? Upon the whole earth? How many would it take to equal the size of a man? And if one grew that big, how fearsome a creature would it be?

His whistling trailed off after he had rendered the part he knew well three times over—the rest of the hymn had left him. That he retained even that much of it seemed remarkable to him, for it was now more than a year and a half since the parish church had closed its doors. Yet how little he missed Mass, he confessed to himself sheepishly, and the haranguing priest who was so miserly in his expenditure of compassion. True, Blake vaguely felt himself a spiritual truant now, ducking about the edges of God's surveillance in sly evasion. Still, the Lord and His worshipers were getting on well enough without the priests to negotiate between them; there had been no plague or famine since the holy fathers were idled; and even the weather had been pleasurably moderate, as if Christ were hovering just overhead in benign majesty yet asking no tithe to minister to the infinite pains of the living.

Thus ruminating during his daily round of the villagers' crops, always made at a different hour, in search for those avoiding their duty to work the manor fields, Blake came upon the selions belonging to the ploughman Griggs's widow, Susan. They looked in better condition than he had supposed possible. He knew she had contracted with another villein to do the heavy work in return for two-thirds of the harvest, which she and her children were to help gather; meanwhile, throughout the growing season her humpbacked boy had been weeding the fields and trying to keep in place their stone boundary markers against the encroachment of neighbors. But even if the plan worked out, the reeve doubted the yield would be sufficient both to help feed Susan's family and to contribute to her other financial needs. Since he had forcibly retired her from the illicit flour-milling business, they were largely dependent on the earnings of Susan's older daughter, Judith, whose smiles and sweetness fetched enough in gratuities from the patrons of the Rainworth alehouse to pay several times over the steep price the steward had fixed for the privilege of her serving there as a barmaid. At best, their economic survival would be a close thing. Yet he could do no more for her—and what he had already done had earned him only her resentment.

As Blake swung around the corner of the farthermost of Griggs's strips, he spotted a parting in the tall rows of grain and the foreign object that had caused it. Dismounting, he warily approached the unfamiliar heap on the ground and drew up short as the crumpled shape took on definition. The little humpback lay there curled in a bloody, nearly naked mass, beaten almost lifeless. His scalp had been gashed in several places, with blood still oozing from a loosened flap; his cheek was torn half-open; one eye was badly bruised and shut; and painted on his bare hump with his own blood was the cross of Christ, apparently to pay back the devil for having inflicted the malformation. On his genitals someone had poured honey, which a swarm of insects was busily attacking.

Gingerly the reeve lifted the pitiful creature, eliciting a moan of protest that was nevertheless a welcome sign of persistent life. He carried the boy to where his horse stood and reset him on the ground within the shadow that the animal cast. Then he stripped off his own tunic, wrapped the beaten child in it, and awkwardly remounted with the living burden in his arms. The mare he kept to a walk all the way back to the village while he soothed the boy and tried to elicit from him in as few words as possible details of the evil that had transpired.

If he knew who it was that had attacked him, the victim would not say. Even after Blake told him the attackers could not be punished unless their names were known and promised that he would try to shield him from further harm, the boy remained mute. The most the reeve could determine was that the lad had been assaulted for allegedly moving the boundary markers in order to expand his family's fields. "One place I did it," the boy whimpered, "to get back what they stole from Pa—nothing more." The real reason, Blake knew, was that the lad was disfigured and defenseless, the perfect prey for brutishness among the progeny of the put-upon.

As they neared his cottage, the boy said through puffed, cracked lips that the reeve should not bother his mother if the window was shuttered with a rag tied to its outer edge. Seeing a bit of yellow cloth fixed in place as the lad had described, Blake asked him what it meant. "She's busy," he said. "Don't bother her now."

"Busy? Busy doing what? You need tending."

"She . . . friends come. She said . . . I shouldn't . . ."

He stroked the back of the boy's head to calm him, then shouted for Susan to come and take her wounded child. Several long moments passed before the disheveled widow flung open her door and looked with horror at the mayhem done to the malformed fruit of her womb. After Blake had carefully handed down the frail child, he began to follow Susan inside to see what help he could lend or obtain, but she snapped at him over her shoulder, "Keep out—I've enough misery without your adding to it!" Saddened by this brusque dismissal, the reeve hovered shirtless in the doorway until forced to make way for Noah the hayward, who, his clothes hastily assembled and still untucked, fled from the cottage as Susan sent up a great wail of lamentation.

He could not bring himself to talk to the hayward the next day, even though they were close friends. It was Noah who took the lead late in the afternoon after the reeve had plainly slighted him twice earlier. "Don't be cross with me, Blake," he said. "The woman needs the money, my organs need the exercise—and she happens to be skilled at her work."

Blake only glared in response and turned away from him again.

"Look, I'm sorry about her cripple—but that wasn't my fault. And you shouldn't turn up your nose at a little commercial rutting—unless you've tried her yourself, that is, and were disappointed—which, with all due respect to Mistress Blake, I doubt."

"Shut your fool's mouth," the reeve shouted.

"When you stop playing the priest. The woman's only human—and so am I. Aren't we entitled to a little pleasure in life? And she gives more than fair value."

Blake collected himself. "Just tell me one thing, please. How could the long-faithful wife of a simple ploughman school herself so well in the whoring arts?"

The hayward shrugged. "Learns a little from each customer, I suppose. Griggs will never know what he missed, poor man."

"Each customer?" Blake's heart fell. "Are there so many?"

"I wouldn't know. But they say she's quite selective—and that her price varies with what you can afford." Noah looked puzzled. "I thought the reeve knew everything. Can all this be news to you?"

"We've quarreled, so I steer clear of her. She resents my thinking better of her than she does herself."

"Oh," said Noah, failing to restrain a smile. "But we all think well of her."

"You all debase her," said Blake, easing his horse into motion, "and yourselves in the bargain."

The reeve came upon her several days afterward while she was returning from the spring on a strange horse heavily laden with water jugs; he paused to ask after her boy's health. At first she would not reply but, remembering the kindness he had done in recovering the lad from the common, finally said, "As best as can be expected, thank you. He eats little and is sullen."

"If it would be any help, I'll stand guard next time he's fit enough to go to the common."

"Don't be foolish, Master Reeve—I can't allow him to go back. They'll kill him."

He turned his horse and rode uninvited alongside hers for a time. "A neighbor's palfrey?" he asked. "She's a beauty."

"Mine," said Susan. "I bought it."

"Oh? Then things are better with you. I'm glad. I hear that Judith is well liked at the—"

"You *know* how things are with us, Master Blake, so don't be coy. I needed a horse, and I earned it. I can't help it if you disapprove of where my earnings come from. There's no other way. Judith's work may pay our tallage, but the steward has made it clear that Sarah's labors at the manor fall far short of meeting our week-work. The balance must be made up in cash—so I work as I can."

He was silent for a time, then risked provoking her anew. "They say you have a talent for your trade." When she did not reply, he waited another moment and then asked, "What do you think they called your boy's mother when they assaulted him?"

She bit her lip and kept her head forward, sliding her eyes toward him with dark malevolence brimming in them. "Did he tell you that?" she asked, voice brittle.

"No," he said, "but I can guess."

"In order to hurt me."

"In order to save you."

"I'm saving myself, reeve—I don't need you to."

"How can you live with yourself, Susan?"

She turned toward him, more in resignation now than in anger. "I pray to God more—you should, too. Now leave me." She rapped her horse's rump so that it advanced at a slightly less sluggish pace.

One assault seemed to spawn the next. Shortly after Michaelmas, the ploughman Paul was found in the hedgerow separating the Swanhill oat fields from the great pasture. His throat had been severely slit, nearly decapitating him, and his testicles had been stuffed into his mouth.

A normally peaceable place, Swanhill was aswarm with the authorities for a week following the crime while the perpetrator was hunted. The dead man had dwelled there nearly his whole life and, though not universally beloved, had no known enemies. Sir Mitchell, the shire coroner, spent several days at the manor gathering particulars, accompanied by the Rainworth bailiff and several of the king's men-at-arms from the castle. Even Sheriff Mark was seen at the manor house in consultation with Lord Lambert. Murder was far from unheard of in the shire, but generally the victims were found discarded along the highway or in Sherwood, their deaths attributed to brigands. The brutal manner of Paul's death suggested, by contrast, that he had been done in by one or more assailants who knew him and nursed a sore grievance against him. Jadwin, the beadle, and Stryker, the steward, were particularly visible in and about the village, eager to ferret out even the meagerest clue, and the reeve himself was pressed into service to inquire of villagers who were especially taciturn.

In the end these investigations yielded but one plausible theory for the crime. Paul, it was learned, had long envied his fellow ploughman Griggs for the face and form of his wife, Susan, who at thirty-five had not yet turned into a crone as his own wife and so many others had by that age. Griggs had spared her not only from his abusiveness but also from as much physical labor as he could in order to preserve her fairness and good humor. Upon Griggs's death, Paul's covetousness grew uncontainable, and his own wife seemed to him all the more shrewish and haggard.

When he learned that Susan was plying the carnal trade to sustain her home and family, he was among her early and most admiring customers. But one day, after enjoying her services, he said he had forgotten to bring money and promised to make it up to her the next time. On the ensuing occasion, though, he again failed to pay her, saying he was temporarily short of funds and next time he would give her interest as well as what he owed. On the third visit, however, he brought only half the usual price for a single pleasuring, contending that as he was a good friend of Susan's late husband, he was entitled to a cut rate; and further, that since he possessed what was undoubtedly the largest and handsomest member of any man in the village, she ought to have been happy to service him for whatever he could afford. If she refused to accommodate him, he added, he would go to the reeve and the beadle and see to it that she was prosecuted in the manor court as a stain on the community. Two mornings later, Paul's body was found, his sex organs mutilated.

His connection with the widow was discovered in long, painful talks with her by the authorities, of whom the beadle was the most unstinting, according to his own account, which he freely gave at the alehouse. Susan herself, of course, was not suspected, given the extreme violence of the murder and the strength it must have taken, but the likely linkage between Paul's behavior toward her and the manner of his dispatch was hard to gainsay. Plainly she had a fierce protector at the manor or in the village; and for Paul's repeated abuses of her, the ultimate price was exacted.

"You must forgive me, reeve," Jadwin said to him shortly after this motive had been more or less established, "but you are known to have been kindly disposed toward the widow. If you have any knowledge whatever of the crime, you had best report it."

"I'm not a violent man," Blake answered. "I suggest you concentrate your efforts on those men around here known for their brutal temperaments. If you're in any doubt, I'll supply the names."

The beadle riddled the reeve with his most hateful stare. "At any rate, you see what's become of your fine, fair Susan—just another degenerate bitch, as I told you she was—laying with the likes of Paul, the worst sort of slime. He used to beat his pigs half the Sabbath for squealing too loud and his wife the other half for the same cause. He's no great loss to the manor—though of course murder can't be excused."

The reeve gained further insight into the crime upon taking his horse to be shoed by Sparks the smith. The proprietor was discreet in his revelations—which was no doubt why so many in the village confided in him; his mother, though, who lived with his family in the ample cottage attached to the smithy, was less so when meeting with those she favored. The reeve was one of them, partially because he came regularly to visit the wizened woman, whose bone disorders had left her crippled and house-bound, and partially because he shared what harmless gossip he could with her in exchange for her more telling news.

Finding her seated as usual on a stool close by the two windows at the rear of their dwelling, where she remained hours on end in rapt study of the comings and goings in the village, the reeve greeted Mother Sparks warmly and asked after the health of her younger son. Jared had clerked at Nottingham Castle for nearly a dozen years now but still visited the manor every month to bring her a portion of his wages and news from the larger world. "He keeps telling me our French sheriff is Heaven-sent," she said after bestowing a toothless smile on Blake, "but cannot help making enemies. One of them must be the coroner, from what I've heard of his recent visit here—speaking ill of Master Mark at every turn for not getting to the bottom of our dreadful murder."

The old woman had other spicy items to retail, not the least of them the besotted disclosure that Lot, the miller's son, had made at the alehouse a fortnight earlier to the always receptive ear of the smith, who passed it to his mother verbatim and in the utmost confidence. Afloat in hatred for his father, who overworked and underpaid him, Lot revealed the chicanery he had uncovered between the miller and Steward Stryker when they had gone off to Lincoln the year before to buy a new millstone for the manor. The pair of them had told Lord Lambert the charge was fifteen pounds six, as the bill of sale stated, but the true price they had bartered down to thirteen pounds, and they then prevailed upon the quarry owner, for a small consideration on the side, to falsify the bill. Afterward the pair of them split the difference, as Lot learned in coming upon the cache of pennies that comprised his father's share. The money was a source of open pride to the miller, who, when questioned, avidly explained the windfall to his son as an example of crafty commerce. On more than one occasion while tippling in public, Lot had wished his father dead for his meanness of spirit—"And in that the lad's not alone," the old woman added.

In further connection with the alehouse, she expressed her forebod-ings about the barmaid Judith, the widow Griggs's older daughter, who was said to be too free with her big eyes and broad smiles in the pursuit of gratuities. "My older boy says he thinks she is still pure, but her knack at coquetry could soon turn her to a strumpet—and she'd have far more takers than her mother."

The allusion to Susan prompted one further revelation by the shriveled story-monger, this one more intriguing to Blake than all the rest. Did the reeve know, she asked, that the Griggs widow was visited every second day by Master Jadwin, who generally arrived on foot, often looking about as if anxious that he enter unobserved? He sometimes remained but a few minutes, at other times up to an hour. "It wouldn't surprise me a bit," she said with a cackle that caused some to surmise she was at least part-witch, "if the beadle takes a plump share of her earnings, bloody beast that he is."

Some instinct as deep within him as his loathing for the beadle drove Blake to ride out that very afternoon to the hedgerow where the murdered ploughman had been found. While his horse grazed nearby and served as sentry, the reeve combed every square inch of earth, plant, and tree in the vicinity, much as the law officers had done earlier, but more intensively. After nearly two hours that revealed nothing irregular, his eye was caught by the merest sliver of something white near the bottom of a clump of thatch he was raking through. He poked deeper and deeper and at last extracted the source, two pieces from what was unquestionably the beadle's broken white wand. Another minute of probing yielded the missing final piece.

His heart raced to keep up with his churning brain. The shattered wand, unearthed some twenty feet from where the body was found, could mean everything—or nothing. It could have fallen unnoticed in the night when Jadwin did the foul deed and delivered the corpse to that spot; his charger might have stepped on the fallen wand and ground it into the underbrush. Or it could have been mixed into the thatch while the coroner and bailiffs' party were rummaging over the terrain. But Jadwin was there among them and could easily claim the wand had fallen then and its loss gone unnoticed until later. Yet who else had so free a rein to roam the manor unquestioned as the beadle? Who else was known to have had regular dealings with Susan, his sly words slandering her to the reeve notwithstanding? Who else was known to have so violent a disposition—and little hesitancy to act on it? And who else had lately spoken to him of the dead man as so much worthless offal?

Still, the reeve could prove nothing. And if he took his suspicions to the bailiff, who was in the manor's pay and sure to report the matter to the steward if not to the beadle himself, Blake would succeed only in further arousing a murderous adversary. He carefully placed the pieces of the broken wand in his saddlebag and resolved to safeguard them against some timely future use.

The ploughman's murder, if intended to avenge mistreatment of the widow Susan, had the companion effect of slowing her trade for a time, as prospective patrons feared that any involvement with her might prove to be their last act. But such anxiety passed soon enough, and by Martinmas eve the alehouse vibrated with leering laughter about the resumption of steady activity in the straw beside her hearth. Before Paul's grisly death, such talk was subdued out of kindness to the callow barmaid Judith, who was said somehow to have been shielded from awareness of her mother's lately learned profession. Susan was reportedly at pains not to practice it except when her daughters were expected to be away; she had even told them to disregard any scurrilous remarks they might hear about her since it was a widow's lot to suffer such. Now, though, after Susan's charms had likely contributed to the loss of a life, such niceties were dropped and Judith heard the lecherous jests, told with hurtful anatomical detail, and the prophecy that, as the apple never fell far from the tree, she herself would soon be ripe for rutting.

The girl, alas, was not strong enough to withstand such incessant brutish talk and one night grew hysterical. She screamed at her foul-mouthed tormentors that they were liars, and when one of them rubbed her buttocks in further provocation, Judith turned uncontrollable with rage. She snatched up the jeerers' cups and goblets from their tables and hurled them full force at their faces. The resulting damage to them was minimal, but to her, catastrophic. Several of the worst men in the crowd pummeled her into semiconsciousness and carried her into the rear room to teach her manners and other unforgettable lessons. Soon some who had nourished dark fantasies about the pretty girl joined in until she was left massively deflowered, pitched out onto the road as close to naked as her little brother had been found in the common the summer previous, and barred from ever returning to the alehouse.

A week passed before Susan interrupted the nursing of her shattered daughter long enough to venture to the village spring for water. While there, with grief written heavily across her suddenly aging face, she saw the reeve but could not bring herself to confront him. Silently he took her jars, filled them, and brought them back to her cottage on his own horse while the widow returned ahead of him. "I thank you, Master Blake," she whispered as he placed the water by her door.

"Mistress Blake would like to help you with the girl," he said.

She closed her eyes, and her whole upper torso seemed to convulse with a single sob. "No one can help," she said softly. "I must care for her—she cannot work as before, nor can I." She glanced up at him, misery contorting the unspoken plea in her expression. "How shall we have the money to survive?" she asked, looking as forlorn as the last leaf on a tree in autumn. Then her head was buried in his chest, and she sobbed uncontrollably without letup. He folded his arms about her warm, trembling form but did not draw her still closer to him.

A.D.
1210

· XX ·

THE SHERIFF'S RECTITUDE, so entirely admirable throughout his early years of service at Nottingham, edged toward a maddening mulishness in the eyes of his devoted clerk as the third year of Philip Mark's tenure unfolded. The problems encountered, Sparks granted him, were not of the sheriff's making. But his stiff-necked character only made matters worse. For the first time the little clerk feared that his master's purity of heart was causing him to misjudge the fragility of his position and the potency of his detractors, whom the kings' policies served to multiply and inflame.

The crisis grew out of that most mundane of civic irritants: taxes. Their perceived oppressiveness had in the past stemmed as much from the king's military failures—why drain the financial life's blood of the realm only to spill it in vain on the battlefield?—as from the takings themselves. Now, at least, John bestrode the British Isles as a triumphant captain of his own destiny, if not precisely a conquering hero in his brother's mold. He had followed up his humbling of the Scots the prior year by summoning a goodly host of English knights and Flemish mercenaries and setting sail at midyear to carry the royal pennon across Ireland. The king's purported objective was the capture of that lately mighty fugitive William de Briouse, wanted for insults paid and debts unpaid the crown, according to the king's calculations. Briouse had been granted asylum by Irish lords who held their baronies by royal charter; John had either to exert his sway over them and their sympathizers or concede that Ireland was lost to freebooters and anarchy. He chose the former course and carried it off, leveling castles as need be and gathering tribute from native chieftains and previously reluctant lords while the royal army swept over the Irish countryside with William the Marshal, restored to full honors, at the king's side.

To pay for this fresh sceptering of the kingdom and its ever-growing military needs since the pope had moved to isolate a greater Britain from the rest of Christendom, the king did not hesitate to tax his subjects more heavily than ever. Beyond all the regular and immutable exactions, the special levies that used to vary in size and frequency were now becoming almost annual burdens of steadily growing weight. The scutage, levied against tenants-in-chief of the crown who owed it military service but elected to send silver instead, reached two pounds per knight's fee, double the '09 figure. The tallage, tribute money that all lords were privileged to demand from their vassals, also climbed to a new high, pinching every tenant of a royal manor—there were thirty-two of them alone at Tickhill, the largest of the king's estates in Nottinghamshire—as well as every holder of a crown custodianship and every occupant of royal boroughs like Nottingham Town. Lest these two exactions fail to replenish the crown coffers adequately, the king also ordered an enormous tallage against the Jews, amounting to a full fifth of their holdings. While this last order would not normally have grieved the realm unduly, it was coupled with the painful insistence that all outstanding debts to the Jews be promptly settled so the crown could have its share of those as well (not to mention its 10 percent fee for enforcing collection). The sum and substance of all these taxes, as Sparks calculated them, was that the sheriff would have to turn over to the Exchequer by Michaelmas an amount more than three times as large as the previous year's.

To succeed at this repellent task, the castle urgently required a leading lord to play the compliant bellwether, however reluctantly. Toward this end, Sparks urged the sheriff to pay a visit to Swanhill. Philip concurred, and brought along only his clerk lest a larger delegation inhibit his freely soliciting Lord Lambert's acquiescence.

The sheriff arrived with hopes unreasonably high because Sir Thomas's son Guthrie had answered the king's call and ridden off with him to Ireland, more for the adventure of the thing than for the politics but zestfully nonetheless. His father, however, finding the king's purpose at its core to be the persecution of Briouse, a fellow baron who dared defy the crown's high-handedness, had declined to send the additional dozen knights enfiefed to him and so owed the crown twenty-four pounds for scutage, as well as previous delinquencies that he was satisfying at a snail's pace.

"But surely this Irish expedition is the king's legitimate business," Philip said soon after their interview began and the baron's reluctance had become manifest, "and a far cry from his warring in France that drew your allegiance from him."

"The same towering pride has prompted both," Lambert replied. "In this instance the king musters the full might of the realm to hunt down a single vassal whose crime is to resist John's craving to humble him without just cause."

"The king may lift up or cast down whom he chooses."

"Not unduly, in either case, if he hopes to retain his subjects' devotion."

The sheriff altered tack. "Yet you paid the full scutage promptly last year. Was that notably different?"

"Quite. First, the Scots needed to be chastened. Second, the fine was half as high as this year's. Third, I paid more out of liking for you than love for my liege lord. But as you see, there's no end to it. Each year there will be some fresh provocation, and each compliance forms the precedent for the next demand, however arbitrary. It's a vicious cycle that I am duty-bound to oppose."

However hard the sheriff pressed him, Lambert said he would not decide what portion of the scutage he might fulfill until a fortnight before Michaelmas, the very deadline. As to abetting Philip's anxiety that the shire's quota would not be met without the full and early cooperation of its leading landholder, the baron regretted he could not play the sheriff's client. "If the king's reach exceeds the castle's grasp, I'll lament for you," he told Philip, "but in that event, you ought not mistake whether it is John or I who did you in."

Others proved comparably resistant to reasoned appeals by the sheriff's agents. Some said they had little money on hand and had to wait for the harvest to get more. Others declined to sell their chattels to raise the tax money, citing the low prices they would fetch at market just then. Still others openly voiced their objection to the soaring demands of an excommunicate king whom they no longer owed absolute fealty. No one could find his purse when the bailiffs first called, and on their second visit only a small partial payment was forthcoming, if any at all. Increasingly, the shirewide grievance was directed against "this thieving Frenchman of a sheriff" and not the far-off sovereign whose creature he was.

His most prudent recourse, Philip decided at this juncture, was to make an example of a current tax delinquent so all would know that while they might delay meeting the king's call on them to the last, woe be to those who failed the test in the end. The plan required a decision whether it would be better to bring to heel a disliked landholder who was unlikely to stir the shire's sympathy or to seize one high in its esteem and thus risk earning its wrath. Not wanting the county to conclude that a rotter had received his just deserts, the sheriff selected as his exemplar in truancy Gilbert de Berri, a knight enfiefed to Lord Lambert and the very embodiment of chivalric virtue. Money being peripheral to his daily concerns, he had slighted his tax debts to the point where the interest charges were now accruing at a rate faster than he was discharging the principal, so that his deficit grew by the year.

Bailiff Manning called upon Sir Gilbert to advise him that unless his delinquency was cured in the interim, castle officers would be obliged to return a week hence and remove such of his grain, stock, and household items as were required to settle his debt to the crown. Nothing was heard from the knight thereafter, but when the bailiff, two deputies, and five sergeants-at-arms appeared with a small caravan of carts to relieve the delinquent of his possessions, Sir Gilbert met them in full battle regalia, reinforced by ten pitchfork-wielding bondsmen. A well-armored Manning, with the undersheriff alongside him in the lead, returned the next day in company with half the castle garrison, only to find that all of Sir Gilbert's chattels had disappeared overnight; the knight himself they apprehended beside his hearth, unarmed now and softly insistent that he was being abused. They carted him off to gaol, where he was temporarily lodged in Master Plunk's apartment.

Lord Lambert himself shortly appeared in the sheriff's closet to decry the seizure of one of his vassals. "It's cowardly of you in the extreme, Master Mark," he stormed, "to carry off an impoverished knight who has harmed no one. Why not seize me if you're so determined to instruct the shire?"

"Sir Gilbert is not so much impoverished as improvident," said Philip, meeting Lambert's fury with calm. "And you at least discharge some part of your debt to the crown each year; his only deepens."

"He's a noble soul, and all you'll do by holding him is arouse the rest of us to fiercer resistance. And if you then arrest others as well, you'll soon have no room in the gaol because the whole shire will rise up and rally against you." Lambert's eye wandered to his old sword tilted against the wall behind the sheriff's chair. "I urge you with all my heart, sire, not to proceed in this fashion."

"But you were the one who declined to accommodate me, my lord, when I peaceably sought a model of knightly devotion to his liege lord our king. And now you fault me for settling on a model of another sort—one who chronically shirks his duty to the crown and is at last forced to submit. You cannot have it both ways, sire."

"I need not be an eager party to the crown's unjust levies. Don't trifle with me, Philip—I'm your friend, and you'll find such at a premium if you persist in oppressive tactics."

Since the sheriff, his feigned dismay aside, had never intended a wholesale ingathering of tax debtors, no harm was done. Sir Gilbert was held only until his missing chattels were traced and seized. Still, it had been far from an idle gesture, to judge by Lambert's response to the castle's display of resolve. Tax collections rose, if only from a few drops at a time to a steady trickle. So apprehensive did Sparks grow that when the Nottingham burgesses inquired into what sort of gift they might bestow upon the castle this year, the clerk suggested that the hundred shillings might best be applied to the outsized shire tax quota.

"But the burgesses might not credit such an explanation," Philip objected, "and suppose instead that I've pocketed the money as a gratuity."

"The burgesses are long since convinced that you're the soul of honor, sire. The trouble might arise from others who are always prepared to think the worst of sheriffs. My view of it is based on the precepts of Baron Brewer—namely, that your sole implacable master is neither the king nor the shire but the Exchequer; disappoint it, and your doom is sealed. So I'd take the town council's shillings and ignore any resulting criticism—come autumn, you're likely to need every penny of it."

Philip sensed impending panic in his clerk's counsel, yet agreed it would be wastrel to bedeck the castle with some bauble or other when the burgesses' silver might help fill a far more pressing need. Master Welles was quick to tell the sheriff what use he made of the money was immaterial so long as the council retained his good will. Their five pounds, while gratefully received, was nevertheless dwarfed by the lengthening specter of a disastrous tax harvest. The castle thus turned its full attention to the affairs of Master Ephraim in the hope of richer gleanings.

Sparks and the other clerks studied the Jew's commandeered ledgers, with particular care to the records of overdue debts that the bailiffs were striving to collect. Although examination of the castle rolls showed that all such contracts had been duly registered by Ephraim, a number of them seemed unfamiliar to Sparks, whose task it had been to enter them before his promotion to the sheriff's first clerk. All of these strange entries, he soon discovered, fell at the end of the listing for the year in which they had been contracted. On scrutinizing the entries still further, Sparks concluded that the script, while bearing a passable likeness to his own, was doubtless a forgery. This could mean nothing other than that Ephraim had withheld these contracts from the castle registry until the lenders fell into arrears, at which point the Jew conspired with one of the clerks to enter them belatedly so the debtors could be assigned to the bailiffs for forceful dunning.

Suspicion settled on Brother Alfred, Sparks's successor as apprentice treasury clerk, whose gifted hand had prompted Prior Clement to nominate him for the post. The stooped cleric, brought before the sheriff and told that the Jew had already confessed to their scheme, broke down at once and promised to restore every penny of the bribe money that he had been squirreling away for a year against the purchase of a gilded reliquary. He knew the wrong of it, Alfred blubbered, but the godless Ephraim had persuaded him that the crown was in no way being denied by his belated registering of the contracts. It was not, after all, as if the bailiffs were being duped into collecting on illicit contracts; it was just that the Jew had neglected to register them until in need of the king's muscle to enforce his claims.

Brother Alfred was packed off to Lenton Priory with a note to Father Clement from the sheriff, respectfully recommending that the dismissed cleric do ample penance and noting that he had been spared the ignominy of the castle gaol only out of regard for the prior's lofty standing. Then Ephraim himself was delivered to the sheriff's closet, for there could be small doubt now that if the moneylender was registering some of his contracts years after the fact—and then only when the need arose—there were many others he had not registered at all. The fifth of the Jew's holdings that the bailiffs had already separated from him under the new tallage was thus a diminished portion of what was truly due the king.

Two of the bailiff's deputies marched Master Ephraim before the sheriff with rather more force than the detainee's slight frame and gentle bearing warranted. Half-dressed when the castle officers seized him, the moneylender struggled to retain what shreds of dignity were left to him.

"May I inquire after my offense, Master Mark, that I should be handled like the hind quarters of a putrid beast?"

"We believe you have deceived the crown," said the sheriff, "by failure to reveal all of your records and assets to us. How say you?"

"I say you are mistaken—and that you have only lately dealt my little business a severe blow by the king's newest tallage—and plead that you let me be, for I harm no one and steadfastly hew to the law."

"You have a few moments to sit yourself in the corner," said Philip, not bothering to look at the accused, "and reconsider your answer. If it is unchanged, Master Manning will escort you to our gaol so that you may perhaps gain a fresh perspective on the matter."

Ephraim, though, would not recant and was swept roughly into captivity like some flailing bug.

"Master Plunk and Master Sunbeam will no doubt oppress him," Sparks pointed out, "unless instructed to the contrary."

"A little oppression may prove useful," offered the bailiff.

"Can they gauge it with precision?" asked the sheriff. "The prisoner is not robust. If they maim him, we may never have the truth."

"I'll urge moderation," Manning promised.

But on the third day of the Jew's detention, Father Ivo reported after his regular morning visit to the dank catacomb that the prisoner was being abused to the brink of his endurance. "They leave him too long in the hot chair," the chaplain told the sheriff, "and wield dreadful instruments over him that they say will enhance his circumcision."

Philip ordered Ephraim brought before him anew and, upon seeing his wasted appearance, offered the half-dead Jew a bench to recline on. But he could not, for the pain of it, and stood slumped and benumbed before his accuser. "Have you more to say to me yet, Master Ephraim?" the sheriff asked.

The prisoner's eyes closed, as if in prayerful meditation, and his head shook slightly, as if the weight of it were a great burden to him.

"Then perhaps it would interest you to know that your accomplice in the castle has fully revealed your deception—and was spared the agonies of gaol for his belated forthrightness."

Ephraim's lowered head slowly lifted, disclosing a flash of hatred in his narrowed eyes. "Why didn't you say as much when I was first brought here?" he asked, his voice a scratchy whisper.

"Because I hoped you might mitigate your crime by revealing the

truth," said the sheriff. "Instead you only aggravated your offense. Pity—
for it will go that much the harder against you now."

The Jew's head recoiled, and he suddenly found his tongue. "I am
oppressed unstintingly by the crown and all its officers, yet when in my
own defense I resist you and your monstrous gaolers, you fault me all the
more. What would you have me do, Master Sheriff, to earn your high
regard?"

"I would have you worship our laws as you do Jehovah's."

"Your laws! They are as the king pronounces them and vary by the
season. And what sort of law is it that says to seize the Jews' belongings
but not others'? We are the crown's playthings—even as I appear to be
yours." His head dropped from the painful effort to justify himself. "Spare
me further misery, sire, and I'll confess the full enormity of my sins."

His secret ledgers, hidden in hollowed panels of several chests in the
great room of his house, showed that nearly a third part of Ephraim's
dealings were unregistered with the crown. Sparks reported his findings
with scarcely veiled pleasure, for they meant that the portion of the Jew's
principal put out at loan illicitly could be confiscated. And since there was
every prospect that the castle's tax collections would come up well short
of the shire quota, Ephraim's loss could be the sheriff's gain. But the
money making up the unregistered loans would not return to the Jew's
hands until repaid under the terms of his contracts—or was pried from
his debtors by the bailiffs' efforts. Here, then, was a sudden windfall to
alleviate Philip's peril, if only a way could be found for the castle to get
hold of the encumbered funds at once instead of awaiting their eventual
repayment.

"Why not just remove the equivalent amount from the remainder of
Master Ephraim's holdings," Sparks ventured, "and reimburse him as the
unregistered loans get repaid—minus the interest, of course, which falls
to the crown?"

"That amounts to stealing from the Jew to lighten our burden," said
Philip. "I will not."

"It is more in the nature of an advance against funds we know will
materialize. And you would be fully justified, sire. He has committed a
heinous criminal act and fully conceded it."

"You surprise me, Master Sparks. Since when does one crime justify
another? The Jew claims mitigating conditions and pleads for mercy. We
have procedures to follow, presentments to make in court. The money
cannot just be snatched to suit our convenience."

"We face pressing circumstances, sire," the clerk persisted. "Sometimes the rules must be bent to serve a higher end."

"The Exchequer does not invite our playing games."

"The Exchequer need never know. It's only a matter of a few short-term adjustments in our ledgers, sire—and who would suffer hurt by it other than the Jew, who has richly earned it and, at any rate, must eventually forfeit the money?"

The sheriff shook his head. "You exhibit a distressingly larcenous turn of mind, Master Sparks, though I appreciate that your purpose is honorable. I will not conduct dirty business, however artfully perfumed."

Sparks gave his head a shake that unwittingly mimicked his master's. "I fear, sire, that your very survival in office is at stake—and to dwell on legal niceties when a God-sent solution is at hand may be to thumb your nose at Providence."

The undersheriff, who had witnessed this exchange, now stepped into it. "Why not," Peter asked his brother, "simply borrow the money from the Jew instead of taking it, as you say, in advance of the law's remedy? A loan is not a theft. A sheriff may borrow like any other man. And for collateral you need only offer the Jew's own unlawfully lent monies, which you have full authority to collect when due. He could hardly cavil at that."

Philip savored the suggestion a moment, glad for a constructive thought from an unexpected quarter. But his clerk was unhesitating in rebuttal. "Yours is a more ingenious approach than mine, sire," Sparks said to Peter, "but infinitely more dangerous. If Westminster were to learn of the arrangement, the sheriff would likely be faulted for meeting his tax quota by artifice instead of competence."

"But Westminster need never know," Peter contended. "It would be a strictly private transaction."

"Unless the Jew disclosed it," Sparks said, turning to the sheriff, "as well he might to thwart you. His very threat to do so could compromise you. No, to do business with the moneylender is to hand him a weapon to use against you. Your position within the shire, furthermore, would be undermined if word spread that you were in Ephraim's debt, whatever the justification. My method requires no explanations, were it to become known, though it ought not to be considered except as a last resort—for why should anyone hurry to pay his taxes when the money can be so readily lifted from the Jew's purse instead?"

"I like neither course," said Philip, waving them both away. "The

Jew will be prosecuted as the statutes direct. The castle will not revert to rule by barbarism so long as I govern it."

But as September arrived and the bailiffs' collections remained lean, Sparks fretted that the castle coffers would fall well shy of what was due the Exchequer by month's end. The very thought nearly dizzied the clerk, who by then was persuaded that the sheriff's unalloyed goodness was creating as many difficulties as it cured for the faithful governance of his shires.

·XXI·

SHE RECEIVED HIM WITHOUT APOLOGY in her bedchamber while a hand-maiden was languorously brushing her black hair with long, practiced strokes. Clad in nothing more than a light blue bliaut of diaphanous silk, Lady Olivia had draped herself across a thickly cushioned bench in a fashion that required her attendant to kneel close beside her to accomplish the ritual. Curled on the edge of the bench and blissfully sharing body warmth with the mistress of Pendrake was a large Manx cat whose fur was as coal-black as her owner's hair.

"I know you will forgive me for greeting you dishabille," she said with a smile while remaining at a slight incline from the horizontal, "but I wanted neither to detain you nor to interrupt my little ménage à trois. Puss is a finicky sleeper and craves her nap time with me."

"I should not have come unannounced, my lady," he said, feeling the heavy-booted intruder in a nest all of gossamer and scrim. "Perhaps another time would be more suitable. It was simply that I found myself not far distant and, having a matter to discuss with you, I supposed—"

"You need be no more apologetic than I about the informality of our meeting, sire. Sheriffs have much to accomplish and little time, I'm sure, to lavish on scheduling." She shifted herself more or less upright, causing the Manx to stir peevishly and the maid to complete her task standing behind her mistress, the better to peek at the prominent visitor. "I fear I know the nature of your business, but Claudia will leave us shortly, at any rate, so that we may pursue the matter in private."

For the next few minutes he stood like an awkward supplicant immobilized before a Grecian goddess preening for a day of earnest immanence. They spoke fecklessly of the season, the harvest, the king's triumphal return from Ireland, and where Philip might best lay his ungirdled sword so it would not be forgotten—"to our mutual embarrassment, no doubt," she added merrily. Then the cat and the maid were summarily dismissed, refreshments were ordered, and Lady Olivia, wrapping herself additionally in a short cape, led him to an open balcony overlooking her private garden. "You must share my secret vice with me," she said, sweetness rising like a soft mist from her flowing hair, as a serving woman delivered wine and a golden bowl with contents he could not readily name. "Chestnut pudding à la Pendrake," she cried, "with a soupçon of burnt sugar—my chief remaining extravagance. It's total ecstasy—and makes me fat as a gravid sow, but I cannot resist taking a small portion each afternoon."

"Then you must subsist on little else, my lady. You are among the least sowlike women of my acquaintance."

She beamed at the obligatory disclaimer and then fell silent while he sampled the rich delicacy. His lip-smacking approval drew her nod as they both avidly spooned the sweet for a time. "Your wife," she said, sated before him and setting her plate aside, "is a great beauty." The remark seemed inspired by nothing that had preceded it. "I meant to compliment you on her at the banquet for the earl."

"My lady is generous with praise."

"It's no more than the truth. Happily, I do not suffer from the malady afflicting most vain women—I enjoy the beauty of others as well." She inclined her head as if to intimate a playful purpose. "And does she please you, my lord sheriff?"

"I . . . To be sure. We are—close."

"I meant, you understand, in the private sense."

His eyes met hers, then flicked by, apprehensive at the unexpectedness of the inquiry. "I . . . would not qualify my—"

"I ask only because great beauties are often said to lack passion—being borne away as they are by narcissism."

"I . . . it is not a subject I hold forth on freely, my lady."

"Especially," she said, delighting in his discomfiture, "with another woman. You are far too much the *chevalier*."

"I'd no more discuss it with a man."

"To your credit, sire. It bespeaks a sensitive nature." She untilted her head and added, "Highly desirable in a lover—and exceedingly rare."

"I wouldn't know, my lady."

"I would—and do." She studied him for another moment, wrestling with indecision, then asked, "Are you faithful to her, Master Mark?"

He searched the horizon line beyond her shoulder. "My lady is—what shall I say . . . ?"

"Unduly direct? Coarsely inquisitive?"

"The former, anyway."

"I concede it. It's a widow's privilege, I've decided. Having reached a certain age and station in life, I'm beyond the need to be coy. So my question, which I persist in, is more blunt than rude."

"I see." He met her glance now. "And has my lady been delegated, perhaps, by Holy Church to seek my confession, now that the priests have abdicated the function?"

Her smile broadened. "My question is ruled by no ulterior design. Simply, you are here of your own accord—we are speaking at our ease—you please me at a time when there is so much in my surround that I find displeasing—and I am riven by curiosity."

"Then I will simply say yes."

She pursed her lips in momentary reflection. "Flawlessly so?"

"I . . . think my lady probes—one degree beyond the permissible."

"Perhaps you have heard that Stephen was not with me—which I took to be merely customary defiling of our vows—nor, as a result, was I with him. Oddly, it strengthened our matrimonial bond."

"My lady?"

"It made me less bitter and discontent at being spurned while allowing me a fulfillment I had not known."

"By taking forbidden fruit?"

"By taking an authentic lover. It has been my experience, you see, that the only true passion is to be found in infidelity—certainly among men, for whom the obligatory nature of the marriage bed quickly slays fascination, and at least among women of noble birth, who by training are slow to arousal. Ah, I see the disapproval already curdling your expression!"

"You would blithely make a virtue out of perversion."

"Not blithely at all, but from hard-learned resignation. And the 'perversion,' as you call it, is imposed upon us. Women like me are rarely able to select our husbands, and when we are, the choice is limited and the alternatives equally daunting. With mutual affection no requisite, our spouses are not much inclined to concern themselves with our erotic yearnings, their own pleasure being paramount—and ours wicked." She stood now and leaned lightly against the balcony railing. "Whereas in an illicit union, the choice is largely ours—and the danger of it heightens the ardor." She turned sideways and presented her slender silhouette to him. "Most men feel their liberty—not to mention their organs—unnaturally tethered by monogamy, so they philander without qualm while demanding that their wives remain chaste beyond their bedchamber. Stephen was more enlightened than most in this regard—and, as I say, his tolerance strengthened our wedlock by permitting me to find elsewhere what he could not, or would not, provide." She glanced back over her shoulder toward him. "As to the perversion of it, I would argue that matrimonial love—or what passes for it—is the more unnatural state in that it forbids other passageways to the enrichment of our feelings. How, in truth, does conjugal love differ from that we bear our children, or our parents, or our friends? It is a matter of nuance."

"I thought it was a matter of heavenly commandment."

"Propagated by priests who devote themselves to denial of their senses and wish to accustom the rest of us to a similar dullness." She swung about and came closer to him, hovering just above his shoulder. "What is truly perverse," she said with a small laugh, "is that widowhood has perforce made me still more circumspect than in marriage in my choice of partners—lest the slander circulate that I am promiscuous, thereby narrowing the likelihood of my ever finding a man of quality and unbrutishness to wed."

"I shouldn't think there would be a shortage of applicants."

"Possibly the better ones apply directly to the king for my hand. The lot I've seen are dreary oxen—so I cling to my widowhood and pray for a deliverer." She fell still, casting him loose in a sea of arousal that had enveloped him since first sight of her filmy attire; every provocative word had only deepened the spell. Then she asked in a softened tone, "Have I appalled you, Master Mark, by all these tactless revelations?" Her hand rested lightly on his shoulder.

"Awakened me," he said, intensely aware of the touch of her fingers, "to the perils of my office, at the least." His head turned back far enough to see her splayed hand enclose and press upon his shoulder bone. "Even

if I conceded all you say—and were eager to engage in—to be so engaged—
a sheriff cannot risk being compromised. Any dalliance can so easily be
turned against him."

"So then it would be even between us—we should each stand to lose
a good deal, if perchance . . . But that is the only true way."

"I cannot, my sweet lady," he said, reaching up and placing his hand
over hers.

"As a sheriff—or as a man? Are you not the latter before the former?
Or do you live only through your office?"

"You would not entertain the thought if I were not the sheriff."

Her hand inverted, deftly weaving her fingers within his. "Say only
that the occasion would not have arisen. Yet that's what all of life is—
accidents of time and place—of birth—and need—and agreeableness found
where none was expected. . . ."

His eyes closed as he struggled to put his one burning thought out
of mind. "I must speak to you of the Jew," he said at last, "and your debt
to him. It is why I've come to you—largely. . . ."

She broke their bond and retreated to the stone railing on which she
perched, arms folded in front of her and gaze directed toward the late-
summer bloom in the garden below. "I've heard. All the Jews' debts are
called by the crown under the tallage, so you can no longer play my hero
by holding him off—thereby leaving you to sorrow for me but without
recourse."

He nodded. "It saddens me that it cannot be said more prettily."

"Sadness seems remote from your nature."

"My lady ought not mistake duty for lack of tenderness."

"If you are so tender," she said, voice rising more in plea than re-
crimination, "then apply to the crown to serve as custodian of Pendrake.
Why should you not have it—and all the rights of the seigneur that go
with it? Far less deserving men are so rewarded." She stretched an
upturned hand toward him. "I cannot think why the crown has not yet
imposed a custodian on me—except there are hundreds of cases such as
mine pending throughout the realm. Mine must be imminent by now,
though, so I beseech you, if you have a grain of tenderness in you, to
ask—for both our sakes."

"I should greatly savor it, my lady—"

"You would of necessity be on these premises often—and become a
yet more pleasing sight to me."

"Your meaning all but turns me molten—but I cannot satisfy your needs. I do not solicit favors from the crown—and will not in your behalf any more than my own. It would be the path to my downfall—placing my head down the wolf's throat, as it were, to cite your own—"

"Speak no more of this," she said, "and come lie with me now—call it a gesture of my gratitude for your concern—and weigh my words after being pleasured and you are gone from me. You cannot know your own mind at this instant."

"Flattered as I am, dear lady, I fear you are moved by desperation. Last I was here, you sought to buy me with silver. Now you offer your whole being. It moves me greatly, yet is unseemly for one in your—"

"What is unseemly? That I bargain for my life, and ask your help—and that you be manly and accept a reward in the fashion I propose? You have much to gain, sire—only I stand to be the loser."

"It grows late," he said, rising. "Will my lady help me retrieve my sword?"

·XXII·

MASTER STUCKEY WOODFINCH, doubling as castle archer and royal huntsman, had proven adept enough at those callings—at least on the irregular occasions he chose to perform them—but his presence in the sheriff's employ was, by all accounts, a highly disruptive one.

Stuckey arose when he wished and reported to duty, if at all, with a nice disregard for the hour. As often, he hid out within the castle confines, eluding the constable until apprehended deep inside the cellar stores or crouched in the pantry, gulping leftovers, or enfolded between the coverlets in a chambermaid's bedding. Other times he fled the castle without sanction, clinging to the underside of a cart or mingling with its cargo of refuse. In the wood, he took game at such a prodigious rate that the cook had to assign a helper to no other task than cleaning and curing the huntsman's takings. Even then there was said to be a surplus that the incorrigible Woodfinch disposed of in a manner known only to himself.

At the Trip, he had become a familiar if not altogether welcome patron, loud and bawdy but of irrepressibly good humor in an establishment that at times took on a funereal air. He drank barrels, paying for no more than half what he consumed while chiding Master le Gyw that his tariff was twice the rate of the Leaping Stag and ought to be the subject of prosecution by the castle. The innkeeper tolerated his presence because it seemed to attract rather more customers than it repelled.

On retiring to the castle dormitory after a night of heroic guzzling, Stuckey was given to singing lustily, either in his deepest bass or affecting a eunuch's falsetto (sometimes alternating between them within the same song), and no end diverting all who had gone to their slumber at the normal hour. Other times, he would retire to the straw with a wide assortment of wenches, both within and beyond the castle, who were said to crave the company of so durable and gymnastic a lover. Among those smitten was the daughter of the president of the tanners' guild, whom Stuckey had taken a-hunting and bedded on the forest floor not five yards from a hart he had felled, the skin of which he later presented with his compliments to the girl's father. He accepted it, after determining its tannable quality, then went straightway to the undersheriff to file complaint against the randy huntsman for defiling his daughter. Peter Mark, one of Stuckey's favored drinking companions, had been assured the maiden was certifiably unvirginal and counseled the tanner to better mind his child's propensities than Master Woodfinch's.

None, or not even all, of these breaches of decorum had upset the sheriff enough to consider cashiering the brassy lout until he was told that Stuckey had thrice offered to sell Master le Gyw some surplus deer meat. The rake plainly needed his handle shortened.

"It's not your venison to sell," Philip lectured him. "You're flirting with the prospect of the hangman's noose, Master Woodfinch."

"I had every intention, sire, of returning the sale price to the castle treasury," said the libertine, looking wounded by the very suspicion he might do otherwise, "less a small service charge, possibly, for wear and tear on the huntsman."

"Any such transaction, even assuming it had been remotely contemplated, is the proper business of the steward. Nobody assigned you to hawk the castle's bounty."

"The steward is dishonest and would have greatly overcharged Master le Gyw—which he'd surely have deserved, now that I find he's a tattle, not to mention a waterer of his ale."

"The innkeeper is chartered by the crown, and keeps his license in part by informing on those who would connive against it. In your case, he said it grieved him deeply because he loves the merriment you splash among his clientele—though he loves not your dicing in the corners or how heavily you're in arrears." The sheriff quenched an impulse to smile at such gaudy intemperance. "What troubles me most in your words is the charge against Master Devereaux. I thought we had reformed him."

"They say your brother had largely checked the steward's extortions, but as undersheriff is too busy now to superintend him, and may even— well, there is . . . some suspicion . . . I cannot say what—"

"Say—or it's the gallows."

"You'll not love me for it."

"And even less if you withhold—"

"Some say the undersheriff collaborates with the steward now in— his unwholesome dealings. But I set aside such talk as rank envy. The Marks are not everywhere beloved in and about the castle—and the more firm your sway, the greater the resentment. I tell you this, sire, as only a jester can speak truth without risk of dismemberment. I beg your leniency for my—small lapses."

Before Philip could settle on a fit reprimand, his clerk intruded to say that the abbess of an impoverished nunnery near Wellbeck Park was on hand to ask the sheriff's aid. It seemed that she had applied to the deputy warden of Sherwood to sell off the underbrush and forty oaks from her abbey's chartered wood for the badly needed revenues; the warden's deputy had unaccountably refused her. "And so she comes to you with her grievance," Sparks reported, "having heard that you are just."

"But the forest is not within my jurisdiction."

"Mother Superior has been so advised, yet she persists."

Philip mused on the case, saying finally, "I can do nothing for her, sad to say—though the deputy warden's hardheartedness beggars understanding. Why deny a straitened abbey so small a benefit?"

"You don't know?" asked Woodfinch, who suffered no qualm at commenting on what he had just overheard.

The sheriff looked over at him with more surprise than annoyance. "Suppose you enlighten me—since you are expert on so many subjects."

"The deputy can make a dozen times as much money selling off the nunnery's wood as he can from the abbess's pittance of thanks."

"But it's not his wood."

"Nor, as you informed me, was it my venison that I sought to peddle to the Trip's innkeeper. But my solicitation was a lark—whereas the deputy warden makes a wholesale business of it. He and his henchmen have sold off thousands of Sherwood oaks over the years."

"They do this?"

"All the time—hither and yon, spreading the waste so as not to be so noticeable."

"What of the regarders? Isn't it their duty to police such takings?"

"The regarders, sire, are the worst thieves of all. They are part and parcel of it, betraying their trust."

"Part and parcel of what?"

"The abuse of the forest and its laws."

"Whose abuse?"

"Theirs—all of them."

Philip was hardly ignorant of such offenses but supposed them commonest in woods far afield. Indeed, the king several years prior had ordered the forest eyre to crack down on malpractices that were reputedly depriving the crown of fees in massive number. Had this measure, then, made no inroads whatever and the tendency now spread to Sherwood as well?

"The forest eyre comes this way but once every third year," said Woodfinch, "and can attend to only what is brought before it. The foresters bring in only those who defy them or neglect to buy them off—and rarely confess to their own guilt."

Only the year before, though, Philip noted, the king had appointed Brian de Lisle, a careerist collector of royal custodianships, to be the new warden of Sherwood, ostensibly to halt all such corruption. Was Lisle a gross malingerer, or worse yet?

"Ah, yes—Sir Brian the Blind. 'De Lisle de lies' is how the saying goes. Either he partakes amply in the loot, as the wardens have always done, or he's ignorant of it. I lean a bit toward the latter view, since his deputy is the real overseer and must surely tell the warden that all is well."

Philip agitatedly massaged his chin. "How do you know all that you tell me?"

"Everyone who's at home in the wood knows it, sire. I saw it firsthand with my father for years and years—and because he wouldn't yield to the foresters' extortions, I was denied a place in their ranks."

So vast a crime against the crown demanded investigation, the sheriff thought, for if he could corroborate its existence, he was bound by his oath of office to see it ended, even though the matter fell beyond his direct charge. Accordingly, he set aside three days and, with Sparks at his side, Woodfinch as his guide, and a pair of sergeants-at-arms as protectors, ranged through Sherwood to familiarize himself with its beauties, perils, and debasement.

They could scarcely begin to compass its 100,000 acres within that brief a span, but for the first time Philip gained a vivid sense of the enormity of the forest and its variety of terrain. At its most glorious, Sherwood was traversed by long, shady avenues of oak, allowing swift and easy passage beneath arcades formed from their mighty boughs. Elsewhere the branches were so densely tangled and laced with thorny vines that the wood was impenetrable on horseback and slow, painful going on foot. In the damp bottoms, stands of lithe, snowy birch, Scotch fir, and Spanish chestnut flourished, and then the forest floor would without warning turn itself into lush fields of undulating meadows tufted gold with gorse and broom. At its western edge, just before the wood drifted across the county boundary into Derbyshire, the earth had heaved up the Cresswell crags and the caverns of Wellbeck Park, where outlaws and misfits were said to take shelter.

Presiding over this dreamlike domain in the name of the king were a warden, his deputy, a steward, a bow bearer, and a ranger; four verderers, who convened three times a year at the court of swainmote to hear abuses against the forest code; twelve regarders, who over the course of three years perambulated the entire forest to certify that it was not being illicitly encroached upon; four agisters, who counted the animals allowed to forage there and collected the requisite fees; and a dozen foresters to keep the peace. This elaborate mechanism served to legitimize an immense usurpation by the crown, dating from the Conqueror's seizure of nearly a full quarter of all England as his royal hunting preserve—an attempt to establish his dominion, as it were, over Nature herself. No taking of game or wood, nor use or expansion of arable soil, even by those living within their borders, nor construction of dwellings, bridges, hedges, ditches or any other intrusion on their natural state, was permissible in the king's forests unless explicitly licensed and paid for. A prime source of crown revenues, the English woods in their entirety functioned as a subkingdom all its own, a kind of royal appendage and not a little despotic under the chief forester, who operated with his own laws, courts, exchequer, and officers. Its net income was ultimately payable to the crown on an annual basis, but far more was siphoned off along the way—just how much had not begun to alarm the king and his counselors until the opening years of the thirteenth century.

The abuses of the wood, Master Woodfinch instructed Master Mark as they cantered among its sweet dells and through its scattered meadows, were of two basic kinds, at which the crown officers were equally gifted: they would, on the one hand, disregard the strictures of the forest code for the proper price, and they would, on the other, ignore the proper price in the levy of fees and fines, charging instead whatever greed dictated and withholding from the royal treasury whatever portion they could get away with. They were masters at a third sort of banditry as well: the fabrication of offenses that could empty a man's purse or curtail his liberty if falsely testified to—an all but irresistible extortion.

Thus, even the most ordinary of transactions—the chartering of a chase, say, for private hunting, or the grant of free warren for the taking of small game uncovered by the forest laws—was an opportunity for endless conniving. The prices and boundaries were not only negotiable but also elastically subject, from one year to the next, to pretexts for altering the bargain. All such sanctioned killing grounds, by way of example, had to be properly fenced to keep out the king's deer, according to the law.

"But who is to say what's a proper fence?" Stuckey asked. Any field within the forest cleared for new cropland was by law to cost the tenant one shilling per acre per year. "But if you cavil at paying the foresters twice or thrice the king's price, who else cares if your fields end up trampled?" Stuckey continued. It was the same with the pannage fee, for having your swine feast on acorns and beechmast, and with the cheminage fee, for the right of passage of a loaded cart. "If you dare to sneak by one porker too many or balk at handing over four pence instead of the pre-scribed two for your cart, the royals make seizures to their hearts' content." Those who would take a tree for use in building or making charcoal were obliged to spread their cuttings or be found guilty of wasting, a crime determinable by sitting on a freshly cut stump, looking about, and seeing five or more other stumps. "Now some sitters and lookers-about don't see too far," Stuckey noted, "whereas others have the eye of a hawk. And does the rule mean looking in one direction only or all about? Depends on the forester and how deep he thinks your pockets."

The severity of the authorized penalties for poaching, while irregularly applied, inspired its own kind of dread. Killing a deer or a boar or even a plover could cost a man his life; merely to give unarmed chase to a stag to the point of causing it to pant was listed as a violation—"and for making it fart they'd as soon separate you from your testicles," Stuckey added. Facing so possibly dire a fate upon being taken into custody, who would not reach deep to avoid false arrest by the vile watchmen of the wood? "Once with my father," Stuckey recounted, "I came upon a yeoman weeping in a copse because the foresters claimed he had allowed his oxen to wander onto the king's meadow. He had to pay three pounds or forfeit the beasts—it came to nearly the same thing, and either way meant ruination."

"Which did he choose?" asked Philip.

"They held his oxen while he went for the money, which he thought he could bargain over, but on his return he found one ox gone and the other heaving its last in the meadow."

Such tales of oppression and morbid cruelty were retold to the sheriff three dozen times as his little party toured the wood, stopping its inhabitants, nearby residents, and random wayfarers to inquire about the foresters' conduct. None of their abuses, as it turned out, provoked more resentment than the scotale, a crown-approved "gracious aid," whereby the officers collected grain from the people of the forest for making into ale, which the victims of the taking were then required to buy at the local alehouse, the proceeds passing directly into their tormentors' hands. "And while we're inside drinking their vomitous stuff," said a swineherd of whom the sheriff had inquired, "they got them an accomplice without who goes sneaking through our saddle sacks for anything of value we're fool enough to leave untended."

Not a fortnight following this instructive journey, the sheriff was in receipt of word that the crown had intervened massively in Essex Forest, where abuses like those in Sherwood had long gone on. With a single hammer blow, the king ordered all incursions in the Essex wood ended, all structures pulled down, all hedges torn up, all charters canceled, all fees strictly enforced, and many foresters cast in gaol or heavily fined. As sobering was the nearly simultaneous report that the chief forester of the realm, Hugh de Neville, had been amerced seven hundred pounds for allowing the bishop of Winchester to enclose a park without a license. Since Neville was one of the king's closest drinking and gambling cronies and had held office a dozen years, and his wife was said to be on intimate terms with the royal bedstead, such a measure made all the more manifest the crown resolve to purge the forests of these noxious practices.

In these circumstances, Philip took it upon himself to render the king a sizable service by trying to bring Sherwood under his sway and end all abuses within it, notwithstanding that sheriffs had no royal authority in the king's wood. However commendable in purpose, this intention was flush with the risks of overreaching. Yet Philip chose to proceed (though sharing his plan as yet with no one at the castle), more from a hatred of corruption rampant under his very nose than from any hope of increment to his power. He thus invited Sir Brian de Lisle to dine and stay the night with him at Nottingham Castle on the pretext of celebrating his first year in office as the warden of Sherwood.

Sir Brian was another in the cadre of modestly born royal retainers who had accumulated offices and wealth by unstinting service to the king and asking no questions. Lisle had done some dirty work for John in Normandy at the outset of the reign and been rewarded with a string of northern custodianships, most notably as castellan of Knaresborough, a military and financial stronghold for the crown some seventy miles above Nottingham. Closer to Philip's ambit, Sir Brian held the royal estates of Laxton and Peverel in Nottinghamshire as well as the wardenship of Sherwood, Bolsover Castle just across the line in Derbyshire, and several manors in Lincolnshire. What he had done to deserve all this was a mystery beyond the confines of Westminster. Philip, supposing him a deft plunderer in the mold of Baron Brewer, moved cautiously toward correcting his lax oversight of the forest.

"I must regretfully advise you," said the sheriff after they had supped and removed themselves to his closet, "that your deputy in Sherwood does you a grave disservice—one that I fear exposes you to the crown's harshest reprimand." He proceeded to spell out the list of abuses he had lately been made aware of and could no longer in good conscience ignore.

Lisle listened, sipping sparely at his wine and on his mettle every moment, then bristlingly replied, "Why is this of your concern, Master Mark?"

"I am the king's magistrate here, he is being deprived of his rightful revenues within my knowledge, and his forest is being irreparably stripped of game and wood. All of this must end."

"Then I shall attend to it—and thank you for instructing me."

"I'm in need of more than thanks, sire—the situation has deteriorated too far to be cured by casual attention."

"Casualness is not in my nature."

"But there is no other explanation for what has been tolerated in Sherwood—except venality, which I attribute to the deputy warden but fault his superior for not quashing. Either you have known of these abuses and been complicitous in them, or you do not know—in which case 'casual' is the kindest word that can be applied to your superintendence."

Lisle suddenly sensed the gravity of the threat that was confronting him. "If the offense is so great as you say and my negligence so apparent, why come to me of all people?" he asked. "Why not take your charges straightway to the crown and be done with it?"

"Because I've no need of your enmity—and because I think the fault truly stems from your being too greatly occupied by other duties."

"I see. And so what is your remedy for this inadequacy of mine?"

"For you to entrust me with the selection of an entirely new roster of forest officers. I'll try to enlist men of the highest scruples—fellows who will strictly enforce the statutes and return to the crown neither more nor less than its entitlement."

Lisle's eyes widened. "You ask me to relinquish my supervisory powers over Sherwood?"

"To delegate them, not relinquish them—with no sacrifice to your financial interest in the legitimate collections."

"You're a saucy fellow, Master Mark."

"My character is not the issue. It's a matter of simple logistics, sire. I'm close at hand while you must constantly reconnoiter to manage your diverse holdings. I'd of course apprise you of every appointment lest any of my nominees prove personally objectionable to you."

Lisle shook his head slowly in muted amazement. "You bargain with cocksureness, Master Sheriff—as if we were equals in rank and access to the crown. I marvel at your courage."

"Our respective positions are altogether beside the point, sire. I have no stake in what I ask beyond the proper conduct of the king's business in my shires."

"And if I politely decline your gracious offer to unburden me?"

"I—cannot say."

"Cannot, or will not say?"

The sheriff remained silent.

"Then it's as I suspect—naked coercion, or thinly veiled indeed. Either I yield to you, or you go to Westminster. Dirty dealing, I call it! How on earth can you expect not to antagonize me by such a tactic?"

"I count on you to grasp that it spares you far more hurtful alternatives that will surely come to pass otherwise. The facts are as I state them, and you cannot gainsay them in good faith. Do nothing about them, and you'll shortly feel the king's wrath, even as it fell on the Essex wood. The arrangement I propose is to our mutual interest, and its precise nature would remain our private business."

Lisle fell back and took a large swallow of wine. "You've thought it through and through, I see, and have me at a disadvantage. Perhaps I need to sleep on it."

"I recommend it, sire. Meanwhile, if you lack for any comfort, you need only say so."

By morning the warden of Sherwood had seen the unrefracted light of pure reason. "The truth is often painful," said Sir Brian, "but I am not one to deny it. I've shirked the forest job yet enjoyed its rewards. And while I do not love you for berating me on that account and should scorn your meddlesomeness, I cannot. Only one concern of mine remains to be addressed before I'll seal our pact—how do I know you won't tolerate the very abuses you denounce and become their beneficiary once your own people take control of the forest?"

The sheriff looked at him for a very long moment and then said, "Because I would die first—or insist you take my life with your own hand if you so discovered."

As a consequence of the foregoing, Stuckey Woodfinch was once more called to the sheriff's closet, where in council with his undersheriff, his bailiff, his constable, his steward, his clerk, and the coroner, Philip dismissed the reprobate huntsman for "ceaselessly uproarious conduct detrimental to the king's service," as the charge against him read.

"Fair enough," said Stuckey when told he was at liberty and strongly urged to mind his antics lest he again run afoul of the laws of the realm. Yet he darted a look at the sheriff that conveyed pique for Philip's not having been more tolerant of his foibles or appreciative of his talents.

As the discharged officer was bidding hearty though by no means tearful farewells about the castle, the undersheriff rode off and stationed himself beside the Great Road North just above the Trent Bridge. When Woodfinch came bobbing along on a swayback mare, a gift of his severance from crown employment, Peter intercepted him and asked, "Can you bear a bit of companionship on the first part of your journey?"

"An unexpected pleasure," said the now serene Stuckey. With polite interest he listened to the tale of how the warden of Sherwood had welcomed the sheriff's advisory on the forest abuses, stated his determination to cleanse them away, and asked the castle to lend a hand in the effort. Bearing that end in mind, Peter explained, the sheriff wished to re-enlist the services of that incomparable woodsman, Master Woodfinch of Blyth, in a unique capacity. "Then why," Stuckey asked, "hurl me out on my rosy derrière with the rest of you turds looking on?"

"To distance you from the sheriff so nobody would suspect your further association with him." Philip wished him to become a kind of permanent monitor among the new foresters, on free-roaming assignment rather than saddled with fixed patrols and duties. This latitude would permit him to mingle freely with the officers in order to gauge how diligently and justly they enforced the code of the wood. He would then report his findings to the newly designated deputy warden, without whose knowledge he would also meet once a month with the undersheriff at Clipstone, the king's rarely used hunting lodge in Sherwood, to pass on the identical intelligence—"in the unhappy event our new deputy should turn into as big a thief as the old one."

"In short, he wants me to be the sheriff's little spy in the wood."

"My brother would not call it that. He thinks it an office of special importance and seeks you for it only because he trusts in your basic goodness of heart."

"But he hadn't the courtesy to say so to me directly."

"Don't be churlish, Stuckey. If he'd asked you before your dismissal, your manner in front of our little tribunal might have reeked of a telltale smugness. And for him to have been seen speaking with you afterward might have served to soften the apparent sternness of his rebuke to you. The entire scheme, don't you see, depends on the seeming estrangement between you."

Woodfinch, equally disdainful of and intrigued by the proposition, mulled it awhile as they rode along the shady highway in silence. "The fly in the unguent is that I don't fancy myself an informer—and surely not one paid for his dirt."

"You'd be very well rewarded indeed—three times what a forester may be expected to earn honestly—"

"Hardly a king's ransom."

"—enhanced by a generous allowance of food, garments, and ale from the castle stores, as well as the right to take venison and wood from the forest, provided you do so in moderation and swear not to sell any of it. And since Sherwood is vast and your mission equally so, you would be invited to hire a few underlings—strictly on an unofficial basis—to serve your needs as surrogate eyes, ears, arms, and legs, so to speak."

"I like your scheme better and better," Woodfinch said, giving his mussed hair a vigorous scratching, "but I fear it suffers from a fatal flaw. Behold my history: at first denied admittance to the royal foresters' ranks, later dismissed for naughtiness from the castle's service, and in between renowned as an upcounty bumpkin of infinite thirst and bulging lewdness. Who would credit such a knave?"

"Ask who would suspect him of policing the policemen, and you'll have hit upon the genius of the plan."

"But why would the warden," Stuckey wondered, "if truly bent on purging the vile sort from among his foresters, have employed such a rascal in the first place? It defies common sense. I'd either be laughed from the newly conscripted corps as a misfit, or else some may smell a rotten egg in my presence."

"Then perhaps," said Peter, conceding the point with a nod, "we have to rechristen you—and alter your appearance somewhat—a beard, certainly . . . a longer head of hair, possibly . . . a dashing cap or some such—"

"And a third eye in the midst of my forehead while we're at it."

"The very thing!"

"We'll bury old Stuckey, that cheeky devil!"

"It's a thought."

"Then come along with me now to his wake. You know the Leaping Stag outside of Blyth? We'll hoist a tankard or two there to the late, lovable lout. There'll be much wailing among the wenches."

"Blyth is a long way off, and I have other duties, alas."

"Your brother is a slave driver—much too somber a sort. He needs a bit of tickling. Come, enjoy a day or two of freedom from that rockpile of a purgatory you Marks inhabit—or rejoice with me in my liberty, at the least."

"Truly, I'd crave it, friend Stuckey, but I fear to—"

"Which would be more in your favor, friend Peter—to return to the castle promptly, bearing my regrets, or to tarry with me a while and carry back my joyful consent to serve as your scheming brother's faithful secret agent?" He reached over and gave the undersheriff a well-knuckled poke in the shoulder, then urged a brisker pace on his dawdling nag. She sprang ahead, and Peter's charger kept apace.

· XXIII ·

"THE CARP IS PARCHED instead of oily as it's meant to be," Father Clement apologized, "and the fowl is undelectably stringy, but these are the wages of austerity. Our splendid cook I had to let go—and most of the bondsmen who provided our victuals have been cast adrift since we can no longer afford them. It has all come to pass as you thought fit, Master Mark. If ever it were true that Holy Church lived in the lap of luxury, she has been rudely bumped off it."

The prior's new tune differed radically from the old but was no less incessant. The sheriff did not doubt that matters stood as Clement professed, what with the Interdict in its third year and the laity so disaffected; Holy Church's former torrent of revenues had dried up, and the clergy was surviving on its crops and endowments. At Lenton Priory, Philip noted with approval, every aspect of the maintenance, from shearing the cloister grass to scraping the trenchers in the scullery, appeared now to be manned by monks. "Forgive me, Father," he said, "but possibly the Lord has visited this spell of hardship on his shepherds of the faith by way of reminding them how dreary most men's lot is. It can only deepen the piety of the brethren and better prepare them for the blessed day when the church doors are flung open and the bells ring anew."

The time was not so long past when a comparable remark would have caused the prior to fly at the sheriff for serving as the ready instrument of oppression against Holy Church. Now the pallid priest merely nodded and preached reconciliation. "I no longer fault you, Master Mark, for your exemplary obedience to the dictates of the crown," he roundly intoned, "nor should you fail to befriend me on the ground of my resenting the king's intransigence toward the Holy Father. But let us not dwell on this—

the pope has pronounced sentence, and the Almighty will resolve the matter."

What Clement wished to pursue instead was the matter of the priory's annual fair, duly licensed by the crown as an outgrowth of its monastic charter. It was a far less tumultuous business than Nottingham's Goose Fair but had the high virtue of generating fees paid in by the vendors to help sustain the priory. With the entire English church hurting for monies, the fair had become a still more important provider for Lenton.

"I regret you did not attend us last year, Master Mark, for it was a colorful occasion—if rather more rowdy than I should have preferred."

"I was not invited, Father."

"You had no need to stand on ceremony. Our fair welcomes all the shire—all of England if we could but entice it."

"Then perhaps I had the mistaken sense that I would not have been altogether welcome in your midst."

"Assign that to our bygones, sire, and do us the kindness of joining us this time. Our fair may be less ambitious than the town merchants' but is a far greater boon to the commoners, especially those with more faith than money. Our prices, you see, are much lower than theirs because we do not admit the middle men, only honest craftsmen who fashion their own wares and charge no more than they need for sustenance, or perhaps a shade above in order to meet life's crueler contingencies." He went on to note that the sainted Augustine had held commerce as an end in itself to be an abomination, "for it turns men from seeking true rest, which is God."

"But not all of us, Father, enjoy Holy Church's faculty for casting aside material concerns to dwell solely on the spiritual—else we should have no need of priests."

"It is, I suppose, a matter of degree more than an absolute proscription—Augustine's point being that excessive concern with self-enhancement will cause the loving heart to shrivel. Seeking one's advantage is the very devil's work."

"Which is to say—what, Father—that any man's material gain comes only at others' expense and must be steeped in sin?"

"It is to say that none should profiteer from God's bounty or the sweat of others."

"You would destroy the nobility at a stroke? They thrive through indentured servitude."

"Only as it is ordained that there should be masters and servants. I speak of those gross strivers who partake in trade, the basest of occupations, for it entails gain without desert and perpetuates the exploitive power of money to foully beget yet more money. So we at Lenton require those who would display their wares with us to sell at the just price, or they would disrupt the divine plan that directs all souls to navigate not by greed but by the stars in Heaven."

To the sheriff, himself a man with his eye ever fixed on a higher station, such a creed sounded suspiciously like the beatification of impoverishment, or at least a hosanna for the established order of mankind, no matter its inequities. But he saw no point in further debating the matter, given the prior's newly accommodating humor. Instead, he agreed to attend the Lenton Fair, absent any other obligation.

"Pray, you will let nothing else intrude, Master Mark, for the sheriff's attendance will signal to the laity that whilst king and pope may feud, the rest of humanity may continue to dwell together in love and understanding." The prior patted his lips to rid them of a residue of fish grease. "And I would respectfully ask that the castle provide us the same degree of protection by the bailiffs as I am told it extended to the burgesses' fair. Since both are royally chartered, I fail to see how in justice you can do less."

In a rare instance of indiscretion, the sheriff's clerk remarked to Bailiff Manning about the prior's request, which Philip had confided to him. Word of it spread so rapidly thereafter that Master Welles, three guild presidents, and Nottingham's foremost silversmith appeared at the castle the next day to inveigh against the Lenton Fair.

"The church is well known to be an avowed enemy of commerce," asserted Master Welles, "for they resent the flow of silver into any coffers but their own. The prior and his *fratres* have long lived a life of received comfort—no doubt temporarily reduced by the current unpleasantness—and because they have no need of it, lack all knowledge of industry, thrift, and material incentive."

"And the priory fair undersells our wares," added the silversmith, "by enlisting merchants and craftsmen who do not work to the standards set by the guilds and pay their workers far less amply. So they gull the populace with the pretense of bargain prices when their articles, in truth, are of far poorer quality."

As to the prior's request of the sheriff to attend the Lenton Fair and extend the castle's protection of it, the guildsmen argued that the crown was in no way obligated during the course of the Interdict to honor the chartered privileges of any monastic house, especially now that the king had been formally sundered from the faith. "We side with our monarch," said the chief of the chandlers' guild, "so why should he not help us and hinder our unfair competitors—especially those who would mulct the common people while professing sacred purposes? Deny the prior's plea, we implore you, Master Mark."

Each side to the argument thus having stated its case, Philip was hard put to choose between them. Nor could he devise a plausible way to split their difference—and coming down on either side would leave the other sorely aggrieved. "Then why not put the matter to Westminster?" Sparks suggested. "We might seek guidance from the Chancery as to whether Holy Church's chartered fairs are meant to be allowed so long as the clergy denies its services to the laity. If yes, then the prior must be satisfied, and if not, then he must not be. Either way, the decision is taken out of your hands—and the losing party's rancor is deflected from the castle."

His clerk's proposal was, as always, both shrewd and commonsensical; yet it troubled Philip, for he preferred to deal with Westminster only when it was an absolute necessity. To yield his sovereignty over shire matters sent the wrong message to its inhabitants; sheriffs were not meant to run to the king each time a hard case came along. To wield his sway in this instance, though, was to make a decision that could only weaken his overall standing. And for him to do nothing at all would likely irritate both sides, hurting him even more. In the end, despite his misgivings, he referred the conflict to the crown in a form that implied he was merely asking clarification, not that a decision be made for him.

Westminster responded promptly by declaring the Lenton Fair suspended for as long as the priory inmates honored the Interdict. The sheriff could not fault the logic of the ruling, but it seemed to him heartless in its failure to acknowledge the relative innocence of the Lenton monks. Their idleness was not of their own making; their fair had next to nothing to do with spiritual matters; there was surely enough commerce in the Nottingham region to sustain two annual fairs—and if Lenton's goods were inferior, as the town craftsmen argued, then no one need buy them. The just course, Philip saw clearly now in retrospect, would have been to leave all as it had been and, although such dissembling appalled him, to have confected inoffensive grounds for absenting himself from the Lenton Fair and otherwise busying the bailiffs on that date. Hindsight availed him naught, though, and he had no choice left but to send the regretful notice of cancellation to the prior. The coroner appeared in his behalf the next day to report that Father Clement was beside himself with un-Christian rage.

"I sympathize with him," said the sheriff, "but I'm powerless to alter the decision."

"There was no need to invite the crown's consent to a traditional event," Sir Mitchell shot back. "It was an inherently base act."

"I did as I thought best."

"Best for you—and for the burgesses, who have bought your favors for five pounds of silver."

"Their money was applied directly to the shire coffers, not my personal use. Our tax collections lag—the situation is alarming."

"For you, Master Mark—not the crown. Amply fleecing the shire is your personal responsibility, so the townsmen's gift benefits you directly, does it not? In gratitude, you punish the priory, to the advantage of those who worship Mammon. You're as corrupt in your way as any of your predecessors—and the crown shall soon learn of it."

"I have no doubt," Philip said, bridling his temper even while reaching behind him to draw his sword away from its resting place against the wall. "And when you make your report, sire, do not fail to say that the sheriff has promised to run his steel through your belly the next time you speak of defaming him."

Sir Mitchell drew back a step and then another. "The crown appoints me to guard against the excesses of the sheriff—I am no less a royal officer than you, and it behooves you to recall as much."

"You leave me no chance to forget it." He gripped the sword firmly and held it toward the window, bringing his eye down close by the hilt in order to test the straightness of the blade. "I weary of your bluster, sire. It must end, I tell you, one way or another."

"To threaten the coroner is a crime," said Sir Mitchell, his voice wavering as he stood his ground.

"To threaten the sheriff is insurrection—and as such is put down forcibly, by and large. The crown would doubtless absolve me of homicide and choose a new coroner more sensitive to the limits of his office." Philip then whacked the sword against the table edge with a sudden snap of his wrist, sending the coroner into headlong flight from the room and its echoing clangor.

·XXIV·

IT WAS HARDLY THE FIRST TIME the reeve had spoken crossly to his wife, but the occasions were rare enough that they invariably plunged him into melancholy. This time it was less than ever the good woman's fault, for he could not tell her the nature of his night-crawling errand beyond that he was visiting the alehouse, which he had taken to attending on a weekly basis. When Mistress Blake chided him about the added cost of his new habit and the perils of indiscretion if drink should loosen his tongue, he replied unkindly. That she had been right only deepened his regret.

He spied the woodward slouched in the corner and tippling alone. Normally Blake would not have intruded upon him, but lately the reeve had heard no end of complaints about the excessive zeal with which the woodward had been enforcing the wood-penny. He was said to be taxing even the least fortunate on the manor for every limb larger than a twig that they took away. Further, he would cut the ration of underbrush whenever he snarlingly detected too full an armload, and only yesterday he had forbade the once-customary hauling off of wind-blown saplings without extra charge. Everyone thought he had a bug in his bunghole, but no one would say so to his face. So they had come to the reeve and appealed to him to intercede.

"I know what you're going to say, but join me anyway," the woodward muttered, not bothering to look up at Blake's approach. "They all hate me—you, too, I suppose. Why not? I even hate myself."

"It's so unlike you," said the reeve, balancing on the stool beside the woodward's. " 'It must be something beyond his sudden souring on the world,' is what I tell them."

"Can it be any secret to you, of all people? It's Stryker. Just saying his name turns my tongue to ashes."

"As the beadle's does mine."

"The beadle's a cherub next to the steward."

"A cherub with fangs and talons—and the heart of a gnat."

"A small gnat, at that. I pray the Almighty will strike them both dead in unison—but if only one, let it be the steward. He taxes me each month now, so I must pass on the cost—and the pain—by grubbing pennies for even the least offense against the wood."

"How can he tax you? Your position is hereditary."

"Unless I'm charged with criminal neglect—which he regularly threatens. There are five others waiting to fill my place, he says."

"He has no right."

"He makes the right. And if I appeal, I'm done for. The lord would doubtless side with Stryker—so I pay the nasty prick. Pray with me that he may drown in swine shit."

At the center of the smoky alehouse, Father Theodorus, the parish priest of Rainworth, was holding forth in a slightly less vulgar vein. Given his long-standing uselessness, the priest had found the Interdict a great blessing. Officially idled, he spent the small allowance he received from the archdeacon on drink and other dissipations, thereby ingratiating himself to his parishioners far more than he ever had in his soiled vestments. While barred from dispensing spiritual counsel, Theodorus was much sought after now for his easy fellowship and expansive homilies. Some said he was never holier than when he was most profane.

As the reeve drifted into his orbit, the priest was adjudicating between two Swanhill bondsmen speculating on whether either of them could ever purchase his freedom. Master Golly, who had broached the subject, was intent on the legal impediments to such a transaction, assuming he could ever assemble the money, whereas Master Piddling was preoccupied with the consequences if the dream ever came to pass. "But why seek it?" asked the latter. "What would you gain?"

"My liberty—to choose my own work, and not be at the constant mercy of the lord, and Master Stryker—may his balls drop off—and our wolf of a beadle, and even our dear Master Blake here."

"Still, what would you do with yourself? Where would you go?"

"Away . . . I don't know where. That's a different question."

"But shouldn't you answer it first before worrying about the rest?"

"I'm not worrying—I'm imagining. I'd go elsewhere, and do something else—anything else."

"You know nothing but the land," said Piddling, "and have none. So how could elsewhere be better than here?"

"Your brain is too wizened to understand," said Golly. "I can't plan for a thing unless I know it's possible." He turned to the priest. "Holy Church always says we must forbear, but why couldn't I buy me a new lot in life, Father? What's the harm?"

"I can't speak for Holy Church, my son," said Father Theodorus, "but for myself only I should say the cost isn't measurable in silver alone. Liberty brings with it woe as well as license, so Master Piddling's question is not altogether idle. As to the practicality of the step, how would you buy your release from the manor? All your possessions—your stock, your tools, your furnishings, the very clothes on your back—are derived from Lord Lambert as surely as your croft is, and are yours only pending good behavior. And what cash you might manage to accumulate comes out of his soil, which he kindly permits you to rent. You would be buying your freedom with his money, in effect—not a bargain he'd take to quickly. I fear he'd see only ingratitude in your offer."

"But it's my muscle and sweat I've applied to enrich him."

"Of course. But you hold body and soul together only by virtue of service to Sir Thomas, who keeps you nourished and covered and usefully busy so that you may earn your passage to Heaven—ergo, you owe him your sweated labor."

Golly summoned a considerable belch, his parry to the priest's eloquence, and swung about to the reeve. "Is that your belief as well, Master Blake—or have you never pondered buying your liberty?"

He had cradled the thought his life long but rarely dwelled on it, for he could contemplate no crueler folly than the ungrantable wish. Now, though, having nearly drained his second tankard of the evening, Blake saw the nature of their bondage with blazing clarity. "I would differ with our esteemed father," said the reeve, "only in that he has it entirely the wrong way around. All that Lord Lambert has and is, I'd warrant, stems from us. Oh, yes, from the king in the first instance, or he'd have no title, but what is land if it goes untilled and untended? There is no manor but for us and our ilk, nor any manor house. Lord Lambert may nourish and protect us, as Father says, but only as chattel and little better than his beasts. Who has the might rules the roost—all the rest is jabber, at which the gentry are skilled where we are mute. Sir Thomas owns our blood, I tell you, and will not part with it for any price."

Theodorus snatched twice at his little spade-shaped beard and then placed a cautionary hand over the top of the reeve's tankard. "*In vino veritas,* Master Blake, but they'll turn you into suet for it. You'd have made a sorry priest."

The widow Griggs appeared just then among the patrons, whose level of rowdiness rose to greet her. As she passed each group, her hands and face were in ceaseless motion—a touch here, a pat there, a smile, a

squeeze, a hearty hug, and always cheerful blandishments to entice business for her daughter Judith on the morrow.

So overwrought had the reeve become upon first learning that Susan
had substituted her eldest child's body for her own in resuming the carnal
trade that he went to her and threatened exposure before the manor court
for so deplorable an act of immorality. "Do as you like," she replied, "but
charred wood cannot be remade whole. Meanwhile, come lie with me—
and for you, my special friend, there's no charge." She saw the instant
flush her tactic had excited in him and added, "Or is it Judith you prefer?"

"I don't lie with children," he said, pity overtaking revulsion, "nor
with the strumpet of the manor—though there was a time, I'll admit, when
I badly wanted you." He looked down into her eyes, dimmer now and
hardened with defeat. "You had a beauty and a strength, Susan, that flowed
from your soul and transformed your body into—"

"You had only to say so, Master Blake, instead of haranguing me
about my bartered virtue." She placed both hands against his genitals and
cupped them fervently. "All might have been different between us."

"There are many things a man wishes for in life but cannot have,"
he said, and turned away.

"You think that any less true of a woman?"

"But you had your dignity—and then sold it."

"My children could not eat my dignity."

"Better for them to have gone hungry than have a slut for a mother."

"Better the devil for a reeve than one who thinks he's God."

He would not even acknowledge her presence now as she worked
her way through the alehouse crowd. Piddling spat at the floor when she
swept by them, his quid catching her hems, and said to the priest, "I'm
surprised she hasn't solicited you yet, Father."

"And who says she hasn't?"

"Perhaps you should take her up on it."

"And who says I haven't?" the priest asked with a laugh, then thought
better of the quip and asserted, "The sin is not in yielding to the pleasures
of the flesh but in buying or selling them. The Lord created joy for the
having but never meant it to be merchanted."

"I'll say this for her," Golly offered in defense of the fallen widow.
"She knew when to quit—her charms vanished practically overnight, and
who would pay to lie with a hag? Her daughter is the lovelier morsel by
far—the fairest loins for sale in all the shire."

"Have you sampled the lot adequately?" Piddling asked with a snort.

"Ah," said Golly, rolling his eyes, "now *that's* what I'll do with my liberty if ever Lord Lambert should part with it."

On the far side of the room Susan emitted a coarse whoop that revealed the depth of her abasement. The reeve wept within himself at the sound and all the mockery, then pulled his aching soul together and withdrew from the giddy company to pursue his evening's true purpose. Lately he had detected thievery from the manor corncrib—no small concern since the crop had fallen off due to light rain throughout the growing season; grain at market was said to be worth its weight in gold just now. When he mentioned his discovery to the hayward, Noah said the reeve was mistaken but promised to guard the crib more closely. And for a time the takings stopped. But they had since resumed, and Blake had resolved to hide in the hayloft on the first moonless night and uncover the culprit.

Even in the dark and blurred with drink, he knew every step of the way by feel. He slipped, though, climbing the ladder to the loft and collected half a handful of splinters. To ease the pain he had the companionship of numberless insects, scurrying small wildlife, two bats, and an owl. After an hour's excruciating wait, he was rewarded by the approaching rattle of a horse-drawn cart. Carefully he crept back down the ladder and hid himself just within the barn door. Through the open slit he watched and listened until it was apparent that sacks of grain were being tossed onto the wagon. "Who steals Swanhill's corn?" the reeve cried, springing from the doorway.

The bandit froze, then bolted, and Blake gave clumsy chase. But luck was with him, and the intruder tripped in the dark, sprawling face down in the mire. The reeve fell on top of him, pinioning his arms, and was about to raise the hue and cry when he recognized his catch.

"For Christ's sake, let me up," the hayward growled. "So you've got your thief—what of it?"

"But why, Noah?"

"Why? Why do you think?" The hayward rolled over and sat up, rubbing his arms. "The corn fetches good money at market, and the manor has more than it needs."

"It's thievery—they could hang you."

"Not if the lord isn't told."

"Stryker's auditors will find out, sooner or later."

"Not if you cause the ledger to be fixed. Just say your count was off."

"Why should I? You've done wrong."

"I'll let you in for half of it—and why aren't we entitled? We slave for years, and the gain all goes to the manor house."

"I'm no thief—and neither are you."

"Taking what you're entitled to from the greedy is no theft."

"Promise me on God's blood you'll quit right now, and I'll remain silent. Otherwise I'll have no choice but—"

"You'd turn me in? I'm your best friend."

"Then you should know I'm answerable if any of the grain is missing. Yet you've risked my neck as well as your own. Some best friend!"

"So," said the hayward, "you mean to say it's you or me—unless I abandon my golden chance to make some money?"

"That's right."

Noah struggled to his feet. "Why don't you stop playing the righteous fool, Blake? It's time you went along with it all."

"All what?"

"The manor is ripe for pickings—and everyone who can grabs his little bit. Why shouldn't I? Why shouldn't you? What has Lord Almighty Lambert ever done for you to deserve your slavish devotion? Let me tell Stryker you're in on it—it'll cost you some shillings, as it does me, but it's worth it—and you can be assured he won't prosecute you."

"Prosecute *me?* For what?"

"For stealing the lord's corn—as I found you doing tonight." So saying, the hayward suddenly pounced on the still recumbent reeve and pinioned his arms even as his own had been shortly before. "You see—I hid in the hayloft awaiting the thief and then nabbed him in the dark, and to my horror it turned out to be none other than our most virtuous—"

"You'd not tell so monstrous a lie!" the reeve cried, wincing from the pressure Noah was exerting against him.

"What choice would I have if you went to the steward? And which of us is he likelier to satisfy—the one who pays him tribute or the one who gives him trouble?" The hayward eased his grip. "Smarten up, my friend—and leave me now to pack my cart before someone else comes along and demands a piece of the pelf."

· XXV ·

"I DO NOT ASK YOU to betray him. On the contrary, I ask you to fulfill your purpose—in baiting me."

"Baiting? I—it's a most unpleasant word—indeed, as barbed as a fish hook. I take it for an insult, Thomas—nothing less—and far from your normal tone of civility."

"Because you try my patience—by your loveliness."

"Now you would charm me—the sequence is unsettling. I have told myself you care for my company without conditions—or unseemly favors— else I would not—"

"Anne, you come to visit me each month without fail, whatever the occasion or even when there is none at all. There must be a reason beyond the purely social."

"Meaning—what?"

"I say you come because you know Philip wants you here—to serve his ends—to befriend me so I will befriend him in turn—support him— promote him among my circle of acquaintances and thereby ease his task."

"And you believe that's the reason I come to you?"

"Among them. I say it eases your mind and permits you to slip the normal restraints—and I find that not in the least shameful. The trouble is that you delude yourself—have convinced yourself you serve his ends alone in being with me—for fear that something more is lurking. . . ."

"I don't wish to—"

"You never wish to—and so our time together always ends like this, because you think it suits your purpose. And then each new invitation to Swanhill tells you the lure is still alive, so you come smilingly and freshen up the bait—and then retract it ever so slowly as our day together wears on."

"Then I'll come no more, if that's how you perceive—"

"You and I are much alike, you know—as are they."

"Who?"

"Philip is cool and remote, as withdrawn as a pinch of gold inside a mountain—much like Cicely."

"You cannot possibly know Philip from spending a few hours in his company. He's a complex man, not easily given to revealing himself."

"Is there—much to reveal?"

"Oh, yes."

"And you adore him for—what?—the revelations made or the ones withheld?"

"Sarcasm scarcely becomes you, Thomas. I . . . care tenderly for him. He has unplumbed depths that—"

"One may care tenderly for a lapdog as well—and the chill sea, too, has depths beyond our knowing. I inquire into passion."

"And I answer as I think it fit."

"You don't gull me for an instant. You're like me, Anne—we're both creatures of raw feelings beneath the gilding. Though slow to burn, we're fiery by nature—and when aroused, make glorious tinder. Yet we are mismatched in our spouses."

"They say opposite temperaments attract—so your point, even if it were apt, says little for our compatibility."

"Isn't it plain we're suited to each other?"

"As friends—nothing more."

"Why is that?"

"There can be no more. More is betrayal."

"Betrayal again! So, we've arrived at full circle. Yet I am more than ever certain you do not come to me when bidden merely to advance Philip's case, but tell yourself so in order to justify your coming, and excuse whatever caring for me has grown—"

"You abandon good grace, Thomas, in making me into so base a—"

"But there's nothing base in it, I tell you. It's nature. Look, my dear girl, if you truly wished to suit only Philip's ends in coming here, you'd seek to please me still more—yet you do not offer to. And when I ask, you pretend I'm ignoble and would defile you and your pure love for him. You sing me the song of Roland, but I am unbewitched by your melody. The truth is, you fear Philip's wrath, else you'd not leave me in this unrequited state. Yet I tell you there'd be no peep from him, for the rewards would be so attractive that he'd not stop to ask why."

"You think he flaunts me, that I should seduce you—so that—?"

"In a manner of speaking. He doesn't even know he does it—not to that extent. But why else does he permit your constant coming to me?"

"It's not a question of his permitting it. I come because I wish to. He trusts me—knows I know the limits of propriety."

"No, you exceed them—and wreak devastation on my heart—and

then will not submit when I implore you. The effect is to fuel a growing rage—the very opposite of what you have both intended. Why not instead truly serve his end and mine as well—or is it that you find me repulsive to you physically?"

"I—you are not—not in the least, Thomas."

"Is it my age? Am I too old? You'd still find fire in my loins, I assure you, my dear Anne."

"I do not doubt it, my dear sire."

"Then you must end this infernal teasing—I cannot bear it any longer. It demeans us both. We must become either more deeply entwined or go our ways. This present course yields me more pain than joy."

She pinched off an apple from the tree nearest them and examined it coolly. "Their color is very good."

"Their taste as well—better than usual, even though the rest of the harvest is slender." He sighed. "Heaven is indeed mysterious—yet as nothing when compared to my lady of Tours."

She caressed the fruit and studied its shape yet more intently. "You spoke of rewards . . . were I—to—"

"Ahhh."

"Don't rejoice yet."

"What is it you would ask?"

"For myself, nothing—beyond the pleasure of your embrace. But I cannot be so selfish—and the sin is grave."

"So the price must be accordingly high?"

"But not so exorbitant as to defy a fair bargain."

"Then speak it."

She drew the apple close to her bosom and searched the sky for a moment. "Pay your taxes to the crown in full—what is past due as well as the current exaction—and promptly."

"You know of such matters?"

"I keep well informed."

"I should not have thought Philip would have shared—"

"Not Philip—his clerk, a devoted servant who often speaks with me in candor when he comes to school my daughters."

"So—I must pay dearly for my pleasure."

"Yet not a fraction of my cost if it be disclosed. Nor is the price any more than the crown is owed, however great your resentment of it. Indeed, I further ask you let it be known that you've paid willingly as a faithful subject of the king—and call upon your fellow magnates to do likewise and in timely fashion, which is to say at once."

"Lest your Philip be cast from office."

"The possibility has been mentioned to me."

"You would spend yourself to save him?"

"As you say, Thomas—there are worse rationales."

He placed his hand atop the apple she cupped, and their fingers meshed about it. "The price is steep and the prize elusive," he said with a weary smile. "Cicely visits our cousin in Lincoln the week after next. My slate with the crown will be clean by then—and word of it well broadcast."

A.D.
1211

·XXVI·

"THE KING COMMANDS that you attend him at his bath," Sparks reported, "and speedily, sire, before the heat wanes and he needs abandon the tub."

"At his bath?" asked the sheriff. "Surely they mean afterward."

"The message was quite explicit, sire." Knowing how edgy his master habitually grew in the course of a royal visit, the clerk added, "They say the most important and confidential business of the realm is conducted at the king's tubside."

"Do they?" His little aide's admirably useful command of intelligence that ought by right to be remote from him seemed busybody when applied to the royal household and was most certainly less reliable than usual, but Philip did not close his ears to it. "Then I'd best hurry to the summons, eh? I shouldn't want to miss the morning's festival of vituperation."

It was wrong to have let the irreverence slip out, even to his most trusted subordinate, Philip thought as he moved through the castle corridors toward the royal wing. Stoicism was required on these delicate occasions, yet he found that insulating virtue most elusive on just those several days a year the king chose to occupy the castle. For one thing, the sheriff suffered from an extreme sense of displacement on every royal visit, so overrun did the castle become with counselors, courtiers, servants, invited guests, and solicitors of favor who swelled the fortress to three times its customary population. He could hardly turn around for fear of colliding with a potentate of the realm or treading on some fresh pustule of court scandal. While he surely relished the drama of the royal presence and all its panoply, Philip was yet more moved by the inescapable awareness that he was far less a participant than a spectator when Nottingham became the temporary seat of crown power—his place among the king's retinue, in truth, was close to its outermost edge. There was distress as well in the inevitable loss of detachment that allowed him to serve so faithfully while the king remained distant from Philip's shires. He preferred to conceive of his sovereign as the immaculate embodiment of earthly authority, as the very essence of majesty, bringer of justice, defender of the peace, as an aura uncomplicated by deficiencies of character and uncolored by any meanness of spirit or expression. In the flesh, this beau ideal was markedly diminished, along with the sheriff's mindless devotion to him.

The banquet the night before had been a perfect instance of why King John's attendance at Nottingham Castle, generally deemed a high honor, was so disconcerting to its custodian. The sheriff, though among the fifteen seated at the dais, was placed far from the king, who was immediately flanked by the earl of Derby, not among Philip's keener enthusiasts, and Baron Brewer, revisiting the castle for the first time since retiring from his sheriffship there eight years prior. Even Thomas de Lambert, but lately returned to royal favor, sat at lesser remove from his liege lord than the sheriff, who consoled himself that he was, after all, simply a soldier of soiled birth and that he ought to bless his stars for inclusion among this gathering of notables.

But even while Philip was massaging such sentiments, the king chose to indulge in a bit of raillery at the sheriff's expense. "We would commend to your attention, Master Mark, the recent action of our subjects in Dorset and Somerset," John said, as the great hall hushed to catch the royal words. "Finding our good Baron Brewer here so loathsome an article in his performance as their sheriff, they proffered the crown the handsome sum of eight hundred pounds to be rid of such a pestilence. What a grand tribute!" The king chuckled richly. "Naturally eager to accommodate our subjects' wishes whenever possible, we painfully accepted this offering in earnest—leaving the poor baron with but four other shires to bedevil, not to mention his pesky function at the Exchequer, hounding the rest of you into solvency, and more custodies than any man ought rightfully to be burdened with." The royal eyes scanned down the table and briefly cauterized him. "So the lesson here, Master Mark, is for you to engender such an abundance of animosity throughout both your shires that the crown may likewise profit by your timely removal."

Philip knew to join in the laughter, which served to certify Brewer's unique position as the court's dark eminence. That mighty counselor came by the sheriff's place at the close of the banquet to assure him that the king was merely flexing his funnybone with the moral he had drawn from the tale of Brewer's purchased resignation in Dorset and Somerset. "You've done admirably here, Master Mark," said the baron, bending close to his ear. "And your bringing Lambert around was a special triumph— the king had been on the verge of strong measures against the thorny bastard. Just keep tending to your chores here, *mon capitaine,* and you'll flourish."

Brewer then invited him to join the banquet's more select attendees in the lesser hall, where the minstrels waged a losing battle to be heard above the playful—and often revealing—talk. The king was at his scalding best as he parried inquiries about the pending visit by the papal legate, intended to ease, if not end, Rome's quarrel with the crown. "Our Innocent's idea of a negotiation," said John, "is that Langton should reign at Canterbury, all the church properties should be restored, and we should immolate ourselves on the holy vicar's sacred crook. Nothing will come of it, you may rest assured."

John's wrath toward the pope was, if anything, superseded by the devouring suspicions and sly vindictiveness he voiced toward his vassals of uncertain fealty. "We will not hurry to confirm that lickspittle Landreau's succession to his inheritance," the king said of a young and volatile baron known to sympathize with the repugnant Briouses, "and in the end his gaining it will fetch us a pretty penny. The brat must come to heel." He was later overheard confiding to the earl of Derby that he had tired of "our sweetest Lord Mowbray's fantasies that he should receive preferential treatment by the crown because he stood hostage for Richard in Austria for four years—that was not our affair." And on the advice that the baron Eustace de Vesci had become agitated because the crown was harassing him for his debt to the Jews, the king asked simply, "And why should we not?" Everyone in the hall, of course, had heard the report that His Majesty had bedded Vesci's wife—and not a few supposed he might have spared the cuckold this added indignity.

His nastiest cracks of all the king reserved for his aging but still venomous adversary Philip Augustus of France, now in the thirty-second year of his reign at Paris. John, who was thought to despise the Capetian dynast less for his martial triumphs over him than for having used him as a pawn, or possibly a rook, against Richard during the crusade, offered a

mock toast now to "our small, thin, hairless, one-eyed, one-balled antag-
onist across the waves for lately irritating the Lowland princes whom our
ambassadors have been busily romancing. Philip thus yields us his northern
flank—we'll catch him yet in a giant vise and squeeze what life remains in
that decrepit frame."

But such words, while drawing the obligatory "Hear, hear" from the
king's closest attendants, were not popular with everyone in the hall and
had the hollow ring of bravado. Only the month before, John had been
dealt a humbling setback in the Welsh highlands and had retreated now to
Nottingham, some hundred miles due east, to plan a vengeful return expedition to Wales the month following. The French at least were a formidable people and worth contending against. But the Welsh were the
merest canker on the western fringe of the home isle, hardly more than
ragtag savages scattered with their flocks among rugged uplands, ever at
odds among themselves and paying, at best, inconstant lip service to the
crown. That such an inferior people, without crops, without settlements,
who knew nothing of armor or horse and would not stand and fight, should
defy his sway had at last driven John from tolerance to rage. South Wales
he had effectively neutralized by dividing it between the two Williams, the
Marshal and Briouse, mighty lords of his creation—until they had grown
so haughty, in the king's estimate, that he had to check them both, with
Briouse failing the ordeal. But the rest of Wales, eluding the royal hegemony, remained a patchwork of shifting alliances among tribal chieftains,
of whom Gwenwynwyn was dominant in mid-Wales, and Llewellyn, prince
of Gwynedd, supreme in the north. For years the king had played the pair
off against each other, alternating his favor whenever either seemed to
grow too pugnacious or chary of what meager tribute the crown demanded.
In time, though, Llewellyn had wearied of the king's game and gave dangerous evidence of trying to reconcile himself with his rivals. Faced with
the prospect of a united and incorrigible pack of jackals on his western
coast, John vested preeminence in Llewellyn by endowing him with marriage to his bastard daughter Joan, by which measure he hoped to pacify
these wildmen.

At first the alliance seemed a success. Llewellyn's rivals were cowed,
and that prince of the barbarians even joined his father-in-law's expedition
against William the Lion of Scotland in '09, bringing along a contingent of
fearsome spearmen and bowmen. Just when the state of Wales seemed
relatively tranquil, however, the king took it into his head that Llewellyn

was growing unmanageable and needed taming, so John smiled anew on Gwenwynwyn, and before long there was fresh fighting, royal outposts were sacked and burned, and an expedition of English foot soldiers and mercenary cavalry had to be sent in May to quell the havoc.

Alas, no one had fully alerted John's captains of the Welsh aversion for pitched battles and set maneuvers. Instead, they struck and ran, luring their foes into pursuit while they took cover in the ever denser wood. Then they leapt in renewed attack from this rocky outcropping or loosed a fierce volley of spears and arrows out of that inclined copse until their pursuers were whittled by surprise, fatigue, and bloodshed. Such a fate befell the May expedition as supplies dwindled with the lengthening, wavering trail of pursuit, and the royal forces were reduced to eating horse-flesh to avoid starvation in the mountain fastnesses of the Welsh.

"This time it will be different!" the king vowed to his listeners at Nottingham Castle. A sizable, battlewise host was to be sent against the barbarians, whose suicidal zealotry in combat had earned only John's utmost contempt. "They fight as if spilling blood were the object, and not the price, of the exercise. They know no fear, which is commendable, but spend themselves in mad disarray—and when their shoddy weapons are exhausted, they'll try to gouge you to death with the talons they have for fingernails." It was as if the king, an Anglo-Norman voluptuary who loved the complexities of statecraft, could not abide the Spartan simplicity of the Welsh and saw in it only a witless primitivism. "Some say they have sweet souls," he rambled on, "but all they do is fight, hunt, tend their flocks—and doubtless fuck them, sing badly, eat roots, and devour flesh they tear off the bone still bleeding. They grow nothing, make nothing, build nothing, read nothing, know nothing, *are* nothing—except such devout Christians that they are positively pagan! We will—we must—grind down these little monsters to a properly servile state!"

The king was calmer by the time Philip was summoned the next morning to attend the royal hide while it was being poached in the bath. The sheriff had exchanged words with the monarch on perhaps half a dozen previous occasions, but they had never gone beyond formalities and were always uttered with others on hand. Remote as he was from the sovereign, he knew the likely price of intimacy, even if it had been within his reach, and so feared the king's recognition as much as he wished for it. And who among his retainers could be more dispensable just now to this king of caprices, the sheriff asked himself, than a low-born outlander with neither resources nor influence? Perhaps he was about to be sent along to help crush the Welsh. Or to restore a crumbling castle in remotest Westmoreland. Only Brewer's commendatory words to him the night before eased his anxiety.

"Ah, our good Master Mark—draw nigh," said the king, a man of the sheriff's own age but pinker and bulkier in appearance, with his still firm, squarish face the more deeply lined from weather, worry, and the refinements of dissipation. "We wish to discuss a private matter."

"Your Majesty."

The dozen servants who were attending the king, equally divided between the sexes, withdrew to the edges of the chamber at the sheriff's appearance, but the royal words, scarcely modulated, echoed throughout. "The lady Pendrake has come to us of late," the king began, his large head tilted back and his eyes closed as if to fix his senses on the last delicious warmth of the bathwater, "and disclosed your vile behavior toward her."

"Your Majesty?"

"Oh, yes—'vile' was the fair Olivia's very word. And her elaborations, unless we choose to discredit them, fully justify it. Shocking business— utterly despicable for a sheriff of our realm. The lady asks for your dismissal forthwith."

The royal tone, content aside, was more bemused than censorious. But the sheriff detected a lurking wolfishness and assumed his peril genuine. "A serious matter indeed, my lord king," he said as neutrally as possible.

The king's body, entirely submerged save for his head, shifted about, sloshing a wave of filmy water overboard. "Have you no more to say for yourself, Master Mark?"

"Only that if the lady had accompanied her request for my removal with eight hundred pounds, Your Majesty could be still more certain I have been well serving the crown's interest in my dealings with her."

The king emitted a bark of a laugh. "You deny it all, then?"

"I don't know that the lady's charges rise to the dignity of requiring a denial, Your Majesty. If I might be told the nature of my vile conduct toward her, perhaps I should—"

"The lady says you two were fast friends, of the intimate sort, and that you had a bargain with her, sealed by your intimacy, yet you betrayed her. And now she asks that the crown redress her grievance—and hang your balls out to dry." There was less mirth now to his words.

"I—see." The sheriff, fully aware for the first time of his accuser's viciousness, vowed to parcel each syllable he spoke with extreme caution.

"We would not tax you on the merely carnal aspects of the lady's charge, Master Mark—for which one man can hardly fault another, especially when the vessel in question is as well shaped as this one, though she is a bit petite for our taste. No, it is the nature of your compact with her that invites our concern."

"There was no compact, my lord. The woman is desperate—and embittered, I suspect, because I spurned her several enticements."

"But she is a fair and highborn lady who says there was a well-understood bargain whereby her loins would be at your disposal in return for your doing as she bid."

"Yes, that I should petition the crown to reduce her fine so she might remain a widow until a satisfactory husband were found for her—and that in the interim a kindly disposed custodian be secured to manage her estate and affairs—"

"Preferably yourself."

"So she professed—and further, that I should hold off the Jew of Nottingham from pressing her to the hilt for her debts to him."

"Precisely. So you concede the arrangement?"

"I concede that is what she asked of me."

"But you deny taking her up on it?"

"Out of compassion for her—misplaced, I now see—I urged patience on the Jew for a season, so he settled for less than his due. I did nothing for her beyond that."

"Yet you accepted your reward from her?"

"I accepted a portion of chestnut pudding, sire—not suspecting that it would be poisoned."

"Pity—you missed a sweeter treat."

"My lord?"

"The lady Olivia brought her case against you while quite shamelessly roiling our sheets last night. She has a passionate nature and delightful body, both plainly in need of exercise." A royal hand emerged from the depths and pointed in dripping accusation. "Our sheriff has badly shirked his knightly duty to succor fair womanhood in distress."

"Alas, my lord, I am no knight—only a simple soldier in Your Majesty's service, and as such, loath to advantage myself at the expense of a titled lady. It was not that I found her enticements unappealing."

"Ah," said the king, "then you're human, after all."

"To that alone I fully confess, sire."

A puckered kneecap arose from the bath surface like a volcanic isle being born. "Then why did you not at least apply to us for custody of Pendrake? It's human to crave a bit of lucre."

"The crown knows my whereabouts and aptitudes. If it had wished to assign me Lady Pendrake's estate to manage, or any other, I should have undertaken the task to the fullest of my powers. But propriety forbids my soliciting additional rewards for service I am honored to render."

The king's gaze, latched to the ceiling, grew wide with disbelief, and his head gave a powerful shake that unsettled the surface of his portable lake. "We erred, Master Mark—you *aren't* human—though possibly Heaven-sent in your perfection. Would the crown could enlist multiples of your selfless ilk!" His head swiveled slightly toward the sheriff. "So then it all comes down to her word as a noblewoman against that of a 'simple soldier,' a breed prone to copulate with anything that moves. If we are to credit her, then you must be disposed of for having taken foul advantage of her, your protest to the contrary notwithstanding. And if you are to be credited, the lady must be punished for bringing wicked stories, albeit wrapped in a sinuous body, to her credulous king. Why should we side with you in this dispute, Master Mark?"

"Because I have no purpose beyond the crown's well-being, sire, whereas the lady dwells on her imagined misfortunes in life and will go to any length to allay them."

"Indeed, the royal length." The king smiled mischievously, then without warning drew his bulky torso upright like some shimmering sea monster about to devour a passing voyager. His ewerer and two serving maids bearing towels and robes hurried to him. "Enchanted as we were with Lady Pendrake's form, we think she doth overly protest. What punishment shall we mete this concupiscent vixen for slandering the king's devoted officer?"

"I . . . would be inclined to let her stew in her own bile, sire."

"You're indeed a man of godly restraint," said the king as his every surface was being delicately assaulted by the royal dryers. "But we have resolved that the time is at hand to reward Lady Olivia with a husband of our choice—not hers. She has forfeited that option by her duplicity toward our most honorable sheriff. What sayest thou?"

"It is, of course, Your Majesty's prerogative—yet I think it less than kind."

"And what has she been to you if not less than kind? Surely your godliness has its limits, Master Mark. No, we hold there is no unkindliness in our act—quite the opposite. She's had several years to find herself a suitable husband, and if more time passes, she will dry up internally and be of no use to anyone. Therefore, having anticipated that you would give the lie to her allegations of your baseness, we have scanned the list of applicants for her hand and are inclined—barring your strenuous objection—to award her to Sir Ralph de Greasley of this shire. His allegiance to our purposes may be assured by the step."

The name stabbed at Philip, who could not mask his chagrin. "Greasley is a two-faced man, my lord, who flouted an edict of your judicial eyre and continued to oppress a poor widow among his own tenants. When I held him to account, he claimed to concede the wrong yet nevertheless privately denounced me to the earl of Derby for mistreating him."

"Yes, the earl confirms your account—yet it does not foil our larger design but advances it, rather."

Philip's face dropped. "I see—the earl sides with Greasley, and Your Majesty quite naturally credits the earl."

"The earl may not be your most ardent champion, but you miss the point altogether."

"Sire?"

"Assuming Sir Ralph to be what you say and still of likely future use to the crown for our bestowing this boon of Pendrake upon him—now see what we accomplish by this marriage. Lady Olivia is matched with a low character, as befits her conduct toward you, while Sir Ralph is gifted with a bitch who will make his life a misery. What could be more perfect?" He rubbed the dynastic jewels dry by himself and donned the lightest of the robes presented to him.

"There is a certain symmetry to it, I grant you, sire."

"More than symmetry, even—a heavenly fit. He offers two hundred for the lady's hand. What does Pendrake yield per annum?"

"Perhaps twice that, if properly supervised."

"Then he should pay that and a hundred more for good measure." He toweled his head and facial hairs with vigor, then lifted a spare, un-bejeweled crown of beaten gold from the hands of a bearing maid and fit it snugly on. "Given the lady's virtuosity at coitus, the price will go to six hundred—if he is greedy and base into the bargain, let him stretch a bit.

But you must not think it untoward of us, good sheriff, if we accompany our award of Lady Olivia in marriage with forgiveness of her debt to the Jew. It will both allay her pain and make her more agreeable to renewing our pleasurable acquaintance whenever we are in the shire, especially after she has had her fill of the unctuous Greasley—who will surely not begrudge us this small privilege of our rank." Philip's shoulder endured a powerful squeeze of dismissal. "Carry on, then, our courageous captain from Touraine. Your work here goes not unheeded."

"Your Majesty." The sheriff bowed badly, telling himself as always that the fault was the battle injury of his youth.

· XXVII ·

WHEN HE AND HIS WIFE APPEARED before the gates of Nottingham Castle and asked for the sheriff's first clerk, the fugitive reeve of Swanhill declined to give his name or state his business. "Master Sparks will know us," he said, as much to his wife as to the gatekeeper, "and vouchsafe our entry."

"God willing," she replied, looking down wanly from his little dappled gray.

The mare was too small to have carried the both of them any great distance, so Blake had made the trip on foot—a considerable journey for a man past his prime and in a hurry. "It's even bigger than it looks from afar," he said, surveying the fortress that bulked gloomily above them.

"And still less inviting," added his wife, weary from their flight and eager to dismount. "I pray you've made no mistake."

"Jared will do what he can—the rest is in Heaven's hands. At any rate, we cannot be worse off."

"So you say, Master Blake."

Sparks hurriedly answered the gatekeeper's summons, saw at once the nature of their unspoken plight in the pleading faces of the reeve and his wife, and directed their prompt admission to the bailey. Three months had passed since the clerk had last seen the couple at Swanhill, where he had returned just before Eastertide to attend his mother's makeshift funeral. At the smithy afterward, Blake had offered devout condolences, bespeaking his long fondness for Mother Sparks; upon inquiry only, the reeve confided the extent of his own troubles. Now, as the clerk led them to the least trafficked corner of the bailey, Blake related the sorry pass to which they had come.

The corruption at Swanhill had proven still more pervasive than he could ever have supposed. The venerable stablemaster, by way of example, was lately detected by the reeve in collusive arrangements with that ceaseless conniver Stryker. Several Swanhill foals and a number of nags claimed to be no longer serviceable were sold off with the steward's blessing and the receipts divided among the manor, the steward, and the stablemaster in equal portions, although only the lord was entitled to any. When Blake confronted him, the stablemaster readily conceded the ruse but said it had been of long standing, as if that had somehow gained it legitimacy, and sanctioned by the baron's auditors, who doubtless were given a reward on their own for the kindness. Even the senior shepherd and swineherd partook in the larceny rampant throughout the manor. They had driven the larger portion of the Swanhill flocks up into the Newstead pastures—with the complicity of the abbot, in view of Sir Thomas's generous benefactions over the years—in order to escape the full brunt of the thirteenth imposed by the royal tax collectors in '07 on all the chattels of the realm; to maintain their silence, the herders were given several animals each. To sustain the bribe in subsequent years, they were allowed to sell off several head annually for their private gain and assisted the steward in doing likewise.

But nothing had more dispirited the reeve, or precipitated the events that were to undo him, than his discovery that the widow Griggs, by now hard and cunning, had inducted her younger daughter, Sarah, into the carnal trade along with Sarah's older sister, Judith, so that the family business might flourish as never before. Charged as he was with supervising the moral conduct of the lord's bondsmen, the reeve at last brought Susan before the manorial court, where every married woman at Swanhill appeared to lend vocal endorsement to her prosecution. Since the charges could hardly be denied, the two girls were ordered scourged and flogged by the beadle—but not to the point of disfigurement, given the vested interest that Masters Jadwin and Stryker maintained in their enterprise. Susan herself was put into the stocks in front of the Rainworth parish church, where in the full summer heat she dripped bodily wastes for three days while the proper women of the manor trooped by, taunting, cursing, spitting, and tossing bloody rags and fecal matter at the reviled prisoner.

In the end, though, it was the reeve who suffered worst. The men of the manor, turning their backs on him for what he had done to their prized concubines, began to direct their sputum in his wake, to disregard his orders, to insult his wife whenever they passed her, to pelt their cottage with slime and refuse—and as soon as Susan and her daughters had sufficiently recovered, to renew their visits with them. Blake could forbear all but this last act of defiance. With scant hope he went to the steward to protest resumption of the degrading practice and to ask that it be curtailed. "The girls perform a highly useful service," Stryker answered, "even as the miller and the smith." The reeve was free to renew his charges at the manor court, "but for your own well-being, I'd not recommend it."

"It's not right," said Blake, "and you know it."

"I'll tell you what I know, Lord High-and-Mighty—someone ordered new fencing built around the vegetable patches. Who could it have been?"

"The rabbits were up to their worst—so I had it done, of course."

"*Of course?* Without my approval?" The steward looked cross.

"But I've always attended to such—"

"Henceforth you will come to me regarding all such uses of material—and present your work assignments to me as well in advance of your giving them out. You're puffed with arrogance, Sir Reeve, and much in need of unleavening."

It was the blow that sent Blake to Lord Lambert's apartment to disclose the enormity of the steward's sins, including extortions that involved the beadle, the miller, the woodward, the hayward, the stablemaster, even the herders, and his oppression of nearly all who dwelt at Swanhill. "He does the entire manor a disservice each morning he arises," said the reeve, "and Your Lordship most of all."

Sir Thomas looked to be wounded by the sweep of the charges but said nothing beyond promising to reflect on them. Within a few days, however, the lord's judgment was manifest. Without explanation, Blake's sheep and other stock were turned away from the manorial pastures, where they had customarily been allowed to forage; soon all the reeve's animals were seized save for one ox, one cow, and his gray mare. Then his access to the lord's food stores was curtailed, and he was told that his cottage needed repairs requiring him and his wife to move to a croft lately vacated by a victim of the consumption—and for the occupancy of which, not incidentally, he would be charged; no more free rent for this reeve. His work orders, moreover, were now regularly countermanded by the steward, who utterly ignored Blake when crossing his path on their daily rounds. These unending humiliations had but one goal: the reeve was to recant his slanders and beg the steward's forgiveness or be deposed and returned to field labor.

Instead, Blake and his wife searched their souls late into the night, prayed for guidance, and, detecting no omen to the contrary, resolved to leave Swanhill an hour before dawn three days hence, hopeful of gaining their liberty in the wide world, which they knew little of and feared greatly. Yet whatever lay ahead could be no worse than their familiar surroundings, which held nothing for them anymore but hatred.

"But why come to me?" Sparks asked as he signaled a stableboy to water the reeve's sad-eyed gray.

"What better asylum?" Blake asked back. The law granted a master four days to recapture any fled bondsman merely by locating his hiding place and demanding his return; if the escapee was not found until a later time, it was a matter for the courts, often a tortuous process and little resorted to. If the bondsman passed a year and a day within the confines of a royal borough the likes of Nottingham or on a crown manor, he was accounted a free man. "If we are at the castle, the date of our having left the manor is fixed beyond all challenge," the erstwhile reeve went on. "And Mistress Blake and I had hoped you might, out of kindness and understanding, help us find work on one of the king's estates. I have strength yet to be a good worker—and much knowledge that might find a use."

"But the castle is not an inn, Master Blake—much as I am moved by your plight and commend your courage in seeking a new life."

"We ask but four days' shelter, sire—we'll pass them in the gaol, if need be. Just keep the beadle from our necks, and we'll be in your debt forever. On your mother's grave, we beseech you."

Since the hour was still early, the clerk hurried to the sheriff's apartment, hoping for a private audience with him. But his wife was on hand as well, so Sparks hesitated, saying, "I do not wish to trouble Mistress Mark with all the details of the matter."

The clerk's very appearance in their private quarters at such an hour signaled the likely importance of the subject and rendered his reluctance to include her transparent. "I have no secrets from Mistress Mark," said the sheriff. "What grim cargo do you lug us on so perfect a morning?"

Sparks began by recalling the reeve's testimony against a Swanhill slacker who, at the sheriff's first tourn three years earlier, had falsely charged the manor with oppressing him. When Philip registered only the dimmest memory of the case, the clerk remarked that Master Blake's devotion to Lord Lambert's interests had, at any rate, always been exemplary, "yet he has now had to flee the manor for the sake of his survival. Aside from my brother, the smith, this reeve was the only honest servant left at Swanhill as of last midnight. He is much like yourself in his way, sire—industrious, forthright, fair, dedicated to right practices—and for all of these has been sorely abused. Alas, but he brings us word that Lord Lambert, too, for all his admirable qualities, has feet of clay that have not stood on the highest moral perch while the baron was venting his ire over the crown's exactions." Sparks quickly outlined the reeve's tale of corrupt and oppressive practices, becoming ever more aware as he went on of the sheriff's growing unease over his disclosures. At the end, urgency coloring his words and routing his usual dispassion, the clerk said, "I ask that we may harbor him and his good wife just long enough to prevent their recapture. If they tread the streets of Nottingham or the byways of the shire unsheltered, they'll not last long. After the fourth day here, perhaps the reeve's skills can be put to work at one or another of the royal manors in our shires. He asks but for liberty and the chance to perform honest labors without backbiting by those he oversees or being abused for his—"

"Enough of this heart-wrenching tale!" snapped the sheriff, who had been studying the vista of ripe countryside beyond the town as his clerk ran on. "You do me no favor bringing such a matter to the castle."

"I did not invite it, sire."

"Nevertheless, it is here because you are."

"I . . . concede as much. Yet that does not alter the merits of—"

"It comes to special pleading, Master Sparks. Your value to me has been enhanced precisely by your powers of icy analysis, yet here they abandon you altogether."

"I . . . am at a loss . . . to . . ." The little clerk hung his head a moment. "I had but three choices, sire. I might have sent the reeve away, which I deemed a heartless act. Or I might have tried to hide him within the confines of the castle for the requisite four days without calling the matter to your attention—a course that would have spared you the dilemma of complicity but surely violated my duty to you, sire. Or lastly, I could come to you as I have, counting on your compassionate sense of—"

"Yes, quite so, Jared—I meant no unkindness. It's only that the more pressing a case you build for these fugitives, the more troubling it grows for me." He drew in a deep breath from the sweet morning.

"May I venture a thought," asked Anne, who had taken in the entire exchange, "before the matter grows unduly complex?"

"Ahh—a divine sunbeam to light my path. Speak, dear lady."

Anne folded her hands on her lap and expressed herself with quiet precision. "Commendable as this reeve doubtless is and fully worthy of Master Mark's charity, does not the sheriff owe a higher debt of honor to Lord Lambert for his several acts of compliance with the castle's needs— and for championing our interests when no one else of rank or potency within the shire would do as much?" She turned her face upward. "He has befriended us, Philip—so would it not be the height of ingratitude to omit advising him that one of his prize bondsmen has fled to us asking asylum?"

The sheriff closed his eyes and bobbed his head.

"If I may offer a word in mitigation?" Sparks inserted, having fully anticipated that the reeve's fate would be thus summarily settled. "Without gainsaying the value of Lord Lambert's cooperation last autumn, bear in mind that it came at the last possible instant—and what he did was no more than he ought to have done but gained heroic stature with us only because it reversed his own prior obstinacy. Furthermore, why must we assume the baron will be distraught over the flight of a disaffected bonds- man who has made charges against the manor officers that Sir Thomas plainly does not credit? Better to be rid of such a troublemaker."

"Master Sparks is disingenuous," Anne put in, less demurely now. "You simply owe it to Lord Lambert, Philip, to ask him his preference in the matter. It's not for us to guess at it and risk a grievous offense to such a useful friend."

"But to ask him," Sparks fought on valiantly, "is to assure that the reeve will be reclaimed."

"Because his flight is a rebuke to the manor," Anne shot back, "and the baron's honor demands his return. All the more reason for us not to stand against him."

Sparks slumped against the wall in dejection, plainly on the verge of surrender. "I recognize the virtue of my lady's position," he said, wist- fulness edging into his voice, "but I owe Master Blake much and must do all I can to spare him further anguish. I appeal to you, sire, on the ground of justice tinged with mercy—and no other."

"Would that the matter could be weighed in the abstract," said the sheriff, turning from the window. "I think I'll have a walk to the river with the chaplain and invite his counsel."

Father Ivo was quick to confess that because Sparks had spoken to him over time about Master Blake, he was biased toward one of such patent goodness. "Yet I see where your larger interests lie and cannot pretend otherwise," he told the sheriff. "Perhaps the wisest course would be for you to take no action whatever, doing what the law says you must—no more or less."

"Harboring the couple is in itself an overt act," Philip replied.

"And expelling them of your own accord is a heinous one. Perhaps you might withhold any order for a day or two while I explore the possibility of shelter elsewhere so the couple might avoid seizure."

"You have a thought, albeit not trouble-free for me."

While the sheriff and the chaplain conferred, Master Sparks reappeared before Mistress Mark and begged a private exchange with her, adding that he hoped he had not offended her earlier by any stridency in his appeal. "I come to you anew, however, on a different matter, yet disturbing in its own way."

"No one may fault you for your earnest advocacy in the reeve's behalf," she said with a smile. "But is it me or the sheriff you wish to apprise on this other—"

"You, my lady. And I come with yet more trepidation."

"Heavens! I cannot conceive what earthly—"

"I'll not be cryptic, madam." Upon returning to Swanhill for several days in connection with his mother's death, said Sparks, he had been made privy to disquieting reports, "much on my mind ever since. I intended to advise you of them at once, yet have hesitated . . . for fear that . . . my lady would take it most unkindly if . . . ."

The sweetness drained from her. "What reports, Master Sparks? Say your piece."

The clerk paused, dreading that he was about to shatter something sacred, then plunged ahead. "It is no secret you are on friendly terms with Lord Lambert."

"None at all."

"But you have been seen from time to time, my lady, on various parts of the manor, walking hand in hand with the baron."

"What of it? He is . . . like an uncle to me—even as in your relationship with Father Ivo. Surely, no one can suppose—"

"Several times the two of you have been seen in an embrace."

"Of fond greeting or farewell, no doubt. There is affection between us, to be certain, but of the most courtly and innocent sort, I can assure you, Master Sparks."

"I—have no doubt, my lady. It is just that—well, with so many prying eyes and forked tongues, wrongful and salacious stories circulate. They cannot be of any help to you, should they gain currency beyond the manor—compromising you and Master Mark with those already all too eager to think or say the worst. I—thought you had best be advised—and, if I may be forgiven my impertinence, urge that you modify your—expressions of fondness for each other so that the ungently born will not mistake them for indiscretion."

Anne sank onto the chest beside her and, having grown still paler than normal, struggled for composure. "You do me a great kindness, Jared," she said, her voice soft and small. "I had never thought that a friendship of—what shall I call it?—of social utility—might be taken for something unwholesome. The matter will be put aright at once." She looked up at the furrow-browed clerk. "And may I ask that your own discretion foreclose this subject from ever again crossing your lips?"

"On my mother's grave, I swear it."

Anne nodded appreciatively and ventured a brief smile. But a further unsettling thought then seized her, and she grappled with it a moment before yielding to it. "Yet why is it, Jared, you have waited until now—the very morning of the reeve's troubling arrival among us—to offer me your counsel in this other matter?"

"I . . . as I said . . . had not the courage."

"But now you have suddenly summoned it?"

"I . . . yes . . . I felt . . . that I must—"

"In no way connected, perchance, with your effort to protect the reeve—and your fear that I stand in your way by whatever sway I exercise with Master Mark?"

"I . . . the thought has—never entered into my—"

"Could it be that you or even the saintly Master Blake himself has it in mind that if I do not take his side, you or he would—divulge . . ."

"I . . . my lady cannot suppose I am so—artless."

She rose and confronted him with the full intensity of her being. "On the contrary, Master Sparks—I think you most artful indeed—if perhaps nakedly so in this instance."

"My lady—" Sparks's voice began to crack. "I should not, for all the world, wish you to believe that—I would attempt to . . . I hold you in the very highest—"

"Then by all means do not ever entertain such a thought as I have so uncouthly broached, or you would find yourself back at Southwell Minster tending the tallow vats within the hour." She spun about and retreated from him. "As to Master Blake, the sheriff is a man of his own mind, as you've surely grasped by now. I have made known my views to him in your presence regarding the reeve, and that is the end of it so far as I am concerned. Do we understand each other?"

"My lady," Sparks said with a bow and retired hastily, contracting an acute case of the hiccoughs as he fled down the corridor.

The reeve and his wife were brought to the castle kitchen, where they were fed and, after an hour's rest, put to work at scullery while the sheriff temporized in deciding their fate. In so doing, Philip confided his dilemma to the undersheriff, who, while greatly admiring his brother's fastidious balancing of the considerations, saw the matter much as his sister-in-law. When he spoke of it in private with her, Anne shrugged and said only, "In the end he must do what he thinks best."

But Peter, with fewer constraints upon him than the sheriff's wife, thought Philip would be better served if his deputy took the case into his own hands. Accordingly, his nephew, Geoffrey, appeared at Swanhill several hours later in his capacity as royal messenger for the castle. "I have come to you, my lord, at the direction of the undersheriff," he said upon being ushered into the baron's presence, "but without the sheriff's knowledge. Master Peter fears that Master Philip, in his resolve to betray no one, faces an impossible choice. The undersheriff therefore begs your compliance with his request that you honor the confidential nature of my visit and its purpose—believing as he does that it suits your ends, which in the last analysis are congruent with the sheriff's."

"Nicely recited," said Lord Lambert. "Tell your Uncle Peter he is a rogue—and a delight—and come refresh yourself before we go on."

The steward and the beadle of Swanhill, joined by the bailiff for the

Rainworth district, appeared at the castle that same afternoon and demanded an interview with the sheriff. "We know our fugitive reeve to be among you," said Master Stryker, "and request you convey him to us as the law directs."

"Who said your fugitive is here?" asked Philip.

"Does my lord sheriff deny it?"

"My question was put first, and my office grants it precedence."

"We have kept the reeve under surveillance of late, sire. He was last seen leaving Swanhill early this morning and followed here. We have held back this long in order to see where he would go when turned away from the castle. Yet he has not been, raising the suspicion you plan to grant him asylum. This would of course violate Lord Lambert's rights to the churl, since we have come to you in timely fashion and request that—"

"I know your master's rights—and the reeve's as well."

"Do you know as well, sire, that Master Blake is no angel? Indeed, he remains in our minds the leading suspect in the murder of our ploughman Paul two years ago."

"On what evidence?"

"That the reeve was enamored of our resident strumpet and could not abide her selling herself—and when she disregarded his call on her to desist, he vented his fury not against his lady-love but a vulnerable customer of hers. He denies it, of course, and now elects to slander us all before he should make a slip and be prosecuted for the crime."

"Why didn't you share your suspicions with us at the time?"

"We wished to give Master Blake every benefit of the doubt—never suspecting he would turn on us in such a—"

"If you will wait in the great hall, Master Stryker, I will investigate the whereabouts of your fugitive to see if I can oblige you."

"The obligation is clear," said Stryker, leading his little party out the door, "along with his whereabouts."

Sparks grew enraged upon being told what had transpired. "The beadle almost surely did the murder!" the clerk piped. "They're rotten to the core!" The sheriff nodded slowly. "I have no doubt. Yet we must surrender your beloved Blake. It is the law."

"But sire, you could say he was here and has fled—or that you no longer know where he is—or that—that—"

"It would not be the truth."

"Close to it. In fact, he is hidden away, in a place not known to you at the moment."

"But *you* know it, Jared—and you answer to my command—which is to produce him promptly and be done with it."

"Please, sire—would you come with me to see this good man—and hear his own words? You will be moved—and in no doubt of his innocence and righteousness. He is worthy of your asylum."

His clerk's quaking words and brimming eyes moved the sheriff, but not to the point of rashness. "Even if so—and even if his master's position were not what it is—I have no choice but to yield the bondsmen. Bring them to the gate."

With heavy heart Philip made his way to the great hall and asked Stryker what fate awaited the reeve upon his return. "He'll revert to an ordinary ploughman," the steward answered. "Our hayward has already been chosen to succeed him."

"See to it that you oppress him no further," said the sheriff, "or you will earn my deepest wrath, Master Stryker. I know you now."

On their journey back to Swanhill, as Sparks later heard and duly related, the beadle insisted that Blake and his wife ride together on his old gray, though any of the other horses could easily have taken an extra rider. Midway back, the little mare lay down from exhaustion in the summer sun and soon died. With visible annoyance, the beadle and the bailiff helped the reeve drag the animal into the roadside ditch, and the reclaimed fugitives were made to complete the woeful trip on foot, at a none too leisurely gait.

· XXVIII ·

NO ONE WAS MORE STIMULATED by the prospect of thirty boys coming to live at Nottingham Castle than the sheriff's two small daughters, the precocious Angelique, now aged nine, and her sister, Julia, not quite seven. The children grew in excitement not so much because the pending arrivals were all male—they were said, at any rate, to range in age from twelve to sixteen, too old and rough to serve as playmates—but simply because they were young people, of whom very few were ever seen within the castle walls. Indeed, the girls had only infrequent contact with any other children, visiting perhaps three times a year at the home of one of the burgesses or a Nottingham merchant seeking to ingratiate himself with the sheriff. Of the offspring of gentry, pretty, animated Angelique and smart little Julia had seen nothing.

"They are not coming to play tag with you," Anne had to remind the girls repeatedly as their anticipation soared the week before the Welsh boys were due. "This is no social call—they're being sent here by the king to assure that their fathers will no longer war against our England."

"But isn't Wales a part of England?" asked Angelique.

"Only if England makes no point of it," her mother answered. "It's its own place—mostly rocky hills and bosky shadows, they say."

"Then why does the king care what they do there?"

"I've wondered the very same, *ma chère*. I believe it's that kings get upset when their subjects become naughty."

"But why should the king punish the Welsh boys," Julia asked, "when it's their fathers who have misbehaved?"

"You'll have to ask Papa that."

"Because," said Philip, unhappy over the large consignment of hostages and unhappier still with having to justify it, "the king thinks that this way their fathers will not dare strike anew at our forces or war among themselves. The purpose is to prevent, not to punish."

"But the boys won't like it," Angelique pointed out, "and may well become beastly."

"They're beastly to begin with," Julia added. "Nurse says the Welsh have hairy palms and scaly feet bottoms, the better to run with the animals."

"Nurse has too vivid an imagination," Philip cautioned, "though the boys will doubtless need a bit of domesticating."

"And what will happen to them if their fathers should act up?" Angelique asked. "That's the part I don't like at all."

"Nor I," her father conceded. "But that's the part that ensures it won't happen. Fathers love their children too much to risk their safety on folly."

"But they may not think it folly to keep Wales for themselves," said Angelique.

He could not deny that possibility, but it had become decidedly more remote since the king's renewal of hostilities beyond the Marcher region had proven such a triumph. The crown host, far vaster and better supplied than the one waylaid in the Welsh uplands in May, stalked its retreating prey relentlessly. When the royal forces reached the cathedral town of Bangor, where the bishop declined to meet with an excommunicate king, the settlement was torched and the prelate seized in his robes on the high altar and ungently held until a large fine was agreed to for his liberty. This brutish dealing sent the unmistakable message to Llewellyn, prince of Gwynedd and foremost among the warrior chieftains of north Wales, that the king of England would hound them into the sea unless his bands ceased their marauding and surrendered. Through the good offices of Llewellyn's wife, Joan, the king's illegitimate daughter, a peace was arranged whereby the crown was ceded substantial territories along the border and the Welsh warriors agreed to restrict their lambasting to a tight haven west of the river Conway. Additionally, Llewellyn was burdened with a heavy tribute in livestock, dogs, and birds—the only currency of Wales—and the requirement that he send to the king's castle at Nottingham thirty sons of his leading families, to be held indefinitely or until their fathers' peaceable intentions had been reliably established. Among the young men selected for the dubious honor, Philip soon learned, was Prince Llewellyn's own son, Gruffydd—King John's grandson, albeit of bar sinister blood.

Fortunate it was that the sheriff's daughters had been disabused of any fancy that the hostages might resemble mythic princes, for in the flesh they proved a disappointing lot at first. Short, broad, well-knit lads with hair and fingernails of exceeding length and dirtiness, wearing crude garments of skin and poorly woven wool, they huddled among themselves and chattered in a strange tongue, with fear and resentment mingling in their quick, dark eyes. Besides the king's guard, the boys had been accompanied on their week-long journey east by Prince Llewellyn's longtime family nurse, a lapsed old nun named Cadi, who was to remain with them at the castle serving as a go-between for the speech and folkways of the hostages and their keepers.

"They're horrid," announced Angelique, rushing to judgment as children are wont. "They should all be dunked in the moat and left to steep for a month—the nurse included."

Neither the appearance nor hygiene of his charges concerned the sheriff a fraction so much as the potential overflow of their youthful energy and any resulting mindless valor. These were a uniquely hardy breed of manchild, reared in rugged terrain and used to toughening their bodies by tracking barefoot through woodlands, scaling mountain ridges, and honing their deadly skills with the bow and javelin. Theirs was a largely portable culture, suitable for packing up at a moment's notice and quickly dispersed, people, livestock, and belongings alike, for easy reassembly wherever and whenever safety dictated. How to cage the offspring of such roving primitives? The king, moreover, was known to view the escape of hostages from a crown keep as a grave dereliction of duty by his royal officers. But if the sheriff treated his juveniles as prisoners of war, he might only encourage a desperate attempt at flight. Too lax a leash, on the other hand, might invite the mistaken belief that they could easily slip the knot.

Philip's solution was to affect a homey setting, with himself cast as a somewhat stern but deeply caring paterfamilias. The Welsh boys were housed barracks-style in four interior rooms in the sheriff's wing of the castle, and a sergeant-at-arms posted as sentinel at either end of the corridor day and night. But the lads could not be penned throughout their waking hours, given their upbringing; nor were there sufficient men in the garrison to keep all thirty hostages under constant scrutiny. Instead, a roster was compiled and a roll call taken twice daily, the times varying and thus unpredictable, to account for all that precious collateral. Each boy, furthermore, was assigned a partner for whose whereabouts and behavior he was held responsible. If any of them fled, Philip asserted to the lot of them assembled in the great hall moments after their arrival, his partner would be held in gaol for an indefinite spell and all the other boys put in irons and confined to the castle for three months. If more than a single boy ran off, or even tried to, all the rest would be gaoled for three months at the least and thereafter confined to the castle for the remainder of their stay. Lest they think escape a game, the sheriff added, affecting his coldest manner while gripping the hilt of his longsword, any escapee would be mercilessly hunted down and surely caught before getting a quarter-way back to Wales.

"Running away would also be cowardly," Philip added, "and a disgrace to your people. In staying, you serve them well by discouraging any uprising that our king in his wrath would be certain to crush." Then he abandoned his chilling demeanor and moved freely among the boys. "If you behave like the sons of noble Welshmen, you'll be treated as such in return. But if you act like rascals or worse, you'll be roughly dealt with here." He placed a hand on the muscular shoulder of the king's grandson,

Gruffydd, at fifteen their natural leader. "I like this arrangement no more than you," he said, looking the hirsute lad in the eye, "but there is a purpose behind it, and we had all best heed it."

Whether they grasped his words as translated by Nurse Cadi and, if so, intended to comply was not discernible by any expression beyond intentness on their young faces, shrouded as they were by their shaggy manes. The cultural gulf that divided them from their captor-hosts became apparent, though, the moment the boys sat down to their first castle meal. The bread and ale, while not unknown to them, were great delicacies at home, since, as Cadi explained to the sheriff and his officers, little grain was grown in Wales and, like salt and iron and other vital commodities, had to be imported at great expense. Fruits and vegetables were similar rarities in the diets of the meat-and-milk-devouring lads, so they fell upon the novel foods hungrily at first, then suddenly held back almost in unison, as if fearful the tasty abundance might be some trick to soften them. When the bailiff's men and one of the clerks came by after the meal to ask each boy his name so the roster might be compiled, they turned mute and glared at the aged Cadi, who, reluctant but powerless, identified each as requested. The boys' hesitancy was neither shyness nor truculence, she disclosed, but the residue of an ancient Welsh tenet that whosoever knew a body's name thereby attained power over it.

Nothing in their taming prompted such consternation as the requirement by Anne Mark and Father Ivo, jointly charged with the boys' domestication, that they should be made less offensive to the eye and nostril. As a first step in this unwelcome regimen, the barber was called with his sharp implements, which naturally enough inspired dread among the Welsh youngsters. The first few bodily resisted being sheared and had to be manacled by men-at-arms. But when no blood was let, the others insisted on attending the spectacle en masse, forming a circle around the barber and sending up a threnody as they awaited their turns. When Anne inquired into the meaning of this dirgelike chorus, Cadi paused at first, plainly fearful that disclosure of too many cultural secrets might render the boys helpless before their gaolers. "They are singing 'March has horse's ears,' " the nurse finally revealed after being pressed for the third time.

"How playful," said Anne, taking the text for boyish teasing. "But this one's name is Gwion, I thought. Why do they call him March?"

The reference, said Cadi, satisfied that her interrogator was no sorceress, was to a legendary Lord March, who was so displeased by his endowment with horse's ears that, in order to maintain his unsightly secret, he immediately slew whoever shaved him. On the spot where this ever larger accumulation of unfortunate barbers was buried, there grew a field of reeds, upon which a bard came one day and made some cuttings to fashion himself a pipe. But when he tried to play it, all that came out were the words "March has horse's ears."

"Ah," said Anne, "so the boys are merely—"

"Anticipating their barber's death," the nurse replied. "They mean it only in mirth, my lady."

But it was no laughing matter when each boy, after his hair had been shorn and his fingernails clipped, stopped to gather every last lock and sliver of the cuttings, which he compressed into a tight ball and secreted on his person. As with the surrender of their names, Welsh lore had taught them that a stranger's possession of their bodily particles, however minute, exposed them to evil spells and imminent doom.

"Why not burn their cuttings?" asked Anne.

"Oh, no," said Cadi. "Ill health would then plague them all their days."

Beyond trying to deal with their superstitions so as not to induce frenzy, the sheriff understood that the surest way to keep his hostages from turning unruly was to channel their incessant energy. His plan for diverting the boys from the fact of their captivity centered on the need to exhaust them physically and, not entirely as an afterthought, on instructing them in the ways of civilization so that upon their return home, they might become a more industrious and less bellicose people.

The first aspect of this program proved easier. Soon after arising, the boys were escorted by mounted men-at-arms on a mile trot to the the Trent, where they swam and frolicked despite the chilliness of the water, and then quick-marched back within the castle gates. After a spell of helping the carters unload arriving supplies and other physical chores that, in some instances, were frankly invented to tax their muscles, the lads were allowed more joyful exercise in the bailey or, under close watch, in the meadow below the castle. They heaved spears thrilling distances and shot arrows with an accuracy that shamed the castle archers; they wrestled furiously, knocked one another dizzy with the quarterstaff, and raced about, some-times aimlessly, sometimes over a prescribed course, until they at last grew weary. To add a seeming purpose to the play, the sheriff divided the boys into two teams, closely matched by skills, and each Saturday they met, competing with a ferocity that both amused and frightened their guards. The score was kept cumulatively from week to week to sustain the boys' enthusiasm, with the eventual winners promised a visit to London and a small silver crucifix apiece. The latter, they allowed, was much the keener incentive.

As to their social skills, Anne sought to instruct the boys, through the services of Nurse Cadi, in how to eat, clean, dress, and comport themselves, all the while urging them to speak English. But hailing from a tribal people of patriarchal dictates, they scorned such an effort as mere maternal nagging and feared it would only nip their budding manhood. "Better a stalk than a blossom," said young Gruffydd, with an attractive toss of his head.

Father Ivo had rather more success ushering the boys through the workshops of Nottingham in the hope of stirring their interest in artisanry. The metalworking, wool dyeing, and barrel making were prime diversions, to the point where several of the boys entered upon apprenticeships in those crafts for a week at a time. Only ignominy, though, was attached by the young Welsh mind to the pleasures of agriculture when the lads were taken to the royal manor at Peverel and several private estates to observe the fieldwork. Breaking the earth's crust to plant crops their people scorned as sacrilege, and the back-breaking labor it required in no way endeared the process to the hostages. But in order to earn their twice-weekly ride in Sherwood, which the boys craved for its beauty and attendant sense of freedom, they were required to submit to a ration of farm work, as much to demystify it as to tire them. Farming was a livelihood, they concluded, fit only for slaves.

Master Sparks contributed to the civilizing effort by offering to teach reading and writing to any Welsh lad with the interest. A smallish fellow from Bethesda, the only one of even remotely bookish bent, applied and did so well that he was himself soon passing on his lessons to others too proud, suspicious, or lazy to avail themselves of the clerk's offer. Even Bartholomew le Gyw, proprietor of the Trip to Jerusalem Inn and himself half a Welshman, advanced the hostages' education by inviting them gratis to his alehouse once a week for an evening of drink, song, and celebration of their homeland. The sheriff saw in this pastime less a dissipation than a means to dispel sulkiness in the boys, provided the drink did not turn them rowdy. Nausea proved the greater menace for youngsters unused to the blessings of fermented grain; they either overcame the peril with a greenish hue to them or yielded to it by vomiting in the corner, calling manfully for another tankard and joining as loudly as before in the next ballad of unrequited love or lusty mayhem.

Familiarity bred neither contempt nor fondness among the Welsh boys for their wardens; an uncranky forbearance, rather, guided their conduct and slowly won the admiration of the castle officers. Each side, though, remained on constant alert against the other. Only the sight of the sheriff's daughters and their sweet smiles caused the lads' eyes to brighten. The girls were endlessly curious, of course, about the rough-hewn young guests in their midst; but their mother hovered in constant vigil, uncertain of the effects of their communing, even in the most innocent manner. A few of the younger boys took to playing tag with Angelique and Julia in the corridor connecting their apartments, and in time Anne invited several of them to attend her nightly storytelling to the girls. After the first week the boys reciprocated by instructing their hosts—in English—in assorted Welsh customs. The girls were charmed to learn, for example, that no self-respecting family would deny hospitality to any wayfarer in Wales; indeed, the traveler's feet would be washed as a sign of welcome, and inquiry as to the likely duration of the visitor's stay could not be even tactfully broached until at least several days had passed. "But if a guest should truly overstay," young Lloyd of Aber related to an accompaniment of giggles, "he may awaken to find that his hosts have moved their whole household away while he slumbered and left him alone in the clearing." The girls were astonished to hear, in a less endearing vein, that robbery of a deserving victim was held among the Welsh to be semiheroic, considering that the price for failure in the attempt was death. "With us, success at thievery is no commendation, even if Lord March himself were taken," Anne told the boys, placing her hands against the sides of her head in her best approximation of horses' ears.

By the third month of the hostages' stay, she and Philip had begun to bring along several of their favorites on the Sunday rides they took with their daughters through Sherwood. One such tangy afternoon in November, while the wind sang above the oaks and the horses pranced cracklingly over the leaf-strewn forest floor, the sheriff's party came to a clearing where they had planned a picnic. Before the girls could dismount, a boar poked its razor tusks out of a nearby thicket and gave a snort that caused Angelique's normally docile steed to bolt from its small rider's control. She shrieked, only quickening the horse's flight toward three of the Welsh boys who, having arrived at the clearing a few moments earlier, were fooling about on foot.

Seeing the onrushing animal and its panicked rider and aware that no one else in the group was positioned to intercept them and prevent a likely injury to the girl, the boys quelled the primal urge to scatter and instead stood their ground. But the horse did not slow until it had first crashed into the lads and left one of them, a white-haired boy of keen athletic skill named Penwyn, gasping for life with a broken rib cage. The collision jarred Angelique's horse back to its senses and allowed the child to be lifted unharmed from her saddle.

So grateful were the sheriff and his wife for this display of sacrificial valor that an antechamber in their apartment was set aside for Penwyn's recuperation, and Anne joined Cadi in ministering daily to the boy. To lift his spirits, the other fellows visited him regularly and could not help noting the affection and kindness that the sheriff's family lavished on Penwyn.

As part of the new comradery that grew among them all, even Gruf-fydd relented in his usual aloofness and began to attend Anne's nightly storytelling sessions. With his presence a barrier fell, and the Welsh boys vied to narrate folk tales of the Tylwyth Teg, called in English the Beautiful People, from the land of Faery. The girls listened with rapt attention to the antics of these small, magical creatures with their ugly faces, sallow skins, and crotchety dispositions, who lived in a country beneath the lakes of Snowdon. These unlovelies were renowned for their limited ability to count, their fondness for stealing babies and breaking crockery, their hatred of iron objects, and so deep-rooted an objection to the greensward being broken up for planting that they would harass any oxen they found at the task, drawing them off into wayward routes, over hill and dale, plough and all.

"They sound like hateful wretches," said Angelique, "who need a good spanking—and maybe more than one."

"If you even dare to dream of such a thing," said Gwion of the lilting voice, "you'll wake in the morning all black and blue."

"Then I should go after them with a big stick."

"And the stick would turn into a snake that bit you in five places."

Angelique gave a delicious shiver and subsided, eager for the next tale of rampant deviltry.

This nearly familial bond that had begun to form between the Marks and the Welsh boys was sorely tried a fortnight before Christmas, when one of the sergeants-at-arms permanently assigned to guard the hostages was found beaten at the end of a remote castle corridor, with his back and buttocks slashed by a knife. Though it was shadowy, the victim had no trouble identifying his attackers as a pair of the Welsh boys, who had been crouching in wait for him. But just which ones they were he could not tell for certain. Their likely motive, the sheriff learned upon pressing the constable, was vengeance. Ever since the hostages' arrival, the sergeant in question had been besmirching them, to their faces and behind their backs, as the issue of a degenerate race of heathens, skulking cowards instead of intrepid warriors, whose fathers couldn't tell in the course of the procreative act whether they were rutting with Welsh women or with goats—and since they habitually performed the act standing up, it made little difference which.

Philip called the whole Welsh contingent to his closet and said that in light of his growing fondness for them, he was much disappointed by their gross misconduct. "You should have come to me and spoken of this man's slanders," he told them sternly, "and not taken brutal measures on your own. All you've done is lend substance to his hateful words."

"Your other officers knew of this man's wretched behavior toward us," said Gruffydd, standing forward from his brethren. "Perhaps they, too, thought we deserved to be continually insulted."

"Their indifference was wrong as well," Philip said, "but you yourselves should have approached me."

"It is not our way," the king's grandson answered.

"Your way is worse. Brute force solves nothing."

"The sergeant has likely been stilled."

"Momentarily, perhaps—but some of his colleagues may take up his hate-mongering." The sheriff scanned their faces. "Now, which of you committed this mean act?"

Their eyes met his but yielded nothing; no one spoke.

"Then you'll stand here until those who did it have the courage to acknowledge as much."

The threat, in view of the expected consequences, was unavailing. The minutes dragged into hours, their strong frames began to slouch, and the room grew close from their animal warmth. Finally the sheriff ordered the boys confined to their quarters and put on half-rations until the attackers came forward. But they would not yield.

On the second day of their confinement, Cadi came to the sheriff, saying that under the Welsh code of honor, silence would forever cloak the identity of the perpetrators, and urged him not to insist upon distinguishing them from the lot. Philip, though, would not bow to their folkways in this regard, explaining to the nurse that English law and custom required the specific culprits to be identified. So the stalemate deepened; the boys' tempers rose with the stench of the excrement in their windowless quarters.

After another week, Philip cut their food rations again, causing Anne to complain that he was being merciless. "They have no room to exercise, so they don't need the nourishment," he answered tartly. The strain was beginning to wear on him as well.

On the morning of the second day before Christmas, Gruffydd asked to see the sheriff. The robust adolescent had become gaunt, his eyes lusterless from fatigue, but his shoulders remained square and his chin high as he presented himself, a fledgling chieftain ready to treat with the enemy. "The attackers were chosen by lot," he said. "Therefore, we ask that you treat us as if we were all the offenders."

"Our law does not deal in wholesale punishment," Philip explained. "Surely you understand that by now."

"But what else are you already imposing if it is not wholesale punishment? Therefore, whatever you would do to those who silenced your soldier, do to all of us—and we will be glad of it."

"You'll not relish the penalty."

"It cannot be much worse than what we're now enduring."

With nothing to be gained, and possibly much to be lost, by hewing to the letter of English jurisprudence, Philip rendered a summary judgment and ordered each Welsh lad to be given ten lashes across the back and buttocks by Master Sunbeam; additionally, the barber was instructed to leech a half-pint of blood from every boy in retribution for the copious amount that had spilled from the soldier's flesh. "But tell the hangman to modify his customary stroke," the sheriff advised his bailiff. "These are not archfelons."

Still sore but finally freed, the boys were readmitted to the great hall the following evening for a holiday banquet at which high spirits overflowed, along with Master le Gyw's happily provided godale. Midway through the festivities, Philip stood to say how glad he was to welcome back "our young guests from Wales, who, though they have done wrong even as they themselves were wronged, we thoroughly forgive. Without condoning their crime, I wish to credit them for their fortitude these past several weeks in standing together as one—and accepting their painful penalty as one. Unlike the officer of our garrison who abused them and is yet nursing his wounds, I say that if I had any Welsh blood within my veins, I should be proud indeed of it." He toasted the lads, who, apparently contrite from the look of them, cheered him back. Later, Angelique and Julia, their voices shy and tiny, sang the boys a Yule song that Cadi had taught them in Welsh. Not an eye in the hall remained dry.

That night in their bedchamber, Anne was stricken with melancholy at the boys' dreary prospect. "They are like caged little animals, wrenched from their homes," she said. "Their being here is not right. What is their crime? Their people despise the English yoke, so the king oppresses them the more for their fervor in resisting it."

"If he didn't, he'd soon have no kingdom left," Philip answered. "Rebellion spreads like fire if not quickly quenched."

"Then let him quench it—but don't steal innocent children to use against their parents. It's cowardly and altogether perverted."

"I am the king's sheriff, my dear—not his moral instructor. Besides, his actions regarding the Welsh, however unpleasant, strike me as hardly more objectionable than the fanaticism of the boys' fathers. Why not use the children for a while to teach their elders civility? Else generation will follow generation in these bloody immersions."

"But stealing off with the cream of their young manhood will not pacify them—it will only breed greater resentment."

"That remains to be seen."

Anne kicked the coverlet aside and sat up. "You always have an answer, Philip—are always quick to justify the crown. I worry that you blind yourself to what the king truly is—and so make yourself his prisoner, not his officer. You render him more than he deserves."

"For my sake more than his," he said, reaching a finger to her lips, to calm rather than to silence them, "the better to bear each day's burdens. Yet in fairness, I think his detractors grant the king too little. He has brought the realm more of order, wealth, and justice than ever it has known."

"At what cost? He rules by caprice, and by pique, and by bludgeoning whom he would. Every tax, every fine, every charter, the very laws themselves—all are what he says and can change like his humor in a twinkling. This is the stuff of tyranny. Yet you never question it—and I've come to doubt you even recognize it."

"If I didn't know better," he said, running a hand lovingly through her hair, "I'd guess the proud lord of Swanhill has you by the ear and fills it with his tiresome rancor. Heed his hawks and not his seditious talk."

"Thomas pines for a just monarch, nothing more. But you will not even concede the king may be something less."

"What would you have me do, my dear—send him letters of instruction to modify his conduct and burnish his charm? All I can do is strike a bargain with him as I have. I do as he commands so long as it's not patently mad or arrantly vicious. And in return for my uncarping service to the crown, I am granted entry to the ruling class. I, Philip Mark, without benefit of high birth or glittering fortune—I rule these shires. In the king's name, to be sure; but then all earthly power is somehow derived. The choice, my darling, is either to live constantly subject to fear and trembling, or to inspire them. Given the choice, I prefer the latter."

She slipped her head away from under his hand. "I think you delude yourself, Philip—and make yourself an accomplice to the king's excesses."

"Perhaps. But don't we all delude ourselves—every day, about a thousand things—to survive in a world so full of pain and strife? We insist it's God's handiwork that the many are ground down to nourish the few— and tell ourselves we cannot know the reason for this inequity. What is that if not sublime delusion, lest we all go mad from cursing the Almighty? Yet you would make the king earth's vilest fiend—and flay me for taking his part. At most, I can strive not to make matters worse. But if I did not persuade myself that my king strives as well, in his no doubt overcunning fashion, to better his realm and not merely fatten off it, I should hire out first thing in the morning for private service—become a steward, say, like the notorious Master Stryker, stealing silver at every opportunity from my lord Lambert."

And you would be entitled to it, thought Anne, rolling over to a restless slumber, and trying to separate lies from delusions, the king from God, and her husband from her lover.

A.D.
1212

·XXIX·

THE SPEED WITH WHICH the king's charger came clattering into the bailey was alarming enough, but the look on the sovereign's face as he dismounted, florid and sweating in the mid-August heat, alerted Philip that a crisis was at hand. The king hurriedly closed the distance between him and his sheriff, on hand to greet the royal party on its return from Wales, and in a voice burning with rage commanded, "Hang the hostages!"

Philip went numb. "Your Majesty?"

"You heard me—hang them! Hang them all—and at once!" The royal eyes were consumed by wildfire.

Dread so constricted the sheriff's throat that he could barely manage the strangled question. "May I—ask Your Majesty—the reason?"

"Reason? You ask the reason?" He pressed his face close by the sheriff's ear and, with a fury so palpable Philip feared he would bite it off the next instant, hissed, "Because your king commands it!"

Disbelief yielded to simple horror as Philip felt himself suddenly drowning in the malevolence that pulsed from his ruler in massive waves and was enveloping the bailey, now the castle, now the entire realm. "My lord, is there some—"

"Because it must be done! Because there is no other way such savages will ever understand!" He pushed by the sheriff. "We shall remain in the royal quarters without taking food or drink until you have sent word that the deed is done."

"Does Your Majesty—mean to include—your grandson as well?"

" 'All' means all!" the king screamed without looking back or slowing his pace. "All of them—and now!"

Philip stood immobilized by the enormity of the sin he had been ordered to commit. The king left him without recourse, with no leeway for appeal or pity. The merciless command, given in white heat, had no margin for cooling, either. Now—he had to act now. The children's lives and souls, their innocence and dearness, were of no consequence. Yet it was scarcely yesterday that all their hopes were so high the boys might soon be released and sent home to their hills.

As recently as Easter the king had met at Cambridge with his daughter Joan and Prince Llewellyn, her husband, to urge more thorough pacification of his rowdy people—and doubtless to remind him of the hostages held at Nottingham against the good behavior of their elders. With such comity in the air, Anne and her daughters had even gone a-Maying in Sherwood with Cadi and a dozen of the Welsh boys, bringing back great armloads of hawthorn boughs to brighten the castle. Indeed, all their spirits had been renewed by the sweet flowering of the earth. The sheriff, though, ever vigilant, had told himself he must not let down his guard; why, the king had just fined a favorite of his, Hugh de Neville, chief forester and preeminent cuckold of the realm, some £1400, equal to the annual profit of four or five plump manors, for allowing two political prisoners to escape. By that standard, anything less than the loss of his head would be a light reprimand if Philip allowed the hostages to flee. But if he had hardly welcomed playing keeper and nursemaid to thirty high-spirited lads—beautiful boys, bursting with good nature, to whom they had all grown attached—how was he now to summon the strength, and deaden his soul, to become their executioner? It had all gone awry because the king, as always his own worst enemy, kept ignoring the past.

His successes in subduing the Scots, the Irish, and the Welsh over the three years preceding had filled John's head with renewed dreams of grandeur even as his ongoing struggle with the pope had filled the royal coffers with the siphoned wealth of Holy Church. His martial potency thus enhanced, along with the sway of his government, the king's ambition to rewin his ancestral Angevin empire burst forth afresh. Every sheriff was ordered that spring to compile an updated roster of who owed the crown military service for the contemplated expedition to France. A sizable quantity of Flemish mercenaries was hired, and the knights of Poitou and Aquitaine were tentatively summoned to a midsummer gathering in anticipation of John's return by sea to French soil.

What the king chose to overlook were the incubating seeds of insurrection among elements of his baronage for whom a renewed call to arms in support of a foreign adventure remote from their interests was like striking flint to tinder. Though cowed by John's domestic conquests, which had solidified his grip on the realm, these malcontents among his leading vassals numbered more than a few friends and kin of the fugitive baron William Briouse, whose long persecution by the king had ended the year before with his death—and that of his wife and the sons she would not surrender to the crown. Enduring bitterness over such oppression was matched by resentment among an important group of northern barons and lords (of whom Eustace de Vesci, son-in-law to King William of Scotland, was the most prominent) over John's penchant for viewing small transgressions against the crown as telltale acts of virulent disloyalty. A third, yet more powerful group of barons, closer to the king's home counties and centered in the person of the proud and arrogant Robert fitz Walter, had likewise wearied of the crown's constant swings from harshness to appeasement to political blackmail. By turning indebtedness into a prime weapon of statecraft, John had managed to estrange his debtors among the nobility, not grapple them to him as he had intended. These three camps, many of whose members were closely tied by marriage, were not known to have become leagued in any formal conspiracy as yet, but the king's summons to war against France had surely deepened the thought. Who wished to carry colors abroad for such a sovereign?

Even as John had shattered the relative tranquility of the realm by moving to restore his lost grandeur on the Continent, so he had unwittingly inflamed it further by abandoning the crown's time-tested, if messy, policy toward the rambunctious Welsh. The king had achieved success against Llewellyn the previous summer by isolating him from his fellow chiefs and penning him up in the northwest corner of the country under a harsh treaty. But instead of continuing to play off the remaining lesser tribal leaders against one another and thereby blunting any unified action against the crown, John turned to a scheme of conquest and occupation. New castles were strategically erected, old royal fortresses strengthened, and crown raiding parties struck preemptively against concentrations of native forces. Seeing their homeland honeycombed with English strongholds, the Welsh feared for their survival as a people and, even with Llewellyn locked away in the north, took to bedeviling the royal garrisons. It was toward quelling such passionate outbursts that the king had summoned Llewellyn to Cambridge at Eastertide. What he had not counted on, according to reports reaching Nottingham, was Llewellyn's learning, in the course of the trip, of the heightened opposition to the king's policies among the baronage. On top of this, the pope had added his share of spice to the Welsh stew by declaring the natives free of fealty to the king and lifting the Interdict throughout Wales. Llewellyn soon persuaded himself that John would be too preoccupied by larger and more immediate concerns to mount a second invasion against Wales if, treaty or no treaty, the natives should rise up massively against the threatened extermination of their nationhood.

Accordingly, with the prince of Gwynedd resuming the leadership, Welsh warriors went on a rampage in June, storming crown fortresses, attacking their troops, and torching the royal stronghold of Swansea. The king, in the midst of preparations for his French expedition, had intended at first to send a small force to relieve his hard-pressed royal garrisons, thinking the Welsh disturbances a mere nuisance likely contrived by France and Rome in tandem to distract him from his planned invasion. But as the reports from Wales accumulated, John realized he could hardly hazard a major thrust at France while his homeland was being harried from the rear. Reluctantly, the French adventure was postponed, and instead the king readied an immense blow against the Welsh to subdue them once and for all time and then meld what remained of that rough race into the rest of the kingdom.

All of these happenings naturally bred trepidation at Nottingham Castle, where the safety of the young hostages was now thought to be imperiled. It was one thing when the rebel attacks had been undertaken by Llewellyn's rival chieftains, for the boys all came from the north of Wales. But once the prince of Gwynedd had cast his lot with the rest, how long would the king's hand be stayed from lashing out at the hostages? "I'm worried sick," Anne Mark told her husband. "He is a vengeful man."

The sheriff, while fearful, told himself that since the hostage taking had been a preventive measure—and had totally failed—there could be no profit in further abusing the boys; the crown's might would now be properly directed against their incorrigible fathers. But it was only a hope. "If the king is vengeful," Philip replied to her, "what shall we say of the Welsh for so lightly regarding their sons' lives?"

Anne, unable to deny Philip his point, put the same question to Nurse Cadi. "The prince has his whole people to think of," the plucky old Welsh woman answered, "and likely believes he must seize the day or it will pass forever—and all of Wales with it."

"And what of the boys?"

"Prince Llewellyn is not an overly sentimental man."

The sheriff's wistful hope that the king had put the hostages out of mind took on some substance as the scale of the planned Welsh invasion was revealed. All in England who held of the crown by knight service or sergeantry were summoned to a great muster to be held at Chester on the nineteenth of August. A thousand soldiers were being sent by William the Lion of Scotland, whose daughters John still held hostage. William the Marshal was due to arrive from Ireland with two hundred knights and a like number of sergeants. Boatloads of Flemish mercenaries were shortly to embark for Chester. And most telling of all, Philip and the other sheriffs were directed by Westminster to help enlist a civilian army of eight thousand ditchers, masons, carpenters, and common laborers who were to trail the crown's vast military sweep across Wales and without delay rebuild whatever royal forts had been destroyed and add enough new ones so that the vanquished could never rise again. To pay for all these troops and supplies, the royal treasury at Nottingham Castle swelled to a sum larger than anyone there had ever seen. "The king means to wipe the Welsh from the face of the earth," said Constable Aubrey, awed as they all were by the size and pace of the preparations.

The king went west to Wales at the beginning of August, accompanied by his half-brother, William Longsword, the bastard earl of Salisbury and John's chief military commander, to assess the need before deciding finally whether to unleash his mighty host later in the month. It was what they found there in the way of bloodied Englishmen that ignited the king's fury and prompted his order, the moment he arrived back at Nottingham, to hang the boy hostages.

"Does he truly mean it?" the sheriff, welling with anguish, asked of Longsword, who had arrived a moment after the king, "or might his seizure abate by morning?"

The earl, a freckled giant of a man, dismounted slowly and gave a grim shake of his oblong head. "I shouldn't chance it if I were you—his determination to see this done has grown, if anything, throughout our journey back. His command is as plain as it is painful."

"But what conceivable good will it do to hang these boys?"

"The king thinks it will send grim tidings to the Welsh—of the pitiless vengeance that shortly awaits them for having broken the peace again. It may well inspire dread, and possibly surrender, thus sparing many other lives—if not the boys'."

"It will inspire only undying hatred and make their resistance that much fiercer."

"I've tried to reason with him just as you say, Master Mark, but the king is persuaded the Welsh are truly degenerate—to behave as they have with such precious hostages held against them. He says the only thing they will understand is spilt blood and broken necks. 'They are a faithless race!' he shouts at me, quite beside himself with rage." The earl's claw of a hand fell sympathetically on Philip's shoulder. "You'd best do as he orders—and ask God's forgiveness."

The sheriff moved off with unwonted torpor, as if spellbound in a cloying mist. Upon reaching his closet, he ordered the constable to assemble all the Welsh boys in their quarters and have them closely guarded by whatever portion of the garrison was not already assigned to securing the king's safety. "See that the lads are told their monarch wishes to meet with them," Philip added, "so they'd best make themselves kempt and be on best behavior." Then he dragged himself to the sheriff's apartment, each step of the stairway a torture to scale, and told his wife that she must pack some things and prepare to take their daughters away from the castle for the next several days.

"What is it, Philip?" she asked, seeing the glazed sorrow in his eyes.

"I—cannot speak the words. You must not be here—nor the children—till it is done with."

She loosed so fierce a wail that the whole chamber seemed to vibrate with her grief. "Philip—you cannot! The king is a depraved monster!" Her tears flowed over his cheeks as she fell against him in a restraining embrace. "You must not do it! They are almost like—our very own children!"

He grasped her tight and felt her whole essence trembling. "What would you have me do? I've questioned him—tried to reason—"

"Beg for their lives! Fall on your knees if you must!"

"I'll be done for from that moment forth—dismissed as sheriff and possibly much worse, for arguing—questioning—"

"Then let me do it. I'll go to him—as a mother—and plead for them. He may listen to a woman."

"He'll think I've put you up to it—that I'm hiding behind your skirts—because it is so distasteful a task."

"Distasteful? Philip, it's an atrocity! You must let me try to—"

"I cannot, my darling wife." He pressed her to him. "It is not your place—or your business. I'll do what I can—I can do no more. Go ready yourself—and the girls."

Returning to his closet at a leaden pace, he summoned his clerk, the undersheriff, the constable, the bailiff, the chaplain—"and yes, let us have Sir Mitchell as well. Death by foul play is every bit the coroner's business," Philip added bitterly. "Being among us will doubtless simplify his task in determining if there be malice aforethought in these murders."

They filed in soundlessly, like shades recalled to life for a moment's judgment on the folly of the quick. Their eyes would not meet his at first, as if to spare themselves even that much contamination by so horrific an act as awaited his word. What pity they could manage for his plight, let alone the hostages', seemed crowded out by the presence within the castle of a pervasive and irresistible evil. "Your hangdog looks mirror my own emptied heart," the sheriff said at last after their collective silence threatened to entomb them. "I ask if you have any counsel for me."

All their eyes turned reflexively to the senior member among them. It was eighteen years since the chaplain had successfully begged for the lives of the castle garrison by prostrating himself before the Lionheart, claiming they had been powerless against the unsheathed swords of Prince John's party. Now that same perfidious prince was the king, and thirty other, no less innocent, lives were on the brink of extinction. Could the castle priest somehow perform a second miracle of entreaty with the ruler of the realm?

"It must not be done in silent submission," said Father Ivo.

"I did not receive the order silently," Philip replied.

"We have no doubt. Nevertheless, the order stands. At the very least, you must go to the king a second time and urge him to reconsider— on humane grounds if no other. He must be told the hangings will cost him far more than they can ever gain—and that eternity is his witness."

"Will the holy chaplain join the sheriff in voicing such a sentiment to the king?" Peter Mark asked, sparing his brother the request.

"He will," said the priest, "but I cannot think the king will credit any plea from one answerable to the pope. He is hate-addled on that."

The sheriff slumped in his chair and closed his eyes. "And if our earnest prayers to the king avail naught—what then?"

No one spoke for a time, and then finally the constable, the least esteemed among them, dared ask, "Could you not offer to resign your office rather than fulfill so hateful an order?"

"The king would decline the offer at once," said the undersheriff.

"Well, then—could you not say your resignation is an accomplished fact," Aubrey went on weakly, "citing fear of damnation of your eternal soul if you were to carry out—"

"What would resignation gain?" Sparks asked impatiently. "The best sheriff in England would be gone, and someone else—likely the under-sheriff or Master Manning—would be commanded to put the hostages to death—possibly followed by Master Mark himself on the ground of treason."

The bailiff nodded. "I hesitate to say so because it is not your way," Manning offered, "but if carrying out this grim command so grieves you, Master Mark, there is nothing for it but flight—and urgently." His words invited the immediate suspicion that the bailiff was seizing on this somber occasion to rid himself of a resented taskmaster. Sensing this, he promptly added, "Though it is no secret we have had our differences, Master Sheriff, I would sorely regret your departure—yet I can think of no other way to spare you the—"

"Where could the sheriff go?" Peter asked. "He is without powerful friends or financial resources—and we are many leagues from the seacoast. The king would soon hunt him down."

"Is there anyone the king might listen to?" Father Ivo asked after sighing heavily. "The Marshal is due in England momentarily—or possibly he would heed the earl of Chester—or even Ferrers—Derby is at least close at hand. Or perhaps a messenger could be speeded to Brewer, whose mastery of cruel remedies is without peer."

"It would take too long to reach any of them and bring them back here," Sparks said after a respectful moment. "Besides, the king's brother is said to be closer to him than anyone; yet Longsword has failed to dissuade him, so what hope is there that anyone else might succeed?"

"And what have you to offer us, Sir Mitchell?" asked the sheriff, having silently followed their wandering colloquy. "You would hold my office—go now if you will and tell the king that I malinger, and fear him to be temporarily deranged for issuing such a command, and dread God's wrath more than his own. Perhaps then he will reward you with the sheriffship, so you may perform this unspeakable act and not have to answer to the buzzing coroner for your oppression."

"Terrible," said Sir Mitchell, for once at a loss for words. "Terrible, terrible, terrible." His head hung low, but whether for the king's cruelty or from the sheriff's savage raillery was unclear.

"I thank you all kindly," Philip said, standing now, his frustration vented at the coroner's expense, "but plainly I must face the truth of my predicament—which is that I am entrapped by the nature of my service to the king. We each of us have heard he is capable of terrible acts of vengeance, merited or not, yet we have not ourselves been asked to perform them for him before now. My choice, then, is simple. Either I do as I am told—with a pretense of dignity and that it is not done in vain— and will be damned equally with him who commands me. Or I deny him to save my soul—in which case I am a dead man, or as good as one, and gain nothing but possibly a firmer niche in Heaven."

Only the bailiff did not concur. "Or you might concede, sire, that the whole regrettable business is beyond your power to alter and not torture yourself with self-recrimination."

Philip glanced at him dully. "It would be your way, I have no doubt, Master Manning—and perhaps it is the saner one. But for my part, one cannot commit an unconscionable act and then shrug innocently that another conceived it. If I must be an accomplice, I must pay the price."

"The price, though," Father Ivo submitted, "is not yours to say. It is to be negotiated between the Lord God Almighty and the devil."

"Would that someday I'll have you to intercede with them in my behalf, Father." Philip reached back for his sword and, while buckling it on, dismissed them all.

In the corridor outside the royal apartment, where the sheriff and the chaplain presented themselves to request a brief audience with the king, they heard the monarch bellow from behind the door, "Has it been done yet?"

The sheriff shook his head. The gesture was promptly relayed by the captain of the royal knight-guards.

"Then send away the priest—we have no interest in his pleadings!" the king roared. "And tell the sheriff he may have a single minute and no more. We weary of weak knees in times of tribulation."

Father Ivo bowed his head in prayer, then made the sign of the cross before Philip's filmy eyes and retreated to the sheriff's closet to await his return.

"Your Majesty," said Philip, with the most abject bow of his life. "I am grateful for this moment of—"

"What is the reason for the delay?" the king demanded from the far end of the chamber.

Philip absorbed at a glance the refinements of beauty and comfort that had been introduced into the royal quarters under Anne's guidance. It grieved him that they should grace the bedchamber of so callous a creature as this. "There are arrangements to be made, my lord."

"Then go and make them."

"We are proceeding—"

"Then why are you here—to ask again about our daughter's boy?"

"About all the boys, Your Majesty."

"What of them?" The king turned his back on the sheriff.

"I ask if you are entirely certain . . . that you wish such a—a grave step to be taken. The consequences could be—dire indeed, sire."

"You dispute an order of your king?"

"No, Your Majesty. I am—only—questioning it—out of—"

"Is there a difference?"

"In that I ask, with the greatest respect, sire, whether the order has—not perhaps been given in an excess of—heat."

"Heat? Of course, heat! How else should such an order be given— sweetly? With mournful hypocrisy?" The king whirled about and took half a dozen strides toward the sheriff. "You forget your place, Master Mark. You're an officer of the crown—whom we plucked from the jaws of death in a Capetian dungeon. Is this how you repay us—by daring to question our most painfully reached decision?"

"Out of the utmost devotion—and belief in Your Majesty's grace."

The king fell silent for a moment and moved within a few steps of Philip. "Man, do you think I don't know this is a nasty job?" In the emotion of the instant, he had abandoned the royal plural.

"I—cannot believe—that Your Majesty is—insensitive to—"

"There are grave issues at stake here, Master Mark." The king's tone had softened. "I felt much the same ten years ago when I had my nephew Arthur put to death. A hideous thing—yet unavoidable—just as in this case."

"Sire, these boys—I have watched them a full year now—and by no means as a doting uncle. They are fine lads, and innocent of any—"

"They are not innocent!" The softness was gone as quickly as it had come over him. "They lost their innocence the day they were born. The sins of their fathers are visited upon them. They are congenitally treach- erous—the whole race of them. I'm sick unto death of dealing with them."

The royal wrath was now fully unfurled; Philip desperately gauged how much further backtalk it would brook. "Sire, I fear you may be . . . unduly harsh in—your judgment of—"

"*We* are harsh? *They* are the ones who break the peace! They burn our castles—they gut our men—and would drink our blood—when they have solemnly pledged not to—"

"The boys have not done this, though, sire. All you achieve by hanging them is to turn their fathers into yet more fiercely crazed beasts."

"Or it may bring the bloody fools to their senses at last. We'll take that chance."

Philip saw the king's final grains of patience trickling away. "I—fear that such a gamble is a grave wrong, sire—a mortal sin in the eyes of God."

The king's head recoiled in anger. "And who are you now—the damned pope? Have we a papist for a sheriff—who lectures the king on his duty to the Almighty?"

"No, sire—just a man entitled to his own fervent beliefs."

"And are they so fervent that you say to us if we would put these hostages to death, we must take your own life first—that you would rather die than yield them up to this butcher of a king?"

A sly bemusement took possession of the royal countenance. The expression appeared yet more horrid to Philip than the mask of wrath the king was capable of donning and discarding on the instant. Was he cruelly testing him? Did he mean he would accept the sheriff's life in exchange for the Welsh boys'? Or that Philip had but to offer it to certify his moral passion, and the king would then relent? It was a dare that, once accepted, could the next moment send him to eternity. "I . . . I have not put it to you thus, sire."

"No indeed. Ergo, the question." The king's tone was nearly playful.

"I . . . had not considered the matter . . . in such terms."

"Nonetheless, if you tell me that, Master Mark, then I'll fully credit the strength of your conviction. Otherwise, it is mere pious flatulence." The king tilted his head sideways and gave his beard a few pensive stokes. "Say it, my devoted sheriff, and I will retire a moment or two to weigh the grave choice your words would leave me." He lowered his head and eyed Philip obliquely. "But we are used to such burdens. Are you going to say it, Master Mark—your life before theirs?"

I could kill him now, Philip thought—draw my sword and plunge it directly through that dark heart, twisting it to such a depth it could be removed only with all his innards clinging to the blade. Longsword himself would hack me to pieces on this same spot, but the world would embrace me for the deed, and all posterity know my name. . . .

"You have turned the issue on its head, Your Majesty." The word "perversion" must not cross his lips, he knew. "Why is my fervor the question? Why pit my courage in a contest against the lads' survival? No man's life is worth thirty others."

"Do you say the price is too dear or too slender for you?"

"I say the commodity should not be up for purchase."

"Ahhh . . . so you shrink from the ordeal, Master Mark."

"The ordeal is invented to evade the substance of my plea, sire." Trying to engage him was like shouting down an empty well; no reasoning presence dwelt at bottom—only a cold hollow.

"Your words mix boldness with discourtesy." There was steel now in his murderously resentful look. "Worse still, they are not yoked to any offer of sacrifice. Has no one told you the gods demand propitiation before they will answer prayers? We know now why you are no knight." The king turned from him with a triumphant snarl. "We might have made the bargain, too, sparing all—had you but tried us. A man willing to die for his convictions, even if they be counterfeit, cannot be blithely dismissed. But your mettle melted when put to the forge. Talk is easy, Master Mark. Now run and see to our instructions, comforted by the illusion you have done your feeble utmost to stunt the sovereign will."

In his closet, the sheriff asked the chaplain to solicit God's forgiveness for what he could not escape from. Ivo shook his head. "Fond as I am of you, Philip, and certain as it is you are honorable and God-fearing, I cannot— any more than you—defy my master. He is in Rome and holds me under the Interdict." The old priest's eyes were bleary. "To the lads I can administer final rites, but that is all."

Philip's mind drained, and the shell containing it hammered. "Then do not deny me this much, Father. Write a note at once to the abbot at Newstead, begging a few days' sanctuary for my wife and children—longer if need be. My brother Reginald will accompany them there within the hour if you will oblige me."

The chaplain nodded. "And then I'll pray for you as I can, sire."

The fatal instructions followed. Master Sunbeam, the shire hangman, was summoned and told to affix a stout rope to the finial atop every fourth merlon on the parapet along the north wall of the castle, beginning above the gatehouse and working around toward the great donjon tower. The hostages, he told Bailiff Manning, were to be brought to the roof three at a time, their legs manacled and their arms bound behind their backs, starting half an hour after sunset, with Gruffydd held for last. The constable was told to have the soldiery at the ready for use as need be. He might as well be arranging his own execution, Philip thought, marveling sourly at his attentiveness to every last mordant detail.

By the time the sheriff mounted the stairs, heart percussive and head pulpy like some massively impacted fruit as he struggled for breath, all was in readiness on the roof. Sunbeam, in his ceremonial mask, was positioned at the noose end of the first rope, ringed by half a dozen torchbearers and a like number of sergeants to assist in the proceedings. The bailiff stood nearby with two deputies while the balance of his officers remained below to guard the hostages and escort them to their doom. The chaplain hovered near the roof edge, lost in prayer. Posted to one side to bear witness to the ghastly spectacle were the coroner and Longsword, the king's surrogate.

Philip came up into the twilight, his eyes closed momentarily as if with reverence for his Maker, then braced his back and strode to the center of the rooftop arena. Through the crenellated ramparts he could see throngs of townspeople carrying torches through the streets and converging like so many jittery sparks in a fiery crescent beneath the castle walls. Their massed excitement over the pending calamity rushed upward on the moist evening air.

Philip glanced at Sunbeam, who was poised, throat aquiver, to undertake the crowning feat of his sorry career. If death-dealing agreed with him, let him gorge at this banquet. "Bring the first three!" the sheriff commanded, his voice unwavering and his manner resigned.

The hatch flew open shortly, and the bailiff's officers marched out the boy hostages, who had not been apprised of their imminent fate but could be in little doubt of it as they confronted that infernal scene. Philip knew them each by now. First came Rhys, who had grown up by the river Ogwen and was the finest bowman of all the Welsh lads; then Wylan of Conway, the handsome one who told their folktales with most relish; and finally blond Penwyn, who by his steadfastness had surely saved the sheriff's older daughter from crippling injury. Their eyes, proclaiming betrayal, fell upon him in unison as the bailiffs, two to each boy, dragged them toward the ropes and stood them a dozen feet from the sheriff.

"By command of the king," he declared, his eyes glittering in the torchlight that was already consuming their young faces, "John of England, Ireland, and Wales, and lands across the sea, in recompense for the extreme violation of his peace by the chieftains and warriors of your people, commands that you are to be hanged by the neck forthwith until you be dead." His tongue thick and parched, the sheriff added, "May God in Heaven take mercy on your souls—and those of your executioners."

That cream of Welsh youth did not quit the world gently. Though their arms and legs were secured, the boys resisted with their last shred of might and will, hurling themselves against their guards, crying out foul murder, yet never begging mercy. In their defiance they displayed such ultimate courage as to belie the king's disparagement of the Welsh as an unworthy breed. Young Rhys drove his shoulder into the hangman's stout belly, knocking him off his feet, and crashed a knee into the groin of one of the sergeants who gripped him, toppling them both. Master Sunbeam struggled upright and walloped the fallen boy in the face with a brass-knuckled glove, stunning him long enough for the hangman to slip the noose over his head and quickly tighten it. It took both sergeants and the hangman to drag Rhys, screaming and flailing the whole distance, to the edge of the parapet, hoist him high in the air, and pitch him out keening shrilly into the bottomless maw of night. The act was greeted by a roar from below, where the fused torchlight of the assemblage played against the castle wall, allowing them all to watch the boy's suspended body twitch and toss in its grotesque death agony until it was at last mercifully still.

Fair Wylan, who followed, lay down so he had to be hauled to the precipice like rubbish, awash in his own excrement. As his last act on earth he bit into the hangman's arm, drawing blood before they managed to hurl him to oblivion. By the time the executioners confronted Penwyn, Sunbeam was in no mood for further violent resistance. An instant after the boy began to scream "England murders Wales!" the hangman reached for a rock from the nearby siege pile and silenced him with so crushing a blow that the boy was almost surely dead before they dumped his limp form over the wall.

Oblivious to the tears that slipped down his face, Philip ordered all the remaining captives gagged as well as bound before being brought to the roof. Thereafter, the terror and fury that coursed through each upon hearing himself condemned was expressed only by his burning eyes and contorted limbs as he fought in vain against his killers.

By the third batch, the hangman, who was no longer a young man and had never been a spry one, was faint from his wounds and exertions and begged the sheriff for a respite. But Philip would not allow the atrocity to become protracted and ordered one of the sergeants standing in reserve to take Sunbeam's place. The soldier, though, stood frozen and, even under repeated command, would not move. The sheriff had the officer promptly borne off to gaol, but when the next in line as well refused to budge, Philip turned to Bailiff Manning himself in an appeal for help. That dour stalwart shot a searing glance at his commander in the tremulous torchlight, gave the merest nod of compliance, and went about the hideous chore with methodical resolve until the hangman had sufficiently regained his strength.

By the time the second dozen of the hostages had been dispatched, the sheriff knew for a certainty the single unsanctioned act he had to undertake, whatever the risk to his own neck. Indeed, his own survival mattered less now than the free exercise of his will to do, finally, as he saw fit. He owed it to his wife and children, to himself, and to whatever spirit passed for the Deity and permitted, for purposes beyond human imagining, a slaughter such as this.

The next-to-last threesome he could scarcely watch being wrestled to their grave. But when the final group emerged from below, with twenty-seven of their brethren already stretched lifeless just beyond their view, Philip stirred himself and moved closer to them than he had been to the others before passing sentence. The king's grandson, their leader from the moment of arrival, stood slightly to one side; he alone made no movement or gesture as the fatal words were pronounced. "In the case, however, of this youth, Gruffydd, son of Llewellyn, prince of Gwynedd," the sheriff went on in a voice growing stronger if hardly exultant, "by the power vested in me as magistrate of these counties of Nottinghamshire and Derbyshire, I hereby commute the sentence of death for the yet heavier burden of returning alive to his homeland with this memory fixed forever in his soul in order to testify to his people of the madness of their unending warfare against the crown."

So startling and perilous to its framer was this utterance that those who heard it relaxed their vigilance just long enough to allow Gruffydd to break loose and, with the tiny, quick steps his manacles allowed, charge toward the roof's edge, plainly intending to cast himself over the side with no hangman's noose to restrain his fall. Philip alone had the presence to knife after him and brought down the scuttling lad with a desperate lunge just a yard shy of the wall. The sheriff's left temple was gashed by the pitted roof surface, and with blood flowing down the side of his face, he ordered the still-thrashing boy carried off below. "Secure him in my apartment," he said to Manning, "and I will apprise the king when we are done."

After the twenty-ninth boy, Gwion of Rhostrifan, the last to die and as valiant as any, Father Ivo fell to his knees, and all the rest in that company of death followed in an impromptu Mass. Philip's lips, as caked as clay, could form no prayer beyond an inchoate murmur of despair. Longsword, who knelt beside him, was the first to rise. "I'll try to ease your path with the king," the earl said, looking down on the sheriff, "but you'd best not tarry in attending him."

Philip directed the corpses be left swaying in the night breeze and recovered at noonday on the morrow, allowing all to behold by stark daylight the full dimension of the crown's savagery. Then he slumped exhausted against the battlement, shock waves of bereavement assaulting him as the others trudged off, save for the chaplain, who prayed on in silent vigil. Against all reason, Philip blamed himself for not having somehow prevented the catastrophe. So benumbed by self-loathing did he grow that he could barely manage to rehearse his apologia to the king. By the time he reached the royal quarters, he was nearly in a trance, his face drawn and blood-caked, dimly supposing that his own death was soon to follow on that same rooftop Calvary.

If Longsword carried weight with his half-brother, it was not evident in the king's demeanor by the time Philip presented himself. "By what right do you defy the crown?" John howled in white heat. "We had this out—'all' meant *all!*"

That grisly night, though, and the massive insult to his humanity that he had endured had transformed the sheriff and made him, if not fearless before his deadly sovereign, at least immune now to ferocious rebuke. "By the right to render my lord king a higher service than any I have yet performed," he said, the words forming themselves from an inner well of becalmed nerve, "even at risk of paying dearly for the privilege."

"What higher service?" the king screamed. "There is no higher service than obedience! Our sheriffs are not asked to approve but to discharge the crown's commands."

"And it was largely done, sire—with the single exception—"

"But we invited no leeway—it was explicitly forbidden. Who are you to countermand the king?"

"A not insensate officer of the crown—"

"Not yet!"

"—who believed Your Majesty to be caught up in the passion of the moment and would be better served if one hostage survived to testify to his people of—"

"You made your repugnance for this task abundantly clear to us," the king interrupted, his fury still high but easing fractionally, "and we acknowledged it. Your choice then was unmistakable—to do as you were commanded or step aside for those man enough to perform a hateful but essential task. Yet you debate your treason with us."

"Is it treason to spare Your Majesty the greater infamy of destroying all the hostages than to leave one of them to bear witness to the crown's humanity?"

"But the one you chose to spare is our grandson—of a sort—and leaving him proclaims only that the king plays favorites with his blood. No, this way is worse than hanging them all. A king cannot favor his own under such circumstances—that's the entire point! A king must be hard, or he will be trampled."

"Hard, Your Majesty, but not heartless. Your reputation already suffers from a perceived want of mercy."

The royal visage purpled. "Who are you, my little upstart French soldier boy, to patronize your king?"

"One who is fool enough to speak the truth, my lord."

The king fell back a step and grasped the side of his neck as if afflicted with a sudden stab of pain. "Will you not honor my command, Master Mark?"

Philip sensed the king's ferocity seeping away, then hemorrhaging massively. "I ask in response that Your Majesty honor my years of unblemished service to the crown by reflecting until dawn on what I have said. And if you still wish the boy dead, then do the deed with your own hand—that is the way to make your point so that all will grasp it unmistakably—and have me hanged right after the boy."

The king shook his head, more in amazement than in refusal, and, having had his estimate of the sheriff's mettle shaken, waved him from his sight.

Philip ordered a keg of ale brought to the roof above the donjon, where he bathed his being in the darkness after dismissing the watchman. The air was still raw from those young, lifeless husks curing in the eternal blackness hardly a hundred feet behind him but as incorporeal as their fled souls, unsummonable now to hear any pleading of sorrow. Sparks sat with him for a time, much as he had on a similar mid-August night four years earlier when they first became acquainted. It was far from certain what fate the sunrise would hold for him, but his clerk speculated aloud that if the king were bent on having his sheriff's neck or the boy's, or both, he would have already done so.

"The bailiff is right," Sparks said after one particularly pregnant silence. "You must not blame yourself."

"The bailiff is an order-taker by nature—and highly skilled at it. What else would he say?"

"His words can still hold merit."

Philip shrugged. "I've been mulling a related matter. What can excuse a man from rendering avid service to a wicked master?"

"The question assumes he can separate the wicked from the good," said Sparks. "But few masters are so unalloyed in their character."

"Assuming a preponderance of wickedness . . ."

"The answer, sire, is that most men yearn to endure this life as long as they are able. But you, if I may be so direct, reach for something beyond. You wish to prevail over all life's seething meanness and, with but few weapons at your disposal, arrive at Heaven's gate still immaculately true to your own lights. Therein lies your torment."

The sheriff slid the ale keg toward him and refilled both their tankards. "So," he said, after taking a deep swallow, "you find me a bit of a simpleton, do you, Master Sparks?"

"A bit disconnected, I should say, sire—and reckless among so many circling serpents."

"Ought I not to have spared the boy?"

"Would that I had such courage, sire."

"But you say mine is misplaced."

"Courage is an impulse. It picks its own place and moment. It cannot be calculated, or it would never be attempted. Alas, I am a calculator."

Philip smiled. "And tell me, Jared, what is the life's ambition of a truly superior calculator?"

The little clerk took up his tankard. "To live long enough to fathom God's ways," he said, "or to die convinced the Almighty is a yet viler monster than our king." He drank and then added, with a trace of mirth, "If that make me either traitor or heretic, I'll follow you over the wall, should the need arise, come morning."

· XXX ·

BARTHOLOMEW LE GYW, though but half a Welshman, had been fond of saying, while hosting the hostages at his inn, that it was the spicier portion of him that derived from Wales.

The morning after the hangings, he was all Welsh, all grief, all loathing for king and crown, and well on his way to consuming the best bottle of thick Rhenish in his shuttered establishment. Having indelibly etched in mind the twisting bodies of the dear lads whose company had so delighted him for the year past, he was soon possessed by the conviction that the king of England had fixed on annihilating every last Welshman on earth—could half-Welshmen be far behind?—and laying waste every rock and rill of Wales. The great muster at Chester was now only four days distant, and if the king could so coldbloodedly dangle the finest of Welsh youth from the walls of Nottingham Castle, what a butchery he was about to inflict on their pastoral homeland! That crushing blow must not be loosed, Master le Gyw told himself. And somehow he had determined that he was to serve as the instrument of its prevention.

This sudden ambition, unimaginable but for his intake of the Rhenish, so moved the innkeeper that he felt compelled to share it with the castle chaplain and the sheriff's clerk, whom he spied from the doorway of the Trip as they threaded along the edge of the meadow on their way to the riverside. He sprang in pursuit and found them torn by revulsion over the preceding night's disaster, relieved by the king's apparent decision not to add his grandson and the sheriff to the toll, and, like himself, profoundly depressed by the immediate prospect of a Wales bled to death by a mighty swarm of royal invaders. "Precisely why we must prevent it," said le Gyw. "Pray God show us the way," he urged the chaplain, "while the king is still among us."

Ivo gave Sparks a glance that said the innkeeper, to judge by his words and aroma, had turned to his stock-in-trade for consolation. "Perhaps you might go directly to His Majesty yourself," the priest suggested drily, "and tell him he has done quite enough already to pacify the Welsh."

"You mock me, Father, but I'm in dead earnest. This king can be outwitted, for all his wiles, if we can but reach that craven heart."

Upon returning to the castle, Ivo and Sparks came upon Cadi, the Welsh boys' nurse, wandering the corridors half-mad with grief and without a comforting shoulder to absorb her tears. Young Gruffydd was locked away from her in the sheriff's apartment, closely guarded by the bailiff's deputies against any change of heart by the king or the boy's renewed impulse to do away with himself. Mistress Mark remained at Newstead Abbey, and no one else about was eager to be seen soothing the stunned Welsh crone for fear of being denounced a traitor by the king's wandering men. Under such circumstances, the chaplain thought it a blessing to guide Cadi down to the Trip, whose proprietor was at least a partial compatriot and a kindred soul, himself in need of condolence.

Lingering in their company for a time, Ivo was struck not so much by Cadi's tearful gratitude that Gruffydd had been spared as by her noting it was the first sign the king had ever given that the boy shared his blood. "Why, His Royal Highness has had next to nothing to do with the lad's mother since the day he gave her to the prince," the nurse remarked, warming with the malmsey le Gyw fed her, "so you'd hardly expect that he'd count the boy a royal grandson. Yet my mistress Joan, for all his coldness, has never ceased to love her father. Every month without fail, through all the years of rancor between the prince and the king, she writes to him of her abiding affection and gives what news she can in the hope it will gladden him."

In her maundering sorrow, Cadi spoke then of a dream she had been having repeatedly of late and which had come to her anew the horrid night before during a brief interlude of slumber. It sprang from an old Welsh tale, she said, about a cruel and oppressive prince who slew at whim. On the lake nearby his palace, an old boatman one day heard a feeble voice whispering, "Vengeance is mine," and a second voice asking, "When will it come?"—to which the first replied, "In the third generation." Soon thereafter, the prince was strolling in his garden when he heard a voice saying to him, "Vengeance will come," but he laughed it away as an idle figment and by no means tempered his conduct. One night a poor harper from the neighboring hills was ordered to come to the palace to play at a party for the birth of the prince's first grandson. Never had the harper witnessed such a gathering of nobles, such fine dress and food and drink and gaiety, and all danced with abandon to his sprightly tunes. At the midnight interlude he sat in a corner to rest himself but was soon startled to hear whispered in his ear the words "Vengeance is nigh," and to see a little bird appear and beckon him outside. It sang to him in a plaintive voice, leading the harper away from the palace and up into the hills on that moonless night. When he wearied and tried to rest, the bird urged him on and on, until finally the harper thought himself foolish and sought to return to the celebration. By then, though, the bird had vanished, and he soon lost his way and had to wait for morning. On waking and turning his eyes in the direction of the palace, he saw that it was no more—and that where it had been, the lake now covered, with his own harp floating upon the surface.

"In my dream," said Cadi, "Master Gruffydd is likewise of the third generation, and when the murderous king's host embarks from Chester, bent on slaying our people, a great flood engulfs him in a valley, and Wales is saved."

"Like Pharaoh's army," said the chaplain, "pursuing the children of Moses."

"Yes, Father. God in Heaven will destroy evil—and this king is surely evil incarnate."

Ivo glanced at le Gyw, whose eyes had grown big as walnuts as the nurse told her tale. "You see," said the innkeeper, "here is an undeniable omen. But we dare not rely wholly on the Lord—we must ourselves work for the disruption of the king's design."

When the chaplain encountered Sparks an hour later and learned of certain disquieting reports reaching the king's men, Father Ivo was possessed of the clinching element in a train of thought that Master le Gyw had set in motion by his intoxicated jabber at the riverside that morning. Insurrectionist rumblings among the northern shires had grown steadily since the king's now postponed plans to wage war anew on France had been made known in the spring. Some of Longsword's men had just lately heard talk of regicide and negotiations linking the malcontents among the English baronage with Philip of France, the papal court, and the Welsh rebels. "A few even contemplate who the new king will be," Sparks whispered to the chaplain, "and Longsword is said to be thankful the Flemish mercenaries are being reinforced momentarily so the king will have a reliable force on hand if mutiny breaks out while he roams the hinterlands."

At Ivo's instigation the pair of them returned to the Trip, whose keeper had closed it to the public out of respect for the hanged hostages, and sat with the commiserating le Gyw and Cadi to consider a notion of the chaplain's devising. "I am too old and feeble for hatching conspiracies," he said, "but not such an invalid I cannot yet do God's work." Since the king's daughter was in the habit of writing to her father from Wales, was it not plausible, he asked, that she would address him with great alarm if she had caught wind of grave evil awaiting the sovereign upon his expected invasion of Wales?

Cadi looked puzzled by the question, but le Gyw, his mind tumbling with anticipation, asked, "What sort of grave evil?"

"Oh, the gravest sort," said the chaplain. "A carefully laid plot to waylay the king and hack him to pieces."

"But the king has an army to prevent that," le Gyw objected.

"Well, then—prominent elements in it will have been bribed to desert him on the battlefield, allowing the Welsh to seize him and do their worst." The chaplain's mind was racing now, too. "And, of course, when word reaches Wales of the hostages' fate, the people's ferocity will know no bounds—and the plotters will become all the more fanatically resolute."

"Good," said le Gyw, "very good. And so the devoted Joan, in reporting this to the king, will naturally implore her father to withhold his forces from Wales, saying she risks all to divulge this dire secret and in this way hopes to save both John and Wales."

"Yes," said Ivo, "yes. It has the catch of conviction about it."

Cadi's puzzlement thickened. "But what letter is this you speak of? Where is it? How do you know of it?"

The chaplain deferred to le Gyw, who explained to the dazed nurse, "We know of it because it is our invention. The king, though, must not know that but think it perfectly authentic."

Cadi's pouchy face tightened shrewdly. "A forgery? You would foist a forgery on the king?"

"With your help, madam," said le Gyw, "so the words will ring with Joan's characteristic phrases and sentiments."

"With *my* help?"

"To save your people, my dear lady."

"Lord God Almighty in Heaven above!" Cadi crossed herself and fell back against the wall. But her compound invocation of the Deity was by no means a withdrawal from the scheme. "I write her letters for my mistress—or did so before being sent here."

"Excellent!" cried le Gyw, and turned to the priest. "Providence is with us."

"Possibly even the Lord Himself," said Ivo.

"You would need a thoroughly reliable messenger, of course," said Sparks, contributing for the first time since the lineaments of the intrigue had taken form.

"I have a nephew visiting with us from Glamorgan," said the innkeeper. "A quick lad—and second to none in his loathing of the English."

"He would need to be intensively schooled by Mistress Cadi," said Ivo, "and play the part to a fare-thee-well in case the king's officers doubt the authenticity of the letter and question him closely."

"A bright boy, as I say."

"Willing to die for Wales," asked Sparks, "and not divulge who put him up to this gross deceit?"

"I'll talk to him. As to divulging, he'd know no names but mine."

"And would you die without divulging?" Sparks pressed him.

"God's blood."

The others fell silent for a time, awaiting an appraisal by the clerk, whose shrewdness all at the castle readily acknowledged. "The notion has merit," he said, "but I doubt that the letter alone, however skillfully composed and properly delivered, would divert the king from so massive an enterprise as this Welsh expedition."

"Then he shall have further cause," said le Gyw. "Another warning, perhaps, hard on the heels of the first—yes, the very thing."

"But from a different quarter," Ivo added. "Scotland might do."

"Scotland," Sparks mused. "Yes . . . the king still holds the Lion's daughters—so William would naturally solicit the crown's favor. Ah, and his son-in-law Vesci is much in disrepute with the king, thus a plausible conduit to Scotland for word of insurrection."

"But how could we manufacture a letter from the Scottish king without his royal seal?" le Gyw asked.

Sparks pondered a moment. "The sheriff's seal, to which I have ready access, might be adapted, with a bit of handiwork, to resemble Scotland's— we have several examples of the latter in the castle annals. We could say—yes—that the seal was desecrated when the letter was intercepted by the king's enemies and opened—and then later recaptured through— through a defecting conspirator who—who asked a goodly price that was met by a friend of the king who insists on remaining nameless—for fear of reprisal. Something on that order."

The chaplain smiled archly. "You've been hiding unsuspected talents back there in the sheriff's closet, Jared—a fox in sheepskin. Thankfully, you are no counselor to the king."

The innkeeper's excitement grew. "There can be yet more fuel to our fire. While Father and our darling Cadi here compose the warning from Wales and Master Sparks tends to the wording and sealing of our Scottish letter, I'll reopen the Trip, offer gratis refreshment to the king's officers, and make sure the timbers crawl with reports of antiroyalist mischief from all quarters. In no time, they'll be resounding against the royal eardrum, discouraging him all the more."

They sat back, looking at one another in amazement at what they had so swiftly conjured. "Dare we do it," asked the priest, "even with the Lord's inspiration?"

"Dare we not?" the innkeeper asked back. "Weigh the risk against the reward—so much cruel and useless mayhem may be prevented, and a mad king thwarted in his warped purpose."

"And repaid for the hangings," said Sparks. Nothing about the plan pleased him more than its being at once preventive and retributive—an inspired piece of subterfuge. It had all flowed from them so effortlessly that he had not until that moment recognized the gravity of what they were contemplating. If the sheriff, though, for all his unswerving devotion to office, had defied the king as a matter of conscience, could his clerk shrink from the same challenge? And what could be a worthier gamble than to try to rescue a whole people, proud and decent, from the scourge of an English Attila? On the other hand—and Sparks specialized in weighing hands—caution had been his byword; why now toss it witlessly away? Again he looked to the sheriff as his moral exemplar. If life did not amount to more than mere survival on any terms it took, a man might as well be a fern. To live was to risk, and a moment such as this one, thrilling beyond calculation, would never come to him again. "It's thoroughgoing treason on our part, of course," he added, relishing the words, "however justifiable."

"A trick, not treason," le Gyw suggested.

"A treasonable trick, if you will."

"Should the sheriff not be apprised of our delicious confection?" the chaplain wondered. "Our failure would likely cost him his life, not to mention ours. So in fairness—"

"It would gain us nothing," Sparks countered at once, "and probably defeat the entire scheme. If he did not bar us outright from attempting it, he would be implicated by complicity. And if we persevered against his will, he might be moved by some perverse principle of duty to reveal the scheme to the crown—and the names of its authors as well."

Father Ivo shook his head. "He would not."

"Why even risk it?" asked the clerk.

"Perhaps well after the fact—if it had achieved its purpose—Master Mark could be advised," the chaplain persisted. "It might be balm to his conscience."

"His conscience is a two-edged sword," said Sparks, "that might even cut off our heads, dearly as he loves us. He knows only straight lines and distinguishes poorly among the categories of deceit. No, we best serve Master Mark, ourselves, and all of England and Wales by omitting the sheriff from this sinuous business. At any rate, we must hurry to it. Bartholomew, fetch your nephew and have Nurse fill him at once with the minutiae of Llewellyn's household."

The innkeeper leapt to his feet and made them all join hands in the center of the table, whereupon the priest and the nurse fell to their knees in prayer while the clerk and le Gyw sought the blessing of Providence in a long swallow of the Trip's finest ale.

At dinner in the great hall that evening, Longsword was seated to the king's right, and the sheriff, in preference to some magnate of the realm or any other royal officer, to the monarch's left. It was the first time Philip had been granted this distinction. What meaning could it have, he wondered, other than that the king had on reflection approved his overall conduct with the hostages, including his unsanctioned sparing of Gruffydd? Doubtless, Longsword had hymned the king's ear well into the wee hours on the subject. If John harbored any rancor toward his sheriff, it was well concealed at table, where his tone was cordial, even buoyant over the preparations for the imminent gathering of crown forces at Chester. Longsword seemed more somber over the likely outcome of the campaign, grumbling at the treacheries of the alien Welsh terrain.

"Our brother would not have sparkled among Alexander's generals, for whom all of Asia was *terra incognita* and thus the greater challenge," the king said to the sheriff with a smirk. A moment later he issued Philip an invitation to join him next morning on a royal hunt. There was nary an allusion to the grim events of the previous night, as if they had amounted to scarcely more than a disagreeable case of royal indigestion.

Toward the meal's end, the king confided to Philip, "All the sheriffs of our realm will be summoned hither shortly and advised of an extensive inquiry by our royal commission into the details of their official conduct. We have received many reports of irregularities and oppressions, especially from the barons of the north country, whom we wish to appease where their complaints are just."

"Aye, Your Majesty," Philip said simply, intending to appear neither apprehensive nor joyful at the receipt of such news.

"The Exchequer will send examiners to each shire—our clerks have too soft a life at Westminster—to audit every roll and tally—"

"Sire."

"—Nottingham Castle excepted, thanks to its exemplary service to the crown. Brewer says you have met every test—and then some."

What now—not only forgiveness but the king's acclaim? More for dangling hostages, if truth be told, than for any virtuosity of governance. Was he to fall to his knees in gratitude before this selfsame sovereign who only the night before had so beset him with murderous words and looks? "Sire," said Philip in modest acknowledgment.

" 'Sire'? 'Sire' is all?" The king's brows vaulted. "You have our commendation, Master Mark."

"I . . . am unaccustomed . . . to such, Your Majesty. Forgive my—"

"There will be an exhaustive inspection, moreover, of every royal forest and wood in the realm—to root out widely reported abuses. Here again, though, your counties are to be excused. De Lisle is said to have undertaken extensive reforms this past twelvemonth, though de Neville grouses his revenues are off somewhat. Have you had some part in Sir Brian's efforts in Sherwood?"

"Merely in an advisory capacity, my lord. Sir Brian deserves all—"

"Your modesty is becoming, Master Mark—if still inhuman. Hew to it—and to your industry in our name—and perhaps someday there will be rewards beyond exemption from our sternest scrutiny."

"I . . . shall be ever mindful . . . of my lord king's—"

At this instant a singularly dusty and bedraggled rider was admitted to the hall and hurried under guard to the dais, where one of the king's knights sought to relieve him of the message he had brought. But the young traveler resisted and whispered urgently to the knight, who reported to the king, "He's direct from Wales, he says, with an urgent letter from your daughter that can be seen by no eyes but yours."

The king glanced over curiously. "Let's have it, then. Our Joan is wont to write us of the heather's bloom and her favorite falcon's latest feat."

The lightheartedness passed the moment the king broke open the letter and began to read it. With each sentence his expression darkened, and by the end he was visibly agitated. He gave the letter to Longsword to read and said to the sheriff, "She writes of impending evil if we proceed on Wales—of a far-flung conspiracy she has learned of, and would-be regicide."

"To what length would she not go to deter Your Majesty?" at once asked the king's second chamberlain, seated beside Philip.

"She would not lie to her father."

"Perhaps to save her adopted homeland?"

The king glared at the deputy. "Say, rather, she may be misinformed or is being craftily used—but lie to us, never."

Longsword looked up on completing his reading. "It may be counterfeit, of course. Does it sound like my niece Joan, sire?"

"Very like. And note where she says the prince would flay her alive if he knew of her alerting us. Can it be doubted?"

The earl called the soiled messenger to him. "A rough ride, lad?"

"Aye, my lord." The youngster looked petrified in the presence of the mighty.

"Why wasn't a more grizzled man entrusted with so grave a letter?"

"I . . . cannot say, sire. My lady wanted speed above all."

"How long were you on the road?"

"Three days and a half, sire. I've had little of food or rest."

"We'll remedy that," said the king's general. "But first, son, tell me the name of the loftiest peak in Wales."

"Sire?"

"The tallest point in your homeland—what is it?"

"I . . . would it be Snowdon, sire? I've heard of no other quite so—"

"And what is the color of your mistress's hair?"

"Her hair, sire?"

"Is there an echo in here?" Longsword loomed vastly over the terrified messenger.

"I . . . sort of—brownish—reddish."

"And the prince's horse—tell me its name."

"Little Jupiter, my lord."

"And Master Gruffydd's pet collie dog?"

"I . . . I know of—no collie—that he . . . perhaps I am not—"

"Go clean yourself, lad," said the earl with a nod, "and we'll see you're well fed and bedded."

Within the half-hour, one of the bailiff's deputies was admitted to the hall bearing a second letter to the king that had been delivered to the castle gate by a rider who would not give his name. "King William's royal messenger was waylaid," the deputy reported, "and the letter regained only by clandestine and expensive means, according to its deliverer."

The word from Scotland, of dark alliances and purchased loyalties, when coupled with Joan's plea to spare both himself and Wales, sent the king into a storm. "There's rottenness in the air!" he cried. "How can we properly put down the barbarians on our frontier when there is the stench of conspiracy in our heartland? We like not fighting with one eye turned over our shoulder."

"I have not wanted to say so, sire," Longsword told him, "but my men are hearing every manner of disturbing report."

"Regarding?"

"They hear Montfort has been chosen by the conspirators to succeed you when—if—it were to—"

"Montfort! Lord help England—another crusader for the throne! And where do such reports stem from, William?"

"From the bottoms of alehouse tankards, possibly, my lord."

"What else do they say?"

"I would not belabor you with—"

"Spill it, dear brother."

"That the queen has lately been ravished at Windsor—and your boy Richard slain—and the royal treasury at Gloucester plundered."

"Have you thought to verify any—"

"I have sent men. So far there is not the slightest—"

"We like it not—not at all," said the king, who rose from his chair and marched off to the royal apartment.

The sheriff was called there an hour later and offered a glass of the best French wine in England. After his second sip, the king invited his assessment of the evening's happenings and how they should affect the planned assault against Wales. In all Philip's years of royal service, his opinion on policy had never before been solicited. Was this yet further reward for his splendid job of it as the crown's hangman? Or possibly a filament of conscience stirring deep within the king's scarred soul? "I would say, sire, that the return of their dead sons should bear adequate testament to the crown's wrath and will bring the Welsh to their senses as nothing else—even the fiery sweep of a great royal host across their perilous land."

"You'd leave be?" asked the king.

"Aye—especially if there be enemies lurking there who cannot be known until it were too late to counter."

"You would disband our gathering forces?"

"Till a later day and for a more promising battle—though I might direct a portion of them against any waverers among Your Majesty's northern baronage. Visitations in strength, so to speak—with blows dealt if proper tribute were not promptly forthcoming." He checked his tongue. "But I'm a mere sheriff, sire, and no high strategist."

"Our brother is, though," said the king, gesturing to Longsword, who hovered benignly over his shoulder, "and he concurs with you. We have more pressing matters than to spend our might squashing insects. Wales will weary itself and yield to our sway soon enough without our having to desolate it. Why devalue our own realm?"

Philip had not thought he would savor joy again for many a moon. Was it possible the Welsh boys had not died altogether in vain? He nodded, not willing to risk a smile, but his sore heart leapt.

"The earl will leave for Chester in the morning," the king continued, "to spread the word of our decampment. We wish our grandson to accompany him. Let the hostages' coffins follow hard on—dispatch a wagon train at the earliest possible moment—our knights and soldiers will escort it. And when the coffins reach Chester, our Gruffydd shall lead the cortege back to his people."

The sheriff struggled to restrain any show of satisfaction at the king's words lest it be seized on as ground for their withdrawal. "May I ask, Your Majesty, that my brother the undersheriff and our chaplain accompany the coffins as far as Chester?"

"If that is your wish, Master Mark."

Philip gave a half-bow and then turned to Longsword. "If I might, Your Lordship, I would urge that the boy remain manacled throughout the trip. He's a spirited lad, and in his grief may yet do something rash—to himself or the king's officers."

"I'll guard the boy myself," said the earl with an appreciative nod.

The sheriff's wife and daughters returned to the castle the next morning, in time to place a hawthorn bough inside each coffin and a kiss upon each lid as it was closed.

· XXXI ·

IN THE WEEK following the Welsh misfortune, the sheriff acquired the habit of taking a solitary ride through the forest, generally late in the day, to clear his head and let his soul be bathed by the deep bouquets of autumnal air. The muted colors of the season matched his browning mood as he meandered down long aisles of ancient oak and chestnut, which seemed more welcoming and surely less querulous than the sampling of humanity he generally encountered.

His sleep, oddly, had not been haunted by crazed visions of the hangings, though they naturally enough set off a flood of remorse in him each time they came to mind during his waking hours. This happened several times each day, for there were reminders of the dead lads almost everywhere—of their lithe movements and gritty laughter and deep resentment over being held captive—and no place more so than in his daughters' accusing eyes. No amount of explanation by their mother could rout their sadness or win their early forgiveness of a father who slew innocents because his king had ordered him to do so.

His dreams, as if in flight from guilt and self-flagellation, dwelt instead on his being summoned to Westminster for dubbing by the king, whose slur against Philip for his never-attained knighthood rankled in retrospect as much as any words spoken during their heated exchanges. This fantasized fulfillment of his innermost wish plainly stemmed from the king's parting remark to him about possible future rewards if Philip remained steadfast in his service. With such a hope seeded, no aspect of his interior life was more muddled now than the sheriff's sentiments toward his monarch. For John, to be fair about it, had never mistreated him, had advanced him while a young crown retainer in France, had rescued him from the living death of a French dungeon and brought him to England and elevated him to sheriff, had in the crisis just past absorbed his backtalk and, in the end, yielded to his partial defiance. True to the king's word, moreover, Nottingham Castle had been spared the plague of royal auditors lately afflicting most of the shires—even the personable and well-regarded Hubert de Burgh, Philip's former comrade-in-arms-and-gaol, was said to be facing censure and likely expulsion as sheriff in neighboring Lincolnshire. The worst that could be said of his own treatment by the king was that

Philip had not gained material wealth as had some others of the crown's imported French captains. But they had been serving as active warriors while he was essentially a castellan and tax-gatherer, an administrator and mollifier, with far less risk to his neck. Beyond that, Philip remained unpersuaded even now that the king was the endlessly scheming despot claimed by his growing legion of maligners. If he was guilty of oppressing some of his leading vassals, how else might he impose discipline on their unruly ranks and construct a cohesive nation? Even the hangings of the hostages, as barbaric as any act of John's reign, owed almost as much to the unmanageable tempers of the Welsh as to the king's avid refinement of the arts of cruelty.

If Philip himself lacked for rewards from high places, his wife had just been proffered one of a peculiarly troubling nature. She had, of course, deferred to him entirely in the matter, resolution of which he had vowed to reach in the course of the afternoon's ride in the wood. Lambert had promised her one of his best young gyrfalcons, a splendid creature she had watched being trained in the course of her monthly visits to Swanhill. Connoting as it did the rank of gentry, the gift somehow struck Philip as one degree too generous, too insinuating, too—well, or was it that the presentation of such a noble bird was the rough equivalent of Anne's being knighted, as if in his stead, and he was secretly cross? Surely he did not wish to appear petty or jealous in Anne's eyes, nor could he afford to insult the baron, whose friendship he deemed still vital to his tenure in office. Yet there was something about the notion that did not sit well with him, something that tampered with propriety. And where, now that he thought about it, would a single falcon be lodged at the castle? And what might Lambert ask in return for this token of high esteem?

These colliding questions filled his head as Philip dismounted and sat himself beneath a huge oak that stood where two of Sherwood's broadest avenues converged. As he peered up through the webwork of half-leafed branches, taking pleasure in the droll configurations of nature, he heard a brief rustling to his left, and before he could right himself, there materialized in front of him, as if from nowhere, that peerless marksman and master mischief-maker, Stuckey Woodfinch.

Since the sheriff had last seen him two years prior, the woodsman was somewhat altered in appearance. His hair was longer; he wore a full if somewhat scraggly beard; his body seemed more willowy; and instead of the foresters' usual woolen tunic dyed Lincoln green, his was the dun of deerskin—"I change to it in the autumn, the better to avoid detection," he explained, "as befits a secret agent of the crown. And as such, Master Sheriff, I seek you out and wish to speak of a troublous matter."

"And I as well, as chance would have it, Master Woodfinch." Several of the district bailiffs, it seemed, had lately reported that a number of villagers living within or on the edge of Sherwood had received gifts of venison and wood from one of the royal foresters who remained nameless because none of the recipients of this largesse was willing to identify him. "It occurred to me," said Philip, "that this admirable donor of the king's resources could be none other than yourself."

"Guilty as charged, sire," said Stuckey, doffing his cap with its snippet of peacock feather and bowing abjectly.

"A nice change, I grant you, from the old days when our officers of the forest specialized in extortion rather than charity—but nonetheless a violation of the king's laws against poaching and wasting."

"Not so, sire. Our arrangement, as your brother Peter put it to me, was that I might take what I wished from the wood, provided only that I did not turn it to profit—as faithfully I have not."

"Your takings were to be within reason."

"And have they not been? Is there a better reason to take than to comfort the needy? But if you find me in violation of our pact on that account, I'll gladly see it voided—indeed, have trailed you here to propose an altered understanding between us." He had done his part to see that the laws of the forest were evenhandedly enforced, he said, and that the foresters made no undue gain as a result. "Only I've decided, my lord sheriff—possibly I grow heady from the tanginess of all this forest air— that the king's rules are mean-spirited in the extreme and deny Sherwood's bounty to those most in want of it. Common folk without large holdings of land or other ancestral wealth require these trees for fuel and shelter, while the game is needed for food and its pelts for apparel. Yet only the rich can afford licenses for obtaining these lawfully, and the crown hoards the rest for itself." The woodsman knelt limberly beside the sheriff and regarded him with cool, clear eyes. "Now your wages, sire, may be plump enough for you to press home the king's laws, be they just or otherwise— mine are not. And lest you think I apply to you for better terms, strike the thought. There's not enough reward in all Christendom—and add the pagan provinces for good measure—to entice me further. My heart commands that I henceforth disregard harsh laws and work to undermine them

as best I can." He scooped up a handful of leaves and sifted through them
with his thumb, as if seeking something glittery or edible. "And so I would
strike a different bargain with you."

"But you cannot pick and choose among the king's laws," said the
sheriff, "any more than I can. The fact is that, by your own admission,
you waste his wood and poach in it—and intend to quicken your pace in
future—which makes you an outlaw. How, then, can I have any further
dealings with you?"

"Ahhh. But as to which of us is more an outlaw in truth, there may
be an earnest argument. Here, let me raise the matter impartially with
several denizens of the wood—boon acquaintances of mine yet much given
to fair-mindedness." So saying, he unslid a small ram's horn tied to his
belt by a thong and loosed a pair of raucous notes three times running
without pause for breath. Within moments, four fellows of robust propor-
tion arrived on foot, each from a different sector of the compass, and
bowed fulsomely before the presiding magistrate of the shire. "My terms
of employment, as you will recall, provided for my hiring several helpers,"
Woodfinch said airily, "and several others as well have flocked to us for
the free and wholesome life of the wood."

The sheriff acknowledged their considerable presence with a nod.

"Actually, you've more or less encountered each of these worthies
at some point in the past," their leader noted. "From the east arises
Master Owen Saffron, who you will doubtless recall prevailed in the quarterstaff contest at the Goose Fair two years ago—or was it three? Time
is a haze out here. Owen and I have hoisted many a tankard together at
the Leaping Stag before our taking to the wood. On the west you have
Master Alan Little, who was previously employed as the tollkeeper at
Rainworth crossing—until, that is, he was prosecuted for burdening travelers with excessive fees, and you found against him on tourn and through
some trickery by your masquerading brother. Rather than submitting to
the sheriff's tender sentence, Alan took refuge in the wood, knowing that
he had been unjustly accused. For while it was true he overcharged those
well able to afford it, he let by many others without means to satisfy the
king's toll."

Masters Saffron and Little rendered Philip a mocking salute, which
he returned from his still supine position.

"To the north you have Lot, son of the swinish miller at Swanhill
Manor," Woodfinch continued, "whose path you crossed in the course of

the castle's investigation of the ploughman Paul's murder some seasons back. And on the south I take pleasure presenting John-a-Dale, our resident troubadour, cook, arrow-maker, and blossom-sniffer. He performed his minstrelsy at the castle, he informs me, on the occasion of your gala banquet honoring His Tiny Greatness the earl of Derby—"

"And a wee old squeak of a fart he was, too," John inserted, "if you'll forgive my saying, sire—or even if you won't."

"John, as you see, has a way of speaking his mind," said Stuckey, "that somewhat reduced his opportunities for employment. Being nearly as fond of eating as dandling his lyre and his peter, he took to the wood and found our company to his liking." He gathered the group closer about him. "Now all of us have taken different names out here, though slyly connected to our old ones lest we forget who we were, so that our former personages cannot be traced by those who might wish us harm. Thus, my lieutenant, Master Owen Saffron, now styles himself Will Scarlet. Alan and John have merely traded their Christian names, and so have become John Little—or sometimes when his girth grows apace, Little John—and Alan-a-Dale. And since a 'lot' is close in meaning to 'much,' we are graced as well now with Much, the miller's son, who is glad to have fled his thieving father's trade." Stuckey bounced to his feet and summoned his colleagues still nearer.

"Good gentlemen," said the sheriff, rising as well in honor of their newly christened identities and managing a jollity he did not altogether feel amid this muscular pack.

"As for me," their captain went on, "your brother agreed from the first that my former identity might hamper my work among the foresters as your secret eye-in-the-wood and raise suspicion of some continuing link to the castle. So I've changed a bit in look and name. My 'Stuckey' always lacked the dignity with which I'm so famously gifted, so I've killed it outright. My 'Woodfinch' I've played around with a bit. 'Hood' rhymes with 'wood' and means a cloak of sorts, which is the purpose of my rechristening, after all. And still being fond of our feathered friends for their freedom of flight and sweetness of song, I sought a birdy name of the same length to replace 'finch'. Only 'eagle,' 'stork,' and 'robin' came to mind, with the first too predatory to suit my kindly nature and the second too ungainly to love. So there you have it."

"Have what?" asked Philip.

"My new name."

The sheriff wore a confounded look. Then it came to him. "What—Master Hood Robin? A bit odd, if you ask me. But I suppose if you're pleased by it . . ."

"No, it seemed to work better the other way 'round."

The sheriff said the rascal's name several times over, as if trying it on for size. "Robin—Hood? Robin Hood. Well, I grant you there is a certain something to it. I salute you, then, Master Hood, as well as the rest."

"And I, you, good sheriff. Yet we must not forget, sire, amid this orgy of mutual respect, the reason I've summoned these stout lads—to settle the matter of which of us is more truly an outlaw."

"And how is it that I qualify?" asked Philip, his feigned gaiety not yet altogether diminished.

"Why, by hanging the Welsh lads from the top of your castle walls, of course, when you had no reason."

The sheriff's face darkened. "I—cannot see how you—"

"We commend you, to be sure, for having spared the life of the prince's son—and in so doing, defying the king at your peril. Yet you first hanged the rest in cold blood, meekly yielding to an unjust command."

"Who are you, of all people, to pass judgment on—"

"Who better, sire, than sturdy yeomen such as we—the salt of the earth—without pretensions or fear of the truth? Besides, we have you heavily outnumbered."

Philip now sensed the gravity behind this surface play. "As it happens," he said in concession to his circumstance, "I did not meekly yield. I did my best to dissuade the king."

"So you tell us. But your 'best' plainly failed, so you performed the hangings anyway, knowing them to be ordered without just cause—making you a murderer in our eyes and of all those who love justice. Therefore, claim no higher moral ground, Master Mark, in telling us we violate the king's laws of the forest, which by God's right ought to be discarded."

The sheriff's discomfiture grew. The cheeky woodsman's words had lost all their comic edge and bristled with indignation. "My choice was nil," he answered softly, "and had I defied the king, another would have done the grim task."

"How can you be so certain?" Robin demanded. "When you finally chose to defy him, you saved the prince's son."

"The enormity of the sin left me ready to die by then. Yet I will say to you the king had a purpose in mind by taking the hostages in the first place—though I would not have endorsed it if asked—which was to spare still more bloodshed by—"

"By subjugating the Welsh and crushing their spirit."

"—discouraging further rebellion, as the Welsh well knew. Yet they defied the king, who in his own mind had no choice then but to make good the threat or forever after abandon hostage-taking as an instrument of—"

"So now you apologize profusely for the king's cruelty?"

"I'm only trying to explain what he must have—"

"The boys were killed to punish their fathers' conduct—and you were the instrument for that inexcusable act, no matter what it was the king, in his viciousness, may have thought he was accomplishing." Robin's voice was firm and prosecutorial. "Without the king at our disposal, we have only you, my good sheriff, to deal with and make pay for this grave offense against nature and humankind." They crowded closer, almost touching him now. "How say you, lads?"

"Hang this spineless sheriff in reprisal!" John Little exclaimed with no hint of mirth.

"This old oak is stout," added the miller's son, "and he is none too weighty. I know weights—falsifying them is my father's specialty."

"I'll strum him a dirge," said Alan, "as sad as ever he's heard."

"How can he hear it if he's dead?" asked Much.

"Then I'll do it while you fit him out with the rope."

"Me? *You* have the rope."

"A musician's fingers aren't meant for ropes, but I'll go back and fetch it if I was the one to bring it."

"We could just slit his throat and be done with it," John put in.

"If you kill me," said the sheriff, suspecting that his fate might be negotiable, "everyone will think it was done by a band of brigands and in no way linked to your true motive."

"He's right," said Robin. "We could write the king a letter to explain it—if we could write. Perhaps you'll do it for us, Master Mark, as your last act of kindness?"

"I say we spare him," Will Scarlet declared, "as he did the prince's son. Only let's exact a dear price for the favor."

And so the terms were unilaterally put. The brazen woodsman and his brassy comrades would quit all pretense of alliance with the royal foresters yet be left free to dwell there, taking wood and venison for themselves and those in utmost need. They could yet prey upon outlaws, evildoers, and the grossly rich—"oppressing only the oppressors as we see fit," was how Robin phrased it. For sparing him his life, the sheriff would agree that, throughout the remainder of his tenure at Nottingham, he would grant these renegades amnesty if ever they were taken by the king's men and prosecuted as common criminals.

"A generous bargain on my side," said the sheriff.

"But cheap for your life," said Scarlet.

"Have I a choice?"

"Surely. Accept or die."

"Then I accept," Philip said, thinking even as he spoke the words that a bargain made under duress was readily cancellable.

A.D.
1213

·XXXII·

SHE LAY STRETCHED AND FLOATING in sated reverie while the fragrant
June breeze played gently over them. His silvered gray mane and finely
pelted torso rose and fell rhythmically next to her as if in deep contentment—well deserved, she thought. The novelty of their passion had
yielded to a keener sense of its rewards and a fuller understanding of its
true place in her life. Their monthly rendezvous was not the center of her
existence but a sublime additive to it, the zest without which she might
have succumbed long before to a mood of dreary entrapment. The pleasure
and danger of their illicit love, each equally cause and effect, generated
an almost perfectly balanced tension within her that instantly induced a
state of arousal at the sight, or even the thought, of him.

Her postcoital imaginings, indulged in while he drowsed beside her,
had at first fixed on the chances of either Cicely, painfully hoisting a battle-
axe, or Philip, on horseback and wielding Thomas's old sword, bursting
in upon them in mid-copulation and bloodying the sheets with vengeful
blows. Her guilt diminished if scarcely conquered by habit, she dwelt now
instead on how her life would be transformed if she were somehow to
become the mistress of Swanhill and not merely its master's plaything.

Conditions at the castle were not straitened, to be sure, but neither
did they abound with comfort and delight. Her dowry had been all but
exhausted, and Philip, to whom the very scent of profit was the threshold
of extortion and dishonor, provided for her only as the sanctioned resources
of the crown allowed. Which was to say that any indulgence in luxury
would render the sheriff immediately suspect, given his renown for high
rectitude. Nothing at Nottingham was theirs, moreover, even their time

together; all was on loan and would endure only as long as Philip's tenure. At Swanhill, her life would surely be of an altogether different sort. It would expand, bloom, glitter. There would be air and light and color—and riches to suit a queen. She would be draped in elegant garments, embellished with gems and gold, wrapped in the warmest furs against the cold and damp. A horde of darting servants would attend her every want; tasty and varied dishes would be served to her nightly until she was surfeited; and once a week she would preside gaily over a banquet thronged by the magnates of the midlands. Best of all, there would be time to loll and play and simply enjoy her station; what good was mastery without interludes for dreamy idleness?

Its very purposefulness was the prime shortcoming of her life with Philip, she thought, and especially of its carnal aspect. It had become a tightly circumscribed and ritualistic act, though not altogether devoid of gratification, for he plied her as he pursued all other facets of his workday— forthrightly, conscientiously, methodically. Which was not to say his ploughing lacked sincerity but that it rarely varied in technique or degree of ardor. Their lovemaking, or what passed for it, was always done late at night, in the suffocating dark, on a bed too close by their children and servants and the entire castle complement to allow the shedding of constraint. And to their sheets he invariably took his office and its worries, with all the day's distractions, and thus often had to be dextrously aroused. Then he would proceed almost furtively, his smooth, dry body creeping about hers with a catlike litheness and pronging her to a point somewhere between a tickle and a marginal thrill but never to a full burst of ecstasy.

With Thomas it was all the other way—the difference between darkness and sunlight, between enclosure and release, between frustration and fulfillment. She was at the manor with him only in the daytime, of course, and only when Cicely was away; the staff was instructed to leave them in private after their ride or hunt together, with a modest table of refreshments and the lord's second-storey apartment at their disposal for the better part of the afternoon. They would embrace wherever and however long the urge dictated, cry out to their hearts' and loins' content, and play like young lovers in a poet's bower of delights. He was a feral but hardly ferocious bedmate who gloried in his physicality. A larger man than Philip in every way, the lord of Swanhill was proud of his endowment and used it with almost chivalric skill as he attended her in loving assault, consuming her every limb and curve and orifice as if the very marvels of creation, moving endlessly beside, over, under, and across her, sustaining his turgidity for long spells, punctuated by great screams and bellows of mutual release, then lulls for regathering energy and the renewal of their pleasure. His was the performance of a virtuoso lover, grown orgiastic in its frenzy by the fact it was partaken of but once monthly so that his muscles and organs might husband their force and fluids for that singular occasion. And yet his caresses were tender, never abusive, and he was not above playfulness when they entwined. Once he referred to his proud member as a little lance, and she tied a ribbon from her hair around the end of it while he roared at the festooning before they resumed lubricious combat.

For all these reasons, she knew, it was unfair to fault Philip as a lover and thereby justify her infidelity. Rather, as she had from the first, she told herself anew that she was serving him faithfully by servicing the foremost lord of the shire—a force to be reckoned with and kept at bay, as she surely had for the past several years. In rare moments of extreme fantasy, she even supposed Philip knew of her waywardness, understood its value to him, and approved.

"Much as I adore our time together and every fiber of your being," Thomas said to her suddenly in emerging from his semislumber, "this can't go on between us if it must depend on my devotion to the king as well as you."

Such great events had unfolded in May that he had had to cancel their liaison that month, thus doubling the passion he had brought with him to the bedchamber this day—and her surprise at his postcoital announcement. Indeed, this ought to have been a time for hope and rejoicing in view of all that had transpired, she thought. But on arriving at the manor, she had found him testy and distracted. Not wishing to cast a pall over their reunion, he promised to withhold mention of his grievances until after they had gone to bed. On their preliminary ride through the wood, he limited himself to recounting his lately completed service to the crown in Kent and the crushing of the threatened French invasion.

"Oh, what a stirring spectacle it was, my dear!" he exulted. "The flower of English soldiery—the massed might of the realm—all crowded together on one vast meadow. It was a sea of bright tents and jaunty pennants, a forest of lances, a mirror of glinting armor—and enough longbows to puncture three times over any maggoty Frenchman who might scale the cliffs at Dover and cast an envious eye over this precious kingdom."

Lambert had taken his son Guthrie and the other knights enfiefed to him to answer the crown's summons to the great muster at Barham Down, a few miles below Canterbury. King Philip Augustus, momentarily expecting the pope's blessing to unleash a holy war on England and its excommunicate monarch for his five years of "impious persecution" of the English clergy, had gathered an immense host in Flanders and an armada of well over a thousand vessels to transport it across the Channel. Sir Thomas rallied gladly to the royal colors; the king was unquestionably entitled to his services to stave off an invader. Never had England been so united in purpose as when its warriors all gathered in that little corner of Kent; never in men's memory had the menace been more pronounced or the excitement keener or so large and ready an army of resistance assembled. "Why, there were too many to be fed properly," Thomas went on, "so we had to be winnowed, with those of us of proven prowess retained and the rest sent home to stand ready if we faltered. And then our bloody ass of a king went and threw it all away!"

It was not just that John surrendered to Innocent; it was the abject manner of his yielding. Not only did he at last accept Stephen Langton as archbishop; he gave the pope his whole kingdom and declared it a vassal state of Rome. All England fell into instant discord as to whether this was a shrewd maneuver to outfox the French and the crown's other enemies by ensuring an end to papal condemnation or was a humiliation that made utterly pointless the kingdom's enduring defiance of Rome. Lambert himself suffered no cloudiness of judgment on this score. "Bad enough the king quit the field on the brink of glory, but why in so doing enslave us to a foreign ruler?" the baron groused to Anne on the last leg of their ride home. "The pope wants our lances and our money as well as our souls— and John has delivered them all up to him on a silver tray."

"But our chaplain, Ivo, no great admirer of the king, thinks it a stroke of genius," said Anne as they drew within sight of the Swanhill stables. "Not only has he ended the war with Rome when prolonging it could gain him little, but he has done it in such a way as to twist the pope around his finger, turning him from implacable foe into an overnight ally. He thus thwarts the French design on England by dashing all hope of papal sanction for war against an unholy state—and he silences the Scottish and Welsh complaint against paying fealty to an un-Christian king. Doubtless, too, His Holiness will now instruct his minions in the English clergy to heed closely the king's preference in all future appointments. A great gain in the aggregate, Ivo contends—albeit grudgingly."

"Yes, but at what a price! The pope as the overlord of us all—I dread the prospect. Let him tend to shepherding our eternal souls, not to siphoning off our earthly wealth and directing our valiant swords."

"But Father Ivo says King Richard did the very same—declared England the pope's fief."

"Which tells you how little Richard cared for England. Yet he did it only for the length of his reign—and remember, we were all crusaders for a season. John gives away England in perpetuity, the blasted dunce!"

"Honorius, the chronicler at Southwell, tells our priest that other nations have placed themselves under papal vassalage without dire results."

"Yes, but what enfeebled states? Poland—Sweden—Sicily—Portugal! For an England to likewise kneel to Rome is unforgivable degradation."

"Ivo says the real point of it all is to save the crown tens of thousands of pounds—that the pope, in return for the king's tender of the realm in expiation, will go easy on him in reclaiming the funds that the crown has stripped from Holy Church."

"I don't question the king's wiles—he is quite the wiliest ruler on the face of the earth, and more's the pity. It's his consummate hypocrisy that I despise. The man is utterly without scruples."

"But there was France poised to strike at us—"

"Then he ought to have let it strike—and hurled it back into the sea. That's what he summoned us all down to Kent to accomplish. And as it turned out, we hardly needed Rome to leash the French for us."

A fortnight after the king's calculated tender to the pope, the earl of Salisbury—that sturdy Longsword—led the navy John had built on a surprise dash across the Channel to where the French invasion fleet sat anchored at Damme on the Flemish coast. While the French army was off besieging Ghent and plundering the countryside, the English chopped the unguarded fleet to bits and brought back a mountain of booty.

"Yes," said Anne, "but if Longsword hadn't caught the French napping, we might have had a bloodbath on our soil—with the outcome far from certain."

" 'If,' you say—if, if, if. The world doesn't operate on ifs. The fact is that it happened, and the pope was not needed to save us."

"But you're judging after the fact, Thomas."

"And you're draining off my desire," he said, and swooped her from the saddle with an iron arm and gross laugh.

His still more pressing grievance the baron did not disclose to her until after their ardent embraces had subsided. "I had the word only yesterday—no doubt you have heard it at the castle. The king summons us all anew for a muster at Portsmouth next month. We are to sail off to Poitou with him, now that the pope sides with us and not the French, and replay that crack-brained dream of his to gain back his father's Angevin empire. But he is no Henry! The man cannot leave well enough alone!" Lambert rolled over and sat up in the bed. "He hasn't even been formally absolved yet, and Langton isn't due at Canterbury until next month—so what's John's almighty rush? He thinks of nothing but his mania. He's called his knights to service the past four years running, and now he calls us a second time within a few months' span. Is the man not plainly demented? He exhausts us—and the crown purse as well. Enough of fools' errands! Let him put his damned empire behind him—it is a chimera. And he has no right to demand our service abroad."

She swiveled on her side and raked a hand lightly and soothingly through the tangled silver hairs matting his chest. "But his father and brother did the same—and you rode to their colors in France."

"We fought then for Normandy and Brittany—many of us stem from there and had property and family interests to defend. England's lifestream courses with Norman and Breton blood, and I might ride there again if that were the king's purpose. But destiny and bad character have denied him those duchies, and so he turns to Poitou; yet what is that to us beyond his private obsession? Still he summons us—and declares that all who will not come must pay his scutage of two pounds per knight owed. He taxes us for war almost every year now—his father did so but one year in five, and even the gore-loving Richard limited himself to one year in three. They were men of valor, at least—this king is a conniver!"

"Shhh," said Anne. "Your temples throb."

"I will not go to Portsmouth!" he roared at the ceiling. "And I will not pay his damned scutage! And I don't care who knows it or what they do to me—or try to." He stayed her hand from its cosseting course and wrapped it within his. "There are many in the north who I know feel the same—men far mightier than I am—and a goodly number in East Anglia, and not a few in the home counties and the west country. John will use the pope to try to flay us who defy him—I see it coming. He enlisted us to side with him against Rome, and like sheep to the bellwether we followed. And now it suits him to throw us to the wolves—employ us as the meat for the carnage so his crazed yearning may be pursued."

She drew a deep breath and sat up shamelessly beside him, declining to drape the bedding over her womanliness. "You're leaping to conclusions, Thomas."

"The king is the one who would have me leap—I'm the one holding fast." He reached a hand to her shoulder, pressed it gently, then drew it down her cheek line and touched a finger to her lips. "I know your concern, my sweet—and the nature of our contract. If I stand firm against my king, I cannot lie down firm with my beloved, for her husband is second to none in devotion to his guileful sovereign." He shook his head. "It was always a sullied bargain but never insufferable to me before this. I think now you shall have to choose. I already have."

She searched into his eyes to gauge the staying strength of his disquiet. "You've known from the first there can be no choice for me, Thomas. I would be a traitor to Philip in every way if you acted against his interests."

"And what of my interests? Anne, I cannot hostage myself to your womb forever! If you cannot come to me because I must do what my heart dictates, then I must lose you. But the doing will not be mine alone."

"Is that what you wish—for us to part?"

"God, no!"

"Then why hasten it? Why not see what happens before you toss away your standing? Remain aloof if you wish, but don't become a hothead—it's not like you. Don't go with the king to France if it galls you so, but pay his scutage. To do otherwise is to declare yourself for insurrection when there may never be the need."

"I don't follow you."

"Philip confides to me that there are but two courses the kingdom can take. If John goes to France and by some chance prevails in his ambition, however addled, he'll return an invincible hero, having out-Richarded Richard. In that case, you would hardly want to be on his list of enemies and risk his mailed fist."

"I'd rather go down fighting than submit to a swinish king!"

"Shhhhh!" she hissed, more insistent now. "On the other hand—and this is by far the likelier course—the king will fail in France and return with his crown tarnished and loosened, his sway badly reduced—in which case he will have to deal with his vassals and meet their accumulated grievances. Then your voice will carry enhanced weight because you will have met your financial obligation to the crown, however unhappily."

He considered her words. "There is some plausibility to what you say."

She eased her palm against the grain of his beard and outlined his mouth with a fingertip. "Let me sweeten our bargain further. The next time there is a new officer to be installed at the castle—and Philip fears our sulky bailiff may leave soon for the army—I'll bend every effort to see that a man of your choice—one of your knights, perhaps, or some captain or sergeant you esteem—gains the post. Why shouldn't you have a hand, even if it's a bit remote, in the running of the shire? I should have to be forthright with Philip about it, of course."

He smiled broadly and drew her to him. "What a clever girl you are, my Anne of Tours—and quite the most manipulative creature on God's good earth."

"You're not entirely maladroit yourself, my lord, in the arts of manipulation," she said, and folded herself into his arms.

· XXXIII ·

"WHEN YOU SEIZED ME three summers ago and I withheld the truth, you were sorely aggrieved with me," said Ephraim, the olive-skinned Jew of Nottingham, "and now that I volunteer it, you are even more so. What would you have me do, sire?"

"Hew to the laws governing your people," the sheriff answered angrily.

"It was my intention. If I did not in these instances, sire, your brother was the cause."

The order from Westminster had been understood to be directly linked to the financing of the king's great military expedition to France. The crown's coffers, overflowing until lately with takings from the clergy, were about to be heavily reduced by whatever repayment settlement might be reached between the finally installed archbishop and the king's negotiators. And while the riches brought home from the smashed and looted French fleet at Damme would surely help defray the cost of the king's imminent adventure in Poitou, they would hardly compensate for the funds the pope was sure to demand for the forgiveness of his new English vassal. Thus, the crown turned once again to its favorite money-cow, the Jews, for a fresh milking. All their outstanding debts to the king were to be paid forthwith—which was to say the funds were to be seized—and all debts owing to the Jews were likewise to be demanded by the sheriffs. Toward that end, Bailiff Manning and his deputies invaded Ephraim's fine stone house without warning and disassembled its interior in search for the Jew's ledgers, official and secret ones alike.

Master Ephraim appeared at the castle the next morning and made sad-eyed confession of what even perfunctory examination of his private records would soon reveal: that a substantial number of loan contracts had once again been undertaken without registry at the castle, as the law demanded. But unlike the Jew's earlier transgression, when he bribed a clerk to enter such contracts as they became delinquent so that the bailiffs might collect the debts in his (and the crown's) behalf, these were turned over directly to a pair of bailiffs acting on their own to enforce the terms and pocket a fee for their services without sharing it with the crown. In effect, the moneylender was hiring his own collectors, who happened to be royal officers acting with the full force of the crown behind them but entirely without its knowledge.

"The undersheriff approached me with the scheme, sire," Ephraim related, "saying he felt I had been badly abused in the past and that he wished to compensate to a point." Peter Mark offered to collect overdue debts on any contracts the moneylender chose not to register for a fee of 25 percent, according to the Jew—"and when I said I welcomed his concern but thought that figure exorbitant compared with the crown's usual share, your brother made clear that this was to be no business of the crown's but our own private transaction, with its attendant risks, so the higher fee from me was necessary. What was I to say or do, sire?"

Philip eyed him coldly. "Why didn't you simply decline with thanks?"

"For all I knew, he was doing your bidding, sire."

"*My* bidding?"

"It's a common enough practice among sheriffs of the realm—though I grant you that your reputation is as an uncommon holder of the office."

"Then why didn't you ask the undersheriff if he spoke for me?"

"He'd have answered as he wished, without regard for the truth."

"Then why didn't you come to me by way of protecting yourself?"

"Because in so doing I would either have gained a mortal enemy in your brother or run the still greater risk of antagonizing you for failure to go along with your game. I was not in an enviable position—indeed, I rarely am."

"Yet you knew you would be doing wrong to cooperate with him."

"I knew I was being used by a castle officer—probably more than one—and that the castle has the power of life and death over me."

"You might have argued with Peter."

"It avails me naught to argue with my rulers and keepers, sire."

The sheriff pressed his lips tightly and strummed his fingertips against the tabletop. "Which of the bailiffs' deputies were a party to this business?"

"I thought it best not to ask. Your brother handled the transfer of information and silver—I dealt with no one else."

Philip's face was grimly contorted as he stood now and asked, "Do you volunteer this noxious intelligence in the hope I'll exempt these dealings from the crown's purview, fearing my brother's involvement will mortify me?"

"I come forward, sire, because you have my records, and I fear still worse pain if I fail to make a clean breast of it. My hope is that you'll fathom my plight and, possibly in view of your brother's hand in all of this, act toward me with some small show of mercy—of the sort rarely shown my people—for, as I say, you are thought to be an uncommon sheriff."

Philip sent the moneylender back to his shattered home and took the matter under advisement. What could the Jew have hoped to gain by inventing such a tale? But could his own brother have been so faithless after the innumerable instances of kindness he had bestowed on Peter? Could his repayment have been this low treachery? It made no sense. Yet Philip's heart ached, and the conviction took root that his younger brother's flawed character had not outgrown temptation and indeed succumbed to greed as he had feared it someday might.

In the privacy of his closet, the sheriff compared the Jew's listing of illicit contracts with the castle registry and saw they were omitted, thus yielding the crown nothing if the delinquent ones among them were pursued privately by the bailiffs. Then he reluctantly called in Peter, who immediately and indignantly denied Ephraim's story.

"Yet you've spoken of the Jew with regret in the past," Philip pressed him, "and urged our kindness toward him in the future."

"A mote of compassion hardly qualifies me as his collaborator—and his seducer, too, does he say?"

"He does." The sheriff managed to look more impatient than perturbed. "But why should the Jew make up such a fable? How can it benefit him?"

"By saving his hide at the expense of mine. Probably he assumes you'll go easier on him for fear that report of my alleged malfeasance would greatly embarrass our family—and you most of all."

Just possibly, Philip thought, but then noted that Peter was speaking more hurriedly than normal and his scalp line wore the sheen of sweat. "What if I were to bring him here to confront you with this accusation," he asked his brother blandly, "just to set the matter to rest?"

"And what would that accomplish? He'd hardly be likely to recant just because I were present."

"Then that would leave me with only your conduct to observe."

For the first time Peter looked genuinely alarmed. "You would entertain the word of a filthy Jew against that of your own brother?"

"Ah, so now Master Ephraim is filthy whereas before he had your commendation. Why so swift a change of heart?"

"I never conceived he would stoop to so low a device. All I ever said in his favor was that I thought him sorely put upon."

"And it didn't occur to you that you might ease his lot even while improving your own?"

"You sadden me, Philip. I know you get carried away by your own righteousness from time to time but never supposed it would extend to your suspecting your own brother of such baseness."

"Spoken with admirable outrage—but your words are hardly conclusive. Suppose, instead of my bringing in the Jew, I were to summon every deputy bailiff, tell them that you've confessed to me—and that they had better do likewise if they want to avoid a lengthy stay in our little purgatory of a gaol?"

"Do as you wish," Peter said, eyes glinting with open anger, "but I can't think how that would enhance your own standing, let alone mine."

"The truth might spring from it," Philip said, and waved Peter away.

The sheriff reported his distress to his wife, who from the first had feared that he was overinvesting love and confidence in his brothers, especially the younger one, by employing them at the castle. "If he has abused your trust, you must deal with him accordingly," said Anne. "But don't cut off your nose to spite your face—it will go far worse for you than for him."

All night the sheriff tossed with indecision, trying to determine what measures he would take if the Jew's charges had been lodged against an undersheriff who was someone other than his brother. And did this infraction, though heinous if true, nullify all Peter's other energetic efforts since being elevated to his office? But who could say if this disclosure of turpitude would prove to be the limit of it? Did the extortionate impulse not feed on its own success?

Determined to uncover the truth of Ephraim's accusation before deciding what to do about it, Philip elected to make good his threat to confront Peter with the moneylender and assess the authenticity of his response to the latter's charges. But when he arrived at his workplace in the morning, he found that the undersheriff, normally on the job before him, was nowhere about. Nor did casual inquiry produce an explanation. Within the hour, though, Deputy Bailiff Reginald Mark, the sheriff's older brother, appeared in his closet wearing the haggard look of a man little fortified by sleep and with much on his mind.

"He came to me in the night and confessed everything," Reginald said hoarsely. "It was all I could do to talk him out of hanging himself."

Philip dropped his head. "He is no true brother of mine anymore."

"He's consumed by remorse—if it's of any interest to you."

"Because of what he did or because he was found out?"

"Cool your fury, Philip—though I grasp it full well."

"Send him to me."

"He fears he'll dissolve at the very sight of you."

"Speed Peter here, or Master Sunbeam will put him out of his misery."

Within minutes the undersheriff was weeping out his tale of misguided ambition. He had wanted to gather only enough funds so he might buy a small freehold against the day he and his brother were cast from office—"as surely we will be someday soon, Philip. They think of us still as scheming Frenchmen—as the crown's vilest henchmen—as upstarts and interlopers—thieving rascals without any—"

"And you were determined to prove them right."

"I'll pay it all back, Philip—every penny. I'll work twice as hard as ever. Do what you will with me, but such a thing will never happen again. My crime is the height of ingratitude to a kind and trusting brother."

He felt more contempt than loathing for Peter's weakness and turned his boot heels from him before they were afloat in tears. "And which of the deputies did you conspire with?"

Now there was only silence from the bent figure on the floor.

"Well?"

"Why does it matter?"

"Because they were accessories and must be rooted out."

"It was my doing—leave them be."

"Perhaps that's another lie. Perhaps they came to you, my suggestible little brother, and said they badly missed getting the Jew's money and lured you into their easy game. Wasn't that it? Tell me something—anything—to mitigate your treachery."

Peter wept afresh for a time and then abruptly checked the flow. "It's of no matter. I was their superior, and supposedly knew better. They're not the ones who betrayed you—I was."

"I want their names, at any rate."

"I . . . will not say them."

"What?"

"Informing is ignoble—and would only double my guilt."

"And defiance will only double my wrath. Tell me which ones!"

"I cannot."

"You suppose I'll think the better of you for this perverse show of loyalty to fellow thieves?"

"Think what you will—I'll take the rack before betraying them."

"But you thought nothing of betraying me?"

"I—thought no harm would come of it. It was only the Jew's money being reduced. I . . . Don't ask me to add to my abominable—"

"You think I won't submit you to torture?"

"I am beyond thinking," Peter said, and dwindled to a puddle of misery.

The sheriff pondered how to clean up the unsightly mess. To send his brother to gaol was to ventilate the scandal and seriously undermine crown confidence in a sheriff who would employ a larcenous brother in the king's service. To sweep the thing into a dark corner and pretend it did not exist was equally unthinkable for a man of honor—and if it were revealed later, the cost would prove so much the dearer. For the moment, his urgent sense of retributive justice would have to be satisfied with an imperfect solution.

"Then I accept your resignation forthwith, Master Mark," Philip said, "and have no wish to lay eyes on you for some time to come." He turned his back on his brother. "We'll tell the world you've tired of your task here and gone on a pilgrimage to Bury St. Edmunds to ponder how best to pass your life henceforth. Now go."

The Jew's guilt was less neatly disposed of. Instigation of the crime aside, the fact remained that he had once again egregiously broken the king's commandment by failing to register contracts and then paying off bailiffs to make illicit collections on them. Seizing the unregistered loans as they were repaid would cure the first transgression; for the second, Philip settled on a month in gaol and promised Ephraim he would not prosecute him further if the Jew remained silent on the particulars. Dismemberment, he added without pause, was the time-tested antidote for a loose tongue.

As if the sheriff's thought were father to the deed, the moneylender did not survive the gaol a fortnight. Manning brought him the news with his usual functionary's dispassion: "Disemboweled, dismembered, and otherwise disfigured—as thorough a job as I've seen of it outside a butcher's shop."

"It was done within the gaol?"

"Entirely. Somebody who plainly wanted the Jew dead must have sneaked in a knife. The other prisoners all profess innocence, of course."

While he had gaoled the Jew for cause, the sheriff was assaulted now by a raging conscience. He had not disposed of the matter with impartial justice. Beyond his dismissal, Peter had been spared; the Jew had been tossed into the vipers' pit. And who more plausibly would have wanted him dead than the bailiffs who had conspired with Peter, supposed Ephraim knew their identities, and feared he would disclose them in return for mercy? Philip could not let the matter rest, he told himself, even while recognizing that to do so was likely his safest course.

The sheriff sent for Master Plunk and asked him why he thought Ephraim had been murdered.

"Why? Because he is—was—a thieving Jew," said the gaolkeep.

"I see. And how was there a knife available for this butchery?"

"It's beyond me, sire."

"I hope not, Master Plunk, or there'll be a new turnkey. I want the man who did this discovered—and whoever supplied him the knife."

"Sire?"

"And speedily."

"If I may, sire—he was only a Jew. The world's better off without their sort of pox."

"What if it were you, Master Plunk? Not all the world loves its gaolers, either. Would you want your guts splattered about the dungeon and not have us learn the evildoers?"

"I've already inquired, sire—no one will talk."

"Then inquire more forcefully—you know the way. And stop winking at them when you ask."

When Plunk returned at day's end with no progress to report, the sheriff told him that unless the killer or killers were identified by morning, he would hold every prisoner in the gaol responsible and charge the lot of them with murder.

"But if they inform, sire," Plunk confided, "they fear they'll be carved up as well."

"Tell them we'll remove the perpetrator from their presence—ready your apartment as a private cell. And tell them how we hang people here for the slimmest of causes—we're specialists at mass execution, remember, Master Plunk?"

By morning there were a dozen willing witnesses to the Jew's slaughter. The killer was a scrawny wretch awaiting trial for sheep-stealing, with scant chance for acquittal; the only question was whether he would fall to the hangman or merely suffer amputation and, possibly, blinding. Why, then, had he made matters worse for himself by slaying the Jew?

"I was told they wanted it done that way," the foul-smelling creature explained to the sheriff, "and it would go better for me if I did it for 'em."

"Who told you that?"

"The one that give me the knife."

"Which one was that?"

"One of the bailiff's men—he didn't say his name."

"If you saw him, could you remember?"

"Anything in it for me?"

Could he bring himself to lie outright, even to such refuse as this? "I can promise you nothing—except certain death if you withhold."

But before the deputy bailiffs could be paraded past this reeking lowlife, Sparks appeared with word that two of their number had fled the castle upon learning that the Jew's killer had been identified. "They took all their belongings from the dormitory without the least farewell," the clerk reported. "Master Manning is dumbfounded—they were two of his best men."

"A puzzlement indeed," said the sheriff, who chose not to inform the bailiff of his powerful suspicions, for the only other person who might have connected Peter's name with the deputies' disappearance was now mutilated carrion.

To replace Peter as undersheriff, Philip briefly considered appointing either the bailiff or the coroner. But he thought better of it, supposing that whatever might be gained in good will from the one selected would surely be lost by the enmity aroused in the other. "Besides, neither of them loves you," Anne counseled, "nor would ease your dealings with the crown."

"And who might serve that purpose?" Philip asked, respectful of her instincts in such matters.

"You might wish to consider Sir Eustace of Lowdham—he's a nephew of Lord Lambert and a doughty sort, the baron has mentioned in passing."

"Eustace is a tenant at Tickhill, which means he pays fealty to John de Lacy, who is well known to have flirted with rebellious elements."

"Yes, but you might thereby keep better track of the antiroyalist sentiment if Eustace plays Lacy well while remaining loyal to the crown— as Thomas says he assuredly is."

"You discuss such matters of state with Lambert? I thought your excursions to Swanhill were entirely social?"

"Social—with an underlay of practicality, bearing in mind the sheriff's interests," said Anne. "I suspect in this instance Sir Thomas wishes to advance the career of a deserving relative and, on hearing of Peter's departure, has not hesitated to use me to do his bidding. It seems a harmless enough stratagem, and to your mutual interest."

"Harmless, perhaps, but hardly innocent."

"At any rate, it can only strengthen your hand with the baron."

"Sir Eustace is said to be haughty," Sparks advised the sheriff when asked of the nominee's reputation, "but otherwise appears beyond reproach. He owes the crown no taxes—and was with the king in Poitou in '06."

"Let's have him in here, then," said Philip.

Before the new undersheriff could be installed, the murdered Jew's son, Benjamin, came to the castle at the sheriff's invitation. Taller and fairer than his father had been, the young man still plainly bore, in his every word and look, the emotional stigmata of the moneylender's slaughter. His wary eyes asked what further misery the king's men wished to visit on Nottingham's tiny tribe of resident Jews.

"Fret not," said Philip, subduing the impulse to offer him consolation. "No harm will come to you this day."

"What of the morrow, sire?" Benjamin asked, averting his eyes in the fear they would betray the depth of his hatred.

"Nor then," said the sheriff. "I summoned you only to advise that I have written Westminster regarding the untoward circumstances of your father's death and urged the crown to ease the usual death levy against his estate. I have done this out of consideration for both the suffering your family endures and an appearance of complicity in the act by castle officers. If we're in luck, they may order me to take no more than half the normal tax on a Jew's demise."

Benjamin gave a nearly imperceptible nod, then asked softly, "And what has luck to do with any judgment applied to our people?"

"I mean only that the matter is beyond my affecting once I have raised it with the king's counselors."

"Then why stir our hopes, sire, by disclosing your kind gesture?"

"I—thought only to ease your grief—if you knew that—"

"It will not resurrect my father."

The lad was bent on making it no easier for him. "I understand full well your bitterness, Master Benjamin—and sorely regret any part our officers might conceivably have played in—in . . ." He could say no more without seeming to confess the castle's gross liability in the case.

"We know of no participation by your men, sire—or even complicity. We know only that a hateful cutthroat set upon my father and none of his fellow prisoners could stay the brute's hand in time—"

"To that extent it's true. Our men were not directly—"

"—nor could anyone have possibly intervened while this depraved assassin struck again and again and completed his methodical desecration of a helpless being before their fascinated gaze. No, we fault none of your men for this isolated act of madness or even the circumstances leading up to it. And yourself least of all, sire—for how could such mayhem have been anticipated when you elected to drop a defenseless member of a reviled race into that cesspool of human dregs—?" He cut himself short and turned up his scornful face. "No, Master Sheriff, we charge no culpability whatever on the crown's part."

The youngster's sarcasm granted Philip no purchase for escaping censure. If Benjamin knew as well of Peter's part in his father's sorry end, he must have sensed more danger than profit in pressing the charge, even by intimation. "Then perhaps," the sheriff said, softly enough to concede the thrust of the lad's irony, "that aspect of the tragedy ought no longer to be dwelled upon."

"Surely not, sire." Benjamin shot a searing look at Philip. "But our God in Heaven knows the whole truth and will make His strict accounting in due course."

"Ours is a more forgiving God," said the sheriff, "and understands human frailties full well."

"Would that His worshipers might someday grant a semblance of understanding—dignity is too much to ask—to those who embrace Him not."

"You have a facile tongue and a clever mind, Master Benjamin—but they may land you in trouble in time if you overwork them."

"Or even if I do not. I thank you, sire, for your considerateness— however belated."

·XXXIV·

MATERIAL REWARDS BEGAN TO FLOW to the sheriff well within the first year of his having hanged the Welsh hostages. That the two occurrences might be causally connected he would not concede, even to himself. He was persuaded, rather, that some prizes were overdue him—and that his conduct of the king's dirty work merely supplied the crown with a pressing reminder to that effect.

At any rate, Philip suddenly found himself the custodian of several small manors, which added marginally to his wealth and self-esteem but greatly to the frequency of his headaches. While these estates held the potential to yield sizable profits to their holder, his first obligation was to reap enough from them to meet the various exactions of the crown; beyond that, it was a matter of close and prudent management of the crops, stock, and peasantry—unless, of course, the sheriff was inclined to treat the properties as booty and exploit them rudely, as most other crown cus- todians did. Such a course was hugely tempting since the grants endured only as long as the king chose to favor the custodian with a license to milk the holding. It was, of course, far easier to waste plump estates, which were usually bid for by the wealthy, who then set about systematically to recoup their investment. What was left for the likes of a modest crown officer such as Philip Mark were the leaner places, thankless chores to run and all but certifiably profitless for the scruple-ridden overseer. Nevertheless, Philip was determined to tend these bestowals faithfully, because he knew no other way—and because he hoped his industry might earn him yet choicer gleanings.

His first two holdings had belonged to Doun Bardolf, a formerly upstanding lord of the shire who had fallen into steep arrearage in his debts, and Robert of Muskham, an invalided knight who was said to have mismanaged his property of several hundred acres after winning it through double-dealing from a foolish scion of the Pendrake clan. Each holding required the sheriff to appear on the premises with some regularity and stir its tenants and villeins into productive labor. In both cases, large portions of the land had lain fallow too long while others had been depleted through overuse. The sheep, moveover, were heavily infected with the murrain, and the pigpens so poorly kept that most of their inmates had run wild.

To compound matters, within a month of his having taken hold of Robert's estate at Muskham, the sheriff learned that Ralph de Greasley had laid claim to it in his new wife's behalf, arguing that careful study of the tangled deed revealed that the Pendrakes had been unjustly deprived of the holding. Lady Olivia proffered the crown fifty pounds to regain it. That this course was being pursued as a vindictive measure against Philip— by Greasley for the sheriff's early censure of him over a tenant whom Sir Ralph had tyrannized, by Olivia for the sheriff's failure to prevent her disparagement in the form of an unwanted and unworthy husband—could not be seriously doubted. If he failed to challenge the Pendrake claim, Philip's clerk advised him, he would lose the property by default, so he instructed Sparks to draw up the necessary pleadings, and the battle was joined at the king's court of Chancery. The contest, with its accompanying fees, was made the more tolerable by a report from Swanhill, where Greasley had confided to Lambert at dinner that the suit over Muskham had frankly been undertaken "to discomfit our pusillanimous sheriff."

More gratifying though scarcely less problematic to Philip were the pair of wardships he was assigned. The elder of the two wards, Matthew of Hathersgate, already a large, loping lad by the age of twelve, had been living with his dissolute uncle, a drunken widower who turned the manor house into a sty, riding his horse through its rooms and corridors and fornicating with the slatternly housekeeper in front of the hearth while the boy went unwashed, unfed, and undisciplined. The uncle's sister, who lived with her commoner husband, a prosperous corn merchant, in a pretty cottage at Newark, a dozen or so miles above Nottingham on the Trent, had petitioned the crown to free the young heir to Hathersgate from such an unsuitable guardian. Since the estate was delinquent in its taxes, Westminster claimed the wardship for itself, awarding it to the sheriff instead of Matthew's aunt, whom Philip graciously invited to live at Hathersgate as his surrogate after expelling her brother, horse, slattern, and all.

Matthew, though, it soon became apparent, was unhappy with the exchange, finding his aunt as prissy and suffocating as she found him coarse and unbridled. The sheriff himself had to pull the boy aside and threaten to whip him if he failed to correct his behavior.

"I want to become a knight," Matthew announced as Philip rode the grounds with him one day in an effort to tame the lad's spirit. "Are you one?"

"A young fellow of quality would ask, 'Are you one, *sire?*' "

"All right, then."

"Say it."

"You already said it for me."

" 'You already said it for me, *sire.*' "

"Yes, *sire*. Sire, sire—but I have no sire—he's long dead. And the one I had in his stead you've driven off. So to hell with it."

Philip slammed the back of his gloved hand against the side of Matthew's face. "Your days of such talk are past."

The boy touched his smarting cheek, then glanced over at his punisher without remorse. "No knight would strike a lad so. Tell me I'm wrong— sire."

"I'm a soldier, Matthew, and not of the gentry. Soldiers thrive only through discipline—and since the king says you are in my charge, discipline is what you'll get, so accustom yourself."

"Yes—sire, sire, sire."

Andrew Lutteral, orphaned at ten, was an altogether different and easier boy. Heir to two modest estates, at West Bridgeford and Gamston, he had lost his mother during the birth of his sister. His father, who married the housekeeper and tried dutifully but vainly to tend to the needs of the family and property, had lately died in bed from overexertion. His wife's parents came to live with the family at Gamston, but all of them being commoners, custody passed to the crown, pending Andrew's coming of age. Having the sheriff named his guardian proved a source of pride to the boy, who gingerly petted Philip's stallion and asked at their first meeting if he might examine his sword and scabbard.

"Is it not too heavy to lift in combat, sire?" the lad inquired, hefting the weapon with both hands.

"A chore," the sheriff answered, "made lighter by urgency."

His wife invited the wards to spend a week at the castle as a gesture of kindness that succeeded in filling the boys with wonderment. From the roof of the donjon, the tallest structure in the shire, they thrilled to the vista of the town's twisting streets, the picket of cliffs edging it on the west, the rolling countryside to the east, with the silver thread of the Trent winding across its lush alluvial plain, and the great dark-green swath of forest to the north. All the mysteries of the brooding castle were revealed to them—the stench of the gaol, the cache of gleaming weaponry, the cellar stores and subterranean passageways, the royal apartment, even the crown treasury room, where hundred-pound barrels of silver pennies bulked in neat and numbered array. The sheriff himself provided the boys a lesson with the longbow (for which Matthew displayed a pronounced aptitude), while his nephew, Geoffrey, lately advanced to the captaincy of the castle guard, instructed them in the first principles of lethal swordplay. Anne and her daughters rode into the forest with the lads and taught them the names and calls of the birds and the shapes and aromas of the shrubs and wildflowers. After supper the children played by themselves for a time in the castle garden, the boys inquiring enviously of the girls' life at the castle and listening to their tales of far-off France, where knights were said still to charge about on heroic errands. "Mostly, though, they slaughter peasants, Papa says," Angelique remarked.

"That's a bunch of shit," said Matthew.

"You have a foul mouth," said Angelique, "and ought to cleanse it."

"Everyone else gives me instructions—I don't need more of them from a piss-ant like you," the boy growled and stormed off.

Andrew, in all innocence, soon afterward asked Julia if it was true that her father had hanged the Welsh boys because they had misbehaved—a reasonable enough question for a ten-year-old but one that managed to send the girl fleeing in tears. Which was to say that fondness, let alone love, failed to bloom at first sight among the youngsters.

But its eventual flowering was a notion not beyond the realm of possibility in Anne Mark's mind. They were nice-looking lads with enough pedigree and property to establish her daughters as gentry yet were not of such grand standing as to place them hopelessly out of the Marks' reach. "Philip," she said, "you must attend scrupulously to your wards' holdings and their upbringing."

"To be sure. It's my duty—and nature."

"I'm not thinking so much of your obligation to the crown as that our daughters will want fit husbands someday not long distant."

"Aren't you being more than a bit previous?"

"Our opportunities are scant. I think we must nurture the prospect."

Not as an idle afterthought, then, did Philip send each boy a splendid bow of yew and quiver of arrows with best goose feathers, while Anne added a volume on loan from the small castle library, accompanied by a weekly visit from Sparks, who tutored them in literacy and numbers. Every second month the wards passed a stimulating few days at the castle, and fondness slowly grew among the children.

Properly cultivating the estates in wardship was a harder problem. The task required a knowledgeable and constant overseer, not Philip's intermittent visits and a few hortatory words to the field men. He spoke of the need to Anne, who had occasion to mention it to Sparks, who said at once, "I know the perfect person—if we can obtain his services. Master Blake withers on the vine at Swanhill."

Yes—who better than a former reeve of a great manor, and one well regarded for his conscientiousness? Yet the idea made Anne uneasy. What knowledge the denizens of Swanhill possessed of their lord's paramour, there was no way of telling; her monthly appearance there, though, must surely have aroused the naturally lascivious bent of their imaginings. "Your concern for Master Blake, while touching, seems inordinate," she said.

"He suffers unduly from the field work," said Sparks. "He's over fifty now and not truly able to—"

"I think it goes beyond that. You'd best confide in me, Jared."

The clerk's eyes tightened with anxiety. "Madam, I beg you not to—"

"I thought we understood each other well."

Sparks nodded and then, almost with relief, quietly disclosed his dark secret. "Master Blake is my own father. I learned the truth of it only when my mother was on her deathbed." Her late husband, the smith of Swanhill, had long been prone to bouts of drunkenness when he beat his wife and abused her in coitus. As the young Blake came to frequent the smithy, discoursing with her amiably from time to time, an attachment formed between them and culminated in a singular act of mutual adultery; Jared was the result. His paternity Mother Sparks never disclosed to her husband; indeed, Blake himself was not told of it until after the boy had left the manor for Southwell Minster and an anticipated career in cassock. "It was the last thing she said to me before she died," Jared told Anne, "and asked that I look after Master Blake as I was able."

She was touched by this revelation and, knowing the erstwhile reeve had been exiled to menial labor and was thus remote from manor-house chatter, saw scant menace to her in his employment by Philip. "I will proffer to Lord Lambert for his freedom," she said, thinking to make a gift of Blake's services to her husband from the waning residue of her dowry and thereby purchase as well a yet firmer seal to Sparks's lips.

The baron proved reluctant to part with his bondsman, however far reduced in rank. "He works well yet, I'm told—no doubt in retribution."

"Philip is in dire need of a man like this. He is worth our investment of five pounds—if you would consider such an offering," said Anne.

"I don't care for your silver, my dear," said Sir Thomas.

"Seven pounds is the most we could manage."

"I'm not a slave trader, Anne."

"Splendid. Then concede you've mistreated the churl and manumit him."

"I concede nothing. The fellow grew puffed with his own importance. Besides, I'm against manumission on principle—there's no end to it once you begin."

"Yet you freed your present smith's younger brother for a career in orders—he is Philip's clerk now, of course."

"That was long ago, and his father paid a proper fine."

"So shall we then—say, three pounds and my undying gratitude."

"Make it five, my little vixen—reeves are hard to come by—and preserve your gratitude," the baron said and, the bargain consummated, brushed his lips along the curvature of her spine en route to further consummate business.

Within the fortnight, the former reeve and his forlorn wife were miraculously retrieved from their daily purgatory and transplanted to Hathersgate, where they were given freedom, a tidy cottage, fresh garments, some stock, and a young gray mare much like Blake's old one in smallish size and easy disposition. He cycled among the sheriff's holdings and, having soon enough regained his command of detail and the workings of the servile heart, had Philip's custodial fields green, flocks healthy, and barns and fences well mended. Mistress Blake, childless as she was, lent a ready ear and kindly temperament to young Matthew, the heir to Hathersgate, who took to her like a newfound mother.

Highly useful as Blake at once became to Philip, he could be of no help to the sheriff when the largest holding yet fell to him—custody of Bulwell Manor, a collection of eighteen contentious tenants and twice that many subtenants each vying to extract every last advantage from his piece of the crown-held estate a few miles north of Nottingham. To superintend this complex property, Philip recalled his younger brother from his three-month penance. "It's a hard job," he said to Peter, "and if I'm right, you'll not thank me for such employment."

"I thank you for the chance to redeem myself in your eyes."

"I don't want your gratitude—I want your faithfulness to my tenets. Sparks will review the Bulwell accounts twice monthly, so be advised. Any irregularities—any partaking beyond your wages—will make us quits for good, Peter, I vow it."

Amid this flurry of dubious prizes coming to the sheriff was word of an expedited ruling by the Chancery court at Westminster that the Pendrakes' claim to Robert of Muskham's estate had prevailed. As a consolation for his lost custodianship, Philip was awarded Lady Olivia's fifty-pound proffer to the crown. He sent his nephew, Geoffrey, to Pendrake Hall with a report of the ruling and the message that title to the holding would be transferred as soon as Philip was in receipt of his award.

This straightforward communiqué brought Sir Ralph de Greasley flying to the castle in protest. "You insult us, Master Mark," he asserted, "and not for the first time."

"No insult was intended, I assure you, sire," said the sheriff.

"Then do you doubt we're good for your grubby fifty pounds?"

"Not in the least. And when I have them, you shall have Robert's fields at Muskham."

"Why not the other way around?"

"Because I am not a wealthy man, whereas such a sum might readily slip the minds of the master and mistress of Pendrake, and I should not relish dunning such prominent residents of the shire."

"Other sheriffs have been known not to surrender properties in their hands," said Greasley, "even when the debt on them has been discharged."

"I am not other sheriffs, as you and Lady Olivia know full well. I await receipt of her proffer."

But the money was not forthcoming, and the sheriff retained the manor and saw to its continued maintenance. The standoff, soon made public knowledge, prompted the coroner to remark to the castle chaplain, "This is the way Sheriff Brewer battened—by holding until he was bribed with a larger payment. With each new bestowal he wins, Master Mark grows more moved by avarice than saintly devotion to duty." Sir Mitchell shrugged and added, "I've always supposed it would just be a matter of time."

· XXXV ·

ON THE FRONT STEPS of Winchester Cathedral the twentieth day of July, King John exchanged an embrace of reconciliation with Archbishop Stephen Langton, lately readmitted to England. The prelate absolved the monarch of past sins against Holy Church and welcomed him back into the fold of dutiful worshipers. In return, a vow was extracted from the sovereign that he would not only deal benevolently with the clergy but also restore the good laws of his predecessors, desist from any vile practices of his own, and render justice to all his subjects according to the judgment of his courts.

Nowhere was this epochal event greeted with greater joy than at Lenton Priory in Nottingham, where Father Clement de Beaupré was inspired by it to the point of fixation. His holy house, he felt, ought to be among the first to commemorate the occasion, along with the lifting of the Interdict, which would soon follow and release a flood of pilgrims across the kingdom. To attract its fair portion of these holy wayfarers, not to mention their long-withheld offerings, Lenton needed some new lure. The miraculous clock in the priory's cloister court was more curio, alas, than the sort of potent talisman that would draw the spiritually needy away from Southwell Minster, where they had regularly flocked before the

Interdict. What was required, the prior decided, was a sacred relic of the first rank, stemming from a figure of such renowned holiness that no pilgrim who would save his soul could underestimate the efficacy of a journey to Lenton.

Accordingly, Father Clement commissioned Sir Mitchell of Rainworth, guardian knight of his monastic establishment, to spread word of his interest in obtaining such a revered object—or possibly several—and his willingness to pay well for the right acquisition. Sir Mitchell, in his capacity as county coroner, naturally enough mentioned the prior's yen to Father Ivo, who lost no time reporting it to Jared Sparks and Bartholomew le Gyw. This triumvirate, seen together frequently nowadays at a private table in a corner of the Trip, began to ponder how to satisfy the prior's pressing need.

"No sooner is Holy Church back to its sacred business than he busies himself profaning it anew," said the chaplain. "The man has learned nothing from our recent tribulations."

"The prior needs an object lesson," Sparks quipped, "so let us find him the objects."

"A threesome like us who could stay the king's host from trampling Wales with a touch of the counterfeit," whispered the innkeeper, "should have small trouble likewise gulling so worthy a victim."

"As a priest, I can perforce be no party to your chicanery," said Ivo, "unless, of course, the Lord were to instruct me to chasten a misguided shepherd."

"Why would He not?" asked le Gyw.

"I have not inquired."

"Then pray God for guidance—and meanwhile counsel with us."

The logistics of the duping rather than the confected relics themselves required the deeper thought. The merchandise had to be credibly presented, and the consequences of the transaction painful but not excruciating. "I've hit upon someone who might suit our needs ideally," Sparks said after long consultation with the bottom of his tankard. He turned to le Gyw. "Do you remember a certain rowdy customer of yours from some years back who was employed for a season or two at the castle—one Stuckey Woodfinch by name?"

"His memory will not fade," said the innkeeper. "That rascal."

"He pursues other ends now under another name," the clerk expanded, "but I know how to reach him and might recruit him for our exercise."

"His mouth rarely shuts, as I recall," said le Gyw. "Could we confide in such a rake?"

"If we make it worth his while, I've little doubt of it."

Not long afterward, a message was delivered to Lenton Priory inviting Father Clement and any other ranking member of his house, accompanied by an armed guard not to exceed four in number, to meet with a certain pair of holy travelers beside a stout oak in Sherwood at noon the third day following. The message, attached to a crude map that located the proposed rendezvous spot, went on to state that its senders were possessed of several hard-won relics of a most rare and uniquely holy nature that were destined to reside at Southwell Minster—unless the Lenton prior wished to intervene. If, after examining the precious artifacts and being satisfied as to their authenticity, the prior wanted to obtain them, he was to be prepared for purchase on the spot, else they should be carried straightway to Southwell for permanent inclusion in the minster's trove of sacred treasures.

The proposal so intrigued Father Clement that, despite advice to avoid the solicitation, he could not. And so on the assigned day, a party consisting of the prior, his sacristan, Sir Mitchell and a fellow knight in full battle regalia, two men-at-arms, and a sumpter horse bearing several sacks of silver appeared at the designated place deep within the shadows of Sherwood.

For a disconcerting while, no one else was to be seen nor any sound heard beyond the occasional plaintive note of a lark, the hum of a combative bee, or the restless snort of the coroner's gaudily caparisoned steed. Finally there came into view a pair of robed and hooded figures, each with a bulging sack and moving at a sluggish pace that suggested they had proceeded there on foot from a considerable distance. The prior's party followed their arrival cautiously, fearful that some larger contingent might be lurking in their wake. But closer inspection of the fatigued and perspiring strangers as they genuflected before the prior disarmed suspicions of their sinister intent.

"I am Brother Will," said the taller of the pair, "and this is Brother Robert. We are not brothers either by birth or as ordained by Holy Church—only in the comradely sense." Friends from boyhood, they had gone off together to the great crusade more than twenty years before, Will as a Knight Templar and Robert as a student of divinity not yet in final orders, serving as Will's squire. What they encountered in the Holy Land had sorely tried their faith, said Will, and their subsequent wandering about the sinks of the Levant and Europe had sullied their virtue to such an extent that only through protracted prayer and painful ordeal had they redeemed themselves. As a means to this end, they acquired the sacred relics they had borne with them to the forest—obtained through many harrowing and complex adventures, not all of them likely to have won Holy Church's blessing. "But you cannot suppose, Father," said Brother Will, his face shrouded by the ample folds of his dusty robe, "that such potent items would not have lured the attentions of the basest sort of brigands, men who would stop at little to profit from their acquisition and sale. We can thus conceive of no more earnest step toward advancing our hopes for eternal salvation than the tendering of these holiest of *objets* to the minster at Southwell in the shire to which we are both native."

"Why give them all to the minster?" asked the prior, by now gorged with curiosity.

"Why not? We hail from here, Father, and Southwell is a great cathedral."

"Not in the true sense," Clement countered. "It is more a business and administrative center than a purely holy house, as ours is."

"Thus we were advised by an informant when we arrived in the vicinity of the minster several days back—and that Your Holiness had a keen interest in obtaining relics. And so before we contributed them to—"

The prior raised a hand and turned to Sir Mitchell. "Does this conform with the arrangement you made in our behalf, sire?"

The coroner nodded, saying he had posted an agent at the minster who, "for a small consideration," was seeking out pilgrims who either trafficked in or might have knowledge of sacred relics, newly available now that England was no longer ruled by an excommunicate king.

Well satisfied with the pilgrims' account thus far, the prior turned back to Will and asked, "Why do we meet in this remote setting instead of at our priory?"

"It would no doubt shock you, Father, to learn of the places we have been and eminences with whom we have dealt in the course of which we have been done dirty. Godliness too often yields to diabolic urges when such goods as these are involved."

That answer, too, seemed plausible to the prior. "But tell me, my young friend, would you not consider donating a portion of your relics to our priory instead of requiring our purchase of them with desperately needed funds? Our prayers for your souls would be yet more ardent than any the minster might dispense. And having far fewer relics than Southwell, we should display yours with a special prominence that would still further ingratiate their donors to Heaven."

"But you would disturb our intended proffer to the minster," Will answered, "lacking as it is in any hope of commercial gain. Being pious men but without the resources of Holy Church to sustain us, we should be foolhardy indeed to succumb to a rival suitor for our rare offerings without receiving what funds we might in return."

"These are nothing but oily-tongued thieves, I think," the sacristan whispered to the prior.

"Or hard-headed merchants hungry for profit," said the coroner.

"Yet their wares may immeasurably enhance our house," said the prior. "Let us see what they bring us."

With great ceremony Brother Robert opened his sack and spread a cloth of rosy-hued silk upon the forest floor while the prior and his party dismounted and drew close. Then, with still greater flourish, the silent partner of the pair plucked the first packet from his collection and carefully unfolded it beneath Father Clement's bulging eyes. "Here we have two teeth from the lower jaw of the prophet Ezekiel," began the talkative brother, "which I obtained in the Holy Land after great travail. Their authenticity was vouched for by a priest who had wrested them from an infidel who had stolen them from a monastery that had obtained them from an apostate old Judean family."

"Ezekiel," said the prior, "is not of our faith, though indisputably a holy man. Go on."

"Next is a most thoroughly Christian relic," Will continued as his collaborator opened a small mahogany box, "of remarkable healing powers—finger bones of Saint Mary's brother, Lazarus, taken between the time of his death and his resurrection by the Saviour."

"Fast work," muttered the sacristan.

"They look to me like pig's knuckles skinned the day before yesterday," Sir Mitchell concurred.

"Lazarus!" the prior repeated, his tone duly hallow. "But how could we know for certain that these were from—"

"It was sworn to us," said Will, "by a caravan master in Anatolia whose mother was a Nazarene—her family had lived there since our Lord's day, and these joints, preserved in a mix of newt droppings and myrrh, had brought them generations of long life."

"Fascinating!" Clement hissed.

Next on exhibit were hairs reputedly exhumed from the scalps of Saint Bernard and Saint Leonard, "though we cannot, in all honesty, Father, swear which are which." When these provoked small excitement, the hooded purveyor quickly unfurled what he said was the perfectly preserved skull of Saint Denis, as fine a relic as was ever spirited out of France.

"But I have been to the monastery of Saint Denis," the prior objected, "and seen his skull—can this be the very same? I could not countenance our holding an article stolen outright from—"

"Possibly these gentle pilgrims are mistaken in the identity of their objects," the coroner ventured.

"Or possibly such objects can miraculously replicate themselves so that this, too, may be the head of Saint Denis," the sacristan theorized whimsically. "The Lord works in wondrous ways indeed."

"I had not considered such a possibility," said the coroner with mock solemnity.

"Astonishing!" said the prior.

For their *pièces de résistance,* the peddlers displayed a bundle of straw, secured with a bow of white lace, which they said came from the Christ child's manger at Bethlehem; a bit of sail said to have been snipped from Saint Peter's last fishing vessel, and a sizable wooden splinter said to have been salvaged from the True Cross. "I tell you with full devotion to our faith, Father," said Will, "that these objects are so precious that they came into our hands in ways no pious man could entirely condone. But it is a fact that thieves have avidly looted the shrines of Christendom, and if we have had to deal with them on occasion in harsh ways of which we are not proud, I ask whether we were not justified in removing such sacred artifacts from the hands of unscrupulous infidels."

The prior was by this point less concerned with the roughness of commerce in relics generally than with the legitimacy of the items at hand. "But would not the straw from Jesus's manger have long since withered, and the sail from Peter's boat shredded, and the wood from Calvary rotted and decomposed?"

"Not," said Brother Robert, breaking his silence, "if they partook of the Holy Spirit—as we are taught."

Father Clement nodded at the theological consistency of the answer. "And what price would you ask for all of these memorabilia?"

"They are worth two hundred pounds," said Will, "if they are worth a penny."

"And would fetch twice that," the sacristan said behind his hand to the coroner, "if only these intrepid vendors might add a feather or two from the wings of the angel Gabriel."

"Leaving aside their alleged worth," the prior bargained, "what price would you accept?"

"Surely not less than their worth," said Will, "and more if you are moved by the Christian spirit, Father."

"And if we desire only several of the items?" the prior asked.

"We cannot fix a price item by item—it would be sacrilege," said Will. "You must proffer for the lot of them or for none."

"Why thus? Your price is dear—and at least several of the objects seem on the questionable side, if I may say."

"Alas," said Will, gathering up the last of his offerings, "the bargain is sealed."

"How so?"

"That's how," said Will, whirling about and indicating the several dozen woodsmen who had materialized in a circle about the Lenton party while it was lulled into unwariness and who now menaced them with leveled bows. "The first of your soldiers who stirs will find an arrow in his throat." Then Will moved to the sumpter horse, undid one of the sacks weighing it down, and slipped a hand inside. When it emerged with a fistful of silver coins, he smilingly replaced them, retied the sack, and signaled his companion to lead away the animal toward their ring of confederates. "A fair exchange is no robbery," Will concluded, and placed his two sacks of claimed relics on the spot where the horse had stood. "None of you is to move a muscle for five minutes—or all of you will be in imminent need of whatever restorative powers these *objets* command. May the Lord bless you and make His countenance to smile on your folly."

Sir Mitchell confronted the sheriff the next morning with a full account of the robbery and added, "You pride yourself on the safety of our wood, yet a heinous and brazen crime has been committed there against an eminence of Holy Church. I tax you with apprehending the thieves and recovering their takings—which amounted to three hundred pounds sterling."

"The prior was ill advised to pursue such a transaction," said the sheriff, fairly bursting within from mirth and all but certain who had perpetrated the outrage.

"The prior was in fact well advised—but chose to ignore his counselors, myself among them, by going to the wood. His imprudence, however, does not forgive the crime."

Forced to concur, the sheriff sallied out that same afternoon to the forest, where he soon confronted its arch-mischief-maker. "Brother Robin," Philip said to the no-longer-shrouded jester, "I fear you've outdone yourself in victimizing the aged prior of Lenton. Such banditry, alas, is against the law—and the spirit of the understanding between us."

"How so?" asked Robin. "We only lightened the load of a fatuous priest who would find godliness in bits of bone and cloth and wood and thus add to his grandeur. We sought to satisfy his needs."

"His irreligiosity can't excuse a barefaced theft."

"Not barefaced at all, sire—we were bearded and hooded. And at any rate, the prior has long been in need of instruction on the nature of piety."

"And so you have given it to him. Now I want the silver returned."

"Then our instruction will not stick to him. Moreover, we have hewn to our bargain with you—to take from oppressors who wander into our leafy lair."

"These didn't wander in—they were enticed. And the clergy has been inoperative for six years, so how can they be deemed oppressors?"

"The silver in question is plainly left over from Holy Church's vintage years of active oppression—which the blessed fathers will doubtless resume in short order. At the least, our purpose was preventive."

"I want all the silver returned to the priory at once."

"Half."

"All."

"Two-thirds—we have expenses and neither pope nor king to fund us."

"Three-quarters," said the sheriff, "and by the morrow."

"Done," said the woodsman, "but you're in want of levity, Master Sheriff."

The prior was said to be secluded in prayer and meditation when Philip arrived at Lenton that evening to advise him that the crime would be substantially mitigated before another sunset. "He takes it hard," the sacristan confided, "knowing now he ought never to have ventured out on such a feckless quest. He does penance in the form of such self-scorn as I have never seen in him."

The sheriff's good news preceded him to the prior's cell, but if it had brought him any balm, Philip had no way of telling. The priest sat wrapped in silent mortification and, aside from a flicker of recognition in his bleary eyes, gave no sign of acknowledgment of his visitor's presence.

"I pray you will not despise me for saying so, Father," Philip began when it was evident the prior had been rendered mute by the events of his own instigation, "but our chaplain at the castle teaches that spiritual purity resides only in the heart and never in objects—and in simplicity, not adornment." Then he fell still, wishing to add no further to the prior's humiliation.

Father Clement withheld all indication that he was sentient for several agonizing minutes. But when the sheriff prepared to leave, the priest slowly struggled to his feet, raised his clouded eyes to Philip's stainless pair, and fell upon him in bony, silent embrace. Then he dropped away, like a sere, windblown leaf, and resumed his immersion in self-torment.

An elaborately scripted document arrived at the sheriff's closet the week following. A burial place had been set aside for him and his family at Lenton Priory, the parchment stated, "should Philip Mark, as pure of heart as any knight and devoted defender of the True Faith, elect to will us his earthly remains." The missive bore the ragged signature and sacred seal of Clement de Beaupré.

· XXXVI ·

FOR THIS ONE SEPTEMBER EVENING, the three most puissant men in England were housed together under the roof of Nottingham Castle.

As he had the year before, the king arrived in some heat and on the verge of violent action. With him had come only a small entourage, but a sizable phalanx of Flemish mercenaries trailed the royal party by no more than a day's march. Among the king's counselors on hand was that longtime mentor to the Plantagenets William Marshal, earl of Pembroke. His holdings in England, Ireland, and Wales likely made him the richest baron in the realm, and his equal virtuosity in the arts of combat and diplomacy sustained his renown as the finest knight of the age. Now fully restored as John's confidant and champion, the Marshal continued to hold his lands in Normandy at the sufferance of Philip Augustus and, accordingly, still would not accompany his English liege lord abroad to war against the French king.

It was in pursuit of that war that John had come north now to Nottingham—seemingly the wrong direction—all the way from Portsmouth, where he had lain much of the summer in wait for his vassals to answer the royal summons for the expedition to Poitou. Some came dutifully, but many balked. There were those, like the Marshal, who, for disparate reasons, declined to serve in person but sent their knights as fealty required. There were others, like Thomas de Lambert, who neither came nor sent knights but paid scutage to satisfy the crown. A dauntingly large number of others, however, especially in the north of England, declined to heed the king's call in any manner, and so he was forced to reschedule his great enterprise against France for early the following year. Meanwhile he set out for the north on a mission of vengeance against those who had thwarted him. In addition to the use of his practiced punishments—privileges abruptly withdrawn, and onerous, if not ruinous, fines imposed for marginal slights—the king now threatened to seize bodily those who had refused him military aid and to ravage their holdings.

Such conduct, while hardly out of the king's character, flew directly in the face of the oath he had taken at Winchester in late July before Stephen Langton. If John had supposed the archbishop to be a wan ascetic and papal lapdog, he had already proven, in the several months since returning to his native land after so many expatriate years, to be as true an Englishman as a churchman. His mandate from the pope, he told any who would listen, went beyond seeking the early restoration of church property seized by the crown and ensuring that all newly installed clerics were men of proper faith and learning as well as loyalty to the king; he was charged equally to insist that the realm be served by a just government. Indeed, the archbishop had extracted a pledge toward that end as a requisite for dissolving the excommunication. If the king had taken this vow for so many hollow words, uttered as a dictate of ceremony, the archbishop had not. And when John came thundering north to lay misery on his recalcitrant vassals, Langton pursued and confronted him at Nottingham Castle.

They spoke privately in the royal apartment, with the Marshal at the king's side to temper his anger at this renewed ecclesiastical intrusion, but half the castle could overhear their heated words. "You swore on Holy Scripture, with the Lord God as your witness, that you would not take men or property without the prior judgment of your courts of law," the archbishop challenged. "Yet you fly to the north country, trailing threats of lawless violence as if in total disregard of your pledge. It is unseemly conduct, sire, in a great king."

"We are the law!" the king cried. "We choose our counselors and our judges, and they craft the statutes as we direct—can it be otherwise and still a kingdom?"

"The laws are the creation of custom and equity as well as the royal will, my lord, and once born, they have a life of their own. They may not be overridden solely at the crown's prerogative."

"We will punish whom we wish among those who betray us—and cannot be stunted by any authority in the land, else we are no king and there is no England."

"With all due regard, Your Majesty, the two are not inseparable. Likewise, the definition of betrayal does not rest with your person alone— that way lies tyranny, and you have pledged not to follow it."

"We have not consented to turn ourselves into a lily."

"The Holy Father has taxed you to deal justly with your barons and lords, and you have consented. Tracking them down and harshly molesting them is not justice."

"Rough justice, perhaps, but justice all the same. Blackguards must be dealt their due!"

"But what is due them the courts must say—not you alone, sire. These men claim their grievances—and have a right to be heard and judged by others."

"By what right is it that you address us thus?"

"By the right you surrendered to my master in Rome. I did not counsel that act—you did as you chose. And now I am returned to my homeland as the agent of your overlord, to whom you've pledged the creation of equitable rule."

"We've had it for some time now—while Your Eminence has been languishing abroad and lending your distended ear to our most unfaithful vassals."

"Emblazon yourself with virtue as you will, my lord king—it is a fact that there are not a few who think your government unjust—that you rule despotically and *ad hominem* and not by equitable principles impartially applied. All these critics you brand traitors, and any man who would confront you risks your swift and sharp rebuke—which is the very business you now pursue, marching hither with your enforcers close behind. This is rule by malice, sire, not by justice—and I will declare excommunicate all who join you in this unlawful hunting-down of your subjects."

"The Holy Father will not sit for such insolence in his archbishop!"

"Insolence is the almost instantaneous disregard of Your Majesty's sacred oath before God—one might well call it betrayal. Persist in it, my lord, and you will swiftly dissipate Rome's lately minted benevolence toward you."

A great crashing sound ensued, as if a quite large and rather fragile object had been hurled against the nearest wall. Immediately thereafter, the archbishop was seen withdrawing from the royal apartment, his dignity compromised by the apparent haste of his leavetaking.

The king's party, joined by the earls of Derby and Salisbury, who could be expected to exert a cautionary influence on him, headed north the following morning without any indication whether John would play the scourge or heed the archbishop and prosecute his foes peaceably. The Marshal was left behind to negotiate with Langton on the size of the settlement over the church property and revenues the crown had seized in the long course of the Interdict.

With the royal party gone, the sheriff thought to arrange an intimate supper party for that evening at which the Marshal and the archbishop would be joined by two of the shire's most prominent residents—Lord Lambert, a lesser baron of the realm but one well regarded by all, and Father Honorius, the Southwell chronicler. The presence of the latter was especially pleasing to the archbishop, who only a few weeks earlier, in the course of a conclave with leading clerics at St. Paul's, had been presented by its resident annalist with a curious document, a copy of the coronation oath taken at the opening of the previous century by the first Henry. In it he had pledged his barons to end the unjust exactions and rapacious behavior of his brother and predecessor, William Rufus. Here, thought Langton, his attention arrested, might be a pregnant precedent for likewise constraining the present king, and he wished to explore Honorius's familiarity with Henry's reign for any possible current pertinence.

After a modest meal, the four of them retired to the archbishop's chamber for a candid exchange. They invited along their host, the sheriff, for his working knowledge of the laws and administrative procedures of the kingdom, and Father Ivo, Honorius's close friend and a wise old head. To the extent it had a structure, the meeting was presided over by Langton, an austere figure who spurned ornamental attire when off the high altar and, other than for the six-inch gold-and-jeweled crucifix that depended from his link necklace, was attired indistinguishably from the two priests. A lean man with a cap of short gray hair, he suffered the perpetual squint of a scholar who had passed a lifetime applying weak eyes to the contemplation of sacred texts and a supple mind to their exegesis. He seemed athrob with nervous intensity that took the form of a slight stammer, which failed to slow the rush of his words once the blocking syllable had been hurdled. The Marshal was a more imposing presence. Approaching his seventieth year, he was no longer the barrel-chested hulk who had once been the dread of every tourney list and battlefield he entered upon. But he still spoke and carried himself with the certitude that he could overcome any adversary in either physical or mental combat. His deepset hooded eyes and the great spread of his powerful arms gave him somewhat the look of an enormous bird of prey, though his speech had about it the easy charm of understatement that belied his immense sway.

"I cannot speak for Lord Lambert," the Marshal said to the archbishop, "but others in the baronage I have met with since your return are more than glad of it—and yet fearful of your alliance—that it seems to come too soon."

"I take no side in temporal disputes, sire," Langton replied.

"To be sure. Nevertheless, it may have that appearance because you would hold the king accountable as no one has before. My confreres' concern is that if Your Eminence is too direct—since you have no need to deal in artifice after your long ordeal of exile—you may only arouse John's heightened resistance, should he perceive you as closely leagued with the barons."

"Would you have me restrict my attention to liturgical matters and the intrigues of our chapter houses?"

"On the contrary," said Earl William. "Your intervention is badly needed. But the king is simply not used to being spoken to in such a fashion."

"Then he ought not to have made the pope his overlord."

"He felt he was confronted by too many enemies—Philip on the verge of invasion, the Welsh perpetually stirring a bloody ruckus, an indeterminate portion of the baronage abandoning him and contemplating rebellion, or worse. To sustain an unwinnable war with Rome in such circumstances was the height of folly—and I so counseled."

"But it was not necessary to hand the pope his kingdom to achieve the king's purposes. Innocent is not lacking in temporal ambition and takes his overlordship in all seriousness. So now John has not only an archbishop at Canterbury instructed to see that he keeps faith with his subjects but a papal legate as well. I know the legate—he will be zealous that all our clerics who would gain advancement mouth loyalty to the king. But his truer concern will lie with doctrinal purity as evidenced by submission to Rome in all matters. The result may well be a spineless clergy and a yet more libertine crown."

Honorius could not restrain himself at this overflow of candor. "Forgive a humble dweller in the sacred vineyard, Your Eminence, but unless I miss the meaning of your words, they seem inimical to the Holy Father. I cannot think you mean disrespect to the head of God's church."

Langton appraised the chronicler for a moment through slitted eyes that had the look of great shrewdness. "I should like you to misconstrue neither the thrust of my remarks, Father, nor the nature of our papacy. Christ is the head of my church—the Holy Father is but His vicar on earth. As such, he is due our boundless love and abject submission in spiritual matters. But here we address the temporal question of vassalage—of turning a kingdom into an appendage of Rome. I say within these four walls that it was a blunder—and rather than reconciling the strife in our realm, may exacerbate it."

"But if Rome is avid in its attention to England," asked Honorius, "will that not put the king on his mettle?"

"Precisely our design," said the archbishop. "But it is no substitute for earnest entreaty and accommodation within the laity—by which I mean to say the king must be checked not by Rome but by his loyal subjects. Thus far I've heard only of complaints and conspiracies—not of any serious, concerted effort to reason with him."

At this Lambert took exception. "To the king, Your Eminence, 'concerted effort' among the nobility smacks of conspiracy and treason. I am no intimate of his, as Earl William is, but my sense of the king is that he sees scant need to reason with us while he retains the whip hand. He deals in power—respects it first and last—husbands it and will continue to ignore mere moral suasion."

"I think, Sir Thomas, the problem is more nuanced than that," said the Marshal, thrusting his long legs out from his seat and then hunching forward to pursue the point. "We all need to understand the nature of this king and why he is as he is. For all his wit and courage—and make no mistake that he is deficient in either—why does he consume himself with suspicions and ambitions that work against his deeper interests? To answer that, you must know his family—and I knew them all. They are a special breed, of remarkable passion and spirit. John is the last of the brood, the runt of the litter, whose parents had little time to attend him and less interest, so he was cast aside and never expected to assume the throne. His whole life since has been but one loud outcry to tell the world he is special and mighty, every bit the equal of his father and brother—and feels the enduring need to prove it by recapturing their French holdings. That he has gone well beyond them in building this Britain into a citadel, a prosperous kingdom well and closely governed, he dismisses as piddling work. And so those who do not bend to him deeply or swiftly enough he turns on with a savage dread that he is neither loved nor feared adequately and can retain his throne only by force. If he thus abuses power, it is not merely for the sake of the exercise."

"Ah," said the archbishop, "now we progress. But if the king demands our respect, even our reverence, to still his fevered brain, then he must be made to grasp that these need be given to his vassals in return—indeed, to all his subjects. The realm is more than his private fief—it is a compact, the essence of which is a mutuality of interest. Yet he does not acknowledge this—seems incapable of even conceiving it. For him the crown is the repository of all might while the obligations vest entirely with his subjects. The barons must press home this central point with him." He turned to Lambert. "But you have no agenda, no plan, no design beyond raging against his excesses."

"I seek nothing from him," said Sir Thomas, "but that he should not drag me into his wars of self-aggrandizement. As his vassal, I gladly serve him in defense of the realm—and did so this spring when France stood on our doorstep. But I will not be his sacrificial lamb for some mad entanglement abroad that slakes his hunger alone, nor will I let my son or my knights be made into—"

"Ah, but you rail against the symptom only and let the root cause escape," the archbishop contended. "Many seize on this so far phantom war of his on France as an excuse to defy him, whereas their true grievances reside in other of the king's excesses. There must be an end to all these separate moanings. They must be gathered and winnowed and transformed into some set of fixed precepts, some durable structure of governance that will outlast the flesh and withstand the poundings of a black heart. The king may be sovereign, but there must be limits set to his sovereignty—for John and all his successors—else each generation will confront anew the crown's compulsion to vie with God for mastery of our souls. Thus, my keen interest in the conciliatory oath taken by the first King Henry at his coronation."

"But it was more than a century ago," the Marshal pointed out, "and who remembers it or its circumstances?"

"Which is why I thought Father Honorius might enlighten us."

The chronicler, who had long fought a losing battle with obesity, gathered up his wattles and cleared his throat twice before rendering history's judgment. "I have read what accounts there are of that age, Your Eminence, and if we may discount certain profligate tendencies of the king, like his siring eighteen known bastards—and likely more, given the undependability of sources from that primitive era—then we may reasonably conclude that the first Henry was an estimable ruler. But his so-called coronation charter must be considered in light of the fact that Henry's immediate predecessor, whose proneness to violence was matched only by the Conqueror himself, was mysteriously slain by an arrow through the head while he was hunting in the New Forest. Henry's pledge of moderate conduct on taking the throne, therefore, might best be thought of as a prudent act of self-preservation. So far as I can tell, the oath had little relevance to the balance of his reign—or to our present king at this point in his."

"But why can it not serve as a useful starting place for us in framing some sort of charter of concessions by the crown?" the archbishop asked.

"The king is used to dispensing charters," said the Marshal, "not having them imposed on him."

"Exactly so," said Langton, "and thus the value of Henry's charter as precedent. We would tailor ours to present conditions, of course, yet look beyond them to enduring concerns as well. But I do not say it should be imposed on the king—that would be rebellion, and he would properly resist. I am thinking more in terms of a contract or a treaty, freely entered into by the sovereign and his subjects."

"I know that Your Grace is renowned as a theologian and scholar,"

Lambert put in, "but you are only lately returned among us, so I must ask as a practical matter whether any of the others of us believes for a moment that our king would honor mere words on parchment, however artfully phrased."

"I am supposing the entire kingdom would bear witness to the pact."

"Even so," said Lambert.

"If your question is meant rhetorically, Sir Thomas, then I am forced to take exception to it," said the Marshal. "The archbishop presents a novel thought worthy of due deliberation. If the king is nothing else, he is unpredictable. The codified redress of his subjects' grievances, provided they are presented in palatable form, may strike him as preferable to perpetual strife. Let us pursue the process—it costs us nothing, and may yet gain us a peaceable kingdom."

And so for the next several hours, as fresh candles were lighted, flagons of malmsey brought, and the sheriff's first clerk summoned in utmost confidence to record the proceedings, that little group bent to the task of composing a memorandum of concerns that, properly refined, might form the basis of concord among the factions of the realm.

At the outset, the Marshal turned to the sheriff, who had sat by in silence to that point, and said, "You're a magistrate of the crown and much involved in its daily dealings—where would you begin, Master Mark?"

Startled by this deferential courtesy from the foremost knight of the realm, Philip grew momentarily flustered. "I . . . would not presume, my lord, to intrude upon your—"

"There can be neither presumption nor intrusion, Philip, if you are earnestly invited to share with us the fruits of your experience."

"But I—I have not been long among you—for as long as . . . I am French-born and naturally uneasy at—have not shared the same—"

"And I am English-born yet far more conversant with France," Langton submitted. "Nevertheless, I thrust forward my views, Master Mark, because necessity commands it—and concentrates the mind wonderfully. Spare us your modesty, sire, and speak directly."

The sheriff stirred uneasily as their collective looks riddled him. "Your true charge, gentlemen, is not simply to speak up but to say something of value to your deliberations. You must understand the nature of my work, though. It is not to appraise crown policy, only to execute it. If I were to stand in constant judgment of it, I would be quickly reduced to paralysis because it is imperfectly—"

"You speak in rings, Master Sheriff," the Marshal intruded. "Is it that you fear any disparaging remarks of yours will be reported to Westminster and taken for disgruntlement? It would not be unnatural, I suppose, in view of the crown's known lack of enthusiasm for those who question it."

"Perhaps I've become overly habituated to discretion, my lord, given the realities of my position as a crown officer."

"We would not imperil that position, Philip—you have our vows as men of God and honor. Give us your guidance in the privacy of this chamber."

The sheriff began slowly and haltingly. "I am uncomfortable, you see, with the notion that doing justice is our paramount purpose. For me, justice partakes more of philosophy than of logic—more of art than of science— and varies markedly with each man's appraisal. Thus, I cannot declare with confidence that the crown is unjust, say, when scrutinizing hereditary rights, if it appears overintent on the beneficiaries' loyalty to the king. Or that it is unjust for the crown to raise the cost of fees and fines and reliefs well above the customary level—or to impose fresh exactions where there were none—in order to meet its own rising costs. Or even that it is unjust for the crown to hold hostages against good behavior—usually there has been some provocation for such a hateful measure—or that it unjustly calls forth warriors to battle when their interests in the purpose of the combat may be at variance with the king's." He scanned their intently following eyes. "All of these, along with other of the alleged oppressions of the king, are arguably vital to the well-being of the realm—and to try to codify what is fit and proper in each instance seems to me to defy the realities of statecraft. What *is* of the essence, though, is that whenever and wherever and howsoever the crown acts, it should do so with con- sistency and constancy—with regularity and orderliness. The fee set for a given kind of charter ought to be the same here as there, the same tomorrow as it was yesterday—and not vary according to the king's mood or affection for the applicant. The government must live by unprejudiced appliance of settled procedures—otherwise, we are as well ruled by the wind—which, without notice, may shift and become a tempest."

His listeners sat for a long moment, raptly drinking in the sheriff's fervent remarks. Finally, the archbishop spoke. "I would not gainsay a syllable of your speech, Master Mark. But I would caution against confusing uniformity with humanity—though I can see, of course, how a crown officer might be preoccupied with regularity of method. A consistent cruelty of governance is scarcely justified by the rigor of its unvarying application. And where is there room for the compassionate heart in such a scheme— or do you say our government must be heartless?"

"No, but there must be limits to its pliancy, or we are back to rule by caprice."

"Very well," said the archbishop. "Plainly we are in need of both substantive *and* procedural justice—decent rules and equitable laws impartially enforced."

Philip nodded. "The formulating of decency and equity, though, is not my profession, sire."

Langton shook his head. "You cannot be exempted from the task— as if your duty does not extend beyond receiving orders. It must be all our doing, and surely not the king's alone. That is the central point."

Yet in their fear of giving such offense as to quash their creation in its germinal state, they stopped short of any sweeping pronouncements or accusatory language. Their stress, rather, was upon general and practical principles, with the refinements left for later. Thus, Sparks was duly instructed to begin their memorandum by recording, "King John concedes that he will not take men without judgment, nor accept anything for—"

"Should it not say, 'he will not take men *or their property*'?" asked Honorius.

"It is implied," said the Marshal. "These are to be but the outline of what may emerge, so let us not torture it at birth."

". . . 'that he will not take men without judgment,' " Langton continued the dictation, " 'nor accept anything for doing justice, nor perform injustice.' And the subsequent corpus of the charter will expand on these. Good."

Since orderly succession in property-holding was the foundation of the social structure—and the custom most often abused by the crown— the Marshal asked that the second point on their list be the king's agreement that "if my baron or my man should happen to die and his heir is of age, I ought to give him his land at a just relief without taking more." A woman or widow who was heir to land, they went on to prescribe, might be given in marriage by the crown but only "on the advice of her relatives, so that she is not disparaged." Lambert's sorest grievance was addressed by the seventh and eighth points, requiring the king's concession that his men "should not serve in the army outside England, save in Normandy or Brittany," and if a scutage were to be imposed, it might not exceed two-thirds of a pound—the current year's exaction was three times that—except by the advice of the barons of the realm.

When the list reached a dozen items, they stopped, well satisfied with their night's work. Sparks was told to be certain of all their emendations and deletions and have two clean copies ready by morning for the archbishop and the Marshal to bear away with them and share in due course with the king and the baronage.

Only Lord Lambert among them was devoid of hope as they prepared to disperse. "Commendable as the effort may be, I greatly fear the king will seize upon the prospect of such a charter only to suit his immediate ends," the baron predicted gloomily. "He will allow that some sort of broad accommodation is worth reflecting upon but only if the baronage first rallies to his banner for the invasion of France. Then, having appeared conciliatory for the time being, he will have his infamous war. If he wins it, he'll ride roughshod over us on his return—our king is not magnanimous in victory. And if he loses, as I fear he is fated to, he will turn choleric in the extreme, blaming those of us who counseled against his mad adventure—and use this nicely conceived document of ours to wipe his royal bung."

Such language, so ripe with cynicism, bordered on the seditious, forcing the sheriff to speak out. "Admiring as I am of you, my lord Lambert, and knowing your sentiments to be heartfelt, I nonetheless must thank you not to profane the king in his own castle."

"Hear, hear," said the Marshal. "You must grant the king clemency for his past shortcomings, Thomas—he's by no means witless, and may have learned more than he is credited for."

"I'll take heart," Lambert replied, "only if he abandons France to history and cancels his spring war there."

"The king must exorcise his demon," said the Marshal, rising to retire, "even at risk of ruination. There will be war in the spring, with or without us, Thomas."

The parley concluded, Father Ivo trailed the Marshal to his chamber and begged a moment's privacy with him. "A small matter, I assure you, Earl William—we are all fatigued."

"I trust your silence at our gathering did not betoken disapproval, Father. You were more than welcome to—"

"On the contrary, I was much heartened. If any two men can affect the dizzying course of events, they are the archbishop and yourself. Would the king had your temperament and discernment as his critical hour draws nigh. But I would speak to you of the sheriff."

"Master Mark? I've not dealt with him before—he seems a bright and worthy fellow, if given excessively to caution."

"He would never ask this for himself, my lord—he is a sincerely modest man—but I am too old to affect shyness and am partial to Philip, besides. He would be a knight, sire—yet his birth and career have denied the honor to him. He is most deserving of it, as all who know him readily attest, save our coroner, who envies and vilifies him. His office prevents his applying openly for the title, fearing as he does to appear too vain or that he may be ridiculed for its unseemly pursuit. But he would gladly receive the blow as reward for long years of most knightlike service."

"There should be no great difficulty in arranging it."

"Alas, his fair wife confides in me that Master Mark is persuaded there are but two men in all of England who might bestow the knighthood on him this late in life so that it would have true meaning—the king and yourself. And he would greatly prefer the blow be given by you."

"I see. Your Philip is as proud as he is modest. But I could not entertain the notion without first consulting the king. He would no doubt think it peremptory of me to do otherwise—the sheriff is his servant, not my vassal."

"To be sure, sire."

"I'll pursue it at the first opportunity, Father. But the king has much else on his mind and is little inclined to—"

"Which is why I applied to you, my lord—thinking that perhaps while you were on the premises—if you saw justice in the request . . ."

"Justice, sad to say, is never simple. Let us get on with saving the kingdom, and then all deserving men may reap their due, the estimable sheriff among them. Pray for us, Chaplain."

A.D.
1215

·XXXVII·

"THE CONFEDERATES PRANCE AROUND down there like a pack of nances," said Lambert, "and the frothing fitz Walter is no more a general than the king is a monk. John should have slain him when he surrendered Vaudreuil to the French without a fight in '02."

Although the rebel barons had mustered a month earlier at Stamford in open disavowal of their fealty to the crown, and their leader, Lord Robert fitz Walter of Dunmow, had taken up the grand title of "Marshal of the Host of God and Holy Church," Sir Thomas persisted in viewing the insurrectionists as more a fraternal band than a subversive militia. Their first overt act of war had been an effort to seize Northampton Castle, but without adequate troops or weapons to hurl against that royal bulwark, they had to quit the site after a fortnight and settle for capture of the secondary stronghold at Bedford.

"If you ask me, they're pissing down their own legs," the lord of Swanhill went on, "and hoping the spectacle will persuade the French to send an expeditionary force and Alexander to come crawling out of the Scottish wood—Heaven help them. A bootless struggle, though I mock neither their courage nor principles."

"For a moment you sounded as if you were going to embrace the king's side of it," said the sheriff, advancing his bishop to pose a clear peril to the baron's queen. Their Saturday-afternoon matches had become a welcome diversion for Philip, now that he felt no discomfort when he won. In truth, the pleasure was derived less from the chess than from engaging Lambert's instinctive intelligence, which he had come to admire increasingly during the past year as events had proven him more seer than fulminator.

"The king has no side and no adherents—only subjects and servants."

"Come now, my lord—if you're to stay above the battle, you'll have to make a better show of neutrality."

"So that's it between us—sheep are to be my only permissible passion? Well, I cannot counterfeit a love for my liege lord for tearing the kingdom asunder. There is no need of it."

The sheriff's clerk hurried toward them just then. "Sir Fawkes is here," he cried, as if heralding one of the horsemen of the Apocalypse, "and asks to see you on the instant."

"That bandy-legged little cutthroat—here?" Lambert's distaste overflowed. "Had you any notice in advance?"

"None," said the sheriff. "It's not his custom."

"It can't be good news. The stench of carrion wafts ahead of him."

Of all the French hirelings the king had brought home with him after the initial loss of his Angevin domain, none was more disreputable—or would rise higher—than Fawkes de Breauté. Said to have been born a serf who as a boy once slew a knight wasting his father's meadow, he was a small man with a fiery temperament that never cooled, a brutal and godless battler of surpassing valor; not for nothing was he nicknamed after the French word for "scythe." He had graduated from janitorial functions when at court in France to become the king's pet killer on a short leash. His company of rowdies was tossed onto the glowing west-country anvil soon after their transfer to England and fought so well that the king knighted him, loaded him down with lush if troublesome holdings, and placed his troop on permanent assignment as the roving royal fist. Those of Lord Lambert's class loathed Fawkes de Breauté as a lowborn little upstart who had been handed too much power and emblemized the crown's ready use of lawless force to tame a truculent subject. For his part, Philip scorned Fawkes for giving all French officers in the royal service a bad name— and for having gained a knighthood solely by virtue of his sword's cutting edge.

He stalked into the courtyard now, barely a moment after being announced—a short, brawny man with unruly hair and burning eyes. The sheriff rose to greet him. "Perhaps you've met Sir Thomas de Lambert," said Philip, gesturing toward the baron, who remained seated in the presence of the uncivil intruder.

"I've not had the pleasure before," said Fawkes, "and alas, I'll have it all too briefly now, for you and I must confer, Master Mark. London has fallen—and there's much to discuss."

"London!" Lambert blurted with more amazement than alarm. "That may change everything."

"For better or worse, my lord?" Fawkes asked him.

"I hardly know. Plainly it aggravates the situation."

"We're beyond mere irritants, my lord—this is civil war."

"Maneuvers, I should have called it before this—but London! It's all different. I would not have thought fitz Walter had the boldness . . ."

"Possibly we have all misjudged him—and his collaborators. The time for wry bystanding is past." Fawkes looked up. "I trust you've chosen your side wisely, my lord."

"I had hoped to avoid the need."

"Yes—and thereby fed the flame. May I assure the king you'll be among those standing fast with him?"

"I've not been summoned to his camp."

"You evade the question."

"I'm not answerable to a captain of the king, sire. When he asks my support, I'll answer—not before."

"I see." Fawkes looked away. "In that case, I hope you will forgive me. If you'll not stand with the king, I must ask you to stand aside— Master Mark and I have business still more vital than your match." The roughneck glanced down at the chessboard. "At any rate, your queen is done for, from the looks of it, so count my intrusion as a draw and rejoice in your luck. Good day to you, my lord."

Lambert squinted down with disbelief at the blatancy of Fawkes's rudeness. "God save our king," the baron snapped and took his leave in heat.

That the king's seat of government had been abruptly snatched from him should have come as no surprise, yet news of the event left Philip shaken. The rebellion itself, certainly, had become inevitable when the king could not be dissuaded from his renewed warring in France, but the scale of the subsequent uprising at home was less foreseeable. John at least had heeded Archbishop Langton's counsel and chosen to appease rather than manhandle those who defied his original call to arms. By promising to address the rebel barons' grievances on his triumphant return to England, he won enough support to wage his war. He sailed for Poitou in February of A.D. 1214 with a sizable, if reluctant, segment of the English nobility and a great store of treasure to pay the army being conscripted for him in France. The kingdom was left in the hands of the justiciar, Peter des Roches, the Poitevin who also served as bishop of Winchester and was among John's most reliable French imports, and the crown's even more faithful henchman Baron Brewer. Neither of them hesitated to exercise rough sway in the monarch's absence.

The king's plan was bold and simple. While his own army was to reclaim Poitou and the adjacent western counties and duchies, Longsword was to take a smaller force and a fat purse with him to the northeast sector of France, join up with troops under the friendly counts of Flanders and Boulogne, and form a still larger host with allies from the Rhineland, a confederation under King John's nephew Otto of Brunswick, candidate for Holy Roman Emperor but hotly opposed in that claim by the French. Their massed army was to drive on Paris and Normandy and then, with John's force advancing from the west, crush Philip Augustus in a massive vise.

The enterprise began well enough as John marched about gathering tribute without resort to real combat until he met resistance at a castle near Angers and pressed a siege. When Louis, the French crown prince, hurried to the rescue with a substantial force, John wheeled about to meet him, only to find his Poitevin recruits abandoning the field in multitudes at the approach of their countrymen and forcing the king to retire to his port at La Rochelle. Unable to mount a pitched battle or score a decisive victory, John could only lie impotently at bay, writing home in an unanswered plea for reinforcements while awaiting better news from the northern front. There, Longsword's troops scored small, pointless gains as precious weeks slipped by before his German allies mustered in force. By then, though, the French king had had time to drive a wedge into the midst of the gathering enemy host, the two wings of which sought to converge upon him on a stifling day late in July on a plain near the village of Bouvines. Within three violent hours, and despite Longsword's heroics, the French had swept the field, the earl of Salisbury had been clubbed from his horse and taken prisoner along with the two counts, Otto's hopes for emperor lay in shards, and King John's grand design for a rebirth of empire was at last clear to all for what it was—a shattered delusion. King Philip was content to let him loll about Poitou for a time and then agreed to a six-year truce. When John's forlorn fleet put in at Dartmouth late in October, no cheers awaited him.

His bristling baronage soon let it be known that even as the king had had to settle his dispute with the pope and abandon his hope of reasserting sovereignty in France, so he would now be obliged to address the complaints of his vassals. Within a few weeks of his return, the crown's most committed enemies journeyed to Bury St. Edmunds, feigning holy pilgrimage but in fact convening a clandestine war council. They numbered about forty-five, a quarter part of the barons of the realm, with not quite half of them from the counties north and east of Nottinghamshire. A somewhat smaller portion of the baronage, though disproportionately large in wealth and influence, remained steadfast for the king. The balance, of whom Thomas de Lambert might have been said to be representative, stood aloof from the contest, disenchanted by the king but unwilling to disavow their oaths to him in open rebellion.

Anxious to cool this bubbling cauldron, the archbishop of Canterbury succeeded in persuading the rebel party to dwell less on their individual injuries in favor of a far broader settlement built on the argument that an arbitrary ruler was not a king but a tyrant. Governments, Langton proposed as the reasonable core of their creed, should not be conducted to the detriment of the governed. Toward enshrining that noble sentiment, he won their close consideration of the draft of a charter of liberties that had grown in scope and detail since the first rough notes for it were put down in the memorandum composed at Nottingham Castle more than a year earlier. What the list amounted to was nothing less than the king's recognition of a web of laws that bound him every bit as much as his subjects.

After refining their document, the barons came to London the second week of the new year and presented it to the king. He asked until Easter to appraise properly so sweeping a demand to moderate his behavior. Meanwhile, John was not reduced to metaphysical hairpulling on the nature of monarchy. His strategy was two-pronged: first, strengthen his hand militarily—at Nottingham Castle Philip Mark received three dozen new knights and sergeants into his garrison, and other crown outposts were similarly reinforced; second, divide his foes by negotiating separately with the most pliable in hope of luring them away from the rebel cadre. As to the retreat from despotism demanded of him, he was quick to promise "our barons who are against us" that he would not take them or their property without judicial proceedings—a chief tenet of the rebel crusade— but beyond that he would not go. A full-dress charter of liberties that turned malleable custom into rigidified law would fatally compromise the crown's ability to act in its own—and the realm's—best interests, John insisted. Instead, he proposed a committee of eight, four from the crown's side and the same for the disgruntled barons, to negotiate their differences, with the pope to act as grand arbiter on issues unresolved. At this the barons scoffed.

By spring the rebel party concluded that the king had been toying with them while buying time and rallying his resources. Their patience exhausted, they took up arms and moved into the field in April. Richer in anger than in manpower, they were naturally cautious in their first direct acts of insurrection, not so much storming as feinting at royal strongholds. The king, with too small a standing army to nip the budding rebellion, sent abroad for mercenaries and meanwhile kept parleying with the enemy. But now, suddenly, the rebels had taken London, where the heavily taxed mercantile class welcomed them with open arms and gates, and what at first had been a minor surface wound was all at once a gaping fissure in the body politic.

"We have no seat of government for the moment," conceded Fawkes de Breauté, the crown's cruelest lash, whom the king had dispatched to the hinterlands to see to their defense, "only a court on horseback." With Westminster under enemy control, all proceedings of the Chancery and the Exchequer were suspended. "The king's men must fend for themselves," Fawkes told the sheriff, "wherever they are—and there is much to do. See to your weapons supply—put your Nottingham smiths to the task—and add amply to your food stores as the growing season progresses. There is no telling the duration of the crisis. We count on our castellans to hold the line from Chester to Lincoln and keep the traitors in the north locked away up here."

"And what of money?" asked Philip.

"What of it? Your castle is a royal depository—act toward it as if you were your own exchequer. Raise the usual levies, keep your accounts intact against a future audit, and commandeer what weapons and supplies you need in the king's name. His Majesty further authorizes his sheriffs to seize the holdings of any tenants of the crown who desert his cause— take possession outright and plunder their chattels at will to fulfill your military needs and maintain the peace."

"And if they resist my men?"

"Kill them—they're vermin." Fawkes clutched at his sword hilt. "My company will bivouac in your meadow this night. I ask you to see that they are well fed. My officers and I would welcome ample quarters in the royal wing." The stocky tempest's tone was unvaryingly imperious.

"Perhaps the king's apartment would suit you, sire," said the sheriff.

"Perhaps the king's sheriff wearies of his office," Fawkes shot back, eyes glinting at the implied rebuke. "I've traveled too far in great haste these past several days on this urgent business, so you must forgive me, Captain, if my manners flag in the solicitation of your courtesy."

"I had not noticed, sire." Here was no one to cross swords, tempers, or chess pieces with. "How do you like your swan prepared?"

"Moist," said the Scythe, "and unrancid."

·XXXVIII·

WITH ITS HOME BASE OCCUPIED, the crown functioned in the ensuing weeks as something of a headless wonder while the rebel camp gained recruits and its hopes soared on the receipt of pledges of military assistance from the French, the Scots, and the Welsh. As a result, the king was pressed by his closest counselors to examine with a fresh eye the barons' proposed charter of liberties as a basis for making peace.

Accordingly, a cleric arrived at Nottingham Castle on the first day of June with greetings for the sheriff from the archbishop and an urgent request that he assemble Fathers Ivo and Honorius and Lord Lambert to examine the exhaustively reworked draft of the charter that Langton's aide had brought them. The archbishop's letter called the document "almost surely our last hope for avoiding Armageddon." He asked their overnight commentary on the text so the cleric could speed it back to Windsor Castle, where Langton was at the king's side.

By sundown the two priests and the baron had joined the sheriff in his closet, with Sparks admitted as well to note down their collective response. Honorius was the first to read the document, racing over it with a practiced eye. He registered immediate pleasure that it began with a pledge of freedom for Holy Church and waxed ever warmer the further he read.

"It appears to be far more than we might ever have hoped," the chronicler exclaimed. Arbitrary rule was to be swept aside by its numerous guarantees. "Hear this," Honorius said. " 'A freeman shall not be amerced for a slight offense except in accordance with the degree of the offense' "— and such fines were to be imposed only "by the oath of upright men of the neighborhood." No crown officer was henceforth to take corn or chattels without paying a freeman "spot cash" for them or to seize any horse or cart or timber without agreement by the king's subject. Nor was any freeman to be "arrested or imprisoned or disseised or outlawed or exiled or in any way destroyed," the bulbous priest read on with growing excitement, "except by the lawful judgment of his peers and by the law of the land." If anyone had been removed by the king "without the legal judgment of his peers from his lands, castles, franchises or his right, we will immediately restore them to him." All unjust fines were to be remitted in their entirety. All hostages and charters "given to us by an Englishman as security for peace or faithful service" were to be returned at once.

"It is an immense triumph," Honorius announced, and handed the document to Lambert.

"I heard nothing of military service," said the baron, who read it at a more plodding pace with Sparks by his elbow to interpret the more obscure Latin phraseology.

"But there is this in the twelfth clause, my lord," said the clerk. "No scutage is to be levied 'unless by common counsel of our kingdom'—and see here, at the fourteenth clause, how that counsel is spelled out. Both the greater and lesser barons are to be assembled on forty days' notice as well as the leading clergy, and their approval solicited."

"Yet it does not outlaw service abroad," Lambert persisted.

"Perhaps not, my lord, but it reaches the very same point by inference," Honorius argued. "For if the scutage can be objected to, then surely the service it stands in place of can be refused to begin with."

Lambert considered the chronicler's logic and could not fault it. "Still, it leaves me uneasy," said the baron. "I cannot believe the king will finally consent to such strictures as these—or if he does so for reasons of tactical advantage, that he will honor this charter for long. These are mere words."

"Plainly you are not alone in that surmise," said Honorius. "If you will look to the very end—the king there gives security against breaching the charter."

Sparks jumped ahead to the sixty-first clause. "Here, my lord, it speaks of the creation of a standing committee of the barons, to number twenty-five and be selected by their own ranks," the clerk summarized. If said committee received complaint of any abuse of said charter by the king or his officers, the crown would be given forty days to rectify it, or the barons would then be entitled to "call upon the community of the whole land" to seize royal properties and injure the crown in any fashion they might choose, excepting only the private person of the king and his family.

"Preposterous!" Lambert declared.

"Furthermore," the clerk concluded, "every man in the land is obliged to take an oath of loyalty to this committee of baronial overseers."

"Now I know it's all a sham!" Sir Thomas cried. "Such a provision would set the barons in judgment over the king. John would never for a moment consent to such a thing if he truly intended that this agreement should come to pass."

"But it would appear ironclad, my lord," said Honorius. "Your brethren in the baronage are scarcely more trusting of the crown than yourself—thus, their requirement of this elaborate protective device."

"The king will think of something—call on the pope to discredit the whole business, probably."

"Even that prospect is taken into account, my lord," said Sparks. "Here, near the end, the king states, 'We shall procure nothing from anyone . . . whereby any of these concessions and liberties might be revoked or diminished; and if such thing be procured, let it be void and null, and we will never use it.' "

Lambert shook his head. "It's simply too good to be true—so it must not be. I say it's a stratagem—the man is too wily to be trusted."

It was only at this point that the sheriff took up the document and began to scan it. His face drained suddenly when he reached the fiftieth clause, one that amidst all the excitement had eluded the others' attention. It stated: "We will entirely remove from their bailiwicks the relations of Gerard d'Athiés . . . Engelard Cigogne, Peter and Guy and Andrew de Chanceaux, Guy de Cigogne, Geoffrey de Martigny and his brothers, Philip Mark and his brothers and his nephew Geoffrey, and all their following."

"What is it, sire?" Sparks asked, seeing his master's blanched look.

Philip indicated the passage to the clerk, who read it aloud to the group. It had the dolorous sound of a death sentence.

The room turned stone-still. "It would seem," the sheriff said with a grim smile, "that I am imperatively expendable."

"Were you never advised of such a possibility, sire?" Ivo asked.

"Never." Philip's eyes narrowed. "I see now why they say His Majesty is fond of springing surprises—they can be highly debilitating."

"Perhaps it's merely a bargaining position, sire," the chaplain offered, "and in the end the king will not agree to it."

"But if not to this," asked Lambert, "why to any of the rest of it?"

Honorius was baffled. "Why should the fate of the king's former French captains be of such paramount concern to the barons that they would specify their dismissal in a document like this?"

"That, at least, is no puzzle to me," said Lambert. "The king has ceded them great power so they have become the instruments of his sway over us; and, Master Mark's skillful conduct of his office to one side, these native Frenchmen have by and large been forceful tormentors of the baronage, used to hound the king's prey. And their being foreigners has made them all the more hateful. Who better to serve as scapegoats when the time comes to settle scores?"

"But why this list?" Honorius asked. "Why omit Fawkes, who is foremost among the king's French captains in inspiring contempt? And if their Frenchness is to the point, why did the barons not ask that the justiciar be stripped of his rank—Bishop des Roches is every bit as egregious an enforcer of the crown's might as the rest, and still more powerful for serving as the king's surrogate."

Lambert shrugged. "Possibly the king holds them indispensable and has drawn the line with them. Our friend Philip, meanwhile, he tosses to his pursuers to devour." The baron turned saddened eyes on the sheriff. "I've warned you repeatedly—he is not a seemly sovereign."

Anne Mark used plainer words on learning of Philip's callously bargained fate. "He's a filthy dog, that majesty of yours—serving up your head on a platter to these ghouls. What is it you've done but labor honorably and tirelessly in the crown's behalf? And they've not even had the courtesy to tell you that you're about to be hurled upon the sacrificial altar."

"I suspect this is their notification," said Philip, dispirited by now to the edge of despair.

"You must not accept this sheepishly. They are testing you by ordeal—you must protest being discarded in this cold-blooded fashion."

"Protest to whom?"

"To the king—who else?"

"And say what? 'Your Majesty owes this devoted servant his utmost solicitude'? 'Your Majesty ought to reward me well for years of exemplary service, not bargain me away like some lumpish chattel'? 'Your Majesty is an ungrateful brute'?"

"The words are not so important. You must register your chagrin."

"What does the king care for my survival when his own is at stake?"

"Precisely," said Anne. "This is the testing time of his mettle—and he cannot wait to abandon you. You must at the least score him for the unkindness—and if they pitch you into the night, go howling and not like some spineless scarecrow." Then her fortitude and fury gave way all at once, and she slumped against him. "Oh, God—that you should have dedicated your life to such a serpent! What's to become of us now, Philip?"

His reply that night to the archbishop expressed consensual warmth among the Nottingham group over the text of the proposed charter of liberties, but near the end of his letter Philip confessed dismay at encountering his own name. "I cannot but wonder," he wrote, "if my elimination is to be so readily conceded, why the crown has retained my services these many years. If they have been valueless, I ought to have been eliminated long since; if not, this flagrant yielding to the king's intemperate foes honors no one, His Majesty still less than those he would so blithely sacrifice."

Nothing more was heard for a time, and speculation grew that the charter had been scrapped. Then the sheriff had a cryptic letter from Brewer. "Ye of scant faith," the baron wrote, "are too quick to cry betrayal. Our enemies called for your outright exile, not merely dismissal, but the king would have none of it. They want you out precisely because you have served so well. If you read closely, you would have noted the so-called charter mentions no date for your detachment from royal service. But if it must someday come to pass, you and your countrymen will be amply compensated."

"My land of birth notwithstanding," Philip wrote back, "my country is and ever shall be England. Otherwise, your words lend comfort and win my gratitude."

But his uneasiness intensified with each passing day. What conceivable compensation might the crown devise for him beyond some menial task at court or commission as itinerant bloodletter à la Fawkes? Yet his heart was not curdled by bitterness. Rather, he asked himself, assuming his hide was to be part of the price for a just and lasting concord throughout the kingdom, how it was any less his duty now to accept this sacrifice than it had hitherto been for him to serve with devotion.

Within a week of his having had Brewer's reassurance, letters patent reached the castle bearing a copy of the Great Charter, duly executed at a meadow called Runnymede by the Thames between Staines and Windsor, and a message from the king stating that peace had been made "between us, our barons, and the freemen of our realm." The charter was to be read aloud to the people of his shires and the oath to the barons' committee of twenty-five duly administered as per the final clause of the agreement.

"Why not have Sparks do the reading in the shire court?" Anne suggested. "It need not become a major spectacle."

"It would be too crabbed an execution of the king's order," said Philip. "Plainly, it's my duty as the chief magistrate."

"It's not your duty to become a laughingstock by announcing your own forced dismissal—as if you gladly assent. It is a perverse expectation. Let the undersheriff do the reading, or the coroner, or even the bailiff—and let the ceremony be circumspect."

"I'll not give them the satisfaction of proclaiming my finish. And the oath-taking must be as public as possible if it's not to be a sham. No, there's no way out of it. It must be done in the town marketplace before the largest throng that can be coaxed to assemble."

"I'll not attend, thank you, and be a party to your humiliation."

"Think of it, my dear, as a tribute. Had I been less of a sheriff, I'd never have earned this distinction—to be cited by name in so momentous a document."

"How dreadfully amusing," said Anne. "The worst of it is that I think you mean it. Please express my apologies to the mob, but I'll be occupied just then tending my herbs."

Word of the event circulated swiftly among all the districts of Nottinghamshire, so that by noon on the Saturday following, an assemblage as vast as that generally on hand for the Goose Fair filled the marketplace and hummed in celebratory humor at the appearance of the sheriff's company. The bailiff positioned his mounted deputies throughout the crowd while two dozen sergeants-at-arms ringed it. A roar arose as the sheriff climbed the steps of the small platform deployed at the center of the market square for such public occasions, and it did not subside until he held up his hand and began to read the charter in a low, even voice.

Each new pledge of liberty, each fresh vow of royal restraint, drew a volley of cheers that the sheriff let echo to the hillsides before he read on. Their enthusiasm did not flag until after an hour, when the summer sun and the more arcane passages of the document began to take their toll. As Philip reached the forty-fifth clause, the first derisive hoots went up. By the forty-seventh, the first round of overripe fruit and eggs sailed through the sky and landed with bright splatters against the platform. By the forty-ninth, the sheriff's coat and tunic were discolored, and the noise and pelting had become so general as to comprise a direct assault on crown authority. Master Manning climbed the platform at this point, hand latched to the hilt of his heavy sword, and stared the crowd into a momentary hush.

But as the sheriff announced the fateful fiftieth clause, proclaiming the realm's deliverance from its French captains, a churl in the front row shouted with bell-like clarity, "Adieu to you, Monsieur Philippe!" and turned, baring his derrière to the platform.

The crowd's ecstasy knew no bounds. The sheriff stood before them in scalding anger, never flinching as the aerial bombardment resumed. Each time a pulpy, putrid object found its mark and dirtied him more, the roars of spiteful joy were renewed. When they at last ebbed and the assemblage strained to hear the sheriff read the words of his own promised ejection from office, it was the bailiff who spoke instead.

"You are swine who insult this man of honor!" he bellowed, the words rolling like a thunderclap over their heads. "He came here a reviled stranger among us, yet has served justly and squarely, without stinting, as no other who ever held his office." A low, uneasy murmuring was stirred by this stout rebuke. "To mock him now in his hour of tribulation, when he merits your acclaim instead, is no conduct for a fit Englishman. Hear him out in silence and show him your respect, not your scorn!"

Just then a spherical missile with a thin, brittle crust arched through the sunlight and crashed against the side of the bailiff's head, depositing a layer of dark, foul liquid over his face and scalp. The cheer it ignited was scotched at once, though, as the bailiff reflexively unsheathed his sword and raised it high in glittering signal to his deputies among the throng to do likewise. The flashpoint of violence had been reached. The marketplace grew still with expectancy.

"Put up your weapon, Master Manning," the sheriff instructed as quietly as he could and without looking at the bailiff.

"They dishonor you, sire."

"Then the pain is mine. Put up your weapon."

"As you are dishonored, so are we all," the bailiff answered, and kept his sword aloft.

Then the sheriff looked out over the motionless throng and declared so all could hear, "If the folk of the shire delight so at my required leavetaking, Master Bailiff, that is their privilege. I pray only that whoever follows me at the castle will abuse them no more roundly than I have done." He turned to Manning. "And now, put up your sword, sire."

The bailiff cast him a brief sideward glance, then slowly lowered his weapon and returned it to its scabbard.

A roar of a new kind greeted the bailiff's compliance, and when the sheriff resumed his reading, the earlier mood of derision yielded to respectful attentiveness, as if in contrite acknowledgment of Manning's reprimand. By the time he completed the task, the crowd had thinned markedly, its revelry reduced to mute awareness that the likes of Philip Mark might never again be seen in Nottingham.

To close the ceremony, Father Ivo held high a crucifix, and Philip exhorted the few hundred remaining spectators to place a hand over their hearts and repeat his words of fealty to the barons' committee. That he regarded the latter as in no way the king's betters mattered little to him; the oath had been mandated by the charter, and so he administered it— with more detachment than fervor, to be sure. That he might be performing his last official act was a far more somber thought as he mouthed the required words. The possibility, even the likelihood, of his imminent dismissal continued to weigh heavily on him during his slow ride back to the castle in garments stained and reeking. But his furrowed brow remained unbowed, and his gaze fixed to the bright ripples of the crown pennon atop the donjon.

On retiring to his closet for a few moments of contemplation, he was met by the waiting bailiff, still more aromatic than the sheriff and looking twice as glum as customary. "Enduring their abuse," Philip said quietly before he could be addressed, "was well worth it to me, Master Manning, to have earned such a tribute as yours. I've had no finer one all the days of my life." It was as close as the sheriff had ever come to an expression of naked sentiment to an underling.

"In that event," replied the bailiff, "I regret all the more having to tender you my notice of retirement. A week tomorrow, shall we say?"

Drained by his public pillorying, Philip was too weary for a fresh emotional encounter. He lapsed into his most laconic manner. "And why is that called for, Master Bailiff?"

"No sooner were my heartfelt words spoken in defense of your honor, Master Mark, than you saw fit to reprimand me before the entire shire."

"I did such a thing?"

"You ordered me to sheath my sword—so that all might hear—as if I were some crazed Goth about to traffic in gore."

"So it seemed. But I made no reprimand—if anything, it was a countermand—and issued aloud only after you had twice defied my private instruction."

"Because the mob was getting out of hand and needed to fear the feel of cold steel in its ribs."

"But you might have incited it still more in the process—you looked ready to kill—and I could not risk the mayhem."

"I would have killed—if any more of them provoked—"

"Then you endorse my point."

"Still, you had no call to make yourself the mob's hero at my expense."

"I had no such intention—and you must surely know it."

"I know only what I am witness to—or am told, sire. I'm poor at guessing what I'm not told."

In that last plaintive remark the sheriff thought he gleaned the true nature of the bailiff's grievance but hesitated to confront him with it. "At any rate, I cannot accept your notice of retirement—not on the ground of some imagined slight. I think perhaps there is some other—"

"You cannot hold me against my will."

"Is it better wages you seek? Alas, I cannot offer you them even if I were so—"

"You already deprive yourself of wealth, sire, so that our pay may be sustained at a tolerable level. I ask no more of you in that regard."

"Is the work, then, too arduous—or your hours of duty too many?"

"None of that."

"Then I think our quarrel is about nothing I may have said to you of a demeaning sort. It's what I've not said that burns you."

"Sire?"

"I will put it to you plainly, then, as I have never before. You cannot leave the castle's service, Master Manning—you must not—because I badly need you at my side."

The bailiff's immobile face softened. It was just such a disclosure of reciprocated esteem that he had been pining to hear from the sheriff, like a maiden who had perilously committed her affection before learning whether its object shared her tendency. "Sire . . . I—"

"Don't abandon me now, friend," Philip said, his words laced with warmth. "We stand together against the world."

The bailiff, looking more relieved than flattered, broke into a gap-toothed smile. The next instant the two men embraced awkwardly about the shoulders, mingling musk and fugitive emotion for an embarrassed moment, then hurried off in separate directions to rid themselves of rankness.

· XXXIX ·

"YOU MUST GIVE YOUR DEVIL HIS DUE," said the sheriff. "The king has been admirably faithful to the agreement."

"He has made a fair enough start of it," Lambert conceded. "But it can all be swiftly halted—which is precisely why the confederates cannot be expected to lay down their arms until he has satisfied the bulk, if not all, of their grievances."

The writs had gone out from the crown's traveling Chancery with an exemplary show of fidelity to the dictates of the Great Charter. Indeed, the claims of the king's most notorious foes among the rebel baronage were the first to be met. Fitz Walter, their ringleader, regained custody of Hertford castle. A young Briouse was given title in wardship to the town of Buckingham. In the north, Vesci was awarded his ancestral hunting rights for the minimum fine. But it could not all be accomplished everywhere at once, and so the barons found it useful to begin grumbling of the king's dilatory tactics.

With regard to the pledge to remove his French officers, the king appeared to be complying equally—so much so, in fact, that the first to be sacrificed was his pre-eminent retainer, des Roches, the justiciar, who had not even been named in the charter. His high-handedness, though, had no doubt driven the barons to wring assurances from the king that he would be promptly replaced. In his stead, surprisingly, the crown named

Hubert de Burgh, Philip's former colleague in the French wars, who had made a speedy recovery from his careless performance as sheriff of Lincolnshire. Sent to Poitou as seneschal just before the king's late, ill-fated campaign in France, de Burgh performed well under inhospitable conditions; and being one of the few of John's men trusted by all sides, Sir Hubert was a sound choice to heal the wounds des Roches had opened. As to the Frenchmen cited in the charter, the king had lost no time in removing Engelard de Cigogne as sheriff of Gloucestershire and Hereford, Geoffrey de Martigny as constable at Northampton Castle, and Peter de Chanceaux as the castellan at Bristol. They, too, must have been told there would be no rush in disposing of them, Philip guessed. Surely his own days at Nottingham were numbered.

Notwithstanding the king's early efforts to honor the charter, the rebels clung fast to their base in London and showed no willingness to affix their seals in corroboration of the spoken vows given when the pact was agreed upon in mid-June. To the crown, this latter step was of the essence, for by it the rebels were to acknowledge "we are bound by oaths and homage to our lord John, king of England, to protect faithfully his life, limbs, and worldly honor against all men and to guard and defend his rights." Instead of formally confirming this oral pledge, many of the barons had set to work fortifying their manors and castles, arguing they were not bound to bend before the throne until all their grievances had been satisfied, all their contested properties restored, all unreasonable fines canceled—and everyone everywhere in the realm had taken the oath to the baronial committee.

"It has become apparent, though," the sheriff said to Lambert, "from what the archbishop writes to Honorius, that regardless of circumstances, your party refuses to submit to any taking from them whatever or the crown's withholding of any rights or privileges—"

"They're not my party, or I'd be in the field with them. The king's further actions will determine what course I follow."

"But if the barons continue to insist on total license and that the king lacks all power to withhold from them—"

"To withhold unjustly."

"Yes, but to determine what is just or unjust often requires careful weighing. The barons reject the need for any such procedure and simply declare, 'Give us our due.' "

"You ignore the overriding point, Philip. The confederates dare not yield London or disband their forces or swear fealty to John until they've won all their reparations and had their rights restored at once and in full, as the charter specifies. For once they submit—once they abandon the field and enter into endless haggling—the crown instantly regains the upper hand, and the baronage is again at the king's mercy, which is what this entire undertaking seeks to rectify."

"But the barons ought at least begin the process of accommodation—the burden cannot be entirely the crown's," the sheriff argued. "Instead, they say only, 'You've not yet done enough.' And to compound matters, they demean the king. Why couldn't they have risen out of respect when he came on gouty legs to parley with them at Oxford the other week? Such a gratuitous insult throws all their *bona fides* into doubt."

Lambert issued a grunt of assent. "It was foolish and provocative. I can explain it only by their years of bridling under the Angevin yoke. These Plantagenets have not been easy rulers, and so for this singular season of retribution, their abused vassals are in their glory. It's understandable, if not commendable."

"But it advances nothing."

"It sustains the illusion of triumph."

Even as Philip was enduring this protracted period of menace to his tenure, instructions arrived from Windsor that, rather than separating him from the crown, gave him new powers. He was to assume oversight at once of the two castles to his east belonging to the bishop of Lincoln—the bastions at Newark and Sleaford—which, together with Nottingham Castle, would form a vital twenty-five-mile line of blockage against the movement of rebel forces in the eastern half of the kingdom. Told to strengthen their garrisons and fortifications, the sheriff dispatched his deputy, Eustace of Lowdham, to take charge at Sleaford and Bailiff Manning to command Newark Castle, while he himself shuttled constantly between the fortresses to supervise their preparations.

On top of this came an order for Philip to seize and hold custody over the honor of Melbourne, in the extreme southern sector of Derbyshire, whose holder had lately joined the rebel ranks. So long as the barons withheld all semblance of compliance with their pledges under the charter, the crown was not about to tolerate fresh defections to their camp. But no sooner had Philip led a small party to take possession of Melbourne unopposed than he had a message of sharp protest from the earl of Derby.

"You violate my bailiwick," Ferrers wrote him, "and act in grasping fashion only because the crown is incapacitated. Melbourne is justly mine. I await your surrender of it to my men." The sheriff, shunning testiness, replied that he had acted strictly under crown directive, urged the complaint be routed to Windsor, and paid the earl his highest respects.

To cap off this puzzling enhancement of his position, so contradictory to the mandate of the charter, Philip was further ordered to take direct control of the royal forests of his counties—the Peak in Derbyshire and Sherwood in Nottinghamshire. No reason was cited, but the king's chief forester, Hugh de Neville, was said to be under suspicion of consorting with the rebels, likely in revenge for having long endured cuckoldry by the royal cock. Revenues from the crown forests, moreover, could not be properly harvested by their regular officers due to wartime conditions and so were best gathered by those sheriffs who maintained a royal treasury at their castles.

Soon after this last instruction was in hand, Philip rode out into Sherwood with a complement of six knights and six sergeants a discreet mile or so to his rear. He was not long in being escorted to the forest's chief resident poacher and sometime outlaw. "Good Master Hood," said the sheriff, on renewing acquaintance with the antic woodsman, "we need further enlist your doughty skills in the crown's behalf."

"Such an honor! Pray tell, sire."

"There is a war of sorts in progress—"

"So they say, but we've not seen it."

"Matters may worsen momentarily if the rebel side does not soon honor its pledges. Our regular foresters are needed in the king's army and to hold his castles, yet we must keep the wood free of the crown's enemies who would invade it for food, fuel, or haven."

"Fair enough."

"Nor can we leave the forests officially unpoliced, however limited our personnel. So here is my proposal to you and your hearty band. Deny all entry here to forces disloyal to the crown—and those enemies who elude you at first, hunt down and turn over to the castle, where they'll be held for ransom. From all the rest who seek passage, take what cheminage you see fit, tailoring your fee to their capacity for payment—"

"You grant us royal license to extort?"

"To aid in the defense of the realm, shall we say—with the proviso that you deliver half your receipts to the castle. The war has hampered our ability to collect levies—few feel obliged to pay tribute to a king at risk of being deposed."

"Sad happenstance. But while I am deeply moved by your appeal for our aid, Master Mark, tell me why it is we should undertake this service for a king whose laws of the wood remain harsh and who is no friend of the common folk."

"Because the kingdom is at war—and the king has pledged reforms."

"It's not our war but his. As to reforms, pledges are not acts."

"He has begun to act."

"Our oaks have not been advised. Will he act to ease the laws of the forest?"

"The new charter requires a royal commission to investigate these."

"Bulls will grow udders before royal commissioners effect a change. And tell me, sire, what if we decline the task you put to us?"

"You'll be driven from the wood by my forces. Sherwood must be kept secure for the king."

"So," said Robin, "you'd go back on our bargain?"

"Our so-called bargain was made under duress, let me remind you— but was nonetheless honored because I thought it in the crown's interest to do so. At any rate, my proposal in no way revokes your privileges. You'd still have the run of the forest, only now I tax you with the duty to earn your keep. Moreover, I'll pledge you my every effort to see that the codes of the wood are made more humane when the peace is restored and the crown addresses the matter."

"You speak like an intimate of the king, sire. But they say you may soon be retired from royal service, so of what worth is your pledge?"

"Report of my retirement is premature—the crown increases my authority by the day as the emergency grows. I could use a bit of respite, frankly."

"If it should prove to be more than a bit," said the woodsman with a sly smile, "there will always be a place for you with us, sire. We'll hone your skill with the bow in no time—and the life out here is wholesome enough, except in the inclement season."

"I'll bear your kind invitation in mind," said the sheriff, "though my wife and daughters might find the rigors of the wood disheartening."

"Neither wine nor women are unknown to us, sire—both seem more mellow and less numbing with nature as their constant companion."

The sheriff smiled. "Meanwhile, I count on your help. Bring what prisoners and collections you take directly to the castle, asking for me or my clerk."

"What check have you on our takings?"

"None but your honor, Master Hood—and it will suffice."

The kingdom's tremulous prospect for peace was roughly shaken near the close of August by the arrival from Rome of a papal letter. It ordered the archbishop to excommunicate forthwith all "disturbers of the realm" and drew attention to the rebel barons who had not yet renewed their vows to the crown.

"Just as I've suspected!" Lord Lambert railed at the sheriff upon learning the somber news. "It was all premeditated—the pope cares nothing for charters, nor does the king. It's the crowning insult, Philip. How can I remain aloof when John engages in blatant subterfuge?"

"You may be overhasty, sire," said Philip. "As Ivo and Honorius read the papal letter, it was written without knowledge of the charter—it bears no reference to it and would thus appear to be outdated and irrelevant. The test will be whether Langton elects to promulgate it or ignore it. He's the architect of the charter if anyone is—and the kingdom's last honest broker. If he bends to the pope, then you'll be well justified in holding that this has all been a plot concocted between the king and Rome."

"How can the archbishop refuse his vicar? I say it's over with."

"Hold your horses a bit longer, my lord."

Within the fortnight, Honorius was aglow with the report that Langton had chosen not so much to defy the papal instruction as to place it to one side, pending clarification of its apparent ignorance of the charter. But soon came the added word that the pope's commissioners in England had reiterated the excommunication order, insisting that, charter or no charter, the barons remained notoriously defiant of their lord king and, by extension, his overlord in Rome. When the archbishop declined the commissioners' order and questioned their authority, they suspended him from his sacred office scarcely two years after he had taken it up. Langton, in a fury at king, barons, pope, and commissioners alike for utterly frustrating his appeals to sweet reason and temporal justice, left for Rome to plead his case.

Father Ivo was in shock. "We plunge from high hope to the edge of the abyss in three short months," he lamented, and turned to say vespers in a despairing singsong, as if not even God could set matters aright.

The arrival of a second papal bull at the end of September sent the kingdom tumbling into the abyss. This time there could be no question whether Rome knew of the charter; indeed, it was what prompted the communication. In excoriating language, the pope decried "concessions . . . extorted from a great prince," who, Innocent insisted, "was forced to accept an agreement which is not only shameful and base but also illegal and unjust." Thus, he went on, casting the kingdom into a vale of grief, "we utterly reject and condemn this settlement, and under threat of excommunication we order that the king should not dare to observe it." The incandescent charter of liberties, that beacon above the battle, that death knell for tyranny and herald of a just governance, was "null and void of all validity for ever."

Whether the king had been dealing in bad faith from the outset, always intending to call upon the pope to quash any unacceptable concessions the baronage might force upon him, was now a secondary issue. The timing of the new papal letter—a speedy courier could make the round trip from Windsor to Rome in two months—was powerfully suggestive that the king had indeed solicited the pope's intervention after the barons frustrated him at Oxford in late July by refusing even to begin fulfilling their part of the bargain until the royal reparations under the charter had become fact.

"But the charter specifies it is insulated from all outside efforts to nullify it," said Father Ivo, crestfallen after reading the papal text.

"Yes," said Sparks, "but the king has set the pope over him and his vassals, so any dealings between them are necessarily subject to Rome's review—a point we all overlooked in our zeal for the charter."

"I see now why the archbishop held the king accountable for yielding the realm to the Holy Father," said Honorius, as glum as the chaplain at the disastrous turn of events. "It was imprudent in the extreme."

"Infinitely calculating, I should think, rather than imprudent," said the sheriff. "There's no pope to be checkmated on the chessboard of statecraft."

"You mean to say the king has manipulated the charter as a game throughout?" asked Honorius.

"I say only there's blame all around—and trust nowhere."

With the charter voided, the last prop to civility between the sides was kicked away, and the war was soon under way in earnest. The rebels seized Rochester Castle, the archbishop's stronghold in Kent, gateway to the kingdom, and the royal forces moved at once to recover it. The English crown was formally proffered by the baronial party to Philip Augustus's son, Prince Louis. And Fawkes de Breauté, that violent tamer of the unruly, was named sheriff in six hotly disputed counties—the surest sign yet that the country had entered on a full wartime footing.

A week after the annulment of the *magna carta* had become common knowledge, a pair of notes from the same correspondent was delivered at Nottingham Castle. The first, to the sheriff, read:

Sire:

    With due regard for our acquaintance of these several years past, I wish to do you the courtesy of advising that I shall have quit my manor by the time you read this and done what is imperative for me to retain my honor. I cannot feign further loyalty to a treacherous monarch. It is self-evident that he has schemed all along with his nominal master at Rome to make a mockery of our famous charter, hoping the baronial confederates would yield and failing to count on their steadfastness of spirit. I salute your own devotion to duty and know it to be other than mindless, so respect me mine. God be with us both.

                                                                    Lambert.

The second note, to the sheriff's wife, was yet more securely sealed and handled by a discreet courier. It read:

My dearest Anne:

    I have done what I must do—my note to Philip explains all. I know not when or if we shall be with each other again, but it plainly cannot be the same hereafter. You have held me longer than I ought to have stayed in vows to a faithless king, but I do not blame you, only myself for yielding to an irresistible passion— and have no regret. My love for you survives unimpaired yet falls victim to the impingements of our separate lives, for neither of us can or will throw away all else. I shall ache—indeed, do so already—each time I let myself dwell on your loveliness and the

forbidden ardor we have shared. Farewell and Heaven's blessings
on you, sweet lady of Tours.

                                                                T.

She read it over three times. At the first reading, she grew flushed
and panicky. It simply could not be. His disaffection from the king was
habitual peevishness, nothing more—surely not enough to drive him beyond ranting into rashness. Something more, something else, had to be
involved for him to have abandoned reason and put his whole fortune at
dire risk. Had she really known the man half so well as she supposed?
Nobility of character required his enduring a hateful dilemma, not fleeing
from it. And how unbearable, after all, had the king made his life? Perhaps
boredom was consuming him all the days of the month that she was not
with him—and the one that she was could no longer compensate.

On the second reading, she became angered. How could he have
parted from her in such an abrupt and cowardly fashion? Was his will so
frail that he feared she would deflect him from his dubious mission? And
how, moreover, could he have been so thoughtless as to imperil her by
committing his sentiments to writing? It was beyond self-indulgence—as
if in discarding her, he had no further care what might befall her. His
profession of sustaining love struck her now as hollow and almost sordid,
the words of an overgrown boy devoid of sensitivity to their context and
effect.

By the third reading, a spasm of relief had begun to pulse through
her. She felt purged of something insidious within her system over which
she had long ago lost control. Since she had not the strength to act—since
there were so many ready excuses to prolong the emotional imprisonment,
even to relish it—ought she not to be grateful to him for casting her aside
and returning her to her senses?

As she fed the letter to the flames in her hearth, her cheeks grew
unaccountably damp and her eyes red-rimmed, requiring half an hour's
application of the cosmetic arts before she again dared venture beyond
the walls of her apartment. As if drawn by a compulsion she had neither
wish nor need to identify, she struggled up to the small, dark loft adjacent
to the castle stables where the gyrfalcon Lambert had given her was
housed—Eurydice, she had named the finicky creature after their infernal
love. She carried the bird slowly to the castle roof, aware of its coiled
density as never before. Once out in the open, she faced north, toward

Thomas's great manor and the darkly quilted forest just beyond, and uttered a prayer for his well-being and a benediction on their enduring secret. Then she unhooded the falcon and felt a rush of fear at the fierceness of its all-seeing look. It blinked several times, shook itself with a tremor that made her recoil, and leapt into space. After a tentative swoop or two, the bird soared toward the sun at a steep incline, then lapsed into an easy gyre for a few moments before heading for the ridge line cut by the cliffs above the town. Anne turned and fled down the steps before the falcon was out of sight.

She languished in the shadows of the waning day, the numb void within her transformed by imperceptible degrees into a single throbbing bruise that by sundown had seemed to take possession of her wholly. Her sole consolation was that the bird had not returned—nor, so long as she did not reveal herself, was it likely to.

There was no way to avoid the topic of Lambert's desertion to the king's enemies on her after-supper walk with Philip that evening. He was the more forgiving of the pair. "I cannot but admire the man's courage," he said, "however greatly to our disadvantage this step of his."

"I'd call it a mindless tantrum," she answered. "What point can he gain by it? Who or what will come in the king's place if Thomas's side prevails? Can the aftermath prove any better for him—or for England? This is a child's petulance—as if he could conceive of nothing better to do with himself and his dwindling vigor!"

"You're too harsh on him. This was no impulsive act. He'd postponed acting for months—years, even."

"And I say you're not harsh enough on him. You've wanted to change places with the man for years, Philip—admit it."

"Places," he said, taking her hand, "but not wives. How great a sin is it to envy a man with nearly every earthly advantage? I only wonder what I'd have done now in his stead."

"Not tossed away your advantages pointlessly."

"Perhaps that's the great luxury of his position—he has no need to calculate where it will all lead, only to act as he thinks right and hope for the best."

"I'd call that the antics of an irresponsible infant or a doddering dimwit—though, I grant you, he seemed neither."

He released her hand. "You're overwrought by his leaving."

"Am I?"

"Heartbroken, almost, I should say—as if he's abandoned us and ought to have moderated his behavior on our account if no other." He glanced toward her. "Or is it that you've developed a deeper attachment to him than you've ever confessed to me?"

Though years late, the question was welcome. She met his glance. "To you or to myself—I cannot say which. The truth is that I am sickened by his flight—I had thought him made of finer stuff."

"Whereas I, oddly, see fineness in the flight—and his willingness to cast aside everything else for—for the love of justice."

For the love of self, she thought, but did not say it.

Next day the sheriff led a fully armed party of ten that rode without resistance through the gates of Swanhill and posted a royal writ of diseissin beside the main entry to the manor house. The steward was on hand to receive them. "Since your lord has entered into rebellion," Philip told him, "this is now the king's property."

"I shall do my utmost to see the manor maintained in the crown's interest, sire," Stryker replied with a curt bow.

"Your solicitude is touching, Master Steward, but the crown will not consort with those sunk to their nostrils in the bogs of corruption. Three days hence, if not sooner, you will quit these premises or find lodgings not to your liking at the king's castle."

Stryker's mouth gaped. "I . . . what is—is my offense—sire?"

"What is not?"

"But—you must have just cause."

"The manor is in crown custody for treason, and I like you not for a steward—or an excuse for a man. There's cause enough." The sheriff turned his mount and, encountering the stablemaster, told him, "Kindly convey my respects to Lady Cicely and assure her no harm will come to her or the manor."

When he returned the week following to be certain that Stryker had gone and to deal as well with Jadwin, the ruthless beadle, the sheriff was greeted by a plea for mercy and an offer of long-withheld testimony. "If you spare me, sire, I'll name you the murderer of the ploughman Paul," the beadle promised, "unless the crime has fled your memory. I ask only that my name not be linked to the disclosure."

"I can promise you nothing," said the sheriff, containing any show of high curiosity. "But if you fail to reveal now what you plainly know, I'll see you languish in prison till Doomsday."

"But if I speak out, who'll protect me?"

"Since when does the beadle need protection?"

"When he would be menaced by his lord."

"Sir Thomas? You can't mean it."

"But it's so, sire."

"Why would he have done away with his own bondsman?"

"Out of rage."

"From what cause?"

"The ploughman's misguided attempt to ingratiate himself." The beadle paused to weigh the effect of his words. When the sheriff impatiently gestured him on, the rest of the story tumbled out at a rush.

Paul had learned that Stryker was bringing the widow Griggs to the manor house—she had caught the lord's eye, which, according to the beadle, was ever on the rove, given Lady Cicely's chilly disdain for his conjugal rights, and so he asked to have her service him. "Master Stryker neglected to tell the lord that Susan was spreading her legs for half the manor at tuppence a toss," Jadwin said. "The ploughman, who craved her for himself and feared her lying with the lord would soon enough spoil her for the likes of a suety churl, thought to win Sir Thomas's favor by approaching him in private and revealing how widely the fair Susan plied her trade." Unfortunately, this tawdry piece of news drove the lord berserk— partly, the beadle supposed, because of the ploughman's impudence in coming to him on so intimate a matter, partly because he could not stand the thought of its being true. "So Paul's blood flowed."

"And how do you know all of this?"

Jadwin nodded confidently. "Still in a fury, the lord summoned Stryker to the site of the murder and threatened to slit his throat in the same fashion for deceiving him about the widow if he didn't get rid of the body in a way to divert all suspicion from the manor house. Knowing of my close familiarity with Susan's business—I took a sliver of her receipts in return for my protective services—the steward ordered me to arrange the corpse so that it would look like a crime of jealous passion. So I carried his carcass to the wood after nightfall, chopped off his balls, and stuffed them in his mouth. Stryker was admiring of that touch but warned me to keep my mouth shut or I'd end up with my own pair down my throat."

The sheriff quelled a shiver at the grisly tale. "Why come to me with this story now?"

"To save my hide. I've no place else to go if you throw me off the manor, and there's war and danger at every turn. At any rate, I pray the baron never returns here—let him perish in the rebellion."

"You sound an ungrateful dog."

"Why should I be grateful to the likes of him? For all his pose of courtliness, he's always been a heartless master. Swanhill's people are no more than fence posts to him—the man would as soon cut a villein in twain as tell him the month of year. And yet I'm the one here reviled for my cruelty. I hate him to the core."

Philip probed the beadle's eyes and longed to find in them a revealing shiftiness. His vilifying words were all the more repugnant because this Jadwin had won such small renown as an earnest peacekeeper. Yet he seemed to bring such uncontrived fluency to his narrative that the sheriff was persuaded there had to be more than a droplet of truth in it. Nor could he avoid asking himself whether Lambert's charm and verve, when added to his rank and riches, had not long blinded him to the baron's darker nature. Had he unwittingly entered into a bargain, Philip wondered, to gain intimacy with the lord of Swanhill by circumspectly avoiding the meaner aspects of his life and ways? Candid or cunning, though, Sir Thomas surely ought not to be indicted *in absentia* solely on the testimony, likely as spiteful as it was opportune, of a desperate retainer.

"If I were to keep you on here," the sheriff said, slowly scanning the great meadow that fell away in dunes of beige stubble below the manor house lawn, "you would have to pledge absolute obedience to the new steward and refrain altogether from your past abuses."

"I hold myself in penance, sire, from this instant forth."

Philip rode straightway to Hathersgate and related the beadle's story to Master Blake. The erstwhile reeve of Swanhill was shocked by the disclosure but would not fully credit it. "Jadwin, I think, might well kill his own mother to advance his interest."

"Perhaps you'll delve further into the matter with him as his new master," said the sheriff. "The manor is in urgent need of a trustworthy steward."

"Me, sire?"

"Who better?"

Words left him, and Blake's eyes watered in the autumn wind. Then he shook his head and said that much as he relished the notion, the great manor held too many torturous memories for him to return to it, even as its overseer. "But there's one man left at Swanhill fit for the post," Blake added.

"Name him."

"The smith—Alden Sparks. But he is a bondsman."

"Then we shall set him free."

The sheriff's clerk wept openly when told that the royal writ of manumission was to bear his half-brother's name. "And what price does the crown proffer for him?" asked Jared as he set to the happy task of composing the document.

"Shall we say—what?—a penny?"

"It cannot be, sire. So small a price will count as wasting the manor and may someday go against you."

"Then what?—a shilling? The castle funds are in short supply."

"Say six shillings. Alden and I will make up the difference between us."

"A decent price," said Philip with a nod, "for a lasting charter of liberty."

· XL ·

AT HIS FUNERAL all who had known him agreed that Clement de Beaupré had undergone an extraordinary transformation the last two years of his life. From a somewhat shallow and showy celebrant of the faith he turned into a genuinely pious ascetic who wasted away in protracted penance. As he ebbed, the brethren of Lenton Priory drew themselves into two camps, the first led by the subprior, who favored Clement's earlier, more indulgent mode of monasticism, and the second by the sacristan, who, thinking Clement an old fool until his last years, endorsed a more austere communal life of worship and contemplation. Emblematic of the division between the two sides were their contrasting views of the great tolling clock the prior had had installed in the cloister courtyard. Those more frankly worldly in their interests hailed the mechanism as a miraculous confirmation of the divine spirit in mankind; those of a more spiritual nature saw in it the devil's handiwork and wished it gone.

For all his withdrawal from earthly considerations, the prior had become aware of this schism within his house. His last will and testament thus contained a surprising request beyond its asking that the sheriff join the earl of Derby, the prior's chief patron, and Sir Mitchell of Rainworth, its knight protector, as his lay pallbearers. It was his further prayerful wish, the prior added, that his service of interment be conducted not by any Lenton inmate but by Father Ivo—and that, moreover, "that same holiest of sons of Holy Church" be elected to succeed him and heal the spiritual rift that was threatening to tear the priory asunder. This message from eternity inspired consternation throughout the monastery and drew the prompt disapproval of the earl, who was known to favor nothing and nobody connected with Nottingham Castle; he tolerated Sir Mitchell only because the coroner had long provided him corroborative evidence that the king's fortress was a perpetual den of thieves and upstarts.

Not long after the prior had been laid to rest, the sheriff summoned Sir Mitchell and solicited his aid on two counts. The first was to ask the use of his good offices with the earl, whose animus seemed likely to doom Ivo's chances to preside at Lenton. "The chaplain is a true man of God, and his election would be a life's fulfillment as well as a boon to the priory," said Philip. "A few words of warmth from you might make all the difference."

"What sway I have," the coroner answered, "is committed elsewhere, sire." He was championing the candidacy of his brother-in-law, the archdeacon for the see of Lincoln—"and a man, I must say, infinitely better qualified to preside at Lenton than our chaplain. Father Ivo, though I regard him well, is too old and frail for the position, and his coming to the priory as its master would be deeply resented. The notion, I fear, was Father Clement's final folly."

"Once more, then, we are at loggerheads," said Philip sadly. "But there is another matter that I trust may prove more congenial to you." The constant press of new duties brought on by the civil war had severely reduced Philip's opportunity to see to the education of Matthew and Andrew, his two wards, and so he wished to commit their chivalric training to Sir Mitchell in the same fashion as the chaplain was attending to their spiritual guidance and his first clerk to their literacy. "I appreciate it would impose a bit on your duties as coroner, yet perhaps not so much that—"

"Why me, sire? There are a dozen other knights on duty here now, most far more skilled than I at wielding arms and pursuing combat."

"There are more than martial skills to be mastered. And none of the others is likely to linger here—and surely none knows the castle or the shire as you. You would honor me by undertaking the task."

The coroner's eyes darted for escape. "I'm moved that you would repose such trust in me, sire, yet the idea leaves me uneasy."

"There cannot be any question of your knightly standing."

"It's none of that."

"Then what?"

"In the past, Master Mark, I have been your frank detractor—"

"My defamer, even—but what of it? It is your impartial practice with all sheriffs, I take it, to view carping as a sacred duty."

The coroner managed a crooked grin. "I cannot believe, sire, that you bear me no malice."

"We've all of us another cheek to turn," Philip said amiably. "Let my wards become a new bond between us. We'll start Matthew as a page— I'll send him to you a week hence, with deepest thanks and the blunt warning he's a spirited lad often in need of reprimand."

"It is my specialty, sire," Sir Mitchell said with a pleased look and a deep bow.

"Indeed."

Despite a certain remaining roughness of appearance and comportment, the boy's coming to live at Nottingham Castle was a cheering prospect to the Mark family, especially Angelique. For Matthew of Hathersgate re-minded her of the Welsh lads whom she had grown to love in the collective and whose ghastly end still scarred her callow memory. Her mother, too, was buoyed by his arrival, and she did her best to make Matthew welcome without seeming to dote on him. Even the sheriff, busy as he was, found a few moments each day for some friendly words with the boy, generally instructive in nature. Still, Philip was surprised when Matthew, while serving dinner in the great hall during his second month at the castle, asked in a whisper if he might accompany the sheriff on his walk to the river at sundown the next day.

They set out in silence as the boy gathered his courage to speak. Philip withheld all pleasantries and chose an easy pace suitable for ruminating.

"I hope you'll not be angered by what I ask, sire," his ward said at last.

"And should I be?"

"You may find it grating, but I can't think how to make it less so."

"Well, let's find out."

"I wish to know, sire," said Matthew, his gaze bolted to the path, "whether you steal—and if it amounts to very much."

"I see," said the sheriff with an inward smile. "You're no pussyfooter, at least."

The lad flicked an upward glance. "How else could I put it, sire?"

"Assuming a need to put it at all, you've done it eloquently."

"I know that tone, sire—you're displeased with me. But I mean no insult. I hear things, you see, that I'd rather not—"

"To be sure. Well, let's address the matter and not worry for the moment about the thinness of my skin." Philip draped a fond hand over the boy's farther shoulder as they walked. "You've put two related questions to me, and while they're equally unattractive, the first is the nub of it."

"Sire?"

"Well, the amount of my thievery would stem from the fact of it— so we need never reach your second question if we dispose of the matter with the first."

"I . . . yes . . ."

"The answer to your first question, then, is no."

The boy nodded without looking up at him and strode on pensively.

"Is that all it was?" Philip asked him after several moments.

"I . . . thought . . . there might be more to it—to be said."

"You sound disappointed."

"Oh, no—I'm glad—and didn't think so—but . . ."

"But someone's put the thought in your head, and you're man enough to come out with it. I like that in a lad."

Matthew looked across the crest of the meadow toward the river. "It was my damned aunt."

"I didn't ask—and you're not to pay her disrespect."

"She did you. She says all sheriffs steal—from the people and the king alike."

"Some have that reputation."

"She says you steal from Hathersgate as well."

"I see. And what is it she says I've taken from the manor—the stock, perhaps?"

"Oh, no—our flocks have burgeoned since Master Blake's arrival."

"Your corn, then?"

"No—that, too, has prospered under your custody."

"The furnishings, could it be—or your jewels or rare wines?"

"She tried to tell me you took our plate, but I happen to know that my uncle sold it off years ago to meet expenses—along with half the other contents of the place. Our wines I watched vanish down his throat."

"Then I must conclude that your aunt is not fond of me."

"Because you're not a knight, she says, but a common soldier—and knights don't steal, whereas soldiers do by second nature."

"I myself would not generalize that way—about either knights or soldiers. A very few of each are saintly."

Seemingly relieved that the topic had been so quickly exhausted, the boy shifted to a further cause for concern. "Sire, is Hathersgate to be truly mine when I come of age?"

"So I understand it."

"But I'll hold of the king—and must do what fealty he demands."

"You'll hold of Lord Sidwell, to be precise, and be his subtenant."

"So the manor will really be twice removed from my ownership?"

"It is your hereditary right, though, to hold it so long as you render your liege lord forty days' service at combat or guard duty each year and meet his fees."

"But what if the combat be against a foe I cannot despise?"

"It would nevertheless be your duty."

"Then I am to be in thrall to the king if I would not lose Hathersgate by default of hateful service to him?"

"Privilege has its price, Matthew—whereas poverty has no reward but anguish. Your lot, whatever its irksome aspects, is not the worst imaginable."

"I should prefer yours, sire. You serve the king for wages and the importance your office lends you. You could always leave it if you found the tasks required of you too loathsome."

"To a man without a birthright, his office is all the more precious, whereas property gives its owner choices in life. But even without the property, you would at least remain a knight and a gentleman. Out of office, I should be hard-pressed to claim even the latter."

"Why did you never receive the blow, sire? You seem most knightly in manner and bearing—far more so than Sir Mitchell, may I say?"

"The ungently born are but rarely knighted—so it behooves those who would be to strive for the effect."

"Is that the whole of it, then? Does nothing matter beyond birthright?"

` "To frame such a question does you honor—even as it betrays your innocence. Pity, you must be taught to abandon it."

"Must I, sire?"

"To survive."

"How so?"

"Why, then you will know that the thief who is asked if he is one is as unlikely to admit it as the innocent man is to welcome the charge."

Near the end of Matthew's third month in residence at the castle, his aunt, a thickset woman with a corresponding gravity of demeanor, came to see the sheriff's wife. "You are most kind to grant me an interview without notice, madam," she said upon entering the garden where Anne Mark was harvesting the last herbs of the season.

"Your nephew is a fine lad, of whom we have grown fond," Anne replied, "so we extend you every courtesy. How may I help, my lady?"

"My mission is awkward, madam—I must count on that fondness you mention to ease my burden." The boy's other relatives had met with her of late, much troubled by his transfer to the castle, and had delegated her to seek his return to Hathersgate forthwith.

"But why?" asked Anne. "He is well looked-after here."

"It is a combination of factors that distress us, the most immediate of which is the danger the boy faces, now that there is war in progress. The castle may well be subjected to siege—they say the rebel forces are already massing in Lincolnshire. For this reason I come to you, as a mother who may share such concerns, rather than appealing to the sheriff directly."

Anne put aside her trowel, brushed her hands free of soil, and guided her visitor to a nearby bench. "The castle is a great fortress, my lady, and my husband experienced in the defense of such structures. The fact is that Matthew is likely safer here than at home, where lawless enemies of the crown might far more readily wreak havoc on loyalists."

The boy's aunt grew more uneasy, not less, at this rejoinder. "Your words are reassuring, madam, but the problem, to be wholly candid, lies deeper. Let me speak plainly. While we are glad of the great kindness you expend on the boy, we detect in it an underlying purpose that cannot be condoned."

"Perhaps still more plainness will allow me to understand you."

"Matthew is wellborn and heir to a respectable legacy, though not so sizable a one that he can afford to be indifferent to the need for a wife of comparable, if not superior, position. He is not fated to wed the daughter of a common soldier, of however exalted a rank in the king's service." The woman swallowed hard, as if to convey that her barbed message was as painful to deliver as to receive. "I cannot blame you for aspiring to such a bond, madam, if that is indeed your design—nor would we expect you to concede as much, however apparent to us your intent. But we cannot accept it, and seek Matthew's removal from these premises before any untoward attachment might be formed between—"

"I'm told you suppose Master Mark an unscrupulous man—of a thieving nature. Is the boy, then, the booty that you suppose the sheriff has determined to steal from Hathersgate?"

Her visitor grew greatly flustered. "I—have not put it in such—harsh—terms. I say only that Master Mark is not a man of fit breeding but a warrior—and a tax collector—occupying a station well below what we can countenance in a—"

"You mistake the nature of my husband's calling, madam. He is a peacekeeper, not a warmaker. As to collecting taxes, they are the very basis of civilized order—more so, I daresay, than jousting knights, though the task be a thankless and repugnant one." Anne rose and looked down with blazing eyes at the pudding-faced woman. "As to your unspeakable presumption that the boy is here to be ensnared in matrimony to a daughter of ours, I'll dignify it with no comment whatever. But I shall report your request for Matthew's removal to the sheriff for what disposition he thinks fit. I bid you good day—madam."

Philip, to Anne's dismay, yielded readily in the matter.

"But you're the boy's guardian," she objected.

"By royal fiat, not blood tie. Taken though I am with him, I'll not hold the lad hostage against his family's wishes."

Sir Mitchell was charged with the task of explaining to the boy the social niceties of the age and riding him home to Hathersgate. But two mornings later, Matthew presented himself anew at the castle, having ridden there through the night with a weighty quarterstaff his sole companion, and asked to see the sheriff.

"You're far from home, young fellow," said Philip, greeting him with nonchalance. "Your people will fear for your safety."

"My home is here now, sire," said the boy, "unless I displease you."

"Didn't Sir Mitchell explain the reasons for your—"

"I've talked with Mistress Blake about it all, and she says that while you're suitably reluctant to give offense to the lordly class, I'm far better off with you at the castle, where my training can be more readily advanced, than at—"

"Mistress Blake is not your aunt."

"My aunt is a great sow."

"Sows have their virtues. You must stay at Hathersgate, Matthew."

"Why, sire? I am fourteen and have a mind of my own. I wish to be here—with people I care for—and help defend the castle if it—"

"The castle can be defended without you."

"If you send me home, sire, I'll only come back again."

"Then we'll take you home and chain you to a tree."

"Then I'll work myself free and desert to the rebels and tell them all I know of the castle's secrets and how best to lay siege—"

"Enough, enough!" Philip cried, abandoning his sternness with a great burst of laughter. "Besides, they tell me you're adept at the crossbow, and we need every well-knit lad we can scrape from the countryside."

The boy's eyes glowed. "I've not had much practice with the crossbow, sire, and would much welcome it."

"Come, then, I'll show you a thing or two about reloading that the constable may have neglected." As they passed his clerk, the sheriff called out, "Master Sparks, send word to Hathersgate that my prodigal ward insists on corrupting himself in this foul den of low life, and there's scant solace I can offer the family beyond forbearance."

· XLI ·

IT WAS NOT ONE CIVIL WAR but many. Skirmishes occurred up and down England's eastern half, which was largely in the hands, if not the grip, of those sympathetic to the uprising, and across the bleak north country, where King Alexander II of Scotland, reasserting his late father's claim to the border counties, marched as far as Newcastle in support of the rebel cause. But the conflict was inevitably centered wherever John of England rested his bones at any given moment, for the whole point of it was the tenure of the crown upon his head—indeed, of that head upon the royal neck.

The king had begun his defense of the realm at its southeast extremity with a seven-week siege to retake Rochester Castle. That effort intensified as the number of crown hirelings slowly swelled through imports from the Continent. Timbered tunnels painstakingly burrowed under the foundations of the great fortress were set afire by greased pigs serving as live torches, and the walls tumbled, allowing the royal forces to surge into the breach and gain a famous victory.

At that inspired moment, John might have marched on to London and tried to crush the heart of the insurrection before reinforcements could arrive en masse from France or Prince Louis prevail upon the papacy to bless his artfully bogus claim to the English throne. But the king, separated from his seat of government and severely limited in the way of human and financial resources, could not risk a decisive battle. He chose instead to stage a war of attrition. Assigning his most ferocious captain, Fawkes de Breauté, and his company to keep the rebels at bay in London, John turned north in mid-December and, contemptuous of the cold, began a march designed to show the barons against him the futility of their cause.

Such royal progresses had been undertaken almost annually in the past, but this one was different. Decidedly a war party, it reaped fines and tribute as it moved through hostile regions where the normal functioning of government had been badly impaired. And where John was resisted, he ravaged. Having circled London, the king reached St. Albans on the nineteenth and then drove on through Northampton and Rockingham, to arrive at Nottingham Castle the day before Christmas. Gout-ridden and saddle-sore, His Majesty nevertheless seemed exuberant over the mounting success of his northward march and thus brought with him an added air of rejoicing to the year's most hallowed festival.

The king, while hardly renowned as a devout worshiper, dutifully attended Father Ivo's Christmas Eve Mass, then fell into a long, restorative sleep and awoke to enjoy a day of merry respite from the struggle to save his crown. Rich foods abounded, rare libations flowed, impious tales were told while musicians strolled from chamber to chamber in ceaseless serenade of the royal eardrum; and on the dais, the king was as gay and frolicsome as any at Nottingham had ever seen him. Seated beside him at dinner, Anne Mark was struck by his buoyancy of spirit—no word of war or gloom crossed his lips, only regret that he could not dispense the usual gifts to his courtiers this troublous Yuletide—and by the attention the king lavished on her.

At the close of the meal he asked the sheriff's permission to engage his wife in a slightly sacrilegious game or two of chess in the royal apartment, explaining he had never had the pleasure of encountering a woman of intellect, as Mistress Mark was said to be, in such a contest.

Philip, catching Anne's eye with a cautionary glance, offered the obligatory response: "If it pleases the lady, Your Majesty, it would indeed be my honor."

Short of a feigned gastric attack or inexplicably brewed headache, she had no way out of the command performance and so smilingly acceded. Once across the royal threshold, though, Anne grew in discomfort and wariness. Although the king's carnal appetite was infamous, it could not have been inferred from his every look or gesture toward her. Nor could she have spurned his attentions at table without risk of appearing inhospitable and the consequent damage to Philip's position. At any rate, the time for evasion was past; her task now was to limit their engagement to the chess table.

The game advanced uneventfully enough until the king interrupted play to polish an invisible speck from his emerald pendant, the size of a hen's egg, and observe, apropos nothing whatever that Anne could detect, that the Irish attributed the gout to a divine immanence. "Thus, we gain in piety even as our spryness wanes and our pain multiplies," he said with a hollow laugh. "It is the very definition of a mixed blessing."

"At the least, I should think it a consolation, my lord."

"The only consolation," said the king, "is that the disease has not yet impaired our other faculties." He leaned toward her. "If madam would not find the subject unduly coarse, let us confide in her. After a fortnight on the road in chill and sullen weather, we long for the intimate company of a good and lovely woman—someone not unlike yourself."

Delicacy of approach was clearly not essential to the art of the royal huntsman. "Your Majesty—is—most flattering," said the sheriff's wife.

"His Majesty is unapologetically randy, madam. Have you an inkling how he might be accommodated within the castle this night?"

Drink had somewhat dulled her usual faculty for deflecting predators, none of whom, as she was perfectly aware, had ever placed her in quite such peril as this one. "It is—not precisely the sort of provision I am in the habit of—seeing to for our honored guests, sire."

" 'Guests,' madam? We are no guests—this castle is ours. It is you who are the guest—and must look to your behavior lest you offend your host." A sly smile of intimidation played across the king's moist lips.

"Quite so, my lord. I meant only that it is not my customary—"

"Custom aside, madam, might your sovereign not be pleasured by your own company this long, cold night? Nottingham is our draftiest castle."

Forewarned or not, her alarm was now deep and urgent. She had always supposed seduction to be equally at the option of the seduced, but unmistakably close beneath the king's surface playfulness lay the royal imperative: submit or suffer. "I . . . it would . . . I should find it most—uncomfortable, Your Majesty, however thankful I am for the high—"

"*Au contraire,* madam. You would more than likely find it thoroughly stimulating."

"Your Majesty plays coyly with words, as is his wont."

"His Majesty would play with more substantial objects—and asks the beauteous chatelaine if he does not merit her reward for his demonstrated consideration of her happiness—"

"Sire?"

"—by having prolonged her husband's tenure in the royal service when harshly put upon to end it."

"Your Majesty is too cryptic by half for my—poor—"

"Spare us, madam. Surely the contents of the late Great Charter were not unknown even here."

"Ahhh."

"Ahhh indeed."

"I . . . had assumed—that Philip's retention traced to Your Majesty's belief in his uses and devoted service to the crown—through every season of adversity—so that payment and reward are now essentially in balance. Which is hardly to express ingratitude for your—"

"Yes, yes, yes—*touché.*" The king fell back. "Let us try it the other way around, then. Let us say the balance has not yet been struck, and the Marks are deserving of reward beyond Philip's retention and those marginal custodianships that have been doled him."

"And that he has zealously superintended, sire, without wasting and with next to no profit."

"Yes, yes—the man's inhumanly scrupulous. We must not corrupt him with a surfeit of spoils. But what further reward this side of extravagance might gratify the devoted spouse of the devoted sheriff?"

She had on more than one occasion dreamt of just such an opportune moment, with comfort, standing, and riches all magically in the offing. In her dreams, the cost of their fulfillment was nil; in the event, the cost was all too evident. What was unknowable was the limit of royal bestowal. To explore it by saying anything at all was to appear to encourage the bargain; to say nothing was likely to squander the opportunity of a lifetime. Perhaps it could be played out as just a game and end with their merely having tantalized each other. In that case, how much could she lose by simply stating her heart's desire?

"It will doubtless seem a smallish matter to Your Majesty," she said after deliberating, "but nothing would more greatly gratify my husband than a royal boon that involves no expense. If you would bestow a knighthood on him as you have done for others of demonstrated devotion . . ."

"And this would gratify madam equally?"

"Indeed, sire."

"Then perhaps we have a nice bargain in the offing—a knighthood for the sheriff and a night's company for the crown."

So trifling a matter to the king; so consuming a one to the sheriff. The discrepancy riled her and stirred resentment: that a mighty sovereign should bargain pettily with his subjects' lives, like so many heavily fingered coins. "The pair seem—what shall I say?—incongruous, my lord."

"Quite so, but intriguing nonetheless. Come, if the knighthood alone will not suffice to sway you, let us sweeten the reward."

That he was playing cat-and-mouse with her she fully understood, but she felt powerless to squelch him altogether lest his legendary temper become excited. She held silent now and prayed for a providential shift in the royal mood, possibly an attack of the gout that might quell his fire.

"You must not hesitate, madam—name a further reward. Perhaps a crown appointment of some sort?"

"I do not wish to encourage the compact Your Majesty has in mind."

"Name your reward, anyway. Perhaps it will be granted in the hope you'll relent in our favor at some future time."

"Well . . . I . . . Your Majesty has such momentous matters to contend with that it seems presumptuous to—"

"Don't trifle with me, Anne." The king's eyes grew heated.

"Our priest Ivo is a good and holy man, sire, who was nominated for the vacancy at Lenton Priory by its late head. The monks there are said to squabble interminably over his successor, and many on the outside vie for the honor. Before his withdrawal to Rome, the archbishop was much in favor of our chaplain's candidacy, as I further understand. A word from Your Majesty to the earl of Derby would doubtless expedite Father Ivo's election."

"We'll explore the matter, and if there is no obstacle beyond the normal intramural strife, the royal will may be made known—"

"It would be a great kindness, my lord."

"—provided madam will succor a weary soldier who perchance wears a crown. Conceive of it, if you will, as patriotic service."

If her embroilment with Thomas de Lambert had been justifiable as a prop to her husband's standing, how could she now spurn Philip's importuning high lord and master? And he was not, to be fair, altogether devoid of charm, and likely even possessed a certain ferocious sensuousness that might happily abbreviate the ordeal. She teetered in indecision.

The king read her mind. "But you must pass the night with us to receive your rewards."

"The whole of it?"

"The whole."

"How can that be done with discretion, sire?"

"Does it much matter—in the larger scheme of things?"

"Philip would naturally inquire into my whereabouts."

"Then you must naturally tell him."

"I could hardly cite our bargain."

"Why not?"

"Surely you can see that a man of his probity would not find the knighthood worth the humiliation . . ."

"We are told, madam, that many men consider it a signal honor to have their wives selected for the royal bedstead."

"Then you must ask the sheriff, my lord king, if he would bestow me upon you—his gift for the Yule season, as it were."

"Your tone hints of confidence that he would not."

"In candor, it would surprise me if otherwise, sire."

"Even if he were advised of your long liaison with Lord Lambert?"

Her stunned eyes turned away from the taunting royal pair.

"In the drunken nights the rebels pass at their camp outside York, or so our spies report, Lambert is often heard to bleat of his love for you and your delectable loins." The king offered a sigh of mock commiseration. "Not a seemly thing, we grant you, madam, but this is the sort of scrofula drawn to their treacherous ranks."

Anne held her head low for a moment longer and then lifted it with defiance in her face. "Does any woman decline Your Majesty's insistent overtures, sire?" she asked with softer voice than looks.

"On exceedingly rare occasion."

"And do those intrepid souls long survive?"

"You take me for such a monster, Mistress Anne?"

"Am I not then commanded to submit, sire?"

"If it would ease your anxiety to have it said, let us say so."

Thus he neatly hemmed her in with every hope of amnesty from Philip. Yet by now she was persuaded entirely that whatever else he was, the king was a supremely vicious creature—nothing else about him mattered just then—and if he was to violate her, she would first have to be rendered insensate. The still greater risk, though, in rebuffing him now was that, in his royal pique, he would reveal her involvement with Lambert—why else had he broached the indecent topic if not for the implied threat of disclosure? In truth, she feared Philip's wrath far worse than the king's. The former she had greatly wronged; the latter, only momentarily frustrated. All the more reason then, actually, to relent and throw herself upon Philip for his understanding of her submission to a royal skewering. Yet she could not. There was nothing for it, finally, but to steel herself with artifice.

"Your Majesty's proposed transaction is both fair and pleasing, but I will not act disloyally to my husband, sire. I am told that loyalty is the virtue of paramount importance to our king."

"Aren't you a trifle late in this chaste resolve, madam—in view of your less than spotless past?"

Anne sat back and drew her arms across her bodice. "Baron Lambert grows old, my lord, and sadder, I fear, over his wife, who I am told has long recoiled with frigidity before his manly needs. While it is true we were friends of a seemly sort, his delusions plainly overtake him now on these bleak winter nights, so he would slander me and mock the sheriff— out of anger, I suspect, for my husband's unswerving faithfulness to his king and, doubtless, the baron's own unrequited longings for a love I never gave him."

Motionless and incredulous, the king studied her for an interminably arrested moment, then with a furious swoop of his hand flung over the table and scattered its chess pieces in a dozen directions. "A king does not beg for a cunt, madam," he snarled through clenched teeth, "and this one wearies of the pursuit. Leave us on the instant!"

Anne rose with dignity, curtsied fully, said, "May God bless you in the trials ahead, my lord," and took her leave at a suitable pace.

By the first week of the new year, word had reached Lenton Priory of the king's preference for the new head of the monastery; Father Ivo's election duly followed. Of a knighthood for the sheriff, nothing further was heard.

A.D.
1216

·XLII·

NOBODY MISSED THE AGING CHAPLAIN at the castle more than Jared Sparks. Ivo had been both spiritual and secular counselor to the little clerk, who, for all his avoidance of religiosity, took comfort in his close acquaintance with a genuine man of God. In a pinch, Sparks had come to feel, the chaplain would intercede with the Almighty in his behalf.

Amid war, the sheriff had not found the time to apply promptly to the bishop at Lincoln to name a successor chaplain for the castle, and so the chapel fell dark and still after Ivo's removal to the priory. Even in its deserted condition, Sparks found himself drawn to the vaulted sanctuary one night after supper when, exhausted from a day of extraordinary labors, he sought the solace of closeness to the spirit of his transferred friend. By the refracted light from a hallway flambeau, the clerk made his way to a rear bench, where he lay down, curled himself into the sheltering void, and, the imagined chant of evensong softly in his ears, soon fell asleep. And dreamed.

It was a very odd dream indeed—a long and vivid one in which he was both spectator and participant. Sheriff Mark, his wife, and their two daughters were romping hand in hand across a great, sunbathed field lately hayed. Suddenly there came a loud beating sound, and the sky grew overcast with doves of the purest white—a whole heavenly host of them— in formation unmistakably resembling the True Cross. For a time the birds seemed to drift almost motionless overhead, and then, as the Marks squinted up at this aerial phenomenon, the doves began to make a steady deposit upon the earth. At first the Marks flinched and ducked, assuming the worst; but as the droppings reached the ground, they saw to their wonderment that it was not excrement with which they were being pelted but silver pennies, the king's currency, looking as if they had been freshly minted. Soon the entire sky was raining pennies upon their vicinity, and to avoid being painfully nicked by them, the family took shelter by burrowing into a nearby haystack. The pennyfall went clinkingly on for a considerable spell, and when it ceased and the doves had flown off, the Marks found themselves amid a carpet of glittering coin, a fortune beyond ready calculation. A moment later, Sparks saw himself appear upon this magical scene, driving a team of smart-stepping oxen before his outsized wagon. By means of wooden shovels the clerk had providentially brought along, every last penny was gathered from the ground and piled onto the wagon. When this gaily performed task was completed, the groaning wagon moved off with the Mark girls seated atop the small mountain of silver and their parents trailing close behind on foot. There endeth the dream, much to Sparks's annoyance, as he was summoned back to wakefulness by some passing clatter in the corridor outside the darkened chapel.

Not much given to dreaming, the clerk was greatly puzzled by this occurrence. It seemed to him too lifelike and particular to have been merely the senseless conjuring of his unleashed fancy. What else could it have been but a divine visitation, he asked himself, and though a profound questioner of God's benevolence, having come upon precious little evidence of His intervention on the side of the good and deserving, Sparks welcomed the dream as an emanation of the Holy Spirit, bearing him some sort of important message. But of what precise meaning, he could not tell.

The events that led him to decipher his remarkable dream began to unfold innocently enough the next day when Julia Mark, a more pixilated child than her older sister, tied a strand of yellow piping left over from her Easter outfit into a small bow and looped it around the clerk's left ear. The playful gesture, made during a lull in the weekly mathematics lesson he taught the two girls, was accompanied by Julia's asking him, "Will you never have a wife of your own, Uncle Jared? Angelique says you're too busy to, but I say you're not so busy you haven't the time for our nasty lessons."

The question, which he evaded by answering that he had dedicated his life first to God's service and then to the king's, so distracted him that he quite forgot about the bow—much to the children's giggling delight. When he appeared at his regular workplace a short time later, Sparks drew the sheriff's compliment for the colorful addition to his usually drab attire. They shared a laugh over his explanation, but the incident prompted the clerk's reflection that evening on how thoroughly his life had become interwoven with that of the Mark family.

Indeed, aside from his monthly assignation with one or another of the prettily lewd wenches whom Master le Gyw let frequent the Trip to drain the primal urge from needy customers, the clerk had no private existence whatever. He devoted himself all day and half the night to the sheriff's business, except Sundays, when he had often been invited to share the family's pew at chapel Mass and sometimes to join them for a picnic outing afterward. On nonceremonial occasions he supped regularly with them on the dais in the great hall. With Father Ivo's departure, Anne became his primary confidant within the castle, even as her children, to whom he devoted five hours per week of formal instruction, had become his playmates as well as pupils. At Christmas and Easter they presented him with fine garments and small, endearing keepsakes, the likes of which he could not afford to reciprocate. When Peter Mark's successor as undersheriff elected to travel back and forth from his manor rather than take up residence at the castle, it seemed altogether natural for Sparks to be offered Peter's former apartment at the other end of the corridor from the sheriff's. Except for the hour or so of recreation he passed at the Trip each night after his labors, generally sharing the innkeeper's shrewd and lively company, the little clerk was so suffused with Marks that from time to time he wondered what would become of his life if they should disappear from it.

That he had come to find this parasitic existence not only tolerable but even desirable was, at bottom, a tribute to Philip Mark's character. Even in his ninth year of service to the sheriff, Sparks still found him to be wise, kind, just, and occasionally needful of protection from his own noble nature. He had repaid his clerk's indefatigable efforts with an extraordinary portion of freedom and power in the conduct of the crown's business. The sheriff and his wife, furthermore, had been instrumental in obtaining the liberty of his father and half-brother. There thus entered prominently into the clerk's thoughts the desire to express his gratitude in some concrete fashion to the family as a whole for the sense of enrichment each member had brought him in a different way.

But how to manage it? And what meaningful gesture could he make in light of their newly complex circumstances? For the war, on the face of it, had greatly strengthened the sheriff's position. The king, with his government scattered and itinerant, was in no position to replace such dedicated officers as his sheriff at Nottingham. His castle there, in fact, now became the hub of the royalist effort in the midlands and north country. With neither side able to afford a sizable standing army—only raiding parties that roamed the open country, exacting tributes but unable to impose control by extended occupation—the castles were the key to the outcome of the war. They remained in command of their regions after an enemy force had swept by, their garrisons ready to pounce on any stragglers. To capture a castle was a major undertaking, at a considerable outlay of time, weaponry, and blood; and since the crown possessed threescore of these fortresses, its hold on the realm depended on the loyalty and ability of its castellans.

In neither regard was Philip Mark deficient, and as his shires were strongholds of loyalist sentiment, Nottingham Castle, at the geographical heart of England, was suddenly a bulwark of the king's cause. It served as a prime depository of crown funds and pay station for roving royal troops and garrisons at other castles. Its gaol was a convenient holding pen for prominent rebel captives awaiting ransom. Its workshops were busy making and repairing weapons and equipage; its stores became a vast larder overflowing with the bounty of the rich Trent valley; its cobbled bailey was aclatter night and day with the comings and goings of commanders and couriers; and the meadow below its stout southern rampart was a favored camping ground for any king's company in the vicinity.

One inevitable consequence of all this frenetic activity was that a great deal of money flowed through Nottingham Castle—and what did not flow accumulated there. The Exchequer had not sat since the Michaelmas audit of 1214, and with Westminster now in rebel hands, funds that would have ordinarily been transferred to the treasury remained instead at Nottingham. Because his garrison had been much enlarged and the surrounding region was secure for the king, the sheriff was able to harvest nearly all the crown's regular exactions despite the austerities of wartime. On top of these local revenues, heavy sums were collected as a result of ransom payments to free rebel prisoners, fines and tributes from political waverers, plunder from the confiscated property of traitors to the king, and extortions in the name of patriotism by irregular outriders of the crown, like the scruffy band enlisted by the sheriff to secure the peace in Sherwood Forest.

With such riches to account for, the sheriff's chief aide had to realign the duties of the clerical staff so that he himself could monitor all revenues and expenditures. Sparks soon discovered, as the war intensified, that despite the heavy increase in disbursements for soldiers' pay and supplies, the surplus in the castle silver vault grew with each passing month. This bulging mountain of pennies resummoned to mind the field full of silver surrounding the sheriff and his family in the clerk's puzzling dream. But it did not much clarify the spectral meaning behind it.

Sparks did not dwell anew on the subject until the delayed word arrived from France that Anne Mark's father, once among the leading merchants of Tours, had died the year before. Through the family's table talk and the twice-yearly letters that found their expensively circuitous way from Touraine to Nottingham (and then into the clerk's nervously prying fingers when his chores sometimes placed him alone in the sheriff's apartment), Sparks learned that the deceased had passed a lonely old age. A widower, he enjoyed an occasional visit with Adrienne, his older daughter, at the nunnery she had joined shortly after Anne's marriage, but he had no other family involvement beyond what news he could glean from England. His letters were full of regret that the hostile climate between the two countries prevented his crossing the sea to visit his sprouting grandchildren.

Word of his passing arrived while the family was at table. After reading the letter over several times, the distraught but practical Anne remarked, "There is no mention of any legacy. It must be that his trade had long been in decline—remember that he once wrote how he was still viewed as an English sympathizer because of us and that his wares languished accordingly?"

"He was too proud, I think, to have dwelled on his plight," said Philip, "but his finances were doubtless in a fragile state these last years."

"Still, the house ought to have fetched something. Perhaps I'll inquire someday if conditions permit."

"Adrienne might know something," said Philip, touching on a tender point, though in truth he had never fully understood the cause of the long estrangement between the two sisters.

"I'd die before soliciting her counsel," said Anne, closing the subject of whether she might have come into money. But it had been firmly implanted in Sparks's brain, haunted as it had begun to be now by his cryptic vision of the Mark family surrounded by a vast field of silver.

The frightening alteration in the course of the war late that spring was the final turn of the key that unlocked the meaning of the clerk's mysterious dream.

If John had supposed victory within easy reach, he underestimated the ambition of Prince Louis, much as he had long miscalculated the resolve of Louis's father to deny the English king hegemony on French soil. Having failed to convince the pope's representative that John had gained his throne underhandedly and thus deserved to be replaced, the prince succeeded in enlisting the French baronage, hungry for English fiefs, to join him in a cross-Channel invasion. Cheered that the French host was now excommunicated for spurning the pope's order not to attack England, John gathered a great fleet of vessels to stave off the enemy, due to embark in mid-May. But if the Lord was now on England's side, He chose a perverse means to show it: a terrible gale scattered the English ships a few days before Louis set sail, and his well-trained troops landed unopposed.

Whereas the king had collected an enormous army to repulse the French when they had threatened to invade three years earlier, now England was hobbled by civil strife, and John could command only a modest force, of mostly French mercenaries, in defense of the realm. Because their pay was in arrears and John feared they might go over to Louis, their countryman, the king would risk no major battle in an effort to hurl the invader back into the sea; he had heard of Hastings. Instead, he hoped the approach of the French force would rally his subjects to his side as the domestic struggle had not, so that the intruders would be harassed and combatted at every turn. Once again, John's calculations were to prove wishful.

Prince Louis's troops, with a crown in the offing for their able commander, swept through Kent, taking castles and wholesale oaths of fealty as they went, and were received in London within a fortnight of their landing as heroic deliverers of an oppressed kingdom. The English countryside seemed to defect to him en masse as he struck southwest from London, through Surrey and into Hampshire, and took the key cathedral town of Winchester with ease. Soon after, as John shrank away to the west country, the king's half-brother and most trusted military adjutant, Earl William of Salisbury—the indomitable Longsword—judged the situation hopeless and surrendered to Louis. Another of the king's mainstays, the chief warden of the forest, Hugh de Neville, gave over his home fortress in Cambridgeshire, and even the Marshal's oldest son, whom John had held hostage during his father's years out of favor, took up the French and rebel cause. By midsummer, two-thirds of the English baronage had declared against the king, and Louis stood as master of the richest and most populous sector of the country.

In these grave circumstances, Jared Sparks determined it was more likely than not that Louis would consolidate his hold on the home counties, capture the king's vital citadels at Dover, Windsor, Corfe, and Lincoln, and soon win the war and the English crown—thereby cooking Philip Mark's goose. Probably the sheriff would be taken prisoner and hanged as a traitor to France; possibly he would only be gaoled. At the least, he would be ignominiously pitched from office, and his devoted first clerk cast adrift, if not into the moat with a lead weight affixed. Certainly the castle treasury would be confiscated for the greater glory of France.

With this appalling assessment heavy on his mind, Sparks suddenly, and finally, thought he understood the meaning of his dream about the Marks—and the perilous course it prescribed to him. Rather than risk approaching disaster, he had been told from on high, better by far that a portion of the castle's current surplus of silver be set aside for the sheriff's ready use and that, if it came to it, he and his family should flee in advance of the French, assume a new identity in some distant place, and live a life of comfort with the silver his clerk had procured for them. If, perchance, John rallied the realm to his banner, then the purloined money would go toward ensuring the Mark family an agreeable existence at the close of Philip's tenure—they might even choose to adopt Sparks into their household—and providing a suitable dowry for their dear daughters.

The sheriff would of course have nothing to do with such a scheme, his clerk knew, so Sparks was obliged to pursue it on his own. The plan was defensible, he posited, because, in the first place, Philip's selfless labors for the crown merited a substantial pension that would surely never be granted him otherwise. And while he would be the prime beneficiary of the funds, the sheriff would have no idea, as Sparks conceived the undertaking, that they had been irregularly obtained. Finally, the actual perpetrator of the act—he could not bring himself to think of it as bald larceny—would gain nothing of substance for himself by it and could therefore not be held guilty of turpitude. Thus morally armed against Satan, the clerk proceeded to do the devil's work, not without immense trepidation, to be sure, but fully confident his mission was justly ordained.

The device Sparks invented to apprise the sheriff of his good fortune was a letter arriving at the castle in midsummer and purportedly written the previous October by a certain lawyer of Tours—his signature was indecipherable, and he gave no address—who claimed he had drawn the last will and testament for Anne Mark's father. In it the old merchant had made a very sizable bequest to his younger daughter, the letter advised, and a minimal one to the holy house where his older child was resident. But because of the parlous times afflicting England and the imminence of war between it and France, the lawyer had ingeniously arranged that the cash and valuables bequeathed to Anne be paid to a leading wine merchant of Paris, who in turn would ship its equivalent in merchandise to a well-known wine importer in London, said wares to be sold in the normal course of his business. As soon as peace returned to the kingdom, the London wine seller would pay for the shipment by sending Anne her legacy in cash. Because her father had grasped, furthermore, that any sudden increment in wealth enjoyed by the sheriff's family would at once open him to charges of extortion, the lawyer had specified that the money would be delivered in Anne's name at Lenton Priory, where, he understood from her father, Philip and his family had been granted burial rights; there it would be held for safekeeping until the Marks chose to withdraw it on demand. This final aspect of the arrangement would naturally require Philip to apprise the prior in advance of the event.

"He mentions no figure," said the exultant Anne. "A most peculiar lawyer indeed."

"Then let's assume it's paltry," said Philip. "That way we can only be happily surprised."

Sparks's chosen means of converting the promised legacy into reality was not simple expropriation, which on its eventual discovery would render the sheriff liable, but a skillful reworking of the castle ledgers so that the removed funds could not be detected in them. There were but two plausible ways to achieve this effect, the clerk calculated—to overstate expenditures or to understate income. Either method would serve to shrink the size of the surplus posted in the ledgers, allowing Sparks to set aside the difference. On reflection, falsifying the figures for outlays, most of them going for pay and supplies, appeared far riskier; the falsely listed numbers might someday be checked against the records of company commanders or suppliers' receipts. By contrast, revenues could readily be reduced by simple omission—what was not listed invited far fewer questions than what was. And since a goodly part of the castle income derived from such irregular sources as seized rebel property, ransoms, tribute, and other *ad hoc* wartime exactions, many of them against travelers and strangers, they would be hard to track down. And even if they were, any shortage could always be blamed on the harried conditions of wartime bookkeeping: too much to do, too few competent clerks, too many orders transmitted orally, and written records lost or destroyed in the press of duties.

And so, working late into the night in his apartment, Sparks painstakingly created a second ledger of castle revenues, omitting or reducing certain selected items until the total was in balance with true expenditures. When the actual surplus accumulating in the castle treasury reached six thousand pounds, as he planned it, his manufactured ledger would report it at only £3500; the difference he would then cause to be removed from the castle and his counterfeit ledger of revenues substituted for the real one, so that reported income and outlay would tally neatly at the point of the theft.

The largeness of the intended taking—enough for the Marks to purchase a sizable manor and still set aside generous dowries for their daughters—Sparks justified by his sense that anything less was not worth the chance of detection. But even that risk, he righteously reasoned, was remote. For if the French won and came to occupy the castle, all its ledgers could be burned first as an act of patriotic defiance. And if King John prevailed, the restored Exchequer would have its hands full trying to re-establish a working government. Should the Westminster auditors ever attempt to trace the unmonitored wartime operations in the shires, it would not happen until years after the fact, when troops had long since disbanded, memories had faded, and nobody would likely care much that some records had not been fastidiously kept in a time of chaos.

This skein of logic left Sparks with but two final gaps to close in the web he was nimbly weaving—how to get the money out of the castle and where to put it until the outcome of the war was known. The second problem was by far the easier to solve, largely because the clerk could conceive of only one possible safe haven. His father's cottage at Hathersgate lay at the edge of the property, within easy access from the highway. The twenty-five barrels, each containing one hundred pounds of the king's currency—600,000 pennies in all—could thus be delivered under cover of darkness without attracting the attention of the manor residents. Master Blake would be told a variation of the story of Anne's French inheritance—namely, that the money had been smuggled up from London through rebel-infested regions but could be deposited at neither the castle nor the priory without endangering the sheriff or high risk of its being confiscated as a wartime expedient. Blake, already indebted to the sheriff for having rescued him from a hellish life at Swanhill, could hardly refuse to let his son bury Mistress Mark's purported fortune beneath his cottage until it might be safely transferred to Lenton at the war's close.

To get the money to Hathersgate from the castle was the real trick. The treasury was a locked and guarded vault at the far end of the castle's maze of subterranean corridors, which Sparks could have traversed in his sleep. Since the clerk was the principal keeper of the key to the vault and had occasion to visit it at various hours of the day and night in the normal course of his duties, the guard on perpetual watch would hardly be suspicious of Sparks's presence; the problem was how to provide the barrels a covert route out of the castle. The solution to this last part of the puzzle lay in the person of the clerk's sometime collaborator in justified mischief— Bartholomew le Gyw.

"Are you altogether mad?" the innkeeper asked on learning of the clerk's ambitious enterprise.

"No one else on earth must know of this but us two."

"Leave me out," said le Gyw, "and your exposure is reduced by a full half."

"If I could, I would. But it cannot be managed alone."

"It shouldn't be managed by any number. It will surely be discovered— and our necks stretched."

"I think not," said Sparks, persuaded by now that he was quite the cleverest clerk in England—and God's darling, besides. "At any rate, you'll get the first hundred pounds for your labors."

"Hmmm," said le Gyw. "Being half-Welsh, I suppose I'm semi-mad to begin with—and so your perfect accomplice. Let's hear all the loony particulars."

A securely sealed opening well up the rear wall of the Trip's wine cellar led to a steeply rising passageway through the castle bedrock that fed into the much broader corridor known to castle denizens as the Hole to Hell. To render the castle impregnable to infiltration from below, the sheriff had ordered the lower end of the corridor barricaded soon after he took charge of the fortress, and the last fifty feet of the tunnel destroyed. The treasury room stood within twenty feet of the timberwork that closed off the castle end of the collapsed tunnel. Thus, three steps were required to accomplish Sparks's purpose: he and le Gyw had to dig quietly through the fifty feet of debris-filled tunnel to clear a passage for the barrels; a hole had to be cut out of the bottom of the timbered barricade so the barrels could be rolled underneath; and the guard had to be absent or unconscious during the last stage of the tunneling, the cutting of the opening, and the removal of the barrels.

The digging, undertaken after midnight when the Trip was closed, consumed the better part of August. It was filthy, tedious work, done under dank, cramped, and nearly suffocating conditions that allowed the diggers, with many small vile creatures for company, to work but two hours per session lest they collapse from exhaustion. As they neared completion of the task, le Gyw did the digging alone while Sparks tended to distracting the treasury guard. This he managed by appearing at the vault late at night to obtain the barrels the castle needed for its regular disbursements the next day. Each time he arrived, the clerk brought with him a bucket of ale to refresh the morale of the thoroughly bored watchman. In doing so, Sparks entered into animated conversation with the grateful guard that echoed sufficiently to muffle the sounds of le Gyw's digging close behind the nearby timbered barricade. The moment the guard began to roll the barrels thunderously up the corridor to the main floor of the castle as the clerk directed, the innkeeper was at liberty to perform the noisier aspects of his work. The yet more arduous task of chopping a hole at the base of the timberwork had to be spread over five nights, and each time the clerk had to apply daubs of a sawdust-and-paste mixture he had brought with him to fill the chinks that le Gyw had carved, lest they attract the guard's attention upon his return from that night's round of barrel rolling.

With these bone-wearying and precarious preparations out of the way, Sparks marked time for a fortnight, by the end of which the treasury surplus reached the six thousand pounds he had targeted—enough so that his subtraction of £2500 would not unduly jeopardize the castle in the event of an unforeseeable call on its reserves. Master le Gyw, meanwhile, through the services of an apothecary who was one of his steadiest customers, obtained a small, mild extract of belladonna, which in its fully potent form was a deadly narcotic. In the reduced strength obtained, it rendered the user unconscious—a necessary remedy, the innkeeper explained to his supplier, for dealing with certain obstreperous patrons of his establishment.

On the assigned evening, Sparks appeared as usual with his gift of ale for the treasury guard, but this time the beverage was enriched with the belladonna extract. No sooner did it take effect than the clerk signaled his confederate on the far side of the barricade, and le Gyw administered a swift kick to the loosely secured piece he had cut from the bottom. It gave way neatly, opening the passageway down to the Trip's cellar. As the watchman fell deeper into his toxic slumber, the two perpetrators hurriedly rolled the twenty-five barrels of silver under the barricade and afterward restored the cut sector. Sparks then tended to it as before with the sawdust compound so the cut edge could not be noticed except on exceedingly close inspection. After the clerk locked the treasury vault and propped the snoring guard against the outside of the door, he was routinely let out of the castle and went to join le Gyw on the Trip side of the barricade. From there they trundled the barrels down to the wine cellar, struggling not to loose great rumbling sounds or get themselves crushed in the process.

"A bloody miracle!" the panting innkeeper whispered as the unpracticed pair of felons, near exhaustion from their labors, sprawled into a corner of the cellar. "A bloody holy miracle!" he repeated, avidly crossing himself.

The barrels remained under lock and key in the Trip's cellar for the next three days while the clerk and the innkeeper collected their strength for the final phase of the ordeal. In that interim, Sparks substituted the counterfeit ledger of castle revenues so that the records since the last Exchequer audit now conformed with the monies actually remaining in the treasury. Instead of destroying the authentic ledger, though, he hid it among his possessions in the locked chest in his bedchamber lest he ever need to refer to it to verify claimed payments or fend off any assault on the legitimacy of the understated version.

Even the innkeeper's sturdy wagon could not bear the great weight of the stolen silver, so it was moved, twelve barrels at a time, on two consecutive nights. The contents of the twenty-fifth barrel, representing le Gyw's share of the taking, remained at the Trip, stashed in diverse receptacles, while the barrel, with its telltale royal insignia, was chopped into firewood.

On the first night, the transfer was made without incident, so the perpetrators had no call for the glinting double-axe and loaded crossbow they carried to discourage lurking highwaymen. On the second night, however, after they had proceeded about halfway to Hathersgate, the moonlit road was blocked by a pair of masked horsemen, one brandishing a lance, the other a broadsword.

"Good evening, gents," said the latter. "What business have carters on a perilous highway well past the witching hour?"

"I'm an honest innkeeper who brews his own ale," said le Gyw, reaching furtively under the straw beside him for the axe, "and delivering my wares as time allows."

"A long workday, eh, my friend?"

"Very—and I'd thank you good souls not to prolong it."

"That depends on you," said the swordsman. "And who's your companion?"

"A friend who keeps me company and indulges in a bit of my brew."

" 'Strue," said Sparks. "I tipple at the nipple of the goddess Ceres, protector of the—" he hiccoughed emphatically—"the harvest and—and—and the blessedly besotted. . . ."

The swordsman drew closer and inspected the clerk by the pale moon. "I know this drunken little snot," he told the lance bearer, "as do you. It's the younger Sparks brother—the one who works at the castle."

Terrified at being recognized, the clerk struggled to sustain the ruse they had rehearsed in the event they were confronted on the road. "And—and—who dost thou be, oh, great shining knight, behind that cowardly mask?" Another hiccough.

"Never you mind, but I'll wager you're not out on the sheriff's business this night. Once a churl, always a churl."

"Whatever they're up to," said the lanceman, "I don't need trouble from any Sparks. Let's leave them be."

By now the clerk had detected a familiar tone in the voices of both masked men, yet he could not, from the thinness of the crescent moonlight, hit upon their identity. "Sparks make fire if—if—if you stir 'em," he said with forced bravado, "so steer on by us, plucky friends."

"What money have you?" asked the swordsman, paying Sparks no heed.

"A few pennies," said le Gyw.

"Then a piss-poor innkeeper you are, indeed. Let's have a look at your cargo." So saying, the highwayman dismounted and, his sword at the ready, clambered onto the rear of the wagon. As the interloper turned his attention to the barrels, le Gyw gripped fast to the battle-axe and lunged backward with a mighty swipe that caught the swordsman full square on the upper arm. His weapon clattered against the floor of the wagon as the force of the innkeeper's blow sent him flying over the side, blood gushing from the wound. A sickening gurgle of pain announced his arrival on the ground, where his arm remained attached by the merest strand of skin and ligament.

Before his accomplice could menace them with his lance, a highly
sober Sparks withdrew their crossbow from its hiding place and leveled
it at him. "One move toward us, and you're carrion!" cried the clerk,
dreading that the snap of his weighty weapon would break him in two.
The threat alone, happily, froze the horseman in place. "And if you fly,
your partner will tell us who you are, and the bailiffs will hunt you down
from here to Cardiff."

"But nothing was taken off you. . . ."

"Any moment you might have slain us, though, and driven away my
wagon," said le Gyw, climbing onto the wounded thief's mount and waving
the bloodied axe above his head. "Now throw down your lance and hold
fast till we decide your fate."

The villain weighed his predicament and, upon hearing his partner
emit the groan of the eternally damned, obliged. Sparks scrambled down
from the wagon, took a tenuous hold on the lance, and heaved it into the
roadside darkness. Then he hurried to the unconscious figure slumped
beside the left rear wagon wheel, blood still pulsing blue-black from his
wound, and lowered the miscreant's mask. "Stryker!" blurted the clerk.
"Lord, how the mighty have fallen!" He turned to the other culprit, menaced now by le Gyw's axe blade. "And who are you?"

"The reeve at Swanhill, sire," he said sadly. "I was the hayward when
last you knew me there."

"Noah!"

"Aye—but you must not tell your brother, or he'll cast me from the
manor. I came with Stryker only out of kindness." After the sheriff had
exiled him from Swanhill, the base steward could nowhere find employment
suitable to his haughty expectations, Noah related, and so turned to a life
of drink and brigandage. The pair of them had collaborated to bilk the lord
of Swanhill more than once, but with Sparks's incorruptibly vigilant brother
now in charge of the manor, the pickings were slim—"and so I thought
to add a bit to my thin purse, seeing how the war has curdled everything.
I know I did wrong. . . ."

Having apprehended these malefactors was one thing; disposing of
them, another. If they were taken to the castle for prosecution as law
prescribed, Sparks knew, there would likely be still more questions about
what their would-be victims were up to on the road at that hour. Their
choice, the clerk saw, was narrow: to silence the pair either by slaying
them then and there or threatening to skin them alive at the very first

peep they made. Lacking all aptitude for murder, Sparks sought instead to register ultimate menace but managed to sound no worse than cordially intimidating. "My master would like this late-night joyride of mine with the innkeeper," he said, "no more than the steward of Swanhill would approve your shameful antics on the highway. Let us agree, then, to go our ways, vowing never to mention this encounter—and hoping that yon Master Stryker has had a lesson he'll ne'er forget."

Noah gratefully agreed and, after tying the former steward's limp body face-down to the saddle of his mount, led the horse and rider off slowly into the alien darkness.

The second day thereafter, the castle learned that Stryker had been found dead on the roadside about five miles north of town, with one arm missing and a dagger hole through his neck. But the coroner noted little bleeding from the latter wound and speculated that death had been caused by the unstanched flow from the severed arm. "Quite peculiar," said Sir Mitchell.

That same evening Sparks spoke to Geoffrey Mark, in his capacity as captain of the castle guard, and asked that the night watch at the treasury be replaced due to a troubling tendency to nod off while on the job. Thereafter, the clerk rarely visited the vault except during daytime hours and never again brought a gift of ale to gladden the guard.

·XLIII·

AS THE KING LAY DYING that blustery October morning at Newark Castle on the eastern fringe of Nottinghamshire, the sheriff of that county paced about his donjon rooftop several leagues to the southwest, pondering the prospect of a kingless realm—John's oldest son had just turned nine—and his own likely fate if anarchy reigned or, worse still, the French. Unless the abbot of Croxton, who had been summoned to the sovereign's bedside, could work his medicinal magic and halt the oozing of the royal bowels, the end was at hand.

Hardly a month earlier, an altogether different outcome to the civil crisis seemed in store. After lying low in the west country all summer while the French invaders began to squabble with the rebel barons, the king had at last bestirred himself. With his small army he skirted north of London, where Fawkes's forces allowed passage, struck at the Scottish troops who had infiltrated as far south as Cambridgeshire, and then swung across East Anglia, vengefully wasting the property of his rebel vassals. By the time he swept into Norfolk, the king had settled on a more ambitious strategy. Prince Louis had presumptuously named his baron Gilbert de Ghent as earl of Lincolnshire, that rich and heavily rebel-infested county, and Lincoln itself had quickly fallen to Gilbert's soldiers. Only the royal fortress there, under its hereditary castellan, the venerable grand dame Nicolaa de la Haye, held out against the king's enemies. But if Lincoln Castle succumbed, the entire eastern side of England would be rendered virtually defenseless, so John resolved to ride hard to Dame Nicolaa's rescue.

His will, though, was sapped by an intestinal illness—spoiled pears were the suspected instigator—that struck him while camped at Lynn, close by the great bay of the Wash. Soon his guts were leaking incessantly, and he could barely sit his horse. To speed him across to Lincolnshire, on the farther shore of the Wash, where he might rest and be treated at Sleaford or Newark Castle, the king's considerable baggage train was directed on a shortcut over the sandy estuary of the Wellstream. The train normally crept along at not even three miles per hour, and to traverse that boggy stretch at low tide would further reduce its pace. Even so, the four-and-a-half-mile route would save considerable time.

But in October the mist hung close above the fens until well after sunrise, so the train was late in starting. And, worse luck, the guides who led it with long poles to plumb the surface against the treacherous quicksand patches grew befuddled; the vanguard advanced at a crawl. By the time the cumbersome caravan reached the midpoint of the crossing, the tidal waters of the Wash had begun to return, further hampering the progress of the bulging wagons. Some of the drivers, sensing disaster, turned back; others pushed forward more urgently against the ever soupier surface; still others seemed to go in circles—and nearly all were assailed by panic. The king, watching on the far shore, had to be restrained from charging into the maelstrom, but whether to rescue his men or the most precious of his possessions, none afterward chose to speculate.

The toll was immense. The raging whirlpools sucked down wagons, carts, horses, men, and with them most of the traveling crown treasury—

coins, gems, plate, regalia, pendants, candelabra, silver flagons and gold goblets, mounds of jewelry the king had accumulated with the eye of an insatiable collector, his favorite golden wand (with a dove attached), the great crown of state, and—or so it was said—the very sword of Tristram. If John had not already been ailing, the calamity of the Wash would have been enough to quell what fight was left in him. As Providence had scattered his fleet when the French were about to embark on their invasion, so now it had poisoned his body and stolen his purse. By the time he reached Newark Castle, the king's decline had turned precipitous.

To the sheriff, buffeted by an autumnal gust as he prowled the donjon battlement, it was fitting that the king, if now he must die, should do so at one of the castles in Philip's charge and in the shire where he presided. He had devoted thirty-five years of service to the Plantagenet rulers of England, nearly half the span to this one. Whatever John's failings, he had given strength and hope and meaning to Philip's life, and his passing seemed certain to darken it.

The sheriff had harbored the conceit that in the end, perhaps even *at* the end, the king would smile broadly on him and bestow a reward in keeping with his cumulative labors. Yet he prepared himself, as the grim hour drew nigh, to see his iridescent dream turn to vapor and resolved not to grow despondent on account of it. For in a real sense, he had surely had his reward already every waking hour that he had been endowed with the crown's might and majesty. To expect more than that, given the obliquely upward path he had trod since youth, was to try the patience of the universe.

As if some transcendent power had read his thoughts, a courier appeared before him out of the mist, bearing a message from Master Manning, his acting castellan at Newark. The sheriff was to hasten there at the king's command—likely the last ever to be received from him. "Hold no wild hopes," Anne cautioned as Philip hurried into formal dress.

"I have none—only wild fantasies I'd as soon be rid of."

"Would a knighthood please you?"

"Dispensed from the royal deathbed? It would be a true fulfillment, but most unlikely. He has a kingdom to bequeath, with little time to—"

"Yet he summons you. I think he will do it."

"I doubt he even knows I wish for it by his hand."

"He knows—or did, at any rate, before taking ill."

"How would you know?"

"I . . . because . . . Ivo sought the honor for you through the Marshal—he told me of his effort in your behalf."

"Why tell you and not me? And he wasn't authorized to pester—"

"He did what love for you commanded—and that same keen regard would not permit him to broach the topic to you unless he had reason to suppose the honor likely."

"The Marshal spurned him?"

"He said he would have to defer to the king's wishes in the matter—and being a man of his word, no doubt did so."

"Equally doubtless, the king gave it no further thought."

On the hard ride to Newark, the prospect of knighthood, remote as his common sense told him it was, consumed him. It was not the honorific nature of the grant but its implied certification of his ascent that fed the craving. Land had its value, but its truest ownership abided with the earth, whereas a knighthood resided only in the bones of its bearer. The two of them together, naturally, would amount to his full investiture as a gentleman, but if a choice between them had to be made, the title mattered still more to him than the sod.

The blurred sight of the castle breastworks, reflected in the ruffled surface of the Trent, broke his reverie and replaced it with dutiful reverence for the dying monarch. Through corridors hushed with funereal gloom he was conducted to the king's bedchamber, a dim grotto sealed fast against the stormy day and heavy with the reek of mortality. Half a dozen priestly wraiths hovered over the royal bedstead; of them, only Bishop Peter des Roches was a ranking eminence of the realm.

"He beckons you," the bishop said just above a whisper on noting the sheriff's arrival. "Do not tarry—he has little strength."

The former robustness of form and manner had faded to a bleached shadow, swimming in and out of cogency. The sorry sight sent a rush of remorse through Philip for his heart's long reluctance to have rendered more than ceremonial devotion to this hard but able master. He knelt in earnest supplication beside the remnant of the king.

"He cannot see you down there," des Roches said. "Stand to and say your name."

"Is that our heroic captain from Touraine?" the king rasped as Philip stood with bowed head close by him.

"It is, Your Majesty."

"You did nobly at Loches—pity 'twas lost."

"Aye, my lord."

"We've had too many losses. . . ."

"En route to the final triumph, sire."

"Well said, *capitaine.*" The king seemed to drift away, his glazed eyes open but a sliver. Philip felt the priests behind him press closer. The dying lips trembled briefly, then found faint voice once more. "Do you love us, Philip?"

"Never more than now, Your Majesty."

"But more at some times than others, eh?"

"I . . . it is perhaps human nature, my lord."

"Ah—still the most honest officer in our service."

"I think there are not a few others, sire, who have—"

"Do you understand now, Philip, about the Welsh lads?"

"I . . . understand that Your Majesty thought the step—essential."

"Yet you disapprove still?"

"I have closed my mind to the matter, my lord."

The king's head gave a series of tiny bobs. "A ruler's lot is not an easy one. We've had many foes—multitudes. . . ."

"But admirers as well, Majesty—legions."

The king's mouth struggled for words. "We—wish to make a final gesture of gratitude for your faithful service. . . ."

Philip's whole being pulsed with anticipation.

"Have you your sword, Captain?" the king asked.

"Aye, my lord."

"Place its hilt in our hand and kneel by us."

Philip awkwardly unsheathed his weapon, carefully fitted the palsied fingers about it, and tremblingly knelt as tears sprang to his eyes. The consummation of his long quest for grace and dignity seemed at hand.

"Besides your present honors," the king said as all strained to catch the quavery words, "we hereby name you our joint sheriff for Lincolnshire."

"Sire?"

"You will serve us equally with Dame—what's-her-name—"

"Nicolaa?"

"Woman's got the balls of Zeus," said the king. "You know of her splendid defense of our castle at Lincoln?"

"Aye—Your Majesty." The flatness of disappointment took hold of Philip's voice.

"Spell her until the siege is lifted, Philip—and afterward serve by her side as co-sheriff."

"To be sure, Majesty."

He felt himself drawn to his feet and, still dazed, gently but decisively shown the door. It opened magically, and he was cast out, chilled and unanointed, back into the commoners' world. For the next hour he dwelt within his private penumbra amid the milling assemblage in the great hall, its collective sound a growing dirge, until at last a priest emerged to say the end had come and bid them all kneel in prayer for the king's freshly fled soul.

"Treacherous to the end," Anne said with venom after the sheriff had ridden home oblivious to the driving rain and told her of his final reward. "A meaningless honorific—to govern an enemy-held shire. And when it is liberated, doubtless you'll get the dirty work and the noble lady will reap the glory—and dare I say the riches?"

"Still," said the sheriff's clerk upon hearing of the new appointment, "it is a decided form of tribute, sire, and a thumb in the eye of those who'd have deposed you."

"Perhaps," said Philip, drained by the finality of his dashed ambition and apprehensive over the ascension to the throne of either a baffled child or a foreign prince, neither of them likely to wish him well.

At the Trip that evening, the mood was irreverently gladsome. Bartholomew le Gyw, recalling for Jared Sparks that dream the good nurse Cadi had had about the evil Welsh prince against whom vengeance was wrought by the sudden rising of the lake in the third generation, likened it to the disaster of the Wash that had struck the king the week before. "His watery end was foreordained," said the innkeeper, "the moment that warped bastard ordered our lads hanged for no cause."

"But he didn't drown," Sparks noted. "His intestines did him in."

"His bowels were liquefied—it comes to the same thing."

Rather than dwell on the dead king's manifold transgressions, though, the clientele ruminated on who would now hold the crown as regent of England until the boy king came of age. The papal legate would surely have a resounding voice in the framing of policy, but all agreed Rome's representative had best remain in the shadow of the throne, not on it, even if he intended only to keep it warm. The justiciar, who in the normal course of events served as the king's surrogate, would not do, either. De

Burgh, while an able captain, as his stout defense of Dover Castle was confirming, would be taken as the tarnished agent of a spent and little-mourned regime; still more so his predecessor, Bishop des Roches, a Poitevin in the bargain. "Which, as I see it, leaves only the three earls," said the innkeeper. "Chester is more ox than fox. Derby is a blusterer who lacks stature in more ways than one. And the Marshal—well, he's the man for it, without a doubt, but he's too old and shrewd to be drawn into the vortex." He hoisted his tankard mirthfully. "There's nothing for it but to cede the realm to Louis."

Before the French prince could claim the vacant throne, des Roches and the papal legate hurried to Gloucester and solemnly anointed John's pretty little boy as Henry the Third, lord of all England, Ireland, and Wales and claimant to half of France. But he was the king in name only. He had no government, no army, no money, and a virulent enemy in control of much of his realm.

Early in November, the leaders of the royalist camp assembled in a regency council composed of the papal legate, eleven bishops, three earls, one count, and eighteen barons. Of them, only one man was universally admired and trusted, and because he was fully in sympathy with neither party in the civil war, albeit unshakably loyal to the crown throughout John's turbulent reign, William Marshal, earl of Pembroke, was the choice for regent by acclamation. Yet the Marshal demurred. It was a monumentally difficult task, he said, and proper work for a younger and more forceful man. But none was swayed against him on this account. Only when the papal legate, with latitudinarian use of his office, promised William that his taking the regent's scepter would serve as penance for his every sin, thereby all but certifying his eternal stay in Heaven, did the Marshal accede. Lest it be said that he had done so with his eye ever on the favorable bargain, the old knight gallantly vowed his allegiance to the young Henry by declaring that "if all should abandon the king except me, do you know what I would do? I would carry him on my shoulders, now here, now there, from isle to isle, from land to land, and I would never fail him even if I were forced to beg my bread."

The first order of business facing the regent and his council was to persuade the realm that the royalist party would not repeat John's errors. By way of demonstrating their commitment to justice—and that the rebels had no sole claim on that cause—the keepers of the crown reissued, within a scant month of John's death, that Great Charter of liberties, *Magna Carta*, which the pope, at the king's incitement, had annulled the year before. Since they did so of their own accord, the new and somewhat altered version was more a government manifesto of good intentions than a treaty between contending parties. Among the other, mostly minor, omissions from the original charter, it was discovered when a copy of the new one reached Nottingham Castle, there was no longer the requirement that the crown's French hirelings, Philip Mark among them, be discharged.

"Thank God the Marshal lives!" said Anne, exultant that the regency council appeared to value Philip's continued service.

"But he does not reign," said the sheriff. "And unless he musters an army and drives Louis into the sea, no charter can warrant my safety."

·XLIV·

"WE CAN HOLD THEM another fortnight at best," Reginald Mark, the acting chief bailiff at Nottingham Castle while Manning remained away at Newark, told his brother at the onset of the Yule season. "Beyond that, the garrison will desert, excepting possibly the knights completing their term of duty."

"Tell them the demands on our treasury have been ceaseless," said the sheriff. "I've had the whole northern half of the nation to look after."

"Our fellows know as much but think it unfair for them alone to bear the burden. They've had not a penny since Michaelmas."

The disaster of the Wash, claiming a major portion of the crown's riches, plunged the kingdom into immediate financial crisis that was compounded by the king's death, with the mounting uncertainties it added to the existing civil turmoil. Nearly all tax payments dried up while the royalist camp tried to organize itself and appealed to the rebel cadres to quit the field, now that the object of their contempt lay dead and buried beside an abbey in Worcester. But so long as the prince of France roamed the land, the insurrectionists retained hope of casting off the Plantagenets' heavy yoke.

The Marshal, meanwhile, with his last reservoir of strength, was determined to rally the crown's forces. This meant, in the first instance, maintenance of the castle garrisons and itinerant royalist companies by disbursing their back pay, which the king had been in the habit of supplying as he traveled the realm. With his baggage train swallowed up by the sandy bogs of the Wellstream estuary, immediate pressure was felt by the royal treasury at Nottingham, where the reserves were rapidly depleted. The regent ordered what crown monies, plate, jewels, and precious cloths were on deposit at monastic houses across the land to be drawn against to meet the costs of sustaining the government and its military arm.

The effect of this desperate salvage was to promote something close to panic at Nottingham Castle, where the larcenous first clerk feared that his unimaginably bold crime could not long escape detection. But he had planned too carefully for the scheme to come undone; for months he had been apprising the sheriff of the slippage in the reserves, and Philip had been too preoccupied with all the other cares of office to demand a close accounting. Quite simply, he trusted his clerk utterly—and would not, at any rate, have been able to follow the intricacies of his ledger books.

Uncertain how long his funds would last, the sheriff expected his garrison to behave as selflessly as he himself did and, as the year's end approached, to be the last to get paid. One unalloyed triumph on the battlefield would likely have renewed the flow of revenues to the crown; but with winter settling over the land and military operations suspended until spring, every penny on hand would have to be husbanded if the crown camp was not to disintegrate. For all his economies, though, Philip could only watch impotently as the bottoms of the barrels in his vault were scraped bare of their pennies; his soldiers and officers grew restless, then defiant, and now prepared to quit the crown's service altogether if their pay was not forthcoming. On the verge of finding himself in charge of an unmanned castle, the sheriff could think of only one reliable source of funds to tide him over the emergency. He hastened to Derby two days before Christmas.

No seasonal expansiveness of heart warmed the greeting William Ferrers gave him as Philip saluted the gnomish earl and asked after his health. "In view of the imperiled state of the realm," said Ferrers, "my system palpitates continuously, and I take my sleep in bits and pieces. But I am surviving, thank you, Master Sheriff—unless, that is, you bring me news of fresh disasters that will do us all in."

Without further ceremony, Philip stated his business, apologizing only for having to approach the earl at such an untimely moment.

"You ask me for one hundred and fifty pounds to keep your garrison intact?" Ferrers looked as if his life's blood had been solicited to save a wounded pup.

"The garrison, like the castle, is the crown's, not mine, my lord—and you are the ranking resident of the shires I superintend as well as a senior member of the regency council. Where else am I to turn?"

"It is no tribute to your abilities, Master Mark, that you have allowed things to reach this unpretty pass."

"You know as well as I, my lord, what befell the king—the calamity at the Wash and its aftermath could not be foreseen—and I have not stinted in supplying others the funds under my command."

"An earl is not a king. You cannot think I have a bottomless chest to be drawn upon whenever your improvidential needs—"

"It is a temporary aberration, I feel. In the spring we shall become self-sufficient again."

"Who can say that matters will not have worsened by then—and you won't be back at me again?" The earl shook his fiery head. "What truly astounds me, though, is that you have the brass to march in here seeking my aid in total disregard of the acrimony between us."

"Acrimony, my lord? The only sore point I know of is the crown command that I hold Melbourne manor."

"It is more than a sore point—it's a matter of honor. I am the lord of the shire, and Melbourne falls within it."

"Why do you continue to tax me with encroachment, my lord, when it was our late king who assigned me to take and hold Melbourne?"

"Our late king took perverse pleasure in tweaking those like me who loved him best—just to see how steadfast we'd remain. I'm still smarting as well from the other act of disrespect he dealt me a year ago that redounded in your favor."

"My lord?"

"The king preferred your chaplain to become head of my priory—how could I have thwarted him?"

"That was none of my doing, sire."

"Do you take me for a fool? Ivo was chaplain of your castle."

"I would not have had the presumption to approach the king on such—"

"But he told me you did."

"I? Soliciting Lenton for Ivo?"

"Precisely so."

"I did no such thing, my lord."

"Either you're a liar or the king was in this instance—and I cannot conceive why His Majesty should have invented such a tale."

"I'll not slander a king I served faithfully all his reign, my lord, but you have my word of honor that I never spoke to him of Ivo."

"I fear you lie, Master Sheriff—because it suits your ends."

Philip fought to muffle the rage welling within him against this inflated flea of a potentate. Then all at once their unfurling rancor revealed to him, as nothing before it had, the altered nature of his position. If the death of the king had weakened Philip by denying him the patronage of that ultimate liege lord of the realm, it had also had the compensatory effect of releasing him to be his own man—and not nearly so degraded a one as it suited Ferrers to suppose. On the face of it, true enough, the earl had to be numbered among the mighty of the land while Philip remained an untitled officer in a corps suddenly bereft of royal command. But with the country in turmoil, its gentry in a divisive uproar, and its would-be conqueror stalking the land, all the lines of power and position had grown tangled, and rank resided with whoever was bold enough now to exercise it. Was this vulgar opportunism or grave usurpation of privilege—or but the newly picked fruit of liberty to act for himself as conscience alone urged? He grew heady at the release without forgetting that if he served no master but himself, his every next word or motion could mean his downfall. All life, more so than ever, was exposure.

"I'll disregard your insult, my lord, only because I've come to you on more urgent business," the sheriff said. "I put it to you again—funds are required to preserve our castle as a vital crown bastion."

"More vital to you than to me, Master Mark."

"If Nottingham falls, Derby does—will you help or nay, sire?"

"Will you yield me Melbourne if I do as you ask?"

"It's not mine to yield. You sit on the regency council—if your confreres direct me to hand it to you, it will be done on the instant."

"No one would object if you simply yielded it to me at your discretion."

"I cannot indulge in such private transactions, my lord. It must be done by lawful procedure and written directive."

"Then our talk is ended," the earl snapped.

"You will not help?"

"Only if the regency council directs me to—I suggest you apply to us in person when next we gather."

Philip studied him with thickening scorn. "Then I will do just as you say, my lord—and tell the council that while the survival of the crown was hanging in the balance, you elected to place petty resentments, totally unfounded as they are, above the pressing needs of the realm. Is that what you wish, sire?" Philip moved closer to him. "I tell you this is no personal matter between us—it is your country that calls upon you for help. Will you be so faithless and selfish as to reject it now in its direst hour?"

The earl of Derby froze in place, knowing he had been bested. "I'll send a cart to you next week with the silver you ask," he said, contempt coating his tongue, "but I invite you never to return here."

"I came to you in person out of courtesy, sire, rather than addressing you a letter of plea. But my mission is no more to my liking than to yours, so I do not deserve your scorn for performing it. I'll absorb your misdirected wrath because I know my duty as you do yours. I see no reason, though, for you to suffer the added expense of dispatching your wagon and men to Nottingham when I can as well—and more safely—send our own vehicle to you."

The earl cast him a glance of undisguised loathing. "Leave off, sire," he said, "and have the grace to let me pay you tribute, now that you would rule our shires like a king."

A.D.
1217

·XLV·

ON THE EVE OF THE GREAT BATTLE to lift the siege of Lincoln Castle, the sheriff somberly concluded that he must join the fray.

Never in his entire career as a soldier had he been part of an attacking host; he had served only among garrisons defending castles. And never again, he supposed, might such a glorious opportunity present itself, an occasion attended by so many notables of the realm. But being a prudent man in his forty-ninth year, altogether unpracticed in the art of assault, and not at heart a warrior, he did not entirely relish the prospect of facing a violent and painful death on the morrow.

Beyond the dubious adventure of it, there were two pressing reasons for his decision. Bearing the title of co-sheriff of Lincolnshire, though largely an empty one until the French and rebel forces could be driven from the county, he surely had the duty to join the offensive aimed at liberating its capital town. Additionally, Philip had somehow taken it into his head that among the reasons fate had denied him a knighthood was that he had never with his own hand slain a man in battle or for just cause. He had almost surely inflicted fatal wounds at a distance by means of the crossbow during the defense of Loches a dozen years earlier—he had estimated three such shots at the time, as well as another eight or ten grievous wounds as the result of his marksmanship. But that was not the same as grappling with a foe face to face, hand to hand, driving home your weapon, watching the life force flow out of him in gleaming rivulets, and savoring the spill of his shattered organs. This brutish feat, he was certain, required still more courage than inviting that very fate upon himself; how much easier to yield one's life than to cut down another's.

Attended by his nephew, Geoffrey, in his capacity as captain of the castle guard, the sheriff went to the armory room to find a suit and lance for the battle. "They're an awkward business at best, Uncle Philip," said Geoffrey as they surveyed the depleted store, "and I cannot help wondering at your wisdom in wanting to join the sort of fight for which you're so little trained."

"I lived with armor much of my youth," said Philip, "and even squired one season for a knight of precious little mettle."

"But you've never donned the suit yourself or fought with it on or withstood the impact of a crashing lance that can send you flying from the saddle. There's scant room to maneuver, locked in all that metal, and it's dreadfully hot-making, besides."

"Then shall I abandon the armor and go as a simple sergeant?"

"And be slashed to ribbons by the first passing knight? Given the choice, you're safer mounted in armor, though it's a close thing."

Geoffrey saw to it that Philip's suit was mended and oiled and polished overnight, that his lance was properly strong and sharp, that his sword— the very one that Lambert had given him—was straight and keen, and that the best charger left in the castle stable was put under his saddle. Only when all that had been arranged did the sheriff go to his wife and tell her of his resolve. "You must not fear for me," he said. "I'll ride close by the Marshal—surely God sits on his shoulder and has seen him through many a battle."

"This is madness," said Anne. "The Marshal is an old man and ought not to risk his life—all England depends on him. At any rate, you can scarcely look to him for help. And what prowess have you in battle?"

"Nevertheless, I must go—it's my duty."

"Your duty is to defend this castle, not to take the one at Lincoln. And it's doubly so, what with the king's being here."

But his bailiff and undersheriff had lately returned home, having been replaced at Newark and Sleaford by more suitable castellans, so his presence was hardly essential at Nottingham during the day of the battle. "Manning and Eustace can direct our garrison capably enough and will guard the boy with their lives if need be. The matter is settled." Philip kissed her tenderly, knowing she would forgive him so long as he managed to survive the battle unmaimed.

The boy king's presence at the castle underscored the momentous nature of the event. As regent, the Marshal had wanted Henry, then nine

years of age, to be close by the scene of battle, but Nottingham, twenty-
five miles distant, was as near as could be risked. The foremost champions
of Henry's cause were on hand as well: the earls of Chester, Derby, and
Salisbury (Longsword had returned to the crown fold, if not in disgrace,
then contrite and eager to make amends with his martial skills); the fiercest
of the royal captains, Fawkes de Breauté; and Peter des Roches, as able
a soldier as he was a churchman and administrator, his hauteur notwithstanding. None of them stirred more excitement about the castle, though,
than the pretty little knight who was their king. The sheriff's daughters,
several years the boy's senior, were greatly amused at the sight of him
dressed in miniaturized lordly finery and pampered at every turn. "Little
Threesticks," they gigglingly called him after the Roman numeral in the
center of his crest, and were not in the least flustered on being summoned
to provide the pink-cheeked child with some youthful companionship. They
curtsied extravagantly and bid him welcome and long life, as their mother
had instructed.

"They tell us your father is the most honest sheriff we have," said
Henry, in his sweet, piping voice.

"Thank you, Your Majesty," said Angelique, "but who are the 'us'
and 'we' you speak of?"

" 'Us' and 'we'? Why—they are me, of course."

"Then why do you say it that way, sire?"

The boy king shrugged. "Because—our father did—and we've been
taught to do likewise. It's what kings say."

"But there is only one person who is king," Angelique persisted, "so
why are you 'we' instead of 'I,' Your Majesty?"

"I—we—cannot say for certain. It's the custom of the realm."

"Perhaps it means the king and queen together," Julia Mark put in.

"Perhaps it does," said Henry, amused by the topic he himself evi-
dently had never thought to probe.

"Where *is* your mother?" Julia asked. "What is she like? Your father
never brought her with him on his visits here."

"She's at Windsor, tending our brothers and sisters. She's very beautiful, we think. Father wished her to suffer the discomforts of travel as
little as possible, so she rarely moved about with him."

"Who will be your queen?" Julia wondered.

"It's not yet come up," said the king. "We must grow a bit first, and
then we'll see. Someone tall and most ladylike, certainly."

"And a princess," added Angelique. "It's de rigueur."

"Prince Louis's daughter," Julia suggested, "so there can be peace between our countries."

"Oh, no," said Henry, "never."

"Why is that?"

"Our father despised the prince—and his father still more."

"But if the families were married, the hating might end."

Henry pondered. "Perhaps—but in the meantime, the prince fights to take away our crown. He must be put down."

"Then it's good your uncle William is back on our side," said Angelique. "Are you partial to him? He was here when the Welsh boys were hanged—he seemed saddened by it, our father said. Do you know about that horrid night?"

"No."

"He was a child then," Julia chastened her sister. "You'd not tell that to a child—and you shouldn't trouble His Majesty about it now."

"Uncle Longsword is our favorite," said Henry, ignoring the bothersome aspect of the matter. "He's very brave and the best soldier in England, now that the Marshal is old."

"Then why," asked Angelique, "did he desert your father in the very thick of things?"

"That's a sore point—and you shouldn't ask your king such a thing," said the king. "He's explained it all to us carefully, but it's truly none of your business, now, is it?"

"Do you trust him?" Angelique persisted.

"They tell us to trust no one but God and the Holy Father."

"Not even the Marshal?"

"He's the one who tells us that."

Diverting as the king's presence was, it was the Marshal, of course, who dominated the preparations at the castle even as he had towered over the royalist camp since becoming regent six months earlier. He had checked the advance of the French and rebel forces into fresh territories and firmed the resistance of the crown's supporters. Prince Louis had set out, once the cold weather broke in February, to seize the last holdout castles in the east of England but was thwarted by Hubert de Burgh's defense of Dover and Dame Nicolaa de la Haye's resolve at Lincoln. When the prince went back to France for reinforcements in March, the Marshal busied himself cutting a swath southwesterly from London, retaking Farnham, Winchester, Southampton, Portsmouth, and Chichester; on his route, more than a hundred barons and knights flocked back to the royal colors, Longsword and the Marshal's oldest son among them. On his return in April, bearing huge siege engines now, Louis vowed to take Dover and Lincoln castles and then reduce the west of England. Toward that end, he split his forces, sending a sizable contingent north under the count of Perche to overwhelm Dame Nicolaa's fortress in Lincolnshire. Catching wind of this deployment while he lay at Oxford, the regent moved to snap off the overextended arm of the French and rebel army. Couriers were dispatched on the thirteenth of May, calling on every loyal earl, baron, knight, and sergeant in the midlands and near north country to muster a week hence at Newark for a sharp strike at enemy-held Lincoln before Louis's troops could seize the castle. More than four hundred knights, three hundred bowmen, and a sizable phalanx of foot soldiers answered the call—a lesser number, to be sure, than the foe had assembled at Lincoln but easily the largest army to take the field for the crown since the civil war had begun.

Saturday the twentieth of May dawned gloriously clear and bright, and with so many knights and fluttering pennons and caparisoned chargers snorting and pawing the ground, the plain near Newark Castle more nearly resembled a tourney site than a war encampment. Gualo, the papal legate, was on hand to grant full absolution to the crown warriors and repeat the sentence of excommunication against their foes, so that the royal army took on the joyfully sanctified aspect of a holy crusade. The regent delivered a hearty harangue to his assembled host, assuring them that with God's blessing, they could not fail to carry the day. Then Fawkes and his company of mounted sergeants and crossbowmen moved out in the lead on the northward march; behind them rode the four main divisions of the king's army, captained by Ranulph, earl of Chester, Longsword, Bishop des Roches, and the Marshal. The sheriff hung close by the regent's right.

Lincoln was built on the crest and southern slope of a hill rising north of the river Withan where it met the Foss Dyke. An old Roman encampment was at the summit, and the castle stood at the southwest angle of the ancient walled town that had grown up beside the Roman outpost. Only on the west did the castle give out onto open country; on all other sides it abutted the streets and dwellings of the town, making it difficult for assailing forces to mass their effort against the citadel.

To lift the siege and win the day, the Marshal, Longsword, and

Fawkes had devised a dual strategy. If the enemy realized its true numerical advantage, it might well sally out from the town and rush boldly down upon the royalist forces as they struggled uphill toward the city walls. To encourage the perception that it was a mightier army than an accurate count would reveal, each loyalist baron brought with him twice the normal number of banners, one set for his troops, the second for his baggage carriers. Should this deception fail and the enemy come pouring down from the town to engage them in open country, the Marshal had instructed the crossbowmen in Fawkes's vanguard to dismount at once, deploy, and shoot down their own horses to form a gruesome barrier that would break the charge of the hostile cavalry and neutralize their advantage.

But if the enemy remained behind the town walls, the royal army had a more intricate plan. It would draw up on the exposed west side of the castle, where a heavily barricaded postern gate had been prepared to allow entry to Fawkes's company. His bowmen would then position themselves on the battlements while his mounted troops charged out of the main castle gate in a diversionary attack on the town. The real thrust of the assault, though, would be felt elsewhere. The earl of Chester's troops would batter their way through the town's north gate. At the same time, a second assault would be launched through a long-abandoned and now thickly overgrown portal in the town wall north of the castle, which Bishop Peter remembered from his days as a young canon at Lincoln Cathedral. By prearrangement, one of the castle defenders was to slip out and unlatch the hidden and forgotten gate from the inside, permitting the royal forces under the regent and des Roches to pour through.

Well before they drew within sight of the ramparts of Lincoln town, Philip was roiling from the discomforts of armored warfare. Under a cloudless sky, his metal suit baked him. His eyes soon smarted from the steady trickle of perspiration off his scalp. His unreachable groin itched without relief. His arm chafed where the elbow joint in his armor fit imperfectly. And he was ever more persuaded, the farther they traveled and the harder he had to fight against heat and dizziness, that he would be a liability on the battlefield and ought not to have undertaken so foolhardy a mission.

When a volley of roars came eddying back to him, though, from the head of the line of march, signaling that their destination was within view, the sheriff felt his entire insides alternately quicken with excitement and contract with dread; he spurred his charger to keep pace with the Marshal's. They forded the Withan at a narrow spot and started slowly up the hill to the town. But no defenders appeared outside the gates to engage them in the open or even to harry their steady climb. Instead, the occupiers of Lincoln redoubled their efforts to storm the castle before the army of relief could reach and reinforce it. Seeing that they were advancing unimpeded, the Marshal used the cautious tactics of his foe to stir his troops at the brink of battle. "It is a prelude to victory," he shouted to his men, "that the French spurn an engagement with us in open combat and hide from us behind their walls. All this is by Heaven's plan! Great glory will be ours this day, so let us now do the right, for God wills it!"

Only at that moment, thrilled by the old warrior's gallantry and stamina, did Philip truly understand why he had joined the battle. Against all reason he had hoped to conduct himself with enough skill and valor to catch the Marshal's attention and, in his last conscious bid for the prize that had so long eiuded him, gain the endorsement of that greatest knight in chivalry. Amid the shouts and cheers and trumpet blasts and all the dusty tumult of the deploying army, he cast aside fear that his quest was arrant folly and urged his mount forward.

After Fawkes and the earl of Chester had moved off with their forces as planned, the Marshal drew his division close by the obscured western portal and awaited the signal that the other royal troops had launched their attacks, Fawkes from within and the earl battering at the north gate. But the great knight soon grew restless and led a small party to the portal to determine if it had been unlatched from within as intended. Then, and only then, did the sheriff dare to call out to the Marshal in reminder that he had not yet donned his helmet. With a look more akin to annoyance than to gratitude, the regent hurriedly drew on his head gear and then instructed his lead knight to test the portal gate.

No sooner had it swung open to the push of his lance than a group of Fawkes's mounted sergeants came charging out, hotly pursued by a squad of French defenders. The sight of his men in headlong retreat at the very outset of the encounter so enraged the Marshal that he could not bear to await the signal to unleash his troops. "Shame on him who delays longer!" he roared, and plunged through the breach in the wall, hurling aside the startled pursuers of Fawkes's men and bounding onto the cobbles of Lincoln.

The virtue of the attack plan became quickly apparent. The Marshal's men, with the advantage of surprise, surged forward against scant resistance. Imperiled from the rear now as well as from the earl of Chester's men, who by then had crashed through the north gate, from Fawkes's freewheeling horsemen, and from the raking fire of the crossbowmen poised on the castle wall, the defending force hardly knew which way to turn. In the narrow, twisting streets, their superiority of numbers was nullified.

At such close quarters, Philip wielded his sword instead of the far more cumbersome lance, emulating as best he could the motions of the Marshal, who slashed and smashed whatever enemy bodies and objects stood in his way. Not until their column reached the open square beside the cathedral did the enemy mass thickly enough to stay the royalist charge. There the count of Perche could be seen rallying his knights in bristling array; and amid all the wheeling, whinnying horses and shrill cries for courage, Philip knew the panic of blind confusion—friend and foe were caught up in a single, swirling cluster of tangled movement—and the expectation of imminent oblivion. The time for prayer had passed.

Suddenly his immediate group was beset by a furious rush. His slitted visor did not allow him to take in the full sweep of the melee, only the flash of thrusting lances and the glint of clanging swords. He lifted his weapon to deliver a sidelong blow at the nearest flailing foe when from the opposite side a mighty force crashed against his armor and wrenched him from his stirrups. He landed face down, momentarily stunned by the impact, and swam through a deep, dark hole at the edge of consciousness. But he soon grew aware of the ooze of blood from where his forehead was cut by his visor as he fell hard against it. Slowly, while hooves and limbs and screams churned the air about him, he drew himself into a kneeling position and reached to recover his sword, which had fallen but a few feet from him. No sooner had he done so than he glanced up to see a great Gascoyne roan bearing down upon the Marshal from behind. Philip wobbled to his feet and struggled to intercept the charging horseman, whose lowered lance was flying pell-mell toward the Marshal's back. He lunged at the enemy horse with his sword, caught it on the flank, causing it to lurch, and drove home his shaft. The animal staggered barely a yard short of the rider's target, emitting a bellow of agony that caused the Marshal to swing about and confront his would-be slayer. By then Fawkes himself, who had witnessed the flashing episode, had come upon the assailant and smote him mightily with his mace. The enemy knight sagged senseless in the saddle, and while the Marshal grabbed the bridle of his attacker's collapsing mount, one of Fawkes's sergeants relieved him of his mace and lifted the felled knight's visor, allowing the Scythe to drive his lance point neatly through the eyehole.

In another moment the battle had swept by him, and Philip found himself unmenaced by any enemy and standing over the gored knight and his dying steed. It was then that he first noticed, stitched to the roan's caparison, a series of small swans of the sort he had once seen adorning the dress of Cicely de Lambert. The knight's squire was by now at his master's side, gingerly removing his helmet. Thrill and revulsion warred within him as Philip pressed close to observe the ghastly remnants. Instead of a head, there was revealed a gray-and-crimson omelette of brains, blood, dashed bone particles, and jellied tissue—yet enough of it remained intact for him to recognize the lifeless lord of Swanhill. His only thought was not a lament but of how easily it might have been he lying there inert and Sir Thomas the one looking down. A rush of exhilaration bathed over him.

By the end of the day, no fewer than forty-six French and rebel barons and some three hundred of their knights had been ushered into the castle bailey at lance point. Those of their supporting forces who had tried to flee the town on foot were set upon by the suddenly patriotic peasantry of Lincolnshire and summarily slaughtered. The rout was total. The Marshal had turned the tide of the war.

The victors passed the night at Lincoln Castle, where the regent toasted his men, the liberated castellan, and, most generously of all, Sir Fawkes de Breauté for having come to his rescue. The recipient of this salute replied with grace but no word of recognition for the part played by the sheriff, who had stayed the enemy lance just as it was about to cut down the regent. Perhaps Fawkes had not seen his desperate effort, Philip thought; more likely, he had no wish to share the glory. At any rate, the subject was closed from that moment forth. Survival was the sheriff's medal.

The triumphant host dispersed in the morning. A small procession headed for Nottingham with Philip in the lead, followed by Sir Thomas's squire, a horse bearing his master's corpse, and Sir Guthrie de Lambert, Thomas's son, who had fought beside him in the insurrectionist cause. The strapping, somewhat witless young knight had been captured in the battle and released in the sheriff's charge, on his honor to pay the crown one hundred pounds for his liberty and withdraw from the war. On the slow ride to Swanhill, Philip and Guthrie exchanged not a word.

News of Lambert's death had preceded their return, so that the great hall of the manor house had been suitably arranged to receive his body. The priests of Newstead Abbey, of which Sir Thomas had been the foremost patron in the shire, were on hand to offer prayers and chants. After the sheriff, the squire, and Guthrie had placed the baron's remains on the bier, still in his armor and helmet because the manner of his mutilation was too horrid to reveal, Philip ungirdled his sword—the one that Thomas had given him long ago and had played its crucial part in his death the day before—and laid it respectfully beside the body.

As the Newstead monks rendered a *Te Deum* that swelled to the rafters of the darkened hall, the residents of Swanhill, each bearing a votive candle, filed by the bier, the folk of the manor house first, with Alden Sparks, the steward, in the lead, then the folk of the field, headed by Noah, the reeve, and the beadle, Jadwin. Lady Cicely and her son knelt close by the baron while the abbot called on Heaven to receive for all eternity the soul of so splendid and devout a Christian knight.

Half-hearing those prayerful words, Philip hovered at the side of the hall and asked himself whether he could have knowingly cut down Thomas de Lambert on a field of battle. True, he knew him now to have been an abuser of his bondsmen and a likely murderer. But the reverse of that coin was that Lambert, a man of rare civility, had stood by him through trying years when many in the shire were quick to assail the sheriff as a cold and mechanical functionary of the crown. Could such a one as the baron be transformed from friend to enemy by the petty play of politics? How much easier the task of the professional warrior, who slays blindly and impersonally. Surely Sir Fawkes, or likely the Marshal himself, would not have hesitated to strike down yesterday's boon companion—or even each other—if today's cause demanded it. Would Lambert, then, have thought twice about butchering the sheriff if he had not been bent on bringing down the Marshal—and the whole royalist cause with him? Philip told himself the question wanted study.

After the cortege had borne away Sir Thomas's remains in the manor's best wagon, driven by the lord's venerable stablemaster, for burial in Newstead graveyard two days hence, only Philip lingered in the hall with Lady Cicely and Sir Guthrie. Mother and son were seated now on a bench before the bier, empty save for the row of candles that provided the sole illumination in the chamber. Satisfied that the widow was dry-eyed and at peace, the sheriff spoke what words he could of earnest condolence, then added yet deeper regret for his own part in the baron's death. "I had not heard of it," Cicely said, unmoved.

"It is nonetheless the case, my lady. There was, of course, no way of my having known—in the heat of battle. . . ."

She nodded slowly. "Would it have made a difference—if you had known it was Thomas? He was your enemy of late."

"Yet it troubled me greatly to think of him as such."

"It should not have."

"I'd come to feel a special fondness for—"

"Indeed, it would have been altogether fit if he had died of your hand alone. You'd have naught but compassion from me, sire."

"My lady?"

"He'd dishonored the both of us for years—and I'll not pretend by his graveside I loved him for that disdain."

"I . . . my lady . . . I cannot say that I . . ."

"Surely you are not ignorant of his enduring relationship with Mistress Mark?"

"They were fond friends, as I always understood it."

"Passionate lovers, Master Mark. I could hear their caterwaulings on days when I remained in the far wing of the house and no doubt Thomas told your wife I was off visiting somewhere or other. He knew I'd not intrude on them—what would have been the point?"

Philip's throat constricted.

"I see your disbelief, Master Mark. Can this really be a shattering revelation to you? Were you truly blind for so long?"

His face dropped, and the color drained from it.

"They played you for a fool—Thomas the more so, I have no doubt. I'd hear him refer to you contemptuously as a drone bee who served his queen slavishly, as befit the bastard son of a harlot seamstress, with a petty nobleman of a father who had scarce acknowledged his paternity. You were never more than a blatant striver to him, albeit a clever one."

Philip finally found his voice. "I . . . believed in him. . . ."

"I stopped believing in Thomas years ago after he'd decided he had what he wanted from me. But a woman's choices in life are limited if she declines to use her body as a weapon."

When he returned to the castle, a dead calm in his eyes, Anne Mark took it to be a kind of benumbment from the unspeakable horrors of the war her husband had just endured. The scabbed wound on his brow testified to the ordeal. She had not heard the details of Lambert's death until Philip quietly retold them and how he had naturally accompanied the baron's body to Swanhill, remaining for the service of worship. It was not until after he had greeted his daughters with adoring hugs, taken a light supper, and given an hour to the business of the castle that the sheriff confronted his wife in their bedchamber.

"Lady Cicely appeared less than profoundly grief-stricken," he began, and then dryly related her charges. "For what it's worth," he added at the end, "she blamed him and not you."

His muted tone belied the enormity of his words. Anne would not meet his eyes, frighteningly harder now, for fear her own would quiver with confession and decompose into a cascade of tears. She groped for words, finally managing to whisper, "It is monstrous of her—to turn her own wifely failings into so base an accusation."

"Possibly in her overwrought state she masked her pain and sought instead to inflict it on me—on us," Philip suggested.

His seeming eagerness to exonerate her lent Anne encouragement, and she rallied her defenses. "I cannot say. He told me only that she had denied him for years—that whatever love they had known was long since turned to poison. I thought it best not to dwell on the topic with him. But to think that at the end she would use their loveless union to slander me and mock you in such a fashion . . ."

"One thing in particular among her words troubled me—Lambert's allusions to my birth."

"Doubtless Cicely was trying to injure you the more—as if by trans-ferring her own self-hatred, she might mitigate—"

"As it happens, though, my dear, she had the particulars precisely right. While I've never made a secret to you of my father's modest standing in the gentry's lowest tier, I've gone to great length to disclose nothing whatever of my mother's station—and her weakness for lovemaking out of wedlock."

"Philip . . . I—"

"How else could Lambert have hit upon such a thing if you had not conveyed it to him?"

"I . . . Philip, you must try to understand the circumstances—and why I would ever—why I felt it—"

"I need not guess who told you our tawdry family secret."

"Peter meant no unkindness. He was muzzy with drink one night—"

"Oh, he never means to wrong me—betrayal just comes naturally to him." Philip rose and, the mask of invulnerability beginning to drop from his face, stepped closer to her. "But it was not his place to have shared such a thing with you—nor yours to share it with Lambert. You must have known it was a subject of utmost privacy and deeply hurtful to me."

"Yes, but I had a decided purpose—that Thomas might better understand what stuff you are made of—your mettle—to have risen as you have from such—mean beginnings—and why you have long wished to become a knight."

"Why should any of it have mattered to him—that you would—"

"I wished him to hold you in awe, not in contempt as some crude soldier the king used to wipe his feet on."

"Yet he scorned my degraded origins and taunted me for them behind my back. You owed me my privacy, Anne—just as I never pressed you for having come to our marriage bed unchaste."

She bowed her head and slumped into the corner of the chamber. His muted rage only made worse this settling of accounts she had ever hoped to avoid. "You were the infinitely greater gentleman," she said softly. "I confess my error in full."

"Not in full—not yet." He turned away from her and moved to the other end of the room, so that when his voice found her now across the void, it came like a crackle of lightning. "If you shared all of that with him, what of yourself did you withhold? Shall I ask it outright—for the truth of Cicely's words that you would so glibly pass off as villainous? Or hasn't the question already been answered by your pallid words and sorrowful looks?"

She was mute at first, as if waiting for the full detonation of his wrath before trying to mitigate her sin. When he said no more, she braced herself and looked full at him across the chamber. "You may think what you will, Philip, but in my mind and heart, I never did anything I thought would dishonor you—precisely the opposite."

"Of course."

"Philip, as my God in Heaven will witness, I went with Thomas only for your own advantage. I . . . it was wrong—entirely—I saw that as time went on—and not a day has passed since it ended—that's almost two years now—that I'm not riven with remorse. It was only that I thought my—my being with him would—"

"You endured his great grunting embraces only out of love for me—to advance my career by the artful application of your sinuous loins!"

"Yes! Scorn me if you will—as you must—hate and punish me as you like—but that's the truth of it."

"You sought to honor me by dishonoring me—while caring nothing whatever for a man you let violate you repeatedly?"

Her head tilted, averting the full lash of his bitterness. "If I had cared nothing whatever for him, my actions would have been altogether reprehensible. As it is, they were only unspeakably shameful—the more so that you've hit upon them, to my utter humiliation. . . ."

"*Your* humiliation? You haven't begun to be humiliated, my dearest Anne—while I've worn horns before the eyes of who knows how many—and you, with your professed bottomless devotion to me, permitted it!"

"I took what precaution I could—that it should be discreet."

"Kept from my eyes and ears, at any rate."

"Philip, my whole purpose was to hold him to your side."

"By betraying me?"

"I never felt it a betrayal—I thought I was sacrificing myself. But I can hardly expect you to believe that. Judge me as harshly as you wish—as you do all others."

"Would you have me hold my own wife to a lesser standard?"

"I would have you grasp that perfection is granted to no mortal—and temper your wrath with understanding—"

He left her in midsentence and took refuge in one of the windowless chambers at the far end of the corridor that had gone unoccupied since housing the Welsh boys. Thrashing sleepless on the straw matting, he passed the night in bewilderment that he could have so grossly misjudged his life's companion. That he had blinded himself with regard to Lambert as well, he saw plainly now, had been largely her doing. He could think only of how best to flay her for her sorcery over him.

The accused sorceress lay awake in terror of the dawn. She knew his stony rectitude could never have compassed the truth: she had been driven into infidelity not by her own unnatural overflow of appetite but by his mere tolerance of the carnal practice. Simply, he rated concupiscence a petty distraction from life's earnest business. Forced to choose between orgy and abstinence, he would have opted for the latter as the lesser inconvenience. But the time to have confronted the matter, she understood now, was before and not after she sought compensation elsewhere for his dispassionate nature. In her heart, though, she was persuaded that if the want of sensuality were correctible merely by due diligence to the defect, all lovers would be prodigies. Thus, she could only wait, defenseless before his ripening rage.

"I no longer want you at my side," he told her within moments of the sun's ruddy arrival, "and wish to look at you, for all your fairness, as rarely as possible." She and their daughters would move within the week to the custodian's ample cottage at Bulwell Manor, occupied at the moment only by his brother Peter.

"I see," said Anne. "And what are the girls to be told?"

"Surely not the truth about their mother. Use your wiles on them rather than me—tell them the manor is far more suitable for rearing young ladies than a chilly old castle. I'll visit with them each week and have them back here from time to time. Meanwhile, you'd best hone your skills as cook and housekeeper."

"You would deny me even a single servant?" she asked.

"As you denied me all honor," he said.

"No knight was ever honored more," she replied, "and asked less of in return."

"I gave you as I knew how, Anne, yet you chose to purchase more. Now the bill has come due to be paid."

She could only nod at the retribution he coldly dealt her and submit with tearless dignity.

·XLVI·

THE FADING OF WAR and rancor across England, paradoxically enough, caused the sheriff's lot to grow more tenuous, not less.

Within three months of the rout at Lincoln, Prince Louis sued for peace. The reinforcements that were his last hope for victory had been slain or captured in the Dover straits by the crown fleet under Hubert de Burgh. The Marshal himself escorted the vanquished French prince to the water's edge and, having doled him a sizable bribe not to savage the English countryside on the way, bid him a costly adieu.

To heal the weary realm, the regent acted with generosity and enlightenment. Blanket amnesty was extended to every rebel baron and knight who pledged fealty to the crown, and their seized property was returned as promptly as vows could be recorded. To re-establish stable government, the regency council retained the services of King John's most efficient officers, even if, as in the egregious cases of William Brewer and Fawkes de Breauté, with their multiple sheriffships, sundry other offices, and vast holdings, they were rough and unlovable men. To prove he was no quasi-king or Caesarean in his designs, the Marshal would grant no charter that ran beyond 1228, the year the boy king would come of age. And he lost no time ushering into law the first reforms of a just regime; by autumn a new forest charter stood beside the Great Charter of liberties as a further refutation of tyrannical rule.

Philip had attended the parley of sheriffs and wardens at Northampton to hammer out the gentler code of the wood. Whatever forest lands had been proclaimed a royal preserve in the threescore years since the last Henry's coronation were returned to the commonwealth. No man would henceforth lose his life or any member for taking the king's game. Any resident of the forest was entitled to let his stock forage in it without payment. No forester could collect forced exactions, nor could any but an officially appointed forester-in-fee take cheminage for passage of persons or cargo through the wood. The permissible number of foresters was to be set by the regarders of the shire, and any officer making an arrest had to present his evidence to the verderers for enrollment and reference to a prosecutor. In short, the forest was no longer to be a place of rampant abuse of the crown's power. This purpose was not lost upon the sheriff, whose irregular patrollers, under a certain bumptious Robin-in-the-wood, had roamed Sherwood throughout the war with the loosest of tethers.

If the success of the rebellion and the French invasion would surely have cost Philip Mark his office, and possibly his life, their failure, ironically enough, enhanced his security hardly at all—and his power not in the least. In fact, his sway began to ebb apace with the waning crisis.

Even before he could reap the slightest gain from the office, the crown party took away from him the joint sheriffship of Lincolnshire and transferred it to the earl of Salisbury—a reward to Longsword for his part in the battle of Lincoln and return to the loyalist cause. Why his fickleness deserved a prize, particularly at the expense of an unshakably loyal officer, Philip could not imagine but was in poor position to ask aloud. As a sop he was given the small tax farms of the royal boroughs at Derby, Edwin-stowe, and Darlton, which yielded him more heartache than profit. Then they stripped from him Doun Bardolf's estate, among the first custodianships he had been granted, just as his years of work refurbishing the property had begun to produce a surplus. In a still unkinder cut, the sheriff was advised without further explanation that his control of Sherwood Forest was at an end and he was to transfer his men from it. Jurisdiction was to revert to its hereditary warden, falling under the authority of the chief forester of the realm, Hugh de Neville, who was now back in that office despite having abandoned the king's cause in the war.

The wrenching of Sherwood from his hands prompted the sheriff's formal protest. He directed a letter to Westminster, once more in operation as the seat of crown government, and questioned the wisdom of returning the royal forests to Neville, a man notoriously permissive of corrupt practices and known to have benefited directly therefrom. But his complaint was dignified by no response. Angered, Philip resolved to retain his grip on the forest until some satisfactory clarification was forthcoming from the regency council. Meanwhile, he would have to curb the conduct of the free spirit to whom he had given dominion of the wood.

"I must begin with a small cavil, Master Hood," the sheriff said after the two of them had exchanged greetings beneath the ceremonial oak at the crossroads of the forest. "You were licensed these past two years to make certain exactions and other takings as could be defended in the name of justice—provided that you shared the revenues equally with the castle. By our last reckoning, your total contribution to our coffers has come to one pound nine shillings and thruppence."

"Is that not a tidy sum, sire?" asked the woodsman, biting into a pear after the sheriff had declined his offer to share it.

"Meager, I'd call it."

"Perhaps there was some misunderstanding, then," said Robin, wiping the overflow of juices from the fruit upon his doeskin sleeve. "I took our bargain to mean we should present to the castle half of what remained after the expenses of our company had been met—and they are vast, let me tell you, sire. The cost of ale alone for forty thirsty men has become staggering."

"Forty? Why so many?"

"Who can say? Some no doubt chose to dwell with us rather than die in combat for the king—or for those who'd have dethroned him. At any rate, all have their uses here. Even our malingerers are, at the least, amusing."

"Then who is the sheriff to gainsay goodfellowship in the wood? I come not to quibble with you, friend, but to report on large events that must, perforce, alter the nature of your dwelling here." The sheriff sketched for him the chief features of the new forest charter, adding, "I'm proud to have had some small hand in this easing of the code, as I promised you I would."

"Oh, this is a considerable gain, I grant you," said the woodsman, having listened attentively while chomping his pear down to the core. "But still it alters nothing basic. The use of the forest is not granted to the common folk."

"By 'use' I take you to mean its openness to be wasted at will. If that were allowed, it would shortly be stripped of all its game and timber and turned into a barren. The crown wishes to preserve the wood as pristine—"

"The crown wishes to preserve its own privileges—and the interests of those rich enough to pay bribes for use of the wood as they will. The crown wishes to preserve the poverty of the needy."

"Your words are misdirected, friend," said the sheriff. "This is a new regime, eager for reform. By your own concession, this charter is a long stride forward, however short it may fall of perfection. I come here, though, not to debate the merits of the thing with you but to advise that the crown has withdrawn my authority over Sherwood. Accordingly, your past activities under my license must end."

Robin studied the remnant of his luscious morsel and then pitched it into the brush with a hint of agitation. "So much," he said, "for the good intentions of the new regime. No doubt all your noble efforts will be reversed by your successor."

"I've lodged a protest—"

"A grand gesture." Robin gave his head a vigorous shake. "Plainly I chose the wrong side in the war. You shouldn't have seduced me into your ranks."

"You weren't seduced—you were dearly purchased. And it grieves me that our bargain must now be undone."

"But why is that exactly? What has their giving you the heave-ho got to do with my little company of hearties?"

"Your presence here has become illegal—the new charter makes it clear. Who may serve as foresters and how many there can be are now beyond my power to determine. Your men may not continue to make exactions as if they were crown officers—or harass wayfarers, however ripe for the plucking, or rob them outright—"

"Rob? You say we rob in the wood—as if in keeping with my name? No, sire, we never rob, not in the thieving sense. Our purpose is but a slight reallotment of riches."

"Banter as you'd like, Master Hood—the point is that you must alter your conduct altogether now. The war is done; I am deposed as master of this wood—or about to be—and there is a new charter. I have no choice but to dismiss you from your service to the crown and deal with you henceforth as any other trespassers."

The shaggy woodsman grew sulky at this advisory. "So you've used us, Master Mark, for your own damned convenience, and now you would discard us as so much rubbish."

"You were fairly rewarded and scarcely oppressed—but now your commission has expired. You never had my perpetual charter to super-intend these woods."

"And suppose I refuse your dismissal, sire?"

"Refuse it? Your choice is not invited."

"But if the crown has dismissed you as overseer of Sherwood, then how have you the authority to dismiss us?"

"I am resisting the order against me and inquiring into it—but in the meantime, I'll enforce the law and new charter to the letter."

"Well, then, if you can resist your orders from the crown, I can do no less. We'll carry on as ever till the outcome of your own effort becomes known."

"But your presence in the wood would only complicate my task."

"Are we so notorious that the crown has moved against you on our account? We're just a band of merry souls who harm none but the wicked and overfed."

"Look here, my friend, I'm not going to quarrel with you further. I hereby order you to cease and desist your unlawful conduct and find haven elsewhere in the realm."

"But we love this wood, sire, and thrive on it—and what grief do we cause the goodhearted?"

"Nonetheless, if you persist in your prior conduct here, Master Hood, you'll be apprehended and punished."

"Not so fast we won't be, Master Mark. First you'll have to catch us—and if perchance your suety fellows manage the trick and you act to prosecute us, it'll prove a sorry day."

"You threaten the sheriff?"

"It's not a threat, sire—it's a promise. I'll turn crown's evidence on the instant. All the world will learn of our illicit pact—of how you've consorted with outlaws and assorted lowlife to wield violent sway over Sherwood—and extract outlandish fees and fines from all who ventured in—not to mention your receipt of half the swag from our banditry. Hearing that, they'll not only take the forest from you but the castle as well—and likely pitch you in your former gaol, if not dangle you by a rope from the donjon tower." He spit out a vagrant seed that had nestled between two rear teeth. "Disturb us not, sire, or you'll rue the result."

· XLVII ·

BY THE TIME THE LETTER CAME in October from the London wine merchant, advising that Anne Mark's legacy from her father was being forwarded in silver for arrival at Lenton Priory the week following, the sheriff had all but forgotten the existence of the promised bequest. The size of it he had ceased to speculate on altogether from the day that word of the inheritance had reached them more than a year earlier. Anne herself, though, adrift on a sea of remorse, dwelt upon the prospect as a sign that Providence had not abandoned her entirely.

The silver reached the priory in two installments delivered a night apart, each packed in a dozen chests aboard a stout wagon. It was driven by Bartholomew le Gyw's Welsh nephew, who was in Nottingham, as luck would have it, for the first time in five years and had altered considerably in appearance. Not by coincidence, Sparks was supping at Lenton with his old mentor as the first shipment of the silver arrived there. When Ivo saw the size of the treasure, his eyes opened wide, and he remarked to the little clerk, "You see, Jared, it's not only the wicked who are rewarded in this life."

"A veritable miracle, without a doubt," said Sparks. "All the more cause, though, to keep the nature of the fortune and the identity of the beneficiary a confidential matter."

"To be certain," said the prior. "It is a specialty of our house."

"I quite forget myself, Father. It's just that Master Mark has more than his share of detractors, many of whom would be eager to put the worst possible face on his family's sudden prosperity. If you'd like, I'd be honored to carry your receipt to him certifying the monies are on deposit here for release as Mistress Mark sees fit."

"No doubt such a document would be in order. I'll have it drawn within the week."

"Still sooner, Father. Should some mishap befall you in the interim and the claimant had no proof, the funds would disappear into the priory's coffers, never to be extracted."

Ivo nodded. "Would that I had half so faithful a servant at my elbow as your fortunate master does."

Discovering the size of the fortune his wife had come into—the precise figure, according to Prior Ivo's note of receipt, was £2380—did little to lift the sheriff's melancholy. Indeed, the sour humor that had taken hold of him from the time of Anne's departure from the castle seemed only to deepen now. While Philip had not confided in his clerk regarding the cause of his dark mood, the latter had connected its origin to the death of Thomas de Lambert and was not so obtuse that he could not guess the nature of his master's grievance. Since Sparks was as fond of the sheriff's wife as of her husband and had, in a different way, worshiped her almost at first sight and sound, to conceive of her as something less than irreproachable deeply troubled him. If, despite his tremulous warning to her, her friendship with the lord of Swanhill had become a vile thing, as was widely rumored at the manor, the clerk had not detected it in any coolness she ever manifested toward the sheriff. Perhaps that merely made her a more cunning enchantress.

Since exiling her to Bulwell, the sheriff had asked himself repeatedly if he might somehow have led Anne to suppose that his advancement was so central to their life that she should sully herself to promote it. On reflection, he was disinclined to blame himself for what he judged her frailty of character or to forgive it by crediting the elemental allure of forbidden love. Deceit had a thousand excuses; fidelity needed none. It did not occur to him, while nursing his wound, that a man could make himself so blameless as to become insufferable, so ardent as to become unfeeling, so purposeful as to become unlovable.

Another man who felt himself so greatly wronged might have been tempted to deprive his sinful wife of the material wealth she had all at once become heir to. But Philip was no conniver at cruel vengeance; the prior's receipt was delivered to Anne promptly, along with a note urging her to deal discreetly with her new fortune. That very evening she appeared at the castle in garments all black for bereavement and came upon him unannounced in his closet. "You must not deny me a hearing," she said gently.

"My ears have no stoppers."

"It is your heart I would open."

"I can't vouch for that region—in its torn state."

"I would mend it," she said earnestly while taking care to leave a proper distance between them. "Philip, it is an unspeakably large sum— I cannot think how my father managed to preserve it. With such means we could live now like people of rank. The girls can have more than respectable dowries. If you'll take me back, I'll do whatever it is you would have of me to prove the genuineness of my regret. I'm no Jezebel, whatever you may think, nor am I ruled by a lascivious nature. You must not judge me so harshly as to deny this God-sent gift to us and what it can augur for our life together."

"The gift is yours, not ours. Where it came from, I'll not hazard."

"It's meant for all of us—to gain a happiness and comfort we've not known, for all your noble efforts. Let us leave this place, Philip, for all our sakes, and now—before they turn on you viciously."

He met her pleading eyes for only an instant. "I want none of your money, Anne. Your having it changes nothing for me."

"What is it you want, then? To see me dead?"

"I cannot say. . . . Some transcendent act of penance, I suppose— but not a ton of silver. It's not my place to prescribe a remedy; it's yours to contemplate. Go ask Father Ivo—shrive yourself before him, at the least."

"I . . . cannot."

"Why not? Assaying shame is his stock-in-trade."

"It's not Heaven's forgiveness that I crave."

"Perhaps it's where to start, though," he said, turning from her.

A.D.
1220

·XLVIII·

IT WAS THE NINTH EASTERTIDE AUDIT he had been subjected to by Westminster and ought to have aroused small anxiety in the sheriff. To that roomful of finicky crown officers who sat murmuring about the great table, its checkered cloth piled high with ledger books and pipe rolls, and their countless subordinates, alternately hovering and scurrying, Philip had long before established the efficient manner in which he ran his castle and the accuracy of its recordkeeping. Since the Exchequer had resumed its semi-annual inspection of each sheriff's accounts in '18, moreover, the burdensome nature of the scrutiny had been further eased by the Marshal's shrewd decision not to force the sheriffs to account for their handling of funds during the wartime hiatus in Westminster's operations. It was enough, during those tumultuous three years, that the sheriffs had been able to maintain a semblance of government in most counties. But on this morning, as he entered the crowded, noisy hall, Philip sensed menace in the air.

For one thing, he and Sparks had been kept waiting at their inn in Lambeth for three extra days before the Exchequer finally summoned them—time enough to conjure a whole menagerie of dragons lying in wait for them. More worrisome, Philip noted at once on scanning the hall, was an unexpected addition to his panel of interrogators. Seated as usual at the center of the table on its far side was the chamberlain, a brash young cleric who had assumed the post at the war's end and plainly relished making powerful witnesses squirm with his snidely hectoring questions. At his right elbow sat that mainstay of the crown, William Brewer, the barons' representative at the council table. The realm's sternest judge of the sheriff's craft, he knew its every trick firsthand and was, by common consent, a past master at not getting caught for any of them. Brewer had long admired Philip's abilities and rarely pressed him unduly during the audit sessions. At the chamberlain's left elbow this morning, however, sat the man who, since the Marshal's death a year earlier, had become the most powerful officeholder in the kingdom.

As regent, William Marshal had restored the peace, braced the crown, and rehabilitated its government, all largely by dint of his irreproachable character. But there was no one of comparable stature to succeed him. Rather than stirring virulent jealousies by designating any one of a half-dozen plausible candidates as *primus inter pares,* the Marshal committed the care and keeping of young Henry the Third and his realm to Pandulph, the new papal legate, and Peter des Roches, the able and crafty bishop of Winchester. The lawmaking power continued to vest in the regency council, operating more or less by collegial consensus. The government apparatus itself was presided over by King John's last justiciar, Hubert de Burgh, who had in the war displayed his notable military prowess. In normal times, the justiciar served as the king's alter ego when the monarch traveled outside the realm; but with a still impotent lad as titular ruler, whoever held that high post was not only chief magistrate of England but, practically speaking, the prime arbiter of all temporal power.

De Burgh did not rise to greet Philip on his arrival at the Exchequer, managing only a half-salute and wan smile of recognition. This stiffly decorous welcome in and of itself should not have been troubling; the sheriff could hardly have expected the justiciar, amidst the adversarial proceedings in that teeming chamber, to embrace him warmly. They had been cellmates fifteen years earlier following their diehard defense of the two prime Angevin castles in Touraine—Sir Hubert at Chinon and Philip, alongside Gerard d'Athiés, at Loches—and, in their shared ordeal, attained a rare comradery. But time and events had naturally eroded it, although the pair had had a brief reunion of sorts during de Burgh's ill-fated sheriffship in Lincolnshire. His somber presence at the Exchequer table, despite Philip's hope that some shred remained of their former bond, was cause for concern; otherwise, the justiciar of England must surely have had more urgent business than the account books of two smallish shires in the midlands.

The sheriff had not long to wait for his foreboding to be confirmed. "Our usual procedures are being waived this morning, Master Mark," the chamberlain began after Philip and his clerk had taken their places and the soaring chamber had stilled with expectation, "in order that we may inquire into a lengthy dossier of complaints lodged against you since our Michaelmas audit." This accumulation of charges, the chamberlain went on with zest in his excoriating tone, suggested the possibility that the sheriff had been abusing his office, and so the Exchequer was obliged to examine the matter.

The sheriff cast a quick glance to his clerk, who turned his palms toward Heaven in ignorance. "Such allegations are disturbing, of course," said Philip, "but I have no fear of them. We have aspired to the scrupulous superintendence of our shires and stand ready to defend our conduct of office to the last detail."

"In that event," said the chamberlain, "would you kindly address the accusation, sire, that you were notably laggard in returning certain estates confiscated during the war upon their former owners' renewal of their vows of fealty to the crown?"

In the dark corner of his mind, Philip glimpsed a conspiratorial gathering of his maligners. But why now, suddenly? Because, he reasoned, the crown resided upon the head of a child who reigned but did not rule, and there was no magisterial regent in his stead, so every royal officer, even the ablest, was vulnerable to harassment. The very fact of his own longevity in office promoted him for targetry. There was no choice but to parry such thrusts and not lose patience or dignity in doing so.

"My lords and good gentles," said the sheriff, "before restoring their property to those in my shires who had turned against the king, I required that they settle all outstanding debts to the crown that antedated the onset of hostilities. This insistence engendered a certain degree of resentment, it is true, but I felt the policy fully justified."

"But there is the added charge, Master Mark, that in several of these cases, your bailiff imposed a surtax—or attempted to—against those whose land the crown had seized. I cite, by way of example, Lord Guthrie de Lambert, who has advised us that your Master Manning would not convey his arrearage to the castle until the bailiff had been paid an additional five pounds—which Sir Guthrie naturally supposed was done at your instruction."

"He was promptly disabused of that suspicion upon his complaint to me," said the sheriff, "and his coming to you with this story thereafter is testimony only to his animus. When I had such a report from Lord Lambert and several others, I confronted my bailiff, who told me he felt treason ought not to be forgiven so lightly and deemed the extra exaction a fit punishment. I told him that, the justice of his sentiments notwithstanding, his demand amounted to extortion—and I dismissed him from office forthwith." When his words had echoed back from the rafters, Philip added quietly, "It grieved me much to do so, gentlemen, for Master Manning had in many ways been an exemplary bailiff."

The chamberlain flicked a look at Brewer for guidance. The baron gave a contemplative nod, and the presiding cleric moved on. "Then what say you, Master Mark, to the charge that you have levied an annual fine of one hundred shillings against the council of burgesses at your royal borough of Nottingham in return for your good will and the maintenance of their liberties—this being done without authority of the crown?"

"I say it is a groundless canard," the sheriff replied at once. "The burgesses insisted from the first, despite my earnest protest, that I accept such a kindness even as my predecessors had done. In yielding to their entreaty lest I offend them, I required that the money go toward improving the utility or comfort of the castle or, if need be, into the general pool of tax revenues. Never a penny went into my own purse."

"You say the gift was voluntary?" Brewer asked blandly.

"Altogether, my lord."

Nonplussed, the chamberlain continued down his list. "A number of your tenants on the crown manor at Bulwell have charged you with harshness in your tallages and other fees and petitioned for your replacement as custodian."

"These are but the classic whines of the reluctant taxpayer," said the sheriff, shaking his head to discredit such pestiness. The Marshal, he reminded his inquisitor, had ordered the financial records of all royal estates inspected, following which each custodian was sent a list of the reliefs and other monies owed. "I had no leeway in this whatever," said Philip, "though my tenants may have supposed me arbitrary in their exactions. True, I imposed some fresh charges in order to maintain the common fields and facilities that had for too long been neglected before I took custody—a new cow shed was needed, the hay barn was badly in want of repair, likewise all the fencing and the well. So they grumble unjustifiably over this, too—though I suspect my brother Peter, who for a time served as my surrogate at Bulwell, may have been aggressive to a fault in demanding payments."

"They say he was attacked for his zeal by one of your tenants,"

Brewer remarked. "The road to Hell, I would suggest to you, sire, is paved by overly attentive relatives."

The sheriff conceded the point with a smile. "A most unfortunate incident, my lord. My brother was set upon one night and suffered a stab wound in the shoulder. The culprit was never caught, so the exact genesis of the attack remains unknown, but Peter has elected—wisely, I think—to seek his fortune in York, where his gifts may be better appreciated."

Two of the leading religious establishments in Nottinghamshire, it next emerged, were among those charging the castle with oppression. The chancellor at Southwell claimed the sheriff had denied the minster its hunting rights unless an unseemly large fine was paid, and a number of the monks at Lenton had reported that the priory's grain was being stolen by castle officers and their wood likewise filched while the sheriff turned his back on the practice. "Can you explain away these reports as blithely as the others, Master Mark?" asked the chamberlain.

Philip studied him intently across the table's narrow width but registered no pique. "At Southwell, it is the chancellor, let me assure you, sire, who has been the oppressor, and not I. He refused to part with his illustrious chronicler, Father Honorius, who had asked transfer to Lenton, where his old friend Father Ivo, our former chaplain at the castle, had become the prior. Having heard that the chancellor had refused the request lest Lenton gain in stature at Southwell's expense by enrolling so renowned a figure, I urged him to relent as an act of kindness—but making no headway, I wrote to Archbishop Langton, now blessedly back among us, and apprised him of the situation. The transfer was subsequently arranged, and the chancellor, in his annoyance, would now defame me. At Lenton, likewise, there is a sector of the house that resents Father Ivo as a stranger imposed upon them by our late king and, supposing my involvement in his election, seeks to embarrass me with concoctions such as these about my approval of thievery. They are eagerly relayed to Westminster, I have no doubt, by our coroner, who wanted the priorship for his brother-in-law—and is eager as always that there be a new sheriff for him to torment."

"Ask him about the earl," said the justiciar, stirring with impatience and looking bored by the ease with which the sheriff had thus far deflected the charges.

"It's next on the list, my lord." The chamberlain leaned forward, as if to bring more vigor to his case. "The earl of Derby is aggrieved that you retain Melbourne manor in his shire against his wishes."

"This is an old story. I was instructed by the crown to occupy and hold the manor as rebel property for the duration of the war," the sheriff related with dogged equanimity. "As its former owner died before peace was restored, the manor became escheat—and so I hold it still while its title remains in dispute."

"The earl says it should be his to hold by right," de Burgh put in.

"Why tax me with the complaint, my lord? Let the earl apply to the regency council if he would serve as custodian in my place."

"He says you hold perversely, having agreed to turn Melbourne over to him as a condition for his lending you funds in the war to pay your garrison," said the justiciar, looking toward the ceiling.

"There was no such understanding, my lord."

The justiciar suddenly cocked his head toward Philip. "You would call the earl of Derby a liar—before an open session of the Exchequer? A perilous business, Master Mark."

"Then let us say instead, my lord, that the earl has never been a fancier of mine—largely, I suspect, because I am not of the Anglo-Norman gentry but a simple officer of the crown who nevertheless fulfills his duty without apology."

The justiciar fell back and waved the chamberlain ahead. "And what are we to make, Master Mark," the questioner ploughed on, "of the accusation by Sir Ralph de Greasley that for six years, you persistently sought his payment of a bribe to release to his wife the manor of Robert of Muskham, which the crown court ordered transferred to her from your custody?"

"You may conclude, as I have, that Sir Ralph and Lady Olivia are mean-spirited and vindictive toward me for not having been more accommodating to their exalted status. They'd have had Muskham the moment they paid me the fifty pounds the crown said I was entitled to for loss of the custodianship; yet they would not pay it, so I held the manor—but never asked an added payment. The matter was settled in our shire court last year to Sir Ralph's satisfaction, though it was reported to me he had threatened the jurors."

"Then why didn't you prosecute him?" asked Baron Brewer.

"No one would vouch for it," said the sheriff.

"Then tax us not with rumor, Master Mark," said the justiciar. "It is beneath your dignity."

"Very good, my lord. But it is an indisputable fact that I have to this day received no payment whatever from them, though they've had the property more than a year now."

"But you held it six years longer than your entitlement," said the chamberlain, "doubtless earning far more on it than you were owed by Greasley and his wife."

"I earned next to nothing on it, sire—it required close tending and high expenditures lest I be charged by Greasley with wasting the estate. They got it much improved, I can assure you."

"Perhaps if your management had been less profligate," said de Burgh, "your profits would have been higher."

"They'd have been higher," said the sheriff, poorly hiding his annoyance now at the unkind thrust, "if I'd been extortionate. But this is not my practice, sire."

The longer the inquiry wore on, Philip sensed, the less tolerance his answers were winning from his interrogators. He felt the tide rising still higher against him when the chamberlain cleared his throat and straightened his back, as if finally prepared to get down to serious business. "We are freshly in receipt of a most unorthodox charge," he said, "lodged by a certain nameless renegade forester who claims you hired him and his company to police Sherwood Forest and make exactions per your directive—as well as certain illicit takings, a goodly portion of which he was forced to turn back to the castle for your personal enrichment. Not a pretty charge, sire—it smacks of arrant piracy and flagrant abuse of high office."

Philip had always viewed the woodsman as an endearing lout who, for all his antic spirit, possessed a soul of honor; now he was exposed as capable of as much treachery as the craftiest of courtiers. "This is a spiteful rogue, gentlemen, who feeds on sour grapes." Philip sat back and crossed his arms in front of his chest in defiance of such low calumny. "It's true I employed his services as a wartime expedient to keep the forest swept clean of the king's enemies and to take such fees for passage as were authorized—and perhaps then some. The monies, you will recall, were badly needed for our soldiers' pay throughout the midlands. But when the new forest charter was enacted and I was asked to relinquish charge of the wood to our—"

"Instructed, Master Sheriff," said Brewer, "not asked."

"Quite so—I stand corrected," said Philip. Were they about to credit the prattle of this faithless woodsman? "At any rate, I discharged this cheeky devil and told him he must heed the new forest charter to the letter—at which point he threatened to come forward with just such a tale as he's now trying to peddle to this honorable assemblage if I did not relent and leave him be."

"Yet you apparently neither expelled these rogues nor gave Sherwood over to Matilda de Caux, its hereditary forester, as the regency council instructed," Brewer said with flint in his voice.

"Because I was awaiting the council's reply to a letter I addressed to it, taking exception to the transfer because I feared far worse would occur if my men were removed. Dame Matilda has scant aptitude for the administration of the wood, so the task would have fallen to the chief warden of the realm, whose crew of rascals seemed certain to me to revert to their old game of abuses. I had expected the courtesy of a reply from the council."

"Who are you," the justiciar demanded, "to question the directives or the civility of the chief councillors of the realm? They are hard-pressed by their business and unable to heed the bleats of every self-serving grumbler in the crown's service. Meanwhile, you held the forest against the council's instruction by not sending these bandits of yours packing."

The sharpness of de Burgh's rebuke caused Philip to mute his manner. "I sought to bring the matter to a head earlier this year, my lord, by conducting an inquiry among the folk of our shire into the appropriate number of foresters we should have and the nature of their duties."

"And who asked you to conduct such a rump inquiry?" de Burgh asked still more sharply than before.

"I . . . why, no one, my lord. But I thought it a prudent—"

"So you proceeded on your own, and your findings were rebuffed by the regency council—and Dame Matilda's jurisdiction over the forest was confirmed—and you were told in no uncertain terms to chase your men from Sherwood."

"Which I've lately done, sire—and this onslaught against me that you now entertain is the result. Plainly, I ought never to have trafficked with such scum as these, who shamelessly register their peeve by trying to degrade me before this body. Nothing of their takings ever entered my pocket, I swear it. I earned only their slander for doing my duty in driving them from Sherwood."

"At long last," said the justiciar with an edge of sarcasm.

"As you say, my lord," said the sheriff with a hint of obeisance.

The chamberlain sat back now with the smirk of a fox about to slip through the side door to the henhouse. "There is, finally, one matter far more serious than all the foregoing, Master Mark, and requires your enlightening us." The beetle-browed cleric hunched forward, reached for a ledger that had been hidden beneath the heap of other documents in front of him, and shoved it across the table toward the sheriff. "In view of these other accumulated charges against you, the Exchequer deemed it imperative to invade your bailiwick the moment you left for London and make an unimpeded examination of your premises for any data of an incriminating nature—thus, the delay of several days in your being called before us." The chamberlain leveled a prosecutorial finger at the ledger, which now sat midway between him and the sheriff. "This document was found in a chest in your clerk's bedchamber. It appears to be a listing of the revenues recorded at your castle during the war years, but the figures in it do not tally with the official set for the corresponding period residing in the sheriff's closet. Those ledgers balance—but if this hidden one is the true record of your collections, then you would appear to have been some twenty-five hundred pounds in surplus—monies nowhere else accounted for—thus making the receipts ledger officially presented to us for inspection by your undersheriff a gross forgery, and yourself a thief on a grand scale."

The vaulted chamber rumbled with undertones of disapproval. Clerks flew in all directions, as if a beheading had been announced for a few moments hence. Philip slipped Sparks the merest sideways glance, enough to determine that his indispensable aide wished to disappear beneath the checkered cloth. Trying to remain calm above the enveloping pandemonium, the sheriff reached out for the indicting ledger and dragged it toward him. As the great room spent itself in hubbub, the accused opened the document and inspected it for several moments. Then he slid it to one side and, after the chamberlain held up a hand to silence the hall, confronted the circle of narrowed eyes drilling into him.

"I cannot say for certain—it was some years ago, and the circumstances of war were perplexing," Philip began in a tone that was deferential yet conceded nothing.

"But they were not an open invitation to robbery," de Burgh put in hotly.

"I need no such reminder, my lord."

"What you need remains to be seen," the justiciar replied.

"Why is it, my lord, that I alone among the sheriffs of the realm am now suddenly subjected to upbraiding for our wartime activities when the Marshal explicitly exempted all such records from inspection?"

"The Marshal has gone to his eternal reward," de Burgh said, "and no longer rules the realm. Nor am I aware that his directive was meant to grant amnesty to any and all instances of abuse that might be brought to the Exchequer's attention."

"Then I would respectfully ask for time to study the matter with care and frame my answer coherently." Philip glanced around the table. "Offhand, I should guess there was a wartime purpose at the root of it and that the charge will prove as groundless as all the rest dredged up by my defamers and hurled at me this morning. Whatever the explanation, though, I feel certain this honorable body will be satisfied by it."

"I hope so, Master Mark," said the justiciar, "for your words today have about them all the slipperiness of a barrel of eels."

The sheriff held his tongue, but the chamberlain was not eager to let his prey wriggle off the hook. "Perhaps your able clerk can shed some light on the matter for us," he pursued, "especially since the document was found among his soiled garments."

"The responsibility is nevertheless mine, sire—I bear the onus for answering to the crown twice yearly in this chamber and ask only for the opportunity to get to the bottom of this matter and clear my good name."

"He is entitled," said Brewer. "And since it's true that none of our other sheriffs has been required to account for his wartime records, let us give Master Mark until the Michaelmas audit to report back to us in full—or pay the price." From the iron in his voice, the price for disappointing the Exchequer would be steep indeed.

The sheriff punished his terrified clerk throughout the five-day ride back to Nottingham with his choicest, frostiest silence, broken only by a biting disclosure their first hour on the road. "I know precisely what you've done," he told Sparks, "now that they've shown me your handiwork."

"Sire?"

Once he had had word of his wife's inheritance, the sheriff became highly suspicious, knowing as he did that her father had suffered greatly as a result of having a son-in-law among the English captains. "And so his bequeathing Mistress Mark a large legacy struck me as implausible," Philip recounted. "But in the midst of war and with connections severed between here and France, I had to bank my concern. When peace came, though, and the legacy materialized as promised, I directed a letter of inquiry to

Mistress Mark's sister, who is in holy orders and, despite their differences, I felt certain, would speak only the truth. She replied as I had feared— that whoever had told Anne she was the beneficiary of a sizable fortune was committing a cruel hoax—that their father had left little more than enough to pay off his debts and meet his funeral expenses, with the tiny surplus sent to her nunnery by way of compensation for the dowry he had given Anne. Who, then, was Mistress Mark's mysterious benefactor? I had no way of knowing, or even exploring the matter, without dire risks to my reputation. And now, thanks to you, that sleeping dog I let lie bids fair to take my head off."

On returning to the castle, the sheriff first of all determined that his deputy was innocent of complicity with the Exchequer auditors. "They descended on us with every manner of writ and demanded full access to your closet," Sir Eustace assured him. "Our resistance would only have fueled their suspicions." The coroner, however, was not so steadfast; it was Sir Mitchell, the undersheriff revealed, who directed the Westminster investigators to Sparks's apartment and urged them to rummage through it for possibly damaging items.

Philip resolved to deal with the coroner if and when the storm clouds so close overhead now ever dispersed. Then he climbed to the donjon tower, dismissed the watch, and summoned his clerk—upon whom, it had become massively evident, he had relied to an unforgivable excess. While awaiting his arrival, the sheriff scanned the springtime countryside, agleam with the greenest green he could remember since being drugged by the overwhelming purity of the hue on his initial trip to Nottingham a dozen years before. Without letting his gaze wander to the north battlement, where the Welsh boys had been put to death, he recalled the hope and promise with which that radiant landscape had first beckoned to him. And for all his tribulations, for all the disappointments and betrayals, his reign at the castle had not been without its rewards. There simply was no better-governed sector of England than his, and there were some few people who knew it. He wished now only that he might escape the infamy of all his known and nameless predecessors in that office.

"But why, Jared," he asked quietly when the clerk had joined him at the breastworks, "would you ever have thought of this evil thing when you knew full well that every particle of my being disapproved of such perfidy? I am altogether baffled by what possessed you."

Sparks gulped wildly for air and prayed for divine intervention lest his knees give way. "Only my love for you, sire," he offered in a breaking voice, "and my mounting distress at watching your noble efforts go unacknowledged."

"Why is it," the sheriff asked after a moment, directing the query heavenward, "that those who profess to love me best vie in schemes of betrayal? What have I done to them to warrant such hurtful kindness?"

After a respectful silence, Sparks said by way of frail mitigation, "You were never to know anything of this business, sire. I kept the authentic ledger only on the odd chance of our need to determine whether some claimed payment had actually been made. I ought to have burned the damned thing years ago."

"You ought never to have whelped such a misbegotten monster!"

"Without a doubt, sire." Sparks turned to him mournfully. "But I could not put it out of mind how sorely you've been abused for your very spotlessness of character. This latest misadventure in London underscored it. The crown habitually hounds you despite your years of proven competence, as if everlastingly eager to show you had been gulling them by incessantly painting your blemishes. And the earl—that nasty little work of greed and pomposity—labors ever against you. Our selfish barons and preening lords condemn you as an upstart and revile you for dutifully imposing the crown's sway. The common folk decry you as their heartless tax-gatherer and a peacekeeper of mean impartiality. The pampered church claims you abuse their holy rites. Your tenants denounce you as their oppressor for trying to maintain your holdings in good order. Your debtors balk that you cruelly seek your due. Your wards' families rate you beneath their exalted station and charge you with coarse social ambition. Half the shire, with no other convenient object for their hatreds, casts you as a grasping foreigner wished on them by a dead and unlamented king. Even outlaws, evildoers, and mischievous dwellers in the wood profane you as their unflagging tormentor." The clerk's apologia grew in passion with each lancing sentence. "And what reward have you had for enduring these savage slanders? The crown grants you nothing in perpetuity nor even for the remainder of your life—only a few endlessly worrisome holdings from which to eke out a pound or two while you try to dodge the offal hurled at you by ungrateful tenants. Of material wealth and chattels you have almost none to call your own. Subtract your wife's magically forthcoming bequest from her father, and your dearest daughters will have no dowry and poor prospects for a respectable marriage." His tears flowed without shame now. "Who are your well-wishers at Westminster, sire, and on the regency council? Who is grateful that you held the midlands for the crown when all was so bleak and desperate? And the masters of the realm have not even had the courtesy to raise you to knighthood. They do nothing for you but spill doubt upon your honor, which is triple any of theirs, and cannot wait now to heap you with ignominy."

"For all that you say," said Philip, not unmoved by this pitiable catalogue, "they have continued me in service. That has been my reward, don't you see?—the confirmation of my rule over these shires."

"They have abused and exploited you, sire, because you are hungry for the regard of men you wrongly suppose to be your betters."

"I've been no more sorely used than you, Jared. What reward have you had beyond the faith I reposed in you?"

"That's a different matter, sire."

"In no way. We are all functionaries of a sort—those of us in want of wealth and privilege—and serve without entitlements. To assume any is rank delusion." The sheriff ran his hand over the wind-smoothed stone of the battlement. "I'll ponder your words and settle on a fit response shortly," he said. "Meanwhile, my infernally inventive friend, what is it you propose we do now to answer Westminster?"

Sparks sighed heavily, grateful for his master's seemingly diluted wrath and continued deference to him. He thought it safe, in such circumstances, to propose the easiest and yet for him most unsatisfactory solution. "I could simply go before the Exchequer, sire, and confess the truth. They'll call it misguided devotion to my master. I must and will accept all the blame, paying if need be with my life."

"Admirable," said the sheriff, "and impossible, as you perfectly well know, Jared. They'll not believe you and will suppose instead I've got you to take the fall—thus thinking that much the worse of me. And even if they credited your story, I'd be held grossly negligent for not having detected the larceny."

Sparks gave an appreciative nod. "Perhaps there is another way, then," he said wistfully. He appeared to ponder for a time and then tentatively brought forth a scheme he had devised during the punishing ride back from London. A second counterfeit ledger might be created, one with expenditures to match up with the higher revenues in the authentic ledger the Exchequer auditors had recovered from his bedchamber. "We might say that this new one had been misplaced but that it, along with the one

I held, were the true set, whereas the pair in your closet, with the lower figures, had been manufactured as a ruse to trick the enemy in the event they'd seized the castle—so that, on seeing the lesser numbers, they would underestimate the size and provisions of our forces and, accordingly, act with imprudent boldness. At war's end, I had simply neglected to replace the true ledgers."

The sheriff emitted a derisive grunt. "What a marvel of perverse creativity you are, Jared. But the extremity of our plight fevers your reasoning. In the first place, such a ledger could be too easily investigated for its accuracy. In the second, the logic of the explanation is skewed. If one were to attempt the ruse, the point would be to fabricate our payments in such a way as to cause the enemy to overestimate our military strength and thereby caution them, not to embolden them by minimizing it. Finally, your plan only compounds the lie and paves our way to the gallows." Philip proposed they both reflect further that night; meanwhile, he had to relate the sad tale of her illicit inheritance to his estranged wife.

How shrill an outcry would she send up against the fates, he wondered, for tricking her so gaudily? In truth, he expected her to fall on her knees, begging him not to turn back the money. With it, she might retain the vain hope of purchasing rank and comfort; without it, her life would remain a struggle to the end.

In fact, Anne greeted his grave report with something less than hysteria. She fell back against the pillowed bench in the parlor of the cottage at Bulwell that had become her home and gave a hollow laugh. "At some depth of my being," she said, far more collected than Philip had imagined, "I feared the thing was tainted. But I had embraced it as God-sent recompense for having lost your affection—and the core of my being."

"Then it served to ease your penance—"

"And so you begrudged me it—I've known all along. Perhaps you're even glad, now the truth is out."

"Since it may well cost me my neck or a long stay in gaol—and my office, at the least—there's little joy in it for me." He sat beside her and fought the impulse to place a comforting hand upon hers. "My devoted Sparks is even now beating his brain trying to explain away the crime so that the money can be retained."

"Tell him to save the trouble," Anne said with a resolute shake of her head. "It has brought me no happiness—I've scarcely touched the money. Our life here without you has lacked all purpose."

"But there are dowries to consider, I thought."

"I'm done with deceptions, whatever their fancied excuse. My daughters shall not have stolen monies for their dowry—better that they have none at all and pine away in spinsterhood. We'll persevere as best we can, surviving on what kindness comes our way."

Her words touched him and made him look deeply into his heart. No longer could he doubt the depth of her remorse or justify his own obduracy. He took her hand and held it within both his own. "If you wish it," he said gently, "I'll send a wagon in the morning for the three of you and your belongings—though our stay at the castle, God knows, may prove short-lived."

She placed her free hand over his and gripped fiercely as tears of joy fell from her pain-worn eyes. "I wish it more urgently than you can ever know," she said, resting her cheek alongside his, "but I'll not consent until first you hear a confession of mine. It deals with Peter."

His brother had lived in the same cottage with them for nearly two years; only one form of villainy could spring to Philip's mind. "It cannot be what I think, Anne—it would be too much to—"

"Shhh," she said, "not that—but horrid enough in its own way." A high-spirited bachelor, Peter had not hesitated to bring wenches to the cottage and cavort with them in an unspeakable manner while Angelique and Julia were in the house and could hardly avoid the spectacle. "I had words with him more than once," said Anne, "but he would not curb his conduct—knowing, I suppose, I'd hesitate to run to you in complaint against your brother, given the divide between us. One day, though, he came home drunk while I was in town on an errand, and he embraced Angelique with something more than avuncular affection. When I learned of it, I drew a kitchen knife in my fury and rushed upon him with it, slashing his shoulder. It was no resentful tenant of the manor as you were told. If he had not left for good when he did, I'd have slain him, come what may." She fixed Philip with a look of strength that he could but marvel at. "He is no rightful brother of yours."

He gave a slow, sad nod and took his wasted wife into his no longer punishing arms.

In the morning the sheriff instructed Sparks that he was to return to London shortly along with a small baggage train and half the castle garrison to guard the silver it would put aboard at Lenton before taking the main highway south. "It is the least abominable lie I can invent," said Philip, "and if they hang me for it anyway, I'll not have gone without a struggle."

The unaccounted for money, Sparks was to explain to the watchdogs of the Exchequer, had lain at Lenton Priory, whence it had been transferred as an emergency reserve during the war years—they would need Father Ivo to vouch for that straining of the truth. The counterfeit ledger of receipts had been created so that if the castle fell, the enemy could not detect the surplus or, since the ledger sheets bore no indication of its transfer to Lenton, the whereabouts of the money. At the priory, in order to sustain the secret, the silver was listed as on deposit to the sheriff's wife—an inheritance, it was said to be, from her wealthy merchant father; the French, it was hoped, would not confiscate such private funds if they invaded the priory as well as the castle. For corroboration of this fable, a few falsely dated letters of receipt issued by the prior would be required—easy legerdemain for so accomplished a counterfeiter as Jared Sparks. Then why, it would be asked at Westminster, had the sheriff taxed the earl of Derby for funds to pay his garrison if there was a reserve for such purposes at the priory? Because, Jared would explain, the earl had volunteered no monies to the crown in its hour of utmost need, and the maintenance of the castle that safeguarded his precinct seemed a sanctionable premise for prying open his purse. And since this whole grand deception had been so unorthodox, it could hardly have been blurted out in credible fashion at the Exchequer table. What Philip had been clearly culpable of was not advising London of the existence of these reserve funds, which were hardly the private preserve of the Nottingham treasury even if the sheriff had elected to treat them as such. The matter was now being remedied by the swift, if belated, shipment of the surplus to Westminster.

There was but one irremediable flaw in this elaborate tale: some one hundred and forty pounds could not be accounted for. Of that amount, one hundred pounds had in fact gone to his accomplice, Sparks confessed, and was not recoverable. "Lest you ask," he added, "I'll go to the gallows before revealing his name." An additional twenty pounds the clerk had set aside to buy his father and stepmother a freehold for when his days of useful labor were done—"and you must not ask me to renege on that pledge to Master Blake." The final twenty pounds Anne Mark had withdrawn from the priory account in her name to buy cloth for herself and her daughters and some articles of creature comfort for the cottage at Bulwell.

"Then you shall say we are frankly unable to account for the shortage," the sheriff proposed, "since so many wartime outlays were made by oral instruction or otherwise irregularly authorized. It will make the story less perfect but more plausible."

Sparks smiled at the deftness of the touch. "What a nimble practitioner in the arts of deception you might have made," he said. "It's the devil's loss."

And so it was done. The overseers of the treasury at Westminster were delighted with the unexpected arrival of silver from Nottingham, and the officers of the Exchequer swallowed the little clerk's carefully documented narrative. Sparks rode north in a mood approaching euphoria. It had been a close thing, certainly—both to disaster and to unimaginable success. Without the coroner's hateful intrusion, it all would have worked, and the Marks need never have known the true provenance of their good fortune. Surely, with the crisis passed now, the sheriff would see clearly that only benevolence toward him and his family had inspired the undertaking, however maniacal it may have appeared to him at its disclosure. Likely, he would make Sparks undergo an extended period of contrition, requiring looks of guilt and sighs of remorse he did not feel. In time, though, he was confident, all would be forgiven.

But Sparks had not reckoned adequately on Philip Mark's unrelenting virtue. The sheriff drew him into his closet shortly after the clerk's return and satisfied himself that their story had been well received at Westminster. Then he added mournfully, "I'm not ungrateful for your performance before the Exchequer, Jared, but I cannot pretend that things remain the same between us." He wandered off toward the window as he always did, Sparks knew, when readying his sternest words. "For all your great devotion to me and my family, I cannot forgive this hopelessly misguided conduct of yours. It was a grave felony, even though the crown will have been little deprived by it." Philip crossed his arms and drew a deep breath. "You are no longer welcome among us here, Jared—the words pain me to pronounce, but there they are. I've spoken with Father Ivo while you were in London and told him everything. He was, if anything, more saddened than I—but he agrees to take you in at Lenton if you wish to undergo penance and apply there for final orders."

Sparks turned faint with disbelief. Then the hiccoughs assailed him, and next gastritis. For an instant he feared that he might void where he stood. Was it possible that a dozen years of worshipful devotion had earned him no shelter whatever from his master's terrible righteousness? "I am anguished, sire," he finally managed to utter, "that you could be so harsh with me."

"I'm no less anguished," Philip answered. "But we differ on our notion of harshness."

"Are you so bereft of compassion, sire, that you cannot distinguish between those who would see you banished and threadbare and those who wish the world for you?"

"If I were, my dearest friend, you'd already have been packed off to gaol."

"Your exiling me into the bruising arms of Holy Church is but one step removed, so far as I am concerned. If I have erred, sire, it was on the side of adoration."

"Fondness turned fanatic can prove at least as hurtful for all concerned as its opposite sentiment."

"Might you not concede, sire, that I've learned that lesson? It will surely not recur."

"So you say—and I'm glad of it. Yet retribution must be exacted. Sorrow is no substitute."

"And why is that, sire? It was not Jesus's way."

"If you have somehow come to mistake the two of us, then the need for your leavetaking is yet more urgent. Your lesson must be lasting—you've been too reckless with my friendship. This was not the first instance that you exposed me to ultimate peril, for all your protestations of fondness."

"Sire? I know not your meaning."

"There was a certain episode long past, another unthinkable plot hatched behind my back."

"Sire?"

"Your bold deception to squelch the king's invasion of Wales."

"You—knew of that? Yet you would not—"

"Because it had a worthy purpose—far worthier than this brainless subterfuge. But hold, I'll not engage now in recriminations. What's past is done and over with—as are we, my kindest little friend."

Confronted by such a palisade of sheer rectitude, Sparks mounted one final effort of manipulative virtuosity. "But sire," he said, hoping to avoid the whimper of desperation, "surely the moment Westminster learns of my dismissal, it will suspect foul play."

"You've not been dismissed, Jared—you've merely chosen this opportune moment to retire from the crown's service and seek God." So saying, the sheriff embraced his unconscionably faithful clerk with a full measure of love and grief before turning him out the door.

· XLIX ·

IN THE FOUR AND ONE-HALF YEARS he had presided over Lenton Priory, Father Ivo had brought amity, piety, and enhanced renown to that monastic house without benefit of dearly bought relics or the showy appurtenances of modernity. Indeed, he pacified the aggrieved chancellor of Southwell for his loss of Father Honorius by dismantling the great loud clock overlooking the priory cloister and contributing it to the minster, where there was rather more need to know the hour of the day; at Lenton, Prior Ivo liked to say, it was enough to know the year.

He succeeded as well in winning over the affections of that often disagreeable tempest William Ferrers, earl of Derby, and even assuaged his long-standing animus toward the sheriff. When the chapter house fell into need of repair, the earl was only too glad to pay for it—on receipt of assurances from the subprior that his pathway to Heaven would be all the more direct. Nor was the life of the mind neglected under Ivo's shepherding; colloquia on both Christian and pagan philosophers were regularly conducted, with the prior, the chronicler, the sacristan, and their lately enlisted prize novitiate, Brother Jared, among the participants. The former first clerk at the castle was also put to the task of reorganizing the muddled registries and account books of the monastery. These revealed such fruits of rampant cupidity that the prior ordered the almoner to double his weekly distributions to the wretched of Nottingham.

This golden age of concord at the priory came to an end early in July when the venerated Ivo succumbed to sudden heart failure in his sixty-eighth year. In no time, the factionalism that had afflicted the house before him resurfaced, and sides were drawn for the impending contest to determine Ivo's successor. Because the boy king was still far too young to mix into ecclesiastical elections, the crown party was inclined to defer in such matters to the wishes of the papal legate and the cassocked membership of the house at issue. These circumstances lent disproportionate influence to Lenton's principal patron, the earl of Derby, with whom the priory's knight protector, Sir Mitchell of Rainworth, strongly pressed the renewed candidacy of his brother-in-law. Since this cleric had won the reputation, while archdeacon for the see of Lincoln, as a highborn voluptuary of the most permissive sort, the prospect of his overseeing Lenton necessarily deepened the conflict within the house.

The mourning period for Ivo's passing had hardly expired when a letter addressed to the sheriff arrived at Nottingham Castle from an inmate of the priory who declined to give his name—"for fear of reprisal," he wrote. The late prior's death had been caused, the letter charged, not by heart failure but by poisoning; the deadly nightshade weed abounded on the monastery grounds. Beloved as Ivo had been by many, the correspondent went on, his austere manner and policies were anathema to a certain element, who conspired to do away with him. These were leagued, moreover, with Sir Mitchell, who, as both the shire coroner and the priory's protector, undertook only the most cursory investigation of Ivo's demise. Here was a fiendish crime in urgent need of prosecution, the anonymous letter concluded.

"Absolutely and utterly preposterous!" the coroner exclaimed when the sheriff invited his attendance and read out the accusation.

"I'm glad of it," said Philip. "But then again, I hardly expected your prompt confession of complicity."

"What is it you're saying, Master Mark?"

"That it is a serious and troubling charge, which I am not at liberty to ignore."

Sir Mitchell's color rose, his nostrils dilated, and his eyes bulged. "This is—is—the most scurrilous sort of character assassination. I see through it at once. And I know the culprit—your former clerk, the little swine. He would avenge himself for my having directed the Exchequer auditors to his chamber when my doing so was clearly a justified act of service to the crown."

"As it is mine," said the sheriff, "to get to the bottom of this charge of lethal doings at the priory."

"Put your Sparks to the rack, and you'll have all the answer you need."

"You are quick to accuse, sire—there are a hundred denizens of

Lenton any one of whom might have written such a letter. No, it cannot be arrogantly waved aside, Master Coroner."

"I think this solicitude stems from your ignoble accusation that I tried to turn your wards against you."

"My accusation? The lads themselves testified to it. There can be no pretense any longer over what manner of man I'm dealing with in you." The sheriff rose and strolled in the window, vacantly noting the carts being unloaded in the bailey. "I'll therefore give you a most generous choice, my inconstant friend. Either I'll undertake a thoroughgoing probe into this matter of Ivo's death and call it prominently to Westminster's attention, with all the resulting damage to your own and the priory's reputation—or you may resign your office of coroner forthwith, and I'll ignore this letter as inflammatory rubbish."

"You connive at my downfall!" the coroner cried hotly.

"Moreover, you will prevail upon your brother-in-law to withdraw his candidacy for the priorship of Lenton." The sheriff glanced over at his prey. "And if you try my patience long, you may yet know the gallows."

A.D.
1224

· L ·

THE CEASELESS RAIN had turned the highway into a mutton stew, doubling the time of his journey. There were thus inordinately long spells during the ten-day ordeal for him to consider what lay in store for him in London. He refused to concede the likelihood that the end was at hand.

"You must be prepared for the worst," Anne had warned him when the summons came from Westminster.

"I have been from the first day," Philip said, "but I cannot think why it should come now. The castle is well ordered—our accounts are squared—both counties have been peaceful."

"For a man so thoroughly experienced, you can be wondrously naive," said his wife, her love for him replenished but her judgment of his prudence admirably detached. "If they have decided you must go, small excuse is needed. The fact is that with Fawkes finally out of the way, you're the last of John's formidable French captains left in high office—and why should you be spared de Burgh's gleaming axe?"

"If he'd wished to do me in, there was ground aplenty four years ago. Yet he kept me on—they all recognize my usefulness still. And it's to Brewer's chamber that I'm called. If the justiciar were about to dismiss me, surely he'd have been the one to do the summoning. Perhaps—perhaps I'm to be promoted—and Brewer wishes to explore the—"

"Promoted to what—the royal food taster? The crown's resident wizard? I don't wish to mock you, Philip, but you must not deceive yourself. It's late in the game, and there are many new players eager for the contest."

"Perhaps you're right—in that my capacity is limited. The truth is I haven't the stamina for a more rigorous assignment."

"Have you the courage, though, for no assignment whatever?"

"I've earned no such rebuke."

"You overinvest your confidence in the justiciar. He's but a variation on John—without the grace of majesty."

"As always, you're too scornful of my masters."

"Because you deserve to have none. And I, for one, relish the prospect. Be careful on the highway, my darling."

While the boy king was advancing through his adolescent years, Sir Hubert de Burgh outstripped him in ambition, knowing his hour of dominion could not run long. Like the Marshal, he had parlayed his prowess as a warrior to gain property and rank, and now he unsubtly exploited every advantage he could as chief magistrate of the realm in order to tame the baronage, outflank would-be rivals, and turn the crown's power into his own. By the year previous, he had gathered sufficient strength to demand that every crown property, from mightiest fortress to the narrowest weir, be surrendered to the king for reappraisal of the custodian's merit; the justiciar, furthermore, ordered an inquest into the behavior of all the sheriffs and the revenue-raising customs in all the shires.

This nervy extension of the justiciar's sway was denounced as most injudicious by the baronage and objected to no less strenuously by every royal officeholder beyond Westminster. None of the latter was more potent and vociferous than Fawkes de Breauté, by then the holder of seven sheriffships, more than a dozen castles and royal manors, and even a modicum of social rank through his marriage into the gentry. Though dreaded for his rampages, Fawkes continued to be employed by the regency council for his brutal efficiency in performing its most unsavory business, like putting down a rebellion in London or ousting Longsword from Lincolnshire after the earl had bullied Dame Nicolaa in order to win mastery of the county.

The inevitable collision between Fawkes and the justiciar occurred when the boisterous, brawling ex-captain refused de Burgh's order to yield all his crown properties, arguing that several had now become his family's by hereditary right. Mad with defiance, Fawkes ignored the threat of excommunication by Archbishop Langton and thereby all but forced Hubert to charge him with treason, murder, infinite breaches of the king's peace, and thirty cases of unlawful confiscation. His home base at Bedford Castle was reduced after a massive siege; and, denounced as a public enemy, the Scythe was lucky to escape alive into exile in France. The kingdom thereafter became the justiciar's to rule unopposed until arrogance drove him to assume royal prerogatives and, in time, assured his downfall. Just now, though, de Burgh was at his apex.

"You're looking lean and square-shouldered for a man of gathering years," William Brewer said upon the sheriff's arrival in his chamber. "How do you avoid the stoop and suet that afflict the rest of us?"

The baron had indeed added bulk in his last several years and was mountainously larger than when he had first counseled Philip at the outset of his sheriffship. The mastiff at his heel, doubtless a different creature from the one at their original meeting, looked no less red-eyed and coiled to pounce at any move or sound threatening his bloated master. "Castle food and a caring wife," Philip answered with a smile. "The first limits my appetite, and the second—"

"Stimulates it. You're a lucky man, *mon capitaine*—in more ways than you know." Brewer leaned back and folded his hands over his outsized belly. "But no one's good fortune can last forever. I'll not protract your agony with banter, Master Mark. You've been sent for to be advised that—how shall I say it?—you're a victim of politics."

"My lord?"

"Can it be a secret to you at this late date that most of my misguided fellow barons have long loathed the lot of you Frenchmen?" The most durable of the Plantagenets' henchmen sniffed and shrugged idly. "They resented you as John's mean lash while the king reigned, and with him eight years gone now, you've come to be perceived as his deathless scourge."

"I have? I've always sought to act with moderation—abiding by our laws and charters to the letter."

"Oh, indeed. You've rendered superior service from the first—which is why you are the last to be relieved of your command."

"But why, my lord—if I perform as justly and faithfully as ever?"

"It has little to do with your conduct in office—otherwise you'd be the justiciar, and justice would reign throughout England. Fawkes's beastly behavior has tarred you as well, I'm afraid, so Sir Hubert finds it that much easier to toss you away like a well-used bone to placate the baronage and shore up his own standing as the exterminator of foreign oppressors."

"But I am no Fawkes, sire! Nothing in my record suggests—"

"You cannot reason with emotion, Philip—and politics is three parts feeling for each one part of logic." The baron leaned forward, not without effort, and gave the table edge a rap. "At any rate, the justiciar has delegated me to do his dirty work—I've been doing it for the crown, it appalls me to admit, for forty-six years now—and turn you out to pasture. And it's time, my captain—it's time. We grow stale grazing the same field too long."

"I . . . would like to hear as much from Sir Hubert himself, sire—if that might be arranged."

The baron's eyes widened. "What has been arranged is that I should let you down gently. The justiciar is exceedingly busy."

"There's little justice in the arrangement, if I may say so."

"To me you may say it—to him, I'd not advise. The matter is not open to appeal." Brewer massaged his wattles for a reflective moment. "Nor would I be too quick to bemoan your fate, Philip. The justiciar was ready to dismiss you four years ago when that slight irregularity in your ledgers came to light. But I told him I believed in you—and that nobody could have invented a story like your devious strategy to befuddle the French. Besides, there was the money back in crown hands to verify it. To be honest, though, the justiciar has never trusted you. Oh, yes, I know—you still think the two of you are fast comrades from your time together in Angers prison. But that's nearly twenty years past now. Even then it was not what you think. Hubert had heard from Gerard d'Athiés that your lack of blood lust made you a mockery of a soldier in the defense of Loches."

"Gerard would not have said such a thing!"

"I tell you what I was told."

"We were—like cousins—brothers, practically."

"Jacob and Esau were brothers, in fact. You have a remarkable capacity to deceive yourself, Philip, regarding other people's sincerity. Gerard's report gained standing with Hubert, at any rate, by your conduct in gaol. He couldn't fathom why you objected to taking your father-in-law's money to meet the French ransom demand, and supposed you must have been spying for them."

"Spying? I've served my life long against the Capetians."

"Nevertheless, you are a born Frenchman, and certain impressions die hard. Further, when Sir Hubert was caught for minor malfeasance while the sheriff of Lincolnshire—by none other than myself and our gimlet-eyed auditors, I might add—he suspected you, too, had to be guilty of venally indulging but were just too shrewd to get caught at it."

Philip closed his eyes and shook his head slowly. "It grieves me deeply to learn of this. I had thought better of him."

"Many have made that mistake," said Brewer. "But I'll thank you not to attribute the remark to me, or I'll see you slain." The baron fell backward in his oak-ribbed chair of office. "Don't grow embittered, though, my friend, at this turn in the road. The crown's not forsaken you, nor will you slide headlong into pauperdom—I've seen to that."

"I can't think what I've done to earn your kindness," said Philip, "but I'll not gainsay it."

"You've done your job well—the proof is that your shires little love you, yet no one has ever justly charged you with oppression. It greatly pleases me to say, therefore, that you are to be confirmed in your custody of Bulwell and Melbourne manors as long as you are able to oversee them. That unpleasant little sum of one hundred and forty pounds that you never accounted for from the war years will be forgiven—we'll say it somehow fell into the cracks amid all the tumult of those dark days. And finally, in consideration of your able and faithful service, the crown awards you a modest manor at Keyworth—it amounts to but a quarter of a knight's fee, but it is yours alone to have and to hold and pass down to your progeny. If you are provident, these holdings should yield you between fifty and one hundred a year—not enough to live like a lord, I'll grant you, but then again, you're not one, are you?"

"I'm grateful for the reminder, sire—but still more so for your part in these—gratifying—arrangements."

Brewer gave a dismissive wave of his hand and then reached it down for a fond tug on his dog's ear. "There is one thing more I can offer you that I'm told has long been your earnest wish. It took more doing than all the rest combined, but the regency council has come around. Archbishop Stephen is among us at Westminster for the week and stands ready to officiate in the abbey at your investiture as a knight. It remains only for us to determine who will strike the blow. They say you're choosy in the matter."

The endlessly elusive prize, suddenly within easy reach, now seemed as stale and alluring to him as a year-old pasty. "I have put the idea out of mind long ago, my lord."

"Then let us revive it. Name your champion for the rite."

"I . . . can think of no one, sire—no one left alive, anyway."

"Mmmm. The Marshal once told me you wished for none other than him or the king to do the dub—apparently you put up your chaplain to seek him out and urge the—"

"I did no such thing, sire."

"No—no, of course, you would not have. The chaplain did it of his own volition—and was rewarded, as I recall, with the priorship of Lenton. Nevertheless, weren't those eminences your choice for the knighting?"

"Possibly I once mentioned something to that effect—just when and to whom, I can no longer remember."

"Sadly, they show how ill advised you were—and remote from both the political and moral realities." The baron struggled to his feet and began to pace about slowly behind his chair. "Once the king found out how badly you wished the honor, don't you see, he vowed not to bestow it on you. All the better to keep you hoping for it and assure your utmost dedication. And there was as well the matter of your conduct with the Welsh hostages."

"Because I defied him in sparing his own grandson?"

"Because you were right to—which, by his lights, was even worse." Brewer clucked at the precision of his thrust at the dead. "As to the Marshal, you were still more deluded. They say he was the best knight of our age, yet I say he was the most corrupt of us all. Oh, I see that look of yours again—I know: *de mortuis nil nisi bonum.* But the truth must out. The Marshal's sin was that he turned all that valor and prowess into money. He bested half a thousand knights on the tourney lists, maiming who knows how many others in battle, and did it not for the glory, I tell you, but for the profit from their armor and ransom. He played off the rulers of England and France to his own great advantage like a chess master—who else do you know that held such vast estates in both realms while we were deadly antagonists? And he used the regency to enrich his family all the more. He was a supremely duplicitous knight—who would not take the trouble to extend you that title because there was nothing you could have done for him in return." The baron swung toward him with an oddly graceful pivot. "Now, then, who is left among us fit to do you the honor? No doubt you'd prefer the justiciar himself to knight you in the abbey?"

Philip shrugged. "I can't think that he would dismiss me one day and ennoble me the next."

"Why not? King John excelled at just such artifice. You're right, though—de Burgh lacks the politesse. Do you know how he rose?"

"Why, by gallantry in combat, I suppose."

"By blackmailing the king. Hubert was assigned the safekeeping—which is to say the imprisonment—of John's nephew Arthur, lest the boy get loose and press his claim to the throne. When the king proposed Arthur be blinded and gelded to assure he would never ascend, Hubert objected that such cruelty would surely redound to the king's disfavor—whereupon John, they say, throttled the boy with his own hands and gave his corpse to Hubert to dispose of in secret. For keeping silent, the king rewarded him steadily ever after, allowing him to plunder his holdings as few others. To have made him the supreme jurist of the realm was possibly John's most cynical act. And doubtless you've heard of the booty Hubert lifted off the French fleet after they finished butchering it in '17. So I'm not greatly enamoured of the justiciar, you see. He keeps me in place, I tell you in candor, only because he knows my skills and has the wit to harness them to his needs instead of avenging himself for my having once revealed his knavery. A fool he's not, but if it were me, Master Mark, I'd want his better to knight me."

"I'm at a loss, then, my lord."

"Let's think. No other earl or baron is kindly disposed to you—you've made too many of their lives more difficult—unless Longsword would suit you. He might be prevailed upon—I know he thinks passingly well of you."

"More so, probably, than I of him. He abandoned the king at the war's darkest hour—and lately oppressed Dame Nicolaa for withstanding his designs on Lincolnshire. I like no knight of his stripe."

"Is there no knight in all the realm you regard highly enough?"

"Truly not, my lord."

"Yet I have in mind one who ought to commend himself to your immaculate taste."

"Who is that, sire?"

"Why, me, of course."

Dismay contorted the sheriff's brow. "You, sire?"

"And why not? I've served four kings closely and faithfully for nearly half a century—and never once been found guilty of abuse of office."

The ultimate proof of his guile, thought Philip. "I . . . do not place you in a knightly context, my lord."

"Name another as meritorious as I."

"With all due deference, sire, I would hope I myself am no less so, though I have not the power or station to certify it."

"So, then—I'm not exalted enough to knight you!"

"I've not said that, sire—only that the whole idea now seems—"

"You reek from pride, *mon capitaine.*" Brewer snapped and halted by the arm of his chair, causing his watchdog to stir. "You'd have been a corpse long since if it weren't for me. I've watched over you all these years like an older brother, and now you would scorn me?"

"Sire, you mistake my—"

"I saved your foul bung from the pyre in '20 only because I admired the daring of your scheme and how you then confected so grand a lie to cover its detection. My chief regret was that you had to give the money back." His tone mellowed. "If only you had come to me with the truth then, Philip—whatever the truth was—we might have worked out something between us. Twenty-five hundred pounds is a lot of money."

"I thought you said earlier that you believed me."

"I said I told the justiciar I believed in you—that's a very different pot of pike."

"You're persuaded that I extorted the crown's silver?"

"Tried to, certainly—in a most enterprising and inventive fashion."

"Then I am to become no knight by your hand, sire—though I thank you roundly for the consideration." The sheriff stood and tendered the baron a stiff little bow. "I hold myself as honorable as any knight who ever lived, my lord, even if God strike me dead for the conceit—and ask no confirmation of that estimate by any mortal man."

"You saddle the Lord with a heavy burden, come Judgment Day," the baron growled, and turned away.

His leavetaking from Nottingham Castle inspired no ceremony of fond farewells. No one of rank who had been there when Philip first arrived survived him now, the sybaritic steward Devereaux having succumbed some years before to gross inflammation of the male organs and the constable Aubrey to choking on a baked lark's-wing. The sheriff's older brother, Reginald, who had succeeded Master Manning as chief bailiff, and Reginald's son, Geoffrey, who had risen to Aubrey's post, retired from the castle along with Philip. Father and son between them bought a tidy freehold near Worksop with the savings from their pay and the many undetected small extortions they had managed while in the castle's service.

Philip moved his immediate family back to the custodian's cottage at Bulwell, where he passed his days tending his properties in a restless quest for serenity. His wife was not sure at first how best to comfort him, for while the scarred tissue of their marital bond no longer throbbed, neither did the pain from it subside in its entirety. Yet compensations grew. Before this, he had always been too hard at work to contemplate life in all its beauty and mystery; only its travails had engaged him to the utmost. Anne now helped him to a deepened understanding of each day's small delights, and even as he recognized that he had never given her an existence of true comfort and leisure, so he came to appreciate her arrival at contentment and the supreme effort she was making to reconcile him to his disappointed ambitions. While her beauty had faded, there bloomed a tenderness that heightened his love for her beyond what it had ever been. They walked the wood together each day that the weather permitted and catalogued its glories. She mastered the lute and played and sang for him each sunset while he carved a new bow of Spanish yew. And when his sight began to dim, she took to reading to him by the firelight—from their Aesop, or some instructive passages from the precious volume of Augustine that Father Ivo had sent them as a gift soon after he was installed at Lenton Priory. Once when Philip confessed to encroaching despair over his reduced vision, she took his hand and remarked, "It's but nature's peculiar form of kindness. By thus losing our faculties gradually as we approach life's end, we resign from it with less regret." He kissed her for the sentiment and blinked back a tear.

The great joy of Philip's life in retirement, though, was his beloved daughters, whom he avidly cosseted. But they seemed never so much alive as when Philip's former wards, Matthew and Andrew, came to the cottage on their monthly visit. On one such occasion, Philip rode through the wood with the young master of Hathersgate, who confided the growing suasion his aunt was applying to him to find a suitable wife and sire an heir while the kingdom remained at peace. For all the lingering affection between the two fine fellows and her daughters, Anne dared harbor only the dimmest hope of a lasting union, in view of her family's diminished circumstances. A tanner's son or, at best, the corn merchant's was the likelier match.

One day a wagon that looked as derelict as its two burly drivers drew up before Philip's cottage, carrying a large chest heavily wrapped in chains. The deliverers said the battered object was a gift from an old friend of

Philip and asked permission to drag it into the Marks' parlor. There they noisily struggled to open the chest, and when the ancient lid at last creaked open, glittering within was a heap of coin, plate, and jewels that could not have been worth less than eight hundred pounds.

The treasure, according to the perspiring wagonmaster, had been removed by a certain band of good-natured woodsmen from an overburdened baggage train belonging to Sir Ralph and Lady Olivia de Greasley as it traversed the forest in Yorkshire, en route from Pendrake to one of their outlying properties near Chester. "Our captain knows these folk to have done you dirt," the senior deliveryman explained, "and holds this trinketry to be yours by entitlement. Besides which, he himself wronged you twice over—once for withholding your full share of his wartime takings in the wood here, and then again for bearing false witness against you to the crown for grievances not of your making. Furthermore, he says you were ever kind to him, and now that you are said to be less than flush, he wishes you to have this chest as a token of his high regard."

Anne fairly burst with joy, and their daughters grew giddy at this gleaming windfall. But the retired sheriff could respond only as his nature dictated. "Please take your refreshment with us, my good fellows," he said, "and then return with your cargo whence you came. Tell your captain that if his gift was sent for charity, most in the kingdom are far needier than we. If sent out of gratitude, tell him that being thought of kindly is more than enough for me. And if as payment on some imagined debt, tell him I cannot share in the plunder of thieves or rogues, however beguiling."

Upon hearing this pretty speech, the drivers spun on their heels and headed for the cottage door. "Our master warned us to brook no refusal," the wagonmaster said in hasty retreat. "The gift is yours, and what you do with it is not our business. Godspeed, sire."

Philip sent Angelique in pursuit of the drivers with sixpence each for their troubles. Then he settled back and began to ponder what to do with the tainted gift. All night he sat by the hearth and thought.

"It cannot be that Heaven would taunt us thus twice," Anne said to him. "It is plainly recognition for your lifetime of virtue." She sat on the floor beside his feet and looked up at him. "Well do I know your dislike of our benefactors' acquisitive habits, but their kindness may purchase for our daughters their hearts' dearest wish—would you deny them that?"

Her words greatly dispirited him. "You told me once you'd rather the girls have no dowry at all," said Philip, "than one derived from stolen money."

"But this comes from none but the wicked—and there is a rightness in your being recompensed for past wrongs and slights."

"But the further wrong of our accepting it gains no virtue for those reasons. It cannot be, my dear—nor can I be other than I am."

While Anne grieved in the darkness, Philip studied the dancing flames and wrestled with his dilemma. The treasure could not be returned to its donor now; there was no telling in what fragrant copse he dwelt or which sour alehouse he frequented. It could be restored to its owners, of course, but they deserved no such kindness, whatever the law prescribed. Indeed, Philip resolved to lighten the chest by the fifty pounds Greasley and his wife had long owed him and put the money, his by right, toward his daughters' dowries. But the problem of what to do with the rest of it seemed insoluble. Shortly before sunrise, though, he hit upon its just disposition and rode into Nottingham that very morning to visit with the proprietor of the Trip to Jerusalem before the inn opened for business.

"If memory serves, you have a nephew from Wales, do you not, Master Bartholomew?" Philip asked after accepting a courtesy dram of malmsey.

"I do," said le Gyw. "He comes on a visit every once in so often—and indeed stays in my house this very moment."

"Excellent. There is a somewhat delicate business proposal I'd have you put to him." Whereupon Philip unfolded his plan. Under suitable guard, his unwelcome treasure was to be carted one hundred miles west to the heart of Gwynedd and there distributed in equal portions among the families of the Welsh lads who had long ago been hanged from the wall of Nottingham Castle. "Your nephew is to say that this belated gift comes from one who is profoundly sorrowful and well knows the money can in no way be measured against their enduring grief. Yet if it might somehow ease the burdens of their lives or be put to some other worthy end, it will have been well expended." For their efforts, the deliverers were to divide ten pounds as le Gyw's nephew saw fit.

The innkeeper nodded admiringly and promised to arrange the transfer. But how, he wondered, had Philip known of his Welsh nephew?

"Ah, yes—that. I know far more of him—and you—than you might have liked." Philip recalled the night after the hangings when a certain road-weary youngster appeared at the castle with an urgent letter for the king, reputedly from his daughter Joan, warning of dire consequences if he persisted in his imminent assault on Wales. "I heeded closely when the earl of Salisbury questioned the messenger to be sure he was who he said and that the letter was authentic. The lad answered persuasively enough to pass for a claimed member of Prince Llewellyn's household—until Longsword asked the name of his nephew Gruffydd's pet collie dog. The earl was just guessing that the boy would have such a dog and afterward asked Nurse Cadi if the messenger had rightly stated he knew no such creature. She confirmed the messenger lad's answer—for reasons I couldn't at once fathom, for I had several times heard young Gruffydd speak of his beloved pet Shortfang, and Cadi once told me the boy and his dog were inseparable."

More than a little suspicious by then, the sheriff ordered the messenger put under surveillance, and when he slipped out of the castle, he was followed to the Trip, where it was not difficult to learn his relationship to the proprietor. Added to that discovery was the notice taken by the sheriff's wife that Nurse Cadi, no doubt in her grief, reeked from potent spirits that must have been fed her by her commiserating half-countryman, Master le Gyw. Knowing, furthermore, of the innkeeper's closeness to his first clerk and suspecting the latter's implication in the plot, Philip searched hurriedly through a pile of refuse in a sack beneath Sparks's worktable and found in it a cloth that had been used to blot the letter delivered to the king that same night, allegedly from William the Lion of Scotland. "By then I understood the nature and purpose of the scheme— and that the messenger had no knowledge of Gruffydd's pet simply because the nurse had forgotten to mention the animal to your nephew while speedily coaching him for his precarious assignment."

Le Gyw, dumbstruck at this disclosure, fetched a pair of goblets and poured them both a generous round of Rhenish. "You knew our game yet did not apprise the king?"

"By the time I grasped the full measure of your daring design, the invasion had been mercifully called off. What could have been gained by my denouncing the subterfuge, save a few more hangings?"

"Then I owe you my life," said the innkeeper.

"And you helped salve my bleeding conscience—I'd call the bargain fair."

Troubled by his daughters' thwarted dreams of matrimony and determined now to see them fulfilled, Philip traveled to the north end of the shire to visit with his brother Reginald and nephew, Geoffrey, on the small farm they worked together. If they could lend him as much as fifty pounds to go with the similar amount he had already set aside from the Greasley money, he would have the beginnings of a not insubstantial dowry for each of his daughters. Philip promised to pay a good rate of interest from the income of his holdings, but Reginald told him with regret that they had nothing whatever to spare, since all their accumulated savings were committed to livestock and grain seed. "It's not our fault you were dismissed from the castle," his brother added, "or were disinclined to make provision for such needs when you had the opportunity."

Chagrined but determined, Philip turned to the one man of rank with whom he remained on cordial terms—his former undersheriff Sir Eustace of Lowdham—and asked a boon of him. Might he enter into a negotiation on the Marks' behalf with Matthew's kin at Hathersgate to determine if they would consent to his marriage to Angelique and how large a dowry they would require? Respectful as he was of Philip, Eustace undertook the task with heavy qualms, which Matthew's hardheaded aunt was quick to detect. "I have no doubt that the two youngsters are deeply and mutually smitten," she said, "but I must ask you in all honesty, Sir Eustace, if you would have your son or nephew marry into a family so common and ill suited as the Marks."

"Philip is the soul of honor, madam," the knight answered, "and his wife and daughters decent and comely people."

"I have no doubt of that, sire, but honor without rank will not ennoble our family line or cause Hathersgate to flourish."

"Philip is prepared to pay to gain the advantage such a union will bring his daughter. He asks what dowry you would require."

"The matter cannot be so lightly bargained, sire."

"I wonder, madam, if you aren't closing your heart to—"

"You have not answered my question, Sir Eustace. Would you approve such a marriage and sully your own family, whatever the price?"

Eustace dropped his head. "If only Philip retained his office, I would argue with you more spiritedly. But removed from the castle . . ."

"He is a petty landholder, on the edge of impoverishment—or no doubt soon would be if forced to raise a dowry suitable to Matthew's needs. What wish have we to drive the man to ruin? It cannot be, both for social and material reasons. Please express my deepest regret to Master Mark—I know that Matthew remains devoted to him."

This interview in its entirety, as it happened, was overheard by a maidservant at Hathersgate, who repeated the essence of the exchange to Mistress Blake. The old woman, whom Matthew loved as if she were the mother he had never known, reported the matter to him at once— and at no small risk to her well-being. Matthew was at first much angered that his aunt had rejected Philip's overtures out of hand without consulting him. "No doubt she's right, though," he said, cooling after some moments. "The burden would prove far too great for Master Mark."

"Then reduce it for him," said Mistress Blake. "You're of age now— if you would have Angelique for your wife, you must not let your family stand in the way."

"But she lacks all rank and wealth."

"You have enough for the both of you—and she is fair and kind and clever. Can you do better?"

Upon due reflection, the still boyish master of Hathersgate rode to Bulwell and met with his former guardian. "Our intermediaries have served us faithlessly, sire," said Matthew. "Let us attack the matter between us." His aunt, he stated straightforwardly, had urged him to consider a dowry of no less than six hundred pounds.

"Possibly that could be managed," said Philip with a sigh. "The problem arises in that I am duty-bound to provide as much for Julia. Her love for Andrew does not go unrequited, I know, but the Lutteral family has raised the same objection as yours. Twelve hundred pounds, alas, is hopelessly beyond my capacity."

Matthew nodded. "We cannot have sweet Julia disadvantaged, I agree. Let me meet with Andrew and see what we shall see."

Two days later, Matthew returned to advise Philip that he and Andrew Lutteral would each accept a proffered dowry of three hundred pounds if it could be managed without severe duress. Elated, Philip presented himself that very afternoon at the door of Benjamin, the moneylender of Nottingham. "I find myself in need of your resources, sire," he said, removing his cap as the Jew led him to his parlor, "though it would come as no surprise if time had not healed your heart adequately to deal with me."

"I am not obliged to love my clients," said Benjamin. "Indeed, I'd no longer be in business if it were requisite. Tell me your needs."

The terms were quickly settled. Philip was advanced five hundred and fifty pounds, which with the Greasley fifty added to it would provide the agreed-upon sum for the two dowries. The interest was set at 14 percent—"I can do no better," Benjamin assured him, "even for the most benign tormentors of my race"—with the principal to be repaid over fifteen years. The transaction left the retired officeholder and his wife scant margin to live in repose.

Through the courtesy of Sir Ralph Nicholson, Philip's successor as sheriff, the double ceremony was performed in the chapel at Nottingham Castle and presided over by Prior Honorius of Lenton, with Brother Jared in attendance as well. The great hall was given over to the wedding feast, throughout the course of which the brides' mother could not help shedding continual tears of happiness. The guests were largely composed of the bridegrooms' families and friends, many of whom had made it a mindless practice to curse Philip during his years as sheriff. Yet on this day of days, he looked on them all with a beamish smile, danced lightfootedly with his wife and daughters, and even sang out robustly to the troubadours' tunes. There came a moment during the banquet, between the serving of the turtle soup and the roast swan, when he stole a bleary backward glance at the map of the world that Anne had caused to be painted on the wall behind the dais. Reflecting on all the lands he had never seen, all the pleasures he had never had, all the glories he had never won, Philip knew then precisely why there was a Heaven.

Near the close of the fete, a pair of imposing white steeds arrived in the bailey ridden by royal messengers; each carried on his gauntlet a hooded peregrine falcon of perfect form and luster. "For the kindness two young ladies extended their even younger monarch on the eve of the battle that saved his crown," read the message the riders bore with them, "he presents them these winged lovelies and best prayers for a long and happy life on this their wedding day." It carried the privy seal and the signature "Hen. III Rex."

Her bird, though, for all its beauty and the high recognition that came with it, did not please Angelique. When her husband twitted her for neglecting the peregrine, she offered it to him; he declined, saying that to hunt in such a fashion required little of the falconer but much of the falcon. She turned for guidance to Master Blake, by then the steward of Hathersgate, who counseled merely, "The bird needs to fly, my lady."

"Then you fly it," she said. "I find it a nasty creature, good only for killing. I remember my mother working with one—a gift like mine from a noble friend—till it flew off one day and deigned never to return."

"Its flight is a lovely thing to witness, my lady."

"Then you must have it, Blake—by all means."

"It's not fit for me, my lady—such fine birds are emblems of the gentry, whereas I am but a freed bondsman. There would be questions."

Angelique regarded him with mock sternness. "You're as fine a gentleman as any I know, Master Blake, save my father and husband. Care for the peregrine or let her go, as you choose—only we'll not tell Master Matthew she's all yours now—or the king, either, if you don't mind."

The former sheriff endured, more happily than not, for ten years after leaving the crown's service. He died still in debt to the Jew of Nottingham, and his holdings had to be surrendered to satisfy the obligation. His widow, as a result, had no place to call her own but gladly accepted an offer to live at Hathersgate, in only slightly strained communion with her son-in-law's people. If, in the caress of her memories, she could not contrive to make of Philip a heroic figure for remaining true to himself, neither did she turn him into a saint or fool for what he sacrificed to honor. Part of that, without a doubt, was a diminished capacity for loving, but what abided was sufficient to sustain her. Life is too brief for bitterness, she decided, and cares nothing for those who waste themselves decrying its unkindness.

All that remained of Philip Mark was the invidious mention of his name in the Great Charter of English liberties and his last resting place at Lenton Priory. His former clerk, by then the aging chronicler of that monastic house, presided at his service of interment. In offering his prayer for the soul of the departed, Brother Jared asked divine forgiveness as well for all those to whom the sheriff had entrusted his heart and his honor and who had, sooner or later, to one extent or another, betrayed him.

None of these, though, as posterity would record, was unkinder to him than the perversity of human nature. The men of his day, invested with original sin and so many more of their own devising, came to resent Philip's unabated rectitude: the better he was, the more glaring their own foibles. And so, in the years after he was gone, they turned on him by collective instinct and tore him down. Among the chief propagators of this unlovely tendency was Alan-a-Dale, the balladeer among the company headed by the sly former woodsman turned outlaw. The *chansons de geste* that Alan performed of their rollicking feats in the forest, sung or recited at many a manor house and inn across the midlands and, in time, throughout the realm and then the world, were just barely true enough to life to escape being outright lies. In these lively ballads, the sheriff was invariably cast as the embodiment of villainy, and even as his rightful name has been lost to the ages, so the office he held has come, by its very mention, to signify evildoing. The man who was that sheriff, though, was as stubbornly virtuous as any ever to serve the crown. The legend embodying him has nonetheless persisted, supremely unjust to the historical presence behind it. Of how many others retained within the common memory of our planet— the good taken for bad and the bad for good—might the same be said if the truth could but be known?

THE END IS NOT YET

Author's Note

IT IS THE STORYTELLER'S AMBITION that the foregoing should conform as closely as possible with—and in no case violate—facts, texts, and events recorded in the documents and chronicles of the age examined. The principal contemporary commentators were, of course, monastics; and their estimates of King John—and, by extension, his royal officeholders, such as our title character—were almost surely colored by the struggle between the king and Pope Innocent III.

   The central fact of the narrative is that Philip Mark (sometimes spelled "Marc" in annals of the time) truly served at Nottingham, apparently with distinction, during the years indicated. The very duration of his tenure, at a highly unsettled time, is the strongest argument that he was an able official. No surviving evidence taints him as an egregious oppressor, and what faults have been attributed to him by modern scholars are open to question in the fashion that the story proposes. Almost nothing is known of Philip's background before he arrived in England.

   Of the residents of Nottinghamshire portrayed, only Philip, his family members, his wards, and Ralph de Greasley were historical personages, as were the primary officials here dealt with, including the Marshal, Brewer, Fawkes, Hubert de Burgh, Longsword, and Archbishop Langton. The geographical locations, religious houses, and Sherwood (if not its most renowned resident) are authentic; Swanhill manor and all who dwelt thereon are inventions. Events involving King John, particularly those set at Nottingham Castle, are known to have occurred, in their essence, on the dates or at the times indicated.

   For those curious or loath to suspend disbelief, let it be further noted that: Langton's thoughts on transubstantiation cited in chapter II are based on his surviving writings. The Inn of the Trip to Jerusalem, mentioned first in chapter V and often thereafter, was in fact an annex of Nottingham Castle, dating back to the end of the twelfth century, and still exists. The Hole to Hell, mentioned first in chapter VI and more importantly in the criminal activities of chapter XLII, was an actual feature of the castle and called Mortimer's Hole in later centuries. The tourn pleas cited in chapter IX are based on cases heard at that time. The events surrounding the Welsh hostages in chapters XXVIII and XXIX are cited in many historical sources; and while paragraph 58 of the Magna Carta seems to corroborate Gruffydd's survival of his stay at Nottingham (testified to by several sources), it also suggests that he, or possibly another son of Prince Llewellyn, and other Welsh hostages were still being held at the time—but just where, there is no telling. King John did receive letters on the night after the hangings, purportedly from his daughter Joan and the king of Scotland, warning against the invasion of Wales, as set forth in chapter XXX, and did cancel the impending invasion. Philip did receive the custodianships cited in chapter XXXIV and later and encountered the difficulties noted, including the dispute over Melbourne with the earl of Derby (who nevertheless advanced him the money to pay his garrison at the beginning of 1217, described in chapter XLIV). The memorandum noted at length in chapter XXXVI as the forerunner of the Magna Carta is based (including the quoted phrases) on the so-called "unknown charter" discovered in the late nineteenth century and thought to have been drafted in the autumn of 1213; who wrote it and where are not known, but there is no other surviving preliminary document to the final charter of 1215. The roles of Langton and Marshal in the creation of the charter are widely suspected and in some small measure documented. Philip is cited by name in paragraph 50 of the charter, as discussed in chapter XXXVIII, and the sheriffs were required to have the charter read aloud in public. Among the king's last acts, as given in chapter XLIII, was Philip's appointment as co-sheriff of Lincolnshire. The loyalist strategy for the battle of Lincoln Fair, as set out in chapter XLV, including use of the forgotten portal to gain entry to the town, is based on historical accounts; the boy king was at Nottingham at the time, as indicated. The Exchequer did discover some £2500 in wartime revenues passing through Philip's treasury to be unaccounted for, as presented in chapter XLVIII, but they were later satisfactorily explained, save for £140, which was forgiven Philip after he left royal service.

Philip's daughters did in fact marry his former wards. And he was buried at Lenton Priory. Of the historical existence of Robin Hood, there is no persuasive evidence. The tales involving him began to be set down in written form in the fourteenth century, with the characters of the friar and Marian appearing several centuries later. Nottingham Castle was razed in the seventeenth century after surviving the better part of six hundred years.

FOR THE BEST IN PAPERBACKS, LOOK FOR THE

In every corner of the world, on every subject under the sun, Penguin represents quality and variety—the very best in publishing today.

For complete information about books available from Penguin—including Pelicans, Puffins, Peregrines, and Penguin Classics—and how to order them, write to us at the appropriate address below. Please note that for copyright reasons the selection of books varies from country to country.

In the United Kingdom: For a complete list of books available from Penguin in the U.K., please write to *Dept E.P., Penguin Books Ltd, Harmondsworth, Middlesex, UB7 0DA*.

In the United States: For a complete list of books available from Penguin in the U.S., please write to *Dept BA, Penguin*, Box 120, Bergenfield, New Jersey 07621-0120.

In Canada: For a complete list of books available from Penguin in Canada, please write to *Penguin Books Canada Ltd, 10 Alcorn Avenue, Suite 300, Toronto, Ontario, Canada M4V 3B2*.

In Australia: For a complete list of books available from Penguin in Australia, please write to the *Marketing Department, Penguin Books Ltd, P.O. Box 257, Ringwood, Victoria 3134*.

In New Zealand: For a complete list of books available from Penguin in New Zealand, please write to the *Marketing Department, Penguin Books (NZ) Ltd, Private Bag, Takapuna, Auckland 9*.

In India: For a complete list of books available from Penguin, please write to *Penguin Overseas Ltd, 706 Eros Apartments, 56 Nehru Place, New Delhi, 110019*.

In Holland: For a complete list of books available from Penguin in Holland, please write to *Penguin Books Nederland B.V., Postbus 195, NL-1380AD Weesp, Netherlands*.

In Germany: For a complete list of books available from Penguin, please write to *Penguin Books Ltd, Friedrichstrasse 10-12, D-6000 Frankfurt Main I, Federal Republic of Germany*.

In Spain: For a complete list of books available from Penguin in Spain, please write to *Longman, Penguin España, Calle San Nicolas 15, E-28013 Madrid, Spain*.

In Japan: For a complete list of books available from Penguin in Japan, please write to *Longman Penguin Japan Co Ltd, Yamaguchi Building, 2-12-9 Kanda Jimbocho, Chiyoda-Ku, Tokyo 101, Japan*.